Praise for the novels of Jeffery Deaver

'Probably the best book he's written . . . Enough of Deaver's trademark twists to satisfy his most diehard fans . . . A great read'   *Observer*

'More than just a spy novel or a "what if" tale, this is a consummate thriller with a sure grasp of history and human emotions'
Maxim Jakubowski, *Guardian*

'The most creative, skilled and intriguing thriller writer in the world . . . [Deaver] has produced a stunning series of bestsellers with unique characterisation, intelligent characters, beguiling plots and double-barrelled and sometimes triple-barrelled solutions'   *Sunday Telegraph*

'Teeth-chattering suspense'   *Daily Mail*

'Brilliant plotting'   *The Sunday Times*

'Deaver is a terrific storyteller, and he takes the reader on a roller coaster of suspense, violence and mystery'
Daily Telegraph

'Engrossing, entertaining, and fizzing with energy, this is a thriller to keep narcolepts awake'
Val McDermid, *Manchester Evening News*

Shallow Graves

Mistress of Justice

Jeffery Deaver

HODDER

Shallow Graves Copyright © 1992 by Jeffery Wilds Deaver
Mistress of Justice Copyright © 1992, 2002 by Jeffery Deaver

Shallow Graves first published in Great Britain in 2001 by Hodder & Stoughton
A division of Hodder Headline
Mistress of Justice first published in Great Britain in 2002 by Hodder & Stoughton
A division of Hodder Headline
This omnibus edition first published in 2006 by Hodder & Stoughton

A Hodder paperback

1

A CIP catalogue record for this title is available from the British Library

ISBN 0 340 93288 0

Typeset in Times by
Palimpsest Book Production Limited
Polmont, Stirlingshire

Printed and bound by
Clays Ltd, St Ives plc

Hodder Headline's policy is to use papers that are natural, renewable and
recyclable products and made from wood grown in sustainable forests. The
logging and manufacturing processes are expected to conform to the
environmental regulations of the country of origin.

Hodder & Stoughton Ltd
A division of Hodder Headline
338 Euston Road
London NW1 3BH

SHALLOW GRAVES

"A man should keep his word."
— James Stewart as Rupert Cadell
in Alfred Hitchcock's *Rope*

SHALLOW GRAVES

1

—◆—◇◆◇—◆—

"I heard this scary story about you one time," Marty said, "and I didn't know whether it was true or not."

Pellam didn't look over. He was driving the Winnebago Chieftain 43 back into town. They'd just found an old farmhouse a mile up the road and had offered the astonished owner thirteen hundred dollars to shoot two scenes on his front porch, provided he didn't mind if a combine replaced his rusting orange Nissan in the driveway for a couple of days. For that kind of money, the farmer said, he'd eat the car if that was what they wanted.

Pellam had told him that wouldn't be necessary.

"You used to do stunt work?" Marty asked. His voice was high and Midwest-inflected.

"Some stunts, yeah. Just for a year or so."

"About this film you did?"

"Uh." Pellam pulled off his black 1950s Hugh Hefner sunglasses. The autumn day had dawned bright as blue ice. A half hour ago it had turned dark and now the early afternoon seemed like a winter dusk.

"It was a Spielberg film," Marty said.

"Never worked for Spielberg."

Marty considered. "No? Well, I *heard* it was a Spielberg film. Anyway, there was this scene where the guy, the star, you know, was supposed to drive a motorcycle over this bridge and these bombs or something were blowing up behind him and he was driving like a son of a bitch, just ahead of these shells. Only then one hits under him and he goes flying through the air just as the bridge collapses . . . Okay? And they were supposed to rig a dummy because the stunt supervisor wouldn't let any of his guys do it but you just got on the bike and told the second unit director to roll the cameras. And you just, like, did it."

"Uh-huh."

Marty looked at Pellam. He waited. He laughed. "What do you mean, 'uh-huh'? Did you do it?"

"Yeah, I remember that one."

Marty rolled his eyes and looked out the window at a distant speck of bird. "He remembers it . . ." He looked back at Pellam. "And I heard that the thing was you didn't get blown clear but you had to hang on to this cable while the bridge collapsed."

"Uh-huh."

Marty kept waiting. It was no fun telling war stories to people who should be telling them to you. "Well?"

"That's pretty much what happened."

"Weren't you scared?"

"Sure was."

"Why'd you do it?"

Pellam reached down and picked up a Molson bottle wedged

between his scuffed brown Nokona boots. He glanced around the red and yellow autumn countryside for New York state troopers then lifted the bottle and drained it. "I don't know. I did crazy things then. Stupid of me. The unit director fired me."

"But they used the footage?"

"Had to. They'd run out of bridges."

Pellam floored the worn accelerator pedal to take a grade. The engine didn't respond well. They heard the tapping of whatever taps in an old engine when it struggles to push a heavy camper uphill.

Marty was twenty-nine, skinny, and had a small gold hoop in his left ear. His face was round and smooth and he had eyelids connected directly to his heart; they opened wide whenever his pulse picked up. Pellam was older. He was thin too, though more sinewy than skinny, and dark complected. He had a scrawny, salt-and-pepper beard that he'd started last week and he was already tired of. The lids over *his* gray-green eyes never lifted very far. Both men wore denim – blue jeans and jackets. Marty wore a black T-shirt. Pellam, a blue work shirt. In clothes like these, with his pointy-toed boots, Pellam looked a lot like a cowboy and if anyone – a woman anyway – would comment on it, he'd tell her that he was related to Wild Bill Hickok. This was true though it was true in some complicated way he'd distorted so often that he couldn't now remember exactly where the gunfighter had figured into his ancestry.

Marty said, "I'd like to do stunt work."

"I don't think so," Pellam told him.

"No, it'd be fun."

"No, it'd be painful."

After a few minutes Pellam said, "So we got a cemetery, we

got a town square, two barns and a farmhouse. We got a ton of roads. What else do we need?"

Marty flipped through a large notebook. "One big, big, big field, I'm talking sonuvabitch big, a funeral home, a Victorian house overlooking a yard big enough for a wedding, a hardware store, a mess of interiors . . . Goddamn, I ain't gonna get to Manhattan for two weeks. I'm tired of cows, Pellam. I'm so damned tired of cows."

Pellam asked, "You ever tip cows?"

"I'm from the Midwest. Everybody there tips cows."

"I've never done it. I'd like to, though."

"Pellam, you never tipped a cow?"

"Nope."

Marty shook his head with what seemed like genuine dismay. "Man . . ."

It had been three days since they'd pulled off the Interstate here in Cleary, New York. The Winnebago had clocked two hundred miles, roaming through knobby pine hills and tired farms and small, simple pastel cubes of houses decorated with pickups in the driveway, cars on blocks, and stiff laundry pinned and drying on long lines.

Three days, driving through mist and fog and yellow storms of September leaves and plenty of outright rain.

Marty looked out the window. He didn't speak for five minutes. Pellam, thinking: *Silence is platinum.*

Marty said, "Know what this reminds me of?"

The boy had a mind that ranged like a hungry crow; Pellam couldn't even guess.

"I was an assistant on *Echoes of War*," he continued.

This was a sixty-three-million-dollar Vietnam War movie that

Pellam had no desire to scout for, now had no desire to see in the theaters, and knew he wouldn't rent when it came to Tower Video in L.A.

Marty said, "For some reason they didn't shoot in Asia?"

"That's a question?"

"No. I'm telling you."

Pellam said, "It sounded like you were asking me."

"No. They decided not to shoot in Asia."

"Why not?"

"It's not important. They just didn't."

"Got it," Pellam said.

"They shot it in England, in Cornwall." Marty's head swung sideways, the grin spreading into his big, oval face. Pellam liked enthusiasm. But enthusiasm went with people that talked a lot. You can't have everything. "Man, did you know they have palm trees in England? I couldn't believe it. Palm trees . . . Anyway, the set designer made this totally incredible Army base, mortar holes and everything. And we'd get up at five a.m. to shoot and I'd get this weird feeling. I mean, I knew I was in England, and I knew it was just a movie. But all the actors were in costume – uniforms – sleeping in foxholes and eating rations. That's what the director wanted. I tell you, man, standing around, I felt totally . . . queasy." He considered if this was the right word. He decided it was and repeated it. "Queasy. That's what I feel like now."

He fell silent.

Pellam had worked on several war movies but at this moment, none of those came to mind. What he was thinking of now was rosettes of broken glass on the side window of the camper, a day after they'd arrived in the area here. Winnebago makes strong windows and it had taken a real good throw to get the bottle through the glass. The note inside had read: "*Goodbye*." The camper'd been subjected to all kinds of creative destruction over the years but nothing so ambiguously disturbing. Pellam noticed the vandals had had the foresight not to pitch the message through the windshield; they wanted to make sure the Winnebago would have an unobstructed view when it drove out of town.

He also noticed the missile had been a bottle, not a rock, and could as easily have held gasoline as a carefully lettered note.

That's what John Pellam was thinking of now. Not stunts, not war movies, not ominous dawns in tropical England.

"Getting cold," Marty said.

Pellam reached for the heater on the dash and turned it up two notches. They smelled the wet, rubbery scent of the warm air filling the cab.

On the floor Pellam's boot crunched several pieces of shattered window glass. He kicked them aside.

Goodbye . . .

Downtown Cleary wasn't much.

Two laundromats, a Chase branch, a local bank. Two bars outfitted by the same prop department. A dozen antique stores, their windows crammed with tea tables, presidential campaign buttons, sconces, trivets, tinware, scraps of faded rugs, elegant Victorian tools. There were two real estate brokerage storefronts, a music store specializing in marching-band instruments, a hardware store. The tea shop – a little, hobbity place – did a bang-up business selling muffins laced with fiber and granola and honey.

An old wood-floored five-and-dime. A couple of drugstores, one with a lunch counter right out of the fifties, so authentic a set designer couldn't have done better. Several houses had been turned into small businesses. *Crystalmere – Original Jewelry Designs by Janine. Scotch Imports, Shetland Wool Our Speciality.*

Two teenage boys, large, with scrubbed faces and pick-a-fight grins, stood outside the hardware store, under an awning, shirts open over their beefy chests, acting like the brisk wind was nothing. One of them lifted his middle finger to the passing camper.

"Assholes," Marty said.

(The locals were friendlier in Mexico, where Marty and Pellam had been last month, though that may have had something to do with the exchange rate; U.S. currency makes for a great deal of international brotherhood and understanding.)

Pellam shrugged.

Marty's eyes remained outside the camper, looking at the sidewalks. He said, "They don't have many women in this town." He was frowning, as if he were disappointed he couldn't find any young ladies in store windows wearing *Sports Illustrated* swimsuits.

"Sent 'em all to the hills when they heard you were coming." Pellam looked for a place to park.

"I haven't seen a movie theater, either."

"You better hope they've got one of those, boy," Pellam told him. "You're gonna have more luck with a movie than with women."

Marty ignored this and asked, almost reverently, "Man, isn't it the best to make love to country girls in strange hotel rooms?"

"Instead of normal hotel rooms?" In fact, Pellam thought that it *was* good, though probably not the best, and he didn't call it making love. He also didn't get all adolescently lustful like Marty. Pellam had to keep an eye on the boy. He tended to lose control and flirt relentlessly with blondes in small-town cocktail lounges – women light-years tougher than the most steely-eyed sleek Manhattanite or Los Angelina.

They hit the middle of town just as the rain had congregated all it could in the thick clouds overhead and poured down, slashing streets and slapping leaves to the ground. Visibility dropped to zero and the camper swayed like a boat in a squall.

"Whoa," Marty said. "I'd say it's 'bout time for us to get drunk."

Pellam pulled into a parking place. In the torrent of rain he missed the curb and rode over it with a grind of metal. He couldn't remember if there were parking meters in downtown Cleary but if so there was one less now.

The rain fell and fell. It pounded like a dozen break-dancers, spinning and tromping and moonwalking across the roof of the Winnebago. It slid in thick sheets down the windshield and windows.

Pellam climbed out of his seat and looked at Marty. "On three."

"Oh, hell, Pellam, no, it's wet out there."

"You wanted a drink."

"Wait till it—"

Pellam opened the door. He jumped out. "Three."

"—lets up."

In the eight leaping steps it took them to find refuge they were completely drenched.

They swung through the door with a hollow ringing of cowbell. Marty stopped short. "This's the diner, Pellam."

"Close the door, boy!"

"It's the diner."

Pellam said, "Too early to drink. Besides, I feel like some cake."

"Cake, Pellam? Damn."

Marge's Cafe was all turquoise and plasticky and unhomey. The fluorescent was green – the light that took you right back to every high school corridor you'd ever walked down.

They sat at the counter and pulled napkins out of a metal holder to wipe their faces and arms.

Two scruffy men in their fifties, maybe grain elevator operators or farmers, stocky, with black grit seated in their pores, sat hunched over bulletproof white coffee mugs. They kept their conversation going, not missing a word, though their eyes followed Pellam and Marty like retrievers sighting birds.

"Yep, had his Massey near upside down."

"On the interstate? I'da paid to see that."

"Addled a whole mess of drivers . . . I ever tell you 'bout the time I took my Harvester over the crick?"

Marty said he'd love a beer and the country girl, pretty face, hugh hips, thirty-three-ish, said she'd love to serve him one but too bad they didn't have a license. "Too bad, too bad," she repeated, trying fiercely to think of something to add. She decided on: "What else kin I gitcha?" She asked the question adoringly. Marty shot a black glance at Pellam then smiled at the girl and settled for a bowl of chili and a Coke. Pellam ordered coffee and a piece of chocolate cake.

"That really homemade?" he asked.

"You'd call A&P a home then you bet."

She added some infatuation to the adoration and said to Marty, "Onions?"

"Yes'm."

"Nope," Pellam told her. It was a small camper.

Marty sighed. She looked at him and he shook his head no. She asked Pellam, "You be wanting that à la mode?"

"Alamo?"

She glanced around. "With ice cream, you know."

"Oh. No. Just the cake."

"That's an all-right camper you boys got yourself." She wasn't moving. "My daddy had us a Travel-All one time but he backed it up the wrong way – we was going to Lake Webster – and cracked the yoke."

Pellam said, "You've got to be careful."

"She never welded proper either."

"There you go."

After a moment she waddled into action. The spherical thighs swung as she stepped to a counter.

Marty was excited. "That five and dime, Pellam? Across the street?" He was looking out the window. "I was in there yesterday. It is a totally excellent place. I mean, they sell wigs there. A couple rows of them. What other store in the world can you walk into, pay nineteen ninety nine and walk out with a wig? I ask you? Can you do that on Rodeo Drive, can you do that on Michigan Avenue?"

"You *are* getting a bit thin on top."

The rain hit the large plate-glass window with a slap and there were several huge claps of thunder. As Pellam turned toward the noise he saw a woman running into the diner, the door flying open, the cowbell dinging. She pulled off a green cape. She was about his age, a year or two more maybe, wearing a faded purple dress, the waist high, just under her ample breasts. A granny dress, he remembered they were called. Her long hair – brown with a silver sheen to it – was parted in the center.

She scanned both Pellam and Marty. To Pellam she gave what could have been a smile then turned back to the counter, wiping the rain from her face.

Pellam and Marty turned back to the counter. They took the Polaroids out of their pockets, lined them up on the counter and started talking about camera angles.

The woman in the granny dress glanced over at them, casually. Then she looked back to the counter girl and ordered herbal tea and a bran muffin. She glanced again at the two men, then away.

The waitress set the coffee and Coke in front of the men and lifted a piece of frothy cake out of a cello-window carton. She disappeared into the back to collect the chili.

She delivered the food – adoringly in Marty's case. They ate. The granny-dress woman ignored them – even when Pellam said, "Hollywood," twice in one sentence.

"How's the cake?" Marty asked.

Pellam had three bites and couldn't take any more. He pushed the plate toward Marty, who dug into it with a spoon still containing a helping of greasy chili.

More thunder, shaking the windows. Huge detonations.

Pellam said, "What else is Lefkowitz doing now?"

Marty thought. "That European thing?"

Pellam shook his head.

Marty said, "Oh, I know. The Western?"

Pellam smiled. He stood and walked to the telephone. He called to Marty, "Look at this." He was genuinely surprised. "Still costs a dime to make a phone call." The granny-dress woman was looking at him now. Smiling. He smiled her way. She turned back to her tea.

Pellam punched in the number and was put on hold, the first of several times.

Finally, the assistant producer came on the line and said, "Johnny, my boy, where you been?"

Pellam knew he was a young man but he couldn't picture him. "Around."

"Ha, 'around,'" he said. "Ha."

"So," Pellam said lazily. "How's the weather in Tinsel Town? Damn hot out here. Close to a hundred."

"Johnny, how's it going?"

"It's going."

"I'm not kiddin' you, friend, the man's got a righteous hard-on for this project and we don't get the locations buttoned up soon all God's chilluns gonna be in serious trouble. Where the hell are you?"

"Think I've got just the spot for you."

"Oh, I love the sound of your voice. Marry me."

"It's perfect."

"Talk to me, Johnny, talk to me. We got pressure, hombre. I'm talking righteous pressure, dig?"

Pellam wondered where you learned producer-speak. Maybe it was at UCLA. He winked at Marty then said into the phone, "Lefkowitz's going to go hog wild. The dawn shots'll be so beautiful . . . Desert for miles around. I mean, you cannot *see* a goddamn tree, I mean, *see* one, unless you look west, then you'd need a telephoto, and—"

"Desert?"

"Then there's this little shack . . . You can't shoot inside—"

From the other end of the line: the silence of the universe's outer reaches. Then: "Shack?"

Pellam continued, "—but don't worry. There *is* a corral. Oh, and I thought you could move some of the interiors out there. The scene where—"

"You ragging me, John."

Pellam sounded hurt. "Ragging you? No, when I say it's perfect, it's perfect. I wouldn't—"

"You're ragging me."

Marty shouted, "Tell him about the arroyos."

"Oh, yeah, the arroyos. You know the scene where the Comanches are sneaking up on the cabin?"

"John, not funny."

Pellam said, "What do you mean?"

"It's not a Western."

"What do you mean it's not a Western?" There was a pause, while Pellam pretended to examine the script. "What do you call Arizona in 1876?"

"You'reinArizona?" The voice was a tenor car alarm. *"Theysentyouthewrongscript?"*

Pellam said, "Uh . . ."

He tried. But he couldn't keep it in a second longer. Marty, who'd heard the assistant producer's cry, had lowered his head to the counter and was shaking uncontrollably. Pellam joined him.

"You goddamn son of a bitch, Pellam," the A.P. muttered.

Pellam rocked against the side of the phone stall, immobilized with laughter, trying to catch his breath. "Sorry," he gasped.

"That . . . is . . . not . . . funny."

Though there was considerable evidence to the contrary. Pellam finally caught his breath then looked at Marty. He lost it again, quivering with laughter. After he'd calmed, Pellam managed to say, "We're in a place called Cleary. Upstate New York. It looks good. I think it'll be perfect. We've got 27 out of 51 setups but we did the principal-shoot first so it's mostly just background and establishing shots we've got left. We'll finish the snaps and get you the report in a couple days." He paused for a moment then said, "I've been looking at the script. Can I talk you into a few changes?"

"No way. It's carved in stone." Now the A.P. was laughing too, an indulgent chuckle, just to show he was a good sport and now it was time to put the joshing aside and give straight answers. "You mean it, John? It looks good?"

"It's—"

"We can't wait any longer. The big man's gonna have my balls for breakfast if we don't move fast. What were you going to say?"

"When?"

"Just now. I interrupted you."

"Just, it's a good town. It'll work." He recited slowly, "Chill out, man."

"Haw, haw."

Pellam said, "I'm gonna be serious for a minute."

"We're listening, dear."

"The script. You're not going to like this but I've been doing some doctoring, and—"

"I don't like, I don't dislike. I ignore."

"The story needs a little help."

"Forget about it. Lefty'll cut your balls off too, you even mention it."

Pellam remembered another Hollywoodism. "The thing is, it's a good property; it's not a great property."

"But it's *Lefkowitz's* property."

"Your loss," Pellam said.

"No, my ass."

"Okay. I tried . . . Oh, before I go I should mention . . ."

"What? Problem?"

"Not really a problem, I don't think. It's just finding the airfield's been tougher than we thought."

"The—"

"Marty and I are flying to London tomorrow. We'll be in Dover by five."

"Dover?"

"That's London time."

"What airfield?"

"You know, the paratrooper scene . . ."

"John, you're a prick, anybody ever tell you that?" He hung up.

He joined Marty and said, "No sense of humor."

Marty began working on the cake again.

A half hour later the rain had slowed to a fine mist and the thunderstorm had passed. The granny-dress woman, after a couple soulful glances at Pellam, was back at the salt mine – the way she phrased it to the waitress, who was herself hard at work adoring Marty.

"Let's roll," Pellam said. The men stood.

"Bye-ee," she called.

"See you later," Marty said. "Thanks for the fine service."

"Anytime," she said.

When the door closed behind them Pellam whispered, "Anytime, anyplace, any way you want it, lover doll."

"Pellam, it's not my fault I'm a stud."

"She wants you, boy. She wants you to be the father of her children. All twelve of them. Look at you, rosy cheeked, cute as a button. Oh, she'll be dreaming about you tonight."

"Hang it up, Pellam."

"Maybe," Pellam said seriously, "you should think about settling down here. Get yourself a NAPA franchise, wear a CAT hat to cover up that thinning hairline of yours, join the Elks . . ."

"You should talk, old man. That other lady checking you out in there reminded me a lot of my mother."

"They're the most experienced."

"They—"

Both Marty and Pellam stopped short, twenty feet in front of the camper.

"Jesus," Marty asked. "Wait. What is that?"

Pellam was surprised the boy couldn't figure it out but then he guessed it was like those optical illusions in science books, the ones that some people see right away and others you've got to explain it to them.

This one seemed pretty clear to Pellam. On the side of the camper, in black spray paint, were crude images of the mounds of two graves with crosses stuck in them. Scrawled beneath them was that word again. *Goodbye*.

"Oh," Marty whispered, getting it at last. "Damn."

They walked closer, then around the camper, expecting some more damage, but, no, there was none – just the artwork. They looked around the street. Deserted.

"Who was it, those kids we saw before?"

"Maybe," Pellam said.

They stood for a moment looking at the crude, feathery lines of the bad drawings. Pellam started up Main Street.

"Where're you going?" Marty asked.

"Buy us some turpentine and steel wool. Can't go driving around looking like an ad for a funeral home."

2

━━━◆◈◆━━━

Pellam said to Janine, the granny-dress woman, "You'd think they'd come up with some more money for that. It's going to represent something, it ought to have a little class."

He was looking at the tiny, overpainted black cannon, donated to the town by the Veterans of Foreign Wars. It didn't seem capable of lobbing a shell more than ten feet. They sat in the town square, where he'd been sitting, marking Polaroids, when she walked past casually and sat on the bench next to his. He'd smelled minty tea – what she'd been drinking yesterday in Marge's diner – and when he'd looked up she'd smiled at him. He'd scooted over four feet of bumpy wood and they'd struck up a conversation.

"Maybe it's valuable," Janine now said. "Looks can be deceiving."

Pellam liked her outfit today better than what she'd worn yesterday: a long skirt, boots, a big bulky-knit sweater. Her hair – in the sun you could see some red – was still parted in the middle. She was an easy forty, looking older straight-on, though she probably wasn't. That happened to a lot of these poor flower children; maybe they're limber and they live a long time, but sun and fresh air can do harsh things to your skin.

"Where's your boyish partner, with the cute little tush, the one who's probably a year or two under my limit?"

"He rented a car and went out to the hinterland, checking out some parks. We've got a lot of scenes left, so we split the troops."

She asked, "What company you work for?"

"Called Big Mountain Studios."

"Didn't they do *Night Players*? And *Ganges* . . . Oh, that was a great film. Did you go to India for that one?"

Pellam shook his head.

"Wow, do you know William Hurt? You ever meet him?"

"Saw him once in a restaurant."

"How about Willem Dafoe? Glenn Close?"

"No and no." Pellam's eyes were scanning the downtown, which almost shimmered in the heat: It was eleven a.m. The temperature was up by twenty degrees over yesterday. Indian Summer.

"Tell me about the film you're working on now."

"We don't like to give too much away."

She socked him playfully on the arm. "Excuse me? I mean, excuse me? I'm a spy? Like I'm going to sell the story to MGM?"

Pellam said, "It's called *To Sleep in a Shallow Grave*."

"Wild. Love the title. Who's in it?"

"It's not cast yet." It wasn't for location scouts to give away too much.

She said, "Come on now. I don't believe you." She tilted her head coyly and her hair fell straight across her face, leaving only her eyes exposed – like a veiled Islamic woman. "Give me a clue."

"A few supporting actors you couldn't possibly know." He sipped his coffee.

They always liked details. Who in Hollywood was playing musical beds. Which actresses had had implants. Who hit their wives. Or their husbands. Who liked boys. Who had orgies in Beverly Hills.

Some people even wanted to know about the films themselves.

He said, "It's about a woman who comes back to her home town for her father's funeral. But she finds out that he might not have been her father after all and maybe he killed the man who was her real father. It takes place in the fifties, a small town called Bolt's Crossing."

He stood up. She watched him toss the coffee carton into a trash basket painted with tulips, and she scolded, "You drink too much of that. Caffeine. Yuck. Don't you have trouble sleeping?"

"Which way's the cemetery? I want to get some more 'Roids."

"Some? . . ."

"Polaroids."

"Follow me." They turned east. As they walked along the road, Janine said, "Tell me more about the film."

"That's it for now."

She gave him a pout with her full lips. "Maybe I won't be your guide if you're not nice to me."

"Aw, I need a guide. I may never get back to civilization without one."

She grimaced dramatically and waved her arm around downtown. "Bad news, Charlie. This *is* civilization. It don't get no better than this."

They walked for a half hour and found themselves in the cemetery.

His reaction to the place was the same as on the day they'd arrived in Cleary, the day Marty had spotted the cemetery from the highway; it was perfect for the film. Tall black trees bordering a small clearing in which battered tombstones tilted at exotic angles. No big monuments, no mausoleums. Just hunks of stone, spilling right out of the forest.

Pellam pulled the camera out of his pocket, took three or four pictures. The cemetery was filled with an odd, shadowy light, which seemed to come from the underbelly of the low wispy clouds. The light accentuated contrasts: bark was blacker than in bright sun, grass and milkweed stalks paler, stone more bleached; it was white like old bones. Many of the tombstones were badly eroded. Pellam and Janine wove through the grass, toward the woods. A rusty barbed-wire fence of taut strands separated the cemetery from the underbrush.

Wait . . . What was that? Pellam stopped suddenly, stared into the trees. He was sure someone was watching him, but as he stepped to one side, the voyeur, if it was anybody at all, vanished.

Janine said, "All I'll say is, if it has Redford or Newman in it and you don't tell me I'll never speak to you again."

"It doesn't."

"I saw *Butch Cassidy* twelve times. I only saw *Let It Be* eight.

"Were you at Woodstock?"

She smiled, surprised. "Yeah, were you?"

"No. But I wanted to go. Tell me about the cemetery."

"What's to tell? Dead people buried here."

"What sort of dead people? Rich, poor, smugglers, farmers?"

She couldn't quite get a handle on what he was asking. "You mean, like what does it say about the history of the town?"

Pellam was looking at a grave.

Adam Gottlieb
1846–1899
A sailor on your ocean, Lord.

He said, "Man missed the century. Bummer. Yeah, that's basically it. The history of the place, the atmosphere."

She danced over a grave, girlish. "Can you imagine what Cleary was like a hundred years ago? Probably only five, six hundred people here, if that."

He snapped several Polaroids.

Janine took his arm and hooked it through hers. He felt the heavy pressure of her breast against his elbow. He wondered what her chest looked like. Was it dotted with freckles? Pellam really liked freckles.

They walked for a few minutes. He said, "I don't see any recent tombstones."

"Is that bad?"

"No. I'm just curious."

Janine said, "There's a new cemetery outside of town. But that's not the answer. The answer is that nobody ever dies in Cleary. They're dead already."

She now grew serious and started playing with the top of her tea carton. "First, there's something I have to tell you. I'm sort of married." She looked up. "But we're separated. We still groove okay, my old man and me, but it's not like on a physical level, you know? He's living with a bimbo runs a motorcycle repair shop near Fishkill. Her husband split too. He comes back now and then but mostly he's split."

Pellam tried to sort it out. There were two husbands, was that it? One of them kept coming back? To who?

Janine said, "Just want the facts out, you know. Like, in case you heard something . . . Well, you know how it is." She was looking at him. He felt the weight of her eyes on him, as heavy as her breasts. A response was in order.

"Sure do," he said.

This seemed to satisfy her. She kicked at some leaves. Pellam hoped she didn't want to go for a leaf fight. There was nothing worse than somebody on the threshold of middle age going zany.

"Tell me about Hollywood. The parties are pretty wild, huh?"

"I don't go to Hollywood very often."

"Isn't that where the studio's at?"

"Century City."

"Where's that?"

"Now it's office buildings. It used to be the Twentieth Century Fox back lot."

"How 'bout that! Super."

They walked back to the town square. Pellam reloaded his camera. He looked up. From three different windows, faces were staring at him. They looked away quickly. One woman paraded her six-year-old daughter past. The woman pushed the girl forward. "This is Josey," she said. Pellam grinned at the girl and kept walking.

The word had spread into all the nooks of Cleary. Somebody was going to make a Movie. David Lynch, Lawrence Kasdan, Tom Cruise, Meryl Streep, Julia Roberts had all been sighted. It would have a cast of thousands. They needed extras. They needed stuntmen. There'd be tickets to Hollywood. Union contracts. Line up for your fifteen minutes of fame.

None of the hoverers had actually asked for a part yet but Pellam was getting a hell of a lot of silent auditions.

"What does everybody do for entertainment around here," he asked, "when they're not trying to get a role in a movie?"

"We all have great fun robbing tourists blind. You sticking around till Saturday?"

"Maybe."

"Wait till you see it then. It's leaf season. Hundreds of cars, everybody gawking at trees like they were mandalas. Totally far out. They spend an incredible amount of money. I had a tea shop for a few years before the jewelry thing took off. I'd charge two dollars for a scone. A granola muffin was two and a quarter . . . They paid without blinking."

"What do you all do when you're not ripping off the *turistas*?"

She paused to consider. "Socializing. Me and my friends usually get together and hang out. Trivial Pursuit or Monopoly. Rent movies a lot. There are carnivals, parades, Future Farmers of America. Down home, middle America. The workers – I tend to think of it in terms of class; I was a Marxist once – they go in for raising kids, Kiwanis, pancake breakfasts, turkey shoots, church in any one of a number of interchangeable Protestant denominations. But we're very tolerant – both Jewish families in town are well liked."

They walked for a few minutes more. Pellam glanced at her; she was preoccupied, thinking of something that would summarize. "It's a hard place to be single."

He let that sit for a thick moment then said, "The film's got a dark side to it, violence in a small town. Any of that?"

"Oh, yeah. A lot of domestic stuff. Last year a man took a shotgun and killed his family. They found him at home, watching *Wheel of Fortune* with the bodies all around him. Then the police found a couple guys from New York City murdered not far from downtown."

"What happened?"

"Nobody's sure. They were just businessmen. Looked like robbery but who knows? Then you have your assorted drownings, car wrecks, hunting accidents. A lot of those."

Pellam took more Polaroids. "Look, they call it Main Street. Great."

"Yeah, they do. I never thought about it. Outa sight."

He paused, looked across the street into the window of the Dutchess Realty Company. The morning light fell on the storefront glass and he thought somebody else was staring at him, a blond woman. But she wasn't like the other supplicants; there was something intense and troubling about the way she studied him.

Then he decided he was just being paranoid.

Goodbye . . .

He looked away, then back. The blond voyeur was no longer there. Just like the imagined spy in the forest overlooking the cemetery. *Maybe* imagined.

Janine said, "I've gotta open the store now but, you want, sometime I can show you the only building that survived the Great Fire of 1912."

"Love to see it."

"You mean that?"

"Sure do," Pellam said.

No, we'll split the worm . . .

Pellam was walking down a side street in Cleary. The red-covered script was in his hand. He made notations, he shot 'Roids.

No, John, really . . . I insist.

He was thinking about the assignment in Mexico last month.

He and Marty had found a great jungle outside of Puerto Vallarta and after the principal photography had started, the two men had hung around and drunk mescal with the crew and watched the director waste eighty thousand feet of film (shot through a Softar filter so the flick would have that smoky soft look of a Nike or IBM commercial). The story had something to do with forgers and Swiss businessmen and skinny dark-haired women who resembled Trudie, a woman Pellam occasionally dated in L.A. (Damn, he'd forgotten to call her. It had been five days. I've gotta call. I'm going to. Definitely.)

In Mexico, Marty had spent time looking over the director of photography's shoulder – the boy wanted to be a DP himself one day. Pellam had been on plenty of sets, too many, he'd decided years ago, and so he hung out mostly in the one bar in town, which was filled not with roustabouts, like the crew in the opening scenes of *The Treasure of the Sierra Madre*, but with urban Americans on seven-night, six-day packages. Pellam avoided them like the local water and spent his time with a senior gaffer, an old bearded guy, who had two intense loves – one was antique generators and the other was emaciated brunettes.

The latter Pellam shared with him – the love for, not the Gold's Gym'd bodies themselves, since he was among the caste of mere hirelings. Oh, a pert little assistant from wardrobe or makeup might make herself available to Pellam but any woman whose name was on a Screen Actors Guild contract was off limits to the likes of location scouts and electricians.

In two weeks, the men had polished off bottle after bottle of greasy liquor, in which agave worms floated like astronauts spacewalking. They shared the worms. The last one they cut in half with Pellam's buck knife and dropped into the last shot of the granular, smoky drink. The gaffer swore it had hallucinogenic effects and muttered some mumbo jumbo as he tossed back the shot.

Pellam told him he was crazy and didn't feel anything but extremely drunk.

The movie stank but Pellam'd had a good time. For Christsake, it was Mexico. How could you lose? The final scenes (*final* scenes? Hell, the whole movie) involved more explosives and machine guns than acting but Pellam was happy to watch the liquor in the bottles sink toward the fat worms and listen to the explosive charges, which were so much quieter in real life than in the final cut of a film itself, after the sound effects were added.

Whump whump whump.

After a while, things got boring in paradise and Pellam, who maybe didn't smile a whole lot and whose eyelids didn't grow as wide as Marty's but who loved pranks, came up with some good ones. On that Mexican trip, he got a lot of mileage out of stuffed Gila monsters and latex rattlesnakes. The best was when he talked a stunt man into hanging from boots bolted to the ceiling of the director's hotel room. When the director, stoned on some powerful ganja, walked into the room, the stunt man shouted, "Man, you're on the fucking ceiling! How do you *do* that?" The director stared at him in shock, frozen like James Arness in the big ice cube in the original version of *The Thing*. The stuntman began to pass out, both from laughter and blood to the brain. Pellam recorded it on videotape and planned to send the tape to selected friends as Christmas presents.

Pellam got away with a lot. Location scouting is to the film busines what Switzerland is to war. Whatever cataclysm, betrayals and victories occur in boardrooms and on sets and casting couches, nobody has much of an opinion about scouts. Producers are thieves, actors are brain damaged, cinematographers are *artistes*, the trades are gorillas. Everybody hates the writers.

But location scouts, they're cowboys.

They deliver then they're gone.

That, or they sat on the sidelines drinking mescal, picking up script girls and trying to pick up actresses, and *then* they're gone. Nobody thinks twice about them. Pellam had had other jobs in film, and no jobs other than in film, but scouting was the only one he'd kept at for more than a couple years.

Mexico last month. Georgia last week.

Now, Cleary, New York. With clear-cheeked blonde-bait

Marty. With a busty former hippie. With a hundred squares of slick Polaroid pictures. With a cemetery.

With some people who weren't too happy to have him in town.

Goodbye . . .

He paused on a small road that led to what looked like a town park. It might have been private property, though; the lots in Cleary were massive. He thought about his place on Beverly Glen, whose lot line you could measure in inches and not end up with an unwieldy number. Pellam stopped and gazed at the property, at the huge robin's-egg-blue colonial in the middle of the beautiful yard. So, it wasn't a park at all. It was a residence. And it was for sale. The sign was stuck in the front yard.

Pellam wondered what it was like to own a house this big in a town this small. He counted windows. The place must have six or seven bedrooms. He didn't *know* five people he'd want sleeping in his house. Not all at the same time.

He started across the road. What would a house like this cost?

What was the backyard like?

He never found out.

Pellam was halfway across the road when a small gray car crested the hill, hit a patch of leaves slick as spilled oil and skidded hard. He tried to dance out of its path but a part of the car – some piece of resonant sheet metal – caught him square on the thigh.

John Pellam saw:

A sea of leaves, mostly yellow, rising to the sky. A flare of sunlight on glass. A huge oak tree spinning, the blue house turning upside down, caught in a tornado. Then someone swung the curb at him, and everything disappeared in a burst of dirty light.

"Where'd you get that scar?"

Pellam opened his eyes. Thinking only that he wanted to throw up.

He told this to the white-jacketed man standing above him, muscular, in his forties. And, as the doctor was telling him that it was normal, Pellam started to.

A bedpan appeared just in time and, while Pellam was busy with it, the doctor continued his calm monologue. "You wake up from a concussion, you always see regurgitation. I don't mean stunned but actually knocked unconscious. Yep, completely normal reaction."

He looked like a veterinarian Pellam had taken a dog to once. A standard poodle, he thought, but he couldn't remember for sure. He liked standard poodles but he didn't think he'd ever owned one. That bothered him, not remembering. Maybe he had amnesia. Or brain damage.

He groaned. After the completely normal regurgitation, he felt burning stomach muscles and a fiery throat join the agony that swelled inside his skull, a balloon that wouldn't stop expanding until the bone cracked and the pressure hissed out like steam from a burst pipe.

He took a mouthful of water, rinsed, and spit into the bedpan. There was no nurse and the doctor disappeared with the pan. He returned with a clean one and set it on the table next to Pellam.

No, it wasn't a poodle, it was a terrier. One of Trudie's he believed (Trudie, Trudie . . . had he called her?).

"That should be about it," the doctor said and didn't explain any further.

Pellam did a self-exam. He wore just his Jockey briefs under a blue cloth robe. He lifted the sheets and checked body parts in descending order of importance. The only sign of damage, apart from the bandage on his head, was a bruise on his thigh the color and shape of a mutant eggplant.

"I wouldn't drink anything for a while," the doctor said.

Pellam said he wouldn't. Then added, "I got hit by a car." He was disappointed that this was the most significant thing he could think of to say.

The doctor said, "Uh-huh." Mostly he seemed curious about the scar. It was a foot long, a gouge of glossy, indented skin across Pellam's right biceps and chest. It was a memento of the time an arms assistant got the charge instructions wrong during a car chase gag and used dynamite instead of smokeless powder in rigging the Oldsmobile Pellam was driving. When the car exploded, Pellam got an eighteen-inch auto part in the chest. The medic told him that if it'd been going straight it would've pinned him to the wall. "Lahk a stuck piyag, Pellam. You a lucky somvabitch."

"Used to do stunt work," he now said to the doctor.

"Oh, you're the movie man, huh?"

Pellam focused on him. He really looked like he should be treating fuzzy terriers and poodles and mending tipped cows.

"I'm the movie man."

"Don't do stunts anymore, I hope."

"Life's exciting enough."

"I hear you," the doctor said.

"How am I?"

The doctor said, "Nothing serious. Concussion but no cracks. You fell good – I guess because you're used to stunts. That scrape on your head is wide, it can get infected pretty easy, so keep an eye on it. I'll give you some Betadine."

"This a hospital?"

The doctor laughed. "It's got me, a mini lab, a podiatrist, an OB-GYN. If that's a hospital, this is Cleary General."

"Can I leave?"

"Nope. You'll have to stay here the night. You'll be pretty dizzy for a while. I wouldn't want you to fall. I've got plenty of magazines. *Reader's Digests*. Some *National Geographics*. Good things like that. A bible, if you're interested."

"I've got to get a message to somebody."

"There's a phone in the lobby. I can make a call for you. If you—"

"No, not a phone call. Somebody'll be waiting for me back at my camper. It's parked on Main Street." Pellam told him that Marty would be returning about six.

The doctor said, "I've got a son works at the IH plant. He's a manager. He can take some time off and leave a note on your camper door."

"Be obliged."

Pellam watched the doctor take a small chart from beside the bed and write on it.

"Who was it? Who hit me?"

The doctor kept writing.

Pellam wondered if it was a hit and run, wondered who the driver was – some hotshot, a kid, probably.

Wondered too if it *really was* an accident.

Thinking of the mural of crosses on the Winnebago.

Thinking: *Goodbye* . . .

Maybe he should call the sheriff. That'd be the smart thing to—

The doctor looked up. "She's outside."

"What?"

"She's here. She's been waiting to see you."

"Who?" Pellam asked. (Did he mean Trudie? Damn, I hope I called her.)

"The driver. The woman who hit you."

"Oh," Pellam said. "With a lawyer?"

"Just by herself."

He said, "Can I see her?"

"You want to see her?"

"I guess."

The doctor said, "Then you can see her."

Pellam's first reaction was that she was pretty but not sexy. Pert 'n' perky, he thought, discouraged. Not his type at all. A girl with a mile-wide smile.

She was maybe thirty-two, thirty-three, but looked older – something about the teased blond hair, the heavy pale makeup, the fleshy pantyhose made her seem matronly. Pellam could picture her as a Miss America contestant, with a baton, sending it sailing up into the height of the proscenium. Her face was blank when she entered the room but as soon as she was over the threshold, she grinned shy crevices around her mouth.

He was expecting: *Goshhowya'llfeelin'?*

But she didn't sound that way at all.

"Welcome to Cleary," she said in a low, sexy voice that almost made him ignore the mask of pancake makeup. She walked right up to the bed and stuck her hand out.

She saw the scar and it threw her. The facade cracked for a minute then the down-home smile returned. "Meg Torrens."

"John Pellam."

Her mouth went tight. "I don't know what to say."

Pellam knew what to *think*: Bummer. He'd done a fast inventory. A cocktail ring that wouldn't quit, wedding band, a fat rock of an engagement ring.

Pellam said to her, "Not a problem. These things happen."

(Pellam had a lawyer one time, a former flower child who'd done a pretty good job for him on a legal matter – at a time when he needed a lawyer to do a pretty good job. The ponytailed man'd been real concerned about what Pellam said in public and he'd drummed into his client's head that there were a lot of things you shouldn't say to people you might be involved with in court. It occurred to him now that he probably shouldn't have said, *Not a problem*.)

Her eyes were on his scar.

He said, "You're not responsible."

She blinked.

He touched his arm. "Not for that, I mean. I'd show you the

bruise that's got your name on it but I don't know you well enough yet."

She said, "That one looks pretty bad."

"Happened a long time ago."

"I don't think I want to know how."

"I was driving an Olds 88 and firing a machine gun out the window. Somebody shot the car with a rocket. I think it was a rocket. I'm not sure. It blew up."

She stared at him, waiting for the truth, then gave a burst of polite laugh, which faded fast. "A machine gun."

"An Uzi, I think." Pellam frowned and thought hard. "No, a MAC-10."

He nodded again. Right, a MAC-10. And a rocket. And a terrier that looked a little like a poodle. He didn't have amnesia. He looked at her. What was her name again?

"A MAC-10," he repeated.

She stared a moment more. She handed him a white plastic bag with handles on it. "Present," she said. Her cheeks were red and Pellam loved that. As much as he loved freckles he loved blushing women even more. He couldn't remember the last time he'd seen a pretty woman blushing. In L.A., all women were like Trudie; genetically incapable of it.

He opened the bag. The present wasn't wrapped but there was a bow on the box. A new Polaroid camera.

"What happened to the old one?" he asked.

"It got kind of mashed."

He laughed. "You didn't have to. The company'll pay for it."

She smiled cautiously, maybe not sure whether he meant her insurance company or his film company. What he'd meant was his company but then he figured it was all going on her tab anyway – camera, the veterinarian's bill and a little moolah for pain and suffering (the eggplant bruise would look great in court and now, thanks to her, he had a new toy to immortalize it with). He said, "Thanks."

He fiddled with the square, sleek camera, not sure what else to say. He loaded it then held the camera up suddenly and took a picture of her. She blinked and for an instant got a nervous look, as if she suspected him of gathering evidence. *Bzzzzt.* He loved that sound.

But he just looked at the picture as it developed – not quite in focus, tilted, washed out; her lids were half closed. He handed the picture to her.

"What?—"

Pellam shrugged. "A present. You can frame it."

She looked at the square. "It's awful." Then she put it into her purse and looked up at the wall, at an eye chart that must've been thirty or forty years old. She was squinting slightly and he wondered if she was giving herself an informal exam or whether she was appraising its value, picturing it in her tastefully paneled dining room she'd share with a husband rich enough to buy her the Hope Diamond's cousin for her petite finger.

She asked, "You're the man making movies?"

"Nope. I just look for locations that the studio decides they don't like."

"Just like me," she said. "I show houses to people who don't buy them."

So, not a housewife. A businesswoman person. Watch it, Pellam. Middle America ain't the same as when you left. Patronize at your own risk.

She said, "What kind of movie is it?"

"An artsy movie," he said.

"Big Mountain Studios. They're famous."

"Sort of famous," Pellam said. "How did you know the name?"

"You had this permit in the window of your trailer thing. Your Winnebago."

Pellam nodded. Wondering when – and why – she'd checked out the camper.

"When will they start shooting?"

"Three weeks, give or take."

Meg nodded. "Guess you've got lots of people asking about getting a part."

"Some, sure. They think it'd be an adventure. You want a part? I'd be—"

"Are you asking me?" She blinked in surprise.

He didn't like women who couldn't tell when he was joking.

"Everybody wants to be in movies," Pellam said, not looking at her directly, but studying her reflection in a round wall mirror. "Everybody wants to be rich. Everybody wants to be young. Everybody wants to be thin."

She – *Meg* he remembered her name (MAC-10, rocket, terrier, call Trudie, Meg, Meg, Meg) – she swallowed whatever she was going to say and instead offered: "I've got a son." Saying that seemed to make her more comfortable, established some boundaries. *Yo, men, secure the perimeter.* Pellam was getting tired of the visit. He had his present, she had her son and her husband's massive rings. Now he wanted her to leave. Meg said, "He'd love to be in a movie."

"You don't want him to be," Pellam said in a tone that said he knew.

"I don't know. He's really into California. We went to Universal Studios last year. He loved it. I did too."

"Universal Studios isn't Hollywood. Except in the most general of senses."

Meg said, "You have any kids?" Now her eyes did the heart-finger scan.

"Nope," he said.

A pause. "I think it'd be tough to have a job like yours and have kids."

"It would, true."

"Or," she said, "be married."

"Also true."

"So, you're not?"

"Divorced."

Meg nodded. He wondered if she was storing this information and, if so, in what kind of file.

"So, you just drive around and look for places to shoot movies?"

He thought for a moment and decided that described his life about as succinctly as anybody'd ever done. "Yep."

A luxuriant silence.

She handed him a piece of paper. "That's my insurance agent."

He put the slip on the bedside table, next to the bed-pan.

"My husband told me not to say anything to you . . . But, I had to come by."

(*"John, cops and insurance companies they're going to eat*

up your words like M&M's. Don't say a goddamn syllable to
the cannibals, got it?")

He told her, "These things happen."

"I hit a patch of leaves. I wasn't expecting to see somebody
in the middle of the street."

He said, "You've acted, haven't you?"

She laughed in surprise. "No. I did some modeling. Just for
a year. How could you tell?"

He said, "The way you carry yourself . . . I don't know. Just
an impression."

He felt she wanted to warm up, but was keeping the tone
conversational. "I lived in Manhattan for a while. I did some
fashion work. But I was too short to get good assignments. I
didn't like it anyway." She folded her arm across her chest and
looked for the door, seemed relieved that it was only six feet
away. "Why are you asking me these questions?"

"I always like to find out from the locals about locations I'm
scouting. It's—"

"Locals?" She tromped hard on the frown, but some of it
escaped.

He said, "I get the feeling you've lived here long enough to
give me an idea of what Cleary's really like."

Meg was grimacing. Whatever was behind the visit – Pellam
didn't have a clue what that might be – wasn't working out. On
cue, she looked at her watch. "I should go. There's someone
covering for me at the office."

"When I get out of here – they're paroling me tomorrow –
let me buy you lunch."

"No, I—"

"Not to worry," Pellam said. "I'll drive."

"Uh, I don't think that's a very good idea. I've got a lot going on. I'm very busy."

"People are busy in Cleary?"

Okay, it was a little over the line with that one. He'd forgotten you have to be real careful when you hit people in their home towns. Especially if you're from one that's a thousand times bigger than theirs. But come on, country folk, you gotta have a sense of humor.

She bristled. "Yes, people are busy in Cleary. There's more to this town than people like you'll ever see—"

"There, perfect," Pellam announced.

She frowned.

"Keep talking. You're giving me a feel for the place. That's just what I'm looking for."

"I should go."

He said, "No, you shouldn't."

"Anyway, I'm not a local. I've only lived here for—"

"Don't tell me, let me guess . . ." Pellam was feeling perverse (hell, why not? She'd run him over). "Ten years."

Her eyes flared. "What makes you think I've lived here that long?"

In for a penny, in for a pound.

"The makeup, the hair, the clothes—"

"What's wrong with—?" Her voice was high, indignant.

"Nothing. You just asked me—"

"Never mind." Meg unfolded her arms and walked to the door.

Pellam asked, "So when can we get together?"

"The word *never* comes to mind." She stepped through the doorway, gripping the knob hard then must've decided she shouldn't be slamming clinic doors and closed it silently. A second later it opened and she said to him, "And for your information, I've lived here for five years, not ten."

The door closed again, harder this time.

Ah, she'll be back.

Pellam heard her low heels tapping on the linoleum, then the grind of the front door and then nothing.

She'll be back. She's on her way now.

A car started.

She'll be back.

He heard a car strew gravel as it hit the road, then the whine of gears.

Okay, maybe not.

Bzzzzt.

Marty stuffed the moist square of the Polaroid into his pocket and squinted as he looked at a bald spot on the small mountain across a ravine. Acid rain'd eaten away at a lot of the greenery. It didn't look good at all. By the time Marty'd gone to college, schools were offering degrees in the environment. Marty could recognize acid rain.

He took four pictures, numbered them and slipped them into his pocket. All location scouts he knew used Polaroids, but Marty was an amateur photographer and would've preferred to use his old Nikkormat 35mm. The variation in the lenses – wide angle, telephoto – would give a better idea of what the scenery and locations looked like through the Panaflex movie camera. But the studio paid his salary and the studio said 'Roids.

So 'Roids were what they were going to get.

Marty wanted to be a cinematographer eventually. He knew

cameras. He liked the murmuring gears and heavy, oil-scented parts that fit together so well. He liked the perfectly ground disks of the Schneider lenses, set into their royal-blue velvet carrying cases. He liked the portable Arriflex 35mm cameras, which cameramen would carry around on sets like rocket launchers. He liked the robotic contraption of Steadicams.

He figured a couple more years of location scouting, then it would be about time for his break (a unit director would call out, "Holy Mother, the director of photography's on a bender – you, kid, get behind the Panaflex. Roll, roll, roll . . .") Until that happened, however, being a location scout would do. Especially being a location scout for John Pellam, where you tended to get a week of experience in the movie business for every day you worked.

Marty wandered back down the hill toward the rented Tempo.

Get the feel.

Marty worked hard at trying to get the feel. Pellam made him read the scripts over and over. Scripts are a bitch to read but he kept at it. Pellam would question him about a story. You gotta get the feel for it, he'd say.

The feel . . . that was the extra ten percent that Pellam – for all his bullshit and fire-me-if-you-want attitude – was always talking about. The ten percent that Pellam delivered. This was the essential lesson Marty had learned from John Pellam.

The day was getting hot. The sun was out. Marty looked at his watch. There were still thirteen locations he had to find but sun like this was too good to miss. Beer break. Marty went to the trunk of the car and took out a Miller. He opened it. He sat on the rear bumper as he flipped through the script for *Shallow*

Grave. He unbuttoned his shirt and let the sunlight fall on his tanned, skinny chest.

He liked sitting in the sun and drinking beer. He liked the country, liked the blond dry grass that hissed when he walked through it. When he was in California he usually stayed in a condo in Van Nuys, but he preferred to travel because there were no seasons in L.A. He loved fall. He wondered if there were more jobs for cinematographers in New York than in L.A.

He wondered—

The bullet hit the back of the car with a huge ringing slap a full second before he heard the rolling boom of the rifle shot. Marty jumped up, eyes wide, dropping the script, the camera and his beer. White, malty foam shot out of the gold can.

"Christ," he whispered as terror and relief oozed through his legs. All he could do was stare, openmouthed, at the hole in the car, remembering a newspaper story about a woman who was killed by a gunshot from several miles away, a hunting accident. "Christ."

He thought: that'd been four feet to the right . . .

The second shot, which he never heard, wasn't four feet to the right at all. It hit the gas tank pretty much dead center.

You could hear, as if on a soundtrack, a huge whoosh, as the flaming ball spread twenty feet in all directions.

You could hear Marty's horrific scream from the tangle of fire.

And, as the Ford burned into black metal, you could hear the honking of geese and swans, fleeing with their imperfect memory of the terrible explosion.

4

At first, Pellam thought the tragedy was his.
Leukemia. A tumor. Hodgkin's.

I'm sorry, sir. The X ray showed something else.

The doctor opened the door slowly. Pellam looked at the man's face and knew something bad was coming. The man sure had the technique down. Pellam had used it himself. When his father had died he'd been elected to break the news to a lot of people. He let the downcast eyes and endless loop of a sigh explain to them that terrible news was impending, before he said a word. The telepathic message of tragedy did a lot of the work for him.

Pellam saw this same expression in the eyes of the strong, young vet of a doctor, pausing in the doorway, looking at Pellam as if he were gazing at the last few seconds of his patient's good health.

"Evening," Pellam said.

Then he saw the deputy, a young man, similar in build to the doctor, baby-faced, crewcut, and he thought – his first fleeting thought – someone had stolen the camper. But their eyes explained too much. And at that moment, Pellam understood.

"Marty?"

The doctor looked at the deputy, who nodded.

He asked, "An accident?"

The deputy said, "I'm sorry, sir."

"What happened?" Pellam found himself breathless. The air had actually escaped from his lungs.

The deputy said, "His car caught fire. I'm sorry to have to tell you he was killed."

"Oh, God." Pellam closed his eyes. He felt an overwhelming, raw sense of loss. Images of the boy flipped through Pellam's head. Like still pictures. That was one thing about himself he'd always thought odd. For someone who worked in film, his memories were always static. Kodacolor snapshots. They never moved.

"Oh, God . . ." His voice faded. Suddenly, he thought of all the things he'd have to do. Who should he call? What should he say? There'd be hours of the grim, official business that he'd have to handle. Pellam, surrogate father to this poor young man. "What happened? A crash?"

The deputy, a boy not much older than Marty, but with that vest of self-assurance most cops seem to wear, said, "Truth be told, sir, appears he was doing some drugs. We found pot and some crack cocaine vials. He—"

"Crack? Marty? No, no, no . . ."

"We found the body next to the gas tank. We think some grass caught fire and he tried to put it out. Before he could, she blew up."

"He didn't do crack."

"Well, sir, I should tell you too that we got a call just before it happened. Couple men said they'd seen him selling some pot to a local boy. They—"

"No," Pellam spat out. "Impossible."

"They described the car pretty good, sir."

"Who was it? Who reported it?"

"An anonymous call. There was a foil package with a goodly bit of grass in it. And some crack. It was in the car. The glove compartment. It wasn't all burnt up."

Pellam lifted his hands to his face. He wondered if he was going to cry. He'd cried twice in the past ten years. Once was just after the funeral of a friend. The second time was when his ex had left. He'd been drunk on both occasions. He was sober now and he didn't think he was going to cry.

"If it's any consolation," the deputy said, "the coroner said it was fast." He looked at the doctor for confirmation that a fast death was better than a slow one.

The doctor handed him a paper cup. Inside were two pills, tiny white pills.

"They'll help you sleep."

Pellam shook his head but he didn't hand them back. He held the cup in both hands and stared at the two dots of pills, studying them carefully, noting the way the light, muted by the side of the paper cup, fell on them, how they were perfectly symmetrical, how they rested against each other – a kind of infinity symbol in three dimensions.

What Pellam couldn't tell them was: one of the things he was feeling was fury. He'd been after Marty for months to give up the pot. Pellam had done his share of controlled substances in his day, but had been shocked to find that Marty had smuggled a few nickel bags into Mexico. When Pellam had found them, he'd pulled the boy from bed, pinning him to the cold metallic sides of the camper just before dawn, demanding to know where the rest of the stash was. He owned up and handed it over to Pellam, who threw it out. Marty promised he'd abstain while they were driving together.

Would the boy have gone back on his word?

And crack? He'd never even mentioned that.

"Uhm, what?—" Pellam started to ask the deputy but his thoughts jammed. The men looked at him patiently. He remembered. "What should I do?"

The doctor said, "You don't have to do anything at all but get some rest. I still don't want you out of bed till tomorrow."

"But—"

The young deputy held teardrop-shaped sunglasses with haze-cutting yellow lenses – right out of a sixties biker movie. The sincere, well-scrubbed man hooked a thumb into a leather mesh belt and said, "The coroner's doing his report right now; we've already called the young man's family. And your film studio."

His family . . .

Hello, Mrs Jacobs. You don't know me, but I worked with your son . . . The two of us, we got our asses thrown out of a whorehouse in Nogales about three weeks ago . . .

The deputy continued, "We're making arrangements to ship the body back to Los Angeles. We figured you'd want to be traveling with him, sir, so we've booked you on the same flight. The local funeral home's agreed to transport the body to Albany airport. That'll be American Eagle flight 6733, day after tomorrow."

"If he's well enough to travel," the doctor said.

Your son, Mr Jacobs, was smoking a nugget of crack and got blown up . . .

"Of course," the deputy said. "Sure." The man leaned forward and Pellam saw a roll of dense fat encroach over the black belt of his Sam Browne harness, Vaseline-shined patent leather. The deputy said, "I don't like, you know, drugs much, sir. Especially if he was into selling them to some of our young people. But I'm truly sorry about your friend. What happened, wasn't fair. All outa proportion, you know what I mean?"

The man's battleship-gray eyes were tight with sorrow and Pellam thanked him. He looked again at the pills. The cup wasn't waxed and he found that his sweat had left fingerprints on the sides.

The doctor said, "Take those now. You need rest."

Pellam couldn't speak. He nodded.

"We'll leave you alone. You want some company or anything, my wife and I live a hundred yards up the road. There'll be someone here all night, a nurse. Just tell her and she'll get me."

"Thanks."

The men left the room. Pellam set the cup on the tabletop. He misjudged the distance and it hit the edge and fell to the floor. He heard one, or maybe both of the pills, rolling somewhere, endlessly. He didn't even look down. He lay back in bed and stared at the ceiling as the dusk turned into night and finally he slept.

The noise.

Sitting in the Winnebago, Pellam remembered the way the

boy would sit sideways in the camper's small bunk and swing his Adidas back and forth. The thud-thud, pause, thud-thud. A monotonous heartbeat.

God, it was quiet. Pellam cocked his head and couldn't hear a thing. A hum, but that was in his head. (Well, he heard Marty's voice and his laugh and the fake heartbeat of his boots but those were in his head too.) No airplane drone, no diesels. No children whooping as they played. Pellam sat in the driver's seat of the camper, looking back into the living quarters. The pain in his back was less when he sat upright. Standing was agony, unless he leaned. For some reason when he moved the pain wasn't as bad as standing still.

Ah, Marty . . .

He stood up. The tragedy tired him out more than the injuries did. He walked stiffly. He'd refused the cane the doctor recommended. There was a black scab on his head and the bruise now had some green in it.

While he still had the courage, he filled a Macy's shopping bag with the boy's belongings. He rested, sitting on the bunk in the camper, looking at the bag for a few minutes, the big brown-red logo, the white, spidery wrinkles. Pellam stood, emptied the bag and packed the contents back into his own leather suitcase, which he'd bought on Rodeo Drive eight years before, folding the boy's shirts and jeans and Jockey shorts as careful as if he were doing piece cleaning in a Beverly Hills laundry.

Then he sat and studied the suitcase for a half hour.

After he'd been released from the clinic a few hours before, the first thing he'd done was shave. He'd passed a mirror, and his face, with the uneven beard laced with gray, had shocked him. He looked like he was a badly abused 50. Then he'd called Marty's father. It had not been a good conversation. The man, a retired studio gaffer, blamed Pellam. He wasn't contemptuous, he wasn't snide, but throughout the conversation, Pellam could hear the pedal tone of suspicion – as if Pellam had supplied the drugs that had killed his son. Pellam wondered what the man looked like, what his house was like, what his relationship with Marty had been. The boy had complained about his parents a lot but most of the examples the boy cited made Pellam think: And the problem is what exactly? Marty bitched about the time they took away car privileges for a month after he'd passed out drunk in a HoJo's off the Eden's Expressway. And the time they made him go to a counselor when he went through a spell of cutting classes.

All high school stuff – bitching and moaning.

Pellam also asked to speak to Marty's mother. He felt a wave of relief when the boy's father said that wouldn't be a good idea. Then he'd hung up and lain back in the camper cot.

He clicked the heavy brass latches back and forth. The suitcase had cost him a thousand dollars.

Pellam felt the bottle of Demerol in his pocket, took it out and tossed it into one of the kitchen drawers. He needed something different. He slowly crouched down and reached into a cabinet. Out came a bottle of mescal, a quarter full, with a bloated white worm in the bottom. Pellam poured a double shot and drank the liquid down in two swallows. He coughed and felt the crackling wave from his chest up to his face and the nearly instantaneous deflating of the pain. He poured one more, smaller, and again began the slow crouch to replace the bottle. He set it in the back of the cabinet but it landed on something and fell forward. The loose cork stopper fell out and a quarter cup of liquor spilled out before he could snatch the bottle up again. "Damn." He managed to save the worm. Pellam reached in the back and felt for what the bottle had landed on. It was soft and crunched. He jerked his hand back, thinking: Rat, mouse . . .

He lookcd. Just a Baggie. He reached in and pulled it out. Filled with Marty's stash. He looked at it for a long moment then wrapped it in paper towels, which he soaked under the low-pressure water tap and wadded up. This he dropped into a brown paper bag, crumpled that up and then stepped outside and tossed the whole thing into a refuse basket.

Pellam hefted the suitcase, wheezing painfully from the effort, and left the camper. He walked stiffly through the cold autumn sunlight to the Greyhound depot, which took up a small portion of a gas station on Main Street. He paid to have the bag shipped to Marty's parents.

The clerk stroked the leather. "That's a fine suitcase."

"Yessir," Pellam said, and as it joined other luggage on a baggage cart, walked listlessly outside.

He was reminded of the last time he went hunting with his father – in his hometown, Simmons, New York, probably no more than sixty or seventy miles from where he now stood.

Walking then through the same stubbly grass he now limped over, smelling the same scent of damp foliage, bathed in the same pale cast of light. Twenty-five years ago Pellam Senior had struggled through the fields, lifting the long Browning shotgun with an effort and missing even the slowest of pheasants. Two days later the man had collapsed with the first of the heart attacks that would eventually finish him.

Pellam associated the hunting trip with his father's death.

That memory came back to him now and would not leave.

He walked slowly, favoring his left foot to ease some of the dull ache in his back. Should've taken the damn cane the doctor had offered him, he thought again.

The top of the park had been roped off by the police. A thin yellow tape that said, "Sheriff's Department," every few inches stretched from one thick rusted pipe to another. There was a chain on the ground attached to one pipe; they could have used that to bar the entrance but Pellam guessed the cops wanted the chance to use all their crime-fighting gear. He walked around the pipe and started to climb toward the summit of this hill.

Pellam, breathing hard against the pain, reached the top of the drive and stopped.

Obliterated.

He walked to the center of the parking area – what had been grass and gravel was now just a pile of rich dark earth and the surrounding mess made by the dozer, whose tread marks he'd seen on the way up but hadn't thought anything of.

Obliterated.

In the exact center – probably just where Marty's car had been – there was no trace of scorch marks, no trace of footprints, no car treads. Just a dry foamy powder of dug-up dirt like a huge round grave. He stayed here for a long time. Mostly just walking around in slow circles, listening to the birds and the whiplashing wind in the leaves; there was really nothing to see. Nothing at all.

"What happened?"

"Happened?" the deputy asked.

They were standing outside the camper, parked on Main Street. The beefy deputy looked familiar. Pellam thought he was maybe the same one who'd helped him to the clinic after his accident. (What was the driver's name? May? Mary? No, Meg. That was it. Meg.) The law enforcer stood with his arms pushed out from his body by a lot of biceps muscle. He noticed the man's .357 had rubberized combat grips. He wondered if the gun had ever been fired anywhere but on a range. This deputy also had teardrop-shaped glasses though his had lavender-tinted lenses.

"I get to where the accident was," Pellam explained, "and the ground's all plowed over."

Lavender?

"Oh, that. What it was, they figured it would be, you know, discouraging for people to see where it happened."

Discouraging? "How do you mean?"

"Wasn't my decision. I don't really know. I just heard, what with leaf season here and all, it might hurt tourist trade."

"Discouraging?" Pellam asked in exasperation.

The deputy answered in a monotone. "It was kind of unpleasant. A bad fire, you know. Blood. We get a lot of hunters too. We—"

"Then why was the tape still up?"

"Tape?"

"The police tape. That'd discourage tourists too pretty fast, you'd think."

"Oh, the tape. You're right, sir. We forgot about it. But thanks for bringing it to our attention."

"You're welcome," Pellam said. "What happened to the car?"

"Car?"

The miniature troops with needles were climbing up and down Pellam's back, working hard. He thought about the Demerol. He thought about tequila, with or without worms. The pain was bad and he was losing patience fast. "My friend's car, the one that burned?"

"Yessir?"

"I'd like to take a look at it."

"Don't think that'd be possible."

"Why not?"

Not a nick in his deputy soul. The man was a real side of beef. "Well, sir, it just wouldn't."

"I see. That explains it." The men stood facing each other, the deputy scanning the street for crime. Pellam scanning the man's face. "If you could just tell me where it might be."

"I really don't know. I just know it was hauled away after the investigation."

"You do any forensics?"

"I really—"

"Got it," Pellam said. "Never mind." They both did the street scan this time. Pellam looked back and asked, "I don't remember what the company was. Would you know?"

"Company?"

"Where my friend rented the car."

"We don't have any Avis or Hertz here. Or nearby."

"It would be more helpful to know where he *did* rent it, rather than where he didn't."

"Sillman's Garage, I think it was. Up the road a quarter mile."

"Thanks."

The deputy said, "Kleman's Funeral Home's made all the arrangements."

"Thank you, officer. Appreciate it."

"Not at all, sir. I was to L.A. once. Me and the wife went to Disneyland. You know, the real one."

"Uh-huh."

"Suspect you'll be going back for the funeral. The mayor's got an airline ticket—"

"No, I won't be going."

There must have been a flicker somewhere in the brain, but there's wasn't one in the eyes. "No?"

"I'll be staying around for a while."

"Around here?"

"That's right."

"Oh. We expected you'd be leaving."

"Yeah, well, I won't be. Now, I'd like to see the police report. And—"

"Can't do it, sir."

"What?" Pellam felt the anger popping like fire-crackers.

"That's not public record material."

"Public record material?"

"That's right, sir."

"Well, I'm not public. I was his friend."

"Sorry, sir."

"How about the coroner's report? Is that public record material too?"

"Nosir, it's not. But all it says is he died as a result of injuries caused by a fire of his own making. I'm pretty much quoting."

"Officer, someone killed my friend. There were incidents of vandalism against our camper before he was killed and . . ."

"In Cleary?"

"That's right," Pellam said.

"I don't recall you reported them."

"We didn't. I didn't think anything of them until this happened."

"Yessir. Let me ask you, you drive into any small town, the local kids probably go fooling around some with your vehicle, don't they? Pranks. That's happened before, hasn't it?"

"Sure, but—"

"There you go."

"But it's never happened the day before one of my friends is murdered."

"Murdered? Nosir. The coroner said it was accidental."

"I guess there's not much more you can tell me."

"That's right, sir." The sunglasses went back on and the big man's eyes turned a delicate shade of purple. He said, "You staying around, sir, I'd be a bit careful. Already, these couple accidents. Maybe you're kind of a bad luck fellow."

Pellam said he'd be careful, but he was thinking there was a good chance the deputy was right.

5

━━━◦◦◦◦◦━━━

Alan Lefkowitz sat in his huge, completely immaculate office, rocking back and forth in a leather desk chair, and looked out the windows, which were also huge and completely immaculate. Beneath him the traffic on Santa Monica Boulevard flowed past Century City. His eyes were on this wide road, full of nice cars, but his thoughts were solely focused on Upstate New York.

President and principal shareholder of Big Mountain Studios, Lefkowitz, 52, put in at least ten sweaty hours a day working on his film projects. A law school graduate, a successful former agent, he took continuing education classes at UCLA and USC in accounting and finance – at an age when many of his friends (well, this was Hollywood; call them *colleagues*), also producers, were delegating the hard work to underlings and spending mucho time engaged in the "Development" work (that is: thinking in Palm Springs and drinking at the Beverly Hills Hotel).

Also on the asset side of the balance sheet: Lefkowitz had integrity. He'd pretty much resisted Hollywood's strongest gravity, which pulled producers toward teenage comedies, buddy cop movies, special effects – fat science fiction and horror films. His own orbit wasn't as lofty as his favorite directors, Bergman, Fassbinder, Kurosawa and Truffaut, but in his heart he wanted to make quality films.

With film schools pumping out students who learned *cinema* (not, no, never *movies*), there was no lack of independent directors in the U.S. making wonderful, small, serious flicks. But Lefkowitz's particular talent was that he worked within the system. His films were mostly financed, and wholly distributed, by major studios, one of which he presently had a five-movie housekeeping deal with (this being one of the better gold rings in contemporary movieland). Balls, a temper and an ability to convince people that he had vision had managed to get him into bed with this huge entertainment conglomerate, which was putting up 80 percent of the money for any five pictures he wished to produce.

Good muscle tone, a beach permit for his Mercedes, and a housekeeping deal for five flicks. It didn't get much better than this. But, although he could legitimately be spending this lunch hour reflecting on his good fortune, what Lefkowitz was in fact obsessing about was New York, the Empire State, while he swung back and forth in a three-thousand-dollar leather chair.

The reason for this meditation sat in front of him on his desk (which was huge but not at all immaculate): a battered, red-covered script, marred with doodles and numbers and words. It was the first flick in the five-movie deal. A dark and lyrical film called *To Sleep in a Shallow Grave*. A picture that had no buddies, no car chases, no wisecracking teenagers, no karate fights, and not a single actor magically turned into a dog, baby or person of the opposite sex.

The property had had a strange history. The film was in turn-around – another studio had bought the script and started production. A month later, though, it had been canceled. Lefkowitz, who'd lusted to do the film ever since he'd read the book it was based on years before, immediately snatched up the rights. But buying a turn-around property meant paying a premium; he had not only to pay for the script itself but he also had to reimburse the first studio for its production expenses. So what should have been a small art film became overnight a big-budget monster.

Then a famous rule in Hollywood proved true: If anybody wants it, everybody wants it. Last week, two other studios started bidding for the film.

Loyalty in Hollywood is a moving target and Lefkowitz's studio would have sold the property out from underneath him in a minute, except that under his contract he had an absolute right to make the movie.

Absolute, that is, *provided* the film met a complicated series of production deadlines. It now seemed there was a serious possibility that these deadlines might be missed. Already the company was two weeks behind schedule and Lefkowitz knew that the studio lawyers had notified the production execs that if principal photography didn't begin in three weeks, all bets were off. Lefkowitz would be in breach, and *Shallow Grave* would disappear from his company faster than a gold chain on the streets of New York.

Lefkowitz was reflecting on this when the assistant producer, a handsome, intense thirty-year-old, walked through the door.

Since he'd been working for Lefkowitz, the young man, who'd been so eager and talked so flippantly about ball-busting when he'd accepted the job, didn't look so young anymore. He definitely wasn't as eager. And the only balls he thought about regularly were his own.

"He's calling at three," the AP announced.

Lefkowitz examined his Oyster Perpetual. Five minutes. "Tell me what happened."

The assistant producer began, "Marty—"

"Who's Marty?"

"Jacobs. Pellam's assistant."

"Okay."

"He was killed, and—"

"Jesus."

"Pellam ended up in the hospital. I'm not sure but the way the sheriff explained it they seem to be separate accidents."

"What happened to Marty?"

"The car blew up."

"Jesus. What about his family?"

"The sheriff called and he told them. I made a call for your office. You don't have to do anything, but—"

Lefkowitz said, "We'll send flowers. You know that florist, the one I mean?"

"Will do."

"I'll write a note too. How's Pellam?"

"I'm not sure. All I know is I got a message saying that he was going to be calling in at three."

"We should get mobiles in all the honey wagons. It's crazy we don't. Look into that, okay?"

"Youwant, yougot."

"Any chance we'll get sued?"

"By who?"

"Marty's family?"

"I don't know . . . But there's something I've got to tell you, Alan. It gets kind of worse."

"How could it get worse?"

"The mayor of the town where it happened? Cleary? He called. Crazy man. I'm talking PMS. They won't issue permits."

"Oh, Christ in a tree. Oh, Christ."

"It's like a real small town. They found the stuff—"

"What stuff?"

"Aw, Marty had a little grass on him. They said some crack too, but I don't think—"

"Brother," Lefkowitz whispered. He looked out at the huge, immaculate highway. He closed his eyes. "Why, why, why? . . ." He spun around and faced the AP. "Any chance we can buy our way in?"

"I tried. Thousands. I practically gave him head."

"And?"

The AP swallowed. "He called me a ghoul. Then he called me a prick. Then he hung up on me. It's cratered, Alan. The whole's project's cratered."

Lefkowitz felt numb. A moment passed. Finally he asked, "Pellam's okay, though?"

The phone rang. Both men looked at their watches. It was three. The AP said, "Why don't you ask him?"

Pellam leaned his head against the glass of the phone booth. Cleary still had booths with squeaky, two-panel doors. He looked at two initials carved into the aluminum; otherwise there was no graffiti. One set of initials looked like *JP*. He listened to the buzz of the phone ringing. He felt the vibration of the healing skin under the bandage on his temple.

Alan Lefkowitz came on the phone himself, something he had never done. No secretary. No AP. Just the soft voice of a tanned, fit, eccentric, multimillionaire producer.

"John, how are you? What happened?"

He sensed some real sympathy.

"Fine, Lefty. I'm okay." Pellam then told him in general terms about the accidents – Meg's running into him, Marty's death.

Lefkowitz said, "The permits. What happened?"

"Permits? What about them?" Pellam was squinting. No, it wasn't *JP* written on the phone booth wall. It was *JD*. Below that, in marker: *Tigers, they're number one!!!* One thing about the country: teenagers were literate. In Manhattan he'd seen a similar sign. *Debbo and Ki there the best!*

"They're not issuing permits. The mayor, or somebody. Didn't anybody tell you?"

Pellam felt the shock. He burned with a wave of sudden fever. A week's work, wasted.

Marty's death, wasted.

"I didn't hear. Did they say why?"

Lefkowitz said, "They found some shit on him. I don't know, pot or something. You guys . . ."

"Alan, Marty wasn't smoking when he died. I don't know what happened but it wasn't that. I found his stash. It hadn't been opened."

"Whatever . . . You know I don't have any choice."

"It wasn't Marty's fault." Pellam focused outside the glass

and found he was staring directly into the window of Dutchess County Realty. The awning was down and the lights inside were on. There was nobody in the office.

"Well, I'm sorry, John. But you understand."

"Sure." Then it occurred to Pellam that there were two conversations going at once. He said, "Actually, no, Alan, I don't understand. What're you talking about?"

"I've got to let you go."

"Alan, what are you saying?"

"I'm saying you're fired, John."

"What?" *Just like that?*

"I thought that little incident a few years ago would have taught you a lesson."

In a low voice Pellam said, "What the hell do you mean by that?"

"I'm back at square one, thanks to you and Marty."

"I'm telling you Marty was murdered. It was a setup."

Lefkowitz seemed distracted. "Get the wagon to the New York office. We'll have your check waiting for you."

"Just—"

Lefkowitz said, "Sorry, John. I got no room for mistakes with this project."

He hung up.

"—like that?"

The first thing Meg Torrens did when she woke up: she put her two-carat diamond ring on her index finger then lay back in bed for fifteen minutes and tried to think about nothing.

It was a form of meditation she'd read about somewhere. It cleared your mind, made you healthier, relaxed you, made you more creative. It didn't always work, but even if not, the discipline required – working with your brain like an unruly puppy – seemed helpful. Marginally helpful. *Mademoiselle* helpful. *Better Homes & Gardens* helpful.

Beside her, Keith stirred slightly. His breathing was slow.

She glanced at him, closed her eyes.

Thinking about nothing.

A bird trilled in the distance, a truck shifted gears on the grade of Lampton Road.

Nothing, nothing, nothing.

An instant before the alarm rang, she sensed it in her mind. An electronic *Bzzzzt*. Meg opened her eyes and just as the Seiko went off, reached over to tap the off button. She patted Keith on his solid shoulders. He was ten years older than Meg and had some serious businessman fat on him. But she didn't mind that. His legs and butt were thin; you could get away with a lot of belly if everything else stayed in line. He had a broad, handsome face, the face of an actor who played kindly merchants and railroad owners. His hair was dense and unruly and he forced it into shape with spray and split it with a ruler-straight part. Meg regularly talked him out of dye; she thought salt-and-pepper was sexy.

Keith reached up and squeezed her hand, muttering something. She moved closer to him, smelling the warm body sleep scent puff out from under the bellows of the sheet and comforter.

The tip-off was his wristwatch.

Keith groggily pulled the Rolex off his wrist and dropped it heavily on the bedside table. When he took off the watch she knew what was coming.

His hands began to wander.

"Honey . . ." she said, something of a protest. But let herself be pulled over to him.

They kissed. She pulled off the violet Victoria's Secret teddy he'd bought for her several months ago, offering the box shyly, as if he was worried she'd be offended.

The familiar routine began. He kissed her long, on her mouth, her chin, working downward. He lingered at her neck, taking her S-link chain in his mouth. He often did this and she wondered if the gold had a taste that he liked. Then his lips found her collarbone and he moved down toward her breasts and, slowly, slowly, to her contracted nipples.

When they made love Keith was energetic, simple, effective.

Meg was ready for him. Although from time to time she let her hands explore herself when she was taking a shower she hadn't done so since the last time they'd made love, a week ago. So now, even though it was morning, even though she wanted to bathe first, to brush her teeth, even though she didn't feel beautiful, even though she had to wake Sam in the next few minutes to get him moving in time for his schoolbus – despite all that, she felt the low kick inside her.

Meg smiled, kissed his chest and nipples, rolled him over on his back. She stroked him then moved down his belly. She felt her own passion swell when he began to grow inside her mouth.

This is what their romantic life had become – usually mornings, usually spontaneous. And Meg Torrens had no real complaints about it. True, they weren't youthfully passionate. But who is, after ten years of marriage? The compensation was that neither of them demanded too much from the other. Sex was comfortable, like browsing through antique stores or trying out new recipes. Diverting pleasures. Silent and a little anonymous. They'd learned not to intrude on each other's fantasies.

He nearly came and he held her head still. Then he sat up, rolled her over and kissed her breasts again, moved down. Licked her navel. He moved further down her trim body.

After five minutes she shuddered violently under the clever effort of his tongue and fingers. She lay gasping and smiling in the near darkness, trying to cement the moment.

Keith waited a gallant minute or two before mounting her. She held him fiercely and she moaned the way she knew he liked but was too shy to ask her for. She bit his ear. She dug nails into his back. She pressed her face against his soft, gray hair, through which a residue of sweat was building.

She curled her legs around him, she moaned again. Then, suddenly, her eyes snapped open.

The intrusion was like a slap. A spray of cold water.

No!

The memory of the sound wouldn't go away.

Bzzzzt.

She couldn't place it, but it intruded unrelentingly. It was spoiling the entire moment. She hated it.

No, no, go away, please.

Then, she remembered. At the same instant Keith gripped her furiously and squeezed the air from her lungs. She felt the contractions and the fierce tensing of his hips.

That was the intrusion – a sound.

Playing in her mind, over and over, was the satisfying whir of the film as it shot out of the man's Polaroid camera. She pictured his narrow face, she heard his voice. She saw the glossy dark scar. *A machine gun. An Oldsmobile. You've lived here how long?*

Keith rolled off. She pressed her legs together tightly and stretched. They lay together for five minutes. (Nothing, nothing, think about nothing!) Then slowly Meg sat up. A *local?* she thought angrily. He thought I was a local?

Who'd lived here *ten* years?

"Love you," Keith said.

"Me too."

She sat for a moment then saw her face in the mirror. A confused, frightened look in her eyes. She smiled at her husband and forced all thoughts of the location scout out of her mind. She swung out of bed and walked into the hall.

The bathroom was carpeted in black shag. The shower curtain was black with red roses on it and the walls were pink. (Meg couldn't decide whether the decor was eighteenth-century country or Victorian bordello.) She shook her head and tossed her light blonde hair with her fingers. It stuck out wildly in all directions from yesterday's spray and the electric curlers she set it with. It would take half an hour of diligent work to turn herself into a blond, bouffanted, real estate agent.

She fixated on the mirror. Her lips had always bothered her. They were nearly flat planes and she used two subtly different shades of lipstick to give them dimension. And, when she remembered, she would keep the bottom lip curled forward slightly. This tended to make her look more pouty than sensuous, but, in her experience, men liked pouting women as much as sexy ones.

Out of the shower, drying her thin legs and waist, Meg stepped on the scale automatically, though she'd never weighed a pound over 105 since a month after Sam was born. She combed her hair straight, pulled on her robe.

She called down the hall, "Sam, let's go, honey."

In the bedroom Keith was still in bed. He seemed asleep. As she passed he groped playfully for her butt. She slapped his hand gently then tugged at his arm. "Up, up!" she called. "The world awaits."

He groaned.

Meg walked down the stairs. She didn't put on her slippers until she stepped into the kitchen. She liked the touch of the carpet on her feet in the morning.

Fifteen minutes later, rolls were warm, coffee was hot. Meg was sipping from a heavy mug and wondering where they got the crazy names for kids' breakfast cereal when Sam came thumping down the stairs. He was his father's son in many ways. In the morning he was groggy, puffy faced, his sandy hair going at odd angles. But unlike Keith (a pudgy boy forty years ago, a pudgy man now), Sam was lean and tall.

And brilliant. This gift *was* from his father. If Meg had said prayers, she would have thanked the generic all-powerful spirit she nearly believed in that Sam had received the gene for Keith's brains, not hers.

Meg Torrens, with two years' community college, was going to be the mother of Samuel K. Torrens, Ph.D., *cum laude*.

Keith came down the stairs slowly, wearing knife-crease gray slacks, a white dress shirt, a green-and-black striped tie.

She poured coffee. He said, "Thanks, darling," and started working on a sweetroll.

They paid the premium for the *New York Times* but Keith preferred the Cleary *Leader*, which if you read it regularly would really scare the hell out of you, and make you think that Dutchess County was filled with nothing but murderers, child molesters and the mournful classmates of teenagers who'd driven the family car into trains while tanked up on their father's vodka. Today was Tuesday, publication day, and he read the thin paper hungrily, boning up on local gossip.

"Hey, Mom," Sam said, sitting forward on his chair, making valleys in his cereal. "What happens when a duck flies upside down?"

Meg knew that success as a mother, just like success as a politician, is largely dependent on cheerful insincerity. She turned to him, thought a moment, then frowned. "I have no idea. What?"

"He quacks up!" He laughed. Meg did too and wiped a bit of Smurf off his cheek. Keith grunted a laugh and ruffled the boy's hair.

Sam dodged away and shook his hair back into place. "Dad!"

Keith looked at him for a moment, an affectionate gaze, then turned back to the paper. There was a shyness about Keith, even with his wife and son, and he didn't look up as he said, "If I don't have to work, how about going to the game on Saturday?" It was as though he was afraid they'd turn him down. He added, "They're playing . . ." He looked at Meg. "Who're they playing?"

The high school team's standing and upcoming opponents were pretty much common knowledge in Cleary. Meg said, "No game this weekend, remember? It's the festival. If you're taking time off we can all go."

"Yeah!" said Sam, his voice breaking.

"Sounds good."

Meg said, "Maybe I should enter my apple butter."

Keith said slowly, "Well, sure. You could."

He and Sam looked at each other.

She said, "It wasn't *that* bad."

"It like tasted good, Mom. It really did."

"Maybe," Keith said delicately, "next time, just some food color."

"Critics." Meg turned to the *Times* classified real estate section and added up the commissions she would have made last year if she were selling houses in Scarsdale or Greenwich instead of Cleary.

At seven-thirty: the bus arrived and Meg pitched Sam his pro-wrestling lunch box. He hugged her then disappeared out the front door.

Keith said, "That guy ever call the insurance company?"

Meg asked, "What guy?"

"Your accident? That guy with the movie company."

Bzzzt.

"Oh, him. I'd forgotten about him. I don't know. I'll call Jim. Find out."

Keith looked at his watch, muttered, "Damn," and walked quickly up the stairs. He returned ten minutes later; he'd added spit-shined shoes and a navy blazer to his uniform of the day.

They brushed cheeks and he walked out the screen door. She called, "Bye, honey."

Keith said something to her and lifted his hand but she missed his words. They were obscured by a sound that started running through her head again, the whir of the Polaroid, which this time, try though she might, she could not force out of her thoughts.

6

---◆·◆·◆---

"Mr Pellam."

Pellam smiled and shook the man's hand, glancing around him.

The scene was something out of a really bad movie – one that Alan Lefkowitz wouldn't have come close to. He was in a little, close-smelling town-government office. A lumber yard calendar on the wall, a dead plant in a drought-struck flower pot, a few yellowing files, a map dated 1964. The smell of bitter old coffee, papers, musty cardboard.

And at the desk: a local pol – looking just like Oral Roberts – with a tight grin he no way in the world meant.

"You're the mayor, that correct?"

"Hank Moorhouse." Silver hair, baby-blue suit, shiny pale green shirt and striped brown and yellow tie. Jowls and chicken skin. His eyes were bloodshot. "Mayor and town magistrate. First, let me say how sorry we are about what happened to your friend. Is there anything I can do?"

Pellam discreetly studied Moorhouse's Sunday-go-to-meeting

outfit. "I'd like to see the coroner's report on my friend's death. The deputy—"

And damn if the man wasn't nodding and looking over his desk. He pulled a file out from underneath a stack of papers. "Sure thing, sir. Here you go."

Pellam opened it. On top of the report were pictures of Marty's body – taken at the scene of the fire and during the autopsy. It was like a jolt of electricity seeing those photos. He closed his eyes for a moment then glanced at Moorhouse's impassive face and shuffled the glossy pictures to the back. He read the short, badly typed report.

The cause of death was shock and loss of blood due to massive burns. There was evidence of some alcohol in the blood stream but no drugs.

"How do you figure he was killed doing drugs if the coroner didn't find any in his system?"

Moorhouse sniffed a cautious laugh. "Oh, well, that's easy. Pretty clear he was killed before he had a chance to smoke anything."

Pellam handed the file back. "I'd like to see the police report, if it's possible."

"Sorry. That's not public—"

"—record material."

Moorhouse said, "Nosir. That's correct."

"Did you consider the possibility he was murdered?"

"That's not my job, sir. The sheriff and the coroner make that determination. Tom – he's the sheriff – he's out of town for a day or so. And as for the coroner, well, what does that tell you?" Moorhouse tapped the file. "County doc seemed to think it was pretty straightforward."

Pellam asked, "What about the permits?"

Moorhouse swivelled back in his green leatherette chair. "Don't need to see me about that. Town clerk can issue them."

"He can?"

"Yep. Deer'll cost you twenty-five. Bear's protected. Geese—"

Pellam smiled. "I understand you decided not to issue obstruction permits to my movie company."

"Oh, that. True."

"Why?"

Moorhouse pulled an inch of Scotch Magic tape off a dispenser, rolled it up and began chewing it. "Your friend, if he'd got himself killed in a car crash or racing out into the street to rescue a little girl we'd put banners up and welcome your outfit to town. But the boy was smoking crack—"

"He wasn't smoking crack. He never did crack. I traveled with him for months."

"Well, we found crack vials – pot there too."

"I doubt it was his."

"Somebody walked up and dropped a foil-wrapped package full of hash in a burning car?"

"If the police found it there then, yes, that's exactly what happened."

"What'd you be suggesting, sir?"

This man, like the town deputies, was getting some serious mileage out of "sir." The word seemed to have a different meaning every time he said it.

"He couldn't have had any with him."

"And why would you be so sure?"

"I just am."

"Yessir, well, doesn't really matter. It's in our discretion to issue permits or not. We chose not to. Nothing more needs to be said. We're a self-sufficient community."

Pellam blinked, wondering what on earth that meant.

"I'm saying we don't need your movie here, sir. We don't need your Hollywood money."

"I'm not suggesting you do."

Moorhouse held his hands up. "So. That's it. There's nothing more to be said."

"I guess not."

Moorhouse's wattles stretched as he broke into a shallow smile. He opened his desk. "Now, we've got a ticket for you . . . Ha, that'd be an *airline* ticket. Not parking."

"Oh, I'm not leaving."

"You're not . . ."

"Leaving."

"Uh-huh. I see."

Pellam said, "Real pretty around here. The leaves and everything."

"We do get tourists from around the world."

Pellam said, "I can understand why."

"So, you're just going to look at some leaves for a while?"

"Well, see without those permits I'm out of a job. So may as well take a bit of a vacation."

"Vacation." The Scotch tape got chewed and the eyebrows moved a fraction of an inch closer. "That's wonderful. I'm glad our little burg made an impression on you. Uhm, one thing I'd mention, for your benefit. You've got that camper of yours. Which you can't park on the town streets two to six a.m. You'll get yourself a ticket, you do." The grin tightened. "That's parking. *Not* airline. Ha."

"And I'll bet that's enforced pretty well."

"Tom and his boys do their best."

Pellam walked to the door. He stopped. "The car?"

"Car, sir?"

Damn, gotta learn how to say that. *Sir, sir, sir, sir . . .* It seemed very Zen. Like a mantra.

"The car Marty was in. The one that burned. You still have it in custody, don't you?"

"Believe it's been sold."

"In two days?"

"Sold for scrap."

"But how?"

"Selling a car's easy, sir."

"I mean, there'll be lawsuits, won't there? There'll be some kind of investigation."

"The police investigation ended with the coroner's report. You curious, you'll have to ask the rental place."

"Obliged for your help . . ." Pellam opened the door. He turned back and nodded. "Sir."

Meg Torrens listened to the familiar squeak of her chair as she sat back. It was the oldest chair in an old office, a teacher's dark oak chair with an elaborate spring mechanism underneath a carved seat that matched no posterior she'd ever seen.

"Wex," Meg said, "I can promise you, they aren't going to go with less than R-1. This is Cleary P&Z you're talking about."

Wexell Ambler sat across from her and looked unhappily at the survey in front of him.

The midmorning lull was in full swing at Dutchess County Realty. In residential real estate evenings and Saturdays were the hectic times though that was an adjective Meg doubted could ever legitimately describe business in Cleary (No, Mr Pellam, you are one hundred percent on point there: people *aren't* busy in Cleary. Never have been, never will be). The small office, littered with three desks and unmatched chairs, scarred bookcases, an eclectic assortment of lamps, which were always illuminated because the window awning had been frozen in the down position for a year. The room was decorated with one yellowing ficus tree, some primitive paintings of houses one broker's daughter had done in grade school and a huge roll-up map of Cleary and environs, which made the town look more impressive than it ever could in person.

Ambler twisted the survey several ways and studied it. None of the positions cheered him up.

Wex Ambler was a tall man – six four. Lean. In his early fifties. He was thin on top, with a few renegade tufts of fine hair going in different directions. He had a long face and he continually reminded himself to keep his chin high; otherwise his neck flesh became a small wattle. He played golf, he jogged two miles a day and was a member of the town council. He believed (one of the few things he had in common with most of the rest of the local population) that he was the wealthiest man in Cleary. He owned Foxwood, the one apartment complex in town, and was the most successful real estate developer in this part of the county. (Real estate and death of a rich relative being the only ways people in Cleary could come by real money.)

Meg's co-broker of the day, a horsy, blond woman named Doris, was ticking off items on her to-do list with a tiny flick of a mechanical pencil. "Ah, huh," she said with each accomplishment. Meg fired a look of irritation at the self-congratulations – Doris missed it completely – and she turned back to Ambler.

"They're not . . ." Ambler searched for a word. "Progressive."

Meg laughed, her expression saying: You just figured that out about Cleary?

She knew that Ambler had told a number of people – his ex-wife, his associates, even virtual strangers – that his life goal was not to amass a huge reservoir of money. What he loved was the entrepreneurial process itself. It didn't matter what he did, as long as the challenge was there. The process held more intrigue and excitement than the capital gains did.

Still, he told her now, "The difference to me between three-quarter acre lots and two acres . . ." He looked up, calculated. ". . . is about eight million dollars. Total. For all lots."

"But that's pretax," she said seriously, frowning. She was trying to joke.

Ambler wasn't amused. "A variance'll take forever."

Meg said, "It's the best land north of the city. It's—"

"Meg," Doris interrupted her jotting. "There. That's him. Didn't squash him so bad, looks like."

She looked up and watched a thin man in jeans walk down Main Street.

"Is that? . . ." Meg asked.

"Yup," Doris said.

Ambler's eyes followed him. "Who?"

Doris turned to him with an excited face. "Didn't you hear? The man from the movie company. Meg ran into him in her car." She smiled at Meg and continued to tick away on her list.

But Ambler said, "I know. I heard. I heard you went to his hotel room."

Meg blinked. Doris's head shot up. She stopped ticking.

Ambler shook his head. "I meant his hospital room."

Meg's eyes flared. "I went to see how he was."

Doris said, "You didn't tell me that."

Meg said, "Did you hear about his partner?"

"No," Doris asked.

"The accident?" Meg continued.

"What accident?" Ambler looked at her.

"I don't know much about it. Just that he was smoking dope and it blew up. Killed him."

"My God," Doris said, "the fire in the park?"

"That was it, yeah."

Ambler said nothing. He stared out the windows.

Doris said, "Tough luck, honey. You know, Mr Ambler, last week, after those boys showed up, all Meg was talking about was trying to get an audition . . ."

"Doris," Meg barked.

Doris said to Ambler, "Meg did some modeling in Manhattan, you know. She was in *Vogue* and *Self* a couple times. *Woman's Day*."

"I think I knew that," Ambler said.

Doris continued, girlishly. "I know you were trying to get an audition, but—"

"Enough!"

"—running him over's a hell of a way to do it."

Meg mouthed *Bitch* at Doris, who blinked and retreated to her ticks.

Ambler's eyes left hers and he looked out the window, staring across the street. Meg noticed this. She zeroed in on Pellam who stood in front of Marge's, opening a Styrofoam coffee cup.

He said, "What's he doing here?"

Meg answered, "They were looking for places to shoot a movie. He's a location scout."

"No, I mean, why hasn't he left town? If his friend died . . ."

Doris said, "Well, I talked to Danny, the guy works afternoons at Marge's? He said he heard from Betty in Moorhouse's office that he's staying for a while."

"He is?" Meg and Ambler asked simultaneously.

"That's what Betty told Danny."

"So they're going to do a movie after all?" Ambler said.

Doris said, "Dunno."

Meg stared out the window, sighting on Pellam through the reversed letters. She kept her eyes there and said, "Look, Wex, I hear what you're saying but look at some of the features. It's practically flat; you're going to need zero grading. And clearing? Only a quarter of the whole package is trees and they're shallow-root pine. You don't even *have* to touch that, unless you build with leaching fields toward the trees."

"I'm not saying I don't want those plots. I'm saying I don't want two-acre zoning. If I had my way I'd want half acre."

She frowned. She said, "Why don't you just do fifty by seventy-fives? Burn out the trees and Lefrack it? Put in cinder block." There was irritation in her voice.

They both realized they'd been negotiating while they were looking out the window. They simultaneously turned to face each other. Ambler stood up. Meg frowned. She wondered if she'd offended him. He said, "I'll have to think about it."

"I've got another developer interested," Doris said.

"Who?"

"Ralph Weinberg."

"Oh. Him," Ambler said. "You'd rather sell to a . . . to someone like him?"

"His money's as good as anyone's."

Ambler was quiet for a moment. "I can't think about it now. I'm sorry."

• • •

TO SLEEP IN A SHALLOW GRAVE/ BIG MOUNTAIN STUDIOS

FADE IN:

EXTERIOR DAY, GRAVEYARD, BOLT'S CROSSING, NEW YORK

CREDITS ROLL, as we see VARIOUS ANGLES on the cemetery. Uneven tombstones of granite, chipped and broken, thumbed down by the weather. The grass is anemic, the lighting bland, ghostly, like the bones buried here.

Pellam tossed back the bourbon and bent over his typewriter.

He had stopped by the funeral home to pay for shipping Marty's casket back to L.A. but had found the charges had already been taken care of, courtesy of Alan Lefkowitz. He'd spent a few silent minutes alone with Marty in the back room of the funeral home that had arranged for the shipment. A loading dock, really. He'd wanted to say something. But could think of absolutely no words. He found a Bible in a small chapel near the room where the casket rested. He looked for three or four minutes to find a passage that he liked. Nothing applied. He put the Bible back, touched the smooth, heavy coffin, and returned to the Winnebago.

Outside, it was a windy night, and the camper rocked slightly, reminding him of a boat, though he'd only been on water once or twice in his life. Subterranean noises rose from his stomach. The dinner of ham with fruit sauce he'd eaten at the Cedar Tap wasn't sitting well.

He returned to his typewriter, a small German portable. He hammered away.

> *. . . the graveyard is on a plateau. One hill eases down to the cemetery from the crest of the piney woods. On the other side the land glides down to the river. From that point of stability you go into the town itself. An old cannon is small and over painted, just like the park benches. The storefronts are bleached out and full of antiques no one wants, hardware that no one needs. The town has managed something remarkable – absorbed fatigue and turned it into a fuel that runs a thousand small-town dreams.*

> *ANGLE: A flagpole rung by its wind-blown rope like a bell.*

> *ANGLE: A roaring 4x4 with exhaust bubbling driven by a YOUNG MAN, who grins at a TEENAGE GIRL. He's your perfect citizen of Cleary: snotty, confident, comforting as*

long as you share his race and ancestry. We FOLLOW
the truck to –

LONG ANGLE: A motorcycle coming toward us, a man
in his thirties driving slowly. There's something ominous
about him. He –

The car door outside the Winnebago startled him. He'd seen
the lights through the curtain, but, absorbed in writing, hadn't
noticed they weren't continuing around the curve and disappearing.

"Hey, Pellam, you in there? I saw the light." A woman's
voice.

He opened the door.

"Hi there," he said and let Janine in.

"I was just passing by . . . You know." She laughed and set a
shopping bag on the table. She surveyed the rooms. "Reminds
me of, know what?, an airplane."

What was that smell? It entered with her. He thought of newly
mown grass. He looked outside then shut the door and locked it.

"This is luxury," he said. "At the studio they call these honey
wagons."

"Why's that?"

"There are several theories," he said. "None of which I really
ought to go into."

"Look, I heard about your friend. I'm so sorry."

"Thank you."

"What happened?"

Pellam believed that grief, like joy, was best explained
simply. "Car accident."

"That's so sad. Terrible." She looked like she meant it and he wondered if she was going to start crying. He really hoped she wouldn't. She said, "What I was saying the other day, about Cleary? You read about car crashes every week in the *Leader*." She surveyed him and nodded toward his thigh (scary about these small-town rumors – man, they spread fast). "How're *you*?"

"Right muscle. Wrong leg. I'll be okay."

The sorrow in her voice was gone; he was grateful that she'd expressed it but hadn't overdone the emotion.

"I'll give it a massage. I studied Rolfing."

"Maybe later. It's a bit tender right now."

She studied the camper carefully. Her eyes lingered on the one decoration: A New York Film Festival poster of Abel Ganz's *Napoleon*. She kept giving faint little laughs, as each new thing she noticed surprised her.

"I heard they aren't going to do the movie here."

"True."

"But you're staying?"

"True also. I got fired."

"No! Why?"

"It's Hollywood."

"What a downer." She didn't look real down, though. She touched his arm. "I'm sorry about the movie but I'm glad about you."

He didn't respond.

She waited a few seconds then let go and looked around again. "Don't you get claustrophobic?"

"It's not bad."

"I'm not disturbing you?" Though as she said it she was

sitting down in the small dining alcove, making herself at home.

There are times to say, Yes, you are, and times to say, No, when asked that question.

He said, "No, not at all."

"I brought you some dessert."

"Dessert?"

"I remember you liked dessert. The cake at Marge's? When you picked me up? On Monday?" Her eyebrows raised with every sentence.

"I remember, yeah."

Picked her up?

"Terrible cake," he added.

"Could've warned you. My desserts aren't terrible."

She unloaded the bag. Carefully wrapped in foil was a small package. Next came a thermos, two mugs, a jar of honey.

"Tea. Herbal tea. Rosehips and lemon grass. It's very relaxing." She opened the foil. "And brownies."

"Ah, brownies." Pellam looked at them closely. Then he grinned. "Wait. Are those . . . ? They aren't really, are they?"

"Uh-huh. They're a little bitter but, hey, so's peyote, right? They're worth it, though. Man, I'll tell you . . . It's not as strong as a Thai stick, but then again you won't wake up with a cough. You have a plate?"

He dug into the cabinet. "Plastic."

"Shame on you. Disposable? What'd nature ever do to you?" Janine cut the brownies – she'd also brought a knife. He tried one. It tasted bitter and left bits of soggy vegetation in his mouth. The tea was awful but you needed it to wash the grass down.

"Honey?" She held up a jar.

"No." He sipped the weed water. He glanced at the bottle of whisky. Was tempted. But he figured that Janine might feel that making liquor was an unnatural thing to do to plants.

"Really great," he said. She'd already finished her piece of brownie. He chewed down the rest of his.

She looked at what he was typing. "You mind?" She pulled it forward and read intently. After a few minutes she gave another of her breathy, surprised laughs. "This is fantastic. It's like poetry. Is this the way they write scripts?"

"It's the way I write scripts."

"I didn't know you were a writer."

"I write scripts that nobody reads, just like . . ." He stopped himself. He was going to say, *the way you sell houses that nobody buys.* Good line, wrong woman. ". . . everybody else in Hollywood."

"I hear you. But aren't you, like, fired?"

"It's a crazy business out there," he said without explaining further.

She read a few more portions. "Damn, Pellam. Poetry."

"The movie's good but it could be a lot better. Also, Guild scale for script doctoring is obscenely high."

"Know what it reminds me of?"

Renoir? Fellini? David Lynch?

Pellam asked, "Who?"

"Kahlil Gibran."

What? He tried to smile. Wasn't he that romance poet? Pellam hadn't read him but he believed that they used his verses in Hallmark cards.

She looked at him wide-eyed. "I really, really mean that."

"Well, thanks."

"The descriptions are fantastic."

He explained, "I think the setting in a film is another lead character. Setting a scene one place instead of another will produce a totally different movie. Like casting Denzel Washington in a lead versus Wesley Snipes. Same lines, same direction, but a different film."

Kahlil Gibran?

"You write like this, why're you just a location scout?"

"Just?"

"You know what I mean."

He did know what she meant. "I like traveling around. I don't like meetings. I don't like California. I don't own a suit—"

"That sounds like you're reciting catechism."

"In nomine Zanuck, et Goldwyn, et spiritus Warner."

"Ha. There a message in this movie?"

"The advertising department will say it's about betrayal and passion. Mostly, it's a love story, I guess."

She squinted and licked honey off her reddish finger. "You guess?"

"Love's a funny thing to pin down." Pellam broke off another piece of brownie. No buzz, no tiny people stuffing cotton in the crevices of his brain. He was disappointed.

She was surveying the inside of the camper again. She opened drawers and nodded. "You don't mind, do you?" Fully prepared to keep going, he sensed, if he'd said that he did. But then she came to a cabinet and opened it. Started to pull out a couple of battered scrapbooks.

He was up fast and lifted them, gently and laughing, out of her hands.

"Oops, sorry," she said, "I'm being nosey, huh?"

Pellam smiled and put the books away.

She looked at him for a moment. "You know, I was thinking about this today. You seem awfully familiar. There's something about you . . . Have I read anything about you?"

"Me?"

Janine shook her head. "Maybe," she said seriously, "it was in a former life."

He'd heard this one before.

Sometimes they said, "You and me, I think we're soul mates."

Sometimes they just said point-blank, "Can I come with you in the camper?"

Sometimes they never said anything but looked at him with hungry, hurting eyes. That was the hardest.

Pellam said, "Past lives, huh? Maybe you were a pioneer woman and I was a cowboy." He told her the Wild Bill Hickok story.

"Holy shit, that's terrific, Pellam, a gunslinger."

"His name – I always have to set this straight – was James Butler Hickok. Not William." He blinked and looked at the brownie. It seemed to be floating in the air. He broke off another piece and ate it. "Anyway, he was a . . ." His mind stopped working for a moment. He retrieved the end of his sentence. ". . . relative. I mean, an ancestor." He added, "On my mother's side."

Janine's eyes danced with enthusiasm. She maneuvered her taut hips out of the booth and stood up. Where was she going? There weren't many options in the camper. She asked, "He was the one with the wild west show? With Annie Oakley?"

"No, no, no – that was *Buffalo* Bill. William Cody. *Wild* Bill

was a gunfighter. Fast draw and all that. Just like in the movies.
Buffalo Bill hired him for a while to be in the show but he wasn't
a very good entertainer. He was good at shooting people. That
was about it. So maybe you knew Wild Bill in a former life."

"Oh, but your former lives aren't the same as your ancestors.
But maybe you were a sheriff that Wild Bill killed and you came
back—"

"He didn't kill sheriffs. He was a scout and a federal marshal."

"Okay, then an Indian warrior he killed. Or a cattle rustler.
Maybe I was a squaw. And we've met a couple of times in the
past . . ."

Pellam lost this train of thought completely. She had disappeared into the back of the camper. He heard her voice, muffled.
"This is very comfortable." Pellam heard the bedside light click
on. "Cozy, you know."

"I guess." He was moving unsteadily toward her. He said,
"Maybe I was the lover of the wife of the cattle rustler . . ."
Pellam stopped speaking.

Janine was lounging back. Pellam found he was staring at
her breasts. She noticed his eyes and he said quickly, "Nice
pin. You make it?" He pointed to a round moon face necklace
made of sterling silver. It had a coy feminine face.

She leaned forward and held it out to him. He tried to focus
on it. "It's a bestseller at my store." Then she frowned.

"What's the matter?"

"Well, here I bring you brownies and tea, and you don't even
ask me to get comfortable."

He clicked the bedside light out. The moonlight came in
through the blinds and the cold illumination was almost as

bright as the lamp. "Sorry. What can I do to make amends?"

"You can start by helping me off with my boots."

She lifted her leg, and he took her calf, taut in the tight denim, in his left hand and gripped the heel of her boot. He looked down.

They were cowboy boots.

———◆———

7

"How many you want?" Billy asked the boy.

Before he could answer, Bobby said, "Have four."

"What's your name again?" Billy asked.

"Ned. And sure, I'll have four."

The pancake somersaulted through the air like the bone in the movie *2001*, the bone that became a space station. What the pancake became, after Bobby maneuvered the plasticized Grand Union paper plate underneath it, adjusting for the trajectory, was just more of the boy's breakfast – flapjacks, sausage, eggs and buttered toast.

"That was, you know, totally fresh," the boy said, his eyes whipping up and down, replaying the flip. Billy nodded toward his brother and said, "Nobody flips 'em like Bobby."

Another flip. Ned, a strapping, seventeen year old, was having five pancakes, it turned out, not four.

Bobby looked shy and pleased about the good review of his talent. He didn't say anything. He wiped his hands on his Kiwanis-supplied apron.

Billy and Bobby were twins. They were about the same size as the boy, a little under six feet and maybe a hundred eighty pounds. But less of them was muscle than in the kid. They were thirty-five. They wore their dark hair similarly, Carnaby look: with long bangs. A fringe came over their ears in a slight curl. They shampooed with coal tar soap and always had a medicinal smell about them. Today, they wore brown. Bobby had on a white shirt because he'd volunteered to cook at the Kiwanis Breakfast. Billy, just hanging around and helping whoever needed help, wore a beige short-sleeved shirt printed with designs that looked like chain links.

"Whatsa time?" he asked the boy, who looked at a big, gleaming watch (birthday present, Billy thought).

"Almost eleven."

"Near quitting time for us." Bobby said. He scanned the site of the breakfast – the basement of the First Presbyterian Church of Cleary – and motioned to a nearby paper-tablecloth-covered card table. "Why don't you sit over there. We'll join you."

"Well, sure," Ned said, turning his round, red-scrubbed face to where they pointed.

Bobby made himself and his brother plates of pancakes and sausage, then plastered the stacks with smears of Parkay. He added a couple extra sausages to his and poured syrup on both plates.

He called across the room to Earl Gibson, the manager of Cleary Bank & Trust and president of the Kiwanis, and asked if it was okay for them to quit and have something to eat. And Earl came by, pumped their damp hands and said, "You bet." Then he thanked them both for doing such a good job. "Whatsyer secret, Robert?"

Bobby winked at the boy and said, "What it is, they get aerated when I send 'em up."

"He makes 'em good, Mr Gibson," Ned told Earl.

Billy said, "Aunt Gee-mima, watch yo black butt. My bro Bobby's in town."

They all laughed and the twins sat down with the boy.

The twins loved to volunteer. They were Little League coaches and they worked regularly at the Cleary Boys' Club and the Future Farmers of America. Their favorite volunteering was for this, the Fall Kiwanis Pancake Breakfast, and the Jay-Cees summer barbecue and, though they weren't married and had no children, the PTA's regular potluck suppers (nothing beat the combo of food and volunteer work).

Ned was one of those teenagers that could talk easily with adults, especially adults like the twins, who knew sports and weren't too geekish to tell an occasional Polack joke or one about girls' periods or boobs. The boy's rambling monologue was up and running by the time Billy and Bobby focused on it.

"Oh, man, I heard it was like totally awesome. Sid, he's kinduva dweeb but, you know, he can be okay sometimes, he was driving by and seen the cloud."

"Cloud?" Billy asked, eating a huge mouthful of pancakes.

"Yeah. Of smoke. He goes, 'It was totally black.' I thought he was a hatter, man, really. Like I go, 'Excuse me, I mean, *excuse* me, but gas doesn't burn black.' But then I figured it must've been tires. You hear about that illegal dump over in Jersey? They had like a million tires there and they caught fire only nobody could put it out."

"Missed that," Bobby said. He frowned. "Did you hear about that?"

Billy said, "Didn't hear about it."

Ned continued. "So what is I went by the park. Stan was there and he wouldn't let us get too close. I mean, the body was gone and everything but the car – you should've seen it. Totally nuked. Awesome!"

Bobby said, "I didn't hear about any car, what happened?"

Ned said, "The guy was freebasing or doing crack. And, man, it went up like an M80. Like what *is* freebasing?"

Bobby shrugged and finished his pancakes. He took half of one off his brother's plate. "I don't know."

"What happened to the dude who was driving?" Bobby asked.

Ned said, "Torched. Like this sausage." He grinned and held it up on a white plastic fork. He put the whole link in his mouth and chewed slowly.

"He was the guy from the movie company, right?"

Ned said, "Yeah, I guess that screws up the chance of 'em making a movie in Cleary. The other one's still here, though. His buddy."

Billy said, "I'd like to be in a movie."

Ned said, "Yeah, both you guys together! I don't think I ever saw twins in a movie." He wiped up syrup with his finger and licked it off slowly. "I think it'd be totally fresh to be in a movie. Only, you know what bothers me?"

"No telling."

"Well, think about it. In a love scene, okay? Some guy's kissing Sharon Stone or Kim Bassinger or some fox, he's gotta have a hard-on, don't you think?"

Bobby said, "You'd think."

"Man, that'd be totally embarrassing. I'd try to think about making a play at second or something but I bet I'd still get a hard-on. Oh, man, what if I *came* while I was kissing her, right in front of everybody? God, I'd die."

The twins glanced at each other. Neither of them looked like they'd die under those circumstances.

Billy said, "I think it would've been fun, have a movie made here. Then go out to the mall, to the Multiplex over in Osborne, and see Main Street up there on the screen."

Ned said, "Oh, you know what'd be great? When they kiss on screen, you know, the girl's gotta kiss you whether she thinks you're a dweeb or not. It's like in the script, so what I'd do is, I'm holding her and the director says, 'Roll it,'—"

"'Action,'" Bobby offered.

"Yeah, right, 'Action,' and what I'd do is I'd tongue her so fast, bang, just like that! And she'd have to put up with it. She'd have to look like she enjoyed it."

"But then you'd get a hard-on," Billy said, "and be all embarrassed. Was there anything left of it?"

"Of what?" Ned sucked his fork.

"The car?"

"Just the metal parts. They were all twisted and burnt up but—"

"So where's that car now?" Billy asked.

Ned said, "Jimmy and me wanted to go take a look at it. It's at Sillman's garage. They're the ones that rented it to him."

Bobby said, "What you think it's worth?"

"Worth? It's pretty totaled, man. It's like nothing's left of the back half. The engine might be okay."

Bobby looked at his brother. "Maybe we should take a look at it."

"Can't hurt."

Bobby looked at the boy's empty plate. "Hey, you want any more?"

"They're closed up," Ned pointed out.

"Hell, for you, we'll open the kitchen."

"Well, just pancakes and sausages. I don't want any eggs."

"Coming right up," Bobby said just as Billy started to say the same thing.

Wexell Ambler's house was on Barlow Mountain Road just South of Cleary. The yard ran at a shallow incline down to what was called a lake on the local maps, though it was really just a pond. A hundred years ago Samuel Bingham, the Hartford insurance magnate, wanted to surprise his wife on her fortieth birthday by giving her something she didn't already own, which didn't leave many possibilities. But he noticed a low-lying spot on their seventy-acre estate and an idea occurred to him. He dug out three hundred apple trees and dammed a small stream that ran through the property.

The result was a shallow, weedy ten-acre lake, now surrounded by houses of the sort Ambler owned: half-million dollar colonials (Ambler's was the oldest, built in 1746) and contemporaries. All two-acre-plus lots. Ambler's ex-wife had landscaped the place; it was trim and simple. Pollen-dusty hemlocks, azaleas, rhododendrons, boxwood. She'd given up on tulips and annuals. ("The damn deer can find their own entrées," the woman had said shrilly.)

Standing now at the edge of this pond, Ambler whipped his fishing rod back and forth, trying to drop the tiny dot of burgundy fly into the yellow plastic hoop floating thirty feet away. Each time he'd flick the willowy rod he came close to his target but there was an uneven breeze and he was having problems compensating. Although he'd hunted all his life and fished frequently with a spinning reel he'd only been fly-fishing for a year, and learning it was hard as hell. Still, he kept at it, patient, squinting at the hoop, which looked white through his yellow-lens glasses.

The footsteps came up slowly behind him. The steps were deliberately loud (and, he decided, male); someone was walking heavier than necessary to announce himself. So he wouldn't startle Ambler.

He glanced over his shoulder at the young man. "Mark."

"Howdy, Wex."

The man wore blue jeans, a plaid jacket, a blue down vest, engineer boots. He was in his late twenties, heavy. His thin lips curved into a sincere smile. His sand-colored moustache was irritatingly meek. He had brush-cut hair, parted in the middle. Put him in a polyester suit and he'd be a model Kmart manager. He didn't look like what he was: a facilitator. Ambler didn't particularly like the young man; on the other hand, labor and accounts receivable problems at Ambler's construction company had nearly vanished since he'd hired Mark.

The boy was chewing tobacco and Ambler hoped he'd spit ugly so he could dress him down for it. But he just kept the wad in his mouth like a New York Yankee pitcher and looked happily across the lake.

"Catching anything?" Just a salutation. Snappers, snakes and algae were the only living creatures in this lake. Everybody knew that.

"Nope."

"I've asked around. Seems like it's right. About that guy."

"He's staying around."

"Yessir."

"What for?"

"Asking questions about his friend was killed."

"Goddamn."

"You don't have to worry, Wex."

"Any chance at all that somebody saw you?"

"No. I'm sure."

"How sure?"

Mark was completely patient. It was funny how calm and patient truly dangerous people could be. "No one saw me."

"When I heard the car burned up I thought it'd be destroyed."

"I wrapped the stuff in foil. It was in the glove compartment. That may have helped."

"Helped? What do you mean?"

"I don't mean helped in a good sense. I mean, that may have kept it from burning up. There was hash and some crack vials."

As if he didn't want to hear the details Ambler asked quickly, "When you called the sheriff there's no way to trace it? Maybe they could do a voice print."

"Tom doesn't have that kind of equipment, Wex. You know that. Anyway, he was out getting his haircut. I left the message with Gladys. She doesn't even know my voice. Said a couple of us had seen him."

"I shouldn't have told Moorhouse to plow the ground over."

Ambler thought of something else. "What about fingerprints?"

Mark didn't say anything, just stared at the band of colorful trees across the pond.

Ambler said, "I'm sorry. I'm sure you thought of that. I just thought Pellam would have left. It's upsetting."

The fly went wide and caught in some reeds. "Damn," Ambler said. He pulled out his complicated fishing knife, with a hook remover and scaler on it. He was going to cut his line but then thought maybe a Canada goose might get tangled. Ambler was wearing two-hundred-dollar L.L. Bean shoes. He had no idea where his wading boots were. He sighed and started walking into the lake to free the line. He felt soft muck under his shoes. Bubbles of soft air rose around his legs.

Mark said, "You want me to do that?"

Ambler said, "No."

He walked unsteadily to the weeds, unhooked the fly then returned slowly to the shore.

"I know the kind of man he is."

"Who?"

"The man from the movie company. He's not leaving till he gets some answers." Ambler sighed.

"You know him?"

"I know his *kind*," he said impatiently.

The young man looked out over the lake, squinting at a phalanx of geese coming in for a landing. It was a wistful look – as if he wished he were sighting down the barrel of a long ten-gauge shotgun, leading a bird by ten feet. "You want me to keep an eye on him?"

"Yes, I do."

A moment passed. A swan floated past. Ambler knew that

however beautiful they were they were also mean sons of bitches.

Finally Mark said, "You want me to do anything else?"

Ambler glanced at him then dropped to his knees and began to undo the tangled fishing line.

"You're the place rents cars?" Pellam asked the young man.

The kid wore dungarees and stood under a yellow Monte Carlo, which was head high on a lift. The garage had two bays and a small office, the whole place stinking of grease and gasoline and burnt coffee. Pellam's eyes watered from fumes.

"Yessir." He was changing the oil and apart from his finger-nails there didn't seem to be a fleck of grime on his body anywhere.

"That's a good trick, staying that clean."

"I don't work that hard."

Pellam yawned. He was tired. Winnebago beds are small and Janine was a big girl. Also, she was an energetic lover. A bit desperate too. It unnerved him the way she kept promising him how much she liked sex with him, how good he was. He didn't believe women were capable of that many orgasms in a two-hour period. At least not in a Winnebago bunk.

He woke up once in the middle of the night and found her crying. He'd asked her what the matter was. She said angrily he wouldn't understand. He sensed he was supposed to pry an explanation out of her but he fell asleep and woke at seven to find her foraging in the small fridge and making a huge omelette she ate out of hunger and he downed from politeness.

Pellam now asked the well-kempt garage man, "You Sillman?"

"Nosir, just work here is all."

"Is there a Sillman?"

"Yessir, but he's down in Florida."

Pellam walked to the front of the bay and looked again for the wreck. He wasn't sure he wanted to see it. It didn't matter because, although he saw a lot of decrepit cars, he didn't see any burnt wrecks.

"I understand you rented that car that got burnt up. The one the other day?"

"Oh, yeah. That was terrible, wasn't it?"

"You know what happened to the car?"

"Was here yesterday. Out back. Then she got sold."

"Sold?"

"That's right, sir. For scrap."

That *sir* again . . . Pellam asked, "Didn't anybody from the insurance company tell you not to?"

"Me?"

"Well, somebody."

"I don't know, sir. Nobody told me not to do anything. I heard that Mr Sillman settled with the boy's family. Paid 'em some good money. I heard a hundred thousand."

Man, for a town where nobody seemed in a hurry, some things got done real fast.

"Why would Sillman settle? Everybody's saying it's the boy's own fault."

"I'm not a lawyer, sir. Just a mechanic."

Pellam asked, "You know who bought it?"

"Nope."

"Who would?"

"Sillman. He's the one who sold her."

"I thought he was in Florida."

"Clearwater."

"But you said—"

"Oh, he left at noon."

"And that's all you know about it?"

"That's about it, sir."

"And Sillman'll be back when?"

"Probably next month."

"It's a stupid question but I don't suppose you know where I could reach him?"

"Clearwater's a big town."

"Stupid, like I said. A month, hm? He always take a vacation that long?"

"Oftentimes he does."

Pellam said, "This garage business . . . must do pretty well, a man can take a month off."

"You'd be surprised, sir. By the way, that's a nice camper you got yourself. You wanta fill?"

"Not today," he said.

Pellam walked over to the three men playing poker, sitting in the back of the Hudson Inn's sour-mash- and beer-scented bar. "Mind if I sit in?"

A little uncomfortable at first, this crew. Then he bought a round of Bud, in the tall bottles. Then he bought another and things loosened up. Fred was the easiest to talk to. Close to seventy, with a red, leathery face. He hadn't been a farmer, which would have been the safest guess, but had worked railroads all his life, retiring early from Amtrak ten years before. Pete – in his mid forties – ran an insurance agency from his split-level a mile outside of town. Before the first hand was dealt, Pete started hanging on everything Pellam said. Agreeing too often, nodding broadly. He'd say, "Wait!" a lot and have Pellam repeat himself, to make sure he understood what was said. The other of the foursome was Nick. Twenty-one and as blasé as anything Cleary had ever produced. He'd roll his eyes, saying, "Shee-it!" and offered a sneer of a smile that Pellam came to decide wasn't as mean as it appeared. It was just part of the topography of his face. Pellam pegged him as a searcher. A successful high school linebacker going to fat as he cast about for a career.

Fred told the others that Pellam was descended from a famous gunfighter. "Wild Bill Hickok."

Pellam closed his eyes for a moment. "Now where the hell'd you hear that?"

Fred shrugged. Pete's eyes widened another few millimeters and said, "Holy Moly." Nick said, "Bet five."

Janine, of course. It had to be Janine. "See you," Pellam said. "Raise five."

Pete said, "Hey, I saw that film. Who was in it? Jimmy Stewart? I don't remember. He was one of the best shots in the west, Wild Bill. He was your classic gunfighter. He shot . . . who was it? I don't remember. Maybe Billy the Kid. Just . . . it was incredible. See your ten. He got shot in the back . . . Oh, hey, sorry, Pellam." He looked down, blushing at his faux pas.

"Christ, Pete, I never knew the man."

"Well, you know."

Fred said, "Dealer sees your ten. Shot in the back. Hey, Pellam, that why you're sitting facing the door?"

He laughed and said, "No." He didn't tell him that the reason he'd picked this chair was so that he could look across the street into the window of Dutchess Realty Company, where Meg Torrens sat, her white blouse ill-defined but evident in the dimness of the office. He'd decided a real estate broker could give him a good run-down on the cast of characters in Cleary – and who might not want a movie made here.

"Shot in the back? Man, fucking cheap shot," said Nick, and tossed in more chips. "Call you."

They played for nearly an hour, Pellam steadily losing fifty bucks, most of it to Fred.

Pete was still staring at him in an irritatingly eager way when Fred said, "Ha, Pellam, you're a poker player. You ever get a deadman's hand?" Then turned to Nick. "You know what that is?"

"What's that? Like so awesome it blows everybody away, a royal flush?"

"That's what Wild Bill had when he got shot. Full house of aces and eights. You ever get that, Pellam?" Fred stacked up his ample inventory of battered chips.

"Not that I can recall."

Nick got up to hit the john and Pellam asked Fred and Pete, "Got a question. Say somebody had a wrecked car. Where'd they sell it for scrap around here?"

"She run at all?" Fred asked.

"Nope, just for steel."

The local men looked at each other. Pete said, "Couple places. I'd go to Stan Grodsky's yard, out on Nine."

Fred said, "He's a Polack and he'll rob you."

Pete blushed again. "He asked who'd buy wrecks. Stan buys wrecks."

Fred said to Pellam, "He'll rob you."

Pete said, "*I* got a good deal there one time."

"Says you."

"Yeah? I got me a hundred bags of Sakreet at three dollars per."

Fred said, "They were forty pounders, not sixties, and how much was solid on the bottom?"

"Not much at all."

Fred scoffed.

As Pellam wrote down the name, Fred grimaced. "There are a couple others. Bill Shecker's Army & Navy, over on 106, about three miles north of here."

Pete was thinking furiously. "Oh, there's also R&W. They're out on Nine too. That's Nine also, I mean. Not Ninety-two."

Fred nodded. "Yeah, forgot about them."

Nick returned. The table was stacked with bottles, a forest of glossy brown. The bartender cleared some away and the game resumed. Pellam watched the cards flying out from under Nick's thick hands.

They played for another twenty minutes. Then Pellam saw motion across the street. Hard to say, vague in the dusk, but it might have been a pretty blonde in a white blouse wearing too much pancake makeup and fleshy pantyhose, locking up a small-town real estate office at dusk. He looked at the three jacks in his hand and folded. He stood up.

Everyone at the table looked at him.

"I'm beat."

Fred said, "Tough work losing money."

Nick frowned. It was too early to leave. Pellam was breaking gambler protocol. "Suit yourself."

"Maybe sit in tomorrow."

Pete said, "Come by sometime. Anytime. I'd like to get your opinion on what we were talking about before. You know."

Pellam had no clue. "Sure thing. Evening, gentlemen."

By the time he got to the sidewalk Meg had finished locking the door and was moving toward her car.

He felt a presence at his side. It startled him. Someone took his arm.

Janine kissed his neck. "It's Cecil B." She squeezed his biceps into her breast, "I just closed up shop and was going to stop by your camper and say hi. How are you, darling?"

"Doing good," Pellam said, forcing himself not to look toward Meg's receding form.

She squeezed his thigh, mindful of the bruise, and said, "You don't look as sore as last night." A sly grin. "I was thinking, love, you still haven't seen my house. Come by and I'll make you dinner. I'll even cook meat, you want."

"How about a rain check? I've got to send a package off to my studio. I'll be working all night."

"I've got an awareness group tomorrow and women's crisis intervention the day after. Maybe I can . . . Oh, hell, then my old man's coming by. He's bringing his new cycle over to show me . . ." She stood back and examined his face. "Hey, you're not jealous, are you?"

"Not a bit."

"That's a good boy." She held his eyes in a vice grip, then leaned forward suddenly and kissed his mouth. Hers was partly open. He recoiled for an instant in surprise, then returned the kiss.

Janine said, "Then the apple festival's on Saturday and I'm working a booth. How would Sunday be?"

"Sure. Good."

Where was Meg? He'd lost her. Goddamn, why'd she worn a black jacket? He couldn't see her. He looked back at Janine, who was saying, "You better not get cramps anywhere but in your writing hand." She punched him playfully on the jaw, though bone connected with bone and he blinked. She said, "And you better not stand me up. Mama doesn't like to be stood up."

"Yes, dear." He smiled and stood hard on the sarcasm.

Not far away Meg's Toyota fired up. He heard the bubble of the exhaust and saw the gray car back out of its stall. He said, "Well, much as I hate it, better go do some work. Sunday, then?"

"I close the shop at four. Why don't I come by the camper after? We'll drive home together. How's that?"

"Sounds great."

He kissed her cheek, broke away. As he started toward the Toyota he saw the little car speed away. The brake lights flashed as it made a fast turn and then was gone.

"Damn."

Pellam slowed his walk. Stopped and headed back toward the camper.

Thinking about junkyards.

He walked to the end of the deserted block and turned the corner onto the side street where the Winnebago was parked.

Thinking about getting something to eat.

Thinking about—

He nearly walked into the car. The little gray Toyota, idling at the curbside.

When he put his hands on the roof and bent down to the window, where she sat holding the wheel in both hands, staring straight ahead, she said, "You're alone."

"Nope. I'm with you."

"I thought you maybe had a date."

"Date?"

"Weren't you walking with . . ." She debated and the catty side won. ". . . Ms 1969?"

"Business," he said.

"Ah. Business."

Pellam asked, "How about a drink?"

He knew she was going to say no but he was curious what form it would take. There were a thousand different ways a woman says no to a man and they all have different meaning.

"I can't. I'm going out with the girls tonight. Bridge."

"How about poker? I can get us into a game up the street."

She laughed. A moment passed. "I wanted to say I was sorry about your friend. I heard about the accident."

"Thank you."

"I also wanted to apologize."

He cocked an eyebrow toward her, and she added. "For the other day. In the hospital."

"Naw. I was out of line," Pellam said. "I hate hospitals. They put me in a bad mood."

"No . . ." She studied the tachometer. "I was rude."

A hotrod car went past, exhaust popping as it slowed for a stop sign, then took off again.

She said, "There's something else."

He smiled. "Is there?"

Meg swallowed and tried to put up a shield against the flirt.

"It's kind of last minute. But you interested in coming over for dinner?"

"You cook like you drive?"

She blinked and tried to think of a comeback. He could see her thoughts racing. But she decided not to play the wittiest-comeback game. "About eight. That's extremely fashionably late around these parts. In fact, it's about bedtime."

"I'll bring some wine."

"No, you don't have to."

"No bother."

Meg gave him directions. He memorized them and repeated them out loud. He said, "See you then," grinning. She gunned the engine. He stepped back and she spun the car into the intersection, scattering gravel. She'd kept it in gear, the clutch depressed, while they'd talked. Planning a fast getaway.

Meg glanced back and, unsmiling, waved. She drove into the darkness.

Meg Torrens, mixing fresh dill weed into sour cream, heard her husband upstairs, moving slowly.

Keith Torrens liked to dress for dinner.

He'd be laying out his clothes on the bed. He'd picked that up from some episode of *Masterpiece Theater*. Almost anybody else in Cleary mentioned that they are going to dress for dinner, it'd make them sound like an idiot. Or it'd be a joke about changing out of sweats. But Keith was a natural at that kind of formality. Meg found it charming. He was moody some and quiet. But he was a scientist. He was brilliant. His mind was different from everybody else's.

Meg liked smart men.

She liked formal men.

She liked successful men.

And Keith was that. She'd never met anyone so devoted to his own business as her husband. He'd always wanted one, a business of his own. Keith the dreamer. Even as head of research and development at Sandberg Pharmaceutical outside of Poughkeepsie (not a job to shake a stick at, she'd reminded him on the dozens of occasions when he wanted impetuously to quit), he'd obsessed about being an entrepreneur.

At first he hadn't been sure how to go about it. First, he'd considered a consulting firm. But that smacked of laid-off middle management. Then he considered for-hire research laboratory. But that was pretty much for losers and academics and – more troublesome – it wouldn't give Keith the income he wanted as badly as he wanted his name on a corporate office.

Then one day, two years ago, he came home and announced he was going to do it.

"Do it?" Meg had asked uneasily.

"I'm quitting."

"We've been through this a dozen times," she'd reminded.

"Dale's got cash."

Keith's friend from Sandberg and his intended business partner.

"How much cash?" Meg had inquired.

"Enough."

And she knew there was no deterring him.

So with a $185,000 mortgage, a son destined for MIT and a wife who in a good year made twelve thousand in commissions, Keith took the plunge.

In a whirlwind of eighty-hour weeks, Keith, Dale and their lawyer bought their way out of stiff noncompete contracts with Sandberg, and opened a company.

It hurt her some that he wouldn't let her in on the deal. Not that she wanted to have anything to do with the technical part, of course: setting up the factory, the financing, hiring employees.

She knew she wasn't smart in those ways. But Meg thought she was a pretty good broker and when Keith bought property through another realtor it really stung. Why, one night she'd even taken a phone message from the bastard, a competitor.

Another broker!

"Honey," she'd said, "that's what I do for a living. Why didn't you ask me?"

And he'd looked at her, surprised, and then forlorn. She could see that he hadn't even thought about using her. He'd confessed that he'd blown it. He'd apologized, looking miserable. Like a boy who'd forgotten Mother's Day. Oozing contrition. She'd smiled and forgiven him.

Brilliant. But sometimes he just didn't *think*. That was so peculiar. How could that be?

Sam wheeled through the kitchen. "Hey, Mom, you know why the dinosaurs went extinct? An asteroid crashed into the earth and this poison gas killed them all." He sniffed the dip. "Yuck." He vanished.

Did that really happen? How could all the animals on an entire planet get killed at once? Did we have to start over again in evolution? Maybe civilization would be millions of years more advanced if not for a single asteroid . . .

Meg filled the dip bowl and set out crackers like flower petals on the plate. She finished setting the table and wandered through the downstairs rooms.

She'd decorated the house herself. Laura Ashley wallpaper – tiny flowers like an airbrushed spray of blue. A three-inch border of burgundy paper around the walls, below carved molding. Braided rugs. Most of the antiques had been bought on a single occasion, at an auction in Vermont. Country rustic some of them, painted and distressed, and a lot of Victorian. (And a whorehouse of a bathroom, she kept thinking. Gotta change that.) Dried flowers, wreaths, vases and doilies were everywhere. On the living room walls were photographs from the 1800s, mounted on sepia paper. She'd bought them in a local antique store for a dollar each and mounted them in old frames. She sometimes told visitors they were her ancestors and made up elaborate stories about them.

Meg dimmed the lights in the sconces and stood looking for a moment at the romantic ambience. She shook her head. She turned the lights back full and trotted up the stairs.

Keith was sitting on the bed, putting a shine on his shoes. Now he examined the loafers like a diamond cutter.

Until she began to undress. One glossy shoe dropped in his hand. He was grinning.

"Hey, boy," Meg said, "we got a guest in twenty minutes. Get that thought out of your mind."

He dropped his shoes, stepped into them, kissed her chastely. Left the bedroom. Meg tossed her clothes onto the hamper, slipped into her robe.

Do Do a Do . . .

She stepped into the bathroom.

Don't Do a Don't . . .

In the shower, her hair protected under a translucent shower cap printed with somber seagulls (a Christmas present from Sam), Meg felt the stinging water and wondered about the Don'ts for this evening.

It became a private joke, Meg's and Keith's, after she'd told him about a movie she'd seen in high school hygiene class. "Don't Do a Don't, and Do Do a Do" was the theme of the film, which warned about sexual risks in such delicate euphemisms that nobody could figure out exactly what the Don'ts were.

She decided that tonight's Don'ts were: Don't talk about the movie, about his friend's death, about Hollywood . . .

Which made her wonder why she'd invited him in the first place.

When she got out of the shower she heard the comforting sound of her husband flipping through the Moebius strip of TV channels downstairs.

She laid out a black angora sweater with a star in pearls above her left breast and black slacks with a razor crease. She sat at her dressing table. She spread the heavy foundation powder over her face and began working with blue eyeshadow. Her hand paused.

What's so Cleary about me?

Five years, not ten, Mr Pellam.

Bzzzt.

Meg walked into the bathroom and cleaned off the makeup with Ponds. From the back of the toilet, she pulled a recent *Vogue* magazine and began flipping through it.

"Hiya," John Pellam said.

In her heart, Meg knew that every man from Hollywood believed fidelity to one's wife was an idea so odd it could be a headline in the *National Enquirer*. But Pellam's weak handshake and chaste cheek kiss told her she may have found an exception.

His eyes, however, did a complicated reconnaissance of her face and she almost laughed as he tried to figure out exactly what was different about her. She could tell he decided it was the French braid of her hair.

Keith did the same scan and said, "New sweater, darling. Looks super." He'd given it to her two Christmases ago.

Pellam was wearing black jeans and a gray shirt, buttoned at the neck, without a tie, and a black sports jacket.

He was smiling steadily, looking around the house and talking to Keith. She heard her husband say, "You look like you're recovering pretty well from your little run-in with my wife, excuse the expression. Ought to be a town ordinance. Everybody *else's* got to wear crash helmets when Meg drives . . ."

"All right, buddy boy," she said, offering a wry smile, "you want to talk fenders? You want to talk body work."

Keith rolled his eyes. Said, "Okay, sometimes I run into things, true."

"You found the place okay?" she asked Pellam.

"Perfect directions."

Keith was looking out the door. "Oh, a Winnebago?" He stepped out on the porch.

"Home sweet home." To Meg, Pellam said, "Brought you a present." He handed her a small, flat bag. "Oh, yeah," he said. He added to it a paper-wrapped bottle, which turned out to be one of her favorite merlots.

Meg looked at the small bag. "What's this?"

Pellam shrugged.

She opened it and began to laugh. "Honey!" she called to Keith. Pellam cracked a grin. She held up a bumper sticker: *So many pedestrians. So little time*.

Keith laughed hard. "That's a good one, sir. That's very good." He said, "Come on. I'll show you around."

Meg glanced up the stairs. A small face was looking through the newel posts at the landing.

"Sam, come on down here."

Her son jumped down the stairs.

He walked right up to Pellam and stuck out his hand. "How do you do?"

Megan felt a burst of pride.

Pellam smiled – maybe at the formality and at the firm shake. Meg knew that childless men and women tended to think of kids as, more or less, pets. Meg had worked hard with her son. He was polite and direct. Meg said, "Meet my son, Sam. Sam, this is Mr Pellam."

Keith said, "Come on upstairs. Sam, we'll postpone your homework long enough so you can show Mr Pellam your room."

"Yeah!" the boy said in a high voice.

The male contingent of the dinner party vanished upstairs.

Meg walked into the kitchen and poured glasses of Pellam's wine for the three of them. She sipped hers and stared at the Winnebago. Should she join them or not?

No, something told her to stay here.

Ten minutes later the creak of footsteps had worked their way back to the top of the stairs. Pellam's camper was next on the tour itinerary. Sam started to burst out the door but Keith made sure he was wearing his jacket. Meg offered wine to the men. Pellam took his, nodded at her with a smile. Keith glanced at the glass but shook his head. "I'll have some later." He was a hard liquor drinker mostly. Scotch.

"Mom, I showed Mr Pellam the computer, then my burglar alarm and my metal detector . . ."

Pellam said, "He made it himself. I can't believe it."

Sam said, "Dad helped."

"But not much," Keith said.

They all moved toward the door. Keith said to Meg, "We're getting a Winnebago tour."

She said, "Dinner's ready."

"Honey," he said patiently, "it's a Winnebago." And a glance at Sam's face told her a cold dinner was worth it.

As they walked onto the porch Sam asked, "Hey, Mr Pellam, do you like bombs?"

"I've worked on a few."

"Huh?"

"Movies."

Meg laughed.

Sam continued, breathlessly enthusiastic. "Sometime maybe I could show you these practice bombs. They're at this junkyard. They're really neat. Mom won't let me buy one but . . . wow, that's so neat. Can I sit in the driver's seat?"

"You can even honk the horn," Pellam told him.

"Cool."

At the dinner table, Pellam looked out over the spread of osso bucco, mashed sweet potatoes, green bean salad, broccoli. How'd she made all this in the two hours since she'd intercepted him downtown?

Sam was in bed, Keith was serving and Pellam kept looking around him. He felt as if he'd never seen a house before.

Keith adjusted his tie and lifted his wine glass. "To my wonderful wife and her superb dinner."

The conversation meandered. Washington politics, Los Angeles smog. Pellam asked Keith what he did.

"I own a little company that makes over-the-counter products. Cough syrup, aspirin, things like that."

"He's too modest," Meg said. "Keith keeps tap dancing on Bristol-Meyer's face. It's an uphill battle but he's getting there slowly."

"It's tough for us small boys. But I like the challenge. That's what's great about growing a business. The competition."

"You a corporation?"

"Uh-huh. You have to be, with all the personal injury suits now. My single biggest overhead expense after salaries is insurance."

"You have a partner?"

Silence. Meg stirred. Pellam had asked something awkward. Keith said, "Dale Meyerhoff. We worked together at a pharmaceutical company near Poughkeepsie. He died not long ago."

"Died? Oh, I'm sorry."

"Car accident," Meg offered.

Keith said, "Last year. It was quite a shock."

Pellam realized that they'd dealt with the loss a long time ago but they were uneasy now for *him* – probably worried that the reference would remind him of Marty. He said, "So you do everything, hm?"

Keith said, "I had a lot of learning to do. Dale – my partner – was sales and finance. Me, I'm just a chemist basically. A scientist. A nerd, you know."

"Studio I used to work for did a film about a chemist one time."

"Really?" Keith smiled. "Usually you just see movies about cops and monsters and private eyes."

"I guess it wasn't really a chemist. It was called *The Surrey Alchemist*. We made it in England. It had very limited distribution over here."

"Witches and sorcerers."

"Alchemists were considered scientists at the time," Pellam said. "We did a lot of research. Turning lead into gold is called base alchemy. True alchemists practice sparygia."

He noticed Meg checking out the plates, pushing bowls toward Pellam when the helpings got too close to empty. Keith seemed fascinated with the story and wasn't eating.

"Sparygia?" Meg asked.

Pellam said, "It means extracting basic properties from things, usually plants. What an alchemist does is try to find the essence of something and that essence supposedly had powers beyond just the chemical composition of the material."

Keith said, "I remember from a scientific history course I took at MIT. What's the movie about?"

"It was based on a real story. In the late 1700s, in England, there was a rich man named James Price. He was like a lot of the wealthy then. You know, dabbling at science. Maybe he was a little more than a dabbler since he got named a Fellow of the Royal Society. He was also kind of a crank. A little bizarre. He set up a lab in his home – in Surrey, out in the country. He does all this secret work then calls a meeting of his friends and fellow scientists. He brought them into his lab, where he'd set up a display – the three basic ingredients of alchemy: mercury, nitrate and sulfur—"

Keith laughed. "Hey, you know what those are?"

Meg said, "Let him finish."

Pellam said to Keith, "What?"

"A formula for a bullet. Nitrate and sulfur are in gun-powder and fulminate of mercury's in the firing cap."

Pellam laughed. "Wish I'd known that. It would've been a nice metaphor for the flick. Anyway, Price also had some other ingredients – something secret – in covered boxes. He got this crowd together and made a grand entrance. He looked awful, though. Sick and pasty, exhausted. Then he mixed a white powder with the three basic ingredients and turned them into an ingot of silver. He did the same thing with a red powder and produced gold. The metals were tested by a metalsmith and were supposedly genuine."

"Then he sold the ingredients on late-night cable TV and made a fortune," Meg said.

Keith hushed her.

Pellam continued, "But here's the interesting part. Price kept up the alchemy and made a huge amount of gold but after a few months his health began to fail. Finally, when the Society insisted he do another experiment under observation, he agreed. Three members of the Society rode to his laboratory one morning. He invited them in, set up his chemicals and drank a cup of poison. He died right in front of them – without revealing what the powders were."

Keith, tilting back his chair, then said, "What was it, a hoax? And he had to kill himself?"

"We left it up in the air. It's tough to make movies based on true stories. You have to pamper reality."

Meg laughed at this.

Keith suddenly squinted at Pellam. "You seem real familiar."

Pellam said, "Really?"

"Were you ever famous?"

Meg said, "Keith—"

Pellam said seriously, "In my mother's eyes."

Meg laughed. Keith shook his head. "It'll come to me." He squinted again in recognition but apparently the thought vanished; he began talking about his company, new product lines. Stories only a businessman would love. Pellam nodded and ground his teeth together to squash the yawns. He was pleased that Keith wasn't a movie hound and hadn't asked for one iota of Hollywood gossip. On the other hand he was a major bore. Pellam hardly listened to a word he said – until he realized Keith was talking about someone dubbed Miss Woodstock, who knew the astrological sign, as well as a few other intimate facts, of every single man in town. Meg leaned forward and with a coy smile caught Pellam's eye. He knew what she was up to and kept his eyes on Keith until she disappeared into the kitchen of dishes.

The womenfolk gone it was time to talk about serious stuff. Keith lowered his head and asked, "Have you talked to the insurance agent? About the accident?"

"Not yet. Meg gave me his name. The doctor said he'd have a bill ready for me in a couple days. He was waiting for the X-ray lab's bill."

"If you have any problems, you come to me, okay?"

"Appreciate it."

"How long you think you'll be in town?"

"Don't really know. I—"

Meg returned. "Coffee's almost ready." She sat down.

"So tell us, you married?" Meg asked.

He'd told her. In the clinic. Maybe the question was for Keith's benefit, to show that she hadn't known. It meant a bit of intimacy existed between them. Pellam's eyes swept over her dress. The pin on above her breast. She looked a lot younger today. The makeup was better. Maybe she had to wear realtor camouflage when she was selling houses.

He realized he was staring at her and still hadn't answered the question.

"Nope," he said. "Was divorced a few years ago."

"That's right. You'd mentioned that."

Oh. A bad memory. That's all.

"There's a girl I've been dating off and on. Nothing too serious. Her name's Trudie." (Damn! He'd forgotten to call. He would tomorrow. Definitely.)

A timer bonged in the kitchen. As Meg rose Pellam glanced at the pin on her dress again. Thought of Janine's pin. And her breasts. She'd had a moon. Meg was wearing a sun.

"Dessert," Meg said, walking back in from the kitchen with a tray.

Keith said, "Meg's a whiz with desserts."

She set the tray down.

"Brownies," Pellam said.

"You like brownies?" she asked.

"Can't get enough."

The beige car pulled off the highway and into an asphalt parking lot, which was slowly turning into black gravel.

Sleepy Hollow Motor Lodge.

"Here we be," Billy said.

The twins got out of the car and Bobby snagged a big bag from the backseat. "Heinekens," he said, proud he'd bought imports in Gennie Ale country.

They inhaled deeply and Bobby said, "Fall. I love it."

Billy looked at his watch. "Late."

Bobby walked past him and opened the door. Inside was an ugly square room, too hot, too brightly lit.

Billy followed him in.

"Toasty," Billy said. He opened a window.

"Fucking hot. Heh."

Neither of them really liked the hotel that much. Cheap, plastic, tacky. It reminded them of Brooklyn, where they'd been born, or Yonkers, where they'd lived until their junior years in high school, when their father had been laid off from the Stella D'Oro bakery and had moved the family up to Dutchess County. He'd bought what he said was an antiques business, but which turned out to be – to the young twins' delight – a junkyard.

They'd finished high school. Bobby, just barely, though he was captain of the rifle team. Billy, with a B average. When their father died they inherited the family's lime-green split-level and the junkyard, which they renamed after themselves, Robert and William. They'd promised each other that they'd only marry another set of twins – which didn't make room for a lot of matrimonial material in Dutchess County – so their social life was pretty limited.

They had a few other business dealings that took them to New York every couple of weeks and they were always glad to hightail it back to their house, which happened to be in the first tract of land that Wex Ambler had ever developed in Cleary. It was a nice house. Big and filled with the things they loved – dark still life paintings of dead birds and rabbits, prints of leaping fish, carved wooden statues of horses and bears, a Franklin Mint model car collection. The twin leather recliners, Sears Best, were aimed right at a huge stereo TV. Within arm's reach of Billy's chair was a Better microwave, which was perfect for heating nachos and chili during *Jeopardy* or *The Tonight Show*.

A perfect home for two boys on their own.

Exactly what this dingy hotel was not.

Billy expressed this sentiment, as he stepped on a silverfish in the bathroom.

His brother shrugged. "We don't have much choice. Can't do this at home."

"Don't mean I have to like it here."

Bobby shrugged in reluctant agreement. Then sat down on the bed and opened two beers. The twins drained them. Billy turned the TV on, grumbling that the remote was broken.

In five minutes there was a knock on the door.

Billy opened it. Ned, the boy from the pancake breakfast, stood there, in jeans, a T-shirt and a varsity football jacket.

"Ned, hey, how you doing? Come on in."

"Hey, guys, what's up?"

"Nothing yet," Bobby laughed, beating Billy to the punch by a millisecond.

Ned frowned, not getting what seemed to be a joke. "Kinda hot in here," he said.

"Yeah, a little. Funny weather."

"Hey, totally fine place here. Totally." Ned looked around.

The twins exchanged wry glances as Ned studied the brown and orange shag, the laminated brown furniture, the prints of flowers bolted to the wall. Looked like he was examining the grand ballroom of a Fifth Avenue hotel.

They cracked open more beers and turned on a rerun of the *Bill Cosby* show.

Bobby said, "He's stupid in this one. Cosby, I mean. He just mugs for the camera and counts his money. I liked him better in *I Spy*. That was some real acting."

"I never saw it," the boy said.

"On before your time. These two CIA guys. White guy, he was Robert Cummings—"

"Culp," Billy corrected.

"Robert Culp. Right. And Bill Cosby. Man, it was a good program. They knew some real shit karate."

"Course, *this* show's got Lisa Bonet," Bobby pointed out.

Billy called, "Hey, Ned, would you get a hard-on kissing Lisa Bonet?"

"I get a hard-on *looking* at Lisa Bonet."

"Hot as hell in here," Billy said. He took off his shirt and wiped sweat from his face with it. Underneath he wore a sleeveless T-shirt. "Hey, Ned, you're one strong dude. See if you can turn the heat down."

The boy pulled off his red and white jacket and dropped it on the bed. He wrestled with the radiator knob for five minutes until he was crimson-faced from the effort.

"Damn, it's frozen."

"Aw, forget it," Bobby said. "We'll just sweat." He unbuttoned his shirt to his navel – no tee underneath – and flapped it to cool himself. The twins dropped into the room's two chairs. Ned started to sit on the floor but Billy said, "Naw, take the place of honor." He nodded at the bed and Ned flopped onto the spongy mattress. Bobby handed him another beer. They watched TV for a half hour.

Bobby said, "Hey, you want to try something?"

Ned said, "I guess. I don't know."

Bobby pulled an envelope out of his pocket, a small manilla envelope. He rattled it. "Surprise."

"What's that?" the boy asked.

He opened the envelope and showed the contents to the boy.

"The hell's that?"

Inside were two dozen bits that looked like rock candy.

"It's sweet," Bobby said.

Billy gently shook the envelope until three or four spilled into the boy's hand. He lifted them and smelled.

"Don't smell like much."

"Yep."

"We're gonna eat fucking candy?"

"Sure, why not?"

Billy and Bobby each took one. The boy lifted his palm to his lips but they touched his wrist. Billy on the right, Bobby on the left. "Uh-uh. Just one at a time."

"Huh?"

"Just one."

The boy dropped the others back into the envelope. Then lifted the single crystal to his mouth. He ate it slowly.

"It *is* sweet. It's—" He stopped speaking. His eyes went wide then suddenly his lids drooped. "Man," he whispered. "This is totally fresh. Man." He brushed at his ears as if they were clogged, a dumb grin on his face. "What the fuck is this?" His words faded into a giggle. "Man. Excellent."

They knew what was happening – how the soft cotton was expanding into the crevices of his mind, the warmth, the coming feeling starting at the fingertips and flowing along the skin like a woman laying slowly, slowly down on your body, dissolving into a warm liquid, flowing, melting . . .

"You happy?" Bobby asked.

The boy giggled. "Man." He opened his mouth and inhaled as if he were tasting air.

Billy caught his brother's eye and a slight nod passed between them. Bobby closed up the envelope and slipped it into the boy's jeans pocket, where his hand lingered for a long moment.

9

The third on his list.

The R&W Trading Post on Route 9, which the poker-playing boys had been kind enough to suggest to him, was the one. The time was 9 A.M. and a faded sign promised the place was open.

Pellam parked the camper in the small lot and walked back along the shoulder, which was gravelly and strewn with flattened Bud cans and cello wrappers from junk food. Occasional cars and pickups zipped past and he felt the snap of their slipstream.

The Trading Post stretched away behind a gray, broken stockade fence, which was decorated with some of the artifacts that were waiting to be traded: A rusted Mobil gas sign, a blackface jockey hitching post, a cracked wagon wheel, a whiskey aging barrel, an antique wheelbarrow, a dozen hubcaps, a bent plow, a greasy treadle sewing machine mechanism. If R&W had put the premier items here in the window Pellam wasn't too eager to see what lay behind the fence.

But that didn't interest him anyway. What had caught his attention was what rested at the far end of the lot, where the chain-link gate opened onto the secrets of the Trading Post: the rental car responsible for Marty's death.

There was a small shack in front of the fence. It leaned to the left at a serious angle, like a Dogpatch residence. When Pellam knocked no one answered. He strolled over to the jetsam of the car.

The wreck was scary, the way bad ones always are – seeing the best Detroit can do, no longer glossy and hard, but twisted, with stretch marks deep in the steel. The front half was pretty much intact but in the back the paint was all blistered or missing and it was filled with black, melted plastic. Pellam could see the gas tank had blown up. The metal had bent outward like foil. Inside of the car nothing remained of the seats except springs and one or two black tufts of upholstery, sour as burnt hair.

Then he found the holes.

At first, he wasn't sure – there were so many perforations in the car. Parts where the metal had burned clean through, dents and triangular wounds where shrapnel from the tank had fired outward. But, crouching down, studying the metal, he found two holes that were rounder than the others, about a third of an inch in diameter. Just the size of a .30 or .303 bullet – which wasn't to say that some hunters or kids hadn't left the holes there after they found the wreck (Pellam himself had spent a number of lovely, clandestine afternoons playing Bonnie and Clyde with his father's Colt .45 automatic and an abandoned 1954 Chevy pickup). But still—

"Help you?"

Pellam rose slowly and turned.

The man was in his thirties, rounding in the belly, wearing overalls and a cowboy hat. He had a moonish face and weird bangs.

"Howdy," Pellam offered.

"To yourself," the man said, grinning. His hands were slick with grease and he wiped them ineffectually with a wad of paper towels.

"This your place?"

"Yep. I'm the R of R&W. Robert. Well, Bobby I go by."

"Got a lot of interesting stuff here, Bobby."

"Yep. Used to be all Army-Navy but surplus ain't what it used to be."

"That a fact?" Pellam said.

"You don't get the deals you used to. My daddy, owned the place before us, he'd buy some all-right from Uncle Sam. Compasses, Jeep parts, tires, clothes. World War Two, you know. Bayonets, Garands, M-1s. Originals, I'm talking. I'm talking creosote and oil paper."

The man's eyes strayed to the wreck. "I got a better set of wheels, you're interested."

"Nope, just happened to notice it."

"I bought it from a garage over in Cleary. A hundred bucks. There'll be something under the hood I'm thinking I can salvage, then sell 'er to somebody for scrap. Could clear three hundred . . . But if you're not after a vehicle what would you be looking for?"

"Just sight-seeing."

"You're not from around here," Bobby said, "but your, you know, accent. Sounds familiar."

"Born over in Simmons. Only about fifty miles away."

"Got a cousin lives there." The man walked back toward the shack. "You need any help, just holler. I don't mark prices on nothing, too much trouble but you see something you take a liking to we'll work something out. I'll listen to any reasonable offer."

"Keep that in mind."

"You price stuff too high," Bobby explained, "people just aren't going to buy it. Never make money unless you make a sale."

"Good philosophy."

This time it was the sheriff himself.

Pellam hadn't even set foot on the asphalt of Main Street before the man was next to him. He smelled of Old Spice or some kind of drugstore aftershave. Unlike the deputies he was tall and thin, like a hickory limb. He wasn't wearing any *Cool-Hand Luke* law enforcer sunglasses either.

"How you doing today, sir?"

Sir, again.

He was wearing that smile, that indescribable smile the whole constabulary seemed to have. Like Moonies.

Pellam stepped out of the camper and answered, "Not bad. How 'bout yourself?"

"Getting by. Hectic this time of year. Crazy, all these people come looking at colored leaves. I don't get it myself. I'm thinking maybe we should open a travel agency here, take tours of people into Manhattan to look at all the concrete and spotlights."

Pellam grinned back.

"Name's Tom Sherman." They shook hands.

"Guess you know me," Pellam said.

"Yessir, I do."

"You're back in town now," Pellam pointed out. "I heard you were away."

"Some personal business. How you feeling, sir, after your little accident?"

"Stiff is all."

"Wanted to let you know, we probably wouldn't be inclined to cite Mrs Torrens for anything. Unless you were thinking of filing a complaint . . ."

Pellam was shaking his head. "No. She's taken care of the medical bills. I'm not looking to make a profit."

"Well, I think that's fair, sir. You don't see much of that. I was reading in *TIME* about people suing people over all sorts of things. This woman – I saw this on TV – *Sixty Minutes* maybe, I don't recall. This woman, what she did was she opened this package of cereal and there was a dead mouse inside and she sued the company and got, I don't know, a half million dollars. She didn't eat it or anything. She just looked at it. She said she had dreams about mice for a year. That a crock, or what?"

"Uh-huh. Say, Sheriff, there's something I wanted to talk to you about."

"What's that?"

"I saw the car my friend was in."

"Your friend? Oh, right – the car got itself blowed up."

"There were two bullet holes in it."

"Bullet holes?" Not one strand of lean muscle in his cheek changed position. "I doubt that, sir."

"I've hunted since I was twelve," Pellam said.

"We went over it real careful and we didn't find any sign of nothing a'tall."

"Two," Pellam said, "by the gas tank."

His face still didn't budge. "Oh, you mean, in the back. Those the holes in the back about three, four feet apart?"

Pellam said, "Believe they were."

The sheriff nodded. "Firemen."

"What?"

"When they got there, the car was still on fire and the trunk was closed. They used this pike, I don't exactly know what it is, a big rod kind of thing with a hook on it to pop the trunk. They do that with a burning car. Open it up as much as they can. They got a lot of good equipment. Always using the Jaws of Life to cut people out of wrecks."

"Oh."

"Where'd you happen to run across this car, sir?"

"Saw it out by the highway. At the junkyard a mile outside of town."

The sheriff looked down at his feet, shoes expertly polished with more Vaseline. "Uh, one of the things I was looking for you for – I wanted to mention: it might not be such a good idea, you doing what you're doing here."

Pellam said, "What would that be?"

"You know, I get the feeling that you don't like the fact your friend got himself killed doing drugs and you're trying to show something else happened."

"Investigation was pretty fast."

"Pardon?"

"The coroner's inquest, your investigation. All happened pretty fast."

The impassive, sunglass-less face nodding slowly. "Maybe you'd be used to city police work. We don't have a thousand homicides a year in Cleary, sir. We get a crime, or an accident, and we take care of it quick."

"I appreciate that. But I doubt my friend was doing drugs . . ."

"Mr Pellam, we don't have an evidence room, like you see on TV, you know. But we have this file cabinet and sitting inside it right now is a foil package with what must be a couple ounces of hashish. Now, I—"

"But—"

"Let me finish, sir. I was in Nam. I've done some smoking in my day. And I should add I've got no axe to grind with movie people or with you or your friend. We found the dope, we found a lighter, we found a brush fire. You yourself can see where the evidence points."

"I've never heard of a car getting blown up because somebody was smoking nearby."

"Well, you think about that Negro comedian a few years ago, set himself on fire."

"Marty wouldn't be freebasing coke in a state park at noon."

A faint smile. "Oh? Then when would he be?"

Pellam leaned forward. He spotted a cautious flicker in the sheriff's eyes. "Listen, Sheriff, let me line it up for you. And you tell me what you think, okay? My camper's vandalized with threatening messages. Then my friend dies in a pretty curious way. And in forty-eight hours the place where it happened is dug over, the car gets sold to a junkyard and the man who rented the car to him goes off to Miami."

"Clearwater. Fred Sillman goes to Clearwater every year."

"I don't honestly give a shit what his leisure schedule is. My friend didn't die the way everybody keeps saying he did. And if you aren't going to find out what happened I am. Simple as that."

"We did our job, sir. We found some facts about your friend that weren't so nice. I'm sorry about him and I'm sorry about your job but there's nothing to be gained by you staying in Cleary."

"You telling me to leave town?"

"Of course not. You're free to visit, to sight-see, hell, you can even buy yourself a house here – I understand you know a local real estate broker pretty good – all I'm saying is, you're not free to be a policeman. And if you start troubling people I'm going to have to get involved."

"Your concerns've been noted." Pellam tried to imitate the smile. It didn't work too well. He had better luck with: "Have a good day, sir."

Wexell Ambler was going to visit his lover.

He walked out of his house – supposedly on his way to a meeting – and strode toward his big Cadillac, parked in the U-shaped driveway. He was looking forward to sitting with her in the Jacuzzi in the glass-enclosed deck of his house in nearby Claverack, New York, from which they could watch the Catskill Mountains in the distance – now a stunning wash of color. He could look forward to enjoying fresh coffee and tasting some of her cooking.

Thinking about making slow love in the hot tub or in the large Shaker bed he'd bought for her because she'd mentioned that she liked the simple lines. She was a strange woman. He often compared the two of them, his ex-wife and his mistress.

And tried to decide what were the differences and what were the similarities. They both were attractive, dressed well, knew how to carry on a conversation at the country club. His wife was more intelligent but she was also less imaginative; she had no spark, no humor. She let him get away with anything. His lover challenged him (perhaps, he now reflected, this made him feel younger. Uncertainty was a quality brought out by one of the first girls he'd been in love with).

He'd just gotten into the Caddie when his housekeeper ran to the door and signaled to him with a wave.

"It's Mark," she called. "Says it's urgent."

Ambler said, "Have him call on the car phone."

He backed the car out of the driveway and waved to her affectionately once more.

Waiting for the call. He was thinking less about what the beefy young man would have to say and more about the woman he was on his way to see.

Ambler was a religious man (on the executive committee of the First Presbyterian Church), and although he understood that Calvinistic predestination did not absolve him from choosing the right path, the moral path, nonetheless the religion instilled in him a tendency toward helplessness on those moral questions the answers to which he did not like. He tended to throw his hands up and follow his instinct.

So although he knew what he was doing was immoral, he felt an addiction to his mistress, and could more or less successfully conclude that he had no control over the matter.

He packaged the infidelity carefully, though. For instance, he never thought of the word "cheating," which gave the whole matter a blue-collar taint. And he always thought of his paramour as a mistress or lover, rather than girlfriend or "the woman he was seeing on the side." (Dignity was important to Wex Ambler.) He never risked embarrassing his lover just to satisfy his own passion and went to crazy lengths to keep the affair secret.

The one problem, though – one he hadn't counted on – was that he'd fallen completely in love with the woman.

Ambler, who was fifty-two, was not so old that he had forgotten love makes people stupid – and in his philosophy, as well as his profession, stupidity was the number-one sin. He had guarded against love but unlike religion and unlike money and unlike power, love had a mind of its own.

It had nabbed him, but good.

At his insistence, their get-togethers had become more and more frequent. And he now felt his center giving, falling further toward her. He was growing hungrier, even desperate – while *she* seemed increasingly aloof.

Was there anything more foolish than a middle-aged man in love? And was there anyone who could care less about that foolishness?

Ambler smelled leaf dust and warm air from the Caddie's heater and wished he were already at the cabin.

The phone buzzed. The noise always disturbed him; it reminded him of the alarm a hospital monitor would make when a patient went into cardiac arrest. He snatched up the light receiver.

"Yes."

"I talked to Tom," Mark said.

"Yes. And?"

"The guy's turning into some kind of private eye."

Ambler concentrated on driving. The roads were narrow and wound in tricky meanderings past horse and dairy farms. He had a tendency to wander onto the shoulder if he didn't think about his driving. He asked Mark, "What do you mean?"

There was a pause and he heard Mark spit. A young man chewing tobacco – it was stupid. Maybe he did it to darken his moustache. Mark continued. "He's been asking a lot of questions about his friend and the car. He was down to R&W."

"The junkyard."

"Right. Looking at the wreck of the car."

Ambler felt the car bobble as the right front tire dipped noisily off the asphalt. "Damn." He forced the car back onto the road, overcompensating. It slipped over the broken yellow line before he got it steady again.

Mark asked, "What should we do? I was thinking maybe we could offer him some money. You know, bribe him to leave."

"Then he'd think I had something to do with the accident."

"Not necessarily." When Ambler didn't answer, Mark said, "But maybe."

Ambler said, "I've got an idea. I don't want to talk about it on the phone. Come see me."

"Now?"

"I'll be busy for a while. I'll call you."

They hung up, and it took Ambler the rest of the drive to the cabin to shake off his concern at Mark's news. In fact, it wasn't until he turned into the leaf-packed driveway and saw his lover's car sitting obliquely in the turnaround of the cabin that his spirits lifted. He climbed out of the Caddie, eager and buoyant as a seventeen-year-old en route to a homecoming date.

10

The Cleary Volunteer Fire Department had a long history of proud firefighting and a photo gallery to prove it.

Dozens of faded pictures of hand-pump, horsedrawn wagons, even a few of bucket brigades, were scattered on the walls of the tiny office – as if the company had had a Matthew Brady protégé on staff to record every major fire before, after and including the big one of 1912. The firemen seemed to have been arranged by the photographer and Pellam wondered if they'd actually stopped working momentarily, smoothed their pushbroom or handlebar mustaches and posed for the leisurely exposures.

"Afternoon," said the man sitting at the desk, rocking back in a metal chair. He was in his early thirties, wearing a black T-shirt over good muscles, blue jeans, a New York Mets cap.

"How you doing?"

"Not bad."

Silence

Pellam looked through a glass window at a big, yellow Seagrave fire truck. "Got some nice equipment there."

"Town don't scrimp, I'll say that."

"You all volunteer, huh?"

"Yep. There's pay for one man on duty to take calls twenty-four hours."

"He must get pretty tired."

The man snagged the joke right away and fired back with, "But makes a hell of a lot of overtime."

Pellam said, "I'm the one with the movie company."

"I know."

"You mind if I ask you a few questions?"

"Nosir."

"You on duty when that car blew up? The one in the park?"

"That your friend's car?"

Pellam said, "That's right."

"I answered that call, yessir. All of us did."

"You tell me what happened?"

"You mean what caused it?"

"Whatever you can tell me."

The man said, "There was most of it in the coroner's report."

"This isn't official or anything like that. I'm just curious. He was a good friend."

"Yessir, I understand." The fireman squinted up at the spotless, red-enameled tin ceiling. "I recall the back end of the car was burning pretty good when we got there. Somebody'd driven past and called it in."

"You know who?"

"Nope. I think it was a call from a pay phone. Anonymous."

"You showed up and then what happened?"

"No hydrants, course, so we had to use the tank on the truck to get things cooled off enough to get close to your friend. Then half the crew started on the brush fire with extinguishers and shovels. That was about it. We got the body away from the wreck and finally got the fire out. He died right away. It was pretty quick."

"The gas tank had blown up?"

"Yessir."

"You opened the trunk?"

"We popped it open, that's right."

"How do you do that?"

"Usually, we just pop out the cylinder, then reach in and flip the release bar. But the steel'd been pushed outward, so what we did was whack it a couple times with a pike. That jarred the bar and popped it open."

"Why'd you open the trunk?"

"The sheriff wanted us to. To see what was inside. Anyway, it's standard procedure. In case there's cans of gas or oil. Also, your spare'll burn for hours you don't douse it good."

"You find anything interesting?"

"Sir?"

"You said the sheriff wanted to look inside."

"I don't know. I was at the hood."

"You have one of those pikes handy?"

He wasn't yet uncomfortable under this questioning but he was growing warier. "They're mounted on the truck, sir. We're not really supposed to let civilians into the house, you know."

Pellam nodded. He looked at the truck through a greasy

window. The pikes looked blunt and heavy. It didn't seem they'd leave holes as small as the ones he'd seen in the car. "What're they made out of?"

"Steel of course."

"One last question. Why was the area dozed over?"

"Sheriff ordered it. Somebody called him up and told him to, I heard. I don't know why."

"You don't know who called, do you?"

"Sure don't."

Pellam thanked him then said, "Aren't you going to ask me?"

"Ask you what, sir?"

"Whether we're going to be making a movie here?"

The man shrugged. "Don't make a lick of difference to me, sir. I work in feed and grain, not movies."

At noon, Meg Torrens walked out the door of the Dutchess County Realty office, set the hands of the *Be Back At* clock at 1:15. She looked around the square. Pellam's Winnebago camper was parked opposite. She looked up and down the street, then crossed over and circled the camper. Taking in the tan and brown paint, the battered fenders, the mud stains, the chips in the windshield.

What the hell was she doing here?

Going shopping on my lunch hour, that's all.

And when was the last time, my dear, you bought anything in one of these rip-off antique stores? Three, four years ago, wasn't it?

She imagined herself in one of the campers, on location. She imagined what it was like to be in a movie. The modeling she'd done had been pure effort – exhausting. And she'd been treated like a dim-witted cocker spaniel. Making a movie would have to be different, she believed.

She caressed the metal skin of the camper. Noticed the faint remains of some graffiti on the side. It looked like two crosses.

Meg slung her leather bag over her shoulder and strolled up and down the street, looking at sights she'd walked past for years and never noticed. A cornerstone dated in late September, 1929 – could that have been Black Thursday? A painted wooden barrel on the side-walk emblazoned with the number 58 in red paint. One building was topped with a weathervane in the shape of a whale – why here, a hundred fifty miles from the ocean? Another was decorated with a beautiful round stained-glass window.

Meg was gazing into the window of Steptoe Antiques when she heard slow footsteps. A voice asked her, "Could use seconds on the brownies."

Meg turned, looking blank at first, the way she'd rehearsed in case this happened. She said, "Should've eaten them while you had the chance, cowboy."

Pellam stepped next to her to look at what she was examining. "How're the driving lessons coming?"

"'Bout the same as your photo classes."

Meg pointed to a tattered rug hanging on the wall in the window. "See that? Price tag looks like it says sixty. Wrong, that's six hundred. They'll sell it for that too."

"What's that supposed to be on there, a dog?"

Meg looked at it closely. "Could be. Maybe a cat. I don't know."

"Dinner was nice," he said. "I enjoyed it."

She lifted an eyebrow. "I did too." She'd chosen the pronoun carefully.

"Your house is beautiful. That was the first dinner I'd had in a house, I mean a real house, in over a year."

"No kidding," she said, though she wasn't surprised. "Sam's done nothing but talk about you. You better make good on that promise."

Pellam said, "The practice bombs. I haven't forgotten."

They walked past another real estate office. Pellam looked at some of the listings.

Meg's voice dropped a half octave. "I've got some wonderful properties, Mr Pellam. Owner financing is available . . ."

They laughed.

Eyes were on them. Cars slowed as they passed. Meg thought, *Go to hell*. But the defiance was shaky. She felt vulnerable, like the time she found herself at a Florida resort wearing a new bikini that turned out to be more see-through than she was comfortable with. As she did then she now crossed her arms over her chest.

"I guess I better get going," she said.

Pellam touched her arm. She froze, then stepped back casually. He said, "I'd like to ask you a question. In confidence."

Her thoughts raced but she just nodded slowly.

He asked, "There any reason why somebody might not want a movie made in Cleary?"

"We say no to drugs."

"Beg pardon?"

"There's some talk that there might be bad influences if your company came to town."

"Okay, granted. I've heard that before . . . But let me be a little blunter. There any reason why somebody might kill my friend to keep a movie from being made here?"

Meg turned to him, her mouth open in shock. "You're serious, aren't you?" She turned back to the window. "That was a stupid thing to say. Sure, you're serious."

"This is off the record?"

"Sure," she said.

"Okay, Marty did have some pot. Except, it was in the *camper*. Along with the rolling papers—"

"What's that?"

"Rolling papers? Cigarette papers."

"Oh. Right."

"So it *wasn't* in the car with him when it blew up. Somebody planted those drugs on him."

She shook her head, but noncommittally, as if he were a lawyer taking down her reactions.

"Then I looked over the car a little while ago."

"You did?"

"And I found two bullet holes in it."

"Bullet holes?"

"I think so. Near the gas tank. I think that's what happened. Somebody shot the tank, it exploded and then they planted the drugs and left before the fire truck got there."

At first she thought this was impossible – in Cleary. But then she remembered the darker side of the town. The murders of those businessmen, the occasional rapes, two high school boys had driven into a tree at eighty miles an hour – they were both stoned on heroin, of all things.

He continued. "I was hoping I could talk to Keith. Maybe

there's a test he could do. On the metal. See if they were bullet holes."

Meg said, "Why don't you talk to Tom? Didn't he investigate . . ." Then she understood. "I see. You think he's involved in some way, do you? The sheriff?"

"I just want to keep it low-key."

Nodding. She opened her purse and handed him one of Keith's business cards. "Well, sure. Give him a call. He liked you."

Across the square she saw a couple staring at them. The woman leaned toward the man; there was an extended whisper going on. Meg felt the burst of discomfort again.

Life in a small town . . .

I've lived here for five years, Pellam. But it feels like ten.

"Lunch?" he asked.

She hesitated. Yes, no, yes, no . . . she said, "Uh, I don't think so."

"Why not?"

Don't Do a Don't. She said, "Because this is Cleary."

He nodded and said, "Got it."

"Good luck, Pellam." She walked to the coffee shop.

"Uhm, one thing . . . All I'm interested in is lunch. Nothing more or less than that."

Meg lifted her hands and dropped them to her sides with faint slaps. "You maybe have the most honorable intentions in the world . . ." She paused, and for a millisecond tried to read his face for his reaction to this. She couldn't tell. She added, "but Cleary's still Cleary."

"Suppose that doesn't change."

"Not in your life or mine," she said and walked into the diner. The screen door snapped shut with a wooden slam.

M&T Pharmaceutical was a one-story cinder block square outside of Cleary. Prefab. It was surrounded by a gravel parking lot, in which sat thirty or forty cars – a lot of old ones, Torinos and Novas, as well as newer Japanese imports. And, Pellam noticed, pickup trucks galore – many of them with back windows smeared from the noses of excited hunting dogs.

Near the main entrance were several marked parking places. *Mr Torrens* was the first. Beside it was an empty space with a sign that had been painted over. It was probably the spot reserved for Keith's late partner. This had been L.A., Pellam thought cynically, that space would have been appropriated five minutes after the funeral.

It was late afternoon, dusky, and just as he eased the Winnebago into two of the visitor's slots, a sodium vapor light on a pole in the middle of the parking lot came on. He walked past the company sign, a swirling design of an M and a T, backlit.

A young receptionist, hair shooting up in a frothy tease, smiled and shoved the Juicy Fruit into the corner of her cheek.

"Hello, Darla," Pellam said, reading the name off her gold-plate necklace.

"Help you, sir?"

"John Pellam to see Keith Torrens."

"Yessir, have a seat."

Pellam sat and thumbed through a pristine copy of *Chemical Week*. In three minutes, a grinning Keith Torrens walked into the reception area.

"John." They shook hands. "Good to see you."

"Thanks for taking the time."

"Come on, I'll give you the fast tour."

Factories generally depressed Pellam – the regimentation, the way machines dictated where people stood and what they did (reflecting some kind of fear, he decided, that if it all fell apart, he'd end up on an assembly line somewhere twisting sheet metal screws into Whirlpools for the rest of his life). M&T, though, was a surprise. It was bright and clean. Filled with spotless white tile, brilliantly lit. The workers wore white jackets, pants and shoes and transparent bluish hats, like shower caps. It looked like a kitchen. Many of the people were bent over conveyor belts, checking machinery, packing cartons, reading computer screens. The machinery was stainless steel and white.

"Quite an operation."

Keith said, "I'm a small guy. To compete with the Pfizers and Bristol Meyers-Squibbs, you've got to be efficient. That's the key word." Light brown cardboard cartons rose to the ceiling on small elevators and moved along a conveyor overhead until they vanished into the shipping department.

Keith was so excited to show off his company that he talked very quickly; that speed, together with the loud pulse from a dozen different kinds of machines, made it impossible for Pellam to catch more than a few phrases. Still, he smiled and nodded enthusiastically.

They finished the tour and ended up outside Keith's office. "It's small but we're proud of it."

Pellam said, "I'll buy your cough syrup next time I get the flu."

"I'll give you enough samples to last for two years." He vanished into a corridor.

Five minutes later – throat lozenges, cough syrup, nasal spray stuffed in Pellam's jacket pockets – they walked into Keith's office, a large sparse room, done in cheap paneling. Keith seemed like the sort who'd sink most of his money into the factory itself. Pellam shut the door and said softly, "I'd like to ask you a favor."

"Meg said there was something on your mind."

"I'd appreciate if you'd keep this off the record."

"Surely."

Pellam said, "It's about my friend. The one who was killed."

"That car accident."

"I'm not sure it was an accident."

"No?"

"I found the wreck and I noticed what looked like two bullet holes in the back. The sheriff said they were caused by the fire department but I checked out their equipment and I don't think that's it."

"Bullet holes." Keith was frowning.

Pellam shrugged. "I was wondering if there was any way somebody could look at a hole and see if it was definitely made by a bullet. Someone like you?"

Keith said, "Possibly. What do the holes look like?"

"The ones I saw were about a third of an inch, so that would mean they're about thirty caliber."

Keith said, "Deer round, so it might be copper jacketed."

"Could be, sure."

Keith was looking up at the ceiling. "Any chance you could find the bullets in the car?"

"Let's assume they disappeared."

"Got you." He nodded knowingly. Then reflected. "The car burned, right?"

"Right."

"If," Keith began slowly, "they were just lead bullets, the odds are that any residue would have been burned away. Lead oxidizes at a very low temperature. Copper, though, that's a different story. It has a real high vaporization point. And going through sheet steel in a car? Yeah, I'd guess enough would have come off in the holes to find traces."

"Now, next question—"

"I'd be happy to."

"I wasn't going to ask you to go to the trouble. Isn't there something you can show me to look for?"

"After about four years of inorganic chemistry, sure. But why don't we just spend a half hour right now? I'll take some samples and we can have it back here in the lab in no time. We'll run it through the chromatograph and spectrometer. Where's the car?"

"Out at a small junkyard on Route 9."

"R&W?"

"Yeah, that's it."

Keith frowned. "I thought it would've been impounded or something."

"See why I'm a little curious about what's going on?"

The camper, followed by Keith's Cougar, pulled into the R&W parking lot, much of which was piled high with twisted copper piping. The pudgy man Pellam had spoken to yesterday – Bobby, he recalled – stood looking at it like a proud father, his hands on his ample hips. He wore bib overalls and a seersucker hat, like a train engineer's.

Pellam and Keith climbed out, walked up to him.

Keith said, "Hey."

"Hey, Mr Torrens. How you doing?"

"Not bad. How's business?"

"Lookit this," Bobby said proudly.

Keith nodded.

Pellam examined the tangle of pipe. "Not bad."

"No shittin'." He laughed at the obvious statement.

Three men, staring down at ten cubic yards of pipe. Nodding, impressed the way men always are at good finds.

Pellam glanced along the front of the fence toward the charred wreck. It was lit by bare incandescent bulbs in mechanic's hand-held light baskets.

With an odd formality Bobby stuck out his hand. "How you doing, sir? You're that movie guy, right?"

Pellam blinked. "That's right. We're here about what I was asking you before. The car?"

"Car?"

"I was talking to you about that wreck." He nodded toward the remains.

The man frowned. "Don't believe so. No."

Pellam glanced at him. "We were talking about that car down there. The wreck."

The man lifted his hat and greasy bangs dropped onto his forehead. "Don't recall that."

Oh, I get it.

Pellam sighed, reaching for his pocket. He found a bill and was starting to pull it out when the man said, "Bobby."

"What?"

"You were talking to my brother. Bobby. I'm Billy."

Oh. The W in R&W. Got it.

Keith laughed. "Billy and Bobby're twins."

Billy said, "But don't let that stop you." He accepted the twenty.

"You mind if we take a look at the wreck?"

"If you're in the market for a car," Billy said, shrugging, "I can do better'n that. But help yourself." He turned back to his precious pipe.

They walked toward the burnt-out car.

Pellam whispered to Keith, "Twins?"

"You do horror films for your company, I'll bet you could get 'em pretty cheap."

They walked around the wreck. Pellam stopped suddenly.

"It's gone."

Keith blinked and leaned forward. Someone had used an acetylene torch to cut off the trunk and rear portions of the fenders.

Pellam called, "Excuse me . . ."

Billy tore himself away from his pipe. "Yessir?"

He wandered slowly to the wreck.

Pellam said, "What happened to the metal here? The back portions?"

"Whatsat?" Billy called.

"Look here," Keith said.

"Shit, it's gone," Billy said.

"I got the gist of that," Pellam said.

"Shit." The twin put his hands on his hips and looked around, like he was searching for a dropped quarter.

Keith said, "Bobby start to cut her up?"

"Naw, he's not into like heavy work. Damn now. Who'd come by and steal half a burnt car?"

Keith and Pellam walked back to their vehicles. "I'm sorry. Wild goose chase."

Keith said, "It's pretty funny, though. You go out to look at the car and find what looks like evidence. Next thing, you come back and that part's gone."

"Yeah, funny."

Billy stood in the shack, waving goodbye to Keith Torrens and the movie man. He picked up the phone and punched in a number. Bobby answered on the first ring. He must have known it was Billy because he just picked up the phone and said, "So what is it now?"

"Hey, guess who was just here."

"Lessee, Elvis's ghost, singing 'Love Me Tender.'"

"Naw," Billy said, "but wish it was. That'd be a fuck of a lot better for you and me."

11

"Are you all right?"

Wexell Ambler's lover didn't answer him.

After a moment, he gripped her buttocks tighter and dug his nails, which were long for a man's, into her flesh. She whimpered. He remembered to relax his grip somewhat.

"Does it hurt?" he asked. "Does it—"

"Wex, oh—"

"—hurt?"

She whimpered again and pressed her forehead against his pulsing neck.

When they'd begun seeing each other it had been awkward. Several problems.

First, neither had ever had an affair before and they didn't know what you did and didn't do. Surely affairs had special protocols – How do you make dates? Do you even call them "dates"? Do you shop at different grocery stores to avoid chance meetings when you're with your spouse? Or is it better to see each other casually like that and avoid arousing suspicion?

Second, there was a funny type of jealousy at work. He accepted that his lover was married but he was occasionally stung by the thought that she'd learned a certain technique – a touch or kiss – from her husband.

Third, neither of them was twenty-five any longer. Ambler had worked in the building trades when he was young and still hunted and fished – the history of physical effort had helped slow the inevitable effects of gravity and sedentary life. But there was no denying that muscle was giving way to fat, that erections that used to last an hour began to fade after fifteen minutes, and that he'd be no good for twenty-four hours after he came. His hair was thin (though in some slight compensation, not too gray) and he'd developed a jowl that he kept poking at as he'd pass the large oval mirror in his dining room until his wife commented on it and he immediately stopped the habit.

Oddly, though, his lover, who was more than ten years younger than he was, had been even more self-conscious than Ambler. Her body could easily pass for a thirty-year-old's, yet she always shut the lights out and drew the shades before she undressed.

But despite these worries, they had quickly fallen into a comfortable pattern and they soon found themselves making good, sweaty love for the first time in years.

Today, in the dark tangy-wood-scented bedroom, Ambler pinned her to the stark oak bed and pressed into her – hard, hard. Almost cruelly. He wasn't sure why. He knew he had a reputation for being a cruel man in business and at other times, but he would never think of being cruel to anyone he loved. But as he felt himself coming closer to the moment, he wanted to hurt his mistress. He wanted her to admit she was in pain but that she didn't want him to stop.

"Does it hurt, love?"

"Yeah," she whispered, her mouth saying the hot word against his skin, a centimeter from his ear.

She gasped twice, then whispered something he couldn't hear, then she said, "Don't stop. No, don't stop. I like it." The words were lyrical grunts. He smelled the aroma of her perfume and sweat.

"You like it . . ."

"Don't stop."

". . . to hurt?"

"Oh, Wex . . ."

Afterwards they lay together. Unlike when Ambler had made love with his wife he and his lover often began to talk immediately, right after they had caught their breath.

Today, though, he kissed her forehead, whispered, "Darling," and then they lay with their own thoughts for five minutes, half dozing.

"He's still here, I heard," Ambler said casually.

"Who?"

"That man from the movie company."

"I heard."

"What do you suppose he wants?"

"Taking time off after his accident, I suppose."

Ambler asked, "They aren't going to make the movie here, after all?"

"Why don't you like him?"

Why do you say I don't like him? But Ambler didn't say that. He said, "Look what happened. With the drugs and everything."

"Wasn't his fault."

"Movie people."

"Are just like everybody else," she countered.

"You're glad he's staying, aren't you?"

"Wex, what's this all about?"

"Drugs and—"

She said, "You take it on your shoulders to be the moral protector of the town and you scare all these people into thinking that the big bad world is going to gobble them up alive."

That made him nervous. He considered. No, there was no way she could know about what Mark had done. She wouldn't be here if she suspected that. He said, "You give me more credit than I deserve."

"You bully people."

"As if I could bully the whole town of Cleary." After a moment, he said, "Did you talk to him about a job?"

"No."

"Would you?"

"I considered it. I thought—"

He scoffed. "You thought you'd be Lana Turner."

"I'm wasted here. My life is wasted. I should . . ."

"You should what?" he asked, edging back toward desperation.

"Nothing."

"You're life's not wasted at all."

"I feel like I'm just drifting."

"How can you say that? You've made *my* life something wonderful."

The lines fell like a lead sinker. She squeezed his shoulder but he was glad for the darkness. His face burned with embarrassment.

He asked, "Have you ever thought about moving?"

A pause. "I've thought about it."

"You'd just leave, without talking to me about it?"

"Don't put words in my mouth. I didn't say that. I've got a lot of possibilities."

"Some of them involve me, some of them don't. I see."

"Wex." There was a bony edge to her voice. Ambler didn't believe he'd heard this sound before. He wondered if they were going to have their first serious argument. That would be very bad – in light of what he was planning to tell her.

She continued, "Don't disrupt things. Between us, I mean."

"Is something wrong?"

"No, nothing's wrong. What do you mean?"

This was sounding like the conversations he used to have with his wife. Before he fell out of love with her.

He backed off. "You just seem . . . I don't know."

She said, "We were just having a discussion. Don't take it personally."

"You're the one who seems to be picking a fight."

"I am not."

After a moment he felt her stiffen and draw away from him. Only millimeters – but it was enough so that he refused to do what he instinctively wanted to and touch her leg in a chaste way, seeking forgiveness for his vague crimes.

The day wasn't going as he'd planned. Not at all. He wished

they hadn't made love. It tilted the balance of power against him. Men and women. Never changes.

He felt a shudder of pain and anger course through him.

There was silence for a long moment. He debated then wiped his sweating palm on the sheet. "Can I ask you something?"

She didn't answer.

Ambler said, "We've been seeing each other now for, what? Six months?"

She said a neutral, "About that."

"I was thinking . . . I'm not good at this." (The same way he hadn't been very good at asking her out the first time, he recalled.)

She softened. He knew that she had a weakness for chivalrous, struggling men. "What are you trying to say, Wex?"

At least the terrible edge was gone from her voice.

His mind went blank, then he blurted: "I think we should get married."

He wanted to be light about it. He wanted to joke. Like middle-aged couples on sitcoms. Snappy comebacks. Rejoinders. Mugging for the camera. He couldn't think of a single thing else to say.

And from her: Utter silence. As if she'd even stopped breathing.

It couldn't have been that she'd never considered this before, could it? Was he so far off base that he'd completely misjudged? His heart pounded. He actually heard it.

Her hand touched his arm. "We said we'd never think about it."

"That was before." He looked futilely for some appropriate milestone in their relationship – the twenty-fifth time they'd had sex? The twelfth candle-lit dinner together? The sixtieth time they'd laughed at a private joke?

She sat up and reached for the night table. The light snapped on. It was a low bulb, which she'd asked him to put in the lamp. He knew she hated bright lights.

Meg Torrens pulled the comforter around her shoulders and said, "Oh, Wex."

And in his name, spoken through a loving, gentle smile, he heard the word No as clearly as if she'd shouted it.

• • •

TO SLEEP IN A SHALLOW GRAVE/
BIG MOUNTAIN STUDIOS

EXT. ROAD TO BOLT'S CROSSING, NEAR FOREST – DAY

ECU: JANICE'S FACE. It is not aged so much as weathered. You can see in it the hampered beauty of a woman at forty. An earth mother. She was at Woodstock. She cried at Woodstock and got stoned there. The long hair falls across her face, subdividing it into patches of ruddy skin. She brushes it aside. The wind pushes it back.

MEDIUM ANGLE: SHEP. He's leaning against his motorcycle. The lights should be gelled magenta to put an aura on the chrome, harmonizing with the sunset that's approaching behind them. He's torn. He's told her he's leaving, and he wants to go. But also wants desperately to find something

about her that will keep him from leaving. Is it pity? Or is it
something more genuine, more mutual? He doesn't know.

Pellam sat in his hot camper – though he was really in Bolt's
Crossing, not Cleary, New York.

Which was where he needed to be at the moment.

In Bolt's Crossing, there was no stinking hulk of a car,
punctuated with scorched tufts of upholstery shooting outward
like patches of hair.

In Bolt's Crossing, the only people lying still in funeral
parlors weren't dead at all and in four scenes would be prowling
around in flashbacks, lusting and ornery and laughing.

In Bolt's Crossing, people like Marty never died.

CUT TO:

MEDIUM ANGLES, CROSSCUTTING between Janice
and Shep

JANICE

I took a chance you might be here.

SHEP

(Avoiding her eyes)
Brakes gave me some trouble. Thought I should fix them
before I left.

JANICE

I was thinking about what you said. Last night?
About me.

SHEP

I was mad. I—

JANICE

You were right. I keep looking for answers in the past. If I'm not careful, there won't be any future left.

Pellam pulled the sheet out of the typewriter with a satisfying buzz of the platen. He wrote *Insert 58A* across the top and slipped it into the script, which he'd unfastened. It was now just a stack of a hundred fifty sheets of wrinkled paper, filled with his handwriting and interleaved with inserts like this one.

He put his hand on it, then picked it up and riffled the pages, feeling the thin breeze on his jaw.

He walked to the front of the camper and sat in the driver's seat, looking out the grimy windshield. Now he wasn't seeing the cinematographer's stunning dusk in Bolt's Crossing but the winding country road that led into Cleary.

The Winnebago's engine turned right over. He drove downtown, parked and stepped out into the brilliant sun. Blinking his way along Main Street he found a stationery store that did photocopying. He gave them the script and asked for a copy. The polite acned teenage boy behind the counter told him the job would take about twenty minutes. Pellam offered to pay now but the boy said, "No, sir, no hurry. Want to make sure you like the job."

Pellam hesitated then said, "Sure," remembering that he wasn't in Los Angeles or New York and that there was no reason to be suspicious of politeness.

He wandered out into the street, blazing with its raw sunlight, to get a cup of coffee. He saw Marge's across the street but, thinking of the day he and Marty had gone there, decided against it. Also, he preferred to go someplace where he wasn't so well known. He didn't want to be adored by the help, he didn't want to talk about Marty, about parts in movies, about Hollywood.

He walked into a drugstore, with its snaking turquoise lunch counter and chrome-and-red vinyl stools.

"Hey, Mr Pellam." From one of the clerks – a middle-aged man Pellam had never seen.

So much for anonymity.

And for hostility too. Whatever the official opinion about drugs and movies, the half-dozen people in the place all glanced at him with meaningful, eye-involved smiles that said, *I'm not asking but if you want to haul me off to Hollywood and put me in a sitcom episode of your choice, go right ahead.*

He nodded, walked to the pay phone and tried to make a credit card call. His company card number had been canceled. He sighed and billed it to his personal card. After five minutes the assistant producer came on the line. The boy was in high spirits.

"Yo, hombre. You better hope Lefty don't have a homing device set up. 'Cause he do, there's a scout-seeking missile aimed for your crotch this minute."

"He hasn't unfired me, huh?"

"Whoa, boy. You came real close to cratering that movie but I think it's going to fly. He bent over for one of the money cows and I guess it worked out okay. Shysters said Marty's accident was a force majeure. So he's got another couple of weeks."

"You got a location?"

"Not yet, but they've got a free-lancer down in Pennsylvania. Season's later. Gives 'em more time to shoot."

Pellam said, "Pennsylvania's all wrong."

"I'll connect you with Lefty. You can tell him."

"You sound pretty calm."

"I'm medicated."

"I'm going to do something and I need your help."

"No." Cheerful, cheerful, cheerful. "Absolutely not."

"Listen to me. I'm going to—"

"John, clue me in – are you trying to get *me* fired?"

"Every assistant producer gets fired. It's a rite of passage." A sigh. "Okay, talk to me."

"I doctored the script."

"What script?"

"*Shallow Grave.*"

"Hmmm. Why?"

"I want you to get the changes to Bob. Is he still directing?"

"Pellam, are you mad?"

"Don't show them to Lefkowitz. Only the director. *Repetez apres moi.*"

"No."

"Answer my question. Has Lefty fired Bob?"

"No, and he can't. He's in too deep. His deadline problems are almost as bad as his herpes."

"Good. I'm sending it by Express Mail."

"John, no."

"To you."

"John, there's no way they're going to hire you back."

"That's not what I care about. I don't even want a credit. It's too good a story to screw up with that half-assed script. Get it to Bob and don't let Lefty see my changes."

"John—"

"Bye."

"—no."

Before he sat down at the lunch counter Pellam noticed a rack of sunglasses. His had met the same fate as his Polaroid, thanks to Meg Torrens's little Toyota. He decided to buy another pair. He noticed some mirrored teardrop shapes. He tried them on, checked them out in the mirror.

He smiled. Perfect. Yep: *Cool Hand Luke*.

The middle-aged man behind the counter said, "They're you."

"How d'I look? Like a small-town sheriff?"

"Yessir, you could man a speed trap any day with those."

"Take 'em," Pellam said.

"You want the fake leather case?"

"That's okay."

He sat at the counter. The clerk didn't seem much interested in a Hollywood career and just talked to Pellam about traveling, of which he'd done a great deal. He told Pellam how he and his wife had taken this year's vacation in Peru and Chile.

"The air is the thing you don't think about. The altitude, you know. You walk a couple blocks – well, they don't really have blocks but you know what I mean – and you've gotta lie down and take a nap. It's exhausting! I mean, I thought I was in good shape. I can chop a couple cord of wood and no problem. But I was beat. And there are all these little old women steaming along like it's nothing to them and trying to sell you pottery and these blankets and jewelry. They see money and they run right at you. They sprint! In air like that. It's all what you're used to." The man summarized: "Everything's relative."

"Suppose so," Pellam said, and listened to the history of Machu Picchu.

Pellam checked his watch, said, "I've got to pick up something."

"We did the Orinoco too but I didn't see one crocodile." He grimaced.

"Life's full of disappointments." Pellam stood and put his deputy glasses on.

"No disappointment at all. Sally and me're going back in October. We'll find one. I promise you that."

Pellam wished him luck.

12

Pellam parked the camper in the driveway of the Torrens house (the word "homestead" came to mind). Meg stepped out onto the porch, then smiled and jumped down the few steps to the walk that led to the driveway, wiping her hands on a scallopy apron and looking just like a housewife out of a 1960s sitcom.

A housewife, however, in a tight, blue silk blouse, the top two (or was it three?) buttons undone.

Eyes up, boy.

My God, she's got a freckled chest.

Pellam just loved freckles on women.

"What brings you here, Pellam?"

"Came to borrow something."

She blinked. To joke, or not to joke? "Butter churn?"

"Naw."

"Bear grease for your muzzleloader?" she asked.

Gotcha.

He smiled indulgently. "As a matter of fact," Pellam said,

"you're talking to one of the only people in the state of New York that's fired a Sharps .54."

And she didn't miss a beat. "A Sharps? Forget about it, boy. That's a drop-block breechloader, not a muzzleloader."

Gotme.

She laughed hard at his jolted expression. "Girls usually melt at gun talk, huh?"

He said, "Nobody in the goddamn world except me and born-again gun nuts know about Sharps anymore."

"I never fired one but my daddy had one. He collected guns. I've got myself a Springfield breechloader in the den."

"No." He laughed. "A forty-five seventy?"

She nodded. "Carbine. With a saddle ring and everything."

"Damn, what a woman. You ever fire it?"

"What good's a gun unless you fire it? But try getting the black powder smell out of your silk undies."

"Not a problem I have."

"Sam and I take it out to the range sometime. Hard to find ammo, of course."

"That's what I wanted to borrow."

"Ammunition?"

"Your son."

"The bomb expedition?" she nodded.

"Yep. It okay?"

Meg said, "You ever known any parent to mind when somebody says he'll take your child off your hands for a few hours?" She called Sam then turned back to Pellam. "Oh, before I forget . . . The Apple Festival is Saturday afternoon. You interested in seeing it?"

"I guess. You'll be there?"

"It's a family thing."

What was that supposed to mean? *You'll be there it's a family thing.* He waited a second for more messages; when he got none, he said, "Sure. Look forward to it."

Sam appeared. "Hey, Mr Pellam, we gonna look at bombs?"

"You bet, Sam."

"All right! Can we go in the camper?"

"That's the only wheels I got."

"Can I, Mom?"

"Sure, just be back by six for dinner."

"Mr Pellam, these are the greatest. They got red ones and green ones and they got mortar shells that Dad says they don't have powder in them anymore and hand grenades . . ."

"Do not, under any circumstances, buy him anything."

Pellam laughed, "Yes, ma'am."

They got into the camper.

"Hey, Sam, you know, one thing'd be fun?"

"What, Mr Pellam?"

"Why don't you bring your metal detector along?"

"My metal detector?"

"I have this collection?" Pellam said. "And whenever I'm in a new town I like to add to it."

"I collect dinosaurs. And baseball cards. And pro-wrestling cards, of course." Sam jumped down out of the Winnebago and ran into the house.

Energy. Where do they get it?

He was back in two minutes.

"You need batteries?"

"Nope. They're recharged. I used ni-cads. What do you collect, Mr Pellam? Coins?"

He said, "Bullet casings."

Sam said, "Wow."

As it turned out, Pellam liked the bombs as much as Sam did.

This particular junkyard was a lot classier than R&W. He remembered it from the poker boys' list. It sold mostly what the name promised: Army Surplus, which seemed to be in pretty good supply despite what Bobby (or Billy) had said. Vehicle parts, cartridge boxes, portable latrines, tools, tents, flashlights. All solid, olive-drab, functional. A lot of things that you couldn't use for much other than paperweights: Bombsights and old altimeters and doughboy helmets that wouldn't even make good planters.

But the bombs, yeah, they were great. All different colors. Different shapes. Some pointed like rockets, some rounded like old-time airplane bombs. Jesus, they were huge. Pellam cautiously tapped one. Hollow.

Sam said, "They're just practice bombs. You don't have to worry."

"I wasn't worried," Pellam said quickly.

"You looked like you were afraid it was going to go off."

"Ha, ha."

Sam showed him mortar shells, concussion grenades and bayonets, mean-looking things with deep blood grooves up the side. Most of them were still wrapped in sticky creosote.

Despite what Meg had told him, he wanted to buy the kid a bomb. They were only fifty bucks. Then he admitted he really wanted one for himself. One of the deep blue ones. He wanted to mount it on the front of the Winnebago.

No – what he really wanted was to buy one and mail it,

C.O.D., to Alan Lefkowitz, c/o Big Mountain Studios, Santa Monica Boulevard, Century City, California . . .

Then Sam decided it was time to look for bullet casings. They climbed back into the camper and drove ten minutes out of town, parked and started hiking.

They walked through the woods, following what was a pretty clearly marked trail. The boy had a box over his shoulder and carried a short metal rod with a disk attached. He had a headset around his neck. They were by themselves. The day was very quiet. Sam kept looking up at Pellam as if he expected him to say something brilliant.

"You think you're going to find bullets here?"

"You never know."

"Like from hunters?"

"Right."

"You hunt, Mr Pellam?"

"Yep. Haven't for a while. My father and I used to go out all the time."

"Where's he live?"

Pellam glanced at him. "He died few years ago."

"Like Grandpa Wold."

"That's your mother's name? Wold?"

"Un-huh. She's got a gun, my mom. Grandpa gave it to her. It's an old one. Mom and me shoot it sometimes down by the river. Wow, it makes this totally loud noise, really loud. And it knocked me over nearly."

He set down the metal detector and illustrated shooting the gun and falling backwards. He lay on the ground, still.

Pellam looked down at him, alarmed. "Hey, you okay? Are you all right?"

"Sure!" He jumped up. "My dad doesn't hunt much. We go fishing sometimes. What'd you hunt?"

"Pheasant, duck, geese."

Sam asked, "You like football?"

"I used to play."

"Yeah, I knew it! Where? Pro, I'll bet."

He laughed loud. "Pro? I'm about a hundred pounds light for that. Naw, just in high school."

"Quarterback, right?"

"Receiver. I figured it was better to get jumped by one or two big guys instead of four or five."

"What's it like to score a TD? Running over the line. I like the way, you know, how they run over the line and then drop the ball like it's nothing to them. That's so neat! What's it like?"

"I didn't score that many. I wasn't that good."

"Sure you were!" the boy countered. "I'll bet you saved the team. When was that? A couple years ago?"

"More like twenty."

Sam rolled his eyes. "Holy cow, you're older than my mom. You don't look old."

Pellam laughed. He'd forgotten how completely kids nuked your careful adult delusions.

"Hey, Mr Pellam, can we like practice passing sometime? My mom tries but she's a girl and all, you know. Maybe you and me could practice, you could give me some tips. My dad, well, he's busy a lot of the time. All he cares about is his job."

Pellam knew enough not to get into that one. He said, "We'll see."

"My mom'd like it if you stayed around for a while. She likes you, I can tell."

Or into that one either.

They came to a ridge that overlooked the parking lot where Marty had died. The lot was about two hundred yards away. There was only one other high point that Pellam could see that had a view of the lot and that one was five hundred yards. Not an impossible shot with a good scope but this would be the more likely spot for a sniper. Also, this faced the rear of the parking lot, and, if Marty had parked head in, would offer the car's gas tank as a target.

Still, it'd be a bitch of a shot in any kind of breeze, and on a warm day – as that day had been – heat waves from the valley beneath would have blurred the line of sight.

"Okay, Sam, go to work. Find me what you can."

The boy wandered back and forth for ten minutes, retrieving two mashed Coors cans and a quarter ("It's yours, son"). Suddenly he shrieked and ran up to Pellam with a .22 long rifle cartridge in his hand.

"Nope, too small. I'm looking for centerfire. You know the difference?"

"No, sir."

"Firing pin hits a .22 on the rim of the shell. So they're called rimfire. Bigger calibers hit the percussion cap in the center. They're called centerfire."

"Wow, that's neat."

"Come here, I'll show you." Sam frowned, then his eyes went wide, as Pellam opened his jacket and pulled a gun from his waistband. It was an 1876 Colt, steel with dark rosewood grips

"Wow," the boy whispered.

Pellam kept the gun pointed at the ground. "Always pretend a gun is loaded, even if you know it isn't, and always pretend that it could go off at any minute. So you never point it at anything unless you're prepared to shoot it. Got it?"

"I got it. That's a cowboy gun."

"It's a Colt Peacemaker, a .45." He opened the thumb cover and with the ejector rod eased the shell out. He held the end up for the boy to see. "There, that's the cap in the center. The pin on the hammer hits the cap and that sets off the powder. The old-time guns like this use black powder. Like the one your mother's got. Newer guns use smokeless."

"Can you take me shooting, Mr Pellam? Please?"

"Let's talk to your parents about it. Maybe."

"Shoot something. Will you?"

"Not now, Sam. It's not a toy." He put the gun back in his waistband. "Let's find me my cartridges."

With even more enthusiasm the boy swept the detector over the ground. Pellam wasn't paying much attention to him, he was looking at the dark patch of plowed-over earth in the distance, the parking lot, where Marty'd died a horrible death. He didn't notice the boy stoop down and pick up something then come racing over to him.

"Look what I found, Mr Pellam. Look!"

Sam dropped the two cartridges into his hand. They were .30 caliber, though the length was odd, stubbier than a .30-'30 or .30-'06, bigger than a Garand. They couldn't have been from a carbine like an M1 because a short-barreled rifle wouldn't have been accurate enough for a shot of this range.

"Good job, Sam." He patted the beaming boy on his shoulders. "Just what I'm looking for." He dropped the cartridges into his pocket.

"You show me your collection some day, Mr Pellam?"

"You bet, Sam. Time to get home."

"Aw . . ."

Together they walked down the mountain, swapping fishing stories.

That night, Sam upstairs, and Keith still at the company, Meg Torrens ate a turkey sandwich with cold cranberry sauce and drank a glass of white wine, reading the headlines and the first paragraphs of all the stories in the *New York Times*.

She heard the clicks and tiny pops of the hundred-year-old house, the muffled roar of the furnace coming on – something reassuring about the way its simple brain kicked the machinery on and coursed hot water through the pipes. It would shut off and there'd be moments of complete, muffled silence.

She finished the Arts section, dropped the paper and walked upstairs to Sam's room.

"Hi, Mommy."

She walked to his computer.

"Tell me again. You dial, then what do you say?" Meg looked at the computer.

"Aw, Mom," Sam said. He was tired, it was nearly nine. "It's a modem. Nobody says anything. You just get a tone. That means you're on-line."

"Show me." In the master bedroom the clock radio played a sad country western tune, an old Patsy Cline song.

Sam bent over the keyboard and typed rapidly. Meg and Keith spent thirty dollars a month for access to a current events database, which Sam had learned contained a sports submenu; they'd ended up with huge overages one month when he'd printed out the starting lineups of every baseball team since 1956.

He picked up the phone, dialed, his mouth twisted with exasperation, though Meg knew he was tickled to show off this esoteric knowledge. A squeal came from the phone. He held it toward her like a ray gun. "Zap, zap, zap!" And pressed a button on a small box. The computer screen came to life.

"You're on-line, Mom. What do you want to look up?"

"A name. I want to look up a man's name."

She typed in some characters. The response come back in five seconds. Meg scrolled through the text. "How do I print it?"

"You either do a screen dump or download the whole file."

Where did they learn this stuff?

"Just tell me what to push."

"Here." Sam happily hit a button, and the raspy matrix printer began its satisfying sound.

Reminded her of the Polaroid.

Bzzzt.

The sound lasted for some time. There was a lot to print.

———— ·••·•· ————

A pples.
     A thousand apples, a hundred thousand. A million.
     Pellam'd never seen so many apples in his life. And in so
many forms. Apple pies, fritters, turnovers, apple butter, jelly,
pickled apples and candied apples. You could dunk for them.
You could buy them fresh by the bushels, buy them dried and
painted and glued together into wreaths and wall hangings
shaped like geese and pigs.
     There were girls dressed up like apples. All the boys seemed
to have round, rouge cheeks.
     A woman tried to sell him a chance to win a Dutch apple pie
by tossing a ring onto a board with apples nailed onto it.
     "I don't really care for apples," he told her.
     The football field was filled with more than a thousand
people, milling through the booths, playing the games and
examining the junk for sale – sweaters, wooden trinket boxes,
clocks made from driftwood, ceramic, macrame. Janine had a

jewelry booth. Pellam had homed in on it right away, waited until she was busy making a sale, and did the obligatory appearance. All she had time to say was "Dinner tomorrow, remember?"

He nodded.

"At four. Don't you forget, lover boy." She winked and blew him a kiss.

Pellam estimated half the crowd was tourists, half was locals. No one older than seventeen seemed exactly sure why they were there. The tourists were catching the tail of some indigenous upstate experience – *the country, the country!* – and holding on for a while, buying vases, jewelry, decorations, food to take back to their Manhattan apartments. The Cleary moms and dads were gossiping and doing some serious eating. The kids, of course, were the only ones really enjoying themselves because for them it was nothing more than tons of apples. And who needed more than that on a nice fall day?

No more 'Roids. He'd left the camera in the camper. Now, he was just another tourist scoping out the leaves, the booths, the scenery.

The Toyota showed up five minutes later, racing through the parking lot and skidding to a stop on the crumbling asphalt. Meg saw him right away and waved. Keith wasn't with her but Sam was. The boy waved energetically. He wondered if Sam had said anything about Pellam's tendency to collect lethal weapons.

Like the other night at dinner, she looked ten years younger than the upstate matron who'd visited him in the clinic. Her hair wasn't teased and stiff but was tied back in a ponytail. She wore tight jeans and a dark paisley high-necked blouse under a suede jacket. A silver antique pin was at her throat.

The boy stayed close. "Hi, Mr Pellam."

"Howdy, Sam."

"Hello," Meg said to Pellam. He nodded in reply.

They were suddenly enveloped in a large crowd of Izod-shirted Manhattanites. The men with curly dark hair, the women in black stretch pants. Everybody had great forearms and calves, courtesy of the New York Health and Racquet Club.

The gang passed and they found themselves alone.

"You made it," Meg said.

"Wouldn't miss this for the world."

"Here," Meg called. "A present."

She pitched him an apple. He caught it left-handed.

"I hate apples," he said.

Sam grinned. "So do I."

"Cleary still a small town?" Pellam smiled.

She frowned.

He asked, "Won't they talk, we walk around like this?" They circled on the fringes of the festival.

"Let 'em," Meg said. "I'm feeling rebellious today. Phooey."

Sam was running sorties to the booths but always circling back to study Pellam with casual awe. Then he'd be off again, hooking up with some buddies from school, conspiring, looking amazed and devious and overjoyed – and always on the move.

"Energetic, aren't they?" Pellam watched an impromptu race.

Meg said, "There's nothing like children for perspective. What they teach you about yourself is the best. Somebody said that the most honest and the most deceitful, the cruelest and the kindest of all people are children." She laughed. "Of course, that's only half true when you're talking about your own kids."

"You think about it, there are very few good movies about children," Pellam said. "Sentiment, mostly. Or revisionism – directors trying to patch up their own childhood on celluloid. Or trying to put adult values on kids' shoulders. Cheap shots, you ask me. I'd like to see a movie about the ambivalence of being a child. That would be a good project."

"Why don't you suggest it to your studio?"

Former studio, he thought, and didn't answer. Meg jogged away quickly to keep Sam from climbing a fence.

Pellam found himself in front of a turkey shoot booth, where you could win stuffed birds, chocolate turkeys, and a fifteen-pound frozen one by plinking tiny sponge rubber ducks – painted to look like turkeys – with a battered Sears pump action .22. Pellam called Sam over to him.

"What do you want, son, one of those little stuffed turkeys or a candy one?"

Sam looked shyly at his mother, who said, "Tell Mr Pellam what you'd like." She looked up, grinning. "This, I've got to see."

"I guess chocolate, okay?" His eyes on Pellam.

Meg said, "If he can win it you can eat it."

"But maybe not all at once," Pellam said. "It looks pretty big."

The booth attendant took a dollar from Pellam, who asked, "How many to win one of those chocolate turkeys? The bigger one?"

The man loaded the skinny gun. "Six hits out of ten."

"Okay." Pellam leaned forward, resting on the chest-high bench, and fired four shots slowly. They all missed, kicking up dust in the sandbag bullet trap.

Sam laughed. Meg did too.

Pellam slowly stood up straight. "Think I've got the feel." He quickly lifted the stock to his cheek. Six shots – fast, short cracks, as fast as he could work the slide. Six ducks flew off the board.

"Holy shit," the booth man whispered. Then he blushed. "Oh, beg your pardon, Mrs Torrens."

Pellam handed the gun back, and Sam took the candy, staring at him. Eyes wide. "Wow."

"What do you say, Sam?"

"Holy . . .," the boy began slowly.

Meg warned, "Sam."

". . . cow. Wow, thanks, Mr Pellam. That was like totally fresh. I mean, totally."

Meg said, "Sam . . ."

Sam said, "Mom thinks I don't speak English."

"I know fresh," Pellam said. He looked at the candy. "I hope that it is too."

Sam peeled back the foil and bit off the bird's head. "Wow," he said through a mouthful of chocolate and walked away, looking back every fourth or fifth step. Another story was about to circulate.

They wandered on. She said, "I thought all you knew was muzzleloaders."

"I drive the L.A. Freeway. You gotta know how to shoot."

"Where'd you learn?"

"My father," he said.

"Where'd you grow up?" she asked.

"Simmons."

She turned to him, "No! Not just across the river?" She nodded west.

"The very same."

"It's a lot like Cleary."

"Little poorer, little scruffier," Pellam said. "And we don't get the tourists for the leaves. It's mostly pine."

They walked in silence for a moment, kicking through the tall grass at the edge of the football field.

"Keith couldn't make it?"

"He'll be coming by later. He's at his company."

"It was good of him to help me the other day."

"He said somebody'd stolen what you were looking for."

"Yep. We got outflanked."

They walked for a few minutes then, as if Pellam had asked about her husband, Meg said, "Keith's changed. When his partner died, it affected him. He got an edge to him."

"Really? I didn't sense anything like that."

"I wasn't sure he'd help you. He doesn't like things that are out of his own, you know, orbit. I'm glad he did."

They were being examined – dozens of heads turned conspicuously away while eyes followed them.

After five minutes of looking at booths, he said, "Why did you leave Manhattan?"

"Keith got a job with a drug company up here. I wasn't getting modeling work and just couldn't break into acting. I had a baby. I always wanted a house."

"And you like Cleary?"

She gave a nervous laugh and looked away. "It's tough for

me to give you an answer. And it won't matter if I live here for another twenty-five years. I'll never know the place well enough to talk about it. These places, towns like this, they're born into you. The roots go way back. You come any other way, you're just a houseguest. You may be the life of the party, you may even get yourself elected to the town council, but places like Cleary don't become part of you. It's in the genes or it isn't. It's not in mine."

Applause not far away. A new Miss Apple had been crowned. Pellam saw a couple of kids gravitating toward him and Meg. Word was out that the location scout could shoot out a sponge duck's eye at fifty feet. The boys kept their distance as Meg and Pellam circled the field. The ripe, rich scent of decomposing grass came to them.

"Your hair looks nice that way."

Her fingers reached toward her ponytail then she stopped the acknowledgment and lowered her hand. Her eyes fled from his and she concentrated on something on the horizon. They walked to the festival's zoo – a sad collection of cows, goats, geese, ducks and a pony – before she said, "Is that why you and your wife broke up?"

"Uh, why's that?"

"Sorry, I was just thinking about you traveling around."

"There were a lot of reasons. Sure, the job had a lot to do with it."

"You were away from home six months, eight months—"

"I didn't travel as much then."

"I'd love to travel," she said. "Maybe do some acting. Not be a star necessarily. Character acting maybe. I'd even like your job."

Even your job.

Just a location scout.

"I don't think you would."

She said, "Well, I love my house. I wouldn't give that up. But seeing all those new places . . . It's like going on vacation, but having a purpose. I think that'd be wonderful."

Women said that. *My* house. Never our house. He remembered his wife saying just those words. Of course, in the end, that was how it worked out. It did become her house. Self-fulfilling prophecy, he guessed.

". . . I guess what I'd want is Sam to come with me for maybe a week or two at a time." After a moment, she said, "Keith too of course." She looked at him but he gave no reaction to the lapse. If a lapse it had been.

Pellam steered away from the domestic situation. He said, "I can't really tell you why I like it. The thing about scouting is, it's not the work itself – finding a spot that'll work for the film. I mean, that's fine, that's what they pay me for. But I like the being on the road . . ." He waved his arm. "Simmons is, what, less than a hundred miles from here? I grew up with colored leaves and Victorian houses. But I was real glad to get that call and hit the road, scout for towns like this."

He waved to Sam. It seemed his fan club had grown to a half dozen.

"One March," he continued, "I'd been sitting home for a month. I got a call from a producer who wanted me to scout for a labour union film. I got in the camper and headed right out to the steel mills in Gary, Indiana. Ugly, cold, gray. Walking through slush. That place was as close to hell as any I'd ever been. But I was so glad to get that call."

She wrinkled her nose. "I'd only go to fun places. Rio, San Francisco, Hawaii . . ."

He laughed. "You wouldn't get many jobs."

"No, but I'd have a hell of a good time on the ones I got."

"They have beer around here?"

"Probably, but don't you want some cider? They make it fresh."

"No, I want a beer. I hate apples, remember?"

"Then I guess an apple festival doesn't have a lot for you."

"I wouldn't say that."

Meg ignored the flirt and they steered toward the food concession.

As his mother and Mr Pellam were walking through the farmyard zoo Sam ran off toward a bow and arrow shoot. He thought about returning to the rifle shoot and winning something for Mr Pellam, but he remembered seeing the bow and arrow game – where you shot at paper targets of deer. One of the prizes was a small plastic football and because Mr Pellam had played in school that's what Sam decided he was going to win.

He gave the man a dollar for ten arrows and the hawker gave him a smaller bow, a straight pull, not one of the pulleyed hunting bows. Sam took it and notched an arrow, the way he'd done at camp. He went into position and pulled the string back. His muscles were quivering and his fingers let go quickly, before he'd sighted properly. He hit the deer in the rump.

"Hey," the voice called, laughing, "Got him in the ass."

Sam turned. It was one of the boys from high school. A senior, he thought. He believed his name was Ned. He was smiling but Sam followed the grade schoolers' general rule that every high school boy was a potential terrorist. They'd take your lunch away from you, tie your Keds together and swing them like gaucho's bolos over electric wires, swear and spit on you, use you for a sparring partner.

Sam swallowed and ignored him. He concentrated fiercely on the target, the way his mother had taught him when he shot – not paying attention to the bow or arrow, but to where the arrow should strike. He drew the bowstring back and fought the agony in his thin arms as he stared at his target. Finally, he released the arrow.

Thwack.

A heart shot.

"Fucking good," the boy was saying, shaking his head. Sam looked at him cautiously. Ned wasn't being sarcastic. "Thanks."

Two more heart shots, a gut shot, and then his strength started to go. The next four hit the bale of hay, but missed the deer. The last shot was another gut shot.

"Okay, you won yourself anything from the bottom shelf, son. What do you want?"

Sam hesitated. The kid was going to take his football away from him. He'd just grab it and run. He muttered, "One of those footballs."

"Okay, there you go."

Sam took the green plastic ball. He started to walk away quickly but the boy was making no moves toward him. He just said, "That was some good shooting. I wish I could shoot like that."

Sam laughed involuntarily. Here was a kid who was, like, seventeen telling Sam he couldn't shoot bow and arrow as good as him! Totally weird. "It's not hard. You've just gotta, you know, practice."

"What's your name?"

"Sam."

"I'm Ned." He stuck his hand out. No high school kid *ever* shook hands with grade school kids. Sam reached out tentatively and shook.

"Hey, you wanta see something?" Ned asked.

"Like what?" Sam didn't feel uncomfortable anymore. The boy could have grabbed the football and pushed him down any time. But no, he was just smiling and seemed to want to talk.

"Something neat?"

"I guess," Sam said, glancing toward where his mother and Mr Pellam were walking slowly, the same way his mother and father walked.

The boy walked off into a thick woods off the side of the football field. "What's here?" Sam asked.

"You'll see."

About thirty feet inside the woods was a small clearing. The boy sat down. He patted the ground next to him. Sam sat. "Let's see the ball."

Sam handed it to him.

"That's all right." He tossed it in his hand. "Feels good."

"I'm going to give it to Mr Pellam. He's the man with the movie company."

"Yeah, I heard about that. Totally excellent, making a film here." The boy handed the ball back to him. "Here you go."

There was silence for a moment.

Ned said, "I like it here. It's kind of secret."

Sam looked around and thought it looked like a clearing in a forest. "Yeah, it's okay."

"You got ten bucks?" Ned whispered.

"Naw," said Sam, who did in fact have eleven dollars and some change in his jeans pocket.

"How much you got?"

"A couple dollars. I don't know. Why?"

"You wanta buy some candy?"

"Candy? Ten bucks for candy?"

"It's special candy. You'll like it. I thought I saw you had ten bucks when you paid the guy at the arrow shoot."

Sam looked away from the older boy and squeezed the football. "Well, that, like, wasn't mine. It was my mom's."

Ned nodded. "I'll give you a sample. Then see if you don't want to buy one." He opened a yellow envelope and shook a dozen cubes of crystal candy into his hand. He held his palm out to Sam, who looked at the tiny bits cautiously. Ned laughed at his wariness and put a candy in his own mouth. "Come on, don't be a wuss."

"I don't really—"

Ned frowned. "You're not a pussy, are you?"

Sam suddenly grabbed most of the candies and slipped them into his mouth, chewing them down.

"No!" Ned shouted in horror. "You stupid shit! You weren't supposed to eat 'em all! They're ten dollars each!"

"I didn't mean . . ." Sam backed away in fear. His mouth was filled with a powerful, numbing sweetness. "I didn't know. You didn't tell me . . ." He suddenly felt warm and giddy and dizzy. In his mouth was a funny aftertaste, reminded him of the chewable vitamins he took in the morning.

Ned stepped close to him, reaching for Sam's collar; the young boy cowered away, feeling the heat and the dizziness flow over his body.

"Sam!" It was his mother's voice and from not very far away.

Then he was being lifted up. Ned had him by the shirt. "You dumb little prick! You tell anybody about this, I'll find you. I'll come get you and I'll beat the living shit out of you, you got that?"

Sam thought he should be afraid but he felt so good. He laughed.

"You hear me?"

Laughing again.

He felt himself falling into the leaves, which seemed suddenly like the ground in the Candyland game he played with his babysitter until he outgrew it. Cotton candy grass, marshmallow rocks. *Candyland.* Hey, just like the candy he'd eaten, he thought. That thought made him laugh too. He felt like laughing forever, he felt so good.

Strange thumping noises. He looked up. Ned was running, running fast, deep into the forest. Sam thought he saw the boy turn into a tree. He stared at the spot for a long time.

He tried to stand.

Laughing.

Fireworks, black sparklers, cascades, and Roman candles, pouring their fire all over him. A huge roaring hum in his ears.

Warmth and humming music.

"Sam?" His mother's voice was both magnified a thousand times and very distant, like she was trapped in an airlock on the Starship *Enterprise*.

Then the fun started to leave. He felt he was going to sleep, only it was a funny kind of sleep, like the way he felt when he'd had his tonsils out and woke up in terrible pain and so thirsty he thought he'd die. He'd been lonely when he awoke in the hospital and he cried for what seemed like forever, until he saw his mother, asleep, across the room.

That's who he wanted now. "Mommy," he called.

Sam managed to struggle to his feet. He walked forward a few steps. "Mommy, help me!"

A man's voice called, "Sam!" Mr Pellam's. And that reminded him of the football. He turned back into the black explosions, the heat, the cracking fireworks, the hum, and stumbled into the clearing, where he bent down to pick up the football. He was certain he had it but as he reached forward his hand came up with nothing more than leaves. He fell to the ground.

Then he saw nothing more; a huge wave of black filled his vision. But he kept patting the ground around him for the football. He *had* to find it.

He'd won it for Mr Pellam.

Her face scared him.

It wasn't just that she'd been crying, which changed the density and texture of her skin and gave her the contours of a battered wife; it was more the fluttering of the irises of her eyes, unable to alight.

What Pellam saw in Meg Torrens's face was panic.

He just stood there, beside her, not knowing what to say or whether he should touch her in a brotherly way. Thinking he should be taking charge but with no idea of what needed to be done.

Meg sat with her legs spread outward, boot tips pointed at an oblique angle, her body forward, elbows resting on her thighs, her hands washing each other absently in invisible water. Occasionally she'd glance up and Pellam would smile in a way that screenwriters would describe as sympathetically concerned.

They'd waited for twenty minutes.

Keith arrived and as soon as he did, Pellam felt himself relax; he realized he'd been standing hunched forward, jaw tight. He watched the couple embrace. Keith nodded to him.

"What the hell happened?" husband asked wife.

Meg brushed aside her hair, which had come undone from the ponytail and was strewn across her face.

"We found him," she said and started sobbing again.

Pellam said, "Sam passed out and we couldn't revive him. The doctor's been in there since we got here. He hasn't said anything."

"Oh, Keith, he was so pale. It was terrible . . ."

With an anger they knew was not directed toward them Keith asked, "What happened? Did he fall? Is it a seizure?"

Meg wiped her face. "We just found him. Keith, it was so horrible. He was just lying there. It was like he didn't have any muscles. I tried to wake him up. He wouldn't wake up." She looked at Pellam with her trapped animal eyes, staring at *him* but undoubtedly seeing the horrific image of her son's pale skin against the autumn leaves. "He wouldn't wake up."

Keith looked like he wanted to hurt someone. It didn't seem to matter to him whether this'd been caused by another human being or an animal or some haywire connections in the boy's bloodstream. He wanted revenge.

Meg pressed her cheek against her husband's chest and didn't say anything. Slowly she calmed.

The doctor who resembled a vet, the one who'd tended Pellam, appeared and walked slowly down the corridor.

The man had such an expressive face that no words were necessary. There was no doubt about the boy's condition. Pellam remembered the way the man looked at him when he'd entered the room to tell him about Marty's death.

This was no tragedy.

The doctor's round jowly face zeroed in on Meg's eyes and he said, "He'll be okay."

Meg began crying again, quieter, but more desperately. "Can I see him?"

"Sure, Meg. In just a second."

Keith's anger vanished at once as if he were afraid prolonged hate might reverse the results. "What happened to him? Was it a seizure?"

"Keith, I need to ask this. Does Sam have any history of drug use?"

"Drug use?" The laugh was explosive.

Meg let go of her husband and turned to face the doctor. "He's ten years old, how could he—?"

"Drug use?" Keith repeated as if he hadn't heard correctly.

"What did—" she began.

The doctor said, "He overdosed on drugs."

With a blustery edge in her voice Meg said, "No! Not Sam."

"Oh, give me a fucking break," Keith growled. "Are you nuts?"

The doctor continued. "It's true, Keith. It looks like it was an opiate of some kind. Probably heroin."

Keith exploded. "Are you saying he was shooting up? That's the craziest, fucking thing—" Meg touched her husband's arm. He calmed. "I'm sorry. But you made a mistake."

"I'm as disturbed about this as you are . . ." The doctor lifted a small plastic envelope out of his pocket. Inside were tiny fragments of crystals. "These were in his mouth. It's extremely soluble. Which means he ingested much more than this."

All three stared at the bag.

"It's a dextrose base – sugar – but it's mixed with something else. I don't know what exactly. A synthetic heroin of some kind. Stronger than Percodan. I've never seen anything like it."

"Somebody put heroin in candy and gave it to my son?" Keith whispered. He looked at Meg and said, almost accusingly, "Who was he with? Did you see anybody, weren't you watching him?"

Pellam bristled, felt defensive for Meg. "We were both with the boy. He'd run off every once in a while but we—"

"For God's sake, Keith, we were at the Apple Festival. I wasn't letting him wander around in the South Bronx—"

He blinked. "I'm sorry, I just—".

She took his hand.

The doctor said, "I've called Tom. I had to. Whatever this is it's a controlled substance and I've got to report it."

"Fucking right you're going to report it," Keith growled. "But I don't want a story in the *Leader*. I don't want it to sound like he was doing drugs."

"I won't say anything to the paper. But this's serious, Keith. I don't know – Tom may want to bring somebody from Albany in."

In a faint voice, Meg said, "Please let me see my son."

"Come on," the doctor said. He glanced at Pellam, then down at the leg where the bruise resided. "How you doing, sir?" he asked pleasantly but without particular interest.

"Fine."

The doctor put his arm around Meg and led her down

the corridor. Keith said, "Excuse me," to Pellam and followed.

Pellam sat down in an aluminum-and-orange-naugahyde chair and looked at a month-old *People* magazine without reading a single word, or seeing a single picture.

An hour later, Sam walked unsteadily out of the room. Meg had her arm around him and Keith was trying to sound cheerful while he recited phrases like, "You're doing great, skipper" and "You're a tougher man than I." Sam would blink and look at his father as if he were speaking a foreign language.

"Hi, Mr Pellam," Sam said. His face brightened a little but there was hardly any color in it.

"How you feeling, son?"

"I got sick."

"You'll be fine in the morning."

"I don't feel too good."

"Well, get better soon. We've got to practice our football, remember?"

"Yeah."

Meg, Sam and Pellam stood together, silently, while Keith paid the bill with a check and took a prescription and instruction sheet from the doctor.

The door opened and the sheriff walked into the clinic.

"Meg, I just heard."

"Tom," she said, nodding toward him.

The sheriff looked stonily at Pellam for a long moment, then glanced down at Sam. "How you doing, young man?"

"Pretty okay, sir."

"Attaboy."

The doctor joined them, along with Keith. Meg told the sheriff about finding her son in the woods and the doctor explained about the drugs.

"What is it, you know?"

"I'm sending the sample to a lab in Poughkeepsie. I'll get you a copy of it. I think it's a heroin derivative."

The sheriff winced. "Yeah, guess I'll have to go to the NYBI."

"Second time we've had an overdose," the doctor pointed out. "That boy last year."

Tom nodded. "He was in high school. They're getting younger."

The sheriff looked down at Sam then said to Keith. "You mind if I talk to him just for a minute?"

Meg asked her son, "You mind, honey?"

"Uh-uh."

"Maybe just you, me and the boy?" Tom asked her.

Pellam and Keith took their cues and stepped outside.

The sheriff crouched next to a jaundiced potted bamboo palm, vainly reaching for a tiny, greasy window in the front door, the only source of natural light in the waiting room.

Meg was struggling to stay calm, struggling to concentrate. All she wanted to do was throw her arms around the boy.

The sheriff looked into the boy's eyes. "What happened, Sam? You remember?"

"I found this envelope. And there was some candy inside. I ate it."

"You ate it?"

"A bunch of it. I guess I shouldn't've. Mom's pretty mad at me."

Meg said, "No, I'm not, honey."

Tom said, "She's just worried about you, that's all. So you don't know where the envelope came from?"

"No, sir."

"You're sure nobody gave it to you?"

"No, sir. I mean, yeah, I'm sure nobody gave it to me."

"You just found it."

"Uh-huh."

"You know what happened to the envelope?"

"No."

"I'm going to ask you a question, Sammie, and I want you to answer it truthfully."

"Sure."

"You know Mr Pellam."

"Sure."

"Did he give you the candy?"

Meg stiffened when she heard this. This hadn't even occurred to her. She started to speak but the sheriff waved her quiet.

"You mean, that he won?"

"What?"

"He won a chocolate turkey and gave it to me."

"When was that?"

"Just before I got sick."

"It was a game," Meg said. "A booth at the fair."

The sheriff ignored her. "Did he give you the candy in the envelope?"

Sam shook his head. "No, sir."

"You found it, right?"

Sam swallowed. "Yeah, it was just lying there. I found it."

"Okay, Sammie. You go home now and get some rest."

"So he gave the boy some candy," the sheriff said.

Meg frowned, repeated, "From the turkey shoot booth. Chocolate. Not . . . that crap."

"Look, Sam claims he found the envelope but he's lying. I can see. All right, not lying exactly. He's confused. You know kids, Meg, come on. What I'm saying is I know somebody gave him those pills and *he* knows who it is."

Meg asked, "You think it was Pellam?"

"Kind of a coincidence, wouldn't you say? His friend's doing drugs and gets himself killed. Then your son overdoses." He asked, "Was Sam alone with Pellam today?"

She didn't answer at first. "No."

"Any other time they may have been together alone?"

She swallowed and shook her head. "I want to be with my son."

"Sure, Meg."

Outside, Pellam watched the two of them push out the door and head toward Keith's car. Meg hugged Sam. "Let's get you home, into bed."

"I don't feel good."

Pellam stepped forward, crouched down and took the boy by the shoulders. "When you're better, young man, you and I're going to—"

Meg took her son's hand firmly in hers and practically pushed the boy into the Cougar. Pellam stared at her. She wouldn't look back. Meg didn't say anything as she walked to her car and started it.

Keith got in the Cougar, put Sam's seat belt on him.

Both cars pulled out of the parking lot, Keith's red Mercury and Meg's gray Toyota. She didn't even look at him. Pellam stared after the import for several minutes. Finally, there was nothing left to see but a residue of haze above the asphalt in the car's wake. It was only then that he realized that while he was looking at the spot where Meg's car had disappeared the sheriff, sitting in his glossy, pristine squad car, had been staring at him.

He walked over to the man. "I drove here in Meg's car from the fairgrounds. My camper's back there. You give me a lift?"

"Sorry, sir. I'm heading the opposite direction."

"Sure," Pellam said, watching his black-and-white pull dramatically out of the parking lot, slinging gravel behind it. "Thanks anyway. Sir."

Bobby sat inside the cabin at the junkyard and read a *National Geographic*. He looked at the stain in the margin and wondered what it was. Grape jelly, maybe. Blood? Beef juice?

R&W was fat with *National Geographics*. Stacks and stacks of them, going moldy. Yellow and green. His brother didn't understand why Bobby continued to buy the old ones. Something about that magazine, people thought you shouldn't throw them out, like doing that was somehow unpatriotic. So what they did was bundle them up and take them to antique stores or tag sales or junkyards like R&W and sell them, all organized by year. Or decade. Didn't matter if they made money on them. The point was, a part of America got preserved and, besides, where else but in articles about Africa or the Amazon could a twelve-year-old boy get a look at tits and not run the chance of getting whipped?

Today, Bobby was reading about Portland, which seemed

like a great place to live. He closed the magazine and tossed it against the wall of the shack. True, they *were* starting to smell. He'd have to get out the Lysol spray.

He heard the car door slam.

Bobby knew right away, even before the door to the shack opened that there was trouble. This was something about twins, at least something about Billy and him. A telepathy thing. So now when his brother opened the door and walked through it, Bobby was staring right into his eyes, frowning with an expression that matched Billy's almost identically.

He said, "So?"

"So our ass is in deep shit," Billy muttered.

"What?"

"Torrens's kid got some of the pills. Almost OD'd."

"Fuck. That little blond kid?" Bobby glanced in a perfunctory way toward the backroom of the shack where several cartons of their special candy were stacked. "How'd he get it?" Then he knew, the message from his brother coming through loud and clear. He nodded grimly. "The pretty boy? Ned. The other day."

"Your playmate."

Bobby said, "*Our* playmate. Just 'cause I saw him first don't go blaming me. Why'd he give them away?"

"Why'd you give him so many in the first place? Damn, I'll ream that boy's ass."

Bobby gave a splinter of a smile. "You already done that."

But his brother wasn't in any mood to joke. "This isn't funny."

Bobby was nodding slowly. "The Torrens kid," he muttered. "They know it was us?"

"They did, don't you think we'd've heard by now?"

"What if Ned said something to the kid? About where he got it?"

"Could be a problemo," Billy said absently. "Too bad the kid didn't take 'em all. And just, you know, die. Would've been better."

"So they've got some? Of the stuff, I mean."

"Yeah," Billy explained.

"Ouch."

"It's at the clinic. They're going to be shipping it somewhere to find out what it is."

"Fuck," Bobby said. "That's bad. Man, that's bad. What're we gonna do?"

And Billy looked at his brother as if he'd just asked the most dumb-ass question in the world. "Well, if you think real hard, maybe a couple things'll come to mind."

He didn't have to wait very long before they did.

"Hello?"

The voice of Wex Ambler's housekeeper answering the phone.

Meg didn't know the woman. She'd seen her several times since she and Ambler had begun their affair – once coming out of the brick and white-trim First Presbyterian Church on Maple Street. But Meg hadn't actually heard her voice before this moment. She sounded older than Ambler.

"Is Mr Ambler there please?" Meg, who had never typed a letter for anyone other than herself or Keith in her life, tried to sound like a Kelly Girl.

"Just a minute, please. Who shall I say's calling?"

This she'd thought about. "Dutchess County Realty."

"One minute."

"Hello?"

"Wex."

A moment later, she was listening to her lover say with a tortured formality, "Yes, Meg. How are you? I wasn't expecting to hear from you." There was a pause at the end of his sentences. She knew that Ambler liked phrases of affection and it would be natural for him to add a "darling" or "dear." Under the circumstances, of course, he'd have to watch himself carefully to avoid these.

Ambler had reluctantly agreed to Meg's demand that not a single soul in town know about their affair.

Meg asked, "Is it safe to talk?" Then she regretted the idiocy of the question.

Ambler ignored it. "What can I do for you?"

"There was an accident. Somebody gave Sam some drugs."

There was a pause. "Is he all right?"

"He'll be okay. But I can't make it today."

"Of course. I understand. What kind of drugs?"

"Heroin, it looked like."

"Are you sure?" His voice sounded flatlined. As if he hadn't even heard her.

"That's what the doctor said."

"Where did he get it?"

Meg hesitated. "I have no idea. He claims he found it."

"Will he be okay?"

"The doctor said he would."

He spoke again slowly. "I'm sorry. I wish I could have been there."

She said, "Yes, that would have been good."

Static growing on the line. She guessed he was on a cordless phone and had moved into a den, or outside. He spoke more freely. "When can I see you? I—"

Then he stopped talking and – his housekeeper undoubtedly approaching – said, "Those prices are a little high."

"I want to talk to you," she said. "There're some things we should talk about."

She was thankful Ambler wasn't alone and wasn't free to ask the questions that she didn't want to answer right now, certainly not over the phone. She heard the frustration in his voice. "I understand. It's a mutual situation. Day after tomorrow?"

"Probably."

"Have you thought any more about my proposition of the other day?"

"I don't want to talk about that now."

"I'm sorry. It's just . . . I'll look forward to seeing you day after tomorrow."

Meg found she was answering as if Keith were in the room, which he was not. "Those would be acceptable terms." She hung up.

"How you feeling, skipper?" Keith asked his son.

"Pretty good, Dad." But Sam's voice was weak and he was huddled in his bathrobe and blanket on his bed. Heartbreaking, the way he was lying, so small and fragile.

The computer's fan whirred softly; the screen was blank except for the C prompt, waiting for instructions. Keith thought about shutting it off but didn't; he figured Sam had left it on for whatever comfort the sound of the machinery might provide.

Keith sat on the edge of the bed and tucked the blankets around the boy. "How's the stomach?"

"I liked the ice cream. It didn't make me feel icky."

Keith nodded and remembered to look the boy in the eyes. Meg had once told him that he looked away from people too much. He'd explained to her that his mind wandered; he couldn't help it. She'd told him that was no excuse. When you had children, you had to give them a hundred and fifty percent of yourself.

There was a lot he wanted to say. About how he knew he wasn't as attentive as he ought to be, how he didn't like sports the way most of Sam's friends' fathers did, how he kept putting off vacations. About how if he hadn't been working today this probably wouldn't have happened. But he thought that talk like that now would just upset the boy, make him think that the incident with the drugs was worse than it was. He told himself that he simply would make it up to the boy. Not after the expansion at the factory was completed, not after the first of the year, not after the cold-season rush, but soon, very soon.

"I'm sorry about what happened, Daddy."

"We don't blame you, Sam."

"I was like pretty stupid."

"Sam," Keith leaned forward. "It is very, very important that you tell me where you got those pills."

"The candy?"

"Right. The candy. I know you didn't just find it."

Tears had started and the little boy was shaking. Keith put his hand on Sam's shoulder and squeezed it. "Don't worry. I won't let anything else happen to you."

"He said he'd beat me up."

"I won't let anyone beat you up. I promise you. Tell me."

"A kid from the high school."

"Who?"

"I don't know his last name. His first name's Ned. I think he's a senior."

"What does he look like?"

"He was like sort of tall. Like a football player . . . Oh, Daddy . . ." Sam bolted forward into Keith's arms. They hugged for a few minutes. Keith stood up. "You want me to leave the light on?"

"Uh-huh. Is it okay?"

Keith mussed Sam's hair. "I'll be up later and look in on you."

"Okay."

"Goodnight, son."

The fire at the clinic wasn't too bad.

Nowhere near the excitement of the Great Fire of 1912.

Only one of Cleary's trucks was needed and the men got the blaze under control with fire extinguishers, which was a big letdown because of all the hours they'd spent at hose drill. Brush fires and burning toasters – that was all they ever got. And at the clinic they didn't even get to use an axe. Like a lot of buildings in Cleary, the clinic was left open even when the all-night nurse went out for coffee, or – as in this case – to buy batteries for her Walkman.

Most of the carnage was confined to the office. A lot of patient records were destroyed as was all the outgoing mail and a number of envelopes bound for the testing lab in Albany. The gushing water had caused the most damage.

The first chief, a lean, chiseled-faced man who ran an insurance agency in town and took both jobs equally seriously, went through the office slowly. He didn't really need to, though; it didn't take any length of time, or great forensic skill, to make the discovery. He put his find into a Hefty trash bag (the Cleary Fire Department wasn't entrusted with evidence bags) and then went to his car to call the sheriff on his CB. He had trouble getting through and went back inside to call him on the phone, which was partly melted but still working.

As he stood at the charred desk and waited for Tom to come on the line he stared at what he'd found. For some reason the fire had not completely consumed the incendiary device. He knew, from the label, that the bottle at one time had held Taylor New York State sparkling wine and, from the smell, that it had more recently held gasoline.

He knew too (from research and continuing education – never having encountered a fire bomb before) that cloth was standard procedure for fuses. But this one was different. He held it up close.

The fire chief was pretty much a humorless man. But as the sheriff came on the line with a "Lo?," the chief was laughing, thinking they must be dealing with some pretty literate arsonists. Who else'd use pages from a *National Geographic* to light a Molotov cocktail?

"Mark," said Mayor Hank Moorhouse, after hearing him out, "it's no crime for the man to wander around and take pictures. If it weren't for assholes taking pictures of the leaves, we'd be a much poorer town. You know that."

It was suppertime. Succulent smells – roasts and fatty potatoes – floated through the Moorhouse's Victorian home. The sound of utensils and muffled voices came from another part of the house.

The heavyset and damn-scary young man, moving a pile of chewing tobacco around inside his cheek, said, "This guy is dangerous. You heard about Meg Torrens's kid? He got his hands on some dope."

"No! I didn't hear about that. Sam?" Moorhouse's eyes flicked down to the blond moustache then up again.

"The word is he got it from Pellam. A couple guys saw 'em together."

Mark moved the chaw around his mouth.

Moorhouse's nostrils dilated at the smell of dinner. He wanted this over with, and fast. But Mark worked for Wexell Ambler and Ambler held the first and second mortgages on Moorhouse's six-bedroom Colonial and was an assemblyman on the town council. He said, "That somvabitch." He tore off a piece of Scotch tape, wadded it up and started chewing. He'd tried to stop the habit but thought now: Better'n tobacco.

"There's more."

Mark dropped a packet of white powder down onto the desk.

"What's that?"

"What do you think it is?"

Moorhouse stared at the package as if it were from the melted core at Chernobyl.

"I saw him drop it," Mark said. "Pellam."

Moorhouse leaned forward carefully. He didn't want to touch the plastic. "We don't get much of this stuff around here. Christ, I worry about my boys –" He nodded toward the dining room. "– drinking beer. They tell me they've never tried pot and I believe 'em. But this . . . What exactly is it, Mark? Cocaine, huh?"

"Speed, I think."

"And it's illegal?"

Mark scoffed. "Illegal? A class IA controlled substance."

"What do you suppose it's worth? What's the, what do they say on the news, what's the street value?"

"You're asking me?" Mark said, his voice high with surprise. "What difference does it make?"

"Can't arrest someone just 'cause you saw him drop it." Though when Moorhouse thought about this, he wasn't so sure. Maybe you *could*. He wondered where you could look that up. Cleary had a town attorney.

Mark smiled amiably and leaned toward Moorhouse in a way that he thought of as doing what he did best. "Then we'll have to think a little harder."

Moorhouse's eyes kept circling in on the packet like a mosquito over flesh. "I don't know."

The brown envelope hit the desk with a slap. Moorhouse jumped, hesitated a moment, then picked it up. He glanced up at Mark, who said, "There's three thousand dollars in there."

Moorhouse thumbed through the bills. "Take your word for it. Where'd it come from?"

"Let's say a bunch of folk took up a collection. We don't think this guy should be here any longer. Movie ain't gonna be made here. No reason for him to hang around."

"So what's this for?" Moorhouse asked, before he realized he shouldn't be asking.

"A magistrate's fee you could call it."

His eyes darted from the money to the white packet.

He slipped the envelope in his desk and poked the powder, soft as baby talcum, with the end of his Cross pen.

He had three shots of Wild Turkey – trying to convince himself that he was celebrating – and lay back in the camper, listening to Willy Nelson sing *Crazy*.

Pellam had this theory that made for a very optimistic life. You kept considering the worst that could happen to you and then, when it didn't, whatever *did* happen wasn't so bad.

Who couldn't be cheerful with that kind of philosophy?

So, close to drunk, Pellam told himself that the worst had happened. *A*, he'd gotten fired from a job he needed and *B*, that was the one job in the world – outside of being independently wealthy – that he was temperamentally suited for. *C*, the rumor would already be burning up Sunset Boulevard that he was personally responsible for cratering a damn fine movie. *D*, he still hadn't found the man who'd killed his friend. And *E*, the woman he was spending a lot of time thinking about was mad at him for some reason he couldn't for the life of him figure out (this would be Meg, not Janine. Or . . . oh, Trudie. Too late to call her today. He would tomorrow).

He heard the car pull up.

He hoped it would be Meg though he knew it wasn't. It'd be Janine. Pellam knew what had happened: the old man was balling his current old lady under a Da-Glo Hendrix poster and somebody got stood up.

Come on, Janine, please, baby. Free love. Give peace a chance. Up against the wall . . .

Pellam was whisky giddy, almost happy. The worst had

happened. He was immune. And here was a big, horsy warm woman to bed down with.

The worst –

He swung open the door.

– had already happened.

The dirt and stones caught him square in the face before he got his hands halfway up to cover his eyes. He went blind. He inhaled a good bit of Cleary debris and started choking.

There were two of them. And one was big, a bear. He grabbed Pellam's shirt and pulled him easily out of the camper. He stumbled and, off balance, went down on his knees. Got dragged a few feet.

His eyes were burning, he was coughing loud and spitting out the bitter dirt.

"Come on, asshole, stand up," a brisk voice whispered. Arms slid under his chest. The bear tugged him up. Pellam uncoiled his legs. The top of his head collided with jaw.

"Shit, motherfucker! Cut my tongue. Shit, shit, shit!"

Pellam kicked out at the other, a smaller guy, who easily sidestepped the boot.

What he'd done – the lunging up – was just a reaction. But he knew it was a mistake. Guys like this, local tough guys, you don't play with. You just stay as clear away as you can, rolling and dodging until you get a good crack. You don't sting them; you hit them hard once or twice, really hard. Try to break their head. Make them think you're going to kill them. They'll leave, cussing you out and making it sound like you're not worth the trouble.

What happened was they'd come to have fun and Pellam had just pissed them off. Now they were mad.

The bear punched him hard on the first offered target – his shoulder, which didn't hurt much, but then he got him in a full nelson, pressed Pellam's chin down to his chest. Pellam was taller – so the bear couldn't lift him off the ground but the huge man kept him immobile. The other one came in for some low gut swings, right into the muscles, which knocked his wind out and sent blasts of nausea up through his chest. The bear said to no one, "My tongue bleeding? Shit, I think it is. God*damn*, that hurts."

Pellam opened his eyes but couldn't see a thing through the mud and tears. He gasped, "What do you want? You want money?"

The bear bent his head down further and the words got lost in a gurgle.

No, what they want is to beat the living crap out of me . . .

The smaller one came in close, aiming for Pellam's face, but couldn't get his fist in because the bear's fat elbows were in the way. "Hey, turn him loose for a second."

Which is when Pellam, gasped, shuddered and went completely limp.

"Shit, what happened?" The bear relaxed his grip. "Is he dead? Fuck. What'd you do?"

"What'd I do? I didn't do nothing. I just—"

Pellam broke free, felt his shirt rip down the back as the bear grabbed for it and swung a feint with his left fist at the smaller assailant, who dodged to the side. Right into Pellam's sweeping right fist. The snap of the man's nose cartilage was real satisfying; the howl that accompanied it was even more delightful.

Pellam turned to meet the bear but the big man was already

on top of him. He picked Pellam up, right off the ground. "So you want to play rough, huh?" he asked.

"I don't want to do anything! I want—"

The bear slammed him into the side of the camper. Something snapped but it sounded more like metal than bone. Pellam fell to the ground, gasping, then got to his knees. The bear was battering him wildly, connecting often enough so Pellam couldn't stand. The pain swirled through his body.

Finally he gave up, he lay still. Exhausted, gasping. "Enough. Okay."

In the distance was a siren. "Let's get out of here," the bear said.

"Oh, God, this hurts," his partner offered. "He broke my nose. He broke my fucking nose."

The bear whispered, "Shut up, will you?"

Pellam, trying to breathe, started to crawl under the camper. He felt the big hands reach down and grab him by the ankle. They pulled him back then reached into his pocket. Not his wallet pocket, which he would've expected, but his front shirt pocket. Why there? It was empty.

The siren wailed closer.

Pellam heard:

"Let's get the fuck outa here. *Move* it."

"My nose, man. You didn't—"

"Move it, asshole."

He heard doors slam, and the throaty, crisp sound of a motor firing up, a squeal of tires.

Pellam spit blood and tried to catch his breath. Fucking odd . . . He supposed it wasn't a robbery – they left his wallet and watch, ignored everything in the camper and only went through one pocket. If they'd been here to deliver a get-out-of-town message they'd had plenty of time to deliver it but hadn't.

He coughed and made it halfway to a sitting position, lay back down.

The cop car skidded to a stop on the other side of the camper. The siren shut off and he saw the strobe of colored lights on the trees.

His hand strayed to the pocket the bear had rummaged through. He felt the present.

Oh, Christ, no . . .

He pulled out the little glassine envelope. Coke or speed. A gram, easy. Oh, Lord. Felony possession. Pellam stared at the packet through muddy eyes.

He heard their voices. "Okay, let's find him. Search everything around the clearing."

Pellam started coughing again, deeply, as the cops rounded the camper. He recognized the two deputies even though neither was wearing their trademark sunglasses.

"Well, sir," the deputy said, "looks like you had some more of that bad luck after all."

No, don't go after the thugs. Stand there and bust my chops, why don't you? . . .

"You all right, sir?" The other one asked.

He helped Pellam to his feet. He was coughing, choking. "Water, please, some water."

"Sure, no problem." The first deputy stepped into the camper and came back with a cup of water. Pellam took it and swallowed the whole thing down. Breathing desperately, his chest heaving, like a nearly drowned man on land once again.

"Can you stand up, sir?"

Pellam was frowning, watching the other deputy going over the clearing with his flashlight, inch by inch.

"Yeah, I can."

"Good." The deputy smiled. "Because you're under arrest." He glanced at his friend. "Read him his rights. And search him."

16

"And you didn't find anything?" Moorhouse asked the sheriff.

The mayor squinted against the brilliant sunlight streaming into his office early on Sunday morning.

"Nothing. My deputies searched like you told us. But they didn't find anything."

"You're sure? No drugs? All these movie people do drugs all the time," Moorhouse said.

Which Tom knew because he and the wife read *People*. But he also knew they'd searched like a son of a bitch and found zip.

"He was out when they found him?"

"Nosir. But he was down, lying under the camper. He couldn't have thrown anything far enough so's we'd miss it. We combed the ground. And I mean combed."

Moorhouse warily asked, "Any idea who he was mixing it up with?"

"Nope. You want, I can ask around."

Moorhouse shook his head. "No. Pellam probably started the fight." He motioned with his head toward the Sheriff's Department, with its small lock-up. "Can't blame some local kid for getting tough with an asshole from the Coast thinks he owns the place. Any evidence of the, you know, the gas bomb in the clinic?"

"Nope."

"Had to've been him though."

"You'd think," the sheriff said. But uncertainly. He kept looking at Moorhouse curiously, playing with the big hammer of his chrome-plated .357.

The mayor grimaced. *Now I got an envelope of LSD or PVC or whatever the hell it is out loose somewhere in town. Where was it? What if some kid gets a hold of it? Christ.*

"What about Pellam?" he asked the sheriff. "He okay?"

"Seems to be. Brought him in last night, blood all over him. He went into the john at the station and puked his guts out. I thought maybe we oughta get him to the hospital, but—"

"The hospital that he tried to fucking burn down."

"Uh," Tom said noncommittally. "He seems okay now."

"We better have a little talk with him," Moorhouse said. "Bring him in."

Handcuffed.

Standing in front of this small-town shine, who was wearing his favorite baby-blue suit.

And handcuffed, for Christsake.

"Mr Pellam, let me say how sorry we are about what happened. Things like this you don't usually see here. Cleary's a peaceful place."

"Surprising," said the sheriff. "That it happened, I mean."

Pellam nodded to him and squinted against the cold, brutal sun that poured in through the smeared windows. The worst pain was in his right hand – the knuckles – where he'd hit bone.

"Why'd I spend the night in jail?"

"Oh." Moorhouse swivelled back in his green leatherette chair. "You were arrested for D&D. Didn't the deputy read you your rights?"

"Sure he did, Mayor," the sheriff offered.

Pellam asked, "D&D?"

"Drunk and disorderly conduct. How do you plead?"

April fool. Had to be a joke. Pellam even gave them a short laugh. "I got jumped by two assholes knocked on my door, dragged me out and beat the hell out of me. That's not D&D."

Moorhouse smiled patiently. "Guilty or not guilty."

"Not guilty. Have you found the two assholes?"

The sheriff's turn: "Seems the other perpetrators—"

"*Other* perpetrators?" Pellam laughed.

"—escaped. We searched for evidence but didn't find any." He turned to Pellam. "You weren't real helpful when it came to the description, sir."

Pellam raised his hands. The chrome bracelets jangled with a dull sound. "Somebody threw a truckload of dirt in my face before they started working on me."

Moorhouse said, "Well, under the law, of course, we don't need the others. We can prosecute the one we caught. And that's you. Now, I'm taking off my mayor's hat and putting on my magistrate's." He consulted an empty wall calendar. "I'm setting trial for one week. About bail—"

"What do you mean, one week?"

"I'm a very busy man."

"Good. Let me go. I'll be one less burden for you."

Moorhouse looked him up and down – the shirt stained with dirt and ruddy-black dots of blood, the blotched jeans, the hair upended from a night on a stiff pillow.

"To be honest with you, sir, we aren't inclined to keep you around here for any length of time ourselves."

Sir sir sir . . .

The sheriff rocked on his thick heels; a board creaked.

The light was painful as a dull razor. Pellam's eyes were watering. He waited. Moorhouse was trying to tell him something. Something he was supposed to be picking up on. Something that was not quite right for the town magistrate to be asking – even *this* town magistrate.

Pellam sniffed and blinked the tears.

"You got a cold, sir?"

"That truckload of dirt I was mentioning."

"Ah." Moorhouse looked at the sheriff. "Tom, why don't you leave us be for a minute."

"Sure, Mayor." The lean man pivoted on his heels and walked out of the room in as near to a march as a man could get without Sousa playing in the background.

"Pellam, your presence here's been, what's the word? Disruptive."

"No more disruptive than two assholes driving around town beating up people who're minding their own business."

"Ha, there you go." Moorhouse shook his head. "Did you know that the clinic near to burned down last night?"

Pellam blinked. Trying to make the connection, how this figured in his case. He asked, "What, exactly—"

"You know what was destroyed in the fire?"

Oh. Interesting. He said, "Those drugs the Torrens boy had."

"Yes, sir." Moorhouse raising an eyebrow.

"Oh, come on, you charging me with arson too? You've got no probable cause for that."

Moorhouse's other eyebrow joined the first and they seemed to be asking: *How come you're so familiar with words like "probable cause"? How come, sir?*

"Mr Pellam, you're the kind of outside influence isn't good for our community."

"Outside influence might be just the ticket," Pellam said, "you being the inside influence."

Moorhouse, smiling, sucked air in through his white teeth. "I may have to add contempt to your growing list of infractions, you aren't careful—"

Pellam put his hands, balled into fists, on the desk, and leaned forward. Light shot off the cuffs. "I want bail set and I don't care if you're busy fixing DWI tickets for the sons of your clients – I want a trial tomorrow. I'm calling my lawyer in Manhattan and getting him up here today with a habeas corpus writ and you fuck around anymore with me and I'll sue your ass for abuse of judicial process and failure to get an injured prisoner adequate medical attention—"

"Now, just let's calm down here. Let's—"

"You tell me," Pellam said between angry jaws, "how easy your town treasury'll afford a judgment of two-, three-hundred thousand?"

Moorhouse kept the false smile. His face reddened and he faked a cough to swallow. His eyes strayed to the phone. Pellam could see he was furious. Somebody'd put him in this tough position. "My, my, you are a touchy one. I'll tell you what. You just leave our town, and I'll drop all the charges."

Pellam said softly. "What's bail?"

The smile twisted and became lopsided. "Bail is set at five thousand dollars."

The door behind Pellam squealed open. A broad trapezoid of light fell into the room. He hardly heard it. He snapped, "*How* much? Where am I going to get that kind of money on Sunday?"

A woman's voice said, "From me. A check'll be okay, won't it, Hank?"

He frowned. "Morning, Meg. What're you doing here?"

She walked up to the desk. "A check?" She was already writing it out.

"You don't have to—" Pellam began. She glanced at his face, which must've been in worse shape than he'd thought since her eyes flashed wide for a second.

Moorhouse was peeling a piece of tape off the dispenser and rolling it up. He chewed on it absently. "Meg, this isn't a good idea."

She finished writing out the check. Pellam said to her, "How did you know?"

She ignored him.

"Meg," Moorhouse tried again. "It really isn't a good idea."

Meg dropped the check onto his desk. "A receipt. I'd like a receipt."

He couldn't find one and had to write one out by hand on a yellow pad.

Meg pushed through the door. Pellam, frowning, looked after her. Moorhouse spit the tape out of his mouth and said,

"Trial is set for Monday morning. I know a local lawyer, you want."

Pellam pushed his fists out toward the man's chest. "What I want is the cuffs off. They're a little disruptive."

Pellam sat in the passenger seat as Meg pushed the little car up through the gears and shot out of town.

He casually slipped the seatbelt and shoulder harness on. He noticed the knob on the manual transmission gearshift was twisted and worn from heavy use, the gear position symbol upside down. As if to show him why, she downshifted on a gentle curve and brought the speed back up to about seventy.

It was a forty zone.

Over the roar of the engine, he said, "Thanks. I—"

Meg shook her head.

He didn't know what she meant: that she didn't want him to talk or that she couldn't hear him. The tach was almost redlined.

Pellam looked around. The streets were empty. The parking lot next to a church was full of small trucks and cars. It was classic American religion – a sweeping white steeple and red brick, symmetrical, unchallenging, simple. He wondered what denomination it was, then decided it didn't really matter; religion in Cleary would be pretty much the same whatever church you happened to be in.

"Where's Sam?"

"Sunday school."

"Where's Keith?"

"Some errand then he was going to the factory."

"Oh."

They drove in silence to the house. To *her* house. In *her* car.

With *her* flinty eyes and taut mouth.

When they got there, she left four-foot skid marks in the gravel and climbed out, slamming the thin door with a crash. She walked up on the porch, leaving Pellam in the passenger seat.

She disappeared inside.

He sat.

She reappeared a minute later and said, "You coming inside or not?"

"Well, I guess I—" he said to her receding back.

The house was quiet. A funny thing, an old house like this – huge and warm with a woody-smelling heat coming up from parquet floors – being quiet. A house that ought to have a dozen kids running around in it, raising all kinds of hell, adults doing their weekend tasks. But it was still, completely still.

He followed her into the kitchen. She was setting up a Mr Coffee. She put rolls in the oven. He crossed his arms. She didn't say anything. He leaned against the counter. He unfolded his arms and sat down. He said, "I—"

She slammed the coffee can down, spun to face him. "I've only got one question."

"You got me out of jail to ask me a question?"

"Did Sam get that shit from you?"

He didn't answer.

She looked at him.

Pellam stood up. "If you think that then I'm just going to walk back to your lockup, thanks."

Meg walked over to him and stood inches away. "I want you to say it. I want you to tell me."

"I didn't give him any drugs."

She turned away.

He said, "I thought you knew me . . . I thought we knew each other better than that."

Then she was digging in her purse, pulling out sheets of paper.

He squinted. His right eye blurred. A renegade bit of dirt from the night before shifted. He wiped tears. Then he was focusing on the sheets of paper, the kind with the holes in the side. She'd printed something out of a computer.

Pellam frowned and leaned forward.

So that was it.

He cleared his throat. Even here. Cleary, New York, population 5800. Even here.

Pellam said softly, "So you know."

Meg pushed the printouts toward him. They were dirty and well read.

Honing in on his eyes, she said, "I thought I'd heard your name. When I was a model in New York I got interested in movies. I used to buy some of the film magazines, the high-brow ones. I knew your name was familiar."

He lifted several of the articles, glancing at newspaper headlines he could recite in his sleep.

Pellam's "Time Out of Mind" – L.A. Film Critics Top Pick for Independents, New Director Pellam Captures Cannes, Sundance. New York Film Festival Must: Pellam's "Sandra's Apartment."

Then the others, with words that often did come to him in his sleep: *Film Director Indicted in Drug Death of Star. Pellam Trial Revelation: Drugs "Flowed" on Set. Director, Associate Indicted in Star's OD Death. Death Movie "Central Standard Time" Shelved as Backers Drop Out.*

He dropped them on the table. He stood up. "Better be going."

17

M eg stepped between him and the door. Took his arm, and held it hard.

"No, please. I don't want you to go. I was so scared about Sam. I was so hurt. I didn't think they came from you but I couldn't help but think about these." She touched the articles hesitantly.

She let go of his arm and Pellam walked to the back window, pulled aside the curtain. He said, "I never sold anything. The man who died was my friend. Tommy Bernstein."

Meg said, "He was a wonderful actor. I saw a couple of the movies he was in. They weren't yours, I don't think."

"He never worked for me. Not until that last movie. *Central Standard Time*. We were just friends. Best friends, I guess you'd say." He laughed. "God, that sounds strange. Adults saying they're best friends." He laughed hollowly. "Well, we weren't very adult."

"What happened?"

"I was directing indies – you know, independent films. Jarmusch, Seidelman. That sort of thing. I met Tommy the first week he got to Hollywood. You're right – he *was* good. But he got famous real fast, *too* fast – he never grew a thick skin. He got shook too easily and the only way he could work was high. We wrote *Central Standard* together – we went out to the desert a couple times and spent the whole day writing. Just the two of us. He was going to star. His first serious film. But the only way he could work was on coke. He wanted a lot and I gave him a lot. And more. He did too much. He had a heart attack and died. He was thirty-one."

Pellam looked at the refrigerator. A construction paper airplane was stuck to the door with magnets. Printed on it: *Love you, Mom!!!*

"It was so strange. At first nothing happened. Nothing at all. It was like the whole incident vanished. I even got up and went to work, trying to find a new star, looking at rough cuts, seeing what we could salvage. Then, everything fell apart. Me included. I couldn't work, I just didn't care. The financing backed out and I didn't have a completion bond – star insurance. So I lost my savings and my house, the equipment. I did a year for manslaughter; my assistant got suspended."

"But it wasn't your fault."

"Yes, it was. I kept supplying him. It was in the film's budget. Under 'Miscellaneous Cast-related Expenses.'"

"Was that when your wife left you?"

He smiled. "No, it was a little after."

Meg said, "That was six years ago, Pellam. You mean nobody would let you work? I don't mean this bluntly but it wasn't the end of the world."

"Well, it's funny what qualifies for the end of the world. A year in the Q – that's San Quentin. That's one way to define it. Believe me, that's *definitely* a way to define the end of the world."

"I'm sorry, John." She touched his arm. This was a different touch. Softer. Closer.

His laugh was bitter. "Hell, there were publicists in L.A.'d shake my hand and say, 'Fucking great promotion idea – you kill the star. Isn't a newspaper in the country won't do a story about you.'" He paused, listening to the mumble of the coffee machine. "Sure, I probably could have gotten it together after I got out. I'd lost a lot of contacts but that wasn't the problem. The problem was I just didn't care. I had no desire to direct any more. So I got a job scouting locations."

"I don't know what to say."

He walked away from her. "It's temporary. Things'll get better."

"You've got to watch that," she said.

"What?"

"Saying that – things are only temporary. Your life could be over before you know it." She said this knowingly.

"I like scouting," Pellam said.

"You don't think your camper's just a place you're hiding out?"

"We all have places we hide out. Mine just happens to have wheels."

"Exactly what *are* you doing here, Pellam? We aren't going to get ourselves a movie here in Cleary. You aren't real interested in colored leaves. What do you want?"

Pellam reached into his sock and pulled out the clear packet of drugs that the bear had planted on him last night.

Meg glanced at it several times, her eyes flipping back and forth between the powder and his face. "What's that?"

"A gift to me. I think from the same place Sam got that stuff he took." He explained to her about the attack the night before. "One of them planted it on me."

"No! Why?"

"So Moorhouse could throw the book at me and have more leverage to get me out of town." He saw her shocked look. "Oh, the mayor's not behind it. Someone else is."

"Who?"

"Whoever didn't want the movie made here." He looked at her. "Whoever's behind those drugs that Sam got. Whoever killed Marty. *That's* what I'm doing here. That's why I'm not leaving until I find out who it is."

"In Cleary . . ." She shook her head. "This is the town where every other car has a red ribbon on the rear-view mirror."

Pellam shook his head, frowning.

"Mothers Against Drunk Driving," Meg said. "The grocery bags at the Grand Union say, 'Say No to Drugs.'"

Pellam opened the packet, sniffed it.

She said, "Why didn't they find it?"

"I swallowed it. Then I got it back last night after they searched me, by a well-known biological process there's no need to go into on this fine morning."

"Jesus, Pellam. What if it'd broken open? You could've died."

"I couldn't really take a felony possession count." He nodded at the printouts.

"Why didn't you just flush it?"

"Sometimes, they test the water in jails."

She smiled. "I can't exactly see Tom testing the john water for drugs."

Pellam laughed. "Who knows what kind of kits he got mail order from *Small Town Cop Monthly* he's just dying to use."

He stepped to the sink, opened the packet and let the contents disappear into the garbage disposal, under the smiling observation of a cut-out wooden goose wearing a bonnet. "I know people'd cry real tears, see me do this."

Pellam dried his hands then walked up to a tall breakfront. He didn't know anything about antiques. He stood awkwardly in front of the elaborate piece. "This is really something."

The breakfast rolls came out and she set them in front of him. He ate two right away. They had a strongly yeasty flavor. Homemade.

They sipped coffee in an awkward silence for a few minutes. He was on his third roll. "The best compliment there is," she said and ate one herself. "I never gain weight. Oh, I'm not being vain. It's just a fact."

Pellam walked into the hall. Looking at the wallpaper, the furniture.

Houses.

He knew what Tommy Bernstein would have said about his little place on Beverly Glen north of Sunset Boulevard. *Shit, you got a fallee house, man. You be in trouble . . .* Houses on the top of the canyons were faller houses; at the bottom, fallee. *You gonna get squashed in the 'quake,* he'd have said. *Sell that sucker now.*

He said to Meg, "I'll bet you have nice holidays here."

"Holidays?" Meg paused. "I guess so. Quiet. Just the three of us. And friends sometimes. A house like this needs big families. It was different when I was growing up. Family all over the place." Her voice faded. Then she said, "I have a confession."

"Okay."

"The accident, when I ran into you?"

"I'm familiar."

"It wasn't an accident. Oh, I didn't want to *hit* you. But I wanted to meet you. I saw you walk up the sidewalk and I drove up there on purpose. I was going to skid the car or something. Pretend to drive off the road. So I could meet you." She was playing with her cocktail ring. Five thousand dollars of pressurized carbon spun obsessively on a beautiful, thin finger.

He asked, "Why?"

"I thought maybe I could get a part in the movie."

"That's why you came to see me in the hospital?"

"No."

He was standing right next to her. She turned, their eyes met. Outside, miles away, the cracks of shotguns rolled into silence. She said, "Well, maybe."

He leaned down and kissed her.

Just like that.

"No," she said. But that was the only resistance she offered. Her arms were around him, kissing back, and pulling him against her.

Then she stepped back.

"No," she said. And this time she was speaking to herself and, unlike him, she decided to obey the command.

She walked back to the kitchen, stood at the window, wiped the sink absently.

Pellam had long ago given up apologizing for impulse. He followed her, picked up his cup, poured more coffee.

"The thing is." Meg didn't look at him, stared out the window. "I'm having an affair."

He set the cup down.

Good job, Pellam. You can pick 'em like nobody else. Fall for a woman whose got two men in her life, while you're being chased around the ginkgo trees by a drugged-out flower child (and you, with an unblushing rail-thin Hollywood businesswoman you never call waiting at home for you).

He saw she was organizing her thoughts. Confession time. Things to get off her beautiful freckled chest. He sat down again. This might take some time. He knew that straying spouses and bad moviemakers share the same obsessive flaw: excessive explanation.

"Who is he?"

"A man here in town."

"Doesn't word get around?"

"We've been excruciatingly careful. See, Keith's a wonderful person. He's Joe solid. He loves Sam. He's never so much as raised his voice to me. He dotes. He provides. But do I feel magic? No. But *should* you feel magic?"

"I heard this line once: a relationship's like a fire. You got a few months of flame, a year of embers, then the rest smoke."

"It's comfortable."

"There's a lot to be said for comfort."

"But I want more, Pellam. Or I thought I wanted more. This thing with Sam, the drugs. It scared me bad. It shook me up. I didn't get an hour's sleep last night."

"He's okay, isn't he?"

"Oh, yeah, he'll be fine. It just made me feel so vulnerable. Here I was looking for some –" She glanced at him. "– for some flame and it almost seemed that Sam getting sick was revenge for that."

"You love him? This other guy?"

A beat of a pause. "I thought I did. But I don't think so."

"You love Keith?"

"I know I love Sam and my house. I *think* I love Keith. I'm tired of having an affair. I shouldn't be saying this to you, should I?" Her eyes were wide, and she seemed very young.

Pellam smiled. "Say whatever you want. I like listening."

"Keith's so smart. He doesn't . . . It's not like he makes me feel stupid, not intentionally, I mean. But I feel stupid."

"Why do you say that?"

"I'm just not, well, intelligent."

"What does that mean?" Pellam asked. "That you can't do calculus in your head? Or recite the periodic table of the elements?"

"Keith tries to tell me about his business, I don't follow what he's saying. I try, but—"

"Meg, he's a chemist. Why should you understand chemistry?"

"Well, politics too. And I don't read a lot. I try but it's just beyond me."

"You're talking in generalities. What's beyond you?"

There was a pop and a flash of light behind them. Meg jumped, then laughed. A bulb in one of the kitchen's wall sconces had burned out. Meg pulled the shade off, blew on the bulb to cool it and unscrewed it. "When I was a girl, I was afraid of the light. Isn't that odd? Most kids are afraid of the dark. But I hated the light. There was no door to my room and the light from the living room, that white-blue light from bare bulbs, would glare and keep me up. Even when I was older, when my mother put a sheet up for a door, that didn't keep the light out. You know why I hated it? It was that when they fought, my parents' voices seemed to come from that light. I'd hide under the blankets. Mother thought I was afraid of ghosts or something. I was afraid of the light. That's what I feel like now. Light is so hard to escape from." Meg changed the bulb. "I feel you're some kind of darkness." She laughed. "I'm sure this is coming out all wrong."

For a time, after he started scouting, Pellam had wondered why this always happened. Why people talked to him as much as they did, bared their hidden secrets and passions. Priests didn't hear the kinds of things Pellam heard. Then he realized it wasn't so much that he was a good listener; it was that he was safe. They could spill their guts and he'd be gone in a week or two. Their secrets with him.

"I knew you didn't have anything to do with Sam," she said. "I really did." The words were halting. Women are usually better apologists than men. But Meg wasn't.

"What're you going to do?" he asked.

"I'm going to stop seeing him, my lover."

"Is that what you want to do?"

"It's what I *have* to do . . ." She looked at her watch. "Pellam, can I ask a favor?"

He didn't think it was going to involve freckles on her chest or anywhere else. He'd given up on that. He said, "Sure."

"Keith's going to be working all day. But Sam'll be home in a while. Could you stay around here? Did you have any plans?"

"Nothing to speak of."

"Would you? We could all have Sunday dinner. Maybe you could do some shooting with Sam. He's got a .22 and a little .410 shotgun we gave him last year."

Pellam said, "I'd love to."

"Really?"

"Really."

Then she was smiling like a sassy schoolgirl. She looked at her watch. "We've got an hour before I pick him up. There's something we could do together – just you and me."

Where was *this* leading?

She took his hand and pulled him toward the door.

"Where're we going?" he asked.

"Raking leaves."

"Are you serious?"

She pulled him outside. "Sure, come on. It's fun."

"I haven't raked leaves for twenty years. They don't have leaves in L.A. And even if they did, I wouldn't rake them."

He resisted at first. But here she was, a beautiful woman with whom he'd shared secrets. And so he said, "I guess."

He paused on the back porch. Looked out on what must've been four or five acres of colored leaves. She tossed him a rake.

He studied it for a moment. Then said, "I don't know how it works."

The glint of light caught the deputy's eye.

He pulled the Plymouth squad car off the road and eased it into the late-morning shade of a sugar maple, scarred from past years' syrup spigots. He climbed out of the car, pulled his lavender-tinted sunglasses on and began walking through the tall grass and forsythia whips. He'd lived in and around Cleary all his life and knew the customs and routines – where people tended to be and when you could expect to see them there and when you couldn't.

And one place you didn't expect to see a car parked was in this field on Sunday morning.

He climbed over what was left of a low stone fence and walked through a row of more maples to a narrow dirt road that led into some woods and just stopped about halfway through.

The car was parked exactly in the center of this road. The deputy paused twenty yards away and looked at it. A cheap Nissan. White. New York plates and a Cleary Tigers bumper sticker. The reason he stopped wasn't because he was noting all these details. He stopped because he didn't want to see what was in the car.

Figuring he'd deduced what had happened. Two high schoolers had spent their last hours on earth making out only to doze off and die, thanks to a bum exhaust pipe. That was the only possible reason anyone would park on this road on Saturday night and the only reason anyone would still be here now.

He took a breath to calm his stuttering heart and walked forward. He found out that he was wrong. There was another reason a car was parked in the middle of this deserted road. Because the driver had been murdered.

The boy had been shot three times in the chest with a small-caliber gun. His face was serene and there was hardly any blood on the body. Which meant he'd died quickly. The boy's face was pressed against the passenger window, away from the deputy, and his hand gripped the door handle. There was no lividity – sinking of the blood to the lower extremities of the body. This meant that he'd died recently.

Damn. His heart sank. The deputy walked around to the other side of the car and looked at the face. He recognized Ned Harper. A high school boy, a football player and, he believed, a one-eighty-division wrestler. He'd remembered that he'd seen Ned's father driving the Nissan around town. He wondered why the parents hadn't phoned him in missing. Maybe when your son was an eighteen-year-old football player, you assumed he'd be out late and didn't start to worry for a day or two. The deputy's daughter was two years old and he worried about her constantly. He didn't think there'd ever come a time when he didn't.

Who'd do something like this?

Maybe the boy'd picked up a hitchhiker. Maybe an escaped prisoner from Sing-Sing down in Ossining. But then why would he leave the car? Maybe it *was* an accident. He'd been hunting with a friend, the gun went off and the other boy panicked. But, no, the deputy realized. That couldn't be it. Not with three separate wounds.

He walked in a slow circle, looking for obvious clues, but he knew the sheriff would take charge of that and call the county in too. Then he realized he was just stalling, not wanting to make the call to report it.

The sun shot off the slanted window, a dove called from deep in the moist forest. The deputy walked slowly back to the car, praying he wouldn't be the one elected to tell the boy's parents.

A t four-thirty Pellam remembered Janine.
    "Oh, hell."

Sam looked up. Probably thinking that he'd pointed the muzzle of the single-shot, break-action shotgun the wrong way or hadn't remembered one of the firearm safety rules Pellam had told him.

For the past couple hours they'd been plinking away with shotguns. Occasionally Pellam would throw a can or two into the air and Sam, sweating with the effort, would calculate the lead. Pellam noticed the determination on the boy's face. Once he overheard Sam mutter something as he fired. "Ned" was what it sounded like. Pellam had asked him what he'd said but he just shook his head and said, "Can you throw another one please?"

"Got to call it quits, son," Pellam now said. "I've got an errand back in town."

Inside the kitchen Sam said, "Mom, you should've seen me."

"I did. I was watching out the window."

"How'd I do, Mr Pellam?"

"Did good, really good," Pellam said. "You've got to clean your weapon, Sam. But I've got to run to town. We'll do it when I get back." He looked at Meg and there must have been something in his words or – goddamn it, was he blushing? He looked at her coy smile and said, "You mind dropping me in town and I'll bring the camper back?"

"Hey," Sam said, his high voice cracking into an even higher register. "Can I come?"

Meg smiled sweetly, "Oh, and can I come too?"

"Probably better if you didn't."

She let him swing for a minute then said, "Maybe you've got some other friends in town. Some people I don't know."

"Shouldn't take more than fifteen minutes."

Meg smiled innocently. "Fifteen? That's pretty fast."

He gave her an exasperated glance.

The phone rang.

Meg kept her eyes on Pellam as she made a slow turn and walked to it.

"Hi, hon . . . Aw, no. Come on. What? Problems?"

"Hi, Daddy!" Sam shrieked, jumping for the phone. "I shot a hundred cans . . ."

Meg winced and waved him down. "I'm making a roast. You can't make it?" She sighed. "Okay. All right. We'll save some for you. Love you."

"Bye, Daddy!"

To Pellam she said, "He's in a bind at the plant. He's got to work most of the night. Sunday, can you believe it? He said he'll be back at eleven . . . So we eat *a trois*."

Sam said, "What's that, Mom? Sounds yucky."

"It means there'll be three of us for dinner."

"Oh, I thought it was this weird food you were going to make." To Pellam he said, "Mom makes this totally strange stuff sometimes. All slippery—"

"Sam."

". . . and these gross colors."

"Young man, that's enough."

"And her apple butter . . ." He headed for the porch. "It starts out brownish. Then it gets kind of green."

"Sam—" Meg began good-naturedly.

Pellam asked Meg, "So, how 'bout that ride?"

"Let's go."

Pellam called to Sam, "Don't clean that gun till I get back, young man."

"Yessir. And then it goes all grayish. Yuck . . ."

Meg dropped him a block away from the camper.

She turned to him but before she could say anything he preempted her. "You don't talk about flower children, I won't talk about apple butter."

She laughed hard. "See you soon." This was a moment when he might've kissed her. But instead he just climbed stiffly out of the tiny car – his wounds still hurt – and walked quickly to the camper. Inside a light was on. He opened the door. Inside, Janine sat motionless, looking down.

She turned to him. "Bastard."

"I'm sorry I ran into some trouble last night and—"

"Bastard." What she was talking about, though, wasn't his being late but the screenplay of *To Sleep in a Shallow Grave*. The binder was open and she'd read most of it.

He closed the door.

"This character you've added. That's me, isn't it?"

He sat down slowly.

"Some of it's based on you. Some. It isn't what I feel about you, it's not the way I see you. It's fiction. A story, nothing more than that. Mostly my imagination."

She lowered her head and read, "'You're living a dream that the past can't justify . . .' 'It's the remoteness of the past that makes it such a safe place for you to live . . .' 'The Age of Aquarius was a long, long time ago . . .' *Janice*. Christ, Pellam, you could at least have done a better job changing my name."

"I didn't—"

"You!" She threw the notebook against the wall. The binding snapped. The pages cascaded to the floor. "*You're* the one living in a dream, not me. You come into people's lives – nobody invited you to Cleary – you come into town with the big fantasy, promising to put people into a movie, promising to take people away from here—"

"I never said that."

She was crying again. Her hair was pasted to her cheeks, she pulled it angrily away. "You didn't have to *say* it. What the hell did you expect people to think? Here you come, with your van and your camera, studying the town, talking to people, getting to know everyone . . . Getting to know *some* of them very well. You don't understand the power you've got. You don't understand how desperate people are. Desperate to get out of places like Cleary. And what do they do? They spill their guts to you and you betray them. Why? In the name of what? What word is sacred to you, Pellam? Art? In the name of Art? Film? Money? How do you justify taking people's lives and making a movie out of them?"

He stood up and reached out for her. She shook his arms away. "You just can't drop into someone's life, take what you want, then leave."

"I'm sorry."

She stood up. Walked to the door then stopped. Waiting for something. Neither of them knew what should come next.

"I thought . . ." Janine's voice faded and she stepped outside, closing the metal door softly behind her.

Pellam sighed. He picked up the screenplay binder then bent to the floor and gathered the pages, one by one.

Driving down Main Street, Pellam passed a grocery store and parked, bought a bottle of chardonnay and walked back outside. He looked up and down the street for Janine. No sign of her. And what would he tell her if he saw her? There was no answer for that.

He looked up the street at an approaching car, an American GT of some kind, maybe ten years old, its rear end jacked high. It came bubbling down the street. The driver parked in front of the Cedar Tap and gunned the engine into a sexy growl before he shut it off. He got out and walked into the bar. Pellam walked over to the car, looked inside.

He returned to the Winnebago, fired it up and drove slowly out of town. He rolled both windows down and felt the cool air fill the cockpit.

He is driving fast in a fast car. A Porsche. A Hun car, because in L.A. you must have a German car. It's not as easy as that, though. You also have to ignore the fact that a German car is the kind to have and it must seem as if you're the first person on the West Coast to think about owning one. Pellam's is black. He drives it hard, with the passion of someone who loves speed though not necessarily the machinery that allows the car to drive fast. Whenever anybody says, "Shit, the Germans make good cars," he always looks surprised, as if they'd just caught on to his secret.

They are going into the desert, Tommy Bernstein and him.

"Thomaso," Pellam shouts over the huge slipstream. "You're going to lose your hat."

And the man does, reaching up too late to keep the stiff, three-hundred-dollar, curly brimmed cowboy hat from sailing into the hundred-mile-an-hour slip-stream.

"Shit, Pellam, turn around."

Pellam only whoops loudly and speeds up.

Tommy doesn't seem to mind. Somehow, it would be wrong to stop the little black car. There is an urgency, a sense of mission. Tommy shouts something about the hat and illegal aliens. Pellam nods.

The sun is a plate of hot pressure above them. The wind, which makes their ears ache, is hot.

Los Angeles is behind them. Ahead is nothing but desert.

"John, give me some!" Tommy shouts. He repeats this twice before Pellam hears and four times before he chooses to answer.

"Please!" A moaning wail, a sound that the wind takes and instantly makes vanish.

Pellam tosses the salt shaker underhand. The wind plays hell with the trajectory, but Tommy catches it in desperate, fumbling grabs.

"Not funny."

"Improves your reflexes."

Tommy was trying to snort. "Too fast, I can't—"

Pellam hits the clutch and brake. The car skids and fishtails. When they slow to sixty Tommy can snort the coke. He gives the high sign. Pellam accelerates and refuses the offered shaker.

Pellam feels philosophical. He shouts, "You think the desert's minimal, right? Bullshit. It isn't. It's goddamn complex. Complex like a, you know, a crystal. Like the way colors spread under a microscope. Remember those science films in high school?"

"Yeah," Tommy shouts. "About gonads and seeds and ovum." He is grinning like the dirty little boy he likes to portray though he is clearly considering Pellam's comment. In fact he is considering it desperately. Pellam wishes he hadn't spoken.

Tommy suffers from terminally ill confidence. The actor had received one L.A. Film Critics' award and one from Cannes when he'd been courted and seduced by a big studio lot producer. The money was incredible, the movies worse than awful. His most recent, a critic wrote, could be stuffed and served at a Thanksgiving dinner for the population of the country. Tommy was trying to think of ways to redeem himself. "Don't be desperate," Pellam had told him. "This city don't love desperate men."

But Tommy snatched up even that advice like a life preserver.

Pellam drives in silence. A half hour later he notices a small road leading off the highway toward a huge rock eased out of the brush and dirty sand. He makes a fast turn and the car skids to a stop out of sight of the road.

They climb out, stretch, pee against rocks.

Tommy asks, "You bring the Geiger counter?"

"What do we need that for?"

"The fucking Army. They test atom bombs here."

"That's New Mexico."

"Fucking no," Tommy says. "Cruise missiles blasting sheep to hell and gone. I'm scared." He looks around cautiously.

Pellam says, "There're no sheep here."

"What I'm saying! They're dead. Got blasted into lambchops. We're in danger. Our kids'll glow in the dark."

"Let's go to work, hombre."

From the car they take two heavy garbage cans that ring with glass falling against itself. Pellam drags them toward the rock. There isn't much shade though there will be in an hour or two. Tommy, now pissed about his hat, rubs suntan lotion on his face and thinning scalp, then pulls a large cooler from the car. This he plants in the sand near the big rise of rock. He returns and struggles to get two lawnchairs out of what pretends to be a backseat.

"German cars, shit," Tommy says. He drives a Chevy Impala.

Pellam takes empty beer bottles out of the green bags and sets them carefully on a ridge of dirt and sand about thirty feet away from where Tommy plants the lawnchairs. He surveys his handiwork then opens a pineapple-printed beach umbrella and sticks it into the ground between the chairs.

Pellam finishes setting out the bottles. He calls, "How many pages?"

Tommy flips through a plastic-bound manuscript. "One seventeen."

"Need one more."

Tommy pulls another bottle from the cooler, pops the lid with a church key and drinks it down. He tosses it to Pellam, who plants it at the end of the row.

One hundred seventeen bottles.

They sit in the chairs, facing the bottles. Tommy takes another snort from the shaker.

He says, "Can I have the Python. Please?"

From a large, battered attaché case, Pellam takes two pistols. He keeps the Ruger .44 for himself and hands Tommy the Colt. He places yellow-and-green boxes of shells between them.

Two copies of the script appear. On the title page: "Central Standard Time. By John Pellam and Tommy Bernstein."

They begin reading aloud and rewriting the script. They correct each other, changing dialogue, argue. Pellam is quieter and grimmer. Tommy is boisterous. He'll shout, then stand and stalk around, sit again.

When they finish eleven pages – the end of the first scene – they stuff cotton into their ears, load the pistols and with fifteen shots between them take turns disintegrating the first eleven bottles. One for each page. The rules of their game.

Tommy says, spinning the cylinder of his gun, "You remember that scene, what was it from? Some old jungle movie? Stewart Granger's aiming at Deborah Kerr's head? She's scared, doesn't know what's going on. Then, blam! He wastes a boa constrictor right behind her. I always wanted to play that scene. Why don't you go sit over next to the rocks, Pellam? They got snakes in the rocks."

"Yeah, hell with snakes," Pellam says, pulling a beer from the cooler. "I always wanted to shoot me an actor."

They work until eleven that night, and blow the last three bottles apart in the headlight of the tiny German car surrounded by the sound of its bubbling exhaust. They are shivering and it takes ten rounds each to hit the last glistening bottle.

"This fucking movie's going to make us, Pellam!" Tommy shouts. "We're going right to the top!" And he empties the gun at the night sky.

The house was completely quiet.

Meg had a little time until Pellam would be back. She took her coffee and walked up the stairs. She paused, then sat on the landing for a long time, looking into the hall and those portions of the den and living room she could see. The parquet floor, the furniture. The house seemed different, a stranger's home. She didn't recognize it. There was nothing unpleasant about the sensation; it was one of those moments when you focus on a familiar object – a doorknob, a chair, your own little finger – and it seems absurd and alien to you. This was her house, the house she'd always loved. Hers and Keith's and Sam's. Only something was different.

Meg went into the bedroom, got dressed. She tied her hair in a ponytail. Her hands paused, holding the ribbon above her neck.

The doorbell rang. She bounded down the stairs like Sam on Christmas morning.

She swung the heavy door open. She'd already prepared a wry comment for Pellam about Janine and was ready to deliver it.

But she blinked in surprise.

Wexell Ambler stood there, looking shy, leaning against the

jamb. "I was driving past. Saw your car was in the drive. The Cougar was gone. I couldn't wait till tomorrow."

Meg instinctively looked back, into the house to make certain they were alone. Then she looked behind Ambler.

"Is it Mr Pellam, Mommy?" Sam called. She wondered if Ambler could hear what the boy had asked. Didn't seem he had.

"No, honey. I'll be outside for a minute," she shouted. Her hand still on the doorknob Meg said to Ambler, "Keith's at work."

"I want to talk to you. I *have* to talk to you."

"I'm expecting some company."

Ambler had no reaction to this. She was trying to decide whether to tell him who the company was if he asked. He didn't. He said, "It won't take long." Though he said it slowly, the words full of meaning, as if he wanted their conversation to last for the entire evening.

She looked behind her again, up the stairs toward Sam's room, then stepped outside and closed the door behind her. It didn't latch.

He kissed her on the cheek and she kissed him back, though he'd have to be drunk or crazy not to sense the hesitancy.

"I had to see you."

"Is everything okay?"

He looked at her in surprise. "Okay, sure. I should be asking how Sam is. You never called to tell me if he's all right."

"He's fine. He'll be fine."

"He's a wonderful boy," Ambler said.

They walked to the end of the porch and stood at the railing, looking out across the moist lawn, glistening in slight radiance from the houselights.

"What is it, Wex?"

"About what I asked. About marrying me."

She turned to him. He was such a tough man. A dangerous man too, she supposed. That bodyguard thug of his, Mark, for instance. Also, the way he liked her to be helpless, almost cowering when they made love. (Meg Torrens believed sex was a window to your soul.) She'd never actually said, No, to him before and she wondered if there was a risk to her if she did. She felt a chill, colder than the air.

What should she say?

She suddenly remembered a line from one of Pellam's movies. A character has to make a decision about turning a friend over to the police. He says to his wife, "The most important decisions are always made by our hearts."

She let her heart answer now.

"Wex . . ." She looked away, fixing her eyes on a fingernail clipping of a moon over a dark wad of trees. "I can't see you anymore."

She wondered if it would be a total surprise. If he'd nod slowly and walk away. If he'd fly into a rage. She honestly didn't know.

He didn't answer for a moment and she heard his breathing, remembered the deep sound from the times they'd lain together.

Tension filled her body, turned her to stone.

"Were you going to come to the place yesterday and tell me that?" he asked. "Or were you just going to let me figure it out on my own."

She hesitated and for the first time in their relationship lied to him. "No, I was going to come."

Meg glanced toward the house and the driveway and then took his arm. He was shaking. Anger? Sorrow? The cold?

Will he hurt me?

She continued. "I'm sorry, Wex. I loved every minute we spent together, but . . ." She was parsing carefully, but she found she had no idea of what words she could attach to her thoughts to express them right. "But it's just time for it to be over with."

"How can you say that?" he spat out.

"It's what I feel."

"What happened?"

She couldn't look into his eyes. "No. It's run its course. I was searching for something. I—"

"You're going back to Keith."

"I don't know."

"You're in love with that man, Pellam. Right?"

The hesitation must have seemed huge to him, though for Meg it lasted only a second. "No, I'm not."

Ambler stepped away from her. "It's him, isn't it?"

"No."

"I knew it," he said bitterly. "I knew from the minute you heard there was going to be a movie in town, you were going after him. What did you want? For him to sweep you away to be a star?"

"Wex, come on . . ."

"Don't you remember? We were lying in bed—"

"Shhh!" She raised her palm to silence him.

"—and it was the first day they came into town, in that damn camper of theirs and all you talked about was making a movie. How much you wanted to act."

"Maybe I did. I want to be successful at something. Why is that so hard for you to understand?"

"Meg, you can't just go start a Hollywood career. You—"

"I don't want to talk about this."

"Did he fuck you?" His voice was loud.

"Be quiet!" She whirled to face him. "You can't come to my house and talk to me that way!"

He grabbed her arm. She winced. Then he calmed, reached forward and touched her face. Her eyes focused behind him, where a fast burst of light from the opening door would warn that Sam was on his way outside. "I love you, Meg. You don't know how much. I want to be with you. I'm *going* to be with you."

"Wex, it's never been right. Not here. Cleary isn't the kind of place for this sort of thing. I see how wrong it was."

"You make it sound cheap. It wasn't that." His whisper was harsh.

"I didn't mean it that way. I don't regret anything. I just . . ."

He stared down at her for a moment then released her suddenly. Ambler turned and walked down the steps.

Meg felt the vacuum of his leaving. There was too much unresolved. Wex Ambler had been her only lover. Was this how affairs always ended? Punctuated more with question marks and ellipses than exclamation points? She leaned against the banister and watched him – without a glance toward her – get into his Cadillac.

He drove slowly away. She saw the flash of his brake lights

as he paused at the road – paused just long enough to let the Winnebago turn up her driveway. Then Ambler hit the accelerator hard and vanished into the night.

They're waiting for me to say grace, he decided.

Meg and Sam were looking at him, expectation in their faces. Pellam cleared his throat. In front of him, on the Sunday-set table, was a veal roast that would have fed enough men to rake up all six acres of leaves on the Torrens estate in half an hour. A huge bowl of beans and one of salad. Another plate was loaded with potato pancakes. He and Meg were drinking the white wine; Sam had a glass of milk.

That's what they're waiting for. Grace. What do I do now?

They'd settled in their chairs, candles were lit, and their eyes turned toward him. Then, as the seconds rolled past slowly, they looked at each other.

Pellam unrolled his sleeves and buttoned his cuffs to buy time. Meg said, "Well?"

"Last time I did this must be twenty years ago. I don't remember it too well."

She was frowning. "Twenty years?"

"Well, I don't say grace in the camper."

And Meg was laughing, her wine glass in her hand rocking, spilling the blond liquid over her fingers.

"Pellam . . . No. We're just waiting for you to carve the roast."

"Oh." He covered his face with his hands and laughed. Sam said, "I can say grace, Mr Pellam. Here goes: Over the lips and past the gums, look out stomach, here it comes! Amen."

Pellam picked up the knife and serving fork and went to work. The first couple pieces crumbled. "Can I at least pray for help in carving?"

It was an hour into the meal when the eeriness settled on him. A feeling he couldn't pin down. It happened when he was laughing at one of Sam's jokes, one that Pellam himself had told to death thirty years before, and he glanced up at Meg. Their eyes met, and for one moment, a pivotal moment, there was no movie, no studio, no camper, no Keith, just a universe centered around the three of them.

And the instant he thought how comfortable and natural it seemed, the moment ended and he became anxious.

Pellam surveyed his massive wedge of blueberry pie. Meg said to his protesting palm, "Pellam, you're too skinny."

He ate two pieces.

When they'd finished dessert Pellam helped Meg clear the table. Sam asked, "Mr Pellam, tomorrow can you teach me to shoot *your* gun?"

"What gun's that?" Meg asked.

Pellam told her about the Colt.

Meg said, "I'm not real crazy about pistols. But . . ." She looked at her son. "You listen to everything Mr Pellam tells you."

As if that needed to be said.

"Totally excellent!" the little boy squealed.

Meg said, "Next you'll be teaching him poker."

Pellam laughed.

The two of them sat in the living room for a while, sipping coffee, the unidentified feeling ebbing and flowing within Pellam. He couldn't tell whether he wanted to stay, wanted to leave. One thing he knew for sure – he definitely wanted to leave before Keith came home.

The phone rang. Meg went to answer it and returned a moment later. She didn't say who the caller was. But now she too seemed uneasy.

What the hell're you doing here? he thought to himself. She's married, she's got a lover . . . You don't need those kinds of troubles. He rose. "I better go."

"You sure?"

No. But he said, "Better. Still have a few things to do."

"Sunday night?"

He nodded. Then asked, "Got a favor."

"Sure."

"You have a bottle of whiskey I can borrow?"

"Borrow?"

"No, now you mention it, make that *have*."

"After-dinner drink?"

"Little more complicated than that."

"Sure." She smiled in curiosity. And dug down under a cabinet and emerged with a half-full bottle of Wild Turkey.

"That's the cheapest you've got?" Pellam picked up the bottle.

"'Fraid so. Say, what're you going to do, teach my little boy to shoot, gamble *and* drink?"

Pellam hefted the bottle, hugged her. "Thanks again, ma'am. You make a mean meal. See you tomorrow."

————◆———

" Ah, it's the gunslinger's grandson," said Fred, who squinted his red, retiree's face and studied Pellam's cuts and bruises. "Hell, what happened to you?" He ordered two Buds.

"Had an accident."

"Another one?"

Pellam said, "I'm an unlucky guy sometimes. What can I say?"

"No fooling – you all right?" the old man asked with genuine concern.

"Fine, no problem."

"Weekends're rough around here. All those tourists. What'd you do, get in the way of somebody taking a picture of a leaf? Hey, how about a game?"

"Can't tonight, Fred."

"What's this shit I hear about you not making a movie here?"

"Talk to the town council about it."

"Buncha old SOBs. Shit, there goes my Hollywood career."

Pellam asked, "Where can I find Nick?"

"The kid we were playing with th'other night?" Fred's head was swiveling. "Was here a few minutes ago. Maybe he's in the backroom. That's where they got what they call the restaurant."

Pellam finished the beer. He lifted the bottle in thanks.

"Hey, Pellam, Burt Reynolds ain't available, gimme a call."

In the backroom Pellam found Nick sitting at a table with another man, skinny, long hair, a couple years his junior – maybe eighteen. Nick had a bowl of soup in front of him. He hunched over it, putting slippery noodles into his mouth.

"Hi, Nick," Pellam pulled up a chair. Nick waved then returned to the soup. It looked like Campbell's. What else at the Cedar Tap? Nick said, "This here's Rebo. This's Pellam, the guy you heard about, makes the movies."

Rebo's eyes went wide. He grinned. "Wow, movie man." They shook hands.

"How you doing?" Pellam asked.

"Wow."

Pellam turned to Nick. "Hey, Nick, why I stopped by, my studio's looking for somebody like you."

"Yeah?" The big man took some more sips of soup. "You still making that movie? I heard you weren't."

"This's another movie. I remembered you're into wheels."

"I'm like sorta into wheels."

"They need a driver, a stunt driver. But he's got to be good."

Rebo, chewing a wad of hamburger, said, "Oh, he's good.

Nick's a good driver." Rebo's T-shirt said *Mötley Crüe 1987 Tour*.

"You interested?"

A grin snuck into the fat in the boy's cheeks. "Well, I guess."

"The only thing is, you think you could show me what you can do? Like an audition?"

"I guess."

"How about now?"

"It'd be Sunday night."

"They need somebody soon. Next weekend. If I can't get anybody we'll have to bring in somebody from the Coast." Pellam tossed him a bone: "You'll get screen credit."

"A credit?"

"And the pay's great. A thousand bucks for one stunt."

Rebo's eyes were getting bigger. "Hey, man, tell him about your car."

"Well . . ."

The Mötley Crüe boy steamed ahead. "Pontiac GT. He put in a Chevy 442 all by his lonesome."

Nick's grin was back, spreading like a sunrise. "Hurst shifter," he said. "Did that myself too."

Pellam whistled. "You sure know your hardware. How 'bout it?"

Nick shrugged. "Let's go."

Rebo stood up but Pellam shook his head. "Just gotta be the two of us. Insurance problems, you understand."

Rebo nodded and dropped back into his seat as if Duane Allman himself had told him to sit.

Outside they walked to the car and Pellam looked around.

The streets of Cleary were deserted. He said, "Oh, let me get something." He disappeared into the camper for a minute and came out with the bottle of Wild Turkey. He handed it to Nick. The boy looked at it but shook his head. "Maybe afterwards, man. Not a good idea if I'm going to be doing high-speed work."

They walked to Nick's black Pontiac.

High-speed work. Like he did it everyday.

Pellam unscrewed the lid of the bottle. Nick watched him, frowning.

"You don't drink and drive?" Pellam asked. "That's funny. You were the other night. I could smell it. On top of your aftershave. That's what I recognized. Brut, right?"

The eyes were fishy and the grin came back. "The fuck're you saying?"

Pellam nodded toward the car. "Heard your car this afternoon, thought it sounded familiar. Then checked it out and smelled that same drugstore aftershave inside. Didn't your mother raise you with any class?"

"Huh?"

"How's your friend with the broken nose? I hope he's in a lot of pain."

"You fucking crazy?" He'd turned solemn as a mortician.

"I know, you're going to tell me it was nothing personal."

"What wasn't personal?" But the eyes disclosed all the facts. Nick paused then said, "You got me good." He touched his jaw. "I won't be eating solid food for a week. My tongue's sore as a whore's tit. Why didn't you tell Moorhouse?"

"What good would it've done? He'd let you go, right?"

"Yeah."

"So he was in on it, right?"

"In on what?"

"Paying you to beat the crap out of me and plant the drugs?"

"I don't know what—"

The Colt appeared in a flash, pointed straight into the boy's belly.

"Shit," he whispered. "Oh, God, mister."

"Who paid you—" Pellam paused. Suddenly he was curious. "How much was it?"

"A hundred bucks."

"That's *all*? That's crap."

"No, man, no. It's totally true. I swear."

Pellam felt insulted. "You should've charged more. Now tell me who?"

"We didn't have nothing against you. We heard—"

"Who?" Pellam whispered viciously and cocked the Colt, praying that his thumb wouldn't slip off the hammer. The gun was loaded with 130-grain, .45 caliber bullets. The boy was fat but he wouldn't even slow up a slug that size.

Both hands in front of him, palms out. "Okay. Fine. Listen, I'm going—"

"Asked you a question," Pellam growled.

"—to tell you. Just put that—"

"Who?"

"Mr Ambler. Wexell Ambler. Well, was a guy works for him – name's Mark, but I don't know his last name, I swear I don't. This guy Mark talked to Mayor Moorhouse and they wanted me and my friend to rough you up a bit."

"Where's he live? The Ambler?"

Pellam touched Nick's chest with the Colt. A good way to get directions fast. Nick became a regular Triple A guidebook. "Barlow Mountain road. Just off Route Nine, north. Past the Shell station. Go two hundred yards past then make a left. Really, mister, I didn't have nothing against you."

"Well, what's *he* got against me?"

"I don't know, swear to God. Please, mister, point that someplace else."

Pellam aimed at the ground before he eased the hammer to half-cock then slowly spun the cylinder to put an empty chamber beneath the hammer, which he then lowered all the way. He held the gun in his right hand while he handed the whiskey bottle to Nick with his left.

"Take a drink."

Nick's voice shook as he said, "I don't want to take a drink."

"We both want you to." Pellam pointed the Colt at him again.

"Oh, shit, come on—"

"Drink it down."

Nick took a swallow.

"Come on, a couple more. Drink like a man. You hit like a girl. At least drink like a man."

"Fuck you, Pellam," he wheezed.

"You tried that. It didn't work. Drink."

When he'd gotten down five, six good mouthfuls, Pellam took the bottle and threw it, open, into the GT.

"Aw, shit, what you want to do that for?"

"Well, I'll tell you. I've evened things up a bit. You're a little bigger'n me but now you're a little drunker. So we're driving out of town and I'm going to whip your ass one on one."

"You got that gun."

"I'll leave it in the car. Drive out toward the highway to the forest preserve. I'll be right behind you. Don't try to get away. I'll be aiming for the tires but I might hit your gas tank."

"You asshole," the boy muttered as he got into the car. The big Pontiac engine exploded to life and Nick pumped the accelerator.

They pulled out of downtown, the camper right behind the GT.

It turned out even better than Pellam'd thought it would be. They'd gotten two miles out of town, to the stoplight, when Nick did just what Pellam knew he was going to do: Looked for cross traffic, slipped the clutch and shot through the red light, running up through the gears with his fancy shifter, sounding like a buzzsaw.

The boy was probably in fourth when the state trooper Pellam had seen on his way into town, hidden in the bushes, a speed trap, started to pull out.

Nick came within two or three inches of taking the front end of the trooper's Chevy with him.

Pellam drove slowly past the scene of the arrest. Nick, handcuffed. The trooper, writing down Breathalyzer results.

He drove past the sign that said *Welcome to Cleary* and continued into the blackness.

Good night, officer.

Good night, sir . . .

Pellam turned the camper off Barlow Mountain Road, and eased along an overgrown side road up the hill that he supposed was Barlow Mountain. He nosed the Winnebago forward into a clump of hemlocks then killed the engine. He pulled the Colt out from under the seat and slipped it into his waistband then stepped outside. His boots made gritting taps as he walked along the asphalt toward the warm yellow house lights that glowed in the fog, a quarter mile away.

A hundred yards from the house he made his way off the road into brush and sparse woods. He smelled wet pine and ripe leaves. A hit of skunk. He saw the glistening lights reflecting on a lake to his right. A late, lone cicada made its deceptively cheerful sound and somewhere a dog barked. He moved slowly toward the house, stepping around branches.

The house was a rambling old monster, easily two hundred years old. A drab, ugly brown, Plymouth Rock chic. He heard water lapping and saw the lake clearly; it came right to the edge of the property. The dog barked again, the sound rolling across the lake. There was no other noise or motion, not even wind. The house was still and the lights were dim; Pellam wondered if they'd been left on while the residents were out to discourage the potential intruders that Pellam now understood Ambler would have good reason to worry about – the state police, for instance.

He thought of the drugs that had been planted on Marty – and on him – and the odd heroin Sam had taken. He recalled that Meg or someone told him about other overdoses and murders in the area. Ambler was probably responsible for it all.

He knelt in the grass and felt the cold dew through his denim. After five minutes, during which he saw no motion, he ran in a crouch to the separate garage, a two-story saltbox, and looked in the window. Only one car inside, a Cadillac. And there was an oil stain on the concrete, about ten feet to the left of the Caddie, which told him that Ambler had two cars.

A family out to dinner on Sunday night? Probably. But even when he walked to the house Pellam stayed in the shadows and edged up to the first-floor windows slowly. He bobbed his head up and looked in one quickly, seeing small rooms, decorated with rough, painted furniture, wreaths of dried flowers, primitive Colonial paintings of spooky children and black-clad wives – everything stiff and spindly and uncomfortable.

He saw no movement at all.

The windows, he noticed, were mostly unlocked.

The third room was the one he wanted.

It was dark paneled and inside were two large gun cabinets, glass faced, set against the wall. Several trophies were mounted near the low ceiling – a couple of antelope and a good-pointed buck. But they were on one wall only, as if the hunter had gotten tired of displaying his kills. Pellam, squinting, saw a number of rifles in the cases. Several looked like they were .30 caliber and at least two of them had telescopic sights.

Pellam lifted his hands up to the window and tested it. Unlocked. He stood completely still for a moment, his face millimeters away from the smooth, expensive paint job. Then he eased up the window, which moved slowly. He opened it about two feet. A hard climb, though, he thought – considering his bruised thigh, his damaged joints.

It was then that he glanced inside and noticed something odd.

What's wrong with this picture?

The second gun cabinet. The third space from the left.

Empty.

Thinking: If a man was as organized as Ambler seemed to be, and he *didn't* have enough guns to fill a cabinet, he'd probably keep the ones he did have centered in the rack. Which meant—

"Don't move," the man said.

The jump was involuntary, though the cold touch of the shotgun barrel at his head brought the movement under control real fast.

The voice was that of a middle-aged man. He asked, "You have a gun?"

"Yes."

"Hand it to me."

If he was impressed with the Colt, the man didn't say so. He slipped it into his pocket and, leaving the Remington over-under at Pellam's neck like a nesting kitten, said, "Let's go inside."

❦

Pellam moved back and forth slowly in the bentwood rocker he'd been politely invited toward by the blunt 12-gauge trap gun. (Pellam hated shotguns. Shotguns were really loud.)

The man – he *was* Wex Ambler, according to his muttered introduction – studied Pellam carefully. Pellam gazed back. It was an odd contrast – hateful dark eyes and an L.L. Bean Sunday gardener's outfit, complete with bright green Izod shirt.

"What were you doing?" Ambler asked.

"Thinking of shooting a movie here. I was—"

"You know I could shoot you now. Blow your head clean off and all the sheriff'd do is tell me how sorry he was I lost a window and bloodied my floor."

Pellam saw the stillness in Ambler's eyes and knew this was a man who could easily kill.

He said, "I wanted to see if you were really the man who was trying to send me to Attica for ten years."

Ambler said, "I didn't want you to go to prison. I wanted you to leave town. Get the hell out and not come back."

"You could've asked."

"You *were* asked. Several times."

Goodbye . . .

Ambler's eyes flashed. "You people . . . We have a decent town and you think you can come here from Hollywood, and make your movies, but you're laughing at us. Behind our backs you're laughing. I hate you people."

Pellam *was* laughing. "Bullshit. I came to town to rent a few houses and stores for a couple of weeks. That's all we wanted. My friend gets killed and I get beat up and somebody plants drugs on me . . ."

Ambler shook his head, whipping Pellam's words off like they were gnats.

Pellam's eyes measured distances, noticing that the shotgun's safety was on, that Ambler's finger was outside the trigger guard, that the muzzle was aimed sixty or seventy degrees away from him. Noticing a carving set on the counter, antler handled, a burnished, well-honed blade on the knife. Even the serving fork looked vicious.

"Sin city," Ambler said.

Pellam rocked forward. His legs tensed, thinking he could probably make it. He wondered what it was like to stab someone. "It's just a business," Pellam said.

Ambler didn't hear him. "People here go to church, they have children, they teach them Christian values, they work hard, they—"

Pellam thought: *Make millions selling smack.*

"—don't need your kind of influence."

Outside influence. So it was a script. Moorhouse and Ambler and the sheriff all had the same script and the lines were terrible. They'd all be in on it, of course. This man with a million-dollar house was probably the ringleader. He'd arranged to bring the drugs in from someplace out of the country. Then he'd distribute them in small towns like this. An untapped market. Moorhouse, Tom the sheriff and the pastel-sunglassed deputies were his enforcers.

Ambler was lecturing. Sin, providence, promises unkept.

The words didn't quite harmonize with the fact the man had killed Marty. Or was seeding God-fearing Dutchess County with exotic drugs. (But Pellam recalled a former acquaintance – E Block, West Wing, San Quentin, California – who went to church every day.)

Ambler kept talking like a crazy person on the street, furious. Flecks of spittle in the corner of his mouth. The muzzle of the gun rose and fell like surf.

But Pellam wasn't paying much attention to Ambler's mania or the moral purity of Dutchess County.

He was thinking about the carving knife.

His feet rested themselves under the sensually curved chair.

Pressing the balls of his feet against the tile. The knife, the knife, the knife.

He felt the tension, like blued spring steel, building in his calves.

The knife . . .

He kept his eyes calm, staring right into Ambler's. That was the give-away in a fight. You could always tell when a man was about to swing or go for a weapon – his eyes. He'd learned that from another acquaintance (D Block, North Wing). Pellam looked at Ambler and kept his eyes very still.

He rocked forward. The chair swung back and then forward, his weight moved with it.

The knife.

On your mark.

Goddamn, shotguns were loud.

Get set.

Blood on the tiles? No, sir, there'd be blood on the ceiling, the walls, the fancy granite countertop . . .

Go.

Ambler's harsh voice asked, "What did you tell her?"

Pellam froze, stopped rocking. "Who?"

Ambler's feverish eyes danced out the window for a moment, as a car drove past. It continued on.

Pellam rocked back. His quaking legs relaxed. Shotguns didn't so much shoot you as obliterate you.

Ambler continued. "That you'd make her a star?"

"What are you talking about?"

Ambler said, "She told you she'd been a model, didn't she? And you promised to get her jobs. Promised to take her out to California. 'Leave this backwater little town. Leave your son'? And then you seduced her, didn't you? You promised her a job and you fucked her."

"I don't—"

"She's just fodder for you, isn't she?"

"I don't know who you're talking about."

His first thought was: Janine. But then he asked cautiously, "Meg?"

Ambler nodded.

Him? He's the one?

Meg, come on . . . *This* guy?

Ambler muttered sarcastically, "Oh, she'd be in good hands with you . . . Jesus. You gave Sam that fucking heroin or whatever it was and practically killed him . . ."

The surprise in Pellam's eyes must have seemed genuine. Ambler stopped talking.

"I didn't give Sam that stuff."

Ambler frowned. Finally he said, "You seduced her, didn't you?"

"Nothing happened between us. We talked. We had dinner."

Ambler looked at him for a moment, a lover's examination of a possible rival. How they hang on every flutter of eyelash, every syllable.

Pellam said, "She's a captivating person."

Ambler said, "Too good for you."

"That's probably true."

Ambler said, "I love her."

"That's why you did it?" Pellam asked. "Why you had me set up? Because you thought I was taking her away from you?"

"Yes! And here you come to threaten me. To tell me to stop seeing her—"

Pellam said, "I didn't even know you *were* seeing her."

"Then what're you doing here tonight?"

Pellam looked at Ambler's face carefully, judging. Tommy Bernstein had said there were times when a man has to make a leap. He meant it philosophically, muttering something about a leap of faith, though when he said it he was drunk and poised to leap off the second story of his Beverly Hills house into the swimming pool that Liberace had supposedly done something scandalous in.

Pellam said, "I'm going to show you something."

"What?"

"I'm going to reach into my pocket, okay? I just want to show you something."

Pellam's hand disappeared into his pocket and it returned with the two shell casings.

"What are those?"

"These were the shells from the shots that killed my partner. Whoever did that is the same person who's been selling the drugs that Sam got. I assumed it was the same person who had me beat up."

"And you thought it was me?" Ambler's face was horrified. Pellam slowly rocked forward, off the balls of his feet. He'd forgotten about the knife. Ambler said, "I'm a Christian."

Pellam laughed. "Well, you vandalized our camper, right? You planted the drugs in the car and you called the sheriff and said Marty was selling stuff, right?"

Ambler didn't answer for a moment. "The day you and your friend came to town I was with Meg. She was so excited. I've never seen her that way. She was obsessed with the idea of being in a movie. That's all she talked about. If you made a movie here, I was afraid I'd lose her. She'd try to get a part, she'd go off to Hollywood. I *did* have somebody plant something in the car. And then, yes, he called the police. But I didn't have Marty killed. I'd never do that."

"You were the one who ordered the parking lot plowed over?"

"When the accident happened – when the car blew up – I was terrified that I'd be accused of it. I told Moorhouse to have it dozed to hide any evidence."

"And Sillman? The rental place."

"I had my man talk to Sillman. We arranged to offer Marty's family some money. A lot of money. It looked like an insurance settlement."

"And you had those two locals pay me a visit? Beat me up?"

Ambler nodded. "I wanted you gone so badly. All she did was talk about you. Talk about movies. I was losing her. I was desperate." He looked down at his hands, studied his long fingers. Ambler broke open the shotgun and put it on the counter. He picked up the bullet casings. "Winchester .300's. But there's something different about them."

"Magnums," Pellam said.

"I don't have a gun that'll take these." He looked up. "You want to check?"

Pellam glanced at the shotgun, which Ambler could still grab, close and loudly obliterate Pellam with before he was halfway to the knife. He said, "I believe you."

Ambler handed the cartridges back. "Those're unusual rounds."

"Used for real long distance shooting."

"What kind of weapon would that be?" Ambler asked.

"You can get a Beretta bolt-action chambered for them. SIG-Sauer has a .300 Magnum and—"

"Beretta, you say?"

Pellam said, "You know somebody who's got one?"

"I do, but I don't think—"

"Who?"

"You don't know them. A couple brothers."

Something flashed through Pellam's mind.

Pellam said, "They wouldn't be twins, by any chance?"

"Yeah, as a matter of fact, they are."

*   *   *

"You aren't gonna like it," the deputy said to the sheriff.

"I don't like a lot of what's been happening around here lately," Tom said.

They were in the police station, Sunday night, though one thing about Cleary: the Sabbath wasn't any quieter than any other day. The only difference now was that all three of them were working – two in the office, and the other deputy in the field – and they were expecting a visit from a detective and another deputy from the County Sheriff's office, who were going to be assisting in the investigation of Ned's murder.

"I was talking to people who had seen him in the past twenty-four hours. Who'd seen Ned, I mean."

The sheriff knew this, since he'd sent the deputy to do just that. "And?"

"A coupla folks saw him with Sam Torrens. At the festival."

"So?" Tom was exhausted. A blown-up car, drugs, arson, fights. And now a high school boy murdered. Life in small-town America. Crap.

"It was just before the kid got sick."

"Kid? *Which* kid? Explain it to me, will you?"

The deputy said, "I'm saying that it looks like Ned was the one who gave the drugs to Sam Torrens. That heroin shit."

"Oh." The sheriff closed his eyes and rubbed them with his knuckles. "What aren't I going to like? You said before I wasn't going to like something."

The deputy continued. "Keith Torrens got his boy a .22 for Christmas last year. I seen him buying shells."

"When?"

"I don't mean recent. I just mean I know he's got a .22 in the house. And had some shells."

"Come on, Randy. Everybody in town's got a .22. They practically come with the house when you buy one."

"I'm just saying."

"And we don't know for certain it was a .22 killed Ned. Could've been a .25 or a .222."

"Maybe. But you'd think there'd've been more damage—"

"We. Don't. Know."

The deputy nodded. Finally he said, "Closest thing to justifiable I've ever seen."

The sheriff wondered where the hell that was coming from. The deputy had worked on exactly one murder in his four years on the force and that had been when Barnie Slater's wife used a deer slug in his sleep to keep him from taking the lamp cord to her anymore. She had fresh coffee for the deputies when they'd arrived. The sheriff said, "Justifiable's the prosecutor's decision, not ours."

After a moment Tom asked, "When was the time of death?"

"About ten this morning."

"Church time. Meg was here bailing out that movie guy – now *that's* a fact I don't want to think too much on. What about Keith? He do church?"

"I don't know," the deputy answered. "We can call. They're in First Presbyterian."

"Who's that? The Minister?"

"Jim Gitting. Good man. Gives a good sermon."

Tom didn't care whether he was the devil's own brother. "Call him. Find out it Torrens was there today."

The deputy picked up the phone. "Reverend Gitting please . . .

Hey, Reverend, how you doing? Look, I'm real sorry to be—"

Tom took the phone from his hand. "Reverend, this is the sheriff. Was Keith Torrens in church this morning?"

"Uhm, no, Sheriff." The voice was whiny. Didn't sound like he'd give a good sermon at all. "Can I ask why?"

"Just looking into some things. He usually attend services?"

"Hardly ever. He was working this morning – like usual."

"Wait. You said he wasn't there. How'd you know where he was."

"He wasn't *in* church. He just dropped off Sam for Sunday school. Is this about that thing with Sam this morning? It wasn't a big thing. Just gave the teachers a little fright is all."

"What 'thing' with Sam?"

"Well, the boy disappearing. Is that what you're calling about?"

"What happened?"

"The boys had a study group outside, the weather was so nice. About a half hour later the teachers noticed Sam was gone. We called Meg but she wasn't home—"

Bailing out that asshole from the movie company.

"—and we called Keith."

"At his office?"

"Right. He was about to leave but then Sam came back. He was upset about something but wouldn't say what. Mrs Ernhelt had a talk with him about going away without saying anything and he seemed okay. It really wasn't anything."

"What time was this, Reverend?"

"I don't know for sure. About nine forty-five or ten."

Brother . . .

"All right, sir, thank you."

"Can you tell me what this is all about?"

"Nothing important. 'Night."

The deputy finally said what he'd apparently been eager to say for some time. "Tom, if somebody gave my kid drugs like that I'da done something to him too. Maybe not killed him. But I'da done something. You can't hardly blame Keith."

"The minister called Keith when Sam disappeared. He was in his office." Before the deputy could nod in relief Tom said, "But his boy wasn't accounted for."

"Sam? Come on, you're not thinking . . ." But the man's voice faded.

Trash.

The mystery of what lay behind the stockade fence at R&W was solved: not surplus, not salvage. Forget about antiques. Not even good junk.

Robert and William owned a trashyard and nothing but.

Pellam had circled far around the back of R&W and was slowly moving through the woods. Unlike the pristine woods surrounding Ambler's house, the air here was raw, pungent, ripe. He smelled garbage and methane, which filled his throat and made him gag. Several times he had to swallow down nausea. Under the dim moonlight, halved by mist, he felt he was plodding through a dead animal's viscera. The ground under his boots was slick and pasty.

He came to the foothills of the junkyard: A doorless refrigerator on its side then ten yards further along, amputated pieces of laminated furniture, plush toys, books, tangles of wire, hunks of iron losing shape to oxidation.

Twenty yards more and he came to the boundary of R&W. He'd brought a small bolt cutter and though he saw now at one time there had been a cheap chain link enclosing a portion of the yard it had long ago sagged or been pulled down by vandals or gravity. Pellam stuffed the cutter into his back pocket and hopped over an indented portion of the fence.

He paused and listened for dogs.

Nothing. No voices either. Just the sour smell and a tangle of vague moonlight reflecting off a thousand varied surfaces. Pellam walked forward slowly toward the shack that must have been the office of the place, looking for footholds through the maze of scabby, broken trash.

Pellam pressed his back against the shack. He looked quickly in the window then ducked below the sill. Empty. He looked again.

A filthy place. Fast food cartons, empty beer cans, more magazines (he expected *Penthouses* but all he could see were *National Geographics*, *Cosmopolitans* and *Readers' Digests*), moldy and stained clothes. Books, dishes, newspapers, slips of paper, boxes.

He also saw two leather guncases in the corner.

He looked around, then tried the window. It was locked. Pellam took the bolt cutter and whacked out a pane of glass, reached up and undid the latch. He lifted the window and after a struggle to boost himself up, the pain shooting from his thigh to his ribs to his jaw, he half-fell and half-climbed over the windowsill.

He listened for a moment. And heard nothing but the rustle of a car moving by. He walked quickly to the corner, and hefted one of the gun cases. Inside was a Colt AR15, the civilian version of the Army M16.

The other case held the .300 magnum Beretta.

A simple-looking gun, a bolt-action. Walnut stock, dark blued metal, a black shoulder guard, a high-riding telescopic sight. There were no iron sights; it was a sniper's gun. The shells Sam had found fit it perfectly.

Cinderella's slipper.

Was it proof enough? Pellam didn't know. His only bout with the law had been on the other side (and from there it looked pretty damn easy to get yourself arrested and convicted). Pellam replaced the gun then began looking through desk drawers, the closet, the battered olive-drab rucksacks stacked on the back wall.

Which is where they had the drugs hidden.

Thousands of little tubes like the kind crack came in. Must've been five, six thousand of them. And inside each one was a little crystal like the doctor had showed them, the crystals someone had given Sam. A little piece of rock candy.

That solved the probable cause problem. If the gun didn't do it then this ought to.

A car went by. It seemed to slow and he quickly shoved the bags back into place, drew his pistol. Then after a moment, when the car was past, Pellam knelt and opened the rucksack again.

21

"Nekkid," Bobby said.

His brother nodded.

They were in the Cleary Inn, eating prime rib. It was a pretty ritzy place for Dutchess County. Not as damn countryish as most places, the inn was filled with chrome and mirrors and plastic all shoved together and cemented down with plenty of money. The twins sat at a table with red linen tablecloths; in their laps were thick napkins that left whitecaps of lint on their matching dark slacks.

They may have owned a junkyard but these boys loved to eat and didn't mind pampering themselves. A goodly part of the money they made – from the drugs, of course, since they'd had a loss on the junkyard every year they'd operated it – a goodly part of that income went into their mouths. Disposable income. ("We own a junkyard – all our income's disposable! Ha, ha, ha.")

Tonight their fingernails were perfectly clean and under the aroma of coal tar shampoo they smelled sweet as the perfume aisle of a CVS Pharmacy.

Bobby said, "So there I was, nekkid as a jaybird." He paused, wondering what a jaybird was exactly. "And the shades were up. She couldn't've been more than fifteen feet away. In the backyard."

"Fifteen feet."

"In a white bra. Like torpedo tits."

"This's a dumb shit story."

"No, no, no," Bobby said. "It gets better."

Billy said, "It ain't got good yet. How can it get better?"

Bobby paused to eat his Yorkshire pudding, which was new on the menu. He'd never had it before. Well, pudding it wasn't. It was like a pancake that got out of hand. Bobby thought he could show the cook here a thing or two about making pancakes.

Billy ate some more Caesar salad.

Bobby continued, "Then she kind of waves. Only it was, she didn't want to come right out and wave. You know, that kind of wave."

Billy chewed.

"And the next thing, I'm turning around to face her full and she was looking at my ding-dong, smiling."

Billy said, "You talk more about that thang than you use it."

"I sure did use it that night," Bobby said. Then, after another triangle of Yorkshire pudding disappeared into his mouth: "How long is he going to be there?"

He didn't explain that he was talking about Pellam being at the Torrens place (they'd seen the camper on their way to the Inn) but Billy knew that's what his brother was talking about.

"I don't know. How would I know?"

Bobby said, "So, we're just going to do it? It'll look kind of obvious, won't it? First his friend in the car. Then him."

"Uhm," Billy muttered and didn't say anything more. Not

because he was chewing salad but because he was thinking.

Bobby looked at a twelve-point mounted above a smoky-glass fireplace. It was weird to have a trophy in a restaurant that looked like it ought to be on Fort Hamilton Parkway in Brooklyn or someplace in Paramus, New Jersey. He studied the animal's dead eyes and slick fur and he began salivating, imagining that he could smell fresh morning air and feel November stub grass under his boots, the heft of a good rifle in his hands.

He said, "I can't picture that, you know. Traveling around the country. I'd get kind of, you know . . ."

"Disoriented," Billy said. Billy often supplied the words that Bobby couldn't think of.

"Yeah. I'd like to travel, though. There's a lot of the world to see. I just mean I wouldn't want to travel all the time."

"Uhn."

"You're not talking a lot tonight." He tapped a crispy part of the pudding with his fork. The thing that was odd was that you were supposed to put gravy on it. Bobby thought they ought to give you Log Cabin and was close to asking for some.

Pancake pudding with gravy on it. Brits were fucking crazy.

Billy said, "There's one thing that still bothers me. The Torrens kid."

"What about him?"

"Ned gave him the candy, right? So they must've spent some time together. What's a like logical question for the kid to ask?"

Bobby couldn't figure it out. "Tell me."

"He's going to ask where Ned got the stuff, and Ned is – was – just dumb enough to tell him."

"The kid's nine or ten. What's he going to know?"

"Sometimes," Billy said, "you just don't think."

That was not exactly true. Bobby thought a lot. It was just that usually his thoughts weren't helpful; they didn't go anywhere. So he was happy to mix up batter and flip flapjacks like bones that sailed through the air in space movies and drill a deer's shoulder from three hundred yards with a shot aimed through his Zeis-Daiwar 'scope and keep the roadsides of Dutchess county free from any trash that had the slightest use and a lot of things that didn't. Beyond that, okay, he left a lot of the thinking to Billy. Who couldn't shoot and who couldn't cook. And who, fuck him, didn't like *National Geographic*.

Billy said, "He could know a lot. Just 'cause he's a kid doesn't mean *he's* stupid."

Bobby, wondering if he'd been insulted. "So, what are you saying?"

But Billy answered by asking, "What do you think of the Missus?"

Torrens. Meg Torrens. Had to be.

"I dunno," Bobby said. "You going to eat your pudding?"

"Huh?"

"Your pudding?"

"I thought it was like a potato or something. Yeah, I'm gonna eat it." Billy added, "Whatcha think about her?"

"I dunno."

"She's no hausfrau."

"Hausfrau? What's that? Like a Nazi?" Bobby pronounced it Nat-see.

"You think she has big tits?" Billy mused.

"I dunno. What're you—?"

Billy asked, "What do you think about Torrens? I mean, *really* think?"

"Think about him?" Bobby often repeated his brother's questions in a tone that made it sound like it was a dumb thing to ask – usually so he could buy time to figure out an answer.

Billy continued, "You think he's smart?"

"Smart enough."

Billy looked at his brother, then laughed. "What does that mean, 'smart enough'? That's like saying his dick is long enough."

"Okay," Bobby said, "he's smart enough not to put his dick where it don't belong. Which it sounds to me is what *you're* considering doing."

There, dude, how's *that* for thinking?

"How much you think Torrens's worth? How much you think he makes?"

"Man, you're asking for—"

"Compared to what, let's say, we, for instance, make?"

"—fucking trouble."

Billy ate his pudding, every last bit. Bobby watched this with disappointment. He thought that thirteen ninety five, which bought you a good-sized slab of wet, red prime rib, ought to buy you a little more in the Brit pudding department.

"They got themselves a real nice house," Billy said, continuing this line of thought that Bobby didn't quite get but knew he didn't like."

"It's okay."

Billy stared at his brother as if he'd just turned down playoff tickets. Bobby said, "Okay, it's fucking wonderful. Happy?"

"Let's just . . ." Billy began.

"I think you're nuts is what I think."

". . . consider a possibility."

————◆————

S he was wondering where Pellam was. What he was up to. Taking the whiskey, disappearing mysteriously like that.

Meg Torrens felt a brief splinter of jealousy, wondering if he'd gone off to see Janine. Then she forced that thought away. Said to herself: You got yourself a pretty full plate at the moment, babe.

Still . . .

That damn sound again. From the day they'd met in Pellam's hospital room. The Polaroid. *Bzzzt.*

For your information I've lived here five years . . .

She thought about him kissing her, about how she wanted to kiss him back.

Enough . . .

She tucked Sam into bed and went down to the kitchen, poured herself another glass of wine and was returning to the living room, turning the lights down. She'd had them up high while Pellam was here, despite her hatred of bright lights.

Didn't know why she'd done that . . . Okay, yes, she did. Less romantic. Less of a message. She—

A knock on the door.

She hoped it was Pellam but was afraid Ambler had returned. She recalled that he must have seen Pellam leave and wondered if Ambler had parked up the road and been spying on them, waiting for him to leave. To return and try his proposal yet again. How could such a strong man be so desperate?

I'm just not in the mood for this . . .

But when she opened the door she found the sheriff standing on the front porch.

"Tom."

"Evening, Meg."

She felt a jolt. "Is Keith okay?"

"Oh, I'm not here about him."

"Pellam?"

"Not him either. Mind if I come in?"

He was grave but then he was always grave. She nodded him in, setting the wine on a nearby break-front. He walked inside, pulling off his hat the instant his boot touched the threshold.

"Coffee or anything?"

He shook his head. Sat down on the couch.

"What is it?"

"Just wanted to ask you a thing'r two about Sam. You know he left Sunday School for a while this morning."

What was this?

"I didn't know that was a crime," she said stiffly.

"Meg, I think we both know it isn't. And I think you know there's more to me asking than that."

"Which is what?"

"Did you know about Sam? Would you tell me please?"

She opted for the truth but it was a close election. "Yes. Keith told me. They tried to call me here but I was out. They called him at the factory. Sam came back after a few minutes."

"After forty-five minutes."

"What is this all about, Tom?"

"And you talked to Sam about it?"

"Of course." The sheriff said nothing more and Meg felt compelled to continue. "He was upset about what happened. With those pills. He said he didn't feel well. It was a nice day. He went for a walk." She was rambling and stopped. "I want to know what you're asking."

Tom nodded. "Meg, not long after he left the church Ned Harper was killed. It was a mile away – that's a bit of a hike but he could've made it in the time he was gone."

"Ned? What does Sam have to do with Ned?"

"We think Ned was the one gave him those pills. And we think Sam might've killed him."

"No," she said firmly.

"We don't know for sure. But it'd make sense for Ned to've threatened the boy. You saw how scared he was. And it'd make sense for Sam to want to get even."

"Sam wouldn't hurt anybody."

"Ned was killed with a small-caliber. Might be a .22. We haven't got the slugs yet. Randy Gottschalk, my deputy, he was telling me that Keith got Sam a .22 last Christmas."

Her eyes strayed to the den – where the small Winchester usually resided. Her heart jumped when she noticed it was gone. But then she remembered that Sam and Pellam had been shooting that afternoon. Had they been using the .22? Or the little shotgun? Maybe they were on the back porch, awaiting cleaning. Or the basement. The only gun in the cabinet was the antique Springfield – the only surviving bequest from her parents, other than the intense dislike of bright lights.

"Tom, you've known Sam since he was born. You think he's capable of killing somebody?"

"I don't, no. But I'm not the only one going to be asking. We've already had more'n our share of trouble in Cleary – those deaths last year, a couple of other overdoses. The state police're going to be handling this one. And they're going to want to talk to Sam and check out his gun. Run some ballistics."

"What that'll prove is that he's not the one." But even as she said these words a terrible doubt was forming. No, her son was incapable of killing anyone.

Yet she remembered his face today – when he was shooting with Pellam. It looked so determined. So adult. Scarey, at times.

"Can I talk to him?"

"He's asleep."

Tom smiled, looked past her. "Doesn't seem to be."

Sam was standing in the hallway, in his pajamas, staring at the sheriff uneasily.

"I heard a noise, I got scared."

"Hi, Sam. How you doing?"

"Hi, Sheriff."

"You feeling better?"

"Yessir, I am."

"You must've heard me. Sorry I woke you up."

"I wasn't asleep. I heard you come in. This was a different noise. Outside my window."

Meg was looking at his round, sleepy face. She thought: No, he'd never kill anyone. Yet . . . His eyes seemed so cold. He seemed so different. She struggled to smile. "Honey, it's probably that owl. Remember."

"Wasn't the owl."

Meg was thinking: Where is that .22? But, no, he *couldn't* have done it.

Tom stood. "How 'bout I take a look?"

"I guess," Sam said.

"Tom—" Meg began.

In a whisper the sheriff said, "Okay, Meg, tell you what. I'll come by tomorrow. You and Keith'll be here and you can have a lawyer too, you want. Okay?"

She nodded.

Tom put his hand on the boy's shoulder and they started up the stairs. "Now let's check out that noise."

"I'll be there in a minute to tuck you in," Meg called.

Where was that gun? She had to find it.

She was halfway to the back porch when the gunshot, from upstairs, shook the house.

A scream burst from her lips. She ran to the stairs and leapt out of the way just as Tom stumbled down them, a terrible wound in his chest.

"I . . ." He glanced at her with unfocused eyes, crawled toward the front door. He got three or four feet. Then dropped to the floor, lay still. Blood soaked the carpet.

"Jesus . . . Sam!" She started up the stairs again.

For a terrible moment she believed that her son had done it all – killed Ned and then lured the sheriff up to the second floor to kill him. And felt too that it was all her fault – for her infidelity, for her not being grateful for the wonderful life Keith had given her.

But then the boy appeared on the stairs, running in panic, tears streaming down his face.

"There was a man! He hurt Sheriff Tom. He shot him!"

"Where is he?"

"I don't know. He was at the window. I'm scared . . ."

Then she heard the noise.

Coming from the basement, the sound reminded her of the time she'd pulled apart an old lettuce crate for the wood, using a claw hammer to pry the nails. The loud squeal from the rusty friction.

Then a snap and the tinkle of glass on stone.

The basement window.

"Mommy! It's him. He's there. He's in the—"

"Shhh."

Meg ran to the basement door. She locked a small brass latch and grabbed the telephone. The line was dead. She tapped the button.

Silence.

She glanced at Tom but the pistol was no longer in his holster. He must have dropped it somewhere or the intruder had stolen it.

"Sam, where are those guns you and Mr Pellam were shooting?"

"I don't—"

"Sam, it's okay, honey. It's going to be fine. Where are the guns?"

He gasped in fear. "I put them in the basement. We were going to clean them. He said he didn't want me to by myself."

"All right, baby."

She led him to the first-floor guest room, which was windowless. She put him inside. "You lock the door when I close it. And don't open it for anybody but Daddy or me."

"I'm scared."

Hugging him hard. So hard it seemed that she'd never be able to let go. "You'll be all right. I promise."

She closed the door and heard it lock.

Meg sprinted into the den, tore open the gun cabinet door. The carbine, smelling of oil and sulfur, was in her hand. The hundred-year-old Springfield (*breechloader, not muzzleloader* . . . Oh, Pellam where are you?). The saddle ring jingled as she blew dust off the brown metal barrel.

She found a dozen of the long, heavy shells, put one in the chamber and the rest in her sweater pocket. She closed the breech with a snap and ran into the hall.

On the first floor she checked the front and back doors. They were locked. The windows on the ground floor? She usually kept them locked but had she aired the house recently? She couldn't remember and she wasn't going to check now.

She paused, heard delicate scraping sounds. Metal and wood being adjusted. She walked to the kitchen. Slow, determined. Okay, asshole, she thought. With both hands pulled the hammer to half-cock.

Footsteps were coming up the stairs.

Meg clicked out the kitchen light. She took a deep breath, reached forward, undid the latch and swung the door open wide. She stepped back so fast she almost tripped.

The man was three-quarters up the stairs. She couldn't see his face. He stopped. There was a laugh of surprise. He held a flashlight in his hand. His high, playful voice – vaguely familiar – said, "Meter reader."

Meg said, "I've got a gun. One more step and you're dead."

The light beam started to sweep toward her.

"Shine that light in my eyes and you're dead."

"Risky place, this house."

"What do you want?" She tried to keep her voice from quivering.

"Just passing Go. Looking for my two hundred. But seriously, folks . . . Tell you what, just let me wander out and I won't report you."

"I want you to lie facedown on the floor."

He laughed. "Uh, nothing personal but it's not real clean. And there might be spiders. I don't like spiders."

"Now!" With one thumb she managed to put the gun on full cock. The click reverberated through the kitchen.

He took a step down the stairs. He was debating. Then he said, "Don't think so. Thanks for the offer but I believe what I'll do is leave. Keep the jewelry, the silver. Wasn't my pattern anyway. Hey, just want to say . . ."

She held the gun up to her shoulder, started to squeeze the trigger.

He took another two slow steps into the darkness. ". . . dinner smells great, lady. Sorry I couldn't stay. Maybe some other time."

Now! Do it!

Her finger was frozen on the trigger. *Shoot, shoot, shoot . . .*

The man disappeared.

"Shit."

She slammed the door, slipped the latch, and heard him

running through the basement. She sprinted to the front of the house. She peered out through the lace curtains beside the door. She couldn't see anyone.

Hell, hell, hell. Where is he? Where'd he go?

Pellam, she thought, please come home . . .

Keith . . .

She started toward Sam's room.

Which is when the other man stepped into the hall from the living room and got his arm around her chest, saying in the same sort of sick voice that his partner had been speaking in, "Whoa my! Big gun for a little girl."

My God, she recognized him! It was one of the twins. The ones who owned that disgusting junkyard outside of town. Billy, or Bobby, had his hand over her face and groping for the stock of the gun, trying to pull it out of her strong, desperate grip.

She felt painful pressure on her breast as he fondled her with his other hand. "Hmmmm," he said with approval. She smelled his cheap musky aftershave and coal tar.

He was very strong but so was she. Neither could wrest the gun from the other's grip.

So she pointed the gun into the kitchen and pulled the trigger.

The explosion filled the hall with sulfur-stinking smoke. The Sanyo microwave blew into a dozen pieces. The recoil slammed Meg backwards into the twin. Through the ringing in her ears she heard him inhale in surprise. With a resounding crack his head hit the front doorknob.

"Ow, damn! Shit, that hurts." He let go and grabbed his head with both of his hands.

Meg dropped to her knees, tore open the breech of the

gun. The spent cartridge, hot and smokey, popped out, and she reloaded the rifle.

The twin blinked, squeezing the back of his head, spun around, undoing latches and locks on the front door. Blood stained the white enamel door and spattered the carpet.

Chain off, one latch, deadbolt.

Meg slammed the breech closed.

The door swung open.

Cocking the gun . . .

"Fucking cannon," he called to his brother, who must've been outside. "She's got a fucking cannon!"

Then a scream behind her.

"Mommy!" Sam had left the guest room and was running down the corridor toward her.

Meg turned toward him. "No, Sam, no!"

She spun back. But it was too late. The twin jumped toward her. Meg couldn't get the gun on full-cock in time and she swung it like a club. He caught it easily and jabbed his fist into her jaw.

"Mommy," Sam cried again as she dropped to her knees.

The brother stepped forward and, furious, hit her again, harder. A burst of electric pain just under her ears. Her vision went black and grainy around the edges. She slid down against the cornflower-blue wall. Tried to get up. Billy ripped the gun from her hands. Her head sagged against the wall.

Sam reached her, put his arms around her head. He screamed, "Go away, go away, you!"

The twin opened the door and shouted. "Yo, Bobby. It's under control. Come on in."

Bobby walked inside. Sniffed the air. "Stinks. Brimstone.

Lookit that thing." He nodded at the Springfield in admiration. Then he saw the sheriff's body. "You have to do that?"

"He seen me coming through the window," Billy said, massaging his head where he'd struck it on the doorknob. "The fuck you think I should've done? Said 'Howdy-do'?"

Bobby closed the door, looked over at Sam. "Hey, young fella. Don't worry. You'll be okay."

His brother muttered, "Son of a bitch, I'm bleeding." He looked with satisfaction at Meg, whose head lolled back and forth against the wallpaper. Her face was white. He asked, "Where's Keith?"

Meg didn't answer. He slapped her hard. Still silence. She was only half conscious.

"No!" the boy cried.

"Where's your father?"

He hesitated then said, "He's at the office but he's coming home any minute and he's going to kill you."

"Any minute," Billy repeated, looking at his brother.

But Bobby was looking over at the little boy. "How 'bout you and me go watch TV or something. In the living room there? While we wait for him."

"No."

"You don't want me to hit your mommy again, do you?"

Sam didn't say anything, just shook his head, wiped tears.

Bobby smiled. "Come on. Let's you and me go in there."

Billy said, "We don't have time for that now."

Feeling good that he'd thought of something his brother hadn't, Bobby said, "We gotta wait anyway, don't we? May as well enjoy ourselves."

———•◆•———

T he roadside signs gave him messages.

The scientist within Keith Torrens would see a yellow warning sign with a curve and a side road painted on it and he'd think of a sigma bond. And his mind would shift into thoughts about electron sharing and the unequal charge distribution in a chloride-bromine molecule.

Or he'd see a yield sign and think, *delta*, and, bang, there it would be in his thoughts: the Gibbs free-energy exchange formula.

Wandering, his mind. Going down those odd paths, just like it did when he was a pudgy kid with a slide rule. The Magic Moments happened then too, didn't they?

Another sign – this one on an old, abandoned White Castle hamburger stand. Castle . . . He saw the faded paint of the parapets as he sped past.

Castle. Medieval castles. Alchemists.

He thought about the location scout.

Pellam . . .

He was tired. It was nearly eleven and he'd put in a full fourteen hours at the plant. Another Sunday gone. Pushing the Cougar along the deserted, dark road, listening to the damn front-end squeak. A scientist. I'm a scientist and I can't fix a noisy hunk of metal.

But none of that mattered: the fatigue, the squeak, the headache. He didn't care. What was there to bitch about? He'd buy a new goddamn Cougar, a Cadillac, a Mercedes.

He was riding on a Magic Moment.

The answer had come all at once. At two that afternoon in a crisp unfolding of thoughts that he fought to put into numbers, Greek letters and scientific symbols. He had run from the factory into his office, closing the door, shutting off the telephone, and wrote furiously – frantic, terrified that he'd miss something. Keith had felt the shock of fear rise up to his scalp, like the first and only time he took speed – in college, struggling to get his master's degree project in on time. That warm clarity, everything focused, sweeping forward.

A Magic Moment.

That the problem solved – a new stabilizer for one of his company's cough syrups – wasn't exactly earth-shattering or in proportion to his euphoria didn't occur to him. And if it had, the excitement wouldn't be the least dampened.

The magic worked. He'd packed a problem into his brain, let it bake and out came a solution. He was high, he was alive. Those moments validated everything – all the business bullshit he put up with, all the long hours, the risks, the ulcers he was sure he was developing. All the time away from Meg and Sam.

All of that was paid for in one moment. A Magic Moment.

Thinking about Meg . . .

And he regretted for the tenth time that day, as every day, that she couldn't really be a part of what he'd done, his business. She'd benefit, of course. She'd be a millionaire too. But she couldn't be a partner.

That was Keith Torrens's greatest regret.

Castles, medieval alchemists.

Alchemy, turning gold into brighter gold.

Rings of gold. Wedding rings. Meg.

He remembered a line from some country-western station – one that she listened to all the time.

If we tell a lie while we're lying together, then that's nothing more than a port in bad weather . . .

He wondered again whether she was seeing anyone. He didn't think so. But Keith Torrens (who'd never cheated on his wife) believed that while men and women both had an equal capacity for deception, women were better equipped to cover their tracks. Keith (empirical, rational Cartesian – a *scientist*) had decided this was because as mothers, with broods to attend to, and possessing less physical strength than men they had honed their skills in guile for protection.

A tertiary basic nitrogen . . .

So, he'd found no circumstantial evidence. Nothing in her eyes. No Amex receipts (he could imagine what bastards those little blue tissue clues must be). Couldn't recall any times she was supposed to be at home when she wasn't (though how would he know? He was at the plant twelve hours a day). Sam had never referred to an uncle who'd come to help mommy with the yard, the gutters, the shopping.

. . . a quaternary carbon . . .

Who could be more devoted than he was? A better father? He never took long business trips, like some of the men who worked for the big companies by the Hudson. He didn't uproot Meg and Sam and drag them around the country. He wasn't like the fellow he'd met at the golf course one Sunday, a friend of a friend, who worked for IBM (I've Been Moved) down in Westchester. Four houses in six years.

. . . an ethylene chain and a ketone . . . Put them in the oven, and let them bake. Bang, a Magic Moment, and out comes something new.

No, she was faithful. Though questions of fidelity were the type you ask yourself in a certain way – fast, distracted – so as to avoid the possibility of a real answer. A scientist is not equipped to ask questions like that. Scientists aren't happy until they find the truth and he wasn't sure he wanted the truth.

Keith Torrens drove toward his home. He'd make it up to her. Make up for what?

He wasn't sure.

How?

He didn't know.

Pellam pulled the camper into the driveway.

He saw the beige car parked in the road just past the drive and thought: Oh, hell. No . . . He recognized the car. Knew who the visitors were.

Thinking about Big Mountain Studio's promise to put mobile phones in all the campers. None of Lefkowitz's minions had ever gotten around to it. And here the nearest house was several miles up the road. No time to get there.

No time for anything.

He doused the lights, parked on the grass, opened the camper door and climbed out.

No one inside seemed to have noticed him.

Everything seemed slowed up, the way they shoot karate fights in those charmingly bad Hong Kong karate flicks, or the way Sam Peckinpah shot his violent scenes. Pellam stepped out of the camper, breathing deeply. He started toward the house, avoiding the gravel.

At least he had surprise on his side.

Man, no question it was fall. That smell of the air's dry coldness, the sweet scent of oak or cherry fires.

Pellam was thinking how seasonless the big cities are. New York, L.A. And it was odd how returning to the country during a blatant time of year – the first deep snow, the week of the most colorful leaves – is more than anything a return to youth. Painful nostalgia, a rearrangement of priorities and possibilities.

Blatant seasons.

Pellam figured that was a pretty good observation and he wondered if he'd live long enough to use it in a film.

The sky was almost completely clear now, swept clean by the cold front. He glanced up, seeing the stars in the black vacuum that domed over him from one horizon of trees to another.

A perfect fall night in Cleary, New York. Home of the perfect cemetery.

That's how they'd ended up in Cleary in the first place, looking for the ideal, A-number-one cemetery.

A perfect fall night.

As he moved over the lawn. He saw shadows inside. The flicker of a TV screen. Keith's car was gone. So the twins were in there alone with Meg and Sam.

He hurried toward the house. He slipped the gun in his waistband. There was an open window to the right of the door, opening into a dark room. He could go up a rose trellis and through the window. Come around from behind.

Two of them, both armed, probably.

At least he had surprise on his—

A car pulled into the driveway, catching Pellam in its beams. It gave a long blare on the horn.

From the house, fifty feet away, security lights clicked on, blinding him.

"What's going on?" Keith called from the driveway. He'd parked and gotten out of the car. Pellam called, "Stay there. Stay back."

He turned back to the house. The front door opened and one of the twins stepped out, holding a pistol at Pellam's chest.

So much, Pellam thought, for surprise.

———

P ellam supposed that he'd known all along it would come
to this.

He walked to the right, out of the glare, onto the driveway,
gravel scrunching beneath the worn sole of his Nokonas. He
stopped and felt an odd sensation – growing into the drive, like
roots going down, solid as the granite slabs the gravel used to
be. "Hey, mister. Hey, Mr Torrens."

"What the hell—"

"Quiet," Pellam ordered Keith. The man froze.

This was definitely the ending of a film – not like one of
his, though, in which viewers felt all that tension, then nothing
happening, the principals moving vaguely off into the credits
(boy, he took flak for those endings. *Resolve it, John, resolve
it*. How the world hates the truth of ambiguity).

But here it was. Pretty damn clear to him. A man slouching
out onto the porch, holding in his hand an automatic pistol. Meg
said she didn't like handguns. They're man-killing guns, she'd
have been thinking, no other purpose for them.

The man slouching.

"You interrupted me," the twin said. "Was just about to sit down and watch some TV with a little friend in there."

And where's the other one, Pellam wondered, his brother?

Behind him?

Behind me?

Inside, with Sam?

"Where's Meg?" Pellam asked.

"Whatcha doin' here, mister?"

"Which one're you?"

"Bobby. Hey, don't you move there, Mr Torrens. You do, I'll have to kill you too."

Pellam asked, "You the one who did it?"

"Did what?"

"Killed my friend."

"S'pose you know if I tell you I'll have to make sure that fact doesn't go any further."

"That's pretty much on the agenda anyway, isn't it?" Pellam asked.

"Heh."

"I just want to know if it was you killed Marty."

"Was a hell of a shot, I do say so myself." Not smirking. Just mentioning the fact.

"Whatcha got there?" Bobby asked. "In your belt?"

"It'd be a Colt Peacemaker."

"No kidding. Smokeless powder? Reproduction?"

"Nope. It's the real thing."

"No kidding. Forty-four?"

"Forty-five."

"Heh."

"Where's your brother?"

"Maybe he's behind you."

"So you'll die first," Pellam said.

"Heh."

"Please . . ." Keith was begging. "Where's my son?"

They both ignored him.

There was no motion. Pellam stood on the wet gravel, his feet, in scuffed black boots, slightly apart.

There was no noise.

There was nothing else in the world except a man standing in front of him with a gun in his hand. A tall Victorian house. With a woman and boy inside, her husband nearby. Under a canopy of a dry, clear fall night.

Pellam had shot ducks and geese and a number of Gila monsters and rattlesnakes and hundreds of Heincken bottles.

He'd never shot a man.

The security lights poured into his eyes, making Bobby a silhouette. (Pellam recalled that, on various target ranges, he'd shot as many silhouette targets as Gila monsters and rattlesnakes combined.)

No face, no motion, no sound.

In the stillness, in this dense peace, a thought came to him. Something he remembered from researching a script about the Indians of the Great Plains. The Sioux, he believed. Waking up on a beautiful day, they wouldn't think how good it was to be alive. What they'd say was, "It's a good day to die."

Good, Pellam. Good thought.

Well, Wild Bill himself hadn't lived to see forty.

Then, finally, motion intruded on the scene. It was a cliché – one that Pellam, if he were directing a Western, wouldn't have allowed the writer to use: He pulled his blue jean jacket open slightly wider to fully expose the grip of his pistol.

The way Bobby saw it (Bobby who *had* shot a man – several of them, in fact – but only in the backs of their heads after being paid ten thousand dollars each to do it) these were good odds. Pellam had glare in his eyes and he had a single-action gun so he'd have to draw and cock it before he could shoot. It was a six-shot gun and it would take probably three minutes to reload. If he had extra ammo on him. Which he probably didn't.

Also, he figured Pellam hadn't shot anybody in the back of the head or anyplace else for any money.

Bobby, on the other hand, was already holding a cocked Browning automatic .380 with twelve rounds in it. Which all you had to do was aim and pull the trigger. The light was behind him. He could reload the Browning in two seconds.

Torrens was in the yard, true, but he wasn't going to do diddly except stand there like a scared rabbit.

He hoped Billy was watching him. He never missed a chance to impress his smarter brother.

What he'd do is let the guy go for the gun then shoot him in his leg. Watch him fall. Then let him crawl a little. Shoot again.

Maybe he'd aim for Pellam's boots. They were a good contrast, black on the white gravel. But so were the man's eyes, which glinted two reflections from the yellow porch light. And his white shirt under the dark jacket.

But then he decided there was something about the way the man had opened his jacket that made Bobby uneasy. Don't play games. Do Pellam, do Torrens. Go back to the boy. Or the mother. Or both.

Go for a chest shot.

Without really deciding, or thinking, Bobby dropped into a crouch.

He swept the gun upward in an arc, keeping his arm straight the way he knew to do and practiced every week. None of this two-hand combat shooting that nobody who knows guns really ever does. Squinting, but leaving both eyes open, as the blade sight rose right toward the white slash of Pellam's shirt. He started to pull the trigger.

Thunk.

A shovel.

Bobby thought: Goddamn . . . who did that?

Somebody'd snuck up and hit him in the chest with a shovel. Or . . . Damn, it hurt. He coughed. Or maybe it was an ax handle. Bobby dropped his unfired gun. He looked down. Where'd it go? He looked behind him. There was nobody. He looked at his chest again and saw the blood. Oh, that hurts. He was getting dizzy. Then he saw Pellam holding the Colt at his hip, surrounded by a cloud of smoke. Bobby reached for his gun. He fell to the porch. He looked for the shovel.

He asked, "Who? . . ."

He died.

Pellam spun around, looked behind him, into the fields to the side of the house.

No Billy.

He whispered to Keith, "Get down. Don't move." And started forward. But he didn't get very far. The door crashed open and Billy, staggering out, dropped to his knees over Bobby, shrieking. He lifted his own gun and fired sloppily at Pellam.

Ragged blue flashes appeared in the man's hand, the huge crack of the shots filling the night. A bullet popped the sound barrier inches from his left ear with the noise of a huge snapping finger.

All Pellam had time for was one shot, from his hip. He felt the kick, smelled the sulfur from the black powder. He saw the slug dig out a chunk of the porch. Billy fired fast and Pellam dove to the ground. He hit hard, landed on his right elbow. There was a loud snap, followed by breath-taking pain. His vision went black and dusty from the dislocation. He rolled onto his back. His shoulder joint popped back into alignment. He fainted for a second. Sweat shot from his forehead and he felt nausea in a bristling wave.

He lifted the Colt. It fell from his hand. His right arm was useless.

"Bobby, oh, Bobby . . ." Billy was moaning.

More shots from the automatic. Bullets dug into the camper and the ground near him.

Six shots, seven, eight.

"Sonabitchsonabitch! Son . . . of . . . a . . . bitch!"

Pellam lifted the Colt again. But it was a replay – the gun did a double gainer to the ground.

Christ, how many shots in that clip?

Ten, eleven, twelve . . .

Click, click, click.

Empty. He was out. Thank you . . . Pellam raised his head and watched Billy reload.

Pellam felt the cold wet touch of the gravel, smelled the sour earthy-oily scent of the stone. He saw Billy coming closer. He lowered his head and heard the crunch of the gravel under the man's loafers.

Pellam grabbed for the Colt. He hit the butt with his fingers and knocked it out of reach.

He heard the man's breathing. Pellam looked up, opened his eyes. He saw the bore of the gun in the man's hand, six feet away.

Billy stopped.

A good day to die . . .

Billy stopped.

He looked behind him as if he'd heard something.

Then he was flying through the air.

Sailing, the way stunt men did, off springboards mounted on either side of black powder charges in the war movies.

Billy sprawled on top of Pellam, knocking the wind out of him with a high, love-making grunt. The twin rolled over, uttered, "Bobby," then studied the gravel an inch away from his face. "Son of a bitch." He closed his eyes. "Son of a bitch." He shuddered once and was still.

Pellam pushed himself up, fainted for a few seconds. He came to then sat up again.

In front of him, on the porch, Meg was crying, clutching the smoking Springfield. She dug frantically into her pockets – for more ammunition, he guessed.

"Meg!" he called. "It's okay. They're gone. They're both gone."

But she paid no attention, dropped to her knees and slid a new shell into the gun, cocked it with both hands. She stood once more, wiped tears and scanned the yard like a sentry then returned to the house, calling to her son.

—◆◆◆—

"You all right?" Keith asked. Pellam nodded, gasping at the pain. And Keith continued into the house, following Meg.

Pellam made sure that Billy was dead then staggered inside.

He found them in the living room, Keith's arm around Meg, standing over Tom, the sheriff. He was dead.

Meg looked toward the front door, at Pellam, with eyes wide in terror.

Keith was on his knees, hugging Sam. Who glanced at Pellam but said nothing. He was crying. "Did they hurt you?" Keith asked.

The boy shook his head.

Meg, crying too, gasped. "He was going to . . . He took him in there. . . ." She nodded toward the living room. "But then they heard the horn and he went outside to see who it was."

"Oh, honey . . ."

Keith stood and Meg lowered her head to Keith's shoulder.

"What happened?" Keith muttered

"Honey, your phone, in the car. We've got to call the police."

"My phone?"

"In the car. They cut the line here. The phone doesn't work."

"I left it at the factory," he said. He seemed numb, unable to say any more than a few words at a time.

"Then drive to the Burkes, use theirs!"

"What happened? I don't . . ." He looked around the house. "I don't understand."

"It was so terrible . . ."

"Why was Tom here?" Keith asked.

Meg glanced at Sam and whispered something to her husband. He frowned. She nodded. "Then one of them shot Tom. They got in somehow. I don't know why. I have no idea why."

Keith said nothing for a moment, just stared at the sheriff's body. He glanced at Sam. "I'm going to take you up to bed. Your mother and I have to talk."

"Keith . . ." Meg started after him. But Pellam, wincing at the pain in his shoulder, stepped forward, touched her arm. "Meg, wait."

Father and son disappeared up the stairs.

She turned. "You're hurt . . ."

"Sit down."

Meg hesitated. "I have to talk to you. I have to tell you why I came back tonight . . ."

She was staring at Tom. "Keith has to call. He has to go to the Burkes."

"Meg . . . Listen to me. Tonight I went to see your friend."

She stiffened and her attention on the body in her living room vanished. "My friend?" she asked.

"Ambler."

She considered this, then asked, "How did you know he was my friend?"

"We had a talk." Pellam paused, looking at the stairs. But Keith was still with Sam. He added, "He likes you. He likes you a lot."

She wasn't sure what to do with this information. She found an afghan, placed it over the sheriff's head and chest. Pellam wanted to put his arm around her but he would probably have fainted; any motion was pure pain in his shoulder.

"Why did you go to see him?" Meg asked.

"I thought he might've been the one who had Marty killed."

"What?"

Pellam shook his head. "He didn't. But he did plant the drugs and he had me beat up."

"Wex wouldn't do . . ." But her voice faded and she obviously concluded that, yeah, he could very easily do that.

"The reason he did it was that he was afraid I was going to take you away with me."

"He did?"

She looked troubled but he wondered if he wasn't seeing a little pride in her face too. There probably isn't a woman in the world who isn't thrilled by a man who goes to those kind of lengths to keep her for himself.

"We decided it was probably the twins who were behind the shooting. I went to their junkyard. That shack of theirs. I found the gun they killed Marty with. Some other things too. I found—"

Footsteps nearby. Keith walked slowly down the stairs. He caught Pellam's eyes and paused. Then continued. "Sam's okay. I gave him something. He's sleeping."

Meg ignored him. Said to Pellam, "Why are you telling me this?"

But Keith preempted her. He'd overheard Pellam and he asked, "What else did you find in the shack?"

Pellam said to Meg, "I found some of that stuff, the drugs Sam got."

"So they're the ones?" she blurted. "They're the ones behind it . . . But why would they come here? Because Sam was a witness?"

"They weren't after Sam."

Keith had stopped walking. He sat down. Pellam said to him, "They had five or six thousand vials there. All packaged and ready to go . . . So, Keith, tell me: Were they distributing? Or were they skimming from you?"

Keith's eyes swam around the room. "Both, apparently."

Meg stared at her husband. "What do you mean?"

"Your partners came here to kill you," Pellam said. "And your family."

"Partners?" Meg gasped.

Pellam said to Keith, "Would they have enough information to make the drugs themselves? Could they do it without your factory?"

Keith didn't say anything.

Both, apparently.

Keith looked at the wall beyond which two of his employees lay. "I paid them enough."

"There's never enough."

"How'd you find out?"

Pellam said, "In one of the bags in their shack were notes from you. Some of your letterhead. Some cash." He nodded. "I came here to tell Meg."

She turned to Pellam. Wanted to say something, it seemed, but couldn't.

Keith said, "They were just punks but they had contacts in New York, New Jersey, Brooklyn. I needed them."

Pellam asked, "What is it exactly? The drug."

Keith explained. "It's an oral synthetic narcotic."

To her husband Meg whispered, "No. This isn't happening."

Keith took a breath and Pellam could see he was running through the inventory of lies he might choose from. A boy in front of a broken window. He looked at both Pellam and Meg and said, "It's not what you think."

"No, no, no . . ." She shook her head.

"Meg, it's just a product. I—"

"Product!" Meg said. "This shit is poison and you call it a *product?*"

"You don't understand, Meg," he snapped. "It's not like that."

"What *is* it like, then?"

"It's a fantastic discovery! It took me two years to perfect it."

"Discovery?"

Pellam said wryly, "State of the art. Normally, heroin you have to shoot up to get the best rush. This stuff, all you do is chew it."

Keith said, "What I developed was a new vasodilator. It's brilliant. The narcotic goes into the blood cells under the tongue in milliseconds."

Pellam continued. "A new Yuppie drug of choice. No need to shoot up. No needles. No AIDS risk . . ."

Keith said, "I was going to license it. I mean I am going to license it for legitimate medical purposes. We just needed a little more capital . . . We were going to distribute samples to medical research companies—you don't need FDA approval for that. But Dale started selling underground to get some cash flow. By the time I found out we were in too deep."

"Liar."

"No, Meg, really—"

She stepped toward him. "Tell me how my poor baby got in too deep! You and Dale had cash from day one. You bought out your contract . . . Oh, you had somebody bankrolling you and knew exactly who you were going to sell this shit to from the day you opened your factory."

"Stop it!"

"Tell me how someone put a gun to your head and forced you to—" She stopped speaking, frowned. "Wait." More horror in her eyes. "And what happened to him, to Dale?"

"He . . ." Keith looked away.

"They killed him. Those twins . . . Why? Was he getting too greedy?"

"It all got out of hand," Keith said furiously. "It wasn't my fault."

She was continuing, "And those other men, the ones from New York . . . And the boy who overdosed last year . . . And Ned! This morning. They killed him too! And Tom thought Sam had done it! Oh, Jesus Christ."

"And Marty," Pellam said.

It took Keith a moment to realize who Marty was. He said,

"That was an accident. I swear to God. Bobby and Billy were trying to scare the two of you out of here. That's all. We didn't want strangers in town. We couldn't risk any publicity."

Pellam said, "Accident? You killed your partner and who knows who else – and you expect me to believe that you just wanted to scare Marty?"

Meg, incredulous. Shaking her head slowly, her ponytail lolling. "And you almost killed our son?"

"I told them –" Nodding in the direction of the front yard. "– never to sell to anybody around here. But they didn't listen to me. It wasn't my fault. I—"

"Not your fault? You made it and now you're selling it. How do you mean it's not your fault? Explain that to me, Keith."

Keith couldn't hold her eyes any longer and looked down.

She simply shook her head. Her rage was too great.

Pellam could see that he'd fallen into a particular persona – one that must have suckered Meg all along: Keith the boy with the thick hair, the round face. Imploring, needing love. The pudgy boy.

"We have nothing to talk about. Nothing at all."

"Please, let me explain."

She turned to look at him as he slouched in the doorway, pressing against the jamb with his shoulder as if he needed the house itself to hold him upright.

Meg said, "You've lied to me all along."

"I didn't want to tell you. For your own protection."

Meg said bitterly, "How did you figure that?"

"If anything were to happen I didn't want you to be involved."

She laughed in astonishment. "How *wouldn't* I be involved?

My husband's making drugs! How *wouldn't* Sam and I be sucked right into the middle of it? I mean, look what happened the other day with Sam. He could've died."

"That won't happen again."

She was crying now. "Oh, God, Keith . . . You sound like you're not going to stop. Tom's dead! There're two bodies in my front yard. It's over with. We're calling the police."

"No, Meg. What I've come up with, it's magic." His eyes gleamed. "Nobody's ever made anything like this before. Nobody else can."

She spat out, "You sound proud of it."

He shouted, "I am proud! You really don't know who I am. You've never made the least effort to see me. I'm not the same as everybody else. My mind doesn't walk, it runs. I was born that way. I'm not like you. Or him." He glanced at Pellam. "Or anybody."

"But we loved each other," Meg cried.

"What does that have to do with anything? Don't sound so self-righteous. I did it for you. And for Sam. Why do you think? You were always harping about a nice house, having money, your fucking jewelry! How was I supposed to do that on a chemist's salary?" He pointed to her ring. "You think I could afford that if I was still at Sandberg?"

"Are you seriously trying to blame me? You should blame whatever's in you that makes you think you've got a different set of rules than everybody else. And, what? We're just supposed to forget everything that's happened? Well, I'm not forgetting. Sam and I are leaving."

"You're going with *him*?" Keith glanced at Pellam. His voice was filled with disbelief.

"I'm just leaving. That's the only explanation I owe you. Sam and I, we're both leaving."

"You can't just desert me."

"Desert you?" Meg laughed.

The tension in the room was like energy itself.

"I'm not going to let that happen!" Keith's voice jarred in the room, a sound to match the glare of light. "You're my wife. You're staying with me. In six months, I'll have the patent and I'll stop selling on the street. We'll get a license from Pfizer or Merck. We'll tell the state police the twins tried to break in and rape you. Tom was here about Sam and they killed him. We can say—".

"No more." Her eyes closed and her head moved back and forth slowly. "No more." She stood up. "We're not staying here tonight."

"Meg, no." He wasn't a boy any longer. He was mean, dark, brooding.

Their words swirled around Pellam. As they talked, husband and wife, he heard what they said and he observed their expressions but it was from a distance.

Here you come, with your van and your camera, studying the town, talking to people, getting to know everyone . . . Getting to know some of them very well. You don't understand the power you've got.

But no, he thought, I have no power. Nothing he could say or do could teach them about happiness and lift them out of the ruts they'd fallen into. He made movies. He helped people escape from their lives, sure, but only for two hours and only in that one special place: a darkened movie theater. "I'm leaving now."

Keith focused on Pellam, said to him, "You mention this to

anyone, I guess you can figure out what'll happen to them." He nodded toward Meg.

"What are you saying, Keith?" she asked.

Pellam said, "He's saying that if I go to the police, even if he beats the murder charges, there'll be a RICO case against him. The U.S. attorney'll close up the factory and take the house and your savings."

Keith nodded. "That'll be on your conscience."

Pellam laughed, said nothing. He looked at Meg. "You want a ride someplace? Family or friends nearby?"

Keith said, "She's not coming with you."

"That's not your decision."

Meg said to Pellam, "Let me get Sam."

Keith said, "Meg, you're my wife! You—"

"Stop it!" she screamed. Keith the boy, Keith the man stopped speaking. "You don't own me. I'm leaving!"

Pellam sensed it then. In an intuitive flash, he knew.

A combination of things told him – the peripheral sight of Keith reaching for his waistband, his gasping breath, the click of spring metal.

The sound of a gun cocking – Bobby's, of course, which Pellam had forgotten about, left lying under the twin's body on the front porch. Keith had retrieved it on his way inside the house.

The click that was almost hidden by a rising shout, a single word.

One word – his own name – filling the night, as Keith shoved the gun toward him and wailed in primitive rage, "Pellam!"

"No, Keith!" Meg cried.

Pellam's left hand shot forward in a futile, automatic gesture to ward off the scalding bullet.

A ringing explosion. The muzzle blast struck him in the face and hand.

Meg screamed, "John!"

They froze, like children playing the game of statue. Three of them.

There was an endless moment of silence, the sweet piquancy of smoke filling the room.

The gun fell from Keith's hand to the floor and with a wail of anguish he dropped to his knees.

Pellam, waiting for the pain, the blackness, the crawl of blood, stood completely still.

Nothing. He was unhurt.

The man had missed. From fifteen feet away Keith had missed.

He whispered to Meg, "It's all right, I'm okay."

She was shaking her head. "What'm I going to do about this?"

"What?" Pellam asked.

Meg didn't answer. Her head was lowered in concentration, frowning as she studied the diamonds on her finger. "Look at this ring. Look at it. What a mess."

Meg held up her hand, covered with the blood that spread from the front of her blouse. "Can you help me? I'll never get it clean." Her smile faded. Her eyes fluttered closed. "Can you help me," she whispered as she spiraled slowly to the floor. "Can you?"

————◆◆◆◆◆————

Trudie, tanned and dark-haired and model-thin (the best calves of any women he'd ever known but, alas, no freckles anywhere on her body), drove east on Santa Monica, moving slowly in the morning traffic toward the expressway.

John Pellam sat on the passenger side of her white Mercedes 450 SL.

He sat silently, with his suitcase (purchased on Main Street, Cleary, not Rodeo Drive) on his lap. Trudie was animated. She was preoccupied with a teleplay Lorimar was kicking around. She had a fifty-two percent interest in the property. He thought that's what she'd told him. The radio was loud and she nodded in time to the beat, smiling broadly, though Pellam knew that what she hummed was the tune of business, not a Top 40 hit.

Pellam thought she was a wonderful woman. He'd enjoyed going out with her. He'd enjoyed staying with her, lying in a huge bed, sipping sweet liquor drinks on a cement patio high above a junglish canyon (Trudie had a fall-*er* house).

316 • Jeffery Deaver

They passed the park in Beverly Hills where one morning –
must have been five a.m. – he'd found Tommy Bernstein, in a
tuxedo, passed out. Pellam himself had been wasted. Tommy
had said to him, "Fuck, it's the U.S. Cavalry. Get me home.
Am I in bed? I don't think so, no, I don't. Get me home!"

After much time and effort Pellam had.

At Tommy's funeral the minister had been a hired gun, which
wasn't too surprising, since Tommy hadn't been inside a church
in thirty years. The somber man said a lot of innocuous things.
Generic-brand sentiments. Not to put that down, of course.
Pellam thought the doughy old guy with the stiff white collar
had done a good job, under the circumstances. "The lively spirit
that Thomas had, the spirit that touched us all with the love for
the characters he played . . ." Well, Tommy'd have said, "Barf
on that," and howled. But that was hardly the minister's fault.
The funeral had been near the intersection they were passing
through just then. Avenue of the Stars.

"I talked to that exec producer."

Trudie liked that, shortening words and slinging them around.
Exec, photog, res, as in *Make a res at a restaurant.*

"Yeah?" he asked brightly.

"He was like beside himself."

"Yeah?" Pellam couldn't remember exactly which exec she
was talking about, or why he was, or should be, beside himself.
They drove in silence, through that brilliant light, California
light, that seems to bring out some essential radiation from
the grass and trees. It gets right in your face, like a beautiful,
obnoxious teenage girl. From behind his sunglasses Pellam
watched the scenery. And the cars – a thousand German cars,
it seemed – moving opposite, toward Hollywood.

"Won't be back for a while, huh?"

"Probably not."

Trudie didn't answer, just squeezed his knee. She turned the radio up. They were in Beverly Hills; sentiment didn't exist.

"So," she said. "You sure you want to do this?"

"Yep," he said and didn't add anything else.

Ten silent minutes later she dropped him at the airport. He didn't want or expect her to get out. They kissed like siblings and the only clues to the deepest moments of their on-again, off-again year together was a shallow shaking of her head and the sad, mystified smile she lapsed into from time to time.

"Call me sometime," she said.

Pellam promised that he would.

He handed his suitcase to the curbside check-in attendant, and when he turned back, Trudie was gone.

John Pellam sat on a hundred-year-old gravestone, looking out over this upstate New York valley, filled with trees gone to vibrant yellow red. The sun had just disappeared under a row of clouds and the beautiful scenery had taken on an ominous nature.

Adding to which was the young man moving stealthily toward Pellam. He was dressed in a dark shirt and jeans. When he was twenty feet away the man paused and closed his eyes, as if finding strength from somewhere, then drew a black pistol from his back pocket.

He started forward once more.

Pellam rose from the cold stone and squinted at the furtive approach.

Suddenly motion on the ground nearby. The man reared back

in surprise and stumbled over a low tombstone. "Jesus Christ," he called, dropping the pistol.

"What?" Came a booming voice from a loudspeaker.

"It attacked me!" the man called, standing up and brushing grass from his slacks.

The electronic voice of God yelled, "Cut it, cut! What the hell happened?"

The field filled with people. The crew walked around from behind the Panaflex camera, makeup went to work on the actor's face. He called, "A squirrel . . . he attacked me!"

A stuntman grabbed his jacket and leapt into the graveyard, crying, "*Toro, toro!*"

"Hilarious," the director called sarcastically through the loud-speaker.

Pellam walked away from the gravestone and sat down in an old green-plaid lawn chair next to his Winnebago. He said, "You cold? You want to go inside?"

Meg squeezed his hand and said, "No, I wouldn't miss this for anything."

"I want a continuous shot," the director sighed and walked back to the camera. Somebody from Wardrobe was rolling up the actor's cuffs so they wouldn't get dark from the moisture on the grass. The continuity girl began making notes of his position when the wild animal had attacked and the location of all the cameras and backgrounds.

"What's the take?"

"That'll be eight," someone called.

"Jesus. And we'll lose the light in ten minutes. What's the weather supposed to be tomorrow?"

"Rain."

"Jesus."

Pellam and Meg watched the crew in the field. He said, "That's the movies for you. Do it over and over then you wait for a while and do it again."

But Sam at least was enjoying himself, even if he would have preferred a space wars flick or something with machine-gunning robots over some stupid love story called *To Sleep in a Shallow Grave*. Mostly, it was the huge, complicated camera that he loved.

"Wow," he'd say to Pellam. "It's like a spaceship." And Pellam got the okay from the director of photography to put him in the operator's seat for a few minutes.

Alan Lefkowitz ducked out of his honey wagon and trooped toward the director. He was wearing his play clothes, his on-set clothes – chinos and a red-and-white striped shirt (Pellam told Meg, "That's what the refs would wear if Hollywood had its own hockey team"). The producer said, "Hey, Johnny." To Pellam he lifted his hand, which held an invisible glass of a very expensive single-malt scotch, and raised his eyebrows.

Pellam said, "Can't. I've got plans."

"Around *here*?" Lefkowitz joked, gazing longingly at Meg's jeans-clad butt, and began waving papers at the director again.

"So," Pellam said, "what's happening in Cleary?"

She laughed and didn't answer. "Let's go for a walk. That'd be okay?"

"They've got the telephoto on. We walk that way, toward the forest, we won't be in view. You feeling okay?"

"Hell, yes."

She took the cane and got up without his help. They walked past the crowd of locals, which had grown by the dozens with each day of shooting; small-town life had skidded to a stop for the duration of the principal photography. The spectators were enthralled with everything – even the squirrel attack – and they stood silent and frozen as if their fidgeting motion might knock the magic camera to the ground.

Meg and Pellam walked a short distance down the road, Meg glancing back every few minutes to keep Sam in view. She said, "The doctor told me if I'd see a physical therapist and get some exercise the limp would go away in a month."

"And?"

"I see all these young professional gals on TV, running and doing aerobics and lifting weights . . . it all looks so silly. I'll wait till it goes away by itself."

"How's the brokerage business?"

"Sold a house last week. Got a couple of maybe-but-let-me-ask-my-wife. Nobody said it's easy."

"How's he doing?" Pellam's head swivelled back toward Sam.

"We keep talking about it. I don't want to, but I think it's for the best. That's what the therapist says. Get it out, get everything out. Maybe it's best for me too. Sam'll say, 'Tell me again about Daddy.' And we have our talk and he understands or he says he does. I don't, of course."

"What do you hear from him? Keith?"

"Trial's next month."

Pellam nodded. "They're going after your house?"

"It's a possibility. My lawyer says there's a chance we'll lose it. But that also means there's a chance we won't."

He felt her eyes turn toward him. A pause then she said, "I'm seeing my friend again."

"Ambler?"

"He was real good after I got hurt."

"He seems like a nice guy."

For a neo-Bircher, rampant capitalist bigot.

"I didn't really want to at first. I mean—"

"You don't have to explain," Pellam said.

She looked at the horizon. "I know I don't." She smiled. "Pellam, you think . . ." Her voice faded.

He had. A great deal.

And concluded that the answer was pretty clear and they both knew it. He didn't answer or look at her and she didn't repeat the question.

They came to a sign on the edge of the road, facing away from the shooting.

> *Welcome to Simmons.*
> *In the Beautiful Catskills.*
> *Population 6300.*

"What was it when you grew up here?" Meg asked. "The population, I mean."

"Oh, I don't remember. I think maybe the same as Cleary."

"How come they're shooting here?"

"It's a dirty little town. That's what I needed for the story."

"They liked your screenplay after all, huh?"

"Most of it. Of course, the director's ignoring my camera directions."

"Why don't you tell him?"

"Writers don't tell directors where to put the camera. Except euphemistically and only after they get paid."

322 • *Jeffery Deaver*

"Why didn't you set the movie in Cleary?"

"We've got a better cemetery here." He nodded back toward the actor. "For the shooting scene. And the funeral later. When Janice confronts Shep."

"Better cemetery than Cleary's? I'm insulted."

Pellam looked at her hair, now cut short (revealing a good dusting of freckles on the back of her neck), the country-girl jeans, a blue Saks work shirt, brown suede boots.

"Tonight," he said, "Let's have dinner at the inn, okay? Just the two of us?"

"She won't mind?" Meg nodded up the road, toward Pellam's childhood home, three miles away. Meaning Pellam's mother.

"She's seen more of me in the past week than she has in the past five years. She'll be glad to get rid of me. She doesn't cotton to men who drink whiskey. We'll loan her Sam for the evening."

A film crew assistant, a young woman in jeans and a brushed-denim jacket, a fringe of curly hair crowning her forehead, patrolled the road like an Israeli soldier. A huge walkie-talkie bounced on her hip.

He asked Meg, "When are you going back to Cleary?"

"Tomorrow. We can only stay the night. I don't want to keep Sam away from home too long. It's better, I think."

Meg was looking down at the long grass. In the coming dusk the day was taking on a sepia atmosphere. Very still. Quiet.

He motioned her to follow and walked slowly into the graveyard. He pointed to a grave, ten years old.

Meg looked at it. "Your father's name was Benjamin?"

"After Benjamin Franklin, he said."

Meg said, "I'm surprised he didn't name you William."

"William?"

"After Wild Bill, your ancestor."

Pellam gave an exaggerated sigh. "His name was James, not William. James Butler Hickok."

"Oh, right. You told me."

They heard the assistant director call through the bullhorn, "Quiet, everybody, quiet down!"

Pellam and Meg paused and watched the scene begin again. The actor stalking slowly through the tombstones, ready to murder.

Meg said, "So you're a writer now?"

"Nope. Still unemployed. Lefkowitz's gotta give me a writer's credit but that's only because of the Guild. I'm just here in case they need to doctor it. I'm still canned. I'm guilty of the worst crime in Hollywood. Aggravating a producer's ulcer."

"So write more scripts."

Pellam laughed and looked at his watch. "When the mood takes me. I've got a free-lance scouting job in Utah."

They heard the rise and fall of the actors' voices.

Then the director's staticky shout in the bullhorn. "Cut, cut! Somebody . . . you, yes *you!* Get that effing squirrel out of here. I don't believe it, I do not *believe* it."

They returned to the camper and sat down in the lawn chairs – slowly. Meg, because of the gunshot. Pellam, because of the popped shoulder.

"Any chance you'd get back east?"

"Lots of movies to be made."

Meg said, "If you do, why don't you come upstate for a visit? Sam'd like it."

Pellam stretched his legs out in front of him, the sharp tips of his stained Nokonas pointed up toward the gray sky.

"Suppose it's a possibility," he said, and they watched the crew fan out into the cemetery to adjust the grass, pluck up leaves, fix makeup, straighten cuffs, chase a squirrel toward the trees. Everyone serious, everyone rushed, trying to get one more take in the can before the November darkness fell.

AUTHOR'S NOTE

John Pellam's comment about fire, embers, and smoke comes from one of his favorite authors, Reynolds Price, whom he was not, under the circumstances, inclined to attribute.

MISTRESS OF JUSTICE

AUTHOR'S NOTE

Two of my most heartfelt beliefs about writing suspense fiction are these: First, it's a craft—a skill that can be learned and refined and improved with practice. Second, we writers of suspense fiction have a duty to entertain and to—as the other moniker for the genre suggests—*thrill* our readers.

In rereading the first version of this book, which I wrote thirteen years ago, I realized that, while it was a perfectly acceptable dramatic, character-driven study of life on Wall Street, it didn't make my—and presumably my readers'—palms sweat.

It didn't, in other words, thrill.

I considered just letting the book stand as a curiosity among the suspense novels I've written but I felt the nag of the second belief I mentioned above—that overarching duty to readers. I know how much I enjoy the experience of reading a roller coaster of a story and I felt that the premise of this novel and the characters I'd created would lend themselves to more of a carnival ride of a book. Hence, I dismantled the book completely and rewrote nearly all of it.

I had a chance recently to write an introduction to a new edition of Mary Shelley's *Frankenstein* and during the course of researching her work I learned that she significantly revised the novel thirteen years after it was first published (how's *that* for a coincidence?). Many of the changes in the later edition of *Frankenstein* reflected the author's altered worldview. Not so in the case of *Mistress of Justice*. The current edition stands true to its view of Wall Street in the chaotic era of the 1980s—takeover fever, uncontrolled wealth, too-chic-for-words Manhattan clubs, ruthlessness in boardrooms and bedrooms ... and the many hardworking lawyers who wished for nothing more than to help their clients and to make a living at their chosen profession.

My special thanks to editor Kate Miciak for giving me this chance and for helping this book realize its potential.

—J.D., Pacific Grove, CA, 2001

ONE

Conflicts of Interest

"Let the jury consider their verdict," the King said, for about the twentieth time that day.

"No, no," said the Queen. "Sentence first—verdict afterwards."

—Lewis Carroll, *Alice's Adventures in Wonderland*

CHAPTER ONE

The drapery man had been warned that even though it was now well after midnight, Sunday morning of the Thanksgiving holiday, there would very likely be people in the firm here, attorneys and paralegals, still working.

And so he carried the weapon at his side, pointed downward.

It was a curious thing—not a knife exactly, more of an ice pick, but longer and made of a blackened, tempered metal.

He held it with the confidence of someone who was very familiar with the device. And who had used it before.

Dressed in gray coveralls bearing the stencil of a bogus drapery cleaning service and wearing a baseball cap, the big, sandy-haired man now paused and, hearing footsteps, slipped into an empty office. Then there was silence. And he continued on, through shadows, pausing for a long moment, frozen like a fox near a ground nest of skittish birds.

He consulted the diagram of the firm, turned along one corridor and continued, gripping the handle of the weapon tightly in his hand, which was as muscular as the rest of his body.

As he neared the office he sought, he reached up and pulled a paper face mask over his mouth. This was not so that he wouldn't be recognized but because he was concerned that he might lose a fleck of spit that could be retrieved as evidence and used in a DNA match.

The office, which belonged to Mitchell Reece, was at the end of the corridor, not far from the front door of the firm. Like all the offices here, the lights were left on, which meant that the drapery man wasn't sure that it was unoccupied. But he glanced in quickly, saw that the room was empty and stepped inside.

The office was very cluttered. Books, files, charts, thousands of sheets of papers. Still, the man found the filing cabinet easily—there was only one here with two locks on it—and crouched, pulling on tight latex gloves and extracting his tool kit from his coverall pockets.

The drapery man set the weapon nearby and began to work on the locks.

███

Scarf, Mitchell Reece thought, drying his hands in the law firm's marble-and-oak rest room. He'd forgotten his wool scarf.

Well, he was surprised he'd managed to remember his coat and briefcase. The lanky thirty-three-year-old associate, having had only four hours' sleep, had arrived at the firm around 8 A.M. yesterday, Saturday, and had worked straight through until about an hour ago, when he'd fallen asleep at his desk.

A few moments before, something had startled him out of that sleep. He'd roused himself and decided to head home for a few hours of shut-eye the old-fashioned way—horizontally. He'd grabbed his coat and briefcase and made this brief pit stop.

But he wasn't going outside without his scarf—1010

WINS had just reported the temperature was 22 degrees and falling.

Reece stepped into the silent corridor.

Thinking about a law firm at night.

The place was shadowy but not dark, silent yet filled with a white noise of memory and power. A law firm wasn't like other places: banks or corporations or museums or concert halls; it seemed to remain alert even when its occupants were gone.

Here, down a wide wallpapered corridor, was a portrait of a man in stern sideburns, a man who left his partnership at the firm to become governor of the state of New York.

Here, in a small foyer decorated with fresh flowers, was an exquisite Fragonard oil painting, no alarm protecting it. In the hall beyond, two Keith Harings and a Chagall.

Here, in a conference room, were reams of papers containing the magic words required by the law to begin a corporate breach of contract suit for three hundred million dollars, and in a similar room down the hall sat roughly the same amount of paper, assembled in solemn blue binders, which would create a charitable trust to fund private AIDS research.

Here, in a locked safe-file room, rested the last will and testament of the world's third-richest man—whose name most people had never heard of.

Mitchell Reece put these philosophical meanderings down to sleep deprivation, told himself to mentally shut up and turned down the corridor that would lead to his office.

———

Footsteps approaching.

In a soldier's instant the drapery man was on his feet, the ice pick in one hand, his burglar tools in the other. He eased behind the door to Reece's office and quieted his breathing as best he could.

He'd been in this line of work for some years. He'd been hurt in fights and had inflicted a great deal of pain. He'd

killed seven men and two women. But this history didn't
dull his emotions. His heart now beat hard, his palms
sweated and he fervently hoped he didn't have to hurt anyone tonight. Even people like him vastly preferred to avoid
killing.

Which didn't mean he'd hesitate to if he were found out
here.

The steps grew closer.

■■■■■

Mitchell Reece, walking unsteadily from exhaustion,
moved down the corridor, his feet tapping on the marble
floor, the sound occasionally muffled when he strode over
the Turkish rugs carefully positioned throughout the firm
(and carefully mounted on antiskid pads; law firms are extremely cognizant of slip-and-fall lawsuits).

In his mind was a daunting list of tasks to complete before the trial that was scheduled in two days. Reece had
graduated from Harvard Law fourth in his class, largely
thanks to lists—memorizing for his exams volumes of cases
and rules of law and statutes. He was now the firm's most
successful senior litigation associate for much the same reason. Every single aspect of the case—the civil trial of *New
Amsterdam Bank & Trust, Ltd. v. Hanover & Stiver, Inc.*—was
contained in a complicated series of lists, which Reece was
constantly reviewing and editing in his mind.

He supposed he'd been reviewing his lists when he'd
neglected to pick up his scarf.

He now approached the doorway and stepped inside.

Ah, yes, there it was, the tan cashmere given to him by a
former girlfriend. It sat just where he'd left it, next to the refrigerator in the coffee room across from his office. When
he'd arrived that morning—well, make that *yesterday* morning at this point—he'd stopped first in this canteen room to
make a pot of coffee and had dropped the scarf on the table
while getting the machine going.

He now wrapped it around his neck and stepped out

into the corridor. He continued to the front door of the firm. He hit the electric lock button and—hearing the satisfying click that he'd come to know so well, thanks to his thousands of late hours at the firm—Mitchell Reece stepped into the lobby, where he summoned the elevator.

As he waited it seemed to him that he heard a noise somewhere in the firm—nearby. A faint whine of a door hinge maybe. Followed by the *snick-snick* of two metal objects faintly colliding.

But then the elevator arrived. Reece stepped in and began once again reciting his scrolls of lists silently to himself.

"I think we may have a misunderstanding," Taylor Lockwood said.

"Not really," returned the voice, also female though much older, from the phone.

Taylor dropped into her squeaky chair and rolled against the wall of her cubicle. *Not really?* What did *that* mean? She continued, "I'm the lead paralegal on the SCB closing. That's at four today."

It was 8:30 A.M., the Tuesday after the Thanksgiving holiday, and she'd just arrived back here after a few hours' sleep at home, having spent most of the night at the firm, editing, assembling and stapling hundreds of documents for the closing this afternoon.

Ms. Strickland, on the other end of the line, said, "You've been reassigned. Something urgent."

This'd never happened that Taylor knew about. It was general knowledge—as solid as Newton's laws—that a law firm partner was incapable of handling a business closing without the presence of the paralegal who'd worked on the deal. Law is manifest in the details, and a firm's paralegals are the gurus of minutiae.

The only reason for a last-minute reassignment was if a major screwup had occurred.

But Taylor Lockwood did not screw up and a cursory

review of her ball-busting work on the case over the past
weeks revealed no glitches the remedy for which would involve her summarily getting kicked off the deal.

"What're my options?" she asked the paralegal supervisor.

"Actually," the word stretching into far more syllables
than it had, "there *are* no options."

Taylor spun her chair one way, then the other. A paper
cut inflicted by a UCC security agreement last night had
started to bleed again and she wrapped her finger in a napkin with a happy turkey printed on it, a remnant from a
firm cocktail party the week before. "Why——?"

"Mitchell Reece needs your help."

Reece? Taylor reflected. So I'll be playing with the big
boys.... Good news, but still odd. "Why me? I've never
worked for him."

"Apparently your reputation has preceded you." Ms.
Strickland sounded wary, as if she hadn't known that Taylor
had a reputation. "He said you and only you."

"Is this long-term? I'm taking a vacation next week. I'm
scheduled to go skiing."

"You can negotiate with Mr. Reece. I mentioned your
schedule to him."

"What was his reaction?"

"He didn't seem overly concerned."

"Why would he be? *He's* not the one going skiing."
Blood seeping through the napkin had stained the turkey's
smiling face. She pitched it out.

"Be in his office in an hour."

"What sort of project?"

A pause, while Ms. Strickland perhaps selected from
among her quiver of delicate words. "He wasn't specific."

"Should I call Mr. Bradshaw?"

"It's all taken care of."

"I'm sorry?" Taylor asked. "What's been taken care of?"

"Everything. You've been transferred and another paralegal—two actually—are working with Mr. Bradshaw."

"Already?"

"Be in Mr. Reece's office in one hour," Ms. Strickland reminded.

"All right."

"Oh, one more thing."

"What's that?"

"Mr. Reece said you're not supposed to mention this to anyone. He said that was very important. Not to anyone."

"Then I won't."

They hung up.

Taylor walked through the carpeted cubicles of the paralegal pen to the one window in this part of the firm. Outside, the Financial District was bathed in early-morning, overcast light. She didn't care much for the scenery today. Too much old grimy stone, like weathered, eerie mountains. In one window of a building across the way, a maintenance man was struggling to erect a Christmas tree. It seemed out of place in the huge marble lobby.

She focused on the window in front of her and realized she was looking at her own reflection.

Taylor Lockwood was not heavy but neither was she fashionably bony or angular. Earthy. That was how she thought of herself. When asked her height she would answer five-five (she was five-four and a quarter) but she had a dense black tangle of hair that added another two inches. A boyfriend once said that with her hair hanging frizzy and loose she looked like she belonged in a pre-Raphaelite painting.

On days when she was in a good mood she believed she resembled a young Mary Pickford. On not-so-good days she felt like a thirty-year-old little girl, standing pigeon-toed, impatiently waiting for the arrival of maturity, decisiveness, authority. She thought she looked her best in imperfect reflections, like storefronts painted black.

Or Wall Street law firm windows.

She turned away and walked back to her cubicle. It was now close to nine and the firm was coming awake, growing busier—catching up with her; this was usually the case; Taylor Lockwood was often one of the first employees to

arrive. Other paralegals were making their way to their
desks. Shouts of greetings—and warnings of impending
crises—were crisscrossing the paralegal pen, war stories of
subway snarls and traffic jams were exchanged. She sat
down in her chair and thought about how abruptly the
course of life can change, and at someone else's whim.

*Mr. Reece said you're not supposed to mention this to any-
one. He said that was very important. Not to anyone.*

Then I won't.

Taylor glanced at her finger and went to find a Band-Aid
for the paper cut.

CHAPTER TWO

On a warm morning in April of 1887, a balding, thirty-two-year-old sideburned lawyer named Frederick Phyle Hubbard walked into a small office on lower Broadway, slipped his silk hat and Prince Albert coat onto a hook and said wryly to his partner, "Good morning, Mr. White. Have you secured any clients yet?"

The life of a law firm began.

Both Hubbard and George C. T. White had graduated from Columbia Law School and had promptly come under the acutely probing eye of Walter Carter, Esquire, the senior partner at Carter, Hughes & Cravath. Carter hired them without pay for a year then turned them into professionals at the end of their probation by paying them the going salary of twenty dollars a month.

Six years later, the two men—as ambitious as Carter had pegged them to be—borrowed three thousand dollars from White's father, hired one law clerk and a male secretary and opened their own firm.

Though they dreamed of offices in the state-of-the-art Equitable Building at 120 Broadway they settled for less.

Rent in the old building they chose near Trinity Church was sixty-four dollars a month, which bought the partners two dark rooms. Still, their quarters had central heat (though they kept the office's two fireplaces going throughout most of January and February) and an elevator that one operated by pulling a thick rope running through the middle of the car with pieces of tapestry carpeting Hubbard's wife had cut and stitched; the felt pads provided by the building management were, Hubbard felt, inelegant, and he feared they might "impress clients adversely."

Over lunch at Delmonico's on Fifth Avenue, where Hubbard and White sunk much of their first profits feeding existing and would-be clients, they would brag about the firm's new letterpress, which used a damp cloth to make copies of firm correspondence. The firm had a typewriter but the lawyers wrote most of their correspondence in ink with steel pens. Hubbard and White both insisted that their secretary fill the firm's ink-blotting shakers with Lake Champlain black sand. The men had looked at, though rejected, a telephone—it would have cost ten dollars a month (besides, there was no one to call but court clerks and a few government officials).

In school both men had dreamed of becoming great trial lawyers and during their clerking days at Carter, Hughes they'd spent many hours in courtrooms watching famous litigators cajole, charm and terrorize juries and witnesses alike. But in their own practice economics could not be ignored and the lucrative field of corporate law became the mainstay of their young practice. They billed at fifty-two cents an hour though they added arbitrary and generous bonuses for certain assignments.

Those were the days before income tax, before the Antitrust Division of the Justice Department, before the SEC; corporations rode like Assyrians over the landscape of American free enterprise and Messrs. Hubbard and White were their warlords. As their clients became exceedingly wealthy so did they. A third senior partner, Colonel Benjamin Willis, joined the firm in 1920. He died several years later of pneumonia related to a World War One mustard gassing but he left as a legacy to the firm one railroad, two banks and several major utilities as clients. Hubbard and White also inherited the matter of what to do with his name—appending it to theirs had been the price for both the colonel and his fat clients. Nothing of the bargain was in writing but after his death the remaining partners kept their word; the firm would forever be known as a triumvirate.

By the time the mantles passed, in the late 1920s, Hubbard, White & Willis had grown to thirty-eight attorneys and had moved into its cherished Equitable Building. Banking, corporate law, securities and litigation made up the bulk of the work, which was still performed as it had been in the nineteenth century—by gentlemen, and a certain type of gentleman only. Attorneys seeking work who were in fact or by appearance Jewish, Italian or Irish were interviewed with interest and cordiality and were never offered positions.

Women were always welcome—good stenographers being hard to find.

The firm continued to grow, occasionally spinning off satellite firms or political careers (invariably Republican). Several attorneys general issued from Hubbard, White & Willis, as did an SEC commissioner, a senator, two governors and a vice president of the United States. Yet the firm, unlike many of its size and prestige on Wall Street, wasn't a major political breeding ground. It was common knowledge that politics was power without money and the partners at Hubbard, White saw no reason to forsake one reward of Wall Street practice when they could have both.

The present-day Hubbard, White & Willis had over two hundred fifty attorneys and four hundred support employees, placing it in the medium-sized category of Manhattan firms. Of the eighty-four partners, eleven were women, seven were Jewish (including four of the women), two were Asian-American and three were black (one of whom was, to the great delight of the EEOC-conscious executive committee, Latino as well).

Hubbard, White & Willis was now big business. Overhead ran $3 million a month and the partners had upped the billing rates considerably higher than the small change charged by Frederick Hubbard. An hour of a partner's time could hit $650 and in big transactions a premium (referred to by associates as a no-fuck-up bonus) of perhaps $500,000 would be added to the client's final tab.

Twenty-five-year-old associates fresh out of law school made around $100,000 a year.

The firm had moved from sooty limestone into glass and metal and now occupied four floors in a skyscraper near the World Trade Center. An interior designer had been paid a million dollars to awe clients with dramatic understatement. The theme was lavender and burgundy and sea blue, rich stone, smoky glass, brushed metal and dark oak. Spiral marble staircases connected the floors, and the library was a three-story atrium with fifty-foot windows offering a stunning view of New York Harbor. The firm's art collection was appraised at close to fifty million dollars.

Within this combination MOMA and *Interior Design* centerfold, Conference Room 16–2 was the only one large enough to hold all of the partners of the firm. This Tuesday morning, though, only two men were sitting here, at the end of a U-shaped conference table surfaced with dark red marble and edged in rosewood.

Amid an aroma of baseboard heat and brewing coffee they together read a single sheet of paper, gazing at it like next of kin identifying a body.

"Lord, I can't believe this." Donald Burdick, the man pinning the sheet to the table, had been the head of the firm's executive committee for the past eight years. At sixty-seven he was lean and had sleek gray hair trimmed short by a barber who visited Burdick's office fortnightly, the old Italian brought to the firm in the partner's Rolls Royce—"fetched," as Burdick said.

People often described the partner as dapper but this was offered only by those who didn't know him well. "Dapper" suggested weakness and a lack of grit and Donald

Burdick was a powerful man, more powerful than his re-markable resemblance to Laurence Olivier and his suede-glove manners suggested.

His was a power that could not be wholly quantified—it was an amalgam of old money and old friends in strategic places and old favors owed. One aspect of his power, how-ever, did lend itself to calculation: the enigmatic formula of partnership interest in Hubbard, White & Willis. Which was not in fact so mysterious at all if you remembered that the votes you got to cast and the income you took home varied according to the number of clients you brought to the firm and how much they paid in fees.

Donald Burdick's salary was close to five million dollars a year. (And augmented—often doubled—by a complicated network of other "investments," to use his preferred euphe-mism.)

"My Lord," he muttered again, pushing the sheet toward William Winston Stanley. Sixty-five years old, Stanley was stout, ruddy, grim. You could easily picture him in Pilgrim garb, cheeks puffing out steam on a frigid New England morning as he read an indictment to a witch.

Burdick was Dartmouth and Harvard Law; Stanley had gone to Fordham Law School at night while working in the Hubbard, White mailroom. By a crafty mix of charm, blunt-ness and natural brilliance for business he'd fought his way up through a firm of men with addresses (Locust Valley and Westport) as foreign to him as his (Canarsie in Brooklyn) was to them. His saving grace among the society-minded partners was membership in an Episcopalian church.

Burdick asked, "How can this be accurate?"

Stanley gazed at the list. He shrugged.

"How on earth did Clayton do it?" Burdick muttered. "How did he get this many in his camp without our hearing?"

Stanley laughed in a thick rasp. "We just *have* heard."

The names contained on the list had been compiled by one of Burdick's spies—a young partner who was not par-ticularly talented at practicing law but was a whiz kid at getting supposedly secret information out of people at the firm. The list showed how many partners were planning on voting in favor of a proposed merger between Hubbard, White & Willis and a Midtown law firm, a merger that would end the life of Hubbard, White as it then existed, as well as Burdick's control of the firm—and very likely his practice of law on Wall Street altogether.

Until now Burdick and Stanley were convinced that the pro-merger faction, led by a partner named Wendall Clayton, would not have enough votes to ram the deal through. But, if this tally was accurate, it was clear that the rebels probably would succeed.

And the memo contained other information that was just as troubling. At the partnership meeting scheduled for later this morning the pro-merger side was going to try to accelerate the final merger vote to a week from today. Originally it had been planned for next January. Burdick and Stanley had been counting on the month of December to win, or bully, straying partners back into their camp. Moving the vote forward would be disastrous.

Burdick actually felt a sudden urge to break something. His narrow, dry hand snatched up the paper. For a moment it seemed he would crumple it into a tight ball but instead he folded the paper slowly and slipped it into the inside pocket of his trim-fitting suit.

"Well, he's not *going* to do it," Burdick announced.

"What do we do to stop him?" Stanley barked.

Burdick began to speak then shook his head, rose and, stately as ever, buttoned his suit jacket. He nodded toward the complicated telephone sitting near them on the conference table, which unlike the phones in his office was not regularly swept for microphones. "Let's not talk here. Maybe a stroll in Battery Park. I don't think it's that cold out."

CHAPTER THREE

His eyes were the first thing about him she noticed.

They were alarmingly red, testifying to a lack of sleep, but they were also troubled.

"Come on into the lion's den." Mitchell Reece nodded Taylor Lockwood into his office then swung the door shut. He sat slowly in his black leather chair, the mechanism giving a soft ring.

Lion's den . . .

"I should tell you right up front," Taylor began, "I've never worked in litigation. I—"

He held up a hand to stop her. "Your experience doesn't really matter. Not for what I have in mind. Your discretion's what's important."

"I've worked on a lot of sensitive deals. I appreciate client confidentiality."

"Good. But this situation requires more than confidentiality. If we were the government I guess we'd call it top secret."

When Taylor was a little girl her favorite books were

about exploration and adventure. The two at the top of her list were the Alice stories—*Wonderland* and *Through the Looking-Glass*. She liked them because the adventures didn't take the heroine to foreign lands or back through history; they were metaphoric journeys through the bizarre side of life around us.

Taylor was now intrigued. *Lion's den. Top secret.*

She said, "Go ahead."

"Coffee?"

"Sure. Just milk, no sugar."

Reece stood up stiffly, as if he'd been sitting in one position for hours. His office was a mess. A hundred files—bulging manila folders and Redwelds stuffed with documents—filled the floor, the credenza, his desk. Stacks of legal magazines, waiting to be read, filled the spaces between the files. She smelled food and saw the remains of a take-out Chinese dinner sitting in a greasy bag beside the door.

He stepped into the canteen across the hall and she glanced out, watched him pour two cups.

Taylor studied him: the expensive but wrinkled slacks and shirt (there was a pile of new Brooks Brothers' shirts on the credenza behind him; maybe he wore one of these to court if he didn't have time to pick up his laundry). The tousled dark hair. The lean physique. She knew that the trial lawyer, with dark straight hair a touch long to go unnoticed by the more conservative partners, was in his mid-thirties. He specialized in litigation and had a reputation of his own. The firm's clients loved him because he won cases; the firm loved him because he ran up huge tabs doing so. (Taylor had heard that he'd once billed twenty-six hours in a single day; working on a flight to L.A., he'd taken advantage of the time zones.)

Young associates idolized Reece though they burned out working for him. Partners were uncomfortable supervising him; the briefs and motion papers he wrote under their names were often way beyond the older lawyers' skills at legal drafting.

Reece also was the driving force behind the firm's pro

bono program, volunteering much of his time to represent indigent clients in criminal cases.

On the personal side, Reece was *the* trophy of the firm, according to many women paralegals. He was single and probably straight (the proof wasn't conclusive—a divorce—but the ladies were willing to accept that circumstantial evidence as entirely credible). He'd had affairs with at least two women at the firm, or so the rumor went. On the other hand, they lamented, he was your standard Type A workaholic and thus a land mine in the relationship department. Which, nonetheless, didn't stop most of them from dreaming, if not flirting.

Reece returned to his office and closed the door with his foot, handed her the coffee. He sat down.

"Okay, here it is—our client's been robbed," he said.

She asked, "As in what they do to you on the subway or what they do at the IRS?"

"Burglary."

"Really?" Taylor again swallowed the yawn that had been trying to escape and rubbed her own stinging eyes.

"What do you know about banking law?" he asked.

"The fee for bounced checks is fifteen dollars."

"That's all?"

"I'm afraid so. But I'm a fast learner."

Reece said seriously, "I hope so. Here's your first lesson. One of the firm's clients is New Amsterdam Bank & Trust. You ever work for them?"

"No." She knew about the place, though; it was the firm's largest banking client and had been with Hubbard, White for nearly a hundred years. Taylor took a steno pad out of her purse and uncapped a pen.

"Don't write."

"I like to get the facts straight," she said.

"No, don't write," he said bluntly.

"Well, okay." The pad vanished.

Reece continued. "Last year the bank loaned two hundred fifty million dollars to a company in Midtown. Hanover & Stiver, Inc."

"What do they do?"

"They make things. I don't know. Widgets, baubles, bangles, bright, shiny beads." Reece shrugged then continued, "Now the first installments of the loan were due six months ago and the company missed the payments. They go back and forth, the bank and Hanover, but it's pretty clear that the company's never going to pay the money back. So, under the loan agreement, the whole amount comes due—a quarter-billion dollars."

"What'd they do with the money?"

"Good question. My feeling is it's still sitting somewhere—hell, they didn't have *time* to spend that much. But anyway, what happens at New Amsterdam—our revered client—is this: The economy melts down and the bank's reserves are shrinking. Now, the government says to all banks, Thou shalt have X amount of dollars on hand at all times. But New Amsterdam doesn't *have* X amount anymore. They need more in their reserves or the feds're going to step in. And the only way to get a big infusion of cash is to get back Hanover's loan. If they don't, the bank could go under. And that results in a couple of problems: First, Amsterdam is Donald Burdick's plum client. If the bank goes under he will not be a happy person, nor will the firm, because they pay us close to six million a year in fees. The other problem is that New Amsterdam happens to be a bank with a soul. They have the largest minority-business lending program in the country. Now, I'm not a flaming liberal, but you may have heard that one of my pet projects here—"

"The criminal pro bono program."

"Right. And I've seen firsthand that the one thing that helps improve shitty neighborhoods is to keep businesses in them. So I have a philosophical stake in the outcome of this . . . situation."

"And what exactly *is* the situation, Mitchell?"

"Earlier in the fall we filed suit against Hanover for the two hundred fifty million plus interest. Now if we can get a judgment fast we can levy against the assets of the company before the other creditors know what hit them. But if there's a delay in enforcing that judgment the company'll go into bankruptcy, the assets'll disappear and New Amsterdam might just go into receivership."

Taylor tapped the pen on her knee. She didn't mean to be projecting the impatience she felt though she knew maybe she was. "And the burglary part?"

He replied, "I'm getting to that. To loan the money the bank made Hanover sign a promissory note—you know, a negotiable instrument that says Hanover promises to pay the money back. It's like your savings bond."

Not like one of *mine,* Taylor reflected, considering what *theirs* was worth.

"Now the trial was set for yesterday. I had the case all prepared. There was no way we'd lose." Reece sighed. "Except . . . When you're going to sue to recover money on a note you have to produce the note in court. On Saturday the bank couriered the note to me. I put it in the safe there." He nodded at a big filing cabinet bolted to the floor. There were two heavy key locks on the front.

Shocked, Taylor said, "*That's* what was stolen? The note?"

Reece said in a low voice, "Somebody took it right out of my fucking safe. Just walked right in and walked out with it."

"You need the original? Can't you use a copy?"

"We could still win the case but not having the note'll delay the trial for months. I managed to finagle a postponement till next week but the judge won't grant any more extensions."

She nodded at the file cabinet. "But when . . . how was it stolen?"

"I was here until about three on Sunday morning. I went home to get some sleep and was back here by nine-thirty that morning. I almost thought of camping out." He gestured toward a sleeping bag in the corner. "I should have."

"What'd the police say?"

He laughed. "No, no. No police. Burdick'd find out that the note's missing, the client too. The newspapers..." He held her eyes. "So I guess you know why I asked you here."

"You want me to find out who took it?"

"Actually, I'd like you to find the note itself. I don't really care who did it."

She laughed. The whole idea was ridiculous. "But why me?"

"I can't do it by myself." Reece leaned back in his chair; the singing metal rang again. He looked at ease, as if she had already accepted his offer—a bit of haughtiness that irritated her some. "Whoever took it'll know I can't go to the cops and he'll be anticipating me. I need somebody else to help me. I need you."

"I just—"

"I know about your ski trip. I'm sorry. You'd have to postpone it."

Well, so much for the negotiations, Ms. Strickland....

"Mitchell, I don't know. I'm flattered you called me but I don't have a clue how to go about it."

"Well, let me just say one thing. We work with a lot of, you know, private eyes—"

"Sam Spade, sure."

"Actually, no, *not* Sam Spade at all. This's what I'm saying: The best detectives're women. They listen better than men. They're more empathic. They observe more carefully. You're smart, popular at the firm and—if we can mix our gender metaphor for a minute—the grapevine here says you've got balls."

"Does it now?" Taylor asked, frowning and feeling immensely pleased.

"And if you want another reason: I trust you."

Trust me? she wondered. He doesn't even know me. He— But then she understood. She smiled. "And you know I didn't steal it. I've got an alibi."

Reece nodded unabashedly. "Yep, you were out of town."

She'd gone to Maryland to spend the Thanksgiving holiday with her parents.

Taylor said, "I could've hired somebody."

"I think whoever was behind the theft *did* hire somebody." A nod toward the cabinet. "It's a professional break-in—the burglar picked the lock and, whatever you see in the movies, that ain't easy. But the point is that you don't have a motive, and motive is the number one reason somebody becomes a suspect in a crime. Why would *you* steal it? You have a good relationship with everybody at the firm. You don't need money. You've applied to law school—three of the best in the country. Besides, I just can't imagine Samuel Lockwood's daughter stealing a note."

She felt a troubled jolt that he'd peered so far into her life. "Well, I suspect Ted Bundy had upright parents too. It's just that this is out of my depth, Mitchell. You need a pro—one of those private eyes you've hired before."

"That wouldn't work," he said bluntly, as if it were obvious. "I need somebody with a reason to be here, who won't raise eyebrows. You'll have to poke into a lot of different places at the firm."

Like Alice on the other side of the looking glass.

Still seeing the hesitancy in her face, he added, "It could work out well for you too." He toyed with his coffee cup. She lifted an enquiring eyebrow and he continued, "I'm a trial lawyer and I lost my delicacy the first time I ever stood up in court. The fact is if that note doesn't turn up and I lose the case then I'm not going to make partner this year and that just isn't acceptable. I might even get fired. But if we *can* find it and nobody learns about the theft then it's pretty likely I'll make partner here or, if I don't want to stay at Hubbard, White, at some other firm."

"And?" she asked, still not certain where his comments were headed.

"I'll be in a position to make sure you get into whatever law school you want and get you a job when you graduate. I've got contacts everywhere—corporate firms, the government, public welfare law, environmental law firms."

As a paralegal Taylor Lockwood had learned that the engine of law ran on many fuels and that it would seize and burn without the delicate web of contacts and networks and unspoken obligations that Reece was not so subtly referring to.

But she also knew that you could always take a higher path and, with luck, sweat and smarts make your own way in this world. She said stiffly, "I appreciate that, Mitchell, but my undergrad professors're writing me all the letters of recommendation I need."

He blinked and held up a hand. "Look, I'm sorry. That was out of line. I'm used to dealing with clients who're either crooks or greedy bastards." A sour laugh. "And I'm not sure which are my pro bono criminal clients and which are the white-shoe folks we wine and dine at the Downtown Athletic Club."

She nodded, accepting his apology but glad certain ground rules were clear.

Reece looked her over for a moment, as if he suddenly saw her differently. A faint smile bloomed on his face. "I'm kind of like you."

"How do you mean?" she asked.

"I get the sense that you *never* ask for help."

She shrugged.

"I don't either. Never. But now I *need* help and it's hard for me to ask. I don't even know how to.... So, let me try again." A boyish laugh. "Will you help me?" he asked in a voice filled with what seemed to be uncharacteristic emotion.

Taylor looked out the window. The pale sun went behind thick clouds and the sky became as dark as its reflection in the choppy harbor. "I love views," she said. "In my apartment, you can see the Empire State Building. Provided you lean out the bathroom window."

Silence. Reece brushed his hair aside then rubbed his eyes with his knuckles. The brass clock on his desk ticked softly.

Taylor mentally asked the opinion of Alice, the young

girl in the English countryside who decided out of summer boredom to follow a talking white rabbit down its hole to a world very different from her own. Finally Taylor said to the lawyer, "All right. I frankly don't have a clue what to do but I'll help you."

Reece smiled and leaned forward suddenly then stopped fast. There's a code of chastity within law firms. Whatever liaisons occurred in hotel rooms or attorneys' beds at home, when you were within the labyrinth of the office, cheeks were not kissed and lip never met lip. Even embracing was suspect. Reece's concession to gratitude was taking Taylor's hand in both of his. She smelled a mix of expensive aftershave and sweat in his wake as he sat back.

"So, first of all," she said, "what does it look like? The note."

"Nothing fancy. One piece of eight-and-a-half-by-eleven paper." He showed her a binder containing a copy of it.

She looked over the undistinguished document then asked, "Tell me what happened and when."

"The bank messengered the note to me at five in the afternoon on Saturday—they were closed on Sunday and since the trial started at nine on Monday I needed it early to make copies for pleadings. Well, I locked it in my file cabinet as soon as it came in. I made the copies about ten or eleven that night, put it back in the cabinet, locked it. I left at three on Sunday morning. I got some sleep, came back around nine-thirty. I noticed some scratch marks on the lock and opened it up. The note was gone. I spent the rest of Sunday looking for it. I appeared in court yesterday, got the continuance for a week from today and then came back here to find somebody to help me."

"Did you see anybody at the firm that night?"

"Not after five or six. Not a soul. But I was at my desk practically the whole time."

"Well." She sat back, reflecting. "You mentioned motive. Who has a motive to steal it? You said it was negotiable. Could somebody cash it in?"

"No, nobody in the world'd take paper like that. Too big

and too easily traced. I'm sure it was just to delay the case—
to give Lloyd Hanover a chance to hide his assets."

"Who knew you had it?"

"The messenger didn't know what was in the bag but it
was an armed courier service so they'd know it was valuable.
At the bank, as far as I know, the only one who knew I took
delivery was the vice president who worked on the deal."

"Could he have been bribed by Hanover?"

Reece said, "Anything's possible, but he's a career officer.
Been with the bank for twenty years. I know him personally.
He and his wife live in Locust Valley and they've got plenty
of money on their own. Anyway, he's the point man on the
deal. If the bank doesn't collect on this note, he'll be fired."

"Who here knew you were working on the case?"

Reece laughed. He slid a memo across to her.

> From: M. A. Reece
> To: Attorneys of Hubbard, White & Willis
> Re: Conflicts of Interest
>
> I am representing our client New Amsterdam Bank
> & Trust in a lawsuit against Hanover & Stiver, Inc.
> Please advise if you have ever represented Hanover
> & Stiver or have any other conflicts of interest in-
> volving these companies of which the firm should be
> aware.

"This is the standard conflicts of interest memo. To let
everybody know who we're suing. If any lawyers here have
ever represented Hanover we have to drop the case or do a
Chinese wall to make sure there was no appearance that we
were compromising either client. . . . So, in answer to your
question, *everybody* here knew what I was doing. And by
checking copies of my correspondence in the file room they
could figure out when I'd be receiving the note."

Taylor prodded the conflicts memo with the fork of her
fingers.

"What do you know about the executives at Hanover?"

"I've had murderers in the pro bono program who're more upright than the CEO—Lloyd Hanover. He's unadulterated scum. He thinks he's some kind of smooth operator. You know the kind—late fifties, crew-cut, tanned. Has three mistresses. Wears so much gold jewelry he'd never get through a metal detector."

"That's not a crime," Taylor said.

"No, but his three SEC violations and two RICO and one IRS convictions were."

"Ah."

Taylor glanced out the window: across the street was a wall of office windows, a hundred of them. And beyond that building were others with more office windows, and still more beyond that. Taylor Lockwood was, momentarily, overwhelmed by the challenges they faced. Needles and haystacks... She asked, "Are you sure we're looking for something that still exists?"

"How do you mean?"

"If nobody's going to cash the note why wouldn't they just burn it?"

"Good question. I've thought about that. When I was an assistant U.S. prosecutor—and when I do my criminal defense work now—I always put myself in the mind of the perp. In this case, if the note disappears forever that implies a crime. If it's just misplaced until Hanover's hidden his assets and then it resurfaces, well, that suggests, just legal malpractice on Hubbard, White's part; nobody looks any farther for a bad guy than us. That's why I think the note's still in the firm. Maybe in the file room, maybe stuck in a magazine in a partner's office, maybe behind a copier—wherever the thief hid it."

Thief.... Lockwood felt her first uneasy twinge—not only at the impossibility of the task but that there was potential danger too.

In Wonderland the Queen of Hearts' favorite slogan was "Off with their heads."

She sat back. "I don't know, Mitchell. It seems hopeless. There're a million places the note could be."

"We don't have the facts yet. There's a huge amount of information at the firm about where people have been at various times and what they've been doing. Billing department, payroll, things like that. I guess the first thing I'd do is check the door key entry logs and time sheets to find out who was in the firm on Saturday."

She nodded at the lock. "But we think it was a pro, don't we? Not a lawyer or employee?"

"Still, somebody had to let him in. Either that or they lent him their key card—or one they'd stolen." Reece then took out his wallet and handed her a thousand dollars in hundreds.

She looked at the cash with a funny smile, embarrassed, curious.

"For expenses."

"Expenses." Did he mean bribes? She wasn't going to ask. Taylor held the bills awkwardly for a moment then slipped them into her purse. She noticed a sheet of paper on Reece's desk. It was legal-sized and pale green—the color of corridors in old hospitals and government buildings. She recognized it as the court calendar the managing attorney of Hubbard, White circulated throughout the firm daily. It contained a grid of thirty days beginning with today. Filling these squares were the times and locations of all court appearances scheduled for the firm's litigators. She leaned forward. In the square indicating one week from today were the words:

> *New Amsterdam Bank & Trust v. Hanover & Stiver.*
> *Jury trial. Ten a.m. No continuance.*

He looked at his watch. "Let's talk again tomorrow. But we should keep our distance when we're at the firm. If anybody asks tell them you're helping me with some year-end billing problems."

"But who'd ask? Who'd even know?"

He laughed and seemed to consider this a naive comment. "How's the Vista Hotel at nine-thirty?"

"Sure."

"If I call you at home I can leave a message, can't I?"

"I've got an answering machine."

"No, I mean, there won't be anybody else there to pick it up, right? I heard you lived alone."

She hesitated momentarily and said only, "You can leave messages there."

CHAPTER FOUR

"I have a breakfast meeting in half an hour then the partnership meeting for the rest of the morning," Wendall Clayton said into the phone. "Get me the details as soon as possible."

"I'll do what I can, Wendall," Sean Lillick, a young paralegal who worked for Clayton regularly, replied uneasily. "But it's, like, pretty confidential."

"'Like' confidential. It is confidential or not?"

A sigh from the other end of the phone line. "You know what I mean."

The partner muttered, "You meant it *is* confidential. Well, find out who has the information and aristocratize them. I want the particulars. Which you might just have found out *before* you called. You'd know I'd want them."

"Sure, Wendall," Lillick said.

The partner dropped the phone into the cradle.

Wendall Clayton was a handsome man. Not big—under six feet—but solid from running (he didn't jog; he *ran*) and tennis and skippering the forty-two-foot *Ginny May* around Newport every other weekend from April through

September. He had a thick bundle of professorial hair and
he wore European suits, slitless in the back, forgoing the
burdened sacks of dark pinstripe that cloaked most of the
pear-shaped men of the firm. Killer looks, the women in
the firm said. Another three inches and he could have been
a model. Clayton worked hard at his image, the way nobility
worked hard. A duke had to be handsome. A duke enjoyed
dusting his suits with pig-bristle brushes and getting a radi-
ant glow on his burgundy-colored Bally's.

A duke took great pleasures in the small rituals of fastid-
iousness.

Aristocratize them. . . .

Sometimes Clayton would write the word in the margin
of a memo one of his associates had written. Then watch the
girl or boy, flustered, trying to pronounce it. *Ar-is-TOC-ra-*
tize . . . he'd made up the term himself. It had to do with attitude mostly. Much of it was knowing the law, of course, and
much was circumstance.

But mostly it was attitude.

Clayton practiced often and he was very good at it.

He hoped Sean Lillick would, in turn, be good at aristo-
cratizing some underling in the steno department to get the
information he wanted.

By searching through the correspondence files, time
sheets and limousine and telephone logs the young paralegal had learned that Donald Burdick had recently attended
several very secretive meetings and made a large number of
phone calls during firm hours that had not been billed to
any clients. This suggested to Clayton that Burdick was
plotting something that could jeopardize the merger. That
might not be the case, of course; his dealings could be
related to some private business plans that Burdick or
his Lucrezia Borgia of a wife, Vera, were involved in. But
Clayton hadn't gotten to his present station in life by assuming that unknown maneuverings of his rivals were benign.

Hence, his sending Lillick off on the new mission to
find out the details.

The Tuesday morning light filtered into his office, the

corner office, located on the firm's executive row, the seventeenth floor. The room measured twenty-seven by twenty—a
size that by rights should have gone to a partner more senior
than Clayton. When it fell vacant, however, the room was assigned to him. Even Donald Burdick never found out why.

Clayton glanced at the Tiffany nautical clock on his
desk. Nearly time. He rocked back in his chair, his throne, a
huge construction of oak and red leather he had bought in
England for two thousand pounds.

Aristocratize.

He ordered his secretary to have his car brought
around. He rose, donned his suit jacket and left the office.
The breakfast get-together he was about to attend was perhaps the most important of any meeting he'd been to in
the past year. But Clayton didn't go immediately to the
waiting car. Rather, he decided he'd been a bit harsh on
the young man and wandered down to Lillick's cubicle in
the paralegal department to personally thank the young
man and tell him a generous bonus would be forthcoming.

████

"You ever been here, Wendall?" the man across the burnished copper table asked.

When Clayton spoke, however, it was to the captain of
the Carleton Hotel on Fifty-ninth Street, off Fifth Avenue.
"The nova, Frederick?"

"No, Mr. Clayton." The captain shook his head. "Not
today."

"Thanks. I'll have my usual."

"Very good, Mr. Clayton."

"Well, that answers my question," John Perelli said with
an explosive laugh. "How's the yogurt today, Freddie?"

"It's—"

"That's a joke," Perelli barked. "Gimme a bowl. Dry
wheat toast and a fruit cup."

"Yessir, Mr. Perelli."

Perelli was stocky and dark, with a long face. He wore a
navy pinstripe suit.

Clayton shot his cuffs, revealing eighteen-karat-
Wedgwood cuff links, and said, "I feel, in answer to your
question, right at home here."

Though this was not completely true. Recently Wendall
Clayton had been coming to this dining room—where
many of Perelli's partners breakfasted and lunched—to
make inroads into Midtown. Yet this was not his natural
turf, which had always been Wall Street, upper Fifth
Avenue, his weekend house in Redding, Connecticut, his
ten-room cabin in Newport.

Clayton had a stock portfolio worth around twenty-three
million (depending on how the Gods of the Dow were feeling at any particular moment). Hanging on the oak paneling
in his Upper East Side den were a Picasso, three Klees, a
Mondrian, a Magritte. He drove a Jaguar and a Mercedes station wagon. Yet his wealth was of the hushed, Victorian sort:
a third inherited, a third earned at the practice of law (and
cautious investment of the proceeds), the rest from his wife.

But here, in Midtown, he was surrounded by a different
genre of money. It was loud money. Acquired from new
wellsprings. This money was from media, from advertising,
from public relations, from junk bonds, from leveraged
buyouts, from alligator spreads and dividend-snatching.
Commission money. Sales money. Real estate money. Italian
money. Jewish money. Japanese money.

Clayton's wealth was money with cobwebs and therefore it was, ironically, suspect—at least around here. In this
part of town, when it came to wealth the slogan was: the
more respectable, the less acceptable.

He tried not to give a damn. Yet here Clayton felt as if he
were "without passport," the phrase whose acronym gave
rise to the derisive term for Italians. Wendall Clayton in
Midtown was an immigrant in steerage.

"So why the call, Wendall?" Perelli asked.

Clayton replied, "We need to move faster. I'm trying to
accelerate the vote on the merger."

"Faster? Why?"

"The natives are restless."

Perelli barked, "What does that mean? I don't know what it means. That your people wanta go forward or that Burdick and his cronies're trying to fuck the deal?"

"A little bit of both."

"What's Donald doing? Setting up an office in D.C. and London to goose up your operating expense?"

"Something like that. I'm finding out," Clayton conceded with a nod.

The waiter set the plates on the table. Clayton hunched over the soft mounds of eggs and ate hungrily, cutting the food into small bites.

Perelli waited until the server was gone then examined Clayton carefully and said, "We want this to work. We've got labor clients we can parlay into your SEC base. We've got products liability cases that are gold mines. You've got corporate people and litigators who'd be a natural fit. Obviously we want your banking department and you want our real estate group. It's made in heaven, Wendall. What's Burdick's problem?"

"Old school. I don't know."

"The fact we've got Jewish partners? The fact we have Eye-talian partners?"

"Probably."

"But there's more to it, right?" the keen-eyed Perelli asked. "Cut the crap, Wendall. You've got an agenda that's scaring the shit out of Burdick and his boys. What?"

Okay, Clayton thought. This is it. . . . He reached into his jacket and handed Perelli a piece of paper.

Perelli read then looked up questioningly. "A hit list?"

Clayton tapped the paper dramatically. "Yep. That's who I want out within a year after the merger."

"There are—what?—twenty-five names here?" Perelli read. "Burdick, Bill Stanley, Woody Crenshaw, Lamar Fredericks, Ralph Dudley . . . Wendall, these men *are* Hubbard, White & Willis. They've been there for decades."

"They're deadwood, has-beens. This is the last piece of the deal, John. For the merger to work they have to go."

Perelli chewed some of his toast and washed it down with

coffee. "You said you wanted to accelerate the merger." He waved at the paper. "But if you're asking us to agree to *this* it'll only slow things up. I've got to run these names by the management committee. We'll have to review each one of their partnership contracts. Christ, they're all over forty-five. You know the kind of trouble they could make in court for us?"

Clayton laughed with genuine amusement. "John, with my connections you really think the EEOC would be a problem?"

"All right, maybe not. But these're still dangerous men."

"And they're the ones who're bleeding the firm dry. They have to go. If we want to the firm to succeed they have to go." He pushed aside his empty plate. "A week, John. I want the merger papers signed in a week."

"Impossible."

"Considering that you might have to move slightly more quickly," Clayton said, "we would be willing to alter our partnership share price."

"You—"

"If we ink the deal next week, Hubbard, White and Willis is willing to reduce our first-year share take by eight percent."

"Are you out of your fucking mind? You're talking millions of dollars, Wendall."

"*Thirteen* million dollars."

This meant that the Hubbard, White and Willis partners would in effect give the incoming partners a huge bonus simply for expediting the deal—and for ousting Burdick and his cronies.

Clayton continued, "We'll claim it has to be done by year end for tax reasons. That'll be our excuse."

"Just tell me: If I insisted that Burdick stay for, say, five years, would you still be willing to proceed?"

Clayton signed his name to the check. He offered no credit card.

"Let me tell you something, John. Twenty years ago Donald Burdick was asked by the President to head a special committee looking into abuses in the steel industry."

"The Justice Department was involved. I heard about that."

"Burdick was picked because he was known in both Albany and Washington. The executive committee at Hubbard, White—it was called a steering committee then—was ecstatic. Publicity for the firm, a chance for Burdick to do some serious stroking on the Hill. Afterward, a triumphant return. Well, Donald Burdick told the committee he'd accept the appointment on one condition. That when he returned he and a man of his choosing would be placed on the executive committee and three particular partners would be asked to leave the firm. Now, John, that was at a time when law firms did not fire partners. It simply was not done."

"And?"

"Three months later, a memo went around the office congratulating three partners who were unexpectedly leaving Hubbard, White and starting their own firm." Clayton pushed back from the table. "The answer to your question is this: The only way the deal works is without Burdick . . . and everyone else on that list. That's the quid pro quo. What do you say?"

"You really fucking want this, don't you?"

"Deal?" Clayton asked, sticking out his hand.

Perelli hesitated for a moment before pronouncing, "Deal," and shaking Clayton's hand but the delay was merely because he had to swallow the piece of bacon he'd snuck off Clayton's plate and wipe his fingers.

███████

Who are these men and women?

What do I know about them other than the baldest facts of their wealth, their brilliance, their aspirations?

In the back of the massive sixteenth-floor conference room Donald Burdick heard the grandfather clock chime and begin its ringing climb toward 11 A.M. The partners were arriving. Most carried foolscap pads or stacks of files and their ubiquitous leather personal calendars.

Over the years I've seen men like this, women now too,

display stubbornness and brutality and brilliance and cruelty.

And generosity and sacrifice.

But those are the mere *manifestations* of their souls; what's truly in their hearts?

The partners took their places around the table in the dark conference room. Some, the less confident, the younger ones, examined the dings in the rosewood and traced the pattern of the marble with their fingers and eyes and made overly loud comments about their Thanksgivings and about football games. They wore jackets with their suits. Others, the veterans, were in shirtsleeves and had no time for chatter or the administrivia of meetings like this. They appeared inconvenienced. And why shouldn't they? Isn't the point of a law firm, after all, to practice law?

They're my partners . . . but how many are my friends?

Donald Burdick, sitting at the apogee of the table, however, understood that this was a pointless question. The real one was: How many of my friends will stab me in the back? If the tally that Bill Stanley had showed him earlier was accurate the answer to this question was one hell of a lot.

To Stanley, Burdick whispered, "Nearly fifteen'll be missing. That could swing it one way or another."

"They're dead," Stanley replied in a growl. "And we'll never find the bodies."

Wendall Clayton entered the room and took a seat in the middle of one leg of the U. He wasn't particularly far away from Burdick and not particularly close. He busied himself jotting notes and, smiling, chatting with the partner next to him.

At eleven-fifteen Burdick nodded for a partner to close the door. The lock mechanism gave a solid click. It seemed to Burdick that the pressure in the room changed and that they were sealed in, as if this were a chamber in the Great Pyramid.

Donald Burdick called the meeting to order. Minutes were read and not listened to, a brief report from the executive committee on staff overtime went ignored. Committee reports were recited at breakneck speed, with uncharacteristically few interruptions and little debate.

"Do you want to hear about the hiring committee's schedule?" asked a sanguine young partner, who had probably stayed up half the night to prepare it.

"I think we'll postpone that one," Burdick said evenly, and—seeing several partners smile—realized that the royal pronoun was an unfortunate slip.

There was silence in the room, punctuated by the popping of soda cans and papers being organized. Dozens of pens made graffiti on legal pads. Burdick studied the agenda for a moment and then it was time for Wendall Clayton to make his move. He slipped his suit jacket off, opened a file and said, "May I have the floor?"

Burdick nodded in his direction. In a rehearsed baritone Wendall Clayton said, "I'd like to make a motion relevant to the proposed merger of our firm with Sullivan & Perelli."

Burdick shrugged. "You have the floor."

Sipping had stopped. Doodling had stopped. Some partners—like the aging, oblivious Ralph Dudley—were confused because the final vote on the merger wasn't scheduled until January. They were terrified that they might have to make a decision without someone's telling them what to do.

"I'm moving to change the date of the ratification vote regarding the merger to November 28, one week from today."

Clayton's trim young protégé, Randy Simms III, whom Burdick detested, said quickly, "Second."

There was complete silence. And Burdick was mildly surprised that Clayton's bid caught some people off guard. But then Burdick and his wife were rumored to have the best intelligence sources on Wall Street and were often one step ahead of everybody else.

One voice called, "Can we discuss it?"

"The rules of order allow for debate," Clayton said.

And debate ensued. Clayton was clearly prepared for it. He met every objection, making a good case for the acceleration—the year-end tax planning, for instance, hinting that the merger would put significant money into the pockets of all the partners and that they needed to know before December 31 how much this might be.

More voices joined in and a tide of comments and tension-breaking laughter filled the room.

Clayton managed to insert into the discussion a comment on Sullivan & Perelli's income cap on the executive committee partners. Burdick observed that this was irrelevant to the immediate motion under consideration but would not go unnoticed by the younger, poorer partners: The gist of the comment was that after the merger the senior partners could earn no more than two million a year, leaving that much more to be distributed to the rest of the partners. Hubbard, White & Willis currently had no such cap, which was the reason that five partners on the executive committee—such as Burdick and Stanley—earned 18 percent of the firm's income and junior partners often earned less than they did as salaried associates.

"What is the cap?" one partner, obviously impressed, asked.

Goddamn socialism, Burdick thought, then he interrupted the youngster to say bluntly, "We're not here now to discuss the substantive issue of the merger. It's merely a procedural matter on *when* the vote should be. And my opinion is that it's impossible to review the material in one week. We need until January."

"Well, Donald," Clayton pointed out, "you've had everything for two weeks already. And I'd imagine you, like all the rest of us, read it as soon as they messengered the binders to us from Perelli & Sullivan."

He *had* read it, of course, and so had the team of lawyers he and Vera had hired.

A new partner at the end of the table made a comment. "I don't think we can debate this too much. It's not inappropriate to talk about the substance of the merger now, I think." His dialect put him within five minutes of the Charles River.

"Yes, it is inappropriate," Burdick said shortly, silencing him. Then to Clayton: "Go ahead with your vote. It makes no sense to me but if two thirds of the partners are in favor—"

Clayton gave a very minuscule frown. "A simple majority, Donald."

Burdick shook his head. A trace of confusion now crossed *his* face. "Majority? No, Wendall, I don't think so. The issue is the merger of the firm and that requires a vote of two thirds."

Clayton said, "No, we'd be voting simply on establishing an agenda and timetable. Under the partnership rules, Donald, that requires only a simple majority."

Burdick was patient. "Yes, but it's an agenda and timetable that *pertain* to a merger."

Each of the two partners pulled out a copy of the partnership documents, like dueling knights drawing swords.

"Section fourteen, paragraph four, subparagraph d." Clayton said this as if reading from the tome though everyone knew he'd memorized it long ago.

Burdick continued reading for a few moments. "It's ambiguous. But I won't make an issue of it. We'll be here all day at this rate. And I, for one, have some work to do for clients."

The senior partner knew, of course, that Clayton was absolutely correct about the majority vote on this matter. However, it had been vitally important to make clear to everyone in the room exactly where Burdick stood on the merger—how adamantly against it he was.

"Go ahead," Burdick said to Stanley.

As the rotund partner growled off names, Burdick sat calmly, pretending to edit a letter though he was keeping a perfect tally in his head of the fors and againsts.

Distraction on his face, agony in his heart, Burdick added them up. His mood slipped from cautious to alarmed to despairing. Clayton prevailed—and by almost a two-thirds majority, the magic percentage needed to win the entire war.

The list Stanley had shown Burdick earlier was not accurate. Clayton was *stronger* than they'd thought.

Clayton looked at Burdick, studying his opponent from behind the emotionless guise of the great. His gold pen danced on a pad. "If anyone needs any information from Perelli—to make a better-informed decision next week— just let me know."

Burdick said, "Thank you, Wendall. I appreciate the time you've spent on the matter." Looking around the room—at both his supporters and his Judases—with as neutral a face as he could muster, he added, "Now, any more issues we ought to discuss?"

CHAPTER FIVE

"Dimitri." Taylor Lockwood's voice was a whisper. "Don't say 'satin touch' tonight. Please."

"Hey, come on," the man replied in a deep Greek-accented voice, "the guys in the audience, they like it."

"It's embarrassing."

"It's sexy," he replied petulantly.

"No, it's not, and all it does is get me moony looks from the lechers."

"Hey, they like to fantasize. So do I. You got the lights?"

She sighed and said, "Yeah, I got the lights."

From the amplifier his voice filled the bar: "Ladies and gentlemen, Miracles Pub is pleased to bring you the silky and oh-so-smooth satin touch of Taylor Lockwood on the keys. A warm round of applause please. And don't forget to ask your waitress about the Miracles menu of exotic drinks."

Oh-so-smooth satin touch?

Taylor clicked the switch that turned the house lights down and ignited the two overhead spots trained on her. Dimitri had made the spotlights himself—pineapple cans painted black.

Smiling at them all, even the moony lechers, she began to play Gershwin on the battered Baldwin baby grand.

It wasn't a bad gig. The temperamental owner of the club in the West Village—a lech himself—had figured that an attractive woman jazz pianist would help sell bad food, so he'd hired her for Tuesday nights, subject only to sporadic preemption by Dimitri's son-in-law's balalaika orchestra.

With her day job at the firm and this gig, Taylor had found a type of harmony in her life. Music was her pure sensual love; her paralegal job gave her the pleasures of intellect, organization, function. She sometimes felt like those men with two wives who know nothing of the other. Maybe someday she'd get nailed but so far the secret was safe.

A half hour later Taylor was doing the bridge to "Anything Goes" when the front door swung open with its familiar D to B-flat squeak. The woman who entered was in her mid-twenties, with a round, sweet, big-sister face framed by hair pulled back in a ponytail. She wore a sweater decorated with reindeer, black ski pants and, on her petite, out-turned feet, Top-Siders. She smiled nervously and waved broadly to Taylor then stopped suddenly, afraid of disrupting the show.

Taylor nodded back and finished the tune. Then she announced a break and sat down.

"Carrie, thanks for coming."

The young girl's eyes sparkled. "You are *so* good. I didn't know you were a musician. Where did you study? Like, Juilliard?"

Taylor sipped her Seagram's and soda. "Juilliard? Try Mrs. Cuikova's. A famous music school. Freddy Bigelow went there. And Bunny Grundel."

"I never heard of them."

"Nobody has. We were all in the same grade school. We'd go to Frau Cuikova's in Glen Cove every Tuesday and Thursday at four to be abused about arpeggios and finger position."

Several men in the audience were restless, about to make their moves, so Taylor did the lech maneuver—positioning her chair with her back to them—and turned her whole attention to Carrie.

Taylor had spent the day looking through documents on the *New Amsterdam Bank v. Hanover & Stiver* case, collecting the names of everyone who'd worked on it: partners, associates and all the paralegals, typists, messengers and other support staff. But the case had been in the works for months and the cast of characters at Hubbard, White who'd been involved totaled nearly thirty people. She needed to narrow down the suspects and to get the key entry logs and the time sheets, as Reece had suggested. But to do this, she'd found, you needed to be a registered user and to have a pass code. Carrie Mason, a friend of hers at the firm, was the paralegal who oversaw the billing and time recording system and so Taylor had asked the girl to meet her here after work.

Taylor now looked at the girl's Coach attaché case. "You've got what I asked for?"

"I feel like a, you know, spy," the girl joked, though uneasily. She opened the briefcase and pulled out stacks of computer papers.

"I wouldn't have asked if it weren't important. Are these the door key logs?"

"Yeah."

Taylor sat forward and examined the papers. On top was a copy of the computer key entry ledger for the firm's front and back doors. Like many Wall Street firms Hubbard, White had installed computer security locks that were activated with ID cards. To enter the firm you had to slide the card through a reader, which sent the information to the central computer. To leave, or to open the door for someone outside, you had only to hit a button inside the firm.

Taylor read through the information, noting who'd used their keys to get into the firm on Saturday and Sunday morning. There were fifteen people who'd entered on Saturday, two on Sunday.

"Where're the time sheet reports?"

More documents appeared on the table. It was on these

time sheets that lawyers recorded in exasperating detail exactly how they spent each minute at the firm: which clients they worked for and what tasks they'd performed, when they took personal time during office hours, when they worked on business for the firm that was unrelated to clients.

Taylor looked through papers and, cross-checking the owner of the key code with the hours billed, learned that fourteen of the fifteen who'd checked in on Saturday morning had billed no more than six hours, which meant they would have left by four or five in the afternoon—a typical pattern for those working weekends: Get the work done early then play on Saturday night.

The one lawyer who'd remained was Mitchell Reece.

Flipping to the Sunday key entries, she saw that Reece had returned, as he'd told her, later that morning, at 9:23. But there was an entry *before* that, well before it, in fact. Someone had entered the firm at 1:30 A.M. But the only lawyer for whom there were time sheet entries was Reece.

Why on earth would somebody come into the firm that late and not do any work?

Maybe to open the door for a thief who would steal a gazillion-dollar note.

She flipped through the key assignment file and found that the person who'd entered at 1:30 had been Thomas Sebastian.

"Sebastian." Taylor tried to picture him but couldn't form an image; so many of the young associates looked alike. "What do you know about him?"

Carrie rolled her eyes. "Gag me. He's a total party animal. Goes out every night, dates a different girl every week, sometimes two—if you want to call it a date. We went out once and he couldn't keep his hands to himself."

"Is he at the firm now, tonight?"

"When I left, maybe a half hour ago, he was still working. But he'll probably be going out later. Around ten or eleven. I think he goes to clubs every night."

"You know where he hangs out?"

"There's a club called The Space. . . ."

Taylor said, "Sure, I've been there." She then asked, "Did you bring copies of the time sheet summaries from the *New Amsterdam v. Hanover & Stiver* case?"

Carrie slid a thick wad of Xerox copies to Taylor, who thumbed through them. These would show how much time each person spent on the case. Those more familiar with the case, Taylor was figuring, would be more likely to have been the ones approached by Hanover to steal the note.

Of the list of thirty people who'd been involved, though, only a few had spent significant time on it: Burdick and Reece primarily.

"Man," Taylor whispered, "look at the hours Mitchell worked. Fifteen hours in one day, sixteen hours, fourteen—on a Sunday. He even billed ten hours on Thanksgiving."

"That's why I love being a corporate paralegal," Carrie said, sounding as if she devoutly meant it. "You do trial work, you can kiss personal time so long."

"Look at this." Taylor frowned, tapping the "Paralegals" column on the case roster. "Linda Davidoff."

Carrie stared silently at her frothy drink. Then she said, "I didn't go to her funeral. Were you there?"

"Yes, I was."

Many people at the firm had attended. The suicide of the pretty, shy paralegal last fall had stunned everyone in the firm—though such deaths weren't unheard of. The subject wasn't talked about much in Wall Street law circles but paralegals who worked for big firms were under a lot of pressure—not only at their jobs but at home as well: Many of them were urged by their parents or peers to get into good law schools when they in fact had no particular interest in or aptitude for the law. There were many breakdowns and more than a few suicide attempts.

"I didn't know her too good," Carrie said. "She was kind of a mystery." A faint laugh. "Like you in a way. I didn't know you were a musician. Linda was a poet. You know that?"

"I think I remember something from the eulogy," Taylor said absently, eyes scanning the time sheets. "Look, in

September Linda stopped working on the case and Sean
Lillick took over for her as paralegal."

"Sean? He's a strange boy. I think he's a musician too. Or
a stand-up comic, I don't know. He's skinny and wears
weird clothes. Has his hair all spiked up. I like him, though.
I flirted with him some but he never asked me out. You ask
me, Mitchell's cuter." Carrie played with the pearls around
her neck and her voice flattened to a gossipy hush. "I heard
you were with him all day."

Taylor didn't glance up. "With who?" she asked casually
but felt her heart gallop.

"Mitchell Reece."

She laughed. "How'd you hear that?"

"Just the rumor around the paralegal pen. Some of the
girls were jealous. They're dying to work for him."

Who the hell had noticed them? she wondered. She
hadn't seen a soul outside his office when she entered or
left. "I just met with him for a few minutes is all."

"Mitchell's hot," the girl said.

"Is he?" Taylor replied. "I didn't take his temperature."
Nodding at the papers: "Can I keep them?"

"Sure, they're copies."

"Can I get any of this information myself?"

"Not if it's in the computer. You need to be approved to
go on-line and have a pass code and everything. But the raw
time sheets—before they're entered—anybody can look at.
They're in the file room, organized by the attorney assigned
as lead on the case or deal. The other stuff . . . just tell one of
the girls what you want and they'll get it for you. Uhm,
Taylor, can you, like, tell me what's going on?"

She lowered her voice and looked gravely into the eyes
of the young woman. "There was a mega mix-up on the
New Amsterdam bill. I don't know what happened but the
client's totally pissed. It was kind of embarrassing—with all
the merger talks going on and everything. Mitchell wanted
me to get to the bottom of it. On the Q.T."

"I won't say a word."

Taylor put the rest of the papers into her attaché case.

"Ms. Satin Touch?" Dimitri called from behind the bar in a singsongy voice.

"Brother." Taylor grimaced. "Gotta go pay the rent," she said and climbed back under Dimitri's homemade spotlights.

A trickle of fear ran through her as she began to play.

Who else had seen Mitchell and her together?

Taylor suddenly gave a brief laugh as she realized the title of the tune she found herself playing, selected by some subconscious hiccup.

The song was "Someone to Watch Over Me."

———

"Hey," the young man shouted over the music cascading from the club's million-decibel sound system, "I'm sorry I'm late. Are you still speaking to me?"

The blond woman glanced at the chubby man. "What?" she called.

"I can't believe I kept you waiting."

She looked over his smooth baby-fatted skin, the newscaster's perfect hair, the gray suit, wing tips, Cartier watch. He examined her right back: red angular dress, paisley black stockings, black hat and veil. Small tits, he noticed, but a lot of skin was exposed.

"What?" she shouted again. Though she'd heard his words; he knew she had.

"I got held up," he explained, hands clasped together in prayer. "I can't really go into it. It's an unpleasant story."

These were lines he used a lot in clubs like this. Cute lines, silly lines. As soon as the women realized that they'd never seen him before and that he was hitting on them in a major way, they usually rolled their eyes and said, "Fuck off."

But sometimes, just sometimes, they didn't. This one said nothing yet. She was taking her time. She watched him sending out Morse code with something in his hand, tapping it against the bar absently, while he smiled his flirts toward her.

Tap, tap, tap.

"I thought for sure you would've left. Would've served me right. Keeping a beautiful woman waiting," said this young man with a slight swell of double chin and a belly testing his Tripler's 42-inch alligator belt.

The process of scoring in a place like this was, of course, like negotiating. You had to play a role, act, be somebody else.

Tap, tap, tap.

The club was an old warehouse, sitting on a commercial street in downtown Manhattan, deserted except for the cluster of supplicants crowding around the ponytailed, baggy-jacketed doorman, who selected Those Who Might Enter with a grudging flick of a finger.

Thom Sebastian was never denied entrance.

Tap, tap, tap.

True, mostly the women roll their eyes and tell him to fuck off. But sometimes they did what she was doing now: looking down at the telegraph key—a large vial of coke—and saying, "Hi, I'm Veronica."

He reacted to the gift of her name like a shark tasting blood in the water. He moved in fast, sitting next to her, shaking her hand for a lengthy moment.

"Thom," he said.

The sound system's speakers, as tall as the six-foot-six, blue-gowned transvestite dancing in front of them, sent fluttering bass waves into their faces and chests. The smell was a pungent mix of cigarette smoke and a gassy, ozonelike scent—from the fake fog.

Tap, tap, tap.

He offered his boyish grin while she rambled on about careers—she sold something in some store somewhere but wanted to get into something else. Sebastian nodded and murmured single-word encouragements and mentally tumbled forward, caught in the soft avalanche of anticipation. He saw the evening unfold before him: They'd hit the john, duck into a stall and do a fast line or two of coke. No nookie yet, nor would he expect any. After that they'd leave and go over to Meg's, where he was a regular. Then out for pasta. After that, when it was pushing 3 A.M., he'd ask her with mock trepidation if she ever went north of Fourteenth Street.

A car-service Lincoln up to his apartment.

Your condom or mine . . .

And later, after a Val or 'lude to come down, they'd sleep. Up at eight-thirty the next morning, share the shower, take turns with the hair dryer, give her a kiss. She'd cab it home. He'd down some speed and head to Hubbard, White & Willis for another day of lawyering.

Tap, tap, tap . . .

"Hey," Thom said, interrupting her as she was saying *something,* "how about—"

But there was a disturbance. Another incarnation of Veronica appeared: a young woman walking toward them. Different clothes but the same high cheeks, pale flesh, laces, silks, a flea market's worth of costume jewelry. Floral perfume. They were interchangeable, these two women. Clones. They bussed cheeks. Behind Veronica II stood a pair of quiet, preoccupied young Japanese men dressed in black, hair greased and spiked high like porcupine quills. One wore a medal studded with rhinestones.

Sebastian suddenly detested them—not because of the impending kidnapping of his new love but for no reason he could figure out. He wanted to lean forward and ask the young man if he'd won the medal at Iwo Jima. Veronica nodded to her other half, lifted her eyebrows at Sebastian with regret and a smile that belied it and disappeared into the mist.

Tap, tap, tap.

"*Quo vadis,* Veronica?" Sebastian whispered, pronouncing the v's like w's the way his Latin professor had instructed. He turned back to the bar and noticed that somebody had taken Veronica's space. Someone who was the exact opposite of her: homey, pretty, dressed conservatively but stylishly in black. She was vaguely familiar; he must've seen her here before. The woman ordered a rum and Coke, gave a laugh to herself.

She was hardly his type but Sebastian couldn't help raise an eyebrow at the laugh. She noticed and said in response, "That woman over there? She's decided I'm her soul mate. I don't know what she wants but I don't think it's healthy."

Instinctively he glanced where the woman was nodding and studied the gold lamé dress, the stiletto heels. He said, "Well, the good news is it's not a woman."

"What?"

"Truly. But the bad news is that I'm betting what he has in mind is still pretty perverse."

"Maybe I better head for the hills," she said.

"Naw, hang out here. I'll protect you. You can cheer me up. My true love just left me."

"The true love you just met four minutes ago?" the woman asked. "*That* true love?"

"Ah, you witnessed that, did you?"

She added, "Mine just stood me up. I won't go so far as to say true love. He was a blind date."

His mind raced. Yes, she *was* familiar. . . . She now squinted at him as if she recognized him too. Where did he know her from? Here? The Harvard Club? Piping Rock?

He wondered if he'd slept with her, and, if he had, whether he'd enjoyed it. Shit, had he called her the next day?

She was saying, "I couldn't believe it. The bouncer wasn't going to let me in. It took all my political pull."

"Political?"

"A portrait of Alexander Hamilton." She slung out the words and Sebastian thought he heard something akin to mockery in her voice, as if he wasn't quick enough to catch the punch line.

"Gotcha," Sebastian said, feeling defensive.

"This drink sucks. The Coke tastes moldy."

Now he felt offended too, taking this as a criticism of the club, which was one of his homes away from home. He sipped his own drink and felt uncharacteristically out of control. Veronica was easier to handle. He wondered how to get back in the driver's seat.

"Look, I know I know you. You're?"

"Taylor Lockwood." They shook hands.

"Thom Sebastian."

"Right," she said, understanding dawning in his eyes.

With this, his mind made the connection. "Hubbard, White?"

"Corporate paralegal. Hey, you ever fraternize with us folks?"

"Only if we blow this joint. Let's go—there's nothing happening here."

The tall gold-clad transvestite had begun a striptease in front of them, while ten feet away Tina Turner and Calvin Klein paused to watch.

"There isn't?" Taylor asked.

Sebastian smiled, took her hand and led her through the crowd.

CHAPTER SIX

The drapery man was having a busy night.

He pushed a canvas cart ahead of him, filled with his props—draperies that needed to be cleaned but never would be. They were piled atop one another and the one on top was folded carefully; it hid his ice-pick weapon, resting near to hand.

This man had been in many different offices at all hours of the day and night. Insurance companies with rows of ghastly gray desks bathed in green fluorescence. CEOs' offices that were like the finest comp suites in Vegas casinos. Hotels and art galleries. Even some government office buildings. But Hubbard, White & Willis was unique.

At first he'd been impressed with the elegant place. But now, pushing the cart through quiet corridors, he felt belittled. He sensed contempt for people like him, sensed it from the walls themselves. Here, he was nothing. His neck prickled as he walked past a dark portrait of some old man from the 1800s. He wanted to pull out his pick and slash the canvas.

The drapery man's face was a map of vessels burst in

fistfights on the streets and in the various prisons he'd been incarcerated in and his muscles were dense as a bull's. He was a professional, of course, but part of him was hoping one of these scrawny prick lawyers, hunched over stacks of books in the offices he passed (no glances, no nods, no smiles—well, fuck you and your mother)...hoping one of them would walk up to him and demand to see a pass or permit so he could shank them through the lung.

But they all remained oblivious to him. An underling.

Not even worth noticing.

Glancing around to make sure no one was approaching, he stepped into the coffee room on the main floor and took a dusty container of Coffee-mate from the back of a storage shelf. In thirty seconds he'd slid out the tape recorder, removed the cassette, put in a new one and replaced the unit in the canister. He knew it was safe in this particular container because he'd observed that the prissy lawyers here insisted on real milk—half-and-half or 2 percent—and wouldn't think of drinking, or serving their clients, anything artificial. The Coffee-mate tube had been here, untouched, for months.

Making sure the corridor was empty again, the drapery man walked across the hall to Mitchell Reece's office and, listening carefully for footsteps, checked the receiver of Reece's phone.

On Saturday night, when he'd been here to steal the promissory note, he'd placed in the handset of the phone unit an Ashika Electronics omnidirectional ambient-filtering microphone and transmitter. The device was roughly the size of a Susan B. Anthony silver dollar. It was, however, considerably more popular and was used by every security, private eye or industrial espionage outfit that could afford the eight-thousand-dollar price tag. This bug broadcast a razor-clear transmission of all of Reece's conversations on the phone or with anyone else in the office to the radio receiver and tape recorder in the Coffee-mate container across the hall. One feature of the transmitter was that it contained a frequency-canceling feature, which made it virtually invisible to most commercial bug-detecting sweepers. He checked the battery and found it was still good.

When he was finished he spent another three or four minutes arranging the drapes so they looked nice. This was, after all, his purported job.

He peeled off the gloves and walked out into the halls, which greeted him once again with their silence and their real, or imagined, disdain.

———

"I suffer from the fallacy of the beautiful woman."

The Lincoln Town Car limo crashed through the meat-packing district in the western part of Greenwich Village, near the river. Taylor leaned sideways to hear Thom Sebastian over the crackly sound of the talk show on the driver's AM radio.

He continued, "Which is this: that because a woman is attractive she can do no wrong. You think, Christ, the way she lights a cigarette is the right way, the restaurants she picks are the right restaurants, the way she fakes an orgasm—pardon my French—is the right way so *I* must be doing something wrong. For instance, we're now on our way to Meg's. The club. You know it?"

"Absolutely no idea."

"There, my point exactly. I'm thinking: Jesus, I'm doing something wrong. Taylor is a primo woman but she doesn't know about this club. *I've* fucked up. *I've* got it wrong."

Taylor smirked. "Does this usually work?"

Sebastian paused then slouched back in the cab seat and lit a cigarette. "What?"

"That line? The one you're using on me now?"

Sebastian waited a few more seconds and must've decided there'd be no recovery from her busting him. "You'd be surprised at some of the lines I've gotten away with." He laughed. "The thing is *women* suffer from the fallacy of the man who knows what he's doing. We never do, of course." He gave her what might pass for a sincere glance and said, "I like you."

They pulled up in front of nothing. A row of ware-houses and small factories, not a streetlight in sight, only the distant aurora borealis of industrial Jersey across the Hudson River.

"Welcome to my main club."

"Here?"

"Yep. I'm here six, seven nights a week."

Sebastian led them through an unguarded, unmarked door into what looked like a Victorian bordello. The walls were covered with dark tapestry. The tables were marble and brass. Oak columns and sideboards were draped with tooling and floral chintz. Tiffanyesque lamps were every-where. The uniform for men was tuxedo or Italian suits, for the women, dark, close-fitting dresses with necklines that required pure willpower to keep nipples hidden. The rooms were chockablock with high-level celebs and politicos, the sort that regularly make *New York* magazine and Liz Smith's columns.

Sebastian whispered, "The three little piggies," and pointed out a trio of hip young novelists whom a *Times* critic had just vivisected en masse in an article called "Id as Art: The Care and Feeding of Self-Indulgence." Skinny women hovered around the threesome. Sebastian eyed the women with dismay and said, "Why are they wasting time with those dudes? Didn't they see the article?"

Taylor said dryly, "You assume they can read." And bumped into Richard Gere. He glanced at her with a polite acknowledgment, apologized and continued on.

"Oh my God." She gasped, staring at the man's broad back. "*He's* here."

"Yes," Sebastian said, bored. "And so are we."

The music wasn't as loud as at the previous club and the pace was less frantic. Sebastian waved to some people.

"What're you drinking?" he asked.

"Stick with R&C."

They sipped their drinks for a few minutes. Sebastian leaned over again and asked, "What's your biggest passion? After handsome men like me, I mean."

"Skiing, I guess." Taylor was circumspect about telling people her second career—the music—and was particularly reluctant to give a robbery suspect too much information about herself.

"Skiing? Sliding down a mountain, getting wet and cold and breaking bones, is that it?"

"Breaking bones is optional."

"I did some exercise once," Sebastian said, shaking his head. "I got over it. I'm okay now."

She laughed and studied him in the mirror. The lawyer didn't look good. His eyes were puffy and red. He blew his nose often and his posture was terrible. The coke and whatever other drugs he was doing were taking their toll. He seemed deflated as he hunched over his drink, sucking his cocktail through the thin brown straw. Suddenly he straightened, slipped his arm around her shoulders and kissed her hair. "Does anyone ever get lost in there?"

She kept the smile on her face but didn't lean into him. She said evenly, "It's true that I had date failure tonight. But I still do things the old-fashioned way. Real slow." She eased away and looked at him. "Just want the ground rules understood."

He left his arm where it was for a noncommittal ten seconds, then dropped it. "Fair enough," he said with a tone that suggested: all rights reserved.

"You go out a lot?" she asked.

"Work hard and play hard. By the time I burn out at forty-five . . ." His voice faded and he was looking at her expectantly.

Tap, tap, tap.

She saw his hand swinging against the bar. A brown vial.

"You want to retire to the facilities with me? Build strong bodies twelve ways?"

"Not me. I have to keep in shape for breaking bones."

He blinked, surprised. "Yeah? You sure?"

"Never touch the stuff."

He laughed. Then put the bottle away.

Just then another man appeared from the crowd and walked up to Sebastian though his attention seemed fixed on Taylor. He resembled Sebastian some but was thinner, shorter, a few years younger. He wore a conservative gray suit but bright red sunglasses, from which a green cord hooked to the earpieces dangled down the back of his neck.

She noted Sebastian's surprise when the young man approached.

Sebastian said, "Hey, Taylor, meet my main man, Bosk. Hey, Bosk, Taylor." They shook hands.

"Will you marry me?" Bosk asked her in a slurred voice. He'd had a great deal to drink and she knew that beneath the silly Elton John sunglasses his eyes would be unfocused.

"Oh, gosh," she answered brightly, "I can't tonight."

"Story of my life." He turned back to Sebastian. "Hey, you never fucking called me back. We've gotta talk. He called and wanted to know where—"

Bosk suddenly fell silent and as Taylor reached for her drink she observed in the mirror behind the bar two very subtle gestures by Sebastian, a nod toward her and a wag of his finger, whose only possible meaning was that the topic Bosk was raising was not to be discussed in front of her.

Bosk recovered, though not very well, by saying, "What it is, I've still got some room on that New Jersey project if you're interested."

"How leveraged?"

Bosk said, "We'll need to come up with probably six five."

"No fucking way." Sebastian laughed.

"Sea Bass, come on. . . ."

"Three eight was the top, dumbo. I'm not going over three eight."

These figures might have referred to percentages or shares of stock or money, in which case, considering that the context was New York metro area business or real estate, they might be talking about hundreds of thousands or even millions of dollars.

And Alice thought Wonderland was topsy-turvy. . . .

"Don't be such a fucking wuss," Bosk muttered drunk-
enly. Studying Taylor.

Sebastian grinned and grabbed Bosk, swung him into a
neck lock then rapped him on the head.

Bosk broke away and shouted, laughing, "You're a fucking cow chip, you know that?" He replaced his gaudy sunglasses. "Hey, you want to come out to Long Island for
dinner on Friday? My mother'll be out with her cook.
Bunch of the gang. Brittany said she, like, forgives you for
not calling."

An electronic pocket calendar appeared in Sebastian's
pudgy hand. He studied it. "Can do, dude," he said at last.
They slapped palms and Bosk vanished.

"Primo guy," Sebastian said.

"He's a lawyer?"

"Among other things. We go way back. We're doing some
projects together."

Projects . . . as vague a euphemism as there was.

"Like real estate?" Taylor asked.

"Yeah." But she heard a lie in his voice.

Taylor turned back to her drink. "I'd like to do some in-
vesting. But I got one problem. No money."

"Why's that a problem?" Sebastian said, frowning, genuinely perplexed. "You never use your own money. Use
somebody else's. It's the only way to invest."

"Hubbard, White lets you work on your own? Don't you
have to clear it with somebody?"

Sebastian laughed, a sharp exhalation of bitterness that
surprised her. "We aren't on such good terms lately, Messrs.
Hubbard, White and Willis and myself." He apparently decided to drop the fast-lane image. Deflated, he sighed and
muttered, "They passed me over for partner." His lips tightened into a bleak smile and she got what she thought was
her first real look at Thom Sebastian.

"I'm sorry." Taylor knew that this would have been a
devastating blow to him. Partnership was the golden ring

young associates strived for. They worked sixty or seventy hours a week for years for the chance to be asked to join the firm as one of the partners—the owners.

Taylor, on the trail of a thief, after all, sensed he might be revealing a motive to lift the promissory note—revenge—and wanted him to keep talking. She said, "Must've been tough."

"After they told me, I tried to convince myself I didn't really *want* to be partner. I mean, Christ, you can make more money at real estate or investment banking. I said, 'Fuck it. Who needs them? It's just a bunch of old men. . . .' Well, that's what I told myself. But, damn, I wanted it bad. I've worked all my professional life to get my name on the letterhead of Hubbard, White & Willis. And this is what they do to me."

"Did they tell you why?"

His pale jaw, round with fat, trembled. "Bullshit. I mean, finances was what they said. 'Effecting economies,' if I may quote. But that wasn't the reason." He turned to her and said, "See, I don't fit the Hubbard, White mold."

"What's the mold?"

"Ha, that's the catch. They can't tell you; they just know whether you've got it or not. And that prick Clayton didn't think I had it."

"Wendall Clayton? What did he have to do with it?"

"I'm not one of his chosen few. Most of the partnership slots this year got filled with his boys and girls. Look at that asshole Randy Simms."

She had a vague memory of a young, square-jawed blond partner.

"Randy Simms III," Sebastian spat out. "The 'third,'" he mused bitterly. "But, hey, he's gotta be the end of *that* family line though. I'm sure the guy doesn't have a dick."

"But Clayton's not even on the executive committee," Taylor said.

He laughed. "What difference does *that* make? He's got ten times more power than Burdick or Stanley think. He's going to ramrod the merger through."

"The merger?" she said. "That's just a rumor. It's been going around for months."

Sebastian looked at her and detected no irony. He snorted. "Just a rumor? You think that, then you don't know Wendall Clayton. Two months from now, you won't be able to recognize our firm. . . ." His voice dwindled. "I should say, *your* firm. Ain't mine no more."

"What're you going to do?"

He was about to say something but grew cautious. She could sense he was selecting his words carefully. "Oh, I'll get a new job. Probably go in-house, become chief general counsel for a client. That's what happens to most senior associates after they cut your balls off."

Okay, Taylor told herself. Go for it.

"Then why're you working so hard?" she asked. "If I got passed over *I* sure wouldn't be working holiday weekends."

A brief hesitation. "Weekends?" he asked.

"Yeah, you were in the firm on Sunday morning, weren't you?"

He took a long sip of his drink then said, "Me? No. I was here all night. I left about three, when they were getting ready to close."

She frowned. "That's funny. I was doing some billing for . . . who was it? I don't remember. Anyway, I saw your key card number. You came in real early on Sunday." He looked at her for a long moment. His face was completely blank but she sensed that his thoughts were grinding hard and fast. Then he nodded in understanding. "Ralph Dudley," he said angrily.

"Dudley? The old partner?"

"Yeah, Grandpa. Yesterday he dropped my key off in my office. He said I left it in the library and he'd picked it up by mistake on Friday. He must've used it on Sunday."

She couldn't tell whether to believe him or not.

Agitated at this news, Sebastian fished in his pocket and found the little vial. He held it up. "You sure?" She shook her head and he looked toward the men's room. "Excusez-moi."

After he disappeared, Taylor motioned the bartender over to her and said, "You working last Saturday night?"

He normally didn't get questions like this. He polished glasses. But finally he said, "Yeah."

"Was Thom in here from one to three or so on Sunday morning?"

"I don't remember."

She slid two twenties toward him furtively. He blinked. This only happened in movies and the man seemed to be considering how his favorite actor would handle it. The bills disappeared into tight black jeans. "No. He left around one—without a girl. That *never* happens. If he's by himself usually he closes the place. He's even slept here a couple times."

When Sebastian returned he took Taylor's purse and slipped it around her—over one shoulder and under the other arm, the way paranoid tourists do. "Come on. I'm wound, I'm flying like a bird. I gotta dance. . . ."

"But—"

He pulled her onto the small floor. After fifteen minutes, her hair was down, streaming in thick, sweaty tangles. Her toes were on fire, her calves ached. Sebastian kept jerking away in time to the reggae beat, eyes closed, lost in the catharsis of the motion and music and the coke. Taylor collapsed on his shoulder. "Enough."

"I thought you were a skier."

"Exhausted." She was gasping.

His brow arched and the surprise in his eyes was genuine. "But we haven't eaten yet."

Taylor said, "It's one A.M. I've been up for nearly twenty-four hours."

"Time for penne!"

"But—"

"Come on. One plate of darling little squigglies of pasta in alfredo sauce with cilantro and basil, one teeny endive salad, one bottle of Mersault."

Taylor was weakening.

"*Belgium* endive! . . ." Then he lowered his head. "Okay."

Sebastian the negotiator was now speaking. "How's this for a deal? We have dinner and you can tell me about the Pine Breath Inn in Vermont or wherever the hell it is you ski and we'll call it a night. Or I can take you home now and you'll have to fight off my frontal assault at your door. Few women have been able to resist."

"Thom—"

"I take no prisoners."

She lowered her head on his shoulder then straightened up, smiling. "Does this place have spaghetti and meat balls with thick red sauce, à la Ragú?"

"I'll never be able to show my face there again. But if you want it I'll force the chef to make it."

She sighed, took his arm and together they made their way toward the door.

CHAPTER SEVEN

The alarm clock wailed like a smoke detector.

Taylor Lockwood opened one eye. Was this the worst headache of her life? she wondered.

She lay still for five minutes while the votes rolled in. Yes, no?

Sitting up decided the contest—a clear victory for the pain. She slammed her palm down on the alarm then scooted gingerly to the edge of the bed. She still wore her panty hose and bra; the elastic bands had cut deep purple lines into her skin and she was momentarily concerned that she'd have permanent discolorations.

Oh, man, I feel lousy. . . .

Taylor's one-bedroom apartment was small and dark. It was located in the Fifth Avenue Hotel, a dark, Gothic building distinguished only by the prestige of the street it was located on and its reputation for being the place that New York's Judge Crater was supposedly on his way to when he disappeared seventy years before—still an open case on the NYPD books.

Her parents had offered to send her whatever furniture

she wanted from their eight-bedroom house in Chevy Chase or from one of their summer homes but Taylor had wanted this apartment to be exclusively hers. It was furnished post-collegiate—Conran's, Crate & Barrel, Pottery Barn. A lot of fake stone, Formica, black and white plastic. A huge pillow sofa. Canvas chairs that, looked at straight on, seemed to be grinning. A number of interesting pieces from the Twenty-sixth Street flea market on Sixth Avenue.

The bedroom was the homiest room in the place, deco-rated with lace tulle, art deco lamps and old furniture—bat-tered but loaded with personality—a hundred books, souvenirs from the trips young Taylor took to Europe with her parents.

On the wall was a large poster—one of Arthur Rack-ham's sepia illustrations of Lewis Carroll's *Alice's Adventures in Wonderland.*

The picture wasn't like the Disney cartoon or the origi-nal Sir John Tenniel drawings but was a masterful work by the brilliant artist. It showed an alarmed Alice lifting her hands to protect herself as the Red Queen's playing card sol-diers flew into the air.

The caption read:

> At this the whole pack rose up into the air,
> and came flying down upon her.

The framed poster had been a graduation present from her roommates at Dartmouth. Taylor loved the Carroll books, and Alice memorabilia were sure bets as birthday and Christmas presents. There were many other *Wonderland* and *Through the Looking-Glass* artifacts throughout her apartment.

Taylor sent her tongue around her parched mouth; she didn't enjoy the trip. She staggered into the bathroom, where she downed two glasses of water and brushed her teeth twice. She squinted at the clock. Let's see, Sebastian had dropped her off at about four. Do the math.... Okay, we're talking about three and a half hours' sleep.

And, more troubling, it turned out that she'd largely wasted her time. Thom Sebastian had denied being in the firm on Saturday or Sunday and had remained tight-lipped about his dealings with Bosk though he'd continued to talk bitterly about the firm's decision to pass him over. He'd had no response when she'd casually mentioned Hanover & Stiver, Inc.

She kneaded her belly, which swelled slightly over the top of her panties, recalling that there were a hundred fifty calories in each cocktail. . . . She squeezed her temples. Her vision swam.

A blinking red light across the room coincided with the throbbing in her head. It was her answering machine, indicating a message from last night. She hit the play button, thinking it might be a call from Mitchell Reece, remembering his asking her if it was okay to call her at home.

Beep.

"Hello, counselor."

Ah, her father, she realized with a thud in her turbulent stomach.

"Just wanted to tell you: You owe me lunch. Earl Warren was chief justice when the case was decided. Call when you can. Love you."

Click.

Shit, she thought. I shouldn't've bet with him.

Taylor didn't mind losing to him, of course; half the lawyers in Washington, D.C., had lost a case or motion or argument to Samuel Lockwood at one time or another in their careers. The *Washington Post* had called him "The Unbeatable Legal Eagle" (the article was framed and displayed prominently in their living room at home). No, it was that even though she could see clearly that he was testing her, she'd weakened and agreed to the pointless bet.

It was very, very difficult to say no to Samuel Lockwood.

He called her two or three times a week but unless he had something specific to ask her he usually picked "safe" times: During the day he'd call her home, at night he'd call the firm, leaving messages—fulfilling his parental duty and making his royal presence felt in her territory but making sure he didn't waste time actually talking to her. (She noted cynically that she might reasonably have been expected to be home last night when he'd phoned—because the purpose of that call had been to gloat.)

Well, she could hardly point fingers; Taylor did the same—generally calling home when she knew he was working so she could chat with her mother untroubled by the brooding presence of her father hovering near the receiver, a presence she could sense from even three hundred miles away.

She winced as the headache pounded on her again, just for the pure fun of it, it seemed. A glance at the clock.

Okay, Alice, you got twenty minutes to get yourself up and running. Go for it.

■

Sitting before Mitchell Reece in the glaringly lit Vista Hotel dining room was a plate of scrambled eggs, hash browns, bacon and a bagel. Taylor was nursing a grapefruit juice and seltzer.

She'd already been stared down by her dry toast.

Reece said, "You feeling okay?"

"I was out dancing last night till four."

"All work and no play..."

Taylor grunted. "The good news is I've got us a suspect." The juice was reviving traces of rum lurking in her bloodstream. This resuscitation was not pleasant. "Thom Sebastian."

She explained to him about cross-referencing the computer key entries and the time sheets.

"Brilliant," he told her, lifting an eyebrow.

She nodded noncommittally and downed two more Advils.

"Sebastian?" Reece pondered. "In the corporate group, right? He's done work for New Amsterdam in the past. He

might even've done some of the work on the original loan to
Hanover. But what's his motive? Money?"

"Revenge. He was passed over for partner."

"Ouch." Sympathy crept into Reece's face, which revealed the fatigue-dulled skin and damp red eyes that Taylor
knew matched hers. Still, his suit of textured charcoal wool
was perfectly pressed and his shirt was as smooth and white
as the starched napkin that lay across his lap. His dark hair
was combed back, slick and smooth from either a recent
shower or some lotion. He sat comfortably upright at the
table and ate hungrily.

Taylor braved the toast again and managed to eat a small
piece. "And he acted real odd about something. He's got a
quote project going on with somebody nicknamed Bosk.
Another lawyer here in town, young kid. But he wouldn't
talk about it. He also claims he was in a club on Saturday
but the bartender there said he wasn't. He left about one. I
asked Sebastian about it and he claims Ralph Dudley took
his computer door key."

"Old Man Dudley? Working on Sunday at one-thirty?
No way. Past his bedtime." Reece then reconsidered. "Funny,
though, I heard Dudley had money problems. He's borrowed big against his partnership equity."

Taylor said, "How'd you find that out?" The individual
partners' financial situations were closely guarded secrets.

As if citing an immutable rule of physics Reece said,
"*Always* know the successful partners from the losers."

"I'll check out Dudley today."

"I can't imagine he was in the firm on legitimate business. Dudley hasn't worked a weekend in his life. But I also
can't see him as our thief. He's such a bumbler. And he's got
that granddaughter of his he's looking after. I don't see how
he'd risk going to jail and leaving her alone. She doesn't
have any other family."

"That cute little girl he brought to the outing last year?
She's about sixteen?"

"I heard that Dudley's son abandoned her or something.

Anyway, she's in boarding school in town and he takes care of her." He laughed. "Kids. I can't imagine them."

Taylor asked, "You don't have any?"

He grew wistful for a few seconds. "No. I thought I would once." The stoic lawyer's facade returned immediately. "But my wife wasn't so inclined. And, after all, it does take two, you know."

"When I hit thirty-eight I'm going to find a genetically acceptable man, get pregnant and send him on his way."

"You could always try marriage, of course."

"Oh, yeah, I've heard about that."

He looked at her eyes for a moment then started laughing.

She asked, "What?"

"I was thinking, we should start a group."

"What?"

"The Visine Club," he said.

"I can get by with seven hours' sleep. Less than that, no way."

Reece said, "Five's pretty much standard for me." He finished the bacon and held a forkful of eggs toward her. She smiled, fought down the nausea and shook her head. She noticed, behind the bar, a stack of wine bottles and felt her stomach twist. Reece ate some of his breakfast and asked, "Where you from?"

"Burbs of D.C. Chevy Chase in Maryland. Well, I was born on Long Island but my parents moved to Maryland when I was in middle school. My father got a job in the District."

"Oh, I read that article in the Post about him last month. His argument before the Supreme Court."

"Tell me about it," she grumbled. "I've heard the blow-by-blow a half-dozen times. He overnighted me a copy of his argument. For my leisure-time reading, I guess."

"So how'd you end up on Wall Street?" Reece asked.

"Very long story," she said with a tone that told him that this was not the time or place to share it.

"School?"

"Dartmouth . . . music and poly sci."

"Music?"

"I play piano. Jazz mostly."

This seemed to intrigue him. He asked, "Who do you listen to?"

"Billy Taylor's my fave, I guess. But there's something about the fifties and sixties. Cal Tjader, Desmond, Brubeck."

Reece shook his head. "I'm mostly into horn. Dexter Gordon, Javon Jackson."

"No kidding," she said, surprised. Usually only jazzophiles knew these players. "I love Jabbo Smith."

He nodded at this. "Sure, sure. I'm also a big Burrell fan."

She nodded. "Guitar? I still like Wes Montgomery, I've got to admit. For a while I was into a Howard Roberts phase."

Reece said, "Too avant-garde for me."

"Oh, yeah, I hear you," she said. "A melody . . . that's what music's got to have—a tune people can hum. A movie's got to have a story, a piece of music's got to have a tune. That's my philosophy of life."

"You perform?"

"Sometimes. Right now my big push is to get a record contract. I just dropped a bundle making a demo of some of my own tunes. I rented a studio, hired union backup. The works. Sent them to about a hundred companies."

"Yeah?" He seemed excited. "Give me a copy if you think about it. You have any extra?"

She laughed. "Dozens. Even after I give them away as Christmas presents this year."

"How's the response been?"

"Next question?" she asked, sighing. "I've sent out ninety-six tapes—agents, record companies, producers. So far, I've gotten eighty-four rejections. But I did get one 'maybe.' From a big label. They're going to present it to their A&R committee."

"I'll keep my fingers crossed."

"Thanks."

"So," he asked, "how's the music jibe with the law school track?"

"Oh, I can handle them both," she said without really thinking about her response. She wondered if the comment came off as pompous.

He glanced at his watch, and Taylor felt the gesture abruptly push aside the personal turn their conversation had taken. She asked, "There is one thing I wanted to ask you about. Linda Davidoff worked on the Hanover & Stiver case, right?"

"Linda? The paralegal? Yeah, for a few months when the case got started."

"It struck me as a little curious that she quit working on the case pretty suddenly then she killed herself."

He nodded. "That's odd, yeah. I never thought about it. I didn't know her very well. She was a good paralegal. But real quiet. It doesn't seem likely she'd be involved," Reece said, "but if you asked me it if was likely somebody'd steal a note from a law firm, I'd say no way."

The waitress asked if they wanted anything else. They shook their heads. "You women, always dieting," Reece said, nodding at her uneaten toast.

Taylor smiled. Thinking: We women, always trying not to throw up in front of our bosses.

"What's up next?" he asked.

"Time to be a spy," she said.

Taylor sat in her cubicle at the firm and dialed a number.

She let the telephone ring. When the system shifted the call over to voice mail she hung up, left her desk and wandered down the halls. Up a flight of stairs. She turned down a corridor that led past the lunchroom then past the forms room, where copies of prototype contracts and pleadings were filed. At the end of this corridor—in the law firm's Siberia—was a single office. On the door was a nameplate: *R. Dudley.* Most of these plates in the firm were plastic; this

one, though it designated the smallest partner's office in
Hubbard, White, was made of polished brass.

Inside the office were crammed an Italian Renaissance
desk, a tall bookcase, two shabby leather chairs, dozens of
prints of nineteenth-century sailing ships and eighteenth-
century foxhunting scenes. Through a small window you
could see a brick wall and a tiny sliver of New York Harbor.
On the desk rested a large brass ashtray, a picture of an unsmiling, pretty teenage girl, a dozen Metropolitan Opera
Playbills, a date book and one law book—a Supreme Court
Reporter.

Taylor Lockwood opened the *Reporter* and bent over it.
Her eyes, though, camouflaged by her fallen hair, were not
reading the twin columns of type but rather Ralph Dudley's
scuffed leather date book, opened to the present week.

She noticed the letters *W.S.* penned into the box for late
Saturday evening or early Sunday morning, just before the
time Dudley—if Sebastian was right—had used the associate's key to get into the firm.

The initials *W.S.* were also, she observed, written in the
10 P.M. slot for tomorrow. Who was this person? A contact at
Hanover? The professional thief? Taylor then opened the
calendar to the phone number/address section. There was
no one listed with those initials. She should—

"Can I help you?" a man's voice snapped.

Taylor forced herself not to jump. She kept her finger on
the *Reporter* to mark her spot and looked up slowly.

A young man she didn't recognize stood in the doorway.
Blond, scrubbed, chubby. And peeved.

"Ralph had this *Reporter* checked out from the library,"
she said, nodding at the book. "I needed to look up a case."
Taking the offensive, she asked bluntly, "Who're you?"

"Me? I'm Todd Stanton. I work for Mr. Dudley." He
squinted. "Who are *you*?"

"Taylor Lockwood. A paralegal." She forced indignation
into her voice.

"A paralegal." His tone said, Oh, well, that doesn't really
count. "Does Mr. Dudley know you're here?"

"No."

"If you need anything, you can ask me for it. Mr. Dudley doesn't like"—he sought the least disparaging term—"anyone in his office when he's not here."

"Ah," Taylor said and then turned back to the book and slowly finished reading a long paragraph.

Stanton shifted then said with irritation, "Excuse me but—"

Taylor closed the book softly. "Hey," she said, offering a concerned glance. "Don't sweat it. You're excused." And walked past him back into the deserted corridor.

CHAPTER EIGHT

 "Dactyloscopy," the man said. "Repeat after me: dactyloscopy."

Taylor did.

More or less.

"Good," the man said. "Now you know the first thing about fingerprinting. It's called dactyloscopy. The second is that it is a royal pain in the butt."

She sat in the office of John Silbert Hemming. His card explained that he was a vice president in the corporate security department at Manhattan Allied Security, Inc.

The man, in his mid-thirties, had been recommended by a friend from the music world who did word processing for Allied Security to support his addiction to the saxophone.

Taylor had spent most of the day at Hubbard, White, poring over records of the *New Amsterdam Bank v. Hanover & Stiver* case, trying to find a reference to anyone who might have shown unusual interest in the promissory note or who'd requested files on the deal when there didn't seem to be a reason for them to do so.

But after nearly eight hours of mind-numbing legal babble Taylor found not a shred of evidence to suggest that Ralph
Dudley or Thom Sebastian—or anyone else—was the thief.

She'd decided to give up on the subtle approach and try
a more traditional tack, à la *Kojak* or *Rockford Files*.

Hence, the tall shamus she was now sitting across from.

When Hemming had come to meet her in the reception
area she'd blinked and looked up. He was six feet ten. His
height had led, he had explained on their way back to his
office, to his becoming a backroom security man—the company technical and forensic expert.

"You've got to be unobstrusive in private detective work.
A lot of what we do is surveillance, you know."

She said, "Tailing."

"Pardon?"

"Don't you say 'tailing'? You know, like you tail somebody?"

"Hmmm, no, we say say 'surveillance.' "

"Oh."

"If you stand out like me that's not so good. When we
recruit we have a space on our evaluation form—'Is subject
unobtrusive?' We mean 'boring.' "

His hair was tawny and unruly and Taylor's impression
of Hemming was that he was a huge little boy. He had eyes
that seemed perpetually amused and that belied a face that
was dramatically long (what else could it be, given that it sat
atop a body like his?). Despite this quirky appearance there
was something rather appealing about him.

Now, John Silbert Hemming was aiming a startlingly
long finger at her and saying, "I hope you mean that, about
wanting to know everything. Because there's a lot, and here
it comes. Let's start with: What *are* fingerprints?"

"Uh—"

"I know. You paid the money, I've got the answers. But I
like people to participate. I like interaction. Time's up. No
idea? I'd suggest you avoid *Jeopardy!* Now: Fingerprints are
the impressions left by the papillary ridges of the fingers
and thumb, primarily in perspiration. Also called friction

ridges. There are no sebaceous glands in the fingertips themselves but people sometimes leave fingerprints in human oils picked up elsewhere on the body. Yes, in answer to the first most-often-asked question, they are all different. Even more different than snowflakes, I can say safely, because for hundreds of years people have been collecting fingerprints from all over the world and comparing them, and nobody—none of *my* close friends, I'll tell you—have been doing that with snowflakes. Go ahead, ask the next-most-popular question."

"Uh, do animals have fingerprints?"

"Primates do, but who cares? We don't give apes government clearances or put them on the ten-most-wanted list. That's not the question. The question is twins."

"Twins?"

"And the answer is that twins, quadruplets, duodeceplets—they all have different fingerprints. Now, who first discovered fingerprints?"

"I have a feeling you're going to tell me?"

"Guess."

"Scotland Yard?" Taylor offered.

"Prehistoric tribes in France were aware of fingerprints and used them as cave decorations. In the sixteen and seventeen hundreds they were used as graphic designs and trademarks. The first attempt to study them seriously was in 1823—Dr. J. E. Purkinje, an anatomy professor, came up with a crude classification system. Fingerprints became sexy in the late 1800s. Sir Francis Galton, who was a preeminent scholar in the field of . . ." He cocked his eyebrows at Taylor. "Daily Double?"

"Dactyloscopy?"

"Nice try but no. In the field of heredity. He established that all fingerprints are different and they never change throughout one's life. The British government appointed Edward Richard Henry to a commission to consider using fingerprints to identify criminals. By around the turn of the century Henry had created the basic classification system they use in most countries. His system is called, coincidentally, the Henry system. New York was the first state to start fingerprinting all prisoners. Around 1902."

While she found this fascinating the urgency of the Hanover case kept prodding her. When he came up for air she asked, "If one were going to look for fingerprints, how would one do it?"

"'One'?" he asked coyly. "You?"

"No, just . . . one."

"Well, it depends on the surface. You—excuse me, *one*—should wear cloth gloves—not latex. If the surface is light-colored one would use a carbon-based dark powder. On dark, one would use an aluminum-and-chalk mixture; it's light gray. One would dust on the powder with a very soft, long-bristle brush. Then one removes the excess—"

"How?"

"Flip a coin," the detective said.

"One blows it off."

"A lot of rookies think that. But you tend to spit and ruin the whole print. No, use a brush. Now, powders only work on smooth surfaces. If you've got to take a print from paper there are different techniques. If the print's oily maybe it'll show up in iodine vapor. The problem is that you have to expose it in an enclosed cabinet and take a picture of the print very quickly because the vapors evaporate right away. Sometimes latents come out with a nitrate solution or ninhydrin or superglue. But that's the big league, probably over your—one's—skill level.

"Now, once *one* has the print, he or"—a nod toward her—"*she* has to capture it. You lift it off the surface with special tape or else take a picture of it. Remember: Fingerprints are *evidence*. They have to get into the courtroom and in front of an expert witness."

"Now," she said, "just speaking theoretically, could someone like me take fingerprints?"

"If you practiced, sure. But could you testify that prints A and B were the same? No way. Could you even tell if they were the same or different? Not easy, mama, not at all. They squoosh out, they move, they splot. They look different when they're the same, they look identical except for some little significant difference you miss. . . . No, it isn't easy. Fingerprinting is an art."

"How 'bout a machine, or something? A computer?"

"The police use them, sure. The FBI. But not private citizens. Say, Ms. Lockwood?"

"Taylor," she prompted.

"Perhaps if you told me exactly what your problem is I could offer some specific solutions."

"It's somewhat sensitive."

"It always is. That's why companies like us exist."

"Best to keep mum for the time being."

"Understood. Just let me know if you'd like another lesson. Though I do recommend keeping in mind the experts." He grew serious and the charming banter vanished. "Should the matter become, let's say, more than *sensitive*—a lot of our people here have carry permits."

" 'Carry'?"

"They're licensed to carry weapons."

"Oh," she said in a soft voice.

"Just something to think about."

"Thanks, John." Then she said, "I do have one question."

The hand in which a basketball would look so at home rose and a finger pointed skyward. "Allow me to deduce. The inquiry is: Where you can get a Dick Tracy fingerprint kit?" Before she answered yes, he was writing an address on the back of his business card. "It's a police equipment supply house. You can buy anything but weapons and shields there."

"Shields?"

"Badges, you know. Those you can buy—*one* can buy— in Times Square arcades for about ten bucks. But you're not supposed to. Oh, not to be forward, but I did happen to write my home phone number on the back of the card. In case any questions occur to you after hours, say."

She decided she liked this guy. "This's been fascinating, John. Thank you." She stood and he escorted her toward the

elevator, pointing out a glass case containing a collection of
blackjacks and saps.

"Oh, and Miss Lockwood? Taylor?"

"Yes?"

"Before you leave I was just wondering: Would you like
to hear the lecture I give to our new employees on the laws
against breaking and entering and invading privacy?"

Taylor said, "No, I don't believe I would."

▬▬▬▬▬

She'll be moody today.

Ralph Dudley sat in his creaky office chair. The nape of
his neck eased into the tall leather back and he stared at the
thin slice of sky next to the brick wall outside his window.
Gray sky, gray water. November.

Yes, Junie would be in one of her moods.

It was a talent, this intuition of his. Whereas Donald
Burdick, to whom he constantly—obsessively—compared
himself, was brilliant, Ralph Dudley was intuitive. He
charmed clients, he told them jokes appropriate to their age,
gender and background, he listened sympathetically to their
tales of sorrow at infidelities and deaths and to their stories
of joy at grandchildren's births. He told war stories of his
courtroom victories with a dramatic pacing that only fiction—which they were, of course—permits. With his
patented vestigial bow Dudley could charm the daylights
out of the wives of clients and potential clients.

He had sense and feeling while Burdick had reason and
logic.

And, sure enough, he was now right. Here came fifteen-
year-old Junie, a sour look on her face, trooping sullenly
into his office, ignoring the woman from the word processing pool who was handling a typing job for him.

The girl stopped in the doorway, a hip-cocked stance,
unsmiling.

"Come on in, honey," Dudley said. "I'm almost finished."

She wore a jumper, white blouse and white stockings. A

large blue bow was in her hair. She gave him a formal kiss
on the cheek and plopped into one of his visitor's chairs,
swinging her legs over the side.

"Sit like a lady, now."

She waited a defiant thirty seconds then slipped on her
Walkman headset and swiveled slowly in the chair, planting
her feet on the lime-green carpet.

Dudley laughed. He picked up the handle of his dictat-
ing machine. "Look, I've got one, too—a recorder."

She looked perplexed and he realized she couldn't hear
what he was saying (and would probably have thought his
joke was idiotic if she'd been able to). But Dudley had
learned not to be hurt by the girl's behavior and he unemotionally proceeded to dictate a memo that gave the gist of
some rules of law he believed he remembered. At the end of
the tape he included instructions to Todd Stanton, his associate at the firm, who would rewrite the memo and look up
the law Dudley hoped existed to support his points.

Ralph Dudley knew they sometimes laughed at him, the
young associates here. He never raised his voice, he never
criticized, he was solicitous toward them. He supposed the
young men (Dudley had never quite come to terms with the
idea of women lawyers) held him in all the more contempt
for this obsequiousness. There were a few loyal boys, like
Todd, but on the whole no one had much time for Old Man
Dudley.

"Grandpa," he'd heard that the associates called him.
Partners, too, although somewhat more subtly, joined in the
derision. Yet though this treatment soiled his days here—
and obliterated whatever loyalty he had once felt for
Hubbard, White & Willis—he was not overly troubled. His
relation with the firm became just what his marriage to
Emma had been: one of respectful acknowledgment. He was
usually able to keep his bitterness contained.

Junie's eyes were closed, her patent-leather shoes sway-
ing in time to the music. My God, she was growing up. Fifteen. It gave him a pang of sorrow. At times he had
flashes—poses she struck, the way the light might catch her

face—of her as a woman in her twenties. He knew that she, abandoned in adolescence, carried the seeds of adulthood within her more fertilely than other children.

And he often felt she was growing up far too fast for him.

He handed the dictated tape to the typist, who left.

"So," he said to the girl, "are we going to do some shopping?"

"I guess."

That question she heard perfectly, Dudley observed. "Well, let's go."

She shrugged and hopped off the chair, tugging at her dress in irritation, which meant she wanted to be wearing jeans and a T-shirt—clothes that she loved and that he hated.

They were at the elevator when a woman's voice asked, "Ralph, excuse me, you have a minute?"

He recognized the young woman from around the firm but couldn't recall a name. It stung him slightly that she had the effrontery to call him by his first name but because he was a gentlemen he did nothing other than smile and nod. "Yes, you're . . ."

"Taylor Lockwood."

"Sure, of course. This is my granddaughter, Junie. Junie, say hello to Miss Lockwood. She's a lawyer here."

"Paralegal, actually." Taylor smiled and said to the girl pleasantly, "You look like Alice."

"Huh?"

"*Alice in Wonderland.* It's one of my favorite books."

The girl shrugged and returned to the oblivion of her music.

Dudley wondered what this woman wanted. Had he given her some work? An assignment?

"I'd like to ask you something."

"What's that?"

"You went to Yale Law School, didn't you?"

"That's right, I did."

"I'm thinking of applying there."

Dudley felt a bit of alarm. He hadn't quite graduated, despite what he'd told the firm, and so couldn't exactly send a letter of recommendation for her.

But she added, "My application and letters and every-thing're in. I just want to know a little about the school. I'm trying to decide between there and Harvard and NYU."

Relieved, Dudley said, "Oh, I went there before you were born. I don't think anything I'd have to tell you would be much help."

"Well, somebody here said you helped them decide to go to law school, that you were very helpful. I was sort of hoping you could spare a half hour or so."

Dudley felt the pleasure he always did at even minor adulation like this. "Tonight?"

She said, "I was thinking tomorrow night maybe. After work? I could take you out to dinner."

A woman taking a man out to dinner? Dudley was nearly offended.

The paralegal added, "Unless you have plans."

He did, of course—plans he *wouldn't* miss. But that was at 10 P.M. He said, "I'm busy later in the evening. But how would seven be?" A charming smile. "I'll take you to my club."

Junie of the selective hearing said, "Like, Poppie, you told me they didn't let women in there."

Dudley said to her, "That's only as members, honey." To Taylor he said, "Come by tomorrow at six, we'll take a cab uptown. . . ." Then, calculating the taxi fare, he added, "No, actually a subway would be better. That time of day, traffic is terrible."

━━━━━

"Now he's going after the clients."

Donald Burdick knotted the silk tie carefully with his long fingers. He liked the feel of good cloth, the way it yielded yet was tough. Tonight, though, the smooth texture gave him little pleasure.

"First he rams through the accelerated vote and now I hear he's targeting the clients."

"The clients," Vera Burdick repeated, nodding. "We should've thought of that." She sat at her dressing table in the bedroom of their Park Avenue co-op, rubbing prescription retin-A cream on her neck. She wore a red and black silk dress, which revealed pale freckled skin along the unzipped V in the back. She was leaning forward studiously, watching the cream disappear.

A resolute woman, in her early sixties, she'd battled age by making tactical concessions. She gave up tanning fifteen years ago and carefully gained a little weight, refusing to join in the dieting obsession of many of her friends, who were now knobby scarecrows. She let her hair go white but she kept it shiny with Italian conditioner and wore it pulled back in the same style as her granddaughter. She'd allowed herself one face-lift and had flown to Los Angeles to have a particular Beverly Hills surgeon perform the operation.

She was now as she'd always been: attractive, reserved, stubborn, quiet. And virtually as powerful as the two men who'd influenced her life—her father and Donald Burdick, her husband of thirty-two years. Arguably she was *more* powerful in some ways than each of these men because people were always on guard with the masters of Wall Street, like Donald Burdick, but tended to get careless around women and be too chatty, to give away secrets, to reveal weaknesses.

Burdick sat on the bed. His wife offered her back and he carefully zipped up the dress and hooked the top eyelet. The partner continued, "Clayton's moving against them. It's pretty clever, I have to admit. While Bill Stanley and Lamar and I've been taking on as much debt as we can to poison the merger Wendall's been spending time with the clients, trying to convince *them* to pressure the partners at the firm to support the merger."

Vera too felt admiration for what Wendall was doing. Although a firm's clients have no official vote in firm affairs

they ultimately pay the bills and accordingly can exert astonishing influence over which way the partners vote. She'd
often said that if clients unionized against law firms it would
be time for her husband to find a new line of work.

"How's he doing it?" she asked, curious to learn his
technique.

"Probably promising big discounts in legal fees if they
support the merger. Those that still don't go along with
him—my clients or Bill's, the ones who won't support the
merger in any case—we're afraid he's going to sabotage."

"Sabotage. Oh, my. What's the vote so far?"

"It's closer than it should be."

"You've got the long-term lease with Rothstein, right?"
Vera asked. "That should slow him up some. When are you
signing it?"

"Friday or the weekend," he answered glumly.

"Not till then?" She winced.

"I know," he said. "The fastest they could get the papers
together. But it's okay—Clayton doesn't know anything
about it. Then I've been talking to Steve Nordstrom."

"At McMillan Holdings," Vera recalled. "Your biggest
client. Steve's the chief financial officer, right?"

A nod. "I'm closer to him than I am to Ed Gliddick, the
CEO. I'm going to get them to lobby some of the other partners against the merger."

"And Steve'll agree?"

"I'm sure he will. Gliddick's in charge. But he listens to
Steve. Wendall doesn't know about that either. I've been excruciatingly discreet. I . . ."

Burdick realized that he sounded desperate and hated
the tone of his voice. Then he glanced at his wife, who was
gazing at him with a savvy smile on her face. "We can do it,"
she said. "Clayton's not in our league, dear."

"Neither was that cobra on vacation last year. That
doesn't mean he's not dangerous."

"But look what happened to it."

Hiking in Africa, Burdick had accidentally stepped on
the snake in the brush. It had puffed out its hood and pre-

pared to strike. Vera had taken its head off with a swipe of a sharp machete.

Burdick found his teeth clenched. "Wendall just doesn't understand what Wall Street law practice is. He's crude, he bullies. He has affairs."

"Irrelevant." She began on her makeup.

"Oh, I think it *is* relevant. I'm talking about the survival of the firm. Wendall doesn't have *vision*. He doesn't understand what Hubbard, White is, what it should be."

"And how do you define 'should be'?"

Touché, Burdick thought. He grinned involuntarily. "All right, what *I've* made it. Bill and Lamar and I. Wendall wants to turn the firm into a mill. Into a big merger-and-acquisition house."

"Every generation has its own specialties. That's very profitable work." She set down the blush. "I'm not justifying him, darling. I'm only saying we should stay focused. We can't make logical arguments against the nature of the legal work he wants the new firm to handle. We have to remember that the risk is that as part of the merger he's going to burn the firm to the ground and then sow the ashes with salt. *That's* why we have to stop him."

She was, as usual, right. He reached for her hand but the phone rang and he walked to the nightstand to answer it.

Burdick took the call and listened in dismay as Bill Stanley's gruff voice delivered the message. He hung up and looked at his wife, who stared at him, clearly alarmed by his drawn expression.

"He's done it again."

"Clayton?"

Burdick sighed and nodded. He walked to the window and gazed outside into the trim, windswept courtyard. "There's a problem with the St. Agnes case."

Donald Burdick's oldest and second-most-lucrative client was Manhattan's St. Agnes Hospital. It had recently been sued for malpractice and Fred LaDue, a litigation partner, was handling the trial, which was in its fourth day now.

The case was routine and it was likely that the hospital was going to win. Stanley had just reported, however, that the plaintiff's attorneys—from a tough Midtown personal injury firm—had found a new witness, a doctor whose testimony could be devastating to St. Agnes. Even though he was a surprise witness, the judge was going to let him testify to-morrow.

The judgment could be for tens of millions and a loss this big might mean that St. Agnes—which was self-insured—would fire Hubbard, White & Willis altogether. Even if the hospital didn't do so, though, the credibility of Burdick and his litigation department would be seriously eroded and the hospital might push to support the merger; John Perelli's firm was renowned for its brutal handling of personal injury defense work.

"Damn," Burdick muttered. "Damn."

Vera's eyes narrowed. "You don't think that Wendall slipped your client's files to the other side, do you?"

"It did occur to me."

Vera took a sip of scotch and set the Waterford glass down on the table. Burdick's eyes were distant, trying to process this news. His wife's, however, had coalesced into dark dots. "One thing I'd say, darling."

The wind rattled the leaded-glass windows. Burdick glanced at the sound.

She said, "With a man like Wendall, we have to hit him hard the first time. We won't have a second chance."

Burdick's eyes dropped to the Pakistani carpet on the bedroom floor. Then he picked up the phone and called the night operator at the law firm. "This is Donald Burdick," he said politely. "Please locate Mitchell Reece and have him call me at home. Tell him it's urgent."

CHAPTER NINE

Taylor Lockwood walked through the breezy evening streets of the East Village, the curbs banked with trash, and thought of a funeral she'd attended several months earlier.

She'd sat in the front pew of the church in Scarsdale, north of the city, a wood-and-stone building built, someone behind her had whispered, by contributions from tycoons like J. P. Morgan and Vanderbilt. Although Taylor had been in black, that color did not seem to be requisite at funerals any longer; any somber shade was acceptable—purple, forest green, even dusk-brown tapestry. She sat on the hard pew and watched the family members, lost in their personal rituals of grief, tears running in halting streams, hands squeezing hands, fingers rubbing obsessively against fingers. The minister had spoken of Linda Davidoff with genuine sorrow and familiarity. He knew the parents better than the daughter, that was clear, but he was eulogizing well.

Most attendees had seemed sad or bewildered but not everyone had cried; suicide makes for an ambivalent mourning.

The minister had closed the service with one of Linda's poems, one published in her college literary magazine.

As he'd read, images of Linda had returned and the tears that Taylor Lockwood had told herself not to cry appeared fast, stinging the corners of her eyes and running with maddening tickles down her cheeks, even though she hadn't known the paralegal very well.

Then the organ had played a solemn cue and the mourners had filed outside for the drive to the interment.

As she'd told Reece, nothing that she'd found suggested that Linda Davidoff had had any connection with Hanover & Stiver or the loan deal. But there was something suspicious to Taylor about the way the girl had worked such long hours on the case then stopped abruptly—and then committed suicide.

She felt she needed to follow up on this question. Alice, after all, had wandered everywhere throughout Wonderland—a place, however, in which you sure wouldn't find the disgusting six-story tenement she now stood in front of. In the foul entry foyer the intercom had been stolen and the front door was open, swinging in the breeze like a batwing door in a ghost town saloon. She started up the filthy steps.

■■■

"It may look impressive, but the bank owns most of it," Sean Lillick said.

The young paralegal was sitting on the drafty floor, shirtless and shoeless, shoving a backpack under the bed as she walked in.

Taylor Lockwood, catching her breath from the climb, was surveying what Lillick was referring to: a wall of keyboards, wires, boxes, a computer terminal, speakers, guitar, amps. Easily fifty thousand dollars' worth of musical equipment.

Lillick—thin, dark-haired, about twenty-four—was smelling socks, discarding them. He wore black jeans, a sleeveless T-shirt. His boots sat in front of him. The only

clue as to his day job at Hubbard, White & Willis were two
dark suits and three white shirts, in various stages of recy-
cling, hanging on nails pounded crookedly into the wall. He
studied her for a moment. "You look impressed or confused.
I can't tell."

"Your place is a little more alternative than I expected."
The apartment was a patchwork. Someone had nailed
pieces of plywood, plastic or sheet metal over cracks and
holes. Joints didn't meet, plaster was rotting, floorboards
were cracked or missing. In the living room: one hanging
bare bulb, one floor lamp, one daybed, one desk.

And a ton of bank-owned musical instruments and gear.

"Have a seat."

She looked helplessly about her.

"Oh. Well, try the daybed. . . . Hey, Taylor, listen to this. I
just thought it up. I'm going to use it in one of my pieces:
You know what a preppy is?"

"I give up."

"A yuppie with papers."

She smiled politely. He didn't seem concerned about the
tepid response and wrote the line down in a notebook. "So
what do you do?" she asked. "Stand-up comedy?"

"Performance art. I like to rearrange perceptions."

"Ah, musically speaking," she joked, "you're a re-
arranger."

He seemed to like her observation too and mentally
stored it somewhere.

Taylor walked over to a music keyboard.

Lillick said, "You're thinking organ, I know. But—"

"I'm thinking Yamaha DX-7 synthesizer with a digital
sampler, MIDI and a Linn sequencer that should store about
a hundred sequences in RAM. You mind?"

He laughed and waved his hand. She sat on a broken
stool and clicked on the Yamaha. She ran through "Ain't
Misbehavin'."

Lillick said, "This machine cannot deal with music like
that. I think it's having a breakdown."

"What do you play?" she asked him.

"Postmodern, post–New Wave. What I do is integrate music and my show. I call myself a sound painter. Is that obnoxious?"

Taylor thought it was but just smiled and read through some of his lead sheets. In addition to standard musical notation they included drawings of pans and hammers, lightbulbs, bells, a pistol.

"When I started composing I was a serialist and then I moved to minimalism. Now I'm exploring nonmusical elements, like choreography and performance art. Some sound sculpture, too. I love what Philip Glass does only I'm less thematic. Laurie Anderson, that sort of thing. I believe there should be a lot of randomness in art. Don't you think?"

She shook her head, recalling what she'd told Reece that morning: How she believed music should stay close to melodies that resonated within people's hearts. She said, "You're talking to Ms. Mainstream, Sean," and shut off the system. She asked, "Got a beer?"

"Oh. Sure. Help yourself. I'll take one, too, while you're at it."

She popped them and handed him one. He asked, "You perform?"

"You wouldn't approve. Piano bars."

"They serve a valuable function."

Irritated by his too hip, and too righteous, attitude, Taylor asked, "Are you being condescending?"

"No. I mean it. I like classics too." Lillick was up, hobbling on one boot to his rows of records and CDs and tapes. "Charlie Parker. I got every Bird record ever made. Here, listen." He put on an LP, which sounded scratchy and authentic. "Man, that was the life," Lillick said. "You get up late, practice a bit, hang out, play sax till three, watch the sunrise with your buddies."

Taylor, lost in one of Bird's solos, mused, "Man died young."

"Thirty-five," Lillick said.

"World lost a lot of music."

"Maybe it wouldn't have been so, you know, deep, so righteous if he'd lived longer."

Taylor said, "Maybe just the opposite. Hooked on smack's gotta affect you."

He nodded at his record collection, which did contain a lot of mainstream jazz. "See, I'm not a snob. We need people like that. If you don't have rules and traditions there's nothing to break."

If it ain't broke, don't fix it, Taylor thought. But she wasn't here to debate the philosophy of music with him.

Lillick retrieved a fat joint and lit it up. He passed it toward Taylor. She shook her head and, examining the musical armada of equipment, asked, "What're you doing at a law firm, you're so into artsy-fartsy?"

"Steady salary, what else. The way I look at it, Hubbard, White & Willis is supporting the arts." He seemed uneasy, as if the conversation was going down paths he didn't want to tread.

He suddenly pulled out a pad of music staff paper and a pencil. "Keep talking. I work best when I'm only using half my mind."

She asked, "What I came to ask you about . . . You took over for Linda Davidoff on the Hanover & Stiver case, right?"

"Yeah."

"What do you know about her?"

Lillick looked at his cracked plaster walls for a moment and wrote a measure of music. She sensed he was performing for her—playing the distracted artist.

"Linda Davidoff?" she repeated.

After a moment he looked up. "Sorry . . . Linda? Well, we went out a few times. I thought she was more interesting than most of the prep princesses you see around the firm. She wanted to be a writer. It didn't go very far between us."

"Why'd she stop working on the Hanover case?"

Silent for a moment, Lillick thought back. "I'm not sure. I think she was sick."

"Sick? What was wrong with her?"

"I don't know. I remember she didn't look good. She was—"

"—pale," Taylor recalled.

"Yeah, exactly. I saw her filling out insurance forms a couple of times. I asked her about it but she didn't tell me anything."

"Do you know why she killed herself?" Taylor asked.

"No, but I'll tell you I wasn't wildly amazed she did. She was too sensitive, you know? She took things too much to heart. I don't what she was doing working for a law firm." Lillick erased and rewrote a line. He hummed it. "Give me a B-flat diminished."

Taylor turned on the DX-7 and hit the chord.

"Thanks." He wrote some more musical notations.

"Where'd she live?"

"I don't know—in the Village somewhere, I think. What's up? Why're you so interested in Linda?"

"Screwup with the New Amsterdam bill, going way back. They were majorly underbilled and I'm supposed to check out what happened. When you took over for her did she say anything about the case?"

Lillick shook his head.

Taylor asked, "You're still billing time on the case, aren't you?"

"Some. But Mitchell's handling most of it himself." Lillick didn't seem to have any reaction to her questions.

"Anybody she was close to?"

"Her roommate, Danny Stuart. He's an editor or something. Lives in the West Village. Over on Greenwich Street, I think." He rummaged in a stack of papers. "I've got the number somewhere." He handed it to her. "Hey, back in a flash."

He ducked into the john.

Which gave Taylor the chance she'd been waiting for. She dropped to her knees and found the backpack that Lillick had been stashing when she'd entered. It had seemed to her that he'd hidden it just a little too quickly when she walked inside.

A fast unzip revealed cash. A lot of it. Taylor had only ten seconds for a fast estimate but figured the total would probably be something on the order of thirty or forty thousand dollars. An amount equal to his yearly salary at the firm—which didn't, of course, pay in greenbacks.

And, a regular of the Downtown performing circuit herself, Taylor knew that, to quote her father, there was no way in Satan's backyard that anyone would ever make any kind of serious money playing music in bars.

Which meant that, no, Sean, the bank *didn't* own most of your equipment.

She'd come here only for information but had found another suspect.

Taylor shoved the bag back a few seconds before the young man returned. "Better roll," she said. "Thanks for the beer."

"You like goat?"

"What?"

"I'm thinking of going over to this place on Fourteenth. The goat's the best in the city. It's a totally happening place."

The thought of another night partying was more than she could handle. Besides, she had a mission back at the firm.

"Not tonight."

"Hey, this place is mondo cool. Bowie hangs out there. It's so packed you can hardly get in. And they play industrial out of one set of speakers and the Sex Pistols out of the other. I mean in the same room! Like, at a thousand decibels."

"Kills me to say no, Sean. But I'll take a pass."

Wendall Clayton liked the firm at night.

He liked the silence, the jeweled dots of boat lights in New York Harbor, liked taking a mouthful of cigar smoke and holding it against his palate, free from the critical glances his secretary and some of the more reckless younger lawyers shot his way when he lit up a Macanudo in the firm.

This after-hours atmosphere took him back to his days just after law school, when he'd spend many of his nights proofreading the hundreds of documents that make up typical business deals: loan agreements, guarantees, security agreements, cross-collateralization documents, certificates of government filings, corporate documents and board resolutions.

Proofreading . . . and carefully watching the partners he was working for.

Oh, he'd learned the law, yes, because in order to be good a lawyer must have a flawless command of the law. But to be a *great* lawyer—that requires much more. It requires mastering the arts of demeanor, tactics, leadership, extortion, anger and even flirtation.

Sabotage too.

He now looked over statements by a witness in a case that Hubbard, White was currently defending on behalf of one of Donald Burdick's prize clients, St. Agnes Hospital in Manhattan. Sean Lillick and Randy Simms, Clayton's head of the SS, had dug up the identity of a doctor who had first-hand knowledge of the hospital malpractice St. Agnes was allegedly guilty of.

Clayton had slipped the identity of this man to the plaintiff—in effect, scuttling the case against his firm's own client.

This troubled him some, of course, but as he read through the witness's statements and realized that the St. Agnes doctors had indeed committed terrible malpractice, he concluded that his sabotage was in fact loyalty to a higher authority than the client or the firm: loyalty to abstract justice herself.

He rolled these thoughts around in his complex mind for a few minutes and reached this conclusion: that he could live with St. Agnes Hospital's extremely expensive loss in the trial.

He hid these documents away and then opened another sealed envelope. Sean Lillick had dropped it off just before he'd left for the night. He read the memo the paralegal had written him.

Clayton's money was being well spent, he decided. Lillick had apparently aristocratized the right people. Or begged them or fucked them or whatever. In any case the information was as valuable as it was alarming.

Burdick was taking an extreme measure. The firm's lease for its present office space in Wall Street would be up next year. This expiration had been a plus for Clayton's merger because it meant that the firm could move to Perelli's Midtown office, which was much cheaper, without a difficult and expensive buyout of an existing lease.

The purpose of the secret talks Lillick had learned about between Burdick, Stanley and Harry Rothstein, the head of the partnership that owned the building, was to negotiate a new, extremely expensive long-term lease for the existing office space.

By entering the lease, the firm would take on a huge financial commitment that would cost millions to buy its way out of. This would make Hubbard, White a much less attractive target for a merger. The full partnership didn't need to approve the lease, only the executive committee, which Burdick's side controlled.

The lease agreement, Lillick had learned, wouldn't be signed until this weekend.

Son of a bitch, he raged. Well, he'd have to stop the deal somehow.

He put Lillick's memo away and began thinking about defensive measures. If Burdick learned what Clayton was up to, particularly with the St. Agnes case and the lease, he and his bitchy wife would strike back hard. Clayton began to worry about loose ends.

He picked up the phone and called Lillick.

The boy's cheerful voice drooped when he realized who the caller was.

"That information was . . . helpful."

This was one of Clayton's highest forms of compliments. *Helpful*.

"Like . . . I mean, I'm glad."

"I'm a little concerned though, Sean. You *are* being careful, aren't you?"

The boy hesitated and Clayton wondered if there was anything more to his uneasiness than a phone call from his boss.

"Of course."

"I'm aware of people asking questions around the firm, Sean. Anybody been asking you questions?"

"Uh, no."

"You are making sure you cover tracks? Being a good Boy Scout or nature guide or something?"

"Yeah, I'm not stupid, Wendall."

"No, of course you're not. Just make sure everything's covered up carefully, no way to trace what you and I've been up to. You know legal defense fees can be *so* expensive. They can eat up all one's savings in a flash."

The boy's silence told him that the threat had been received.

Clayton looked up into the doorway, where a young woman stood at attention. "Better go, Sean. Be in early tomorrow. Snip any ends, okay?"

"Sure."

The partner hung up, his eyes on the woman. She was one of the night stenographers from the word processing department. Her name was Carmen and she was slim and had a complexion like a week-old tan. She wore tight blouses and dark skirts that would be too short for the day, but on the evening shift the dress code was more relaxed.

"I got your call, Mr. Clayton. You need some dictation?"

Clayton looked at her legs then her breasts. "Yes, I do."

Carmen had a five-year-old son, fathered by a man who was currently in prison. She lived with her mother in the Bronx. She had a patch of stretch marks on her lower belly and a tattoo of a rose on her left buttock.

"Why don't you close the door," he said. "We don't want the cleaning staff to disturb us."

She waited until he'd taken his wallet from his suit jacket pocket and opened it up before she swung the door shut and locked it.

CHAPTER TEN

It was nearly 8 P.M. but for some reason the closing of a corporate merger that had begun at 2 that afternoon ran into difficulties and was not yet completed—some delay in Japanese regulatory approvals.

The Hubbard, White & Willis lawyers and paralegals working on the case, clutching stacks of documents, scurried back and forth between the several conference rooms devoted to the closing like ants stealing bread crumbs from a picnic though with considerably more content faces than their insect counterparts—presumably because ants don't make a collective $4,000 per hour for carting around bits of soggy food. The clients, on the other hand—the *payers* of those legal fees—were nothing but frustrated.

Back from her trip to Lillick's apartment, Taylor Lockwood had learned many intimate details about the closing because she'd been dodging the lawyers and clients for the past hour. Like the clients in the delayed deal, Taylor had her own frustrations.

John Silbert Hemming had neglected to tell her that dactyloscopy powder didn't come off.

She'd just finished fingerprinting Reece's burglarized file cabinet and painstakingly transferring the sticky tape of the two dozen latents she'd found to cards. She thought back to what Hemming'd told her. Yes, he'd mentioned the different kinds of powders. He'd mentioned how to spread it around and how to brush, not blow, the excess away.

But he hadn't told her the stuff was like dry ink.

Once you—once *one*—dusted it onto the surface the damn stuff didn't wipe off. The smear just got bigger and bigger.

She wasn't concerned about the file cabinet that had contained the note. She was concerned about Mitchell Reece's coffee mug, emblazoned with "World's Greatest Lawyer," which she'd dusted to get samples of his prints to eliminate those from the ones she lifted off his cabinet.

Fingerprinting powder coated the mug like epoxy paint. She did her best to clean it then noticed she'd gotten some on her blouse. She pinched the midriff of the shirt and fluffed the poor garment to see if that would dislodge the powder. No effect. She tried to blow it away, and—as her tall private eye had warned—spit into the smear, which immediately ran the powder into the cloth. Permanently, she suspected.

Taylor sighed and pulled on her suit jacket to cover the smudge.

She hurried down to Ralph Dudley's office, where she lifted samples of his fingerprints, then on to Thom Sebastian's, where she did the same.

Finally, back in the paralegal pens, she took samples of Sean Lillick's prints from several objects in his cubicle. Then back in her own cubicle she put the fingerprint cards in an envelope and hid it under a stack of papers in the bottom drawer of her desk.

She found the phone number that Lillick had given her—Danny Stuart, Linda Davidoff's roommate—and called him. He wasn't in but she left a message asking if they could meet; there was something about Linda she wanted to ask him about.

She hung up and then happened to look down at her desktop and, with a twist in her gut, noticed the managing attorney's daily memo. In the square for Tuesday of next week were these words:

> *New Amsterdam Bank & Trust v. Hanover & Stiver.*
> *Jury trial. Ten a.m. No continuance.*

As she stared there was suddenly a huge explosion behind her.

Taylor spun around, inhaling a scream.

Her eyes met those of a young man in a white shirt. He was standing in the hall, staring back at her. He held a bottle of French champagne he'd just opened. "Hey, sorry," he said. Then smiled. "We just closed. We finally got Bank of Tokyo approval."

"I'm happy for you," she said and snagged her coat then started down the hallway as he turned his groggy attention to opening more bottles and setting them on a silver tray.

▄▄▄▄▄▄

The drapery man watched her pull her overcoat on and step into the lobby, the door swinging shut behind her.

He patiently waited a half hour, just in case she'd forgotten anything, and when she didn't return he walked slowly down the corridor to Taylor Lockwood's cubicle, pushing the drapery cart in front of him, his hand near his ice-pick weapon.

Upstairs the firm was bustling like mid-morning—some big fucking business deal going on, dozens of lawyers and assistants ignoring him—but down here the place was dark and empty. He paused in the Lockwood woman's cubicle, checked the hallways again and dropped to his knees. In two minutes he'd fitted the transmitting microphone, like the one he planted in Mitchell Reece's phone, into hers.

The drapery man finished the job, tested the device, ran a sweep to make sure it wasn't detectable and walked to the entranceway of the paralegal cubicles.

Nearby was a conference room, in which he saw a half-dozen open bottles of champagne sitting on a silver tray. When he touched one with the back of his hand he found it was still cold. He glanced behind him, pulled on his gloves and lifted the first bottle to his mouth. He took a sip then ran his tongue around the lip of the bottle. He did the same with the others.

Then feeling the faint buzz from the dry wine—and a huge sense of satisfaction—he returned to the hallway and started pushing his cart toward the back door.

███████

"Never take a job," Sean Lillick said pensively, holding the door open, "where you have to hold things in your teeth."

Carrie Mason, standing in the door of his shabby East Village walk-up, blinked. "Never what?" she asked, entering.

"That's a line from a piece I'm working on right now. I'm, like, a performance artist. This one's about careers. I call it 'W2 Blues.' Like your W2 form, the tax thing. It's spoken over music."

"Never take a job that . . ." Pained, she said, "I don't think I get it."

"There's nothing to get," he explained, a little irritated. "It's more of a social comment, you know, than a joke. It's about how we're defined in terms of what we do for a living. You know, like the first thing lawyers say when you meet them is what they do for a living. The point is we should be human beings first and then have a career."

She nodded. "So when you just said you were a performance artist, that was, like, being ironic?"

Now, *he* blinked. Then, even more irritated, he nodded. "Yeah, exactly. Ironic."

He examined her from the corner of his eye. The girl was hardly his type. Although on the whole Lillick preferred women to men (he'd had his share of both since he came to New York from Des Moines five years ago) the sort of

women he wanted to fuck were willowy, quiet, beautiful and
passed cold judgment on anyone they bothered to glance at.

Carrie Mason didn't come close to meeting his specifica-
tions. For one thing, she was fat. Well, okay, not fat, but
round—round in a way that needed pleated skirts and bil-
lowy blouses to make her look good. For another, she was
polite and laughed a lot, which was evidence that she would
rarely pass moody judgments on anyone at all.

Lillick also suspected she blushed frequently and he
couldn't see himself getting involved with anybody who
blushed.

"You know," she said after a moment, "tailors hold pins
and things in their teeth. Fashion designers too. And car-
penters hold nails when they're building houses."

That was true. He hadn't thought of that. And her comment made him even angrier with her. "I meant more like,
you know, maybe holding bits of tape or tools or something." Then he added quickly, "The point is, like, just to
make people think about things."

"Well, it *does* make you think," she conceded.

Lillick took her coat. "You want a beer?"

She was studying the keyboards and computers. "Sure."

"Have a seat."

She ran her hand over the tie-dye bedspread and
glanced at her fingers to make sure the coloring didn't
come off.

Excuse me, your royal highness. . . .

She sat down. He opened a Pabst and handed it to her,
thinking only after he did that he probably should have
poured it into a glass. But to take it back and find a clean
mug would now seem stupid.

"I was surprised when you called, Sean."

"Yeah?" Lillick punched on a Meredith Monk tape. "I've
been meaning to. You know, you work with somebody and
you think, I'm going to call her up, yadda, yadda, yadda,
but you get caught up in things."

"That's sure true."

"Anyway, I was thinking of going over to this place for

goat...." But he stopped speaking fast, thinking what the hell would his buddies from the East Village say if they saw him at Carlos' with a fat preppy princess?

But he didn't need to worry; Carrie wrinkled her nose at the food. "Goat?"

"Maybe," he said, "we'll find someplace else. Whatta you like?"

"Burgers and fries and salads. Usual stuff, you know. I usually hang out at the bars on Third Avenue. They're fun. You know, sing along."

"When Irish Eyes Are Smiling..." God in heaven save me.

"You want me to...," Carrie began.

"Huh?"

"Well, I was going to say: If you want me to iron your shirt I'm, like, way good at that sort of thing."

The garment was a tan shirt printed with tiny brown scenes of European landmarks. It was one of his favorites and the cloth was wrinkled as a prune.

He laughed. "You iron this poor thing, it'd curl up and die."

Carrie said, "I like ironing. It's therapeutic. Like washing dishes."

In his five years in Manhattan he'd never ironed a single piece of clothing. He *did* do the dishes. Occasionally.

Outside a man's scream cut through the night. Then another, followed by a long moan. Carrie looked up, alarmed.

Lillick laughed. "It's just a hooker. There's a guy turns tricks across the air shaft. He's a howler." He pointed to a machine. "That's a digital sampler. It's a computer that records a sound and lets you play it back through your synthesizer on any note you want."

Carrie looked at the device.

Lillick continued, "I recorded the screaming one night. It was totally the best!" He laughed. "I performed a piece from Bach's *Well-Tempered Clavier,* only instead of the harpsichord sound it's a gay hooker shouting, 'Deeper, deeper!'"

She laughed hard. Then looked out the window toward

the diminishing wails. "I don't get downtown as much as I'd like."

"Where do you live?"

"East Eighty-fourth."

"Ah."

"I know," she said, blushing, as he'd predicted. "It's not so cool. But I kinda ended up there and I've got a three-year lease."

"So, how's Mexican?" he asked. He glanced down at his shirt. It wasn't *that* fucking wrinkled. "There's a place around the corner. I call it the Hacienda del Hole. Kinda a dive but the food's good."

"Sure, whatever." Then she suggested, "Or we could just hang out here. Like, maybe order pizza, watch the tube." Carrie nodded at his dusty TV set. "I like *Cheers,*" she said. "And *M*A*S*H.*"

Lillick only watched TV to pick up on pop culture icons he could trash in his performance pieces. He had to admit, though, he liked *M*A*S*H.* Well, and *Lucy* reruns. And *Gilligan's Island* (though not a soul in the universe knew *that*).

"It's kinda broken. I mean, the reception's pretty shitty."

He walked over to his Yamaha keyboard and turned it on. The amps sent a moan of anticipation through the warm air. "I'll show you how the sampler works. I'll play something for you."

"Good, I'd like to hear it. Hey, got another beer?"

He went to the fridge. "Those were the last. How 'bout wine?"

"Sure."

He poured two large tumblers and handed one to her. They tapped glasses. She picked a piece of cork or lint or something out of hers and they both drank.

Then she slipped off her white plastic headband and lay back on the bed. She ran her hand over the middle part of the mattress. "What's this?"

"What?"

"This lump?"

"I don't know. A pillowcase, I think."

But Carrie was frowning. "No, it's, like, weird. You better check it out."

He stood up and sat on the bed next to her, rummaged under the covers to find the lump. It turned out to be not a pillowcase but a woman's red high-heel shoe.

"How'd that get there?" Carrie laughed, teasing.

"I used it in one of my pieces."

"Uh-huh," she said, not believing him.

It's true, goddamn it, he thought angrily. I'm not a fucking transvestite. . . .

She looked into his eyes and, without even thinking about it, he leaned forward and kissed her. He tasted lipstick and the Binaca she'd sprayed into her mouth when he was busy pouring the wine.

Then she lifted the red shoe away, dropped it on the floor and directed his hand to her breasts.

This is weird. . . .

Carrie reached up and turned off the skewed floor lamp. The only illumination in the room was from the display lights on the synthesizer.

Weird. . .

He began to kiss her hard, desperately, and she kissed him right back.

She pulled off her jeans and sweater. Lillick stared at the huge breasts defined by the netlike cloth of her bra, nipples dark circles.

He kissed her for a full minute.

Weird.

Lillick realized that he'd left the recorder on the sampler running; it would store every sound in the room for the next twenty minutes. He supposed he should shut it off but in fact he didn't really want to get up. Besides, he figured, you never knew when you could use some good sound effects.

CHAPTER ELEVEN

Taylor wasn't sure when the idea occurred to her—probably 4 or 5 A.M. as she lay in bed, listening to the sounds of the city. She was in a half-waking, half-dreaming state—in Wonderland or on the far side of the looking glass.

She'd been thinking about the evidence she'd gathered. A brief comparison of the prints on the safe with her suspects—Sebastian, Lillick and Dudley—wasn't conclusive but it was more likely than not that Sebastian had left several prints on the safe.

But was there any way to verify that he—or someone else—had been in the firm that Saturday night, other than through the time sheets and key card entry logs?

Sure, she realized, there was: The thief might've taken a cab or car service limo to the firm that late at night. And he might've just used his real name and employee number on the reimbursement or payment voucher.

And copiers too. If he'd been in the firm for some legitimate reason he might've used a copier—you had to use a special key, with your number on it, to activate the machine.

Or, she thought, excited about these leads, the thief might have logged onto one of the Lexis/Nexis computers.

Or used the phone.

Every service or function within the firm that can be charged to a client (plus a delightful 300 percent markup for overhead) is recorded in the firm computers.

She glanced at the clock: 7:40 A.M.

Brother.

Exhausted, she rolled out of bed. At least she didn't have a hangover—and she'd managed to change into boxers and a T-shirt last night, saving her skin from more stigmatas of Victoria's Secret.

Let's go, Alice.... This is getting curiouser and curiouser....

At 9 A.M. exactly Taylor was standing in the accounting department at Hubbard, White & Willis.

"I'm doing a bill for Mitchell Reece," she told the computer operator. "Can you let me see the copier card, taxi and car service voucher ledger, phone records and Lexis/Nexis log-ons for last Saturday and Sunday?"

"It's not the end of the month." The operator snapped her gum.

"Mitchell wants to give the client an estimate."

Snap.

"An estimate of disbursements? It couldn't be more than a thousand bucks. Who'd care?"

"If you don't mind," Taylor said sweetly. "Please."

Snap. "I guess." The woman hunched over the keys and typed several lines. She frowned and typed again.

Taylor bent over the computer screen. The screen was blank.

Snap, snap...

"I don't know what's going on. There's no taxi vouchers. There *always* are on Saturday." Taylor knew this very well. The rule was if you had to work on Saturday the firm paid for your taxi to and from your apartment or house.

Alarmed, Taylor said, "How about the copiers?"

The fingernails tapped. The operator squinted, tapped some more and stared at the screen. "Well, this's damn funny."

"Nobody made any copies either."

"You got it."

Snap.

"Phones? Lexis/Nexis?"

The clattering of keys. "Nothing."

Taylor asked, "You think the files were erased?"

"Hold on a minute." Her fingers tapped as noisily as her popping gum.

Snap, snap...

The young woman looked up. "That's it. Erased. Must've had a software hiccup or something. The disbursement and incidental expense files for the past week've been deleted. Taxis, meals, copiers, even the phones. All gone."

"Has that ever happened before?"

"Nup. Never."

Snap.

Sean Lillick stopped by Carrie Mason's cubicle to say good morning to her.

He could tell immediately how pleased she was to see him comply with the famous morning-after rule.

They talked for a few minutes and then he said how much he wanted a cup of coffee and, as he'd expected, she was on her feet immediately and asking him, "How do you want it?"

"Black," he answered because even though he liked a lot of sugar it was cooler to say "Black."

"Sure. I'll be right back."

"You don't have to—," he started to say.

"No problem."

She trotted off down the hallway.

Which gave him the chance to put her computer room access card back into her purse.

That's what'd been so weird last night.

The fact that the sex had been initiated by *her*.

Because the whole point of calling her up was to get her over to his place, get her drunk, seduce her and when she was dozing afterward steal her access card, which would allow him to erase the telltale files of expenses—like the taxi he'd taken from the firm to the office of the plaintiff's lawyer in the St. Agnes case, or the phone calls he'd made about the new lease with Rothstein. After he'd talked to Wendall Clayton earlier Lillick had realized that he *had* been pretty careless and needed to, as the partner had said, "snip some ends."

Hence, the grand seduction last night.

Weird...

Carrie now returned with the coffee and when she handed it to him their hands met and they looked into each other's eyes for a moment. It took perhaps two seconds for the guilt to prod him into looking away and he said quickly, "Got a big project. Better run. I'll call you."

Donald Burdick believed that bringing one's first client into a law firm was the most significant milestone in the career of a Wall Street lawyer.

Unlike graduation from law school, unlike admission to the bar, unlike being made partner—all of which are significant but abstract stages in a lawyer's life—hooking a money-paying client was what distinguished, in his metaphor, the nobility from the gentry.

Many years ago Burdick—a young, newly made partner at Hubbard, White & Willis—had just finished the eighteenth hole at Meadowbrook Club on Long Island when one of the foursome turned to him and said, "Say, Donald, I hear good things about you. Legal-wise, I'm saying. You interested in doing a little work for a hospital?"

That had been on a Sunday afternoon and two days later Burdick had presented to the executive committee of the firm his first signed retainer agreement—with the huge St. Agnes Hospital complex in Manhattan.

At nine-thirty this morning Donald Burdick sat in his office with the chief executive officer of St. Agnes, a tall, middle-aged, mild-spoken veteran of hospital administration. Also present were Fred LaDue, the senior litigation partner handling the malpractice case against the hospital, and Mitchell Reece.

Three of these four appeared very unhappy, though for different reasons. Burdick, because of what he'd learned last night—that with the new witness St. Agnes would probably lose the malpractice trial, which would make the hospital throw its support to Clayton and the pro-merger crowd. The CEO, of course, because his hospital now stood to lose millions of dollars. Lawyer LaDue, because Burdick had summarily ordered that he stand down today and that a young associate Mitchell Reece, take over the cross-examination of the new witness.

Reece, on the other hand, was calm as a priest though it was clear the man hadn't had more than a few hours' sleep. He'd been preparing virtually nonstop since Burdick and LaDue had briefed him last night around 9 p.m.

"Who is this guy?" the CEO asked. "The witness?"

"That's the problem. He was working at St. Agnes when they brought the plaintiff in. He didn't treat the patient himself but he was in the room the whole time."

"One of our own people? Testifying against us?" The CEO was dumbfounded.

"Apparently he was a visiting professor from UC San Diego."

"Can't we object?"

"I did," LaDue said plaintively. "Judge overruled me. The best he did was give us a chance to depose the witness before he goes on."

Reece said, "I'll do that in a half hour. The guy goes on the stand at eleven."

"How bad do you think his testimony's going to be?" the administrator asked.

"From what the other side's lawyer said," Reece explained bluntly, "it could lose you the case."

Burdick, who realized he had been squeezing his teeth together with fierce pressure, said, "Well, Mitchell, perhaps it isn't as hopeless as you're painting it."

Reece shrugged. "I don't think it's hopeless. I never said it's hopeless. But the plaintiff's lawyers've upped their settlement offer to thirty million and they're holding firm. That means that this witness is the smoking gun."

LaDue sat and stewed. The doughy man was as pale as always though at this particular moment his waxen complexion was largely due to the fact that he'd done a very clumsy job at the trial so far.

Burdick played with a manicured thumbnail. He was furious that Clayton had probably spent thousands of dollars to track down this witness and had anonymously sent his name to the plaintiff's attorney.

"What do you have in mind, Mitchell?" LaDue asked. "How're you going to handle the cross?"

Reece looked up and started to answer but then Burdick's secretary walked into the doorway. "Mr. Reece, your secretary said you've just got an important call. You can take it in the conference room there."

"Thank you," he said to her. Then glanced at his watch. "I'll be busy for the rest of the morning, gentlemen. I'll see you in court."

CHAPTER TWELVE

If she hadn't been initiated, Taylor Lockwood would never have known she was watching a trial.

She saw a bored judge rocking back in his chair, distracted lawyers. She saw clerks walking around casually, no one really concentrating on what was going on. She saw dazed jurors and few spectators—a half dozen or so, retirees, she guessed, like the unshaven men who take trains out to Belmont or Aqueduct racetracks in the morning, just for a place to spend their slow days.

She'd found Reece in the hall at the firm earlier and wanted to update him on what she'd learned—the fingerprints and the erased files. But he was jogging from the library to his office, two huge Redweld folders under his arms. He paused briefly to tell her that he'd been called in to handle an emergency cross-examination and that he could see her at the courthouse on Centre Street later, around noon.

Taylor had decided to sit in on this portion of the trial and catch him in the hall afterward. Maybe they could have lunch.

She now looked around the courtroom in which *Marlow v. St. Agnes Hospital and Health Care Center* was being tried and located the plaintiff. Mr. Marlow sat in a wheelchair, pale and unmoving. Unshaven, his hair disheveled. His wife was nearby, with her hand resting on his arm. Taylor's father, a trial lawyer himself, had instilled enough cynicism in his daughter to make her believe that, while undoubtedly the man had suffered a serious injury, the wheelchair might just be a prop and there was no need for him to be looking as destroyed as he did here.

The door opened, and in walked a man she recognized from the firm. It took her a moment to place the name. Randy Simms—either the III or the IV. She recalled that he was a protégé of Wendall Clayton. He sat in the back row, by himself, putting away a cellular phone. He put his hands in his lap and sat perfectly still, perfectly upright.

She scanned the rest of the visitors and was surprised to find Donald Burdick himself in the gallery. He too glanced at Randy Simms, a faint frown on the old partner's face.

Finally, papers were sorted out and the judge pulled off his glasses. In a gruff voice he told the plaintiff's counsel that he could present his witness.

The lawyer rose and called to the stand a handsome, gray-haired man in his mid-fifties. He gazed pleasantly out at the jury. Under questioning from the plaintiff's counsel, he began his testimony.

Taylor Lockwood worked primarily for corporate lawyers at Hubbard, White & Willis but she knew the basics of personal injury law. This man's testimony was clearly devastating to St. Agnes.

Dr. William Morse's credentials were impeccable and, unlike many expert witnesses, who testify based only on what they've read in reports long after the accident, he was actually present at the hospital when the alleged malpractice occurred. The jury members took in his comments and looked at each other with lifted eyebrows, obviously impressed with the man's demeanor and by what he was saying.

"Let's reiterate what happened here," the plaintiff's lawyer said. "In March of last year a doctor at St. Agnes treated a patient—Mr. Marlow there in the wheelchair, the plaintiff in this case—who was suffering from arthritis and adrenal insufficiency with seventy milligrams of cortisone acetate in conjunction with one hundred milligrams of indomethacin."

"That's correct," Morse said.

"Did you observe him do this?"

"I saw the injection and then looked at the chart afterward and told him immediately the mistake he'd make."

"And why was that a mistake?"

"Mr. Marlow had a preexisting ulcerous condition. Everyone knows that such a patient should absolutely not be treated with the drugs he was administered."

"I'd object, sir," Reece said politely. "The witness can't speak for, quote, everyone."

Dr. Morse corrected, "The medical literature is quite clear that such a patient should not be treated with those particular drugs."

The plaintiff's lawyer continued, "What was this doctor's reaction when you told him that?"

"He said that I was not on the staff, I was a visiting physician and, in effect, I should mind my own business."

"Objection," Reece called again. "Hearsay."

The plaintiff's lawyer said, "I'll rephrase. Sir, after you called attention to what you perceived as a dangerous condition, did anyone take any steps to correct it?"

"No."

"What happened then?"

"I told a nurse to monitor the patient carefully and that I thought he might have serious adverse reactions. Then I went to see the chief of staff."

"That would be Harold Simpson?"

"Yessir."

"And what was his reaction?"

"Dr. Simpson was not available. I was told he was playing golf."

"Objection. Hearsay."

"He was not available," the witness corrected.

"What happened then?"

"I returned to Mr. Marlow's ward to see how he was doing but he was unconscious, comatose. The nurse I'd left to monitor his condition was gone. We stabilized his condition. But he remained comatose."

"Would it have been possible, when you called attention to the drugs that had been improperly prescribed, to administer an antidote—"

"Objection," Reece called. "He's suggesting that we poisoned the plaintiff."

"You *did*," Dr. Morse snapped.

"Your honor?" Reece asked.

"A more neutral term, counselor," the judge said to the plaintiff's lawyer.

"Yessir. Dr. Morse, would it have been possible to administer other drugs to counteract the damaging effects of the drugs that the St. Agnes staff doctor administered?"

"Absolutely. But it would have to be done immediately."

"And what happened then?"

"That was my last day at the hospital. I returned to California the next day and as soon as I arrived I called the hospital to check on the status of the patient. I was told that he'd come out of the coma but had suffered irreparable brain damage. I left messages for the chief of staff, the head of the procedures committee and the head of the department of internal medicine. No one ever called me back."

"No further questions."

A murmur from the peanut gallery at the deadly testimony. Taylor concurred with the apparent reaction. She thought, Okay, we just lost the case.

The judge rocked back in his chair and said, "Mr. Reece, cross-examination?"

Mitchell Reece stood and—in smooth motions—buttoned his jacket, straightened his paisley tie.

"Thank you, your honor. First of all"—he turned to the jury—"I'd like to introduce myself. I'm Mitch Reece. I work for Hubbard, White & Willis, along with my friend and colleague, Fred LaDue, who I think you know. And he's been gracious enough to let me visit with you for a few hours to-day." He smiled, creating a camaraderie with six men and women bored numb from days of medical testimony.

Hunkered down behind two octogenarian trial buffs, Taylor watched him pace back and forth slowly.

Reece said, "Now, sir, you know I'm getting paid for asking you questions."

The witness blinked. "I—"

Reece laughed. "It's not a question. I'm just telling you that I'm getting paid to be here, and I assume you're getting paid to testify. But I don't think it's fair to ask you how much *you're* getting, if I'm not prepared to tell you how much *I'm* getting. And I'm not. Lawyers're overpaid anyway." Laughter filled the room. "So we'll just let it go at the fact that we're both professionals. Are we all together on that?"

"Yessir."

"Good.

The plaintiff's lawyers grew wary at this. One of the first ways cross-examining lawyers attack experts is to make them sound like mercenaries.

"Now, Doctor," Reece said, "let me ask you, how often do you testify at medical malpractice cases like this one?"

"Rarely."

"How rare would that be?"

The witness lifted his hand. "I've probably testified three or four times in my life. Only when I feel a terrible injustice has been done and—"

Reece held up his hand and, still smiling, said, "Maybe if we could just stick to answering my questions, please."

"The jury will disregard the witness's last sentence," the judge mumbled.

"So it's safe to say that you spend most of your time *practicing* medicine. Not testifying against other doctors."

"That's right."

"That's so refreshing, Doctor. I mean that. It's clear you care about your patients."

"Helping patients is the most important thing in the world to me."

"I applaud that, sir. And I welcome your appearance here—I mean that. Because these are very tricky technical matters that my friends on the jury and I have to wrestle with, and cooperative witnesses like you can make the issues clearer."

The witness laughed. "I *have* had a bit of experience."

"Let's talk about that, sir. Now, you practice internal medicine, correct?"

"That's correct."

"You're board-certified in internal medicine?"

"I am."

"And you have occasion to administer various drugs?"

"Oh, yessir."

"Would you say you have great experience administering them?"

"I would say so, sure."

"Those ways of administering them would include sublingual—that's under the tongue, right?"

"That's right."

Reece continued, "And rectally as well as administering injected medicines, like the sort that the plaintiff received."

"That's true."

"I don't want you to think I'm up to anything here, sir. You've testified that my client did something wrong in administering certain medicines and all I want to do is make it clear that your observations about what my client did are valid because of your expertise. We're all together on that?"

"All together, yessir."

"Good."

Taylor could see that the jury had brightened up. Something was happening. Reece was being *nice* to the witness. Shouldn't they be screaming at each other? The jury was confused and because of that they'd started paying attention.

She noticed something else: Though she hadn't seen him change his appearance, Reece's jacket, at some point, had become unbuttoned and in lifting his hand to straighten his hair he'd mussed it. He looked boyish. She

thought of him suddenly as a young Southern lawyer—a
hero in a John Grisham book.

The witness too had relaxed. He was less stiff, less cautious.

Taylor, though, thought that Reece had gone too far
with the good-old-boy approach. The witness was looking
good in the eyes of the jury; the credibility of his testimony
was improving. By now, she reflected, her father would've
cut the balls off this doctor and had him cowering on the
stand.

Reece said, "Now, let me quote from the record as best I
can." He squinted and recited, "'In March of last year a doctor from St. Agnes treated a patient—Mr. Marlow there in
the wheelchair, the plaintiff—who has arthritis and adrenal
insufficiency with seventy milligrams of cortisone acetate
in conjunction with one hundred milligrams of indomethacin.'"

"That's right."

"And you testified that you wouldn't have done that."

"Correct."

"Because of his preexisting ulcerous condition."

"Yes."

"But I've looked through his charts. There's no record of
his having an ulcer."

The witness said, "I don't know what happened with the
charts. But he told the doctors he had an ulcer. I was there. I
heard the exchange."

"He was in the emergency room," Reece said. "Generally
a busy place, a lot of doctors trying to cope with all kinds of
problems. I've been in them myself—cut my thumb bad last
year. . . ." Reece winced and smiled at the jury. "I'm a real
klutz," he told them. Then back to the doctor: "So will you
agree that it's *possible* that the person Mr. Marlow told about
his ulcer wasn't the person who administered the drugs?"

"That doesn't—"

Reece smiled. "Please, sir."

"It's possible. But—"

"Please. Just the question."

Taylor saw that Reece was preventing the witness from reminding the jury that it didn't matter who knew before the injection because Dr. Morse had brought it to the staff's attention just *after* the injection, when there was still time to correct it, but the staff had ignored him.

"It's possible."

Reece let this sit for a moment. "Now, Dr. Morse, there's been a lot of talk in this trial about what is and is not an accepted level of medical treatment, right?"

Morse paused before answering, as if trying to figure out where Reece was going. He looked at his own lawyer then answered, "Some, I suppose."

"I'm thinking that if, as you say, you wouldn't've treated the patient with these medications then I assume you feel that St. Agnes's treatment was below the standards of proper medical care?"

"Certainly."

Reece walked to a whiteboard in the corner of the courtroom, near the jury, and drew a thick line horizontally across it. "Doctor, let's say this is the standard-of-care line, all right?"

"Sure."

Reece drew a thin dotted line an inch below it. "Would you say that the level of care St. Agnes provided in administering those drugs was this far below the standard level of care? Just a little bit below?"

Morse looked at his lawyer and was greeted with a shrug.

"No. It wasn't just a little bit below. They almost killed the man."

"Well." Reece drew another line, farther down. "This far?"

"I don't know."

Another line. "This far below?"

Dr. Morse said in a solemn voice, "It was very far below."

Reece drew another two lines then stopped writing. He asked, "Once you get below a certain level of the standard of care . . . well, how'd you describe that?"

Another uncertain look at his lawyer then the witness answered, "I'd say . . . I'd guess I'd say it was malpractice."

"You'd characterize St. Agnes's treatment of Mr. Marlow," Reece said in a sympathetic voice, "as malpractice."

"Well, yes, I would."

A murmur of surprise from several people in the courtroom. Not only was Reece befriending the witness but his cross-examination was having the effect of making the witness repeat over and over again that the hospital had made a mistake. He had even gotten the witness to characterize the staff's behavior as malpractice—a legal conclusion that no defense lawyer in the world would have accepted from a plaintiff's witness. Yet it had been Reece himself who elicited this opinion.

What was going on here? Taylor glanced at Burdick and saw him sitting forward, clearly troubled.

A dozen rows behind him Clayton's representative, Randy Simms, sat immobile though with a slight smile on his face.

The judge looked at Reece, opposing counsel looked at Reece.

"I appreciate your candor, Doctor. Malpractice, malpractice." Reece walked back to the table slowly, letting the word sink into the jury's consciousness. He stopped and then added brightly, "Oh, Doctor, if you don't mind, I just have a few matters of clarification."

"Not at all."

Reece said, "Doctor, where are you licensed to practice?"

"As I said before, California, New Jersey and New York."

"No other state?"

"No."

Reece turned to look into Morse's eyes. "How about any other *country*?"

"Country?"

"Yessir," Reece said. "I'm just curious if you've ever been licensed to practice in any other country."

A hesitation. Then a smile. "No."

"Have you ever *practiced* medicine in another country?"

"I just said I wasn't licensed."

"I caught that, sir. But what I just asked was 'practiced,' Doctor, not licensed. Have you ever *practiced* medicine anywhere outside of the United States?"

The man swallowed, a look of horror in his eyes. "I've done some volunteer work. . . ."

"Outside of the country."

"Yes, that's right."

"And would you be so kind as to tell us which country, if that isn't too much trouble, Doctor?"

"Mexico."

"Mexico," Reece repeated. "What were you doing in Mexico?"

"I was getting a divorce. I liked the country and I decided to stay for a while—"

"This was when?"

"Eight years ago."

"And you practiced medicine in Mexico?"

Morse was looking at his fingertips. "Yes, for a while. Before I moved back to California. I set up a practice in Los Angeles. I found Los Angeles to be—"

Reece waved his hand. "I'm much more interested in Mexico than Los Angeles, Doctor. Now, why did you leave Mexico?"

Dr. Morse took a sip of water, his hands trembling. The plaintiff's lawyers looked at each other. Even the poor plaintiff seemed to have sat up higher in his wheelchair and was frowning.

"The divorce was final. . . . I wanted to move back to the States."

"Is that the only reason?"

The witness lost his composure for a moment as a time-lapse bloom of anger spread on his face. Finally he controlled it. "Yes."

Reece said, "Did you run into some kind of trouble down in Mexico?"

"Trouble, like the food?" He tried to laugh. It didn't work and he cleared his throat again and swallowed.

"Doctor, what is Ketaject?"

Pause. Morse rubbed his eyes. He muttered something.

"Louder, please," Reece asked, his own voice calm and utterly in control of himself, the witness, the universe.

The doctor repeated: "It's the brand name of a drug whose generic name I don't recall."

"Could it be the brand name for ketamine hydrochloride?"

The witness whispered, "Yes."

"And what does that do?"

Morse breathed deeply several times. "It is a general anesthetic." His eyes were joined to Reece's by a current full of fear and hate.

"And what is a general anesthetic, Doctor?"

"You know. Everybody knows."

"Tell us anyway, please."

"It's a solution or gas that renders a patient unconscious."

"Doctor, when you were in Mexico, did you have a patient, a Miss Adelita Corrones, a seventeen-year-old resident of Nogales?"

Hands gripped together. Silence. He wanted water but was afraid to reach for the glass.

"Doctor, shall I repeat the question?"

"I don't recall."

"Well, I'm sure she recalls you. Why don't you think back to the St. Teresa Clinic in Nogales. Think back seven years ago. And try to recall if you had such a patient. Did you?"

"It was all a setup! They set me up! The locals—the police and the judge—blackmailed me! I was innocent!"

"Doctor," Reece continued, "please just respond to my questions." His tie was loose, his face was ruddy with excitement, and even from the back of the courtroom Taylor could see his eyes shining with lust.

"On September seventeenth of that year, pursuant to a procedure for the removal of a nevus—that is, a birthmark—from Miss Corrones's leg, did you administer

Ketaject to her and then, when you perceived her to be unconscious, partially undress her, fondle her breasts and gen-
itals and masturbate until you reached a climax?"

"Objection!" Marlow's lead lawyer was on his feet.

The judge said, "Overruled."

"No! It's a lie," the witness cried.

Reece returned to the counsel table and picked up a
document. "Your honor, I move to introduce Defense
Exhibit Double G: a certified copy of a complaint from the
federal prosecutor's office in Nogales, Mexico."

He handed it to the judge and a copy to the plaintiff's
counsel, who read it, grimaced and said in disgust, "Let it in."

"So admitted," the judge intoned and looked back to the
witness.

Dr. Morse's head was in his hands. "They set the whole
thing up. They blackmailed me. I paid the fine and they said
they'd seal the record."

"Well, I guess it's been unsealed," Reece responded.
"Now, the report goes on to say that the reason Miss
Corrones was aware you were molesting her was that you
not only administered the wrong dosage of Ketaject but that
you injected it improperly so that most of the drug didn't
even reach her bloodstream. Is this what the prosecutor's report says?"

"I—"

"True or not true? Answer the question."

"They set me—"

"Is this what the report says?"

Sobbing, the man said, "Yes, but—"

"Wouldn't you say, sir, that you can hardly state my
client is guilty of malpractice because of the improper administration of drugs when you can't even knock out a
teenager enough to rape her?"

"Objection."

"Withdrawn."

"They set me up," the witness said. "Just to blackmail
me. They—"

Reece turned on him. "Well, then, Doctor, did you at

any time contact the law enforcement authorities in Mexico City or in the United States to report that you were being blackmailed?"

"No," he raged. "I paid them the extortion money and they said I could leave the country and they'd seal the record. I—"

"You mean," Reece said, "you paid the *fine* for your *punishment*. Like any other criminal. No further questions."

Taylor found herself sitting forward on the edge of the pew. She now saw Reece's brilliant tactic. First, he'd gotten the jury's attention. Expecting petty bickering, they'd seen Reece befriend the witness, surprising them and getting them to sit up and listen. Then he got the man to say the magic word that, by rights, Reece or LaDue or anyone on the St. Agnes legal team would try never even to allow into testimony, let alone elicit themselves: "malpractice."

And then, in a masterful stroke, he'd linked that characterization—that one magic word—to the witness's terrible behavior and completely destroyed his credibility.

Taylor saw a gleam in Reece's face, a flushing of the cheeks, fists balled up in excitement.

Reece turned. He noticed Donald Burdick in the back of the courtroom. The two men looked at each other. Neither smiled, but Burdick touched his forehead in a salute of respect.

Taylor turned and looked at Burdick then behind him. Finally Randy Simms showed some emotion. His lips were tight and his eyes bored into the back of Donald Burdick's head. He rose and stepped out of the courtroom, which was utterly silent.

Except for the sobbing of the witness.

CHAPTER THIRTEEN

She stopped him in the hallway of the court.

Reece smiled when he saw her.

"How'd I do?"

"How do you think? I'd say you mopped up the floor with him."

"We'll see." Reece continued, "What most lawyers don't realize is that cross-examination isn't about being an orator. It's about having information. I called a private eye I've used out in San Diego and he dug up the dirt on the guy. Cost me—well, cost St. Agnes—fifty thousand. But it saved them a lot more than that."

"You enjoyed it, didn't you?"

"Handling the cross? Yep." He hesitated a moment, and finally spoke, though whether it was what he'd originally intended to say or not she couldn't tell. "I sometimes feel bad for them—people like that witness—when I tear apart their testimony. But in this case it was easy. He was a rapist."

"You believe he did it? What happened in Mexico?"

He considered. "I *chose* to believe he did something

wrong. It's a mind-set thing. Hard to explain but, yes, I believe it."

Taylor reflected: You could certainly argue that their
client, the hospital, had done something wrong too—destroying the plaintiff's life; and she wasn't sure if the rape, if
it had actually occurred, undermined the legitimacy of
Morse's opinion about that.

She said nothing about any of this though and, indeed,
she secretly envied Reece his fervent view of right and
wrong. For her, justice wasn't quite as clear as that. It was a
moving target, like the birds she'd watch her father hunt
every fall. Some he hit and some he missed and there was
no grand design as to which.

"Listen," she said. "I've got some leads. Have time for
lunch?"

"Can't. I'm meeting one of the vice presidents from New
Amsterdam. I've got to be at the Downtown Athletic Club
fifteen minutes ago."

He looked around. "Let's talk later. But tell you what:
Come over to my place for dinner."

"I'm playing Mata Hari tonight. What's tomorrow?
Friday—how's that?"

"Make it Saturday. I'm meeting with the bank people all
day tomorrow and I'm sure it'll go into dinner." He fell silent
as someone walked by, a sandy-haired man in coveralls,
who glanced at them quickly and then continued on.
Reece's eyes followed the man uneasily as he walked away.

"Paranoid," he muttered with a smile, gave her hand a
fast squeeze and then left the courthouse.

On her way back to the firm Taylor's willpower faded,
her lust for a fast-food burger won and she decided she'd get
something to eat.

This was how she found out that Mitchell Reece had
lied to her.

Instead of going back to the office she'd headed north,
to a Burger King, and as she turned the corner she saw
Reece ahead of her. But he was walking *away* from the

Downtown Athletic Club, where he'd said he was going for lunch. She slowed, stung at first, then thinking, No, he probably meant another athletic club: the *New York* Athletic Club on Central Park South in Midtown.

Only, if that was so, why was he disappearing into the Lexington Avenue subway stop? The train went uptown but there were no stops anywhere near the NYAC. And why was he taking a train in the first place? The rule on Wall Street was that if you went anywhere on firm business, you always took the car service or a cab.

Taylor had had four or five serious relationships in her life and one thing about men that irked her was that their fondness for the truth fell far short of other appreciations. Honesty was her new standard for love and she didn't think that it was too much to ask.

Reece, of course, was nothing more than her employer—but still the lie hurt; she was surprised at how much.

Well, maybe his plans had changed—maybe he'd checked his messages, found the witness had canceled and was on his way to Tripler's to pick up a couple of new shirts.

But on impulse she found herself pulling a token out of her purse and hurrying down the subway stairs.

Why? she wondered.

Because she was Alice. That was the only answer. And once you slip into the rabbit hole, Taylor Lockwood had learned, you go where fate directs you.

Which happened to be Grand Central Terminal.

Taylor followed the lawyer, climbing up the stairs, skirting a small colony of homeless. She watched Reece buy a train ticket and walk toward the gates. She stopped.

Squinting though the misty afternoon light that spilled across the huge cavern of the terminal, she caught a glimpse of him standing at a vending cart in front of a gate. A crowd of passengers walked between them, obscuring him.

She jockeyed aside to get a better view. Then she laughed to herself when she saw what he'd bought.

One mystery of Mitchell Reece had been solved.

He was walking to one of the commuter trains carrying a large bouquet of flowers.

He had a girlfriend after all.

Digging another token from her purse, she descended once more into the piquant subway to return to the firm.

━━━━━

Sometimes he felt like a juggler.

Thom Sebastian was thinking of an off-Broadway magic show he'd seen some years ago.

Sebastian remembered the juggler most clearly. He hadn't used balls or Indian clubs but a hatchet, a lit blow-torch, a crystal vase, a full bottle of wine and a wineglass.

From time to time, Sebastian thought of that show, of the tension that wound your guts up as the man would add a new object and send it sailing up in an arc, a smile on his face, eyes at the apogee. Everyone waited for the metal to cut, the torch to burn, the glass to shatter. But nope, the man's no-sweat smile silently said to the audience: So far, so good.

Sebastian, sitting in his office this afternoon, feeling de-pleted, coked out, 'phetamined out, now told himself the same thing.

So far, so good.

When he had learned that Hubbard, White & Willis had chosen not to make him a partner Thom Sebastian had held a conference with himself and decided after consider-able negotiation to cut back on his working hours; he was going to relax.

But that didn't work. Clients still called. They were of-ten greedy, they were occasionally bastards, but a lot of times they were neither. And whether they were or not was irrelevant. They were still clients and they were scared and troubled and needed help that only a smart, hardworking lawyer could give them.

Sebastian found to his surprise that he was physically incapable of slowing down. He continued at a frantic pace, his hours completely absorbed by two refinancings, a lever-aged buyout, a revolving credit agreement.

By his own real estate transactions, by his special project with Bosk, by his girlfriends, by arranging buys with his drug dealer, Magaly, by his family, by his pro bono clients, all in motion, all spinning, all just barely under control.

So far . . .

He desperately wanted sleep and that thought momentarily brought to mind another: The brown glass vial hidden in his briefcase. But it was no more than that—a passing image. Sebastian did not even consider slipping into the men's room to partake. He never did drugs within the walls of Hubbard, White & Willis. That would be a sin.

. . . so good.

He closed the door to his office then pulled a manila envelope out of his desk. He removed the computer printouts and began to read—all about Ms. Taylor Lockwood.

He found the information fascinating. He jotted a few notes and hid them under the blotter on the desk then fed the printouts themselves and the envelope through the shredder in his office.

Sweeping the phone from the cradle, Sebastian dialed her number from memory.

"Hello?"

"Hey, Taylor . . ."

He heard tension and anxiety in his own voice. This was bad. Take charge.

"Thom?"

"Yeah. How you doing?"

"Fine, but guilty. I'm finishing a Whopper."

With any other woman he'd have jumped on that line with both feet and flirted relentlessly. But he resisted and said casually, "Hey, you survived an evening with me. Not a lot of girls can make that claim. Oops, women. Meant to say 'women.' Have I offended you yet?"

"You're not even on the radar screen."

"I'll try harder." In fact he wasn't really in the mood to joke but he forced himself to maintain a certain level of patented Sebastian banter. "You realize that we're leaving for the airport in a half hour."

"And the 'we' would be who?"

"You and me."

"Ah. Our elopement. Your friend Bosk was first in line. You can be best lawyer."

Damn, she was fast. He'd run out of jokes. "Listen, speaking of your betrothed, I'm going out to dinner in the Hamptons tomorrow with him and a few other folks."

"I remember you mentioning that."

She had? That was interesting. Why'd she been paying attention to their offhand comments? "Hey, it's totally last-minute, I know, but any chance you'd like to come? It'll give me the chance to kill him so that I can move to the number one spot."

"Chivalrous."

He added gravely, "I have to warn you . . ."

"Yes?"

"It's not a stretch limo."

"That's not a deal-breaker. What's the occasion?"

"It's Take Someone to Dinner in the Hamptons Day. You *do* know about that, don't you?"

"I saw the card rack at Hallmark. I thought I'd have to celebrate by myself with popcorn and the tube."

"How 'bout it? Leave early, five-ish. We'll be back by midnight, one."

"Fair enough. Dress?"

"Business."

"Cool," she said. "I'll come by your office."

Sebastian set down the receiver and closed his eyes. He breathed deeply. He relaxed.

The motion of his imaginary juggler slowed. Unnecessary thoughts fell away. Projects that weren't immediate dissolved. The image of the Chinese-American girl he'd picked up last night and would be meeting at The Space tonight vanished. Some technical financial aspects of his project with Bosk rose then faded, as did a nasty, dark portrait of Wendall Clayton. Finally Sebastian was left with two thoughts, tossing them around slowly. One was the loan agreement he was working on, spread out on his desk before him.

The other was Taylor Lockwood.

He pulled the agreement toward him and looked at the words with a grave intensity. But ten minutes passed before he started to read them.

For Donald Burdick there was no square in New York City more beautiful than that at Lincoln Center.

The buoyant fountain, the soaring white rock architecture, the energetic Chagall ... these all came together as a testament to the power of culture and moved him now, as they always did. It was especially stunning on fall nights like this, when the concert halls radiated their rich glow into the misty dimness of the city.

Burdick, his hands in his cashmere coat pockets, paced slowly in front of the fountain. It was chilly but waiting inside the Metropolitan Opera, where he and his wife had tickets for Stravinsky later that night, would undoubtedly require him to speak to any number of other box holders, who like him were major patrons of the arts and arrived early for dinner in the private dining room.

At the moment he didn't want to be distracted.

He glanced up and saw the Silver Cloud ease to the curb and Sergei leap out to open Vera's door. She stepped onto the pavement in her sable coat. He remembered how a few years ago, as Vera had waited for a light to change on Madison Avenue, an animal rights activist had sprayed her mink with orange paint. His wife had grabbed the young woman's arm and wrestled her to the ground, pinned her there until the police arrived.

They hugged and she took his arm as they walked to the private entrance that led to the club reserved for the most generous patrons. Burdick had once calculated that, even adjusted for the charitable deduction, each glass of champagne here cost him roughly two hundred dollars.

They let another couple go ahead of them so they could take an elevator alone.

"St. Agnes?" Vera asked abruptly.

"Mitchell won. Well, they dropped their settlement offer to five million. We'll pay one. That's nothing. Everybody at the hospital's ecstatic."

"Good," she said. "And the lease? Did you sign it up?"

"Not yet. It's on for Monday now. Rothstein . . . I *hate* dealing with him. And we have to keep everything hush-hush so Wendall doesn't find out."

"Monday," she said, troubled, then his wife glanced at her reflection in the elevator's metal panel. She turned back to her husband. "I made some calls today. Talked to Bill O'Brien's wife."

This was an executive of McMillan Holdings, which was Hubbard, White's biggest client. The company was Burdick's client alone and he took home personally about three million a year from McMillan.

"Trouble?" Burdick asked quickly.

"Apparently not. Wendall hasn't approached them about the merger."

"Good," Burdick said. "He doesn't even know the board's meeting in Florida this week or if he does he hasn't made any rumblings about going down there."

Burdick had assumed that Clayton wouldn't waste the time trying to sway McMillan since it was so firmly in the antimerger court.

"But the board's been talking among themselves. They're wondering if the merger'd be good or bad for them."

"Bill's wife knows that?"

Vera nodded matter-of-factly. "She's sleeping with one of the board members: Frank Augustine."

Burdick nodded. "I wondered who he was seeing."

Vera said, "I think you have to get down to Florida and talk to them. As soon as possible. Hold their hands, rally them against the merger. Warn them about Clayton."

"I'll go this weekend. It'll be a good excuse to miss

Clayton's party on Sunday. Last thing in the world I want to do is spend time in that pompous ass's house."

Vera smiled. "I'll go," she said cheerfully. "One of us should be there, I think. Just to keep him a little unsettled."

And, Burdick thought as the elevator door opened, you're just the woman to do it.

CHAPTER FOURTEEN

■■■■■ *Ms. Lockwood:*

We cannot thank you enough for the opportunity to review your demo tape.

Taylor hurried to her apartment from her building's mailroom, clutching three return envelopes from three record companies. She'd called Dudley and told him that she wanted to change before seeing him for dinner at his club in Midtown and that she'd meet him there.

As she walked down the hallway she fantasized about the contents of the envelopes.

It so captivated the initial screener that he sent it to our A&R department, where it made the rounds in record (forgive the pun) time. Your masterly reinterpretations of the old standards in juxtaposition with your own works (masterpieces in fusion) make the tape itself worthy of production, but we would propose a three-record project of primarily original material.

Enclosed you will find our standard recording contract, already executed by our senior vice president, and, as an advance, a check in the amount of fifty thousand dollars. A limousine will be calling for you. . . .

Not able to wait until she got inside, she ripped the envelopes open with her teeth, all of them at once. The torn-off tops lay curled like flat yellow worms on the worn carpet behind her as she read the form rejection letters which were a far cry from the one that her imagination had just composed.

The one that said the most about the music business, she decided, began with the salutation "Dear Submitter."

Shit.

Taylor stepped out of the elevator and tossed the letters into the sand-filled ashtray next to the call button.

Inside her apartment, she saw a blinking light on her answering machine, and pushed the replay button as she stripped off her coat and kicked her shoes in an arc toward the closet.

Her machine had a number of messages:

Ralph Dudley, giving her the address of his club again.

Sebastian, confirming dinner tomorrow.

Reece, confirming dinner on Saturday.

Danny Stuart, Linda Davidoff's roommate, apologizing for not getting back to her but suggesting they meet for lunch in the Village tomorrow.

Three dinners and a lunch. Damn, how *do* spies manage to stay trim?

One more message remained. She hit play.

"Hello, counselor. Got some news. I'll be in town in a week or so and I'm going to take my little legal eagle out to dinner. Call me and we'll make plans."

Taylor instantly looked around her room to see how straightened up it was—as if the phone contained a video camera beaming the images directly to her father's law office.

She sat down slowly on the arm of the couch, Samuel Lockwood's call reviving a question Mitchell Reece had asked yesterday.

So how'd you end up in New York?

Taylor recalled perfectly sitting in front of her father two years ago, the man of medium build, jowly and pale—by rights, he should have broadcast an anemic image, but he filled the living room of their house in Chevy Chase, Maryland, with his powerful image.

She tried to gaze back at him.

But couldn't, of course.

Finally, the sound of spring lawn mowing from outside was broken by his asking, "You can simply try it, Taylor."

"I have other priorities, Dad."

"'Priorities,'" the lawyer said quickly, pouncing. "See, that very word suggests that there are several directions you'd want to go in." A smile. "In the back of your mind you're already entertaining the possibility that you'd like to be a lawyer."

"I mean—"

What *had* she meant? She was too flustered to remember.

"My talent—"

"And you *are* talented, darling. I've always recognized that. Your grades . . . Honey, A's in every government, politics, philosophy course you've ever taken."

And in music composition, music theory, improvisation and performance.

"Music too," he added, with perfect timing, diffusing her anger. Then he laughed, "But there's no way in Satan's backyard that anyone would ever make any kind of serious money playing music in bars."

"I don't do it for the money, Dad. You know that."

"Look, you should pursue everything. Lord knows I do."

And he had. Law, business, golf, tennis, skydiving, sailing, teaching.

"It's just that it's easier to get your law degree now. Going back after you're older . . . it limits your opportunities."

Reduced to a child before him, Taylor could think of no logical retorts. Well, the best legal minds in the country had engaged in forensic battle with Samuel Lockwood and lost. She said weakly, "I just feel alive when I play music, Dad. That's all there is to it."

"And what a feeling that must be," he said. "But remember that we go through stages in life. What excites us now isn't necessarily what sustains us all forever. I pitched a dozen no-hitters in college. And I never felt higher than being on the pitcher's mound. What a thrill that was! But making that my life? A pro ball player? No, I had other things to do. And I found getting up in court gave me exactly the same thrill. Even better, in fact, because I was in harmony with my nature."

"Music isn't a sport to me, Dad." She believed she was whining and hated herself for it.

"Of course not. I know it's an important part of your life." He then tactically reminded, "I was at every single one of your recitals." A pause. "I'm only saying that it would be better to excel in a profession—doesn't have to be the law, not by any means."

Oh, right . . .

"And work at the music part-time. That way if the . . . you call them gigs, right? If they *don't* happen, well, you'd still have something. Or you could do both. Your music could come first and law could be second."

He seemed to have forgotten that he'd absolved her from the practice of law just a moment earlier.

Continuing, Samuel Lockwood said, "There's a whole different approach to practicing nowadays. There are part-time arrangements. A lot of women have other 'priorities'— families and so on. Firms are flexible."

"I'm supporting myself playing, Dad. Not a lot of people are." Not that the eighteen thousand a year she'd made in clubs and playing weddings and a few corporate shows last year could be considered supporting herself.

"And what a feather in your cap that is," he said. Then frowned. "I've got a thought. How about a compromise? What if you got a job as a paralegal at one of the firms in Washington, one of our affiliated firms. I'll get you in. You can try out law firm life, see if you like it. I'll put aside some funds for school."

She'd said no at first but Samuel Lockwood was relentless and she'd finally given in.

"But I'll get a job on my own, Dad. I'll support myself. If I like it I'll apply to law school. But I'll play music at nights. Nothing's going to interfere with that."

"Taylor . . ." He frowned.

"It's the best I can do. And not in D.C. I'll go to New York."

He took a breath and then nodded his concession to her victory over him. "You've got backbone, counselor."

And he gave her a smile that chilled her soul—because it unwittingly revealed that this "spontaneous" thought of his had been born some time ago and nurtured over many nights as he lay in his twin bed, three feet from his wife's, trying to figure out exactly how to manipulate her.

Taylor was furious with herself for letting her guard down. He'd never intended that she work in Washington, wouldn't have presumed to link her with him by getting her a job and would never have threatened her music directly—out of fear that he'd push her away completely.

In the end, even though she'd defiantly resisted him, it turned out that Taylor had played right into his hand.

"You understand I'm doing this because I love you and care for you," he said.

No, she thought, I understand you're doing this because the thought of being unable to control the slightest aspect of your life is abhorrent to you.

She'd said, "I know, Dad."

But, as it turned out, the paralegal life was not as bad as she'd anticipated. Smart, tireless, unintimidated by the culture of Wall Street money and Manhattan society, Taylor had made a reputation for herself at the firm, quickly becoming one of the most popular paralegals, always in demand. She found that she enjoyed the work and had considerable aptitude for it.

So when a cycle came around for applying to law schools and Samuel Lockwood asked her which schools she'd decided to apply to (not *if* she intended to apply), she said what the hell and plunged forward with a yes and basked in the sunlight of her father's approval.

Taylor, lost in this complex answer to Reece's simple question, now realized that she was still frozen in place, perched on a sofa arm, her hand floating above her answering machine.

Why exactly was her father coming here? Where could they eat? Would the place she picked please him? Would he want to come see her perform? They sure couldn't eat at Miracles or one of the other clubs she played at; he'd make a fuss about the menu. Want to know what kind of oil they cooked with, send food back if it wasn't prepared just right.

The electronic woman in the answering machine told her, *"To save this message, press two. To erase this message, press three."*

She hit two and walked into the bedroom to dress for her Mata Hari date.

━━━━━

This is a Midtown club? she thought.

Taylor had expected that it would be more, well, spiffy. More of a power, platinum-card corporate watering hole and less of a tawdry college lounge. Well, maybe old money was allowed a little shabbiness. In any case, Taylor Lockwood looked at the fiercely bright lighting, the dusty moose head sprouting from the wall, the threadbare school banners and uncarpeted floor, and asked herself again, This is a club?

But Ralph Dudley was excited about the Knickerbocker Businessmen's Club. He was at home here and buoyant at showing off his nest to a stranger.

"Come along now," the partner said. And he ushered her into the club's dining room. He walked to what must've been his regular table and, amusing her beyond words, actually held the chair out for her and bowed after she'd sat.

"Have the steak, Miss Lockwood. They have chicken, too, but order the steak. Rare, like mine." The old partner's excitement was infectious, his eyes gleaming as if he were back in the arms of his alma mater.

They ordered. Dudley took instantly to his task as mentor and launched into a series of stories about his law school. It seemed an endless tumble of hard work, harmless collegiate pranks, chorale singers, respectable young gentlemen in suits and ties and tearfully inspiring professors.

All forty years out of date, if it wasn't complete fiction.

She nodded, smiled till she felt jowls and said "Uh-huh" or "No kidding" or "How 'bout that" every so often. She got good mileage out of "That's very helpful, just what I was wondering."

The waiter brought the steaks, charred and fatty, and although she wasn't particularly hungry, she found hers tasted very good. Dudley made sure she was looked after. He was a natural host. They ate in silence for a few minutes as Taylor took in the young men at the tables around them—recent grads, she assumed. In white shirts and striped ties and suspenders, they were just beginning the journeys that, in four decades, would take them to the destinations at which Donald Burdick and Ralph Dudley and Bill Stanley had arrived.

She looked at her watch. "You said you had some plans tonight. I don't want to interfere with them. I hope you're not working late?"

He gave her a charming smile. "Just meeting some friends."

The mysterious W.S.

Taylor took a sip of the heavy wine he'd ordered. "I'd rather work late than on weekends."

"Weekends?" He shook his head. "Never."

"Really?" she asked casually. "I was in on Saturday night. I thought I saw you. Actually I think it was early Sunday morning."

He hesitated a moment but there was nothing evasive about his demeanor when he answered. "Not I. Maybe it was Donald Burdick. Yes, that was probably it. I'm told we look alike. No, I haven't worked on a weekend since, let's see, '79 or '80. That was a case involving the seizure of foreign assets. Iranian, I think. Yes, it was. Let me tell you about it. Fascinating case."

Which it may very well have been. But Taylor wasn't

paying any attention. She was trying to decide if he'd been lying or not.

Well, looking at his frayed cuffs and overwashed shirt, she observed a motive for stealing the note: money. Dudley was a charming old man but he wasn't a player in Wall Street law and probably never had been. His savings dwindling, his partnership share decreasing as he made less and less money for the firm, he would have been an easy target when somebody from Hanover approached and asked him to let a man inside the firm—an industrial spy, they'd probably said.

Dudley finished his story and glanced at his watch.

It was nine-thirty and he was meeting W.S. in a half hour, she recalled.

He signed the bill and they wandered out of the club into the cold, damp ozone of a New York evening on the shag end of November.

Taylor hoped the cool air would wake her but it had no effect. The narcotics of red wine and heavy food numbed her mind. She groggily followed the partner down the front steps, half-wishing she partook in Thom Sebastian's magic wake-up powder.

She thanked Dudley for his insights and for dinner and said that his school had slipped into the front-runner spot.

This seemed to genuinely please him.

He said, "You all right, Taylor?"

"Fine, just a little tired."

"Tired?" Dudley said, as if he had never heard of the word. "I'll walk you to the subway." He started down the sidewalk in long, enthusiastic but gentlemanly strides.

CHAPTER FIFTEEN

"Wait."

Sean Lillick's voice was sufficiently urgent that Wendall Clayton stopped, frozen in the back entrance of the Knickerbocker Club.

"What is it?" the partner asked.

"There, didn't you see them? It was Ralph Dudley and Taylor Lockwood. They were going out the front."

Clayton frowned. It was a constant source of irritation that a has-been like Dudley belonged to the same club that he did. He resumed his aristocratic stride. "So?"

"What are they doing here?" Lillick wondered uneasily.

"Fucking?" Clayton suggested. He glanced toward the stairway, which led to the club's private bedrooms.

"No, they came out of the dining room, it looked like."

"Maybe he bought her dinner and *now* he's going to fuck her. I wonder if he can still get it up."

"I don't want them to see us," Lillick said.

"Why not?"

"I just don't."

Clayton shrugged. He looked at his watch. "Randy's late. What's going on?"

Lillick said, "I've got to leave about midnight, Wendall. If it's okay." His suit didn't fit well and he looked like a college boy out to dinner with Dad.

"Midnight?"

"It's important."

"What's up?" Clayton smiled. "Do you have a date?" He dragged the last word out teasingly.

"Just seeing some friends."

"I don't think it's 'okay.' Not tonight."

Lillick said nothing for a moment. Then: "It's pretty important. I've really got to."

Clayton examined the young man. Like most denizens of the East Village, he seemed damp and unclean. "One of your performances?"

"Yeah."

"Yeah," the partner mocked.

"Yes," Lillick corrected himself instantly though in a tone that approached rebellious.

"We've got so much to do. . . ."

"I mentioned it a week ago."

"And what a busy week it's been, don't you agree?"

"It'll just be a few hours. I'll still be at the office at six if you want."

Clayton had let him dangle enough. He said, "This once, I suppose, it's all right." He had plans of his own tonight and didn't give a rat's rosy ass what Lillick did after they were finished here.

"Thanks—"

Clayton waved him off and gave a reserved smile to Randy Simms, who now walked through the revolving door of the club.

Ignoring Lillick, as he always did, Simms said, "I saw Ralph Dudley outside. With a woman."

Piqued again by the reference to the old partner, Clayton snapped, "Appreciate the weather report, Randy."

Simms was six feet three, thin and solid. Ralph Lauren
might have designed a line of Connecticut sportswear
around him. A mother and her teenage daughter entered the
lobby. They eyed the young lawyer with similar degrees of
desire.

"How'd they get the lowdown on our witness?" Clayton
was referring to the evisceration of Dr. Morse on the witness
stand in the St. Agnes Hospital case.

"Reece used some private eye in San Diego."

"Fuck, that was good," Clayton said with admiration.
He didn't know Reece well but he'd make sure the associate
was guaranteed a partnership slot next year or the year after.

"When's our guest arriving?" Clayton asked him.

"Any minute now."

"Give me the details."

"His name's Harry Rothstein. Senior partner in the general partnership that owns the firm's building. He's got full
authority to go forward or pull the plug. He and Burdick are
planning to sign the new lease on Monday. Rothstein doesn't
seem to have any mistresses but I found some accounts in
the Caymans. Son's got two drug convictions."

"What kind?"

"Cocaine."

"I mean what kind of *convictions*?"

"Felony. One sale, one possession."

"Is he a good friend of Burdick's?"

Simms's face eased into a faint smile.

"What's that supposed to mean?" Clayton snapped
again.

"How can he be a friend of Donald's?" Simms asked.
"Rothstein's a Jew."

A tall, bald man walked through the door and looked
around.

"That's him," Simms said.

Clayton's face broke into a huge smile as he strode forward. "Mr. Rothstein. I'm Wendall Clayton," he called.
"Come join us, my friend."

At the corner of Madison Avenue and Forty-fourth Street Taylor and Ralph Dudley paused and shook hands.

He inclined his head toward her in a Victorian way she found quaint and said, "Which train're you taking?"

"I'll walk."

"I'll cab it, I suppose. Good luck to you. Let me know how you fare with Yale." He turned and walked away.

Taylor had thought she'd have to do a private-eye number: *Hey, follow that cab; there's a fiver in it for you.* But no: Dudley didn't flag down a taxi at all. He was on foot, going to meet the mysterious W.S., whom he had visited the night the note was stolen.

When he was a half block away, Taylor followed. They moved west through the eerie illumination of a city at night—the glossy wetness of the streets and storefront windows lit for security. Still plenty of traffic, some theaters letting out now, people leaving restaurants en route to clubs and bars. Taylor felt infused with the luminous energy of New York; she found that she'd sped up to keep pace with it and had nearly overtaken Dudley. She slowed and let him regain a long lead.

Out of the brilliant, cold, fake daylight of Times Square. Only now did Taylor feel the first lump of fear as she crossed an invisible barrier, into pimp city. The public relations firms hired by New York developers called this area Clinton; almost everyone else knew it by its historical name—the more picturesque Hell's Kitchen.

Taylor continued her pursuit even when Dudley hit Twelfth Avenue, near the river, and turned south, where the streetlights grew sparser and the neighborhoods were deserted, abandoned even by the hookers.

Then Dudley stopped so suddenly, catching Taylor in mid-thought, that she had to jump into a doorway to avoid being seen.

The concrete reeked of sour urine. Hugging the shadows,

she felt nauseous. When she looked again Dudley was gone.
Taylor waited for five minutes, breathing shallow gasps of
cold air, listening to the sticky rush of traffic on the West Side
Highway. Then she walked toward the spot where Dudley
had disappeared: the doorway of a small two-story building.
There were no lights radiating from the windows; she saw
they were painted over. An old sign, faded, read, *West Side Art
and Photography Club.*

W.S. on his calendar. So, a place, not a person.

He'd come here on Saturday night and then—possibly—gone to the firm around the time the note had disappeared.

But was there a connection?

Or was this just his hobby? Taking pictures or attending
lectures on Ansel Adams and Picasso?

She cocked her head and listened. She thought she
heard something. Wait, wait. Taylor tried to block out the
rush of the cars and trucks and believed she heard music,
something syrupy, full of strings, like Mantovani. Standing
in the doorway, her feet stinging from the unaccustomed exercise in very unsensible Joan and David heels, she leaned
against the stone and watched a cluster of intrepid rats
browse through a garbage pile across the street.

He goes in, she figured, he's got to come out.

Forty minutes later he did.

The door swung wide. Taylor caught an image of pink
and lavender. Soft music and softer light spilled out into the
street. A radio cab—owned by the company that the firm
used—pulled up. Dudley vanished immediately into the
car, which sped away.

The question was, what would Mitchell do?

No, that wasn't the question at all. She *knew* what he
would do. The question really was, did she have the guts to
do the same thing?

The grapevine says you've got balls.

Yeah, well . . . Taylor walked to the front door and
pressed the buzzer.

A handsome black man, large and trapezoidal, opened the door. "Yes?" he asked, poised and polite.

Taylor said, "Um, I'm here. . . ." Her voice clogged.

"Yes, you are."

"I'm here because a customer—"

"A member?"

"Right, a member referred me."

The bouncer looked past her and then opened the door. Taylor stepped inside.

It was like the lobby of an exclusive hotel. Smoky pastels, brushed copper, leather furniture, a teak bar. Three Japanese men, all in dark suits, sat on a plush couch, smoking furiously. They looked at Taylor briefly—hopefully—then, when she met their gaze with chill defiance, looked away fast.

A woman in her forties, wearing a conservative navy suit and white blouse, walked silently up to her. "How may I help you?" The smile of a maitre d'.

"I had a little time free tonight. I thought I'd check the place out."

"Well," the woman said, now playing tour director, "the West Side Art and Photography Club is one of the oldest art appreciation clubs in the city. Here's some literature." She handed Taylor a glossy brochure. There were programs of music, art shows, classes.

But how could she find out who Dudley met here?

Taylor nodded. "Ralph can't say enough good things about you."

"Ralph?"

"Ralph Dudley's a friend. I was going to meet him here earlier but—"

"Oh," the woman said quickly, "you just missed him. You should've said you knew him." She took back the brochure and tossed it in a drawer. "Sorry. I didn't know he'd referred you. ID, please."

"I—"

"Driver's license or passport."

What was Alice to do?

Play by the rules of topsy-turvy, what else?

She handed the license over and crossed her arms as the woman compared face and picture then went to a computer and typed in some information.

Apparently favorable results came back and the woman returned the license. "Can't be too careful, you know. Now, our membership fee is one thousand, and the hourly fee is five hundred per model. If you want a man, he'll have to wear a condom. Oral sex is completely up to the individual model; most do, some don't. Tipping is expected. The fee includes any standard toys but if you want something special it can probably be arranged. Will that be cash or charge?"

"Uh, American Express?"

"It'll show up as art instruction on your statement. One hour?"

"One hour, sure."

The woman took the card and asked, "Do you have any special requests?"

Taylor said, "Actually, I was thinking about something a little unusual. Could I have the, uh, model that Ralph Dudley sees?"

The hostess, trained to be unflappable, didn't look up from the charge voucher but hesitated for a millisecond. "You're sure?"

Thinking she'd never been less sure about anything in her life, Taylor Lockwood gave a slight smile and said, "Positive."

"There's a premium. Double."

"No problem." Smiling, Taylor took the credit card slip and a pen.

See the steadiness of my hand as I sign for the *two thousand Jesus Christ what am I doing dollars....*

The hostess disappeared into the back room. Muzak played quietly, a guitar rendition of "Pearly Shells." She returned a moment later with a key. "I've talked to her. She hasn't been with too many women but she's game to try."

"Good."

"I think you'll find her quite nice. Up the stairs, last room on the right. Liquor's free. Coke we can give you at cost."

"That's okay." Taylor walked into the cool corridor.

Topsy-turvy...

She knocked on the door. A voice called, "Come on in."

Taylor took a deep breath, exhaled and pushed into the room. She stopped, total shock in her eyes—an expression that perfectly matched the one on the face of the girl who stood, topless, in the center of the room.

It was the teenage girl she'd met in Dudley's office, Junie. His granddaughter.

The garter belt in the girl's hand fell to the floor with a dull clink. She said, "Oh, shit. Like, it's you."

CHAPTER SIXTEEN

 "You gotta, like, close the door," Junie said, regaining some composure. "It's a rule. Johnny, he's the bouncer, comes around and gets pissed, you don't."

Taylor stepped into the room, shut the door.

Junie said darkly, "Like, Ralph isn't going to be so happy this happened, you know."

Taylor whispered, "You're his granddaughter?"

"Like, helloooo. Whatta you think? Of course not. That's only what he tells people."

The girl was heavily made up, with dark streaks of brown and blue eye shadow that made her face sleek and serpentine. She retrieved the garter and began untangling it. "What it is, he's one of my oldest customers." Then she laughed. "I mean one of the dudes I've been seeing for the longest time. But, you know, he's one of the oldest, too. Probably, like, *the* oldest."

Taylor looked at a plush armchair. "Can I sit down?"

"It's your hour. Have a drink, you want."

Taylor poured sparkling wine into a crystal champagne glass. "You want any?"

"Me?" Junie looked horrified. "I can't drink. I'm under-age, you know."

Taylor blinked.

The girl laughed. "That's, like, a fucking joke. Of *course* I drink. Only they don't let us when we're working."

Taylor said, "You mind?" as she eased her shoes off. A swell of pain went through her feet then slowly vanished.

"Mind? Usually people take off a lot more than their shoes."

"So tell me about you and Ralph."

"I guess I oughta ask why."

"He could be in trouble. I need to find out whether he is or not."

The girl shrugged, meaning: That's not a good enough answer.

"I'll pay you."

This was a better response.

"I guess I oughta see the duckets."

"The what?"

The girl held her palm out.

Taylor opened her purse. She hadn't brought much of Reece's bribe money. She wadded together about two hundred dollars, keeping twenty for herself for cab fare home.

"I get that as a tip for a blow job," Junie said. "If the son of a bitch's cheap."

Taylor handed her more money. "That's all I have."

Junie shrugged and put the money in a dresser drawer. She pulled out a T-shirt and worked it over her head. "So, Poppie—that's what I call him—he likes girls my age. He came to the house last year and we had a date. It was like to-tally bizotic but we kind of hit it off, you know?" She whispered, "We started meeting outside the club. They get really pissed, they find out. But we did it anyway. He brought me some totally def clothes. Nice shit, you know. From the good stores. Anyway, we did some weird things, like, he took me to this art museum, which was a real bore. But then we went to the zoo. . . . Like, I've never been there before. It was way

wild. We just kept hanging out more and more. He's lonely.
His wife died and his daughter is a total bowhead."

"Junie . . . is that really your name?"

"June. I like June."

"June, last Saturday night, was Ralph here?"

"Yeah."

"When?"

"Around ten or eleven, I guess. We had our regular appointment, you know. I'm his on Saturday night. Sorta a tra-
dition."

"Then what?"

She fell silent. Shrugged.

"Another two hundred."

The girl said, "I thought you don't have any more
money."

"I can give you a check."

"A check?" Junie laughed.

"I promise it won't bounce."

"That was, what, five hundred, you said?"

Taylor hesitated. "You have a good memory." She wrote
the check out and handed it to her. Mitchell, you're going to
see a very weird expense account for this project.

Junie slipped the check into her purse. "Okay, but he
didn't want me to tell anybody. . . . He went to your company."

"The law firm?"

"Yeah."

"What was he doing?"

"That's the thing: He wouldn't say. I'm, like, what're you
going there for this time of night? I mean, it's midnight or
whatever. He said he had to—something about a lot of
money. But he wouldn't tell me what. And he told me never
tell anybody."

At least anybody who didn't pay her seven hundred dollars.

Taylor asked, "Has he ever mentioned a company called
Hanover & Stiver?"

"Naw, but he don't talk—I mean, he *doesn't* talk about his business too much. He's always correcting what I say. It's so mundo-boring."

Taylor stood slowly, slipped her swollen feet back into her shoes. She walked painfully to the door. She paused.

"How old are you?"

"Eighteen. And I've got a driver's license."

"I've had fake ones too, honey."

"Okay, I'm sixteen. But I tell Ralph I'm fifteen. He likes it that I'm younger."

"Do you go to school or anything?"

A laugh. "Where're you from? I made sixty-eight thousand dollars last year and have a hundred Gs in a, you know, retirement fund. Why the fuck would I want to go to school?"

Why indeed?

Taylor let herself out into the hallway, through which echoed a cacophony of voices and sounds very different from those she was used to at Hubbard, White & Willis.

At lunchtime the next day, her feet only marginally recovered from their abuse the day before, Taylor Lockwood was sitting across from a diminutive young man in a West Village diner: Danny Stuart, Linda Davidoff's former roommate.

The menu of the place, which had been Stuart's choice, was heavy on foods that had swayed in the wind when alive, and light on main courses that had walked around on two or four legs, the latter being by far Taylor's favorite.

"So," she asked, "you know Sean Lillick too?"

"Not at all really. I met him through Linda and went to some of his shows. But he's a little avante-garde for me."

"You're an editor?"

"That's mostly a hobby. Some of us put together an alternative literary magazine. I'm a computer programmer by profession."

Taylor yawned and stretched. A joint popped. The walls of the place were badly painted, swirls of dark paint didn't cover the lighter enamel underneath. The decorations were à la *Mother Jones* and Woodstock. But the space, she knew, had been a Beat club in the fifties. William Burroughs and Allen Ginsberg had hung out here—the ancient floor felt spongy under the chairs and the wooden columns were carved with the initials of hundreds of former patrons. What these walls have heard, she thought.

Danny ordered sprouts and nuts and yogurt; Taylor, a garden burger. "Bacon?"

"No bacon," the waitress replied through her pierced lips.

"Ketchup," Taylor tried.

"We don't have ketchup."

"Mustard?"

"Sesame-soy paste or eggless mayo."

"Cheese?"

"Not your kind of cheese," the waitress responded.

"Plain'll be just fine."

The woman vanished.

Stuart said, "I think I remember you from Linda's funeral."

Taylor nodded. "I didn't know many people there, except the ones from the firm."

"You a lawyer?" he asked.

"Paralegal. How did you meet her?"

"Just a fluke. You know, your typical New York story. You come to New York from a small town, look for a place to live, you need a roommate 'cause the rents are so high. The guy I was rooming with got AIDS and moved back home. I needed to split the rent and Linda'd been staying at some residence hall for women. She hated it. We roomed together for, I guess, about nine or ten months. Until she died."

"Did you know her well?"

"Pretty well. I read some of her pieces and did some editing for her. She wrote reviews for us and I was hoping eventually to publish some of her poems."

"Was she good?"

"She was young; her work was unformed. But if she'd kept at it I know she would've gone someplace."

"What was her style like? Plath?" Taylor had read some of Sylvia Plath's poetry and recalled that she too had committed suicide.

Stuart said, "Her poetry was more traditionally structured than Plath's. But her personal life? Yep, just as turbulent. The wrong men, always heartbroken. Too stoic. She needed to scream and throw things more. But she kept it all inside."

The food came and Danny Stuart dug eagerly into his huge mass of rabbit food. Taylor started working on the sandwich, which she decided should be named not the garden but the cardboard burger.

"How did it happen, the suicide?" she asked.

"She was up at her parents' summer house in Connecticut. The back deck was above this big gorge. One night, she jumped. The fall didn't kill her but she hit her head and got knocked out. She drowned in a stream."

Taylor closed her eyes and shook her head. "Did she leave a note?"

He nodded. "Well, it wasn't really a note. It was one of her poems. When you called and said you were curious about her I thought you'd like to see it. I made you a copy. It's dated the day before she died. It talks about leaving life behind her, all the cares. . . . I was going to publish it in my magazine but, you know, I haven't had the heart."

He handed her the Xerox copy. Taylor read the title: "When I Leave."

She looked at Danny and said, "I hope I can ask you something in confidence. Something that won't go any further."

"Sure."

"Do you think Linda killed herself because of something that happened at work?"

"No."

"You sound pretty certain."

"I am. I know exactly why she killed herself."

"I thought no one knew."

"Well, I did. She was pregnant."

"Pregnant?"

"I don't think anybody knew except me. She got an EPT kit? It was just a couple of weeks before she died. I saw the kit in the bathroom and asked her about it. You know, we were like girlfriends. She confided in me."

"But why would she kill herself?"

"I think the father dumped her."

"Who was the father?"

"I don't know. She was seeing somebody but never talked about him or brought him around the apartment. She was real secretive about him."

"Breaking up . . . that upset her so much she killed herself?"

Stuart considered. She thought, studying his face: poet's eyes, artist's eyes. Unlike Sean Lillick, this was the real thing. He said, "There's more to it. See, Linda had no business working at that law firm. She was too sensitive. The business world was way too much for her. She got thrown too easily. Then when her personal life came crashing down I think it pushed her over the edge."

"But you don't know if there was anything specific at the firm that upset her? Anything she might've felt guilty about?"

"Nope. She never mentioned a word about that. And she probably would have. As I said, she and I were like, well, sisters."

So, the rabbit hole of Wall Street had proved too much for poor Linda Davidoff.

Without the heart to read the girl's suicide poem, Taylor put it in her purse and continued to eat her bland lunch while she and Danny talked about life in the Village.

Her face broke into another major yawn. She laughed and Stuart joined her.

"Not getting enough sleep lately?" he wondered.

"The problem," she explained, "is that I've been living an after-hours life when I'm not an after-hours person. I'm a during-hours person."

CHAPTER SEVENTEEN

Alice was on another trip through the looking glass.

This time, in a limo.

Taylor and Thom Sebastian were speeding down the Long Island Expressway Friday after work. The driver's eyes flicked to the radar detector needle as often as they glanced at the highway.

"I'm totally psyched you came," Sebastian said with apparent sincerity. "I thought you were going to boogie in with the Big E."

"E?"

"Excuse, you know. I—"

"Get that a lot?" she filled in.

"Yeah." He grimaced. "Now let me tell you about Bosk."

"What's the story behind the name?"

"His real handle's Brad Ottington Smith. B-O-S. Bosk. I'm Sea-bastian. Sea Bass. Get it? Okay. His father and mother have been separated practically since he was born. She has a house in Boston and his father has an apartment on the Upper East Side. They kept the summer place in the

Hamptons and have it on alternate weeks. They—that's the parents they—can't talk to each other without bloodshed so they have their lawyers schedule the visits to the house."

"And we're the mother's week."

"Right."

"Sounds like it's going to be a bucket of kicks and giggles. What is she, a wicked witch?" Taylor asked.

"All I'll say is she's more powerful than his father."

"What does *he* do?"

"Dad? What he does is he's rich. He's a senior partner at Ludlum Morgan, the investment bank."

"Bosk." She laughed. "I feel like I want to give him a Milk-Bone when I call him that. What firm does he work at?"

As he'd done the other night, though, he grew reluctant to give much away about Bosk professionally.

"Little shop in Midtown." Sebastian busied himself opening a Budweiser, handed it to her. Popped another.

"The mother?"

"Ada travels, entertains, does what any fifty-five-year-old sorority sister does: manages her portfolio. It's about a hundred million." Sebastian sipped the beer and let his hand stray—accidentally on purpose—to her knee. "Ho, boy, Taylor. This's gonna be primo. Good food, good drink, good people."

She lifted his pudgy fingers off her skirt. "And good behavior."

Sebastian moaned, then sat back in silence, and they gazed out the dim windows as dusk enveloped the flat, sandy landscape.

The Ottington Smith family manse was a three-story Gothic Victorian house, white with dark blue trim, about a hundred miles east of New York on the South Shore of Long Island. Two towers rose to widow's walks, which overlooked a huge yard and three connected outbuildings. The house itself was covered with skeletons of vines and wisteria. A spiked, wrought-iron fence surrounded a labyrinth of grounds. Much of the property had been reclaimed by tangles of forsythia, which sported sparse tags of brown and yellow leaves.

"Addams Family," Taylor said.

The circular driveway was full of cars. The limo paused and they got out. "God, more German cars than in Brazil," Sebastian said.

"Porches. I love porches," Taylor said. She sat on a wooden swing and rocked back and forth. "Wish it were thirty degrees warmer."

He rang the bell. A woman in her mid-fifties came to the door. Her dry, blond hair swept sideways Jackie Kennedy–style and was sprayed firmly into place. She wore a lime-green silk dress woven with pink and black triangles that pointed feverishly in all directions. Taylor bird-spotted Chanel.

The woman's face was long and glossy, the high bones holding the skin like a taut sail. Her jewelry was large. A blue topaz on her tanned, wrinkled finger was easily fifty carats.

"Thomas." They pressed cheeks and Taylor was introduced to Ada Smith—introduced, then promptly examined: the dynamics of the eyes, the contour of skin. The mouth especially. The review was mixed and Taylor believed she understood why: Bosk's little girlfriends—age twenty-three or twenty-four—could be forgiven their youth. Taylor had broken the three-oh barrier and yet had hardly a crow's foot or defining jowl.

She hates me, Taylor thought.

Yet Ada's smile and charm didn't waver; she'd been brought up right. "Call me Ada, please. I don't know where Bradford is. The others are in the den. Bradford's the cocktail and cigar director. I'm in charge of dinner. That will be at eight."

Then she was gone.

From the back hallway, a bellowing voice: "Sea Bass, Sea Bass!"

Sebastian ran toward him and grunted. "Bosk-meister! Yo!"

They slapped fists, reminding Taylor of bull rams smacking horns.

Their host was in chinos, Top-Siders and a green Harvard sweatshirt. His hands and face were red, his eyes watering from the cold. "We've been chopping wood for the fire."

A girl giggled at the apparent lie.

"Well," Bosk said, "carting it in. Same as chopping it. Just as much work."

Bosk leaned forward, his arm on Sebastian's shoulders. He whispered, "Jennie's here and she brought Billy-boy, you can believe it."

"No way! Is she totally fucked, or what?" Sebastian looked around uneasily. "And how 'bout Brittany?"

"Couldn't make it."

The lawyer's eyes were immeasurably relieved and Taylor remembered something from the club about unreturned phone calls.

Then Bosk's eyes danced to Taylor. " 'Lo. You're . . .?"

"Taylor Lockwood."

"Right, you're the one who won't marry me."

"True, but you're in good company." She nodded at Sebastian. "I won't marry him either. You have a nice place here."

"Thanks. I'll show you around later. Come on inside. We've got a fire going."

After she'd washed up she joined the crowd in the den. They were mostly in their twenties. Names went past—Rob and Mindy and Gay-Gay and Trevor and Windham and MacKenzie (the latter both female), clusters of contemporary syllables more distinct than the faces of the handsome men and pretty women they identified.

Taylor smiled and waved and forgot the names instantly. They were friendly but reserved and Taylor wondered what they were thinking of her—a woman with more wop and mick in her than Brit, with a mass of kinky black hair, not a pert ponytail, and wearing a long paisley skirt and a black blouse, not a J. Crew stitch upon her body.

Suspicion . . . That was the message from the women.

From the men there was something very different. Something between casual flirtation and a knee-jerk invitation
to hump. Taylor supposed that soon there'd be a lot of female fingers twining possessively through the belt loops of
their men.

Bosk made martinis for the crowd but Taylor stuck with
beer.

"Are you a lawyer?" one blonde asked.

"A paralegal."

"Oh," the woman said, blinking. "That's interesting."

"We need you folks," one handsome young man said as
he tinkered nervously with his Rolex. "You save our butts
every day." It seemed he wasn't being condescending; he
was simply embarrassed for her and trying to salvage her
pride.

"Where're you from? Boston, right? I detect Bostonian."

"Born on the North Shore."

"Oh, Locust Valley?" a pretty blond woman asked. The
residence of the crème de la crème. J. P. Morgan's home.

"No, Glen Cove." A pleasant but strip-malled city. "But
we moved to Maryland when I was twelve."

"Is your father or mother in the business?"

"Which business would that be?" Taylor asked innocently.

"Law, banking?" As if no other businesses existed.

"He manages a convenience store," she replied.

Sebastian, who'd already commented about her father and
his renowned law practice, glanced at her with a cryptic look.

"Well, retail," one girl finally said, nodding with robust
approval. "Good margins in retail lately."

"Very good," somebody else added.

And to her relief, Taylor Lockwood ceased to be a human being as far as they were concerned and their own conversation—the real and important conversation—resumed.

⬛

Dinner was Ada's jurisdiction.
She presided with the quiet authority of someone

for whom social propriety is statutory. Somewhere, in a three-decades-old volume of Emily Post, this very layout of Waterford and Wedgwood was represented. Though the clothing was supposed to be casual, Ada's appearance in a rustling silk dress, black-velvet headband and necklace gripping a lemon-colored stone the size of a fat thumb made it clear that, whatever happened in the frat dining halls or eating clubs these youngsters were accustomed to, dinner in this particular house would be governed by a respectable modicum of formality.

Taylor tried a vain end run around the seating ("Oh, I'm sorry, was I supposed to sit there?"); Ada smilingly steered her away from Bosk's girlfriend (a potential source of information about the "project"), scolding, "Boy, girl, boy, girl..."

Lobster bisque, a pear-and-Camembert salad, tiny veal chops surrounded by a yin-yang swirl of pureed peas and carrots, a green salad. A real butler served the meal.

Between polite words with the young man on her right Taylor tried to overhear the conversation between Bosk and Sebastian but Ada's voice was too loud—she was a lock-jawed caricature of Long Island money. She touched the men's arms with her dark, bony fingers and flirted fiercely. Yet their hostess knew this game as well as she knew the proper wording for bread-and-butter notes. She had no intention of seducing these boys; the only organ at play here was her ego—though sex was a strong undercurrent of the meal and crude jokes, some of them really disgusting, flew back and forth. (The upper class, Taylor remembered, had by and large not been Puritans.)

Halfway through the profiteroles and espresso with anisette, the doorbell rang. Bosk rose and a few minutes later returned with a man of about forty-five. He was introduced as Dennis Callaghan.

Taylor disliked him at once.

She wasn't sure why. What she might in fairness have read as groomed, discerning and charming she believed was vain (spun, sprayed hair combed forward, a close-fitting suit with shot cuffs, gold bracelet), pompous (a disdaining look

at the children around him) and dishonest (a broad smile he
could not have felt).

He was also insulting: He ignored Taylor while he studied the bloused or sweatered breasts of every woman
younger than herself at the table before turning a flattering
smile on Ada with the respect due a matriarch.

Taylor then noticed that the climate at the table had
changed considerably. Sebastian's expression was one of
anger. He shot a dark, mystified glance at Bosk, who
shrugged with a look that meant, It wasn't my fault. When
she saw that, Taylor's interest immediately perked up. Perhaps Callaghan had some connection with the "project."

The visitor, whose beach house was apparently nearby,
announced that he'd played hooky from Wall Street today to
hold a couple of meetings out here and happened to notice
the cars as he was driving back to the city. He thought he'd
stop in and see Bosk and Sebastian.

The man glanced at Sebastian, and Taylor saw another
finger wag, just like the other night. Callaghan nodded
subtly.

And so the conversation remained social. As he sat
down at the table and took a glass of wine—he'd eaten already—they talked about problems in finding grounds-
keepers and the advantages and risks of helicoptering into
Manhattan. Sebastian remained nervous as hell and when
Taylor asked Callaghan what he did for a living the young
lawyer answered for the businessman, offering quickly,
"Wall Street, darling. *Everybody* out here's on Wall Street.
Well, you've got an artist or two from time to time—Taylor's
a musician, by the way."

"Really?"

The conversation turned back to her momentarily and
before she could ask anything more about Callaghan, dinner was over and Sebastian had quickly shepherded Bosk
and the businessman downstairs, explaining that they were
going to check out Bosk's cigar cellar.

No one else was invited but the herd of preppies didn't

take any offense. Ada nodded toward the port, sherry and liqueur and, armed with yet more alcohol, this contingent ambled into the panoramic living room for more gossip.

It was then that Taylor recalled: She hadn't told Sebastian that she was a musician.

███████

Soon several people lit up cigarettes, Ada among them.

The smoke gave Taylor an excuse to drain her Grand Marnier and say she was going to step outside to get some air. Whether anyone thought this was rude, or suspicious, didn't matter; they all seemed relieved that the 7-Eleven heiress was leaving and they could spend some time dishing in earnest.

She took her leather jacket from the closet and walked out the front door, then strolled around the house until she spotted a four-foot-deep window well. She climbed down into it. A piece of glass was loose and she worked it free. She could not see the three men downstairs but their words, carried on the warm air, streamed up to her with the awkward-sounding hesitancies of conversations overheard but not witnessed.

"Got to be more careful," Sebastian said. "Jesus, I shit when I saw you here."

Callaghan said, "We've still got some details to work out. And you're impossible to get ahold of, Thom."

"Well, we can't just fucking waltz into each other's office and take a meeting now, can we? We've got to be careful about it, set it up ahead of time, keep everything secret."

Callaghan sighed. "I've been doing this sort of thing a lot longer than you have, Thom. We're going to get away with it. Stop worrying so much."

"I'm thinking about the phones," Bosk said. "You really think they're bugged?"

Sebastian said, "Of course they're fucking bugged. Jesus, don't be so naive.

Bosk: "Well, I can't run downstairs to make a call from a

pay phone every time I want to talk to you. Somebody sees me doing that a couple of times and what're they going to think?"

Sebastian: "Well, that's what you're going to have to do. You can pick up cell phone transmissions even easier than landlines."

Callaghan: "What we could do—I've done this before—what we could do is get an answering service. You call and leave messages. I'll call on a separate line and pick them up. We'll have a second answering service going the other way."

Clever, Taylor Lockwood thought, though being truly clever, Thom, would have meant wearing gloves when you check out the file cabinet you're about to break into so you don't leave fingerprints.

Suddenly she felt a curious thrill. What was it? The excitement of the pursuit, she supposed, getting closer to her quarry. What Reece felt in the courtroom yesterday. What her father undoubtedly felt—in court, on the golf course, with his beloved shotgun out in the fields.

When she was young her father would take her with him when he'd go hunting on Saturday mornings in the fall. She'd hated those times, wanted to be back home in bed, watching cartoons or playing on her upright piano, shopping with her mother. But Samuel Lockwood, eyes keen and hungry for a kill, had insisted she come along. He'd carried the tiny, still-warm corpses of the birds back to the car, where came the moment she dreaded: To make her understand that the dead birds couldn't hurt her, he had her touch each one with her index finger.

There, that wasn't so bad, was it? Didn't hurt. They can't bite when they're dead, Taylie, remember that.

Dennis Callaghan now said, "Look, yeah, we have to be careful but we can't let this paralyze us."

"We're fucking thieves," Sebastian said. "Am I the only one taking this seriously?"

Bosk's laugh was flinty. "Well, whatta you want, Thom? You want to get walkie-talkies and scramblers? Disguises?"

"I'm just a little paranoid, okay? There was a weird fuckup."

"What?"

"Well, last Saturday night, when I was in the firm?"

"Right," Callaghan offered.

"I made sure nobody knew I was there—on Friday I taped the back door latch down so I could get in without leaving any record I was in. But what happens is this old asshole, a partner, cops my key and uses it to get in early Sunday morning. So now I'm in the system."

Gotcha, thought Taylor Lockwood. John Silbert Hemming, her tall private eye, would be proud of her.

"Shit," Bosk said. "Why'd he do it?"

"How the fuck do I know? Alzheimer's."

Callaghan said, "Not the end of the world. They don't know what you were doing there, right?"

"I don't think so."

"Well, relax. You've covered up everything real well, Thom. . . . Oh, here. Got a present."

"Ah, nectar of the gods," Sebastian said.

"Sure," Bosk said. A long pause.

Then a sniff. Another.

The magic powder boosted Sebastian's spirits considerably. When he spoke next he said with a laugh, "I like this—fucking the firm that fucked me and getting rich in the process."

"You want a Lamborghini?" Callaghan asked.

Bosk said seriously, "I don't like the ride. Rough, you know."

Sebastian: "I live in Manhattan. What'm I gonna do, alternate-side-of-the-street parking with a two-hundred-thousand-dollar car?"

"Keep it out at your summer house, Thom, like we all do."

"I don't have a summer house. And I don't want one."

The wind was dicing her face and ears. She closed her eyes against the cold. Her legs and thighs, the last stronghold

168 J e f f e r y D e a v e r

of heat, were going numb. She touched the glass that separated her from a room that was fifty degrees warmer, where
she heard the sounds of two chubby, spoiled boys sniffing the
residue of cocaine into their nostrils.

Bosk said, "So what's with this Taylor cunt? She put out?"

"Fuck you," Sebastian said unemotionally.

"No, does she fuck *you*? That's what I'm asking."

Callaghan sniffed his white powder then said, "You've
got gonads for brains, Bosk. Is that all you think about? Sex?"

"Money, too. I think a lot about money but mostly I
think about sex. Tell me about Taylor."

"I don't want to talk about her," Sebastian said menac-
ingly.

"Does she have big tits? I couldn't tell. . . . Hey, chill, will
you, man? That's a fucking scary look. I was just curious."

There was a pause. And with an ominous tone in his
voice Sebastian said, "Well, don't get too interested in her.
You hear me?"

Taylor felt a ping of fear at that.

"I'm just—"

"You hear what I'm saying?"

"Hey, chill. . . . I hear you, Sea Bass, I hear you."

Then the conversation turned to sports and, stinging
with cold, Taylor left them to their banter. She walked inside and rejoined the crowd in front of the fireplace, observing how the conversation grew sedate when she entered the
room. She nudged herself into the center of the group and
sat on the hearth with her back to the fire until the pain
from the cold became a fierce itch and then finally died
away.

Around 10 P.M. the drapery man walked through
Greenwich Village under huge trapezoids of bruise-purple
clouds, lit from the perpetual glow of the city.

He was concentrating on the buildings and finally arrived at the address he sought.

At the service entrance, which smelled of sour garbage,

he inserted his lock gun and flicked the trigger a dozen times until the teeth of the tumblers were aligned. The door opened easily. He climbed to the fourth floor and picked another set of locks—on the door of the particular apartment he sought.

Inside, he slipped his ice-pick weapon into his belt, handle up, ready to grab it if he had to, and began to search. He found a bag of needlepoint (one a Christmas scene that sure wouldn't be finished in time for the holiday), a box of Weight Watchers apple snacks, a garter belt in its original gift box, apparently never worn, cartons of musty sheet music. An elaborate, expensive-looking reel-to-reel tape recorder. Dozens of tape cassettes with the same title: *The Heat of Midnight. Songs by Taylor Lockwood.*

Inside the woman's briefcase, in addition to sheet music, he found time sheets, key entry logs and other documents from Hubbard, White & Willis. He looked through them carefully and memorized exactly what they contained.

He found and read through the woman's address book, her calendar and her phone bills. He listened to her answering machine tapes. His client had hoped that she'd have a diary but very few people kept diaries anymore and Taylor Lockwood was no exception.

The drapery man continued his search, walking slowly through the apartment, taking his time. He knew his client would grill him at length about what he'd found here and he wanted to make sure he overlooked nothing.

CHAPTER EIGHTEEN

██████ Taylor dropped into the chair in her cubicle.

It was six-thirty, Saturday morning. The gods of the furnace had decided that not even Type A attorneys would be in the office yet and so Hubbard, White & Willis was cold as Anchorage.

She shivered both from the temperature and from exhaustion too. She and Thom Sebastian had arrived back in the city late last night. The lawyer had been subdued. She'd sensed that he was worried she'd ask about Callaghan and he wouldn't be able to come up with a credible story. But there was something else troubling him. His jokey self was gone. And once she caught him looking at her with an odd, troubled expression on his face.

She had an image of herself as a condemned prisoner and him as a prison guard, distancing himself from someone about to die.

Ridiculous, she thought. Still, she could hear his words in her head:

Well, don't get too interested in her.

What did *that* mean?

And how the hell had he known she was a musician?

She noticed a flashing light on her phone, indicating that she had a message. She picked up the receiver to check voice mail.

Reece had called again to remind her about dinner at his place that night.

There was one other message.

Beep.

"*Hey, counselor, how you doing? Saw an article about your shop in the* Law Journal. *About the merger. You've probably seen it but I'm faxing it to you. Always stay on top of firm politics. . . .*"

If you only knew, Dad, she thought.

"*We're planning Christmas dinner and we've got an RSVP from a Supreme Court justice; I'll let you guess who. I'm putting him next to you at the table. Just keep your more liberal views to yourself, counselor. I'm serious about that. Okay, I'll be in town week after next. Your mother says hi.*"

Supreme Court? Samuel Lockwood never did anything without a purpose. What did he have in mind? Was the dinner table placement intended to help her career? she wondered.

Or *his?* she appended cynically.

Taylor found the fax her father had sent about the merger of the firms, scanned it quickly. It described the vicious infighting among the partners at Hubbard, White & Willis—Burdick v. Clayton—and how, despite the animosity, the merged firms would probably succeed much better in the new business climate than if they remained separate. The picture featured Burdick and his wife.

An idea occurred to her.

She wrote on the top, "Thom, FYI." And signed her name.

Using this as an excuse, she hurried to his office, propped the article on his chair and, with a glance into the deserted corridor, proceeded to search the room like an eager rookie cop on crime scene detail.

In his desk she found: condoms, Bamboo paper, an unopened bottle of Chivas Regal, matches from the Harvard

Club, the Palace Hotel and assorted late-night clubs around town, dozens of take-out menus from downtown restaurants, chatty letters from his brother and father and mother (all neatly organized, some with margin notes), brokerage house statements, checkbooks (Jesus, where'd he get all this *money?*), some popular spy and military paperbacks, a coffee-stained copy of the *Lawyer's Code of Professional Responsibility,* assorted photographs from vacations, newspaper articles on bond issues and stock offerings, the *Pennystock News,* candy bars, crumbs and paper clips.

Nothing about the note, no information linking him, Bosk or Callaghan to Hanover & Stiver.

On Sebastian's bookshelves were hundreds of huge books, bound in navy and burgundy and deep green. They'd contain copies of all the closing documents in a business transaction that Sebastian had worked on. They would be great places to hide stolen promissory notes and other incriminating evidence. But it would take several days to look through all of them. She saw Sebastian's name embossed in gold at the bottom of each one.

It was then that she noticed the corner of a piece of paper protruding from beneath Sebastian's desk blotter. Another glance into the corridor—still no signs of life—and she pulled the paper out.

The jottings were brief and to the point.

Taylor Lockwood. 24 Fifth Avenue.

Her age, schools attended. Home address in Chevy Chase. Phone numbers at the firm and at home. The unlisted one too.

Father: Samuel Lockwood. Mother: housewife. No siblings. Applied to law school. Employed by HWW for two years. Merit raises and bonuses at top levels.

"Musician. Every Tuesday. Miracles Pub."

The son of a bitch, she whispered. Then replaced the sheet exactly where she'd found it.

She left his office and returned to the chilly corridor, hearing echoes of footsteps, hearing the click of guns being cocked and the hiss of knives being unsheathed.

And hearing over and over Thom Sebastian's words:
Well, don't get too interested in her.

In the firm's library she logged on to several of the computer databases that the firm subscribed to, including the Lexis/Nexis system, which contains copies of nearly all court decisions, statutes and regulations in the United States, as well as articles from hundreds of magazines and newspapers around the world.

She spent hours trying to find information about Dennis Callaghan, Bosk and Sebastian.

There wasn't much that was helpful. Bradford Smith had been admitted to the New York and federal bars and currently practiced at a Midtown firm, which didn't, however, seem to have any connection to Hanover & Stiver or New Amsterdam Bank.

Dennis Callaghan wasn't a lawyer but a businessman. He dabbled in dozens of different activities and had been under investigation for stock fraud and real estate scams though he'd never been indicted. He was currently connected with about twenty different companies, some of which were incorporated offshore and which, she guessed, were fronts.

But still no connection between any of them and Hanover & Stiver.

The information about Sebastian—found in alumni magazine archives and legal magazines he'd contributed articles to—wasn't incriminating either, though she found, interestingly, that the Upper East Side preppy image was fake. Sebastian had grown up outside of Chicago, his father the manager of a Kroger grocery store (hence, she realized, another reason for the funny look when he'd heard her tell the youngsters at Ada's that Dad managed a convenience store). Sebastian did have an undergrad degree from Harvard but it had taken him six years because he'd gone part-time— presumably while working to support himself.

The Yale Law School certificates she'd noticed on his

wall must have been for continuing education courses; he'd
gotten his law degree from Brooklyn Law at night while
working as a process server during the day—serving sub-
poenas in some of the toughest parts of the outer boroughs.

So, there was a different Thom Sebastian beneath the
jokey party animal. One who was driven, ambitious, tough.
And, Taylor knew, recalling the conversation in Ada's downstairs den, also a thief—fucking the firm that fucked him.

More associates were filing into the library now and she
didn't want anybody to see what she was doing so she logged
off the computer and went to the administrative floor.

There she walked into the file room Carrie Mason had
told her about, a large, dingy space filled with row upon
row of cabinets. It was here that the billing department kept
the original time sheets that lawyers filled out daily.

Making certain the room was empty, Taylor opened the
"D" drawer—where Ralph Dudley's sheets would reside—
and found the most recent ones. They were little blue slips
of carbon paper filled with his imperial scrawl, describing
every ten-minute period during working hours. She read
through and replaced them and then did the same in the "L"
drawer for Lillick and the "S" for Thom Sebastian.

Taylor rose to leave but then paused.

The "R" cabinet was right next to her.

She rested her fingers on the handle and after a moment's hesitation, pulled it open and looked inside. She
stared in astonishment at the booklets with Mitchell Reece's
name on them. There were hundreds of them. Christ
Almighty . . . nearly twice as many as for most other lawyers.

She pulled one out at random—September—and
thumbed through it, looking at a typical day in the life of
Mitchell Reece:

> New Client relations—½ hour.
> New Amsterdam Bank & Trust v. Hanover &
> Stiver—4½ hours (depositions).
> Westron Electronic et al. v. Larson Associates—3¼
>   hours (motion to quash subpoena, J. Brietell).

State of New York v. Kowalski—½ hour *(conference with DA's office; pro bono).*

State of New York v. Hammond—½ hour *(meeting with defendant; pro bono).*

In re Summers Publishing—2½ hours *(research, briefing Chapter 7 bankruptcy issue).*

She skimmed ahead.

Lasky v. Allied Products... Mutual Indemnity of New Jersey v. New Amsterdam Bank... State of New York v. Williams.

She totaled the hours: Sixteen were billed to clients. That was sixteen hours of *productive* work, not commuting time, lunch, trips to the rest rooms and the water fountain.

Sixteen hours in one day!

And every day was pretty much the same.

Arguing motion, arguing motion, on trial, writing brief, on trial, on trial, settlement conference, arguing motion, on trial, pro bono meetings with criminal clients and prosecutors.

On trial on trial on trial...

He never stopped.

A thought occurred to her and she smiled to herself. Yes, no?

Go for it, Alice.

She opened the binder containing the most recent of his sheets. She flipped through them until she found the day that she'd followed him to Grand Central Station.

For the three hours he was out of the office he'd marked the time Code 03.

Which meant personal time.

The time you spend at the dentist's office.

The time you spend at PTA conferences.

The time you spend in Westchester, with your girl-friend.

Taylor felt her skin buzzing with embarrassment as she flipped through other lunch hours over the past several months. In September he'd done the same—taken long lunches—only usually it was two or three times a week. Recently, in the month of November, for instance, he'd done so only once a week.

Three hours in the middle of the day for a workaholic like Reece?

Well, Taylor Lockwood understood; she'd had lovers herself.

She put the time sheets back and closed the drawer.

Outside, the air was cold but the city was ablaze with Christmas decorations and she decided to walk home. She slipped her Walkman headset on, then her earmuffs, and began to walk briskly, thinking about the evening ahead, dinner with Mitchell Reece—at least until the hiss of the cassette grew silent, Miles Davis started into "Seven Steps to Heaven" and the rest of the world was lost to Taylor Lockwood.

CHAPTER NINETEEN

Well, look at this.

Mitchell Reece could've been a professional interior designer.

Taylor would have thought he'd have no time for decor—or interest in the subject. So when he opened his door and ushered her into the huge loft, she exhaled a sharp, surprised laugh.

She was looking at a single room, probably twenty-five hundred square feet. There was a separate elevated sleeping area with a brass railing around it, containing an oak armoire and a matching dresser—and a bed, which caught her attention immediately. It was dark mahogany, with a massive headboard that would have dwarfed any smaller space. The headboard was carved in a Gothic style and the characters cut into the wood were cracked and worn. She couldn't tell exactly what they were—perhaps gargoyles and dragons.

She thought of the mythical creature in *Through the Looking-Glass*.

Beware the Jabberwock, my son!
The jaws that bite, the claws that catch!

Around the loft were plants, sculpture, antiques, tall bookshelves, tapestries. Pin spots shot focused streams of light onto small statues and paintings, many of which looked ugly enough to be very valuable. The walls were brick and plaster, painted mottled white and gray and pink. The floors were oak, stained white.

If this boy cooks, she joked to herself, I may just reconsider my baby-by-mail plan and marry him.

"You did this just to impress me, I know."

He laughed. "Let me take your coat." Reece wore baggy pants and a blousy white shirt. Sockless slippers. His hair was still damp from a shower.

Taylor had chosen noncommittal vamp. Black stockings but shoes with low, functional heels. A black Carolina Herrera dress, tight but high-necked. (Cleavage? A roommate had once bluntly assessed, *Forget boobs, Taylor. Avoid low-cut. But the rest of your bod—it's to die for. Wear short and tight. Remember that. Short and tight.*)

Taylor noted the sweep of Reece's eyes all along her body. He was subtle, but not subtle enough; she caught him in reflection in one of the mirrors near the Jabberwock bed.

Okay, Ms. Westchester, she thought to Reece's mysterious girlfriend, can *you* shoehorn into a dress like this?

She followed him across an oriental rug. The dinner table had feet, and on the side, carved faces of the sun. They were solemn.

"Your table looks unhappy."

"He gets bored. I don't have much company. He'll be happy tonight."

As Reece took the wine she'd brought she looked at him carefully and decided he wasn't very happy either. His eyes were still bloodshot and he seemed to be forcing himself to relax, to push the intruding distractions of the law firm away.

He walked into the kitchen area and put the chardonnay into a refrigerator. She looked inside; it contained nothing but wine. "You should try groceries sometime," she said. "Lettuce, oranges. You can even get chicken, I'm told, ready to cook."

"Wine cellar," Reece said, laughing. He pulled out a bottle of white, a Puligny-Montrachet. Her father's favorite Burgundy, Taylor recalled. Reece added, "The fridge's over there." He pointed to a tall Sub-Zero then took two crystal goblets in one hand and carried the wine and a ceramic cooler out into the living area.

Man, she thought, he's really slick at this.

He poured and they touched glasses. "To winning."

Taylor held his eye for a moment and repeated the toast. The wine was rich and sour-sweet, more like a food than a drink. The goblet was heavy in her hand.

They sat and he told her how he'd found the loft. It was raw space when he'd moved in and he'd had it finished himself. The project had taken nearly a year because he'd had three full-fledged trials that year and had been unable to meet with the contractors. "I slept in sawdust a lot," he explained. "But I won the cases."

"Have you ever lost a trial?" she asked.

"Of course. Everybody loses trials. I seem to win a few more than most people. But that's not magic. Or luck. Preparation is the key. And will to win."

"Preparation and Will. That could be your motto."

"Maybe I should get a crest. I wonder what it'd be in Latin."

Taylor rose and walked toward a long wooden shelf. "My mother," she said, "would call this a knickknack shelf. I used to think 'knickknack' was French for 'small, ugly ceramic poodle.'" He laughed.

She found herself looking at an army of metal soldiers.

"I collect them," Reece said. "Winston Churchill probably had the biggest collection in the world and Malcolm Forbes's wasn't too shabby either. I've only been at it for twenty years or so."

"What are they, tin?"

"Lead."

Taylor said, "One year my father got the idea that I should get soldiers, not dolls, for Christmas. I must've been eight or nine. He gave me bags and bags of these green plastic guys. He gave me a B-52 too so I nuked most of them and went back to Barbie and Pooh. You have other things, too? Like cannons and catapults?"

"Everything. Soldiers, horses, cannons, and caissons..."

She sipped the wine and was thinking: Sometimes in life this craziness falls right on top of you and you find yourself almost floating up and away from your body like a guru or psychic, looking down at yourself, and all you can say is, Shit a brick, this is *so* weird. I mean, here I am, Alice in Wonderland, in a fab loft, next to a handsome man I'm playing detective with, drinking hundred-dollar wine and talking toy soldiers.

Taylor told herself not, under any circumstances, to get drunk.

Reece played with some of the figures. "I have a British Square. I made it when I was sixteen."

"Like a park? Like Trafalgar Square?"

Reece was laughing. "Taylor, British Square? A fighting formation? You know, Gunga Din."

"Kipling," she said.

He nodded. "The ranks divided into two lines. One stood and reloaded, the other knelt and fired. The fuzzy-wuzzies were the only warriors to break through the square."

"The, uh..."

"Zulus. African tribal warriors."

"Ah. Boer War."

"That was twenty years later."

"Oh, sure," she said seriously, nodding in recognition.

"You're laughing at me, aren't you?"

She shook her head but couldn't keep a straight face and said through the grin, "Definitely."

He hit her playfully on the arm and let his hand pause on the thin cotton of her blouse for a moment.

He put on some music jazz.

"Any word about your demo tapes?"

"The responses ain't been jim-dandy."

"It only takes one record company."

She shrugged. And glanced at an antique clock. Eight-thirty. She could smell nothing simmering. Well, scratch one: He can't cook. Maybe they were going out. But—

The door buzzer sounded.

"Excuse me."

He let a young man into the loft. He nodded politely to Taylor and, from a large shopping bag, took out plates wrapped in stippled foil. Reece set the table with bone china plates, silver and a candlestick.

The portable butler said, "Would you like me to pour the wine, Mr. Reece?"

"No, thank you anyway, Robert." Reece signed the proffered slip of paper. A bill changed hands.

"Then good night, sir."

Dinner turned out to be blini with beluga caviar and sour cream, veal medallions with slivers of fresh truffles in a marsala sauce, braised endive and cold marinated green beans.

No fake burgers and sprouts for this boy...

They sat at the table and began to eat. Reece said, "Now, tell me what you've found out about the note."

Taylor organized her thoughts. "First, somebody got into the computer and erased all the disbursements, expenses and phone call logs for Saturday and Sunday."

"All of them?" He winced.

She nodded. "All last week, actually. Everything that'd link a particular person to the firm—except the door card keys and the time sheets."

"Okay." He nodded, taking this in. "Who can get into the system?"

"It's not that hard. You need an access card but it'd be

easy to steal one." More of the wonderful wine—he'd opened a second bottle. "Let me go through the suspects. First, Thom Sebastian."

He nodded. "Go ahead."

"Well, I fingerprinted your safe and found his on the top and side."

He laughed. "You did what?"

"I got a private-eye kit—deerstalker cap and decoder ring, the works. I dusted the scene of the crime and came up with twenty-five latents—that's prints, to you. Fifteen completely unrecognizable. The other ten, most were partials but seven seem to be the same person—you, I'm pretty sure. I dusted your coffee cup—I owe you a new one, by the way; the powder didn't come off too well. I threw it out."

"I wondered what happened to it."

"And three others. A couple of prints are unidentified but there are a dozen or so that're smooth smudges, as if somebody'd worn gloves. Thom's're pretty clear."

"Thom?" Reece frowned. "Son of a bitch."

She said, "I don't think he actually broke into the safe; from the position on the metal it looks like the guy who did that was the one wearing the gloves—the pro. But Sebastian may have checked it out before—or tried to open it that night and when he couldn't called in an expert. Is there any reason why he'd've been going through your files?"

"He's worked for New Amsterdam in the past though not on the Hanover & Stiver deal—not that I've *heard* about. Anyway, he'd have no business going through anybody's office without asking." He laughed and looked at her admiringly. "Fingerprints . . . That never occurred to me."

She continued, explaining to him that Sebastian had lied about how late he'd stayed at the club on Saturday night and that she'd confirmed he was in fact in the firm. She told him too about Bosk and Dennis Callaghan. How they'd talked about stealing something from the firm and how they were going to spend their money.

She asked, "You ever hear the name Callaghan in connection with the Hanover & Stiver case?"

"No." Reece shook his head. "But what about Sebastian's
motive? He's risking prison just to get even with the firm?"

"Why not? The firm was his entire life. Besides, he's got
a dark side to him. He was a process server in Brooklyn and
Queens."

Reece nodded. "Yeah, those guys are tough."

Sebastian's implicit threat echoed in her mind again.

She said, "I think he wants revenge. But mostly I think
he looks at the money Hanover'd pay him to lose the note as
something the firm owes him—for not getting made partner. Think about it: He's a product of Hubbard, White—
which's been training him for six or seven years to go for the
throat, look only at the bottom line. He's also been checking
me out."

"You?"

She nodded. "He's got a little dossier on me."

"Why?"

"Know your enemy?" She then continued, "Remember I
mentioned Dudley? Well, are you ready for this?"

She told him about Junie and the West Side Art and
Photography Club.

"Whoa," Reece blurted. "That little girl's a hooker?
Dudley's mad. They'll put him away forever for that.
Statutory rape, contributing to the delinquency."

"And it looks like he's paying a thousand bucks a week
cash for her. You told me he's got money problems to start
with. That's *his* motive. And as for being in the firm on
Saturday I know he was there and he told Junie that some
project he was working on was going to mean a lot of
money. I checked his time sheets and he didn't bill any time
Saturday or Sunday. So whatever he was doing at the firm
then was personal. . . ."

Taylor added, "Now, we've got a third-party candidate."

"Who?"

"Sean Lillick."

"The paralegal? Hell, he's been working for me on the case—he knows all the details about the note. But what's his motive?"

"Also money. I found thousands of dollars hidden in his apartment. He didn't get it from a paralegal's salary. And he *sure* didn't make it doing that performance art crap of his."

"But he wasn't in the firm when the note was stolen, was he?"

"I'm not sure. He did come in Saturday morning, according to his key entry card. I assumed he left, because he only billed a few hours to a client. But he might've stayed all night."

Reece had a thought. "Something interesting . . . Lillick hangs around with Wendall Clayton a lot."

She nodded. She'd seen them together.

"But you know what's curious?" Reece mused. "Lillick's assigned to the litigation department. Not corporate. Why'd he be working for Clayton?"

"I don't know."

A frown on the lawyer's face. "Lillick'd be familiar with the St. Agnes files too. He might've fed Clayton some information that led him to that surprise witness from San Diego."

"You think *Clayton's* behind that?" she asked.

Reece shrugged. "St. Agnes is Donald's client and so's New Amsterdam Bank. All Clayton cares about is getting the merger through, and sabotaging Burdick's clients is a pretty efficient way to do it."

He stood, walked into the kitchen and returned with two glasses of cognac. He handed one to Taylor, the liqueur leaving thin, syrupy waves on the glass. "Tomorrow, Wendall's having a party at his Connecticut place. Why don't you come along. You might be able to find something."

"Oh, I couldn't go. I'm just a paralegal."

"It's a *firm* function; they just have it at his house. A party for the new associates, an annual thing. You can come with me."

"We shouldn't be seen together."

"We'll split up once we get inside. We'll get there late and just slip in." He tipped his glass to her. "Good job, counselor."

They clinked glasses but she must've winced a bit.

"What?"

" 'Counselor.' "

"You don't like that?"

"My father's pet name for me. Fingernails on the black-board."

"Noted," he said. "I can imagine it's tough being Samuel Lockwood's child."

If you only knew, she thought, echoing the words she'd just directed to her father's phone message earlier that day.

They sipped the cognac and talked about the firm, part-ners, affairs, who was gay, who was on partnership track and who was not. She supplied most of the information and was surprised he knew so little about the gossipy side of the firm and its politics.

It was more astonishing to her that he knew so little about the merger. Although the lawyers and staffers of Hubbard, White spent more hours debating the merger than billing time for clients, Reece seemed oblivious to the whole thing. She mentioned the rumor that Clayton had a German lawyer inquire about accounts Burdick might have opened in Switzerland.

"Really?" Reece asked with what seemed unsophisti-cated surprise.

"Aren't you worried about it?" Taylor asked. "About what'll happen if Wendall wins?"

He laughed. "No. Doesn't make a bit of difference to me—as long as I can try cases, good cases, that's all I care about. Whether it's Donald in charge or Wendall or John Perelli, doesn't matter."

Together they cleared the dishes. He nodded toward the leather sofa and they walked over to it, sitting and sinking into the deep, supple piece of furniture.

There was a moment of quiet. The ticking clock. A siren far away. A distant shout.

That was when he kissed her.

And she kissed him back.

They embraced for a moment, his right hand sliding down the side of her face but coming to rest, ambiguously, at her collarbone.

His palm started downward but it stopped.

Perhaps because he sensed something coming from her—the reserve, the caution, that she in fact suddenly felt.

"Sorry," he said. "I'm impulsive and pushy. Tell me to go to hell."

"I would if I wanted to."

If you only knew . . .

He sat back and after a moment said, "There's something I wanted to say."

"Sure."

"It's nothing really. But it's been bugging me. Remember when I said I couldn't have lunch after the cross? Yesterday?"

"Right." She found her heart beating hard.

"I didn't have a meeting."

She pictured the three-hour lunch reference on the time sheet. The flowers.

"I went up to Westchester."

Taylor nodded, said nothing.

He continued. "There's something I don't talk about too much. My mother's in a home up there."

"Oh, I'm sorry, Mitchell."

He was stoic but she believed she could see pain somewhere behind his eyes. "Schizophrenia. It's pretty bad. I go to see her a couple times a week. Sometimes she remembers me." He smiled. "Yesterday she was pretty good. I took her some flowers and she went on and on about them for a long time."

"She's on medication?"

"Oh, yeah. And the nurses at the home are real good to her. The thing is, it's hard for me to talk about it. In fact, you're the only one I've told."

She felt a burst of pleasure at this confidence, even more than being singled out by Reece to help him find the promissory note. "I won't say anything. . . . If there's anything I can do—"

"Hey, how 'bout just a kiss to forgive me for not being honest."

She laughed and squeezed his arm. And leaned forward. Kissed him quickly.

Then eased her arms around his neck and kept kissing him.

Hard.

Where are we going with this? she wondered.

As she kissed and was kissed, as she touched and was touched, her mind counted her marriage proposals (two), the live-in boyfriends (three), the men she'd slept with (thirteen).

She thought of the ones she felt mere fondness for who'd claimed they were madly in love with her. And the flip side: the ones she'd lusted or pined for who hadn't cared she existed.

But maybe *this* time would be different, she thought. Maybe getting older, maybe simply getting by, *surviving* in this world had changed her, made her more discerning, given her better judgment.

Maybe she'd broken into a different place—that Wonderland where her father and Mitchell Reece resided. Where she was their equal.

But be careful, she thought. Remember Thom Sebastian's myth of the beautiful woman? Well, beware the myth of the absolute moment, a moment like this—when we sit, or lie, close together, muscles ticking, limbs at their most relaxed, bathed in the certainty of love. The absolute moment, when conversation soars, confidences are shared, coincidences between you and your lover pop up like crocuses in April.

The absolute moment—when we forget that most loves aren't forever, that most words are mere vibrations of insubstantial air, that most unions are a nest of comic and aching differences that no other animal in the world would tolerate, let alone desperately pursue.

She eased back slightly, wiped the war paint of lipstick off his cheek. He glanced down at her empty glass. He stood up and filled both of theirs again and returned, sat down, slouching back into the leather, playing with the top button of his shirt. His hair was mussed. He tried to brush it back but the thick comma stayed put.

"Know what?" he asked.

"What's that?"

"I'm glad."

"About what?" Taylor felt it then, that unwinding feeling within her. Despite the keen warning to herself a moment ago, the spring had been set loose.

Was it going to be good or bad? The time was coming soon, quick as a wet-leaf skid. Okay? Decide, good or bad? Decide fast, Alice, you've got about three minutes.

"I'm glad we haven't caught our thief yet. I like working with you." His voice was husky.

Reece held his glass up.

Come on, this is the moment. Now. You going, or staying? You've still got the power. It hasn't tipped yet. You can do it easy, diffuse the whole thing. Thank him for dinner. Stand up. That's all it would take.

One way or another, decide: In the end, is this good or bad?

She lifted her glass too and tapped but as he sipped, some of the cognac spilled onto the front of his shirt.

"Oh, hell," he muttered.

Come on, good or bad? Make it your decision. Choose. . . .

"Here, let me clean it up," she said.

Good or bad?

She thought that question to herself a dozen times in the space of five seconds or maybe two seconds or maybe just one but it never got answered; his mouth closed on hers and his hands—surprisingly large and strong for a bookish man—were covering her breasts and she felt the heat in his fingers as they then slid inside her dress, probing for fasteners.

Taylor in turn sought the smooth cloth of his shirt, gripped it hard and pulled him down on top of her.

Good or bad, good or bad . . .

███████

This Saturday night, late, Donald Burdick and Bill Stanley sat beside each other in tall-backed leather chairs and looked into the valet room of their private club on Broad Street.

It was in that room that every morning one of the club employees would iron the *New York Times, International Herald Tribune* and *Wall Street Journal* for the members. This had been a perk ever since the club had been founded in the mid-1800s. At that time, of course, when New York City boasted more than a dozen papers, the valet was busy all day long. Now, however, with no evening papers of worth, the room was used at night only for its junction box, to which telephones on long wires were connected. When a call came in these phones were carried to members; cellular phones were, of course, forbidden in the club.

Burdick and Stanley watched the poised black man, in a dinner jacket, now carrying one of these phones to Burdick, who took it with a nod of thanks.

The conversation lasted only four minutes.

Burdick absorbed the information, closed his eyes and, thinking that in Roman days the messenger would have been killed had he delivered news like this, nonetheless politely thanked the caller.

He dropped the receiver into the cradle. The valet appeared instantly and removed the phone.

"What the hell was that?" Stanley asked.

"The lease," Burdick said, shaking his head.

"Oh, no," Stanley grumbled.

Burdick nodded. "He did it. Somehow Clayton deep-sixed the lease."

The caller had been an underling of Rothstein's, the head of the real estate syndicate that owned the building where Hubbard, White & Willis was located. The syndicate had suddenly withdrawn from the negotiations for the expensive long-term lease and was going to let the current lease lapse.

This meant that it would now make much more financial sense to merge the firm with Perelli and move into the Midtown firm's space.

Damn . . . Burdick clenched his fist.

"*Clayton's* telling *Jews* what to do with their Manhattan real estate?" Stanley barked. There was no need to lower his voice. The only non-Protestant sect represented in the club was Papist and none of the three Catholic members was here tonight. "How the hell did he do it?"

Burdick didn't know and didn't care but, as his wife had admitted not long ago, he couldn't help but admire Clayton. He hadn't thought that the partner even *knew* about the negotiations, let alone that he could put together some bribery—or extortion—plan to sabotage the lease this quickly.

Now, with the lease gone, all Burdick had left to use as leverage was urging McMillan Holdings to take a stand against the merger.

"I'm going down to Florida tomorrow," he said.

"McMillan?" Stanley asked.

Burdick nodded. "Their board meeting. I'll do whatever I have to to make sure they let Perelli know where they stand."

"That'll help some, I guess." Then Stanley muttered something that Burdick couldn't hear.

"What was that?" the partner asked him.

"I said, 'Remember the days when all we had to do was get clients and practice law?'"

"No," Burdick replied sourly. "That must've been before my time."

CHAPTER TWENTY

The law professor and legal philosopher Karl Llewellyn wrote a book called *The Bramble Bush*. The foliage in his title was a metaphor for the study and practice of law and his meaning was that this field, in all its many incarnations, is endless. In that book he wrote that "the only cure for law is more law," by which he was suggesting that you cannot dabble at the profession. When you are overwhelmed by the case, the business deal, the jurisprudential study, when you are exhausted, when you cannot bear the thought of proceeding one more moment, you can find salvation only by pushing forward, deeper into the tangle.

The law, he was suggesting, is an infinitely complex, uncompromising mistress.

Wendall Clayton thought of Professor Llewellyn's writing now as he sat across his desk from Randy Simms, late Sunday morning at the firm.

The smarmy young lawyer had just delivered troubling news. They had managed to sabotage the long-term lease that Burdick had been trying to put into place. But some of the old-guard partners at the firm were refusing to vote in favor

of the merger. Burdick's win in the St. Agnes trial had heart-
ened them and a bit of cheerleading on Bill Stanley's part had
gotten them to switch their votes back to Burdick's camp.

Which meant that there was now some doubt that
Clayton would have enough votes, come Tuesday, for the
merger to be approved.

"How close is it?" Clayton asked.

"Pretty evenly balanced. Right down the middle, more
or less."

"Then we have to make it less 'pretty even.'"

"Yessir."

"Stay on call. I'll be right back." Clayton rose and walked
down the stairs to the paralegal pen.

To his surprise he found Sean Lillick was not alone.

The pretty boy was standing with a girl, another paralegal in the firm.

Clayton didn't understand what Lillick saw in her. She
seemed shy, timid, unassertive. A bit, well, rotund too.

A consolation fuck at best.

When they saw him coming they stepped apart and
Clayton noticed, though he pretended not to, that they'd
been fighting about something. The girl's eyes were red from
crying and Lillick's otherwise pasty face was flushed.

"Sean," the partner said.

The boy nodded. "Hi, Wendall."

"And you are? . . ."

"Carrie Mason."

"Ah."

"I hope I'm not interrupting anything," Clayton said.

"No. Not at all."

Carrie said quickly, "We were just talking."

"Ah. Talking. Well, if you'll excuse us, Carrie. Sean and I
have some business."

Neither of them moved. Lillick looked at the floor.
Carrie cleared her throat and said, "We've got some documents to copy. For the SCI deal."

Clayton didn't say anything. He just stared from one to
the other.

Lillick said to her, "Why don't you get started."

She hesitated then hefted an armful of papers and walked moodily down the hall on her solid legs.

Clayton said, "You'll be at my party tonight, won't you, Carrie? My place in Connecticut."

The girl looked back and said to the partner, "Yeah, I'll be there."

"I'm so pleased," the partner said, smiling.

When she'd vanished, Clayton said to the young man, "We've got some problems. About the vote. I need some information. Good information. And I need it fast. The vote's day after tomorrow."

It was, of course, the paralegals—and the support staff—who had the best access to information at the firm. As with the butlers and maids on *Upstairs, Downstairs,* the higher echelons of the firm babbled like schoolgirls in front of the hired help at Hubbard, White & Willis. This is why Clayton had swooped down on poor Lillick last year and began bribing him for information.

Lillick swallowed and looked down. "I think I've already done enough."

"You've been very helpful," the partner agreed smoothly.

"I don't want to help you anymore." He looked in the direction Carrie had disappeared.

Clayton nodded. There were times to push and times to placate. "I know it's been tough for you. But everything you've done has been for the good of everybody who works here." He rested his hand on the boy's shoulder. "We're very close, Sean, close to winning. And if we win, well, that'll be . . . rewarding for the whole firm, you included."

When the paralegal said nothing more Clayton said, "There've been some defections. I need any unusual phone calls that Burdick might've made. Travel plans. Anything like that. He's a desperate man and desperate men are his enemy's best friends. Know why? Because they make mistakes. You understand that?"

"Yessir."

"You're grasping it, you're committing it to memory?"

"Yes."

"Good. Find something and it'll be worth a lot of money. I mean five-figure money."

Clayton said nothing further but just leveled his eyes at the boy. After thirty seconds Lillick said slowly, "Let me look around. See if I can find something sort of helpful."

"Ah, wonderful," Clayton said. "Actually, though, it really has to be *very* helpful. I don't have any time left for subtleties."

Every color clashed.

Taylor Lockwood looked over the apparel of the crowd milling in the living room of Wendall Clayton's country home in Redding, Connecticut. She saw plaid. She saw lemon yellow with orange. She saw lime shirts with red slacks.

She saw madras!

Her mother had told her about madras: In the ancien régime of the sixties, star-burst tie-dye marked the hippies; madras flagged the nerds.

To be fair, the collision of hues was almost exclusively on the frames of the older lawyers. The younger crowd of associates were in chinos and Izod shirts or skirts and sweaters. A lot of pearls, a lot of blond hair, a lot of pretty faces.

It was Sunday, around five-thirty, and Reece and Taylor had cruise-controlled their way here along the wide parkway in a car he'd rented. They had found Clayton's place after asking directions twice and, after they'd parked, had walked into the house without knocking. They stood, unnoticed, in the entrance foyer.

"We're overdressed," she observed.

Reece pulled his tie off and stuffed it in his pocket. "How do I look?"

"Like an overdressed lawyer who lost his tie."

He said, "I'll take the first floor. You take the second."

"Okay," she said quickly. Then she hesitated.

"What's wrong?" Reece asked.

"We're kind of like burglars, aren't we?"

He recited quickly, "Burglary is entering a dwelling without permission with the intention of committing a felony." He gave her a fast smile. "We've got permission to be here. Therefore, it's not burglary."

If you say so . . .

Reece disappeared and Taylor found the bar. The bartender was doing a big business with mugs of sweet, mint-laced Southsiders. Taylor shook her head at the offered drink and got a glass of Stag's Leap Chardonnay. Before the first sip a man was right beside her, gripping her arm.

Thom Sebastian.

She shivered, hearing in her mind's ear Sebastian's comment to Bosk, his warning not to get too interested in her, the dangers it implied.

"Hey," the pudgy associate said, "you recovered okay?"

"Recovered?"

"From a night out with me."

"Nothing to report to any official governmental bodies."

"Excellent." His eyes were evasive, almost as if he had something he wanted to confess to her. After a glance around the room he asked casually, "You doing anything tomorrow night?"

What was on his mind?

"I think I've got some time free."

"Maybe dinner?"

"Sure," she said.

"Great. I'll call you." He gazed at her, expressionless, for a moment and she believed suddenly, as she looked into his cryptic eyes, that if he *was* the thief he wanted to come clean with her.

And if he confessed and produced the note? What then? she wondered.

Reece or her father . . . well, they would, of course, destroy Sebastian's life: force him into leaving the practice of law in New York. But *her* inclination would be to reward a confession with anonymity and to let him go.

But, as she watched him walk down a corridor in search of more liquor, she realized that she was getting ahead of herself.

Find the note first, then we'll consider justice. . . .

Taylor made her way through the hallway. As she did she noticed an older woman scrutinizing her carefully, with a look of almost amused curiosity. The woman reminded her of Ada Smith, Bosk's mother. Taylor tried to avoid her but once their eyes met and held, she felt the power of a silent summons and she remained where she was as the woman approached.

"You're Taylor Lockwood," the woman said.

"Yes."

"I'm Vera Burdick, Donald's wife."

"Nice to see you," Taylor said recalling the name from the newspaper article her father had just faxed to her. They shook hands. The woman must have seen the surprise in Taylor's face—surprise that the Burdick camp would be represented in enemy territory. Vera said, "Donald had business tonight. He asked me to come in his stead."

"It's a nice party," Taylor said.

"Wendall was kind enough to donate his house for the evening. He does the same for the summer associates in July. It's a sort of fresh-air outing for lawyers."

Silence filled the small space between them.

Taylor broke the stalemate with "Well, I think I'll mingle a little."

Vera Burdick nodded, as if her examination of Taylor had produced all the information she needed. "A pleasure seeing you again, dear. And good luck."

Taylor watched the partner's wife join a cluster of associates nearby. *Good luck?* As the woman's voice rose in laughter Taylor started again for the stairs. She'd gotten halfway across the hall when she heard another voice—a man's voice, soft, directed at her. "And who are you again?"

Her neck hair bristled.

Taylor turned to look into the face of Wendall Clayton.

She was, at first, surprised that he was only a couple of inches taller than she. Then she noticed that he was much more handsome up close than he seemed from a distance.

And then her mind went blank. For three or four seconds she was utterly without a conscious thought. Clayton's eyes were the reason. They were the eyes of a man who knew how to control people, a man to whom it would be excruciating to say no, even if he made his demands with silence.

A man exactly like her father.

"Pardon?" Taylor asked.

He smiled. "I asked who you were again?"

She thought: The same person I've always been, no "again" about it, hotshot. Then she got lost in his eyes once more and didn't try a snappy comeback. She said, "Taylor Lockwood."

"I'm Wendall Clayton."

She said, "Yes, I know. I'd thank you for inviting me, Wendall, but I'm afraid I crashed. Are you going to kick me out?" She found a smile somewhere and slipped it on, reminding herself to resist the urge to call him "Mr. Clayton."

"On the contrary, you're probably the only person in this crew worth talking to."

"I don't think I'd go that far."

He took her arm. She had never been touched in this way. His grip wasn't a disciplinarian's or a friend's or a lover's. In the contraction of the muscles was a consuming pressure of authority. As if he'd squeezed her soul. After a moment he lowered his hand.

Clayton said, "Would you like a tour of the house?"

"Sure.

"It's an authentic 1780s. I—"

"Taylor! You're here!" Carrie Mason trotted up to them.

"Hello, Carrie."

"Welcome." Clayton took Carrie Mason's hard-pumping hand. "Sean's not here?"

Carrie hesitated and said, "No, he had something else to do." It seemed there was a darkness in her face.

"Ah, maybe one of his performances."

"Carrie," Taylor said, "Wendall was just going to give me a tour of his house. Join us."

"Sure," the chubby girl said.

Clayton didn't appreciate that they were now a three-some but his reaction vanished as Vera Burdick walked past.

The woman stopped and extended a hand to Clayton.

He smiled and shook it graciously, clasping hers in both of his. "Vera. How good to see you again. Donald made it, I hope."

"Unfortunately not. That fund-raiser at City Hall?"

"When the mayor summons you—" Clayton said.

"The governor actually," she corrected.

"—you better go."

Taylor felt the tension between them like sparking wires. Vera Burdick clearly detested the partner, and while Clayton obviously returned the feeling, it was she who easily held his eye and the lawyer who looked defensively away as he made trivial conversation.

In this tableau Taylor recognized a truth about Clayton: While the partner knew men and how to handle them, he was only comfortable with women he could sexualize or control as his lessers.

She was nearly queasy, observing a man like this feeling threatened—a powerful man and, considering that he might have engineered the theft of the New Amsterdam note, one who was quite dangerous.

"I'll leave you to your friends," Vera said, the disdain visible like breath on a cold spring day. A glance at Taylor and Carrie. A meaningless smile.

Clayton said, "I hope Donald enjoys the fund-raiser."

■

"Donald, you're white as snow. Damn it, man, you've got to get more fresh air. Brought your racket, I hope?"

Burdick leaned against the railing of the penthouse suite in the Fleetwood Hotel in Miami Beach and looked at the cool disk of the setting sun. "More business than pleasure today, I'm afraid, Steve."

Burdick was tired. The firm's private Canadair jet hadn't been available—some maintenance problem—and he'd had to fly down to Miami in a commercial airliner. First class, of course, but he'd still had to stand in lines and then there'd been a delay on the runway that put him an hour off schedule.

He'd arrived exhausted but had ordered the car service to bring him directly here before checking in to a room.

Steve Nordstrom, shaking martinis like an ace bartender, was the president of McMillan Holdings. He was thick and square, with gray hair trimmed so impeccably it might have been injection-molded in the company's Teterboro plant, and was wearing a purple Izod shirt and white slacks.

"Drink?"

Burdick didn't want alcohol but he knew he would take the offered glass from Nordstrom, a man of fifty, whose face was already in bloom from the damaged blood vessels.

"How's the board meeting going?" Burdick asked.

Nordstrom licked martini off his finger. He grinned happily. "We're cutting a melon this year, Donald. Three sixty-three a share."

"Ah," Burdick said approvingly.

"You read the *Journal,* you read the *Times*—everybody's cratering but us. Hey, tomorrow, we're meeting on the new industry association. You want to sit in?"

"Can't. But tell your people to watch what they say. I told you that Justice is heating up again and Antitrust is looking at price-fixing. Don't even mention dollars. No numbers at all. Remember what happened in '72."

"Always looking out for your client, Donald?" Nordstrom's question contained the silent modifiers "biggest" and "most lucrative."

They sat down at a table. The bellboy, who had been waiting patiently, brought out lobster salads in half pineapples

and set them on the balcony table. The men ate the salad and
raisin rolls—the lawyer struggling to down the food, which
he had no appetite for—while they talked about vacations
and family and house prices and the administration in
Washington.

When they were finished eating, Burdick accepted another martini and pushed away from the table. "Which of
our boys is down here helping you with the board meeting,
Steve?"

"From Hubbard, White? Stan Johannsen is here and
Thom Sebastian did most of the advance work last week.
He's covering the front in New York. I understand he didn't
make partner. What happened? He's a good man."

Burdick looked out over the flat scenery at a line of cars
shooting flashes of glare from the expressway. After a moment he realized he had been asked a question and said, "I
don't remember exactly about Thom."

He wished Bill Stanley were with him. Or Vera. He
wanted allies nearby.

Nordstrom frowned. "But that's not what you're here for,
is it? About the board meeting."

"No, Steve, it's not. . . ." Burdick stood and paced, hands
clasped behind his back. "Hubbard, White's been doing
your legal work for, let's see, thirty-five years?"

"About that. Before my time."

"Steve, I'd ask you to keep what I'm going to tell you between you and me and Ed Gliddick. For the time being, at
least. No bullshit between us."

"Never has been." The businessman looked the partner
over coyly. "This's about the merger, I assume?"

"Yes. And there's more to it than meets the eye." Burdick
explained to him about Clayton and his planned massacre
after the merger was completed.

Nordstrom said, "So you'd be out? That's crap. You've
made the firm what it is. You *are* Hubbard, White."

Burdick laughed. "I hate to put it this way, Steve, but
McMillan is our largest single source of revenue."

"Well, you give us good service. And we're happy to pay for it."

"So when you or Ed talk, partners at the firm listen."

"And you want me to talk against the merger."

"It'd be bad for you and bad for dozens of other clients. Wendall Clayton has no vision of what a law firm should be. He wants to turn us into some kind of assembly line. Profit's all he thinks about."

Nordstrom picked up a fat piece of lobster and sucked it clean of dressing, then chewed and swallowed it slowly. "What's the time frame?"

"Clayton ramrodded the merger vote through early. It'll be this Tuesday."

"Day after tomorrow? Fuck me," Nordstrom said. "That man is crazy." He probed for more lobster. He settled for raisins. "Ed's in a dinner meeting right now but he should be free in an hour or so. I'll have him call and we'll have after-dinner drinks. About ten or so? By the pool over there. Don't worry, Donald. We'll work *something* out."

CHAPTER TWENTY-ONE

Clayton moved them quickly through his old manse like a tour guide goosed by a tight schedule.

It was a rambling house—big, though the rooms themselves were small and cockeyed. Beams were uneven, floorboards sprung. Much of the furniture was painted in drab Colonial colors. The gewgaws were of hammered tin and wicker and carved wood.

He led them upstairs. Taylor pretended to be studying portraits of horses, Shaker furniture and armoires while in fact she looked for places where he might have hidden information about Hanover & Stiver or the note. She glanced into a small room that seemed to be an office and saw a desk.

"Are you with us, Taylor?" Clayton asked and she hurried to join them. He continued the tour. "...Mark Twain's house, the house he died in, isn't far from here."

"Are you a Son of the American Revolution?" Carrie asked.

Clayton spoke with a feigned indignity that rested on real pride. "The Revolutionaries? They were *newcomers*. My family was one of the original settlers of Nieuw Nederlandt. We came over in 1628."

"Are you Dutch?"

"No. My ancestors were Huguenots."

Taylor said, "I always got those mixed up in school—the Huguenots and the Hottentots."

Clayton smiled coldly.

Ooooh, doesn't like potshots into the family tree.

"The Huguenots were French Protestants," he explained. "They were badly persecuted. In the 1620s Cardinal Richelieu ordered a siege of La Rochelle, a large Huguenot town. My family escaped and settled here. New Rochelle, New York, by the way, is named after La Rochelle."

Carrie asked, "What did your ancestors do when they got here?"

"There was considerable prejudice against the Huguenots, even here. We were barred from many businesses. My family became artisans. Silversmiths mostly. Paul Revere was one of us. But my family were always better merchants than craftsmen. . . . We moved into manufacturing and then finance though that field had largely been preempted by . . . other groups." For a moment he looked wily and Taylor suspected he was suppressing an opinion about early Jewish settlers.

"My family," he continued, "ended up in Manhattan and stayed there. Upper East Side. I was born within a five-block radius of my father's and grandfather's birthplaces."

That touched Taylor. "You don't see that much anymore. Today, everybody's spread all over the world."

"You shouldn't let that happen," Clayton said sincerely. "Your family history is all you have. You should keep your ancestry and be proud of it. This year I'm steward of the French Society. . . ."

Carrie, of the front row in law school, blinked. "Oh, I've heard of that. Sure."

Clayton said to Taylor, "After the Holland Society it's the most prestigious of the hereditary societies in New York."

The chubby paralegal was impressed but another need intruded. "Say, Mr. Clayton, where's the little girls' room?"

Oh, honey, don't fail me now.... Taylor wanted Carrie to keep Clayton busy, giving her a chance to take a look in the office.

But he said, "We've been having problems with the one up here. Why don't you go downstairs. We'll meet you there in a bit."

Carrie trotted off, and it was then that Taylor realized they had ended the tour at Clayton's bedroom. The room was dramatic, filled with Ralph Lauren rust and red florals, English-hunt green, brass. This was the room of a nobleman.

Beware the Jabberwock, my son....

Clayton closed the door. "You're very attractive."

Taylor sighed. Doesn't go much for subtlety, does he? She said, "I should be getting downstairs."

He took her hand. To her astonishment she let him and the next thing she knew some undefinable pressure overwhelmed her. She found herself sitting on the bed next to him.

"Wendall..."

"Look at me."

Taylor did, feeling a growing power from the partner, a magnet tugging at her soul—and at everything around her. It seemed to Taylor that her hair actually stirred in this invisible wind.

She thought of the playing-card soldiers swirling around Alice. *Beware the...*

"Wendall—"

"I want to tell you one thing," he said calmly. "This has to be completely clear. Whatever happens—or doesn't happen—has no affect on your career at Hubbard, White. Is that understood?"

She pulled her arm away. "I don't even know you. I've never even spoken to you before." But she was shocked to hear that her words seemed weak, as if she were wavering.

He shrugged. "Spoken to me? I don't want to have a discussion. I want to make love to you."

There was no physical impediment to her leaving. He wasn't even standing in her way. One foot, then the other, and she could troop right out the door. Yet she didn't.

Clayton crossed his legs. He brushed the tassel of his hair off his forehead.

"I have commitments," she explained.

No, no, no . . . Don't say that. You're meeting his argument. It's like making excuses to your father. Tell him to fuck off. Forget who he is. Forget the case. Just say it now: Fuck off. Fuck. Off.

Say it!

"Well, Taylor, we all have commitments. That's not really the issue."

She felt her throat thicken.

Don't swallow. It's a weakness.

She swallowed. "We don't even know each other."

Clayton smiled, shaking his head. "Hey, look, I don't want to marry you. I want to make love to you. That's all. Two adults. I'm telling you that you're an attractive woman."

"I have to go."

"It's not a compliment," he continued. "It's an observation. I know how to make love to women. I'm good at it. Don't you find me attractive?"

"That's not the point—"

"So you do?" he said quickly. He stroked the bed and repeated, "I want to make love with you. Harmless and simple."

Taylor smiled. "You don't want to make love at all. You want to fuck me."

"No!" he whispered harshly. Then he smiled. "I want us to fuck *together.*"

Mistake, girl. He likes dirty talk.

"Look." He waved his hand in front of his crotch like a magician. He was erect. "You did this. Not everybody does."

She found herself leaning back, first her palms on the rich bedspread, then her elbows.

"Do you know the first thing I noticed about you?" Clayton whispered, touching a renegade strand of her hair. "Your eyes. Even from across the room."

She rolled onto her side. She glanced down between his legs and said, "You're a pretty gifted man, Wendall. I would have thought that with all the excitement at the firm you'd be more distracted."

He hesitated then asked, " 'Excitement'?"

"The merger."

He didn't move for a moment. She'd thrown him off stride. He laughed seductively. "I've got a pretty big appetite."

Taylor scanned his face, which was no more than twelve inches from hers. "I read somewhere that hunters make love before the hunt," she said. "Sex is supposed to steady the hand." She shook her head. "Me, I think it's dissipating."

"Ah, dissipate me, dissipate me. . . ." But the words fell short of their intended playfulness and he sounded like a college boy making an inappropriate joke. And suddenly the balance of this contest shifted—barely—to her.

He whispered, "Lie down, put your head on the pillow." He spoke in a mesmerizing voice and Taylor was suddenly aware of his penis pressing through layers of cloth against her leg. Clayton said, "I have some toys."

"Do you?"

"I can make you feel very, very good. Like you've never felt before."

She laughed and more power slipped to her side of the board. When the spell wasn't working, his lines began to sound silly. She asked, "Why do you hate Donald Burdick?"

"I'm not interested in talking about him. Or about the merger."

"Why not?"

"I'd rather make love to you."

"The merger is all everybody's talking about."

"Are you worried about your job? You won't have to be. I promise you that," he said.

"I haven't worried about a job for years. I'm mostly just curious why you dislike Donald Burdick so much."

She sat up. Clayton seemed befuddled. The evidence of his passion hadn't diminished but he seemed uncertain—as if he had met and overcome all types of reluctance in seducing women over the years yet had suddenly run into a new defense: a barrage of questions.

"Go on," he said. "Tell me why."

"Well," Clayton finally offered, "I don't dislike Donald personally. He's one of the most charming men I know. Socially, I admire him. He's a fine representative of old money."

"The rumor is that you want to destroy him."

Clayton considered his answer. "I hear lots of rumors at the firm. I suspect those that I hear aren't any more accurate than the ones you hear. The merger is solely business. Destroying people is far too time-consuming. . . ."

Finally the partner's spell broke completely.

Taylor Lockwood rolled off the bed and ran her fingers through her hair. "You should go downstairs, I think. You are the host, after all."

Clayton tried one last time. "But . . ." His hand strayed across the bulging front of his slacks.

"You know, Wendall," Taylor said, smiling, "that's the best compliment I've had in months. Does a girl's heart good. But if you'll excuse me."

After leaving the bedroom Taylor walked into the upstairs bathroom (which, she noticed, seemed to be in perfect working order). There she waited until Clayton was out of sight. Then she slipped into his office.

Inside, in addition to the desk, were an armchair, a Victorian tea serving table, several floor lamps, two large armoires; there were no closets. She turned on a lamp and pushed the door partially closed.

The desk was unlocked. Its cubbyholes were filled with hundreds of slips of paper. Bank statements, canceled checks, memos, notes, personal bills, receipts. Taylor sighed at the volume of material she'd have to look through then sat in the red-leather chair and started going through the items one by one.

She'd been doing this for fifteen minutes when she heard a voice in the doorway say, "Ah, here you are...."

The man speaking was Wendall Clayton.

CHAPTER TWENTY-TWO

Taylor spun around and stood up, knocking a stack of papers to the floor. The sheets spread like spilled water.

Wendall Clayton was outside the door, talking to someone else. Just out of his line of sight, she reached toward the papers then heard Clayton say, "Let's go inside here for a minute, shall we?"

Desperately she kicked the papers under the desk; they disappeared—except for the corner of one letter. She reached down for it but the door was swinging open. Taylor leapt behind the largest armoire. She pressed herself flat against the wall, her head pressing painfully into the hard, cold plaster. Another voice spoke. A man's voice, one she recognized. Ralph Dudley asked, "What is it exactly you wanted to see me about, Wendall?"

The door closed. Clayton said, "Have a seat."

"Is something wrong?"

Clayton's voice was curious. "I don't remember this light being on."

Taylor eased back harder against the wall.

Silence. What were they doing? Could they see the tips of her shoes, the corner of the paper under the desk? Was the chair she'd sat in still warm?

Clayton said, "Ralph, you're part of, I guess I'd call it, the old guard, the old-boy network at the firm."

"I go back a ways, that's true."

"You and Donald started at about the same time, didn't you?"

"Bill Stanley, too. And Lamar Fredericks."

"I see you at the DAC with Joe Wilkins and Porter quite a bit, don't I?"

"Yes, we go there often. What do you—"

"Enjoying yourself tonight, are you?"

"Quite, Wendall." The old partner's voice was filled with anxiety as Clayton asked these pleasant questions with a slightly sadistic edge.

Silence. Feet shifting.

Clayton continued. "Young people here tonight. Lots of young people. It's funny, isn't it, Ralph? When I was their age I was making . . . fifty, seventy-five dollars a week. These youngsters make ninety thousand dollars a year. Amazing."

"Wendall, is there something you want?"

"Ralph, I want you to vote in favor of the merger on Tuesday. That's what I want."

A long pause. The old man's voice was trembling when he said, "I can't, Wendall. You know that. If the merger goes through I lose my job. Donald loses his; a lot of people do."

"You'll be well provided for, Ralph. A good severance."

"I can't. I can't afford to retire."

"No, of course not. You've got expenses."

Dudley sounded very cautious now. "That's right. It costs a lot to live here."

"Manhattan . . . most expensive city on earth."

"I'm sorry, Wendall. I'll have to say no to the merger."

Silence again. Taylor imagined Dudley's thoughts racing to catch up with Clayton's. Taylor's, however, had already arrived at their sad destination.

"You don't mind blunt talk?" Clayton asked.

"Of course not. I appreciate candor and—"

"If you don't vote in favor of the merger I'll go public with your affair with a sixteen-year-old girl."

The choked laugh didn't mask the despair. "What are you talking about?"

"Ralph, I respect your intelligence; I hope you'll respect mine. The little whore, the one you dress up and parade around as your granddaughter, which makes it all the more disgusting. You—"

Taylor heard the slap of a blow, a laugh of surprise from Clayton, feet dancing in the awkward shuffle of wrestling. Finally: a sad, desperate groan from Dudley—a sound filled with pain and hate and hopelessness.

Clayton laughed again. "Really, Ralph...Are you all right? There, sit down now. Are you hurt?"

"Don't touch me," Dudley said, his voice cracking. The sounds of the older man's sobbing echoed softly in the room.

Clayton said patiently, "Let's not be emotional. There's no reason for me to tell anyone. Let's negotiate a little bit. You're the firm's charmer, aren't you? You're suave, debonaire. You're a holdout from the days when a lawyer's manners were as important as his intelligence. So, now, how's this? You and three of your cronies switch your votes in favor of the merger and I won't share your secret."

"Three others?"

"Say, Joe, Porter, pick somebody else. But—here's the good part—you bring me any *more* and I'll kick in fifty thousand each to your severance package. That should keep you in teenage pussy for another year or so."

"You're vile," Dudley spat out.

"More vile than you?" Clayton asked. "I wonder. The vote's day after tomorrow, Ralph. Why don't you think about it." Clayton's was the voice of luxurious moderation. "Just think about it. It's your decision. Come on, go downstairs, have a drink. Relax."

"If you only understood—"

J e f f e r y   D e a v e r

Clayton's voice cut through the room like a knife. "Oh, but that's the point, Ralph. I can't understand. And no one else will either."

The door opened. Two pairs of feet receded. Both slowly. One pair in triumph, one in despair, but the sound they made was the same.

━━━━━

Still in the quiet den Taylor was concentrating on a single noise.

Rhythmic and soft.

She had stayed here, hiding behind the armoire, after the partners had left because Clayton had remained upstairs; she'd heard his voice from nearby.

Then after five minutes or so the sound began. What is that?

A voice chanting? Primitive music?

She couldn't place it at first. It seemed very familiar but she associated it with an entirely different place.

Rhythmic and soft.

No, couldn't be. . . .

She walked to the far wall and pressed her head against the plaster again. The sound was coming from the other side—Clayton's bedroom.

Oh, Taylor realized. *That's* the sound. Of course. Not one voice, but two.

The nature of the activity didn't surprise Taylor much, considering what she now knew about Wendall Clayton. What did surprise her, however, was that the other participant was Carrie Mason, who was contributing half of the sound effects.

"Fuck me, fuck me, fuck me. . . . I'm almost there. . . . Yeah, yeah, yeah. . . ."

Carrie may have finished quickly but it took Clayton considerably longer. Long enough, in fact, for Taylor to go through the partner's desk carefully. The sound track conveniently helped her gauge how much time she had.

She found only one thing that interested her: an invoice

for a security firm. The bill was for ongoing services, which had begun last month. The job description was "As directed by client."

She debated stealing it. What would her detective friend John Silbert Hemming do? He'd use a spy camera, she guessed. But ill-equipped Taylor Lockwood did the next best thing: She carefully copied all the information and put the invoice back.

Downstairs she noticed the crowd had dwindled considerably, as you'd expect for a Sunday night party. Only the hard-core partyers remained. Thom Sebastian, for instance, who swooped in for another sloppy bear hug. She ducked away from it. He said good-bye and reiterated his dinner invitation for tomorrow. Taylor ambled through the house, aiming toward the buffet and listening to the snatches of muted, often drunken, conversation.

He's going to do it. For sure. Next month, we're going to be Hubbard, White, Willis, Sullivan & Perelli.

You're out to lunch, dude. No way'll Burdick let it happen.

Do you realize the vote is Tuesday? Day after tomorrow.

You hear about the detective that was going through Burdick's Swiss accounts?

You hear Burdick had somebody check Clayton's law review article to see if he plagiarized?

That's bullshit.

You want to talk bullshit, this merger is bullshit. Nobody's getting any work done.

Where's Donald?

He doesn't need to be here. He sent Himmler instead.

Who?

His wife. See, Burdick would charm a man out of his balls; Vera'd just cut 'em off. You know the stories about her, don't you? Lady Macbeth...

Taylor noticed that Burdick's wife was no longer here.

She then surveyed the long table where there'd once sat mounds of caviar, roast beef, steak tartare and sesame chicken. All that now remained was broccoli.

Taylor Lockwood hated broccoli.

On the patio deck of the Fleetwood Hotel's penthouse on the Miami Beach strip Ed Gliddick sent a golf ball near the putting cup embedded in the roof's AstroTurf.

"Hell," he said of the miss and looked at the trim young man near him, who watched the shot without emotion. Standing ramrod-straight, he offered Gliddick no false compliments and said only, "I play tennis, not golf."

The man was Randall Simms III, Wendall Clayton's protégé. It was he who'd pirated the Hubbard, White & Willis chartered jet to beat Donald Burdick down to Florida to meet with the executives of McMillan Holdings.

While Burdick himself was cooling his heels with the second-in-command of the company, Steve Nordstrom, Simms had been meeting with Gliddick, the chairman of the board and CEO of McMillan.

McMillan was a company that did nothing but own other companies, which either manufactured obscure industrial parts or provided necessary though obscure services to other businesses or in turn owned other companies or portions of them. The vagaries of this structure and function, however, were not to suggest that Gliddick didn't know how to satisfy a market need when he saw one. McMillan was consistently in the top twenty of the most profitable companies in the world.

At sixty-five, Gliddick was stooped and paunchy amidships. His ruddy skin was wrinkled from years of sun on golf courses and tennis courts around the world. Sparse gray hair, a hook of a nose.

So he said to Simms, "Wendall didn't come down to see me. He sent you instead."

Simms said nothing.

Gliddick held up a hand. "Which means only one thing. You're the muscle, right?"

Unsmiling, Simms folded his arms and watched Gliddick miss another easy putt. "Wendall wanted a little distance between himself and what I'm going to say to you."

"This's all about that fucking merger, isn't it?"

"I'd suggest we go inside," Simms said. "Somebody could have an antenna trained on us. They really make those things, you know. They're not just in the movies."

"I know."

Gliddick walked into the room, shut the window and drew the curtains. Simms mixed whiskey sours for them both. Gliddick wondered how this man, whom he'd never met, had known that this was his drink.

The chairman sipped the sweet concoction. "You know Donald Burdick's meeting with Steve Nordstrom right now."

"We know."

We.

"So what is it that you want, I mean, Wendall wants?"

"We want you to let it be known around the firms—ours and John Perelli's—that you want the merger to go through."

"Why would we *not* want it to go through?"

Simms said bluntly, "Donald and his cronies won't be there afterward."

"Ah." Gliddick nodded. "I see."

"You might feel some loyalty to him," Simms said.

"Fuck, I do feel loyalty to him."

"Of course you do. You've been friends for years. But putting that aside for a moment, let's talk about why you *would* want the firms to merge," Simms said.

This is one slick boy—I like him, Gliddick thought, but immediately gave up the idea of trying to wrest him away from Hubbard, White to work for McMillan. Wendall Clayton was not somebody you stole employees from.

Simms continued, "We've gone over your billings, Ed. Burdick's robbing you blind. Your legal costs are totally out of control. You're paying two hundred bucks an hour for first-year associates who know shit. You're paying for limo deliveries when messengers can take public transportation. You're paying premium bonuses for routine legal work. If you help the merger along we'll pare your expenses by an easy five million a year."

"Five?"

"Five. And if the merger goes through, Perelli can take over your labor law work. Right now you've got Mavern, Simpson handling it and, frankly, they're idiots. They didn't do shit to keep the unions out of your subs' Oregon and Washington State operations. Perelli's the toughest labor lawyer in New York. He'll fuck your unions in the ass."

Gliddick shook his head. "Donald was on our board for I don't know how long. He's got friends all over the company. There're a lot of people won't take it kindly that we've sold him out."

" 'Kindly'?" Simms said the word as if it were in a foreign language. "Well, loyalty's important. But it works both ways. I'd think you'd have to *earn* loyalty. And do you think a lawyer who misses a takeover plan against his client deserves it?"

"A . . . What're you talking about?"

"There's a rumor. . . . Only a rumor but Wendall and I think it's valid."

"We're always hearing that. Hell, we beat projections every quarter last year. Everybody'd love to acquire us."

"But does everybody contact your institutional investors on the sly?"

Gliddick's glass froze halfway to his mouth. "Who?"

"GCI in Toronto."

"Weinraub, that fucking Jew prick." A glance to Simms to see if the young man was Semitic but the results of the scan came back reassuringly Aryan. "I saw him just last week in London. He gave me the great stone face."

Simms continued, "We're thinking four months till a tender offer. If you wait you'll pay a takeover firm a million or two to defend. Perelli can preempt it for a quarter of that. And he can handle it in a way that your stockholders and key employees won't get nervous and bail out. That's what he does best."

"Donald doesn't know about it?"

"Nope. We found out through Perelli.

He finished his drink. Simms poured another.

"Randy, I don't know. I can't argue with what you're say-ing, with the numbers. It's a moral decision. I don't like moral decisions. Maybe—"

There was a knock on the door. A young woman. Blond, about five-two, wearing a short leather miniskirt and tight white blouse, walked into the suite.

"Mr. Simms, I've got the file you asked for."

"Thank you, Jean." He took a thick manila folder. "Jean, this is Mr. Gliddick."

They shook hands. Gliddick's eyes skimmed the white silk over her breasts, the lacy bra clearly visible beneath.

"Jean's an assistant with a firm we use down here occa-sionally."

"Nice to meet you, Jean."

Simms tapped the folder. "There's a lot of other material in there about how the merger'd be good for your company, Ed." He looked at his watch. "Say, I've got a conference call scheduled now. I'll make it from my room so I don't bother you. Look over that stuff, think about what I'm saying."

"Sure," Gliddick said, eyes still scanning Jean's figure. She smiled broadly at the paunchy businessman.

"Say, Jean," Simms said, "you know Miami, right?"

"Well, now, I've lived here all my life" came the lilting accent.

"Then maybe you could help Mr. Gliddick figure out a place where he and I could go listen to some music. Jazz or Cuban or something."

"I'd be happy to." The young woman sat on the bed and picked up an entertainment guide. Her skirt hiked up high. "If that's all right with him."

"I'd appreciate your input," Gliddick said.

Simms said, "We're off-duty now, Jean, how 'bout you fix yourself a drink. And another one for Mr. Gliddick too."

"Thanks, Randy. I believe I will."

"I'll be back in about an hour," Simms said.

"That'd be fine," Gliddick replied, setting the file on the table and watching Jean scoot pertly off the bed and walk to the bar. Somehow her shoes had come off in the process.

Moral decision . . .

As Simms was about to step through the door, Gliddick said, "One thing, Randy?"

The tall lawyer turned.

"Maybe you could call first—before coming back to the room?"

"Not a problem, Ed."

At 10 P.M., as Reece was accelerating south onto the highway that would take them from Clayton's Connecticut home back to the city, Taylor stretched out in the reclining seat of the rented Lincoln.

She was listening to the moan of the transmission. The flabby suspension swayed her nearly to sleep. She'd told him about Clayton's blackmailing Dudley and then about the invoice she'd found.

"'Client-directed' security services?" Reece asked. Then he nodded. "A euphemism for industrial espionage. Good job, finding that. How much was it for?"

"Two thousand a month."

"That's pretty low for stealing a note. Maybe it's for spying on people for the merger."

"Did you hear the talk at the party? My God, these are first-year associates and all they were talking about was the merger. Wendall's out on a limb. If he doesn't get it through he's lost a lot of credibility. . . ."

Reece laughed. "Ha, if he doesn't get the merger through he's lost his *job.* . . ." He looked over and caught her in the midst of another huge yawn. "You okay?"

"I used to sleep."

"I tried it once," Reece said, shrugging. "It wears off."

He reached over and began massaging her neck.

"Oh, that's nice. . . ." She closed her eyes. "You ever made love in a car?"

"Never have."

"I never have either. I've never even been to a drive-in movie."

Reece said, "One time when I was in high school, I—
Jesus!"

A huge jolt. Taylor's eyes snapped open and she saw a
white car directly in front of them. It'd veered into their
lane. Reece swerved onto the shoulder but the Lincoln
slipped off the flat surface and started down a steep em-
bankment.

"Mitchell!" Taylor screamed and threw her arms up as
trees and plants raced at them at seventy miles an hour. The
undercarriage scraping and groaning, metal and plastic sup-
ports popping apart. Then brush and reeds were flashing
past the car's windows.

Reece called, "That car, that car! He ran us off the road!
He ran us—"

He was braking, trying to grip the wheel as it spun furiously back and forth, the front tires buffeted by rocks and
branches. The car slowed as it chewed through the underbrush, the buff-colored rushes and weeds whipping into the
windshield.

Taylor's head slammed against the window; she was
stunned. She felt nausea and fear and a huge pain in her
back.

Then they were slowing as the slope flattened out. The
car was still skewing but the wheels started to track, coming
under control.... She heard Reece say reverently, "Son of a
bitch," and saw him smile as the car started a slow skid on
the slippery vegetation. Thirty miles an hour, twenty-five ...

"Okay, okay...," Reece muttered to himself. He steered
carefully into the skids, braking lightly, regaining control,
losing and then regaining it. "Okay, come on," he whispered
seductively to the huge Lincoln.

The car slowed to ten miles an hour. Taylor took his arm
and whispered, "Oh, Mitchell." They smiled at each other,
giddy with relief.

But as she looked at his face his smile vanished.

"God!" He shoved his foot onto the brake with all his
weight. Taylor looked forward and she saw the brush disappear as they broke out of the foliage and dropped over a

ridge, onto a steep incline that led down to the huge reservoir, a half mile across, its surface broken with choppy waves. The locked wheels slid without resistance along the frost and dewy leaves.

"Taylor!" he called. "We're going in, we're going in!"

With a last huge rocking jolt, the scenery and the distant gray horizon disappeared. A wave of black oily water crashed into the windshield and started coming into the car from a dozen places at once.

CHAPTER TWENTY-THREE

At eleven that night, in Miami, the phone in Donald Burdick's hotel room rang.

The partner had been waiting for Ed Gliddick all evening and had fallen asleep, fully dressed, on the couch in his room.

"Yes, hello?" he asked groggily.

"Mr. Burdick?" a woman's voice asked.

"That's right. Who's this?"

"My name's Jean. I'm calling for Mr. Gliddick."

Jean? Burdick wondered. Who was this? Ed Gliddick had had the same secretary, Helen, for twenty years and never traveled anywhere without her.

"Yes, Jean, well, I've been waiting to see Ed all night. Is he all right?"

"Mr. Gliddick asked me to call you and apologize. He won't be able to see you, I'm afraid."

Burdick was angry and disappointed but he said, "Well, it's late anyway. We can meet for breakfast. I'll—"

"Actually, sir, I'm afraid he won't be able to see you at all this trip. He's got meetings nonstop for the next two days and then he's got to get home to Battle Creek."

Burdick closed his eyes and sighed. So, ambushed by Clayton yet again.

"I see. By any chance was there another attorney from Hubbard, White & Willis in town tonight?"

"I wouldn't know, sir."

"Okay," Burdick said wearily, realizing it would be pointless to call Steve Nordstrom—the coward wouldn't even pick up the phone. "If you could deliver a message to Ed for me."

"I'd be happy to."

"'And you too, Brutus?' Do you have that?"

"Uhm, I do, sir. Will he know what it means?"

"I'm sure he will." Burdick dropped the phone in the cradle then picked it up once more to call his wife.

In front of them the huge reservoir extended in faintly lapping waves to the trees on the opposite shore. The moon reflected off the water, broken into a thousand crescents on the textured surface. It would've been quite romantic if they hadn't been wet and freezing.

Taylor Lockwood and Reece sat in the front seat of the rental Lincoln, legs crossed to keep their feet out of the six inches of water that filled the bottom of the car's interior.

After the skid to the bottom of the hill, with its dramatic conclusion—a braking splash like a Disneyland ride—the Lincoln had settled into about eighteen inches of water and stopped sinking.

The reservoir was huge but here, apparently, very shallow.

They'd laughed—edgy and a bit hysterical—but then the humor wore off quickly when they realized that while they could open the door, they'd have a thirty- or forty-foot trek through freezing water up to a deserted road, where they'd have to wait for help with no way to keep warm.

Reece called the police on his cell phone and then they curled their legs up and huddled in their coats.

The dispatcher had assured them that a squad car and rescue truck would be there in ten minutes. But that had been some time ago and, since Reece had been unable to tell them exactly where they'd run off the road, he guessed their rescue might not be imminent even now.

"Who was it?" Taylor asked.

"The thief, I assume. I didn't get a good look at him. Middle-aged guy, white, hat, collar turned up. I didn't even see what kind of car it was. Just a white streak."

"An accident?"

"No way," Reece answered. "He was steering for us."

"Who was at the party—who'd know we were there?"

Reece shrugged. "Thom Sebastian, Dudley. And most of Clayton's little goose-stepping clones, except Randy Simms." Then he fell silent for a moment, finally saying, "I'm thinking it's time to tell the police what happened. Tell them everything."

"No." She shook her head.

"I didn't think this was going to happen, Taylor. I never thought it could turn violent."

She said, "It wouldn't make sense to kill us. That'd bring the police in for sure, and he doesn't want that any more than we do. He didn't know we'd go off the road. He was just scaring us."

Reece considered.

Taylor scooted closer to him. "We're almost there. I can feel it. The trial's day after tomorrow. Let's just hold out until then." She took his head in both her hands. "Just until then?"

"I don't know."

But he was weakening. She repeated, "Just until then," though when she said the words this time, they were not spoken as a question but as a command. He opened his mouth to protest, but she shook her head and touched his lips with her finger.

He leaned close, following the motion of her finger to

her own lips. They kissed hard and their arms wound
around each other.

A moment later this embrace was interrupted by several
probing flashlights, their fierce halogen beams converging
on the car. As Reece and Taylor leapt apart they could hear a
laugh and an amused voice. "Whoa, lookit that car! Looks
like it's floating. Hank, lookit! I mean, you ever seen anything like that?"

To which another voice replied, "I surely haven't. Not in
a month of Sundays."

━━━━━

At lunch on Monday, the day before the New Amsterdam trial, Taylor Lockwood sat in Mc Sorley's Old Ale
House in Manhattan and watched John Silbert Hemming
down a mug of ale.

He may not've been the traditional private eye who
tossed back Scotch on the job but this boy loved his beer.
The tall man finished his sixth mug of dark brew and called
for three more. "They're small."

True, they were, though Taylor was having trouble with
her second. She'd drunk more wine than she'd intended at
Clayton's and had not gotten much sleep, thanks to the dip
in the reservoir—and Reece's presence in bed next to her.

She told Hemming about the Supreme Court case that
required the pub to allow women in; for many years it had
been a men-only establishment.

"Some achievement," Hemming muttered, looking at
the carved-up bare wood tables, the wishbone collection
growing a dark fur of dust and the crowds of young frat
boys shouting and hooting. He glowered at a drunk, beer-
spilling student stumbling toward them. The boy caught the
huge man's gaze and changed direction quickly. With some
true curiosity in his voice the detective asked Taylor, "Are
we having a date?"

"I don't think so."

"Ah," he said and nodded. "How did the fingerprints
work out?"

"Not bad. I'll send you a postcard."

"If you want I'll show you how to do plantars."

"Vegetable prints?"

"Very good but no—feet, Ms. Lockwood."

"Taylor."

"Feet."

Taylor handed him the piece of paper with the information from the invoice she'd found in Wendall Clayton's desk. "John, have you ever heard of this company?"

He read, "Triple A Security? They're not around New York. But we can assume it's a sleazy outfit."

"Why's that?"

"It's an old trick to get in the front of the phone book—to have your listing first. Name your company with a lot of A's. You want me to check it out?"

"Can you?"

"Sure." A waiter carrying fifteen mugs in one hand swooped past and dropped two more, unasked-for.

"Would somebody from a security service—say, this disreputable Triple A outfit—commit a crime?"

"Jaywalking?"

"Worse."

"Stealing apples?"

"That category. More valuable than fruit."

He sat up and towered over her for an instant then hunched forward again. "At the big security firms, like our place, absolutely not. You commit a crime, you lose your license and your surety bond's invalidated. But these small outfits"—he tapped the paper—"there's a fine line between the good guys and the bad guys. I mean, somebody's got to *plant* the bugs that my company finds, right? And planting bugs is illegal."

"Any funny stuff?"

"That's not a term of art in my profession."

"Say, hypothetically, trying to run somebody off the road."

"Run somebody off . . ."

Taylor whispered, " . . . the road."

Hemming hesitated a moment and said, "This sort of

place—Triple A Security—yeah, you could possibly find somebody there who might be willing to do that. Worse too."

Taylor finished the bitter dark ale. She opened her purse, pulled out a twenty and signaled the waiter.

"Is there a Mr. Lockwood?" Hemming asked.

"Yes, but you wouldn't really like my father."

"Well, anything in the fiancé-boyfriend category. You know, those pesky fellows that tend to get there first?"

"Not exactly."

John Silbert Hemming said, "How about dinner?"

"Can't."

"I was going to let *you* take *me* out so you could deduct it."

She laughed and said, "I've got plans for the immediate future."

"Plans are what contractors and shipbuilders use."

"Some other time?" she asked. "I mean it."

"Sure," Hemming said. Then, as she started to stand, he held up a finger, which returned her to her seat. "One thing...there's this friend I have. He wears a badge and works at a place called One Police Plaza and I was thinking maybe it's time you gave him a call. Just to have a chat."

Taylor replayed the drive through the foliage down to the reservoir last night and thought Hemming's was an excellent idea.

But she answered, "No."

CHAPTER TWENTY-FOUR

They walked together through Battery Park.

Ralph Dudley's eyes were on the Statue of Liberty, rising from the harbor like a sister of the figure of blind justice. Junie walked silently beside him. He wanted to hold her hand but of course he did not. Like tourists, they were on their way to see the monument up close.

Dudley wondered how many people Junie's age knew the lines carved on the base of the statue, knew they were from a poem called "The New Colossus" by Emma Lazarus.

> *Give me your tired, your poor,*
> *Your huddled masses, yearning to breathe free,*
> *The wretched refuse of your teeming shore....*

Hardly any.

But, he also wondered, how many Wall Street lawyers knew it?

Not many of them either.

"Is it, like, cold on the boat?"

"You're saying 'like' again a lot. Remember, you were going to watch it."

"Whatever."

"I'm sure we can sit downstairs where it's warm. We'll get some hot chocolate."

"Or a beer," she muttered.

"Ha," Dudley said. "Come on over here for a minute."

He nodded to a bench and they sat down, Dudley wondering, as he had for a thousand times that year, why he was so taken with this little creature.

"Yo, so wassup?" she said. Sometimes she talked black and there was nothing he could say to get her out of this mode. He'd learned that it was best to ignore her affectations. They went away sooner or later.

"I've got some papers here. For you to sign. We couldn't do it in the firm."

She put her Walkman headsets on. He took them off her and smoothed her hair. She wrinkled her face.

"You've got to sign them."

"Like, okay."

He dug them out of his briefcase and handed them to her.

"Okay," she said, snapping her gum. "Gimme a pen."

Dudley reached into his jacket pocket and found that he'd accidentally picked up his Cross mechanical pencil. "Damn, I forgot mine."

"I, like, have one." She reached into her purse and pulled it out. But as she did a piece of paper fell to the ground. Dudley had picked it up and started to hand it back when he looked at the check.

He saw Junie's name.

He saw Taylor Lockwood's name.

His hand froze in midair between them.

Dudley looked at her with rage in his face. "What is this?

"I—"

"What the hell have you done?"

"Poppie?" she asked, dropping her Walkman. It broke apart on the asphalt.

"How could you?" he whispered. "How could you?"

The going rate to get Alice into the rabbit hole of a Manhattan apartment was a sob story.

I feel so stupid, Ralph Dudley's my uncle? And my aunt— that's his wife—passed away two years ago today and he was feeling really lousy. I wanted to make him dinner, just to cheer him up.

She held up the Food Emporium bag as evidence.

Here's fifty for your trouble. Don't say anything, okay? It's a surprise.

Taylor Lockwood had dressed in her business finest, to allay the doorman's concerns. He looked her over, pocketed the money, slipped her a spare key and turned back to a tiny television.

She knew Dudley wouldn't be here. She'd run into him in the halls and he'd told her that he was taking the afternoon off to show Junie the Statue of Liberty. The sullen girl had been in the lobby, waiting for him. Taylor shivered at the thought of the two of them together. For the girl's part, she looked from Dudley's face to Taylor's and back again. And just seemed bored.

Taylor now walked inside and found that Dudley's apartment was much smaller and more modest than she'd expected.

Although she knew about his financial problems, she'd assumed that an elderly Wall Street law firm partner like Dudley would be living at least in simple elegance, jaded though it might be. In fact, the four rooms in the prewar building didn't not have much more square footage than her own apartment. The walls were covered with cheap paint, which blotched where it was thin and peeled where the painters had bothered to apply several coats. There was no way the windows would ever open again.

She gave a cursory once-over to the living room, which was filled with old furniture, some of whose tattered, cracked arms and legs were tied together neatly with twine. She saw chipped vases, lace that had been torn and carelessly

resewn, books, afghans, walking sticks, a collection of
dented silver cigarette cases. Walls were covered with old
framed pictures of relatives, including several of Dudley as a
young man with a large, unfriendly-looking woman. He was
handsome but very thin and he stared at the camera with
solemn introspection.

In his bedroom, beside a neatly made bed, she found
what looked like a wooden torso with one of Dudley's suit
jackets hanging on the shoulders. A clothes brush rested on
a small rack on the torso's chest and on the floor in front of it
was a pair of carefully polished shoes with well-worn heels.

His fussiness made her job as burglar easy. Each of the
pigeonholes in his oak rolltop desk contained a single, well-
marked category of documents. Con Ed bills, phone bills,
letters from his daughter (the least-filled compartment),
business correspondence, warranty cards for household ap-
pliances, letters from his alumni organization, receipts. He
separated opera programs from symphony programs from
ballet programs.

Taylor finished the desk in ten minutes but could find
nothing linking Dudley to the note or to Hanover & Stiver.
Discouraged and feeling hot and filthy from the search, she
walked into the kitchen, illuminated with pallid light from the
courtyard that the room's one small window looked out on.

Taylor leaned against the sink. In front of her was
Dudley's small kitchen table, on either side of which were
two mahogany chairs. One side of the table was empty. On
the other was a faded place mat on which sat an expensive,
nicked porcelain plate, a setting of heavy silverware, a wineglass—all arranged for his solitary dinner that evening. A
starched white napkin, rolled and held by a bright red napkin ring, rested in the center of the plate. The gaudy ring was
the one item glaringly out of place. Taylor picked up the
cheap plastic, the kind sold at the bargain stores in Times
Square where tourists buy personalized souvenirs—cups,
dishes, tiny license plates.

She turned it over; the name sloppily embossed in the
plastic was *Poppie*.

A present from June, the object of his perverse desire.

Her hour was up. Book on outta here, Alice. . . .

Nothing, she thought angrily. I didn't find a thing. Not a single hint as to where the note might be. She stuffed the grocery bag, which had been filled only with wadded-up newspapers, into the trash chute and left.

So, can we eliminate Dudley? she wondered.

No, but we can put him lower on the list than Thom Sebastian.

Well, don't get too interested in her. . . .

She'd charm the young lawyer, interrogate him—the prick who'd been collecting information on her. She remembered his troubled expression yesterday. Maybe a confession *would* be forthcoming at dinner tonight. She still held out that hope.

Outside, she paused for a moment, rubbed her eyes.

Tomorrow, she thought in alarm, the trial was tomorrow.

Taylor stepped into the street to flag down a cab.

█████████

Thom Sebastian sat at the bar of the Blue Devil on the far edge of West Fifty-seventh, near the Hudson River.

An excellent place, he assessed, it had a mostly black audience, dressed super-sharp. He was working on a vodka gimlet, imagining his juggler and thinking, So far, so good.

But also thinking *goddamn,* I'm nervous.

He was considering what was about to happen tonight.

Was this a way-major mistake?

For a while he'd thought so. But now he wasn't so sure. Had no idea.

But it *was* going to happen; the die had been cast, he thought, phrasing the situation in a cliché that he found unworthy of a lawyer of his caliber.

He found himself coolly considering partnership at Hubbard, White & Willis and he remembered—almost with amusement—that he'd always considered achieving partnership a matter of life and death.

Death...

After Wendall Clayton had called him into his office and told him in that soft voice of his that the firm had concluded it would be unable to extend the offer of partnership to him, Sebastian had sat motionless for three or four minutes, smiling at the partner, listening to the man describe the firm's plans for Sebastian's severance.

A smile, yes, but it was really a rictus gaze, what to Clayton—had the fucking prick even noticed—must have seemed like a grin of madness: teeth bared, eyes crinkling in a psychotic squint. .

"We'd like to make you a partner, Thom—you're respected here—but you understand that economies have to be effected."

Meaning simply that Sebastian was not a clone of Wendall Clayton and was, therefore, expendable.

Effecting economies...Oh, how that term—pure corporatespeak—had inflamed him like acid.

Listening to Clayton, he'd lowered his head and had seen something resting on the partner's desk: an inlaid dish of Arabic design. Sebastian's eyes had clung to the dish as if he could encapsulate the terrible reality in the cloisonné and escape, leaving his sorrow trapped behind him.

And now he thought about the problem of Taylor Lockwood.

But he tried as hard as he could to push her away, put her out of his mind, and replaced her with the image of the juggler once more.

He glanced at his watch.

Okay, let's do it. He stood up from the bar, told the bartender he'd be back in five.

So far...

Without really thinking about it, the man in the Dodge reached over to the passenger seat and felt the breakdown— a Remington automatic 12-gauge shotgun.

Six shells in the extended magazine. Six more wedged into the seat, business end down.

He wasn't concentrating on the hardware, though; his eyes were on the woman walking down the street toward the fat boy, Thom Sebastian, who waved at her, smiling a weird smile. Looking all shit-his-pants.

All right, so this bitch was the one.

The man in the Dodge watched her, wondering what kind of body she had underneath the overcoat. He would've liked it if she'd been wearing high heels. He liked high heels, not those stupid black flat shoes this broad wore.

The man in the Dodge checked for blue-and-whites and pedestrians who might block the shot.

Clear street, clear shooting zone.

He eased the car forward then braked slowly to a halt twenty feet from the woman. She glanced at him with casual curiosity. Her eyes met his and, as he lifted the gun, she real- ized what was going down. She screamed, holding up her hands.

Nowhere for her to run . . .

He aimed over the bead sight and pulled the trigger. The huge recoil stunned his shoulder. He had a fast image of the woman as she took one load of buckshot in the side, a glancing hit. He fired two more toward her back but the way she fell, it seemed that only one cluster struck her and even that wasn't a square hit.

Well, if she wasn't dead yet she probably would be soon. And at the very worst she'd be out of commission for months.

People screamed and horns wailed as cars screeched to a halt, avoiding the pedestrians who dived into the street for safety.

The man in the Dodge accelerated fast to the next inter- section, skidded through the red then slowed and, once out of sight of the hit, drove carefully uptown, well within the speed limit, diligently stopping at every red light he came to.

CHAPTER TWENTY-FIVE

Thom Sebastian, hands cuffed, was led into the precinct house by two uniformed cops.

Everybody stared at him—the cops, the drunk drivers, the hookers, a lawyer or two.

"Man," somebody whispered.

It was the blood, which covered Sebastian's jacket and white shirt. Nobody could figure out how somebody could be covered with this much blood and not have a dozen stab wounds.

The chubby lawyer slumped on a bench, waiting for the booking officer to get around to him, staring at his brown wing tips. A girl sat next to him, a tall black hooker with a tank top and hot pants under her fake fur coat. She looked at the blood then shook her head quickly, a shiver.

"Jesus," she whispered.

Sebastian felt a shadow over him, someone walking close. He looked up and blinked.

Taylor Lockwood said, "Are you all right? The blood . . ."

Sebastian nodded then closed his eyes and lowered his head again slowly. "Nosebleed," he muttered.

The desk sergeant said gruffly to her, "Who're you?"

Taylor said, "What happened?"

He looked over her black nylons, short black skirt and leather jacket. "Get outta here, lady. He's missin' his date for the night."

A bit of her father's temper popped within her. "And I'm making the trip down here to meet with my client. So I guess I'm missing mine too. Anything else you'd like to put on the record?"

The man's face reddened. "Hey, I didn't know you was a lawyer."

She had no idea what had happened. She'd shown up at the restaurant and found a crime scene investigation under way. Somebody'd been shot and Sebastian had been arrested.

She barked, "What's he been booked on?"

"Nothing yet. The arresting's on the phone to the medical examiner." He turned back to a mass of papers.

Man, that was a lot of blood.

A uniformed officer came up, a thin man, slicked-back hair, gray at the temples. He looked over Taylor and was not pleased. His would be a joint prejudice: against defense lawyers in general (who spent hours tormenting cops on the witness stand and reducing them to little piles of incompetence) and women defense lawyers in particular (who had to prove they could torment more brutally than their male counterparts).

Taylor Lockwood cocked her head and tried to look like a ballbuster. "I'm Mr. Sebastian's lawyer. What's going on?"

Suddenly a roar of a voice filled the station house. "Hey, Taylor!"

She froze. Oh, brother—why now? It was one of those moments when the gods get bored and decide to skewer you just for the fun of it. Taylor gave an inaudible sigh and turned toward the voice, now booming again, "Taylor Lockwood, right?"

A huge cop, a faceful of burst vessels, tan from a vacation in Vegas or the Bahamas, stalked across the room. He was off-duty, wearing designer jeans and a windbreaker. Early forties, thirty pounds overweight. Trim, razor-cut blond hair. A boyish face.

There was nothing to do, she decided, but go all the way. Her father's advice: If you're going to bluff, bluff like there's no tomorrow.

"Hey," she said, smiling.

"It's Tommy Blond. Don'tcha remember? Tommy Bianca, from the Pogiolli case."

"Sure, Tommy. How you doing?" She took his massive, callused hand.

The man was looking down at Sebastian. "He okay?"

"Nosebleed is all," the arresting said. "We thought he'd taken one, too. EMS looked him over, said he'll be okay, he keeps an eye on his nostrils."

Tommy Blond looked at the arresting and the desk sergeant. "Hey, treat this lady right. She's okay. She was working with the lawyer got off Joey, youse remember—Joey Pogiolli from the Sixth? Got him off last year some asshole sued him, said Joey worked him over on a bust. . . . Hey, Taylor, you was a paralegal then. What, you go to law school?"

"Nights," Taylor said, grinning and wondering if the nervous sweat that had gathered on her forehead would start running down to her chin and carrying her makeup with it.

"That's great. My kid's applying to Brooklyn. Wants to be FBI. I told him agents don't got to have law degrees anymore but he wants to do it right. Maybe sometime he could talk to you about school? Got a card?"

"None with me. Sorry."

She glanced at Sebastian, staring at the floor.

Tommy Blond said, "Whatsa story, Frank?"

The arresting said, "We got a vic got took out outside the Blue Devil, name of Magaly Sanchez. Upscale coke dealer moving into the wrong territory. We think whoever did her wasn't sure what she looked like and was using him"—he nodded toward Sebastian—"to ID the hit. Or

maybe they wanted to whack her in front of a customer.
Send a message, you know. She had about ten grams on her,
all packaged and ready for delivery. And Mr. Sebastian had a
quarter gram.... That's why we brought him in."

Taylor rolled her eyes. "A quarter gram? Come on, you
guys."

"Taylor, I know what you're asking...." Tommy Blond
said, then: "That's a lot of blood. You're sure it's just a nosebleed?"

She remembered a buzzword. "What was your probable
cause for search?"

"Probable cause?" The arresting blinked in surprise. "He
was waving at a known drug dealer who got whacked right
in front of him? That's not probable cause—that's for-damn-
fucking-sure cause."

"Let's talk." She walked over to the bulletin board.
Tommy Blond and the arresting looked at each other and
then followed her. She stood with her head down and whispered harshly to the arresting, "Come on, he's never been arrested before. Sure, the guy's an asshole, but a quarter gram?
You and I both know a collar like that's optional."

Taylor was making this up.

The arresting: "I don't know.... Everybody's pissed off
about these assholes from Wall Street think they can buy
and sell blow and we're not going to do anything about it."

"Let's cut a deal," Taylor continued. "Tell you what. Give
him back to me and he'll give you a statement about the late
Miss Sanchez and her friends—as long as it's anonymous
and he never has to testify in court against anybody. And I'll
make him promise to get off the stuff."

"Whatta you say?" Tommy Blond said to the uniformed
officer.

"Look," Taylor pushed, "he works for the same firm got
your buddy Joey off. That oughta count for something."

Joey, Taylor remembered, was the patrolman who
maybe *did* get a little carried away with his nightstick on
that black kid who maybe lifted a wallet but maybe didn't.
And who maybe reached for that tire iron, even though,

funny thing, it was found twenty feet away from the scuffle. Took the ER fifty-eight stitches to repair Officer Joey's hand-iwork on the kid's face.

The arresting gave Taylor a look that's shorthand in law enforcement. It translates to: I don't need this shit.

"Okay, get him out of here. But tell him to clean up his act. I mean, like really. Next time they won't leave *nobody* around. Have him down to Narcotics at the Plaza next week and give 'em a statement." He wrote a name on a card. "Ask for this detective here."

Taylor said, "Thanks, gentlemen."

Tommy Blond shook her hand again. "Proud of you, lit-tle lady. A lawyer. That's all right." He walked off toward the locker room.

Taylor walked back to Sebastian, who'd been slumped in his seat, out of earshot of the bargaining. He didn't yet know he was free.

She knelt down next to him, looked at the blood on his face and shirt. It was quite brilliant. She said, "Thom, I may be able to help you out. But I've got to ask you something. I need an honest answer. . . . Look at me."

Boy's eyes. Indignant, hurt, scared boy's eyes.

"You went through Mitchell Reece's file cabinet some-time recently. Why?"

A furrow ran through his bloody forehead as he frowned. He sniffed. "What are you talking about?"

Taylor said brutally, "Fuck it, Thom, I can get you out of here or I can make sure they book you. That'll be the end of your life in New York. Now, it's your call."

He wiped tears from his cheeks. "Mitchell does trial work for New Amsterdam. I handle a lot of their corporate work. I probably needed some files he had."

"You've been in his safe file?"

Sebastian frowned again. "That thing he's got in his of-fice with the locks on it? Yeah, a few months ago I got some files out of it, some settlement agreements from a secured-loan suit a couple of years ago. I needed them. It wasn't locked and Reece was out of town on business. What's this all about?"

"You know New Amsterdam pretty well?"

"What's this—"

"Answer me," she snapped.

"Know them?" He wiped his face with a tissue and looked at the blood. He laughed bitterly. "I've worked for them for years! I baby-sit them! I hold their hands and walk them through the deals. While Burdick's collecting their fucking check *I'm* the grunt doing all the work for them. While Fred LaDue takes 'em out to dinner and plays tennis with them *I'm* the one who's up till three A.M. doing the documents. *I'm* their lawyer." He sighed. "Yeah, I know them pretty well."

Taylor looked into his eyes and she believed him. But she persisted. "You were in the firm on Saturday night, a week ago. You lied to me about it. You snuck in through the back door."

"How did you know that?" he asked. But his voice faded as he noticed her gaze grow cold again. "I'm sorry. Yeah, I was there. I did lie . . . but I had to. Look, when I got passed over for partner I decided to start my own firm. That's what Bosk and I're doing. Dennis Callaghan's doing the real estate for us, brokering some office space downtown. I just don't want anybody at Hubbard, White to know yet. That's why I lied."

"Prove it."

Numb, he pulled out his cell phone and placed a call. "Dennis? It's Thom. I'm putting somebody on the line. Tell her exactly what you're doing for Bosk and me."

She took the phone and said simply, "Go ahead."

Callaghan hesitated a moment then told her the same thing Sebastian had. "Okay, thanks." She disconnected and handed Sebastian back the phone.

"Why'd you get all that information about me? The stuff under your desk blotter."

Another blink. Another dip of the head. "You showed

up in my life all of a sudden. You were just *there* and I didn't
know why. You were ... interesting. I liked you. I was trying
to find out about you. That's what I do—I'm a lawyer. That's
how I work."

She looked over the miserable fat boy and knew he was
innocent. He glanced at her once but had to look away
quickly as if he were frightened by what he saw.

An odd feeling swept through her. Her face burned; she
felt queasy. And she understood that for the first time in her
life she'd done what her father would have done, what
Mitchell Reece would have done: She'd been brutal in victory.

Power.

That was what she sensed. Sebastian, defeated in front
of her, bloody and fearful as a child, was hers. The cops
were hers. The sensation was exhilarating.

"Can you tell me what's going on?" he asked.

"No," she replied firmly. "I can't." She stood up. He
looked uneasily at the cops.

"It's okay," she said. "You can go home."

"I can—"

"You can leave. It's all right."

Sebastian rose to his feet slowly and she took his arm to
steady him. They started toward the door.

The hooker watched them leave and said cynically, "My,
my, this be some justice system we got ourselves. Anybody
gotta ciggie?"

Late Monday evening—the merger vote a mere fifteen
hours away—Wendall Clayton sat in a conference room
across across from John Perelli.

Fatigue had settled on Clayton like a wet coat. But, unlike Perelli, Clayton had not loosened his tie or rolled up the
sleeves of his white, Sea Island cotton shirt. He sat the way
he had been sitting for the past four hours: upright, only occasionally lowering his head to rub his bloodshot eyes or to
stretch.

Beside him sat Randy Simms and another of Clayton's young partners. Perelli too had several of his lieutenants here.

Simms and the other young man were on the executive committee of Hubbard, White. Burdick had rallied hard to keep them off but Clayton had maneuvered their elections through, though Burdick had retained control. Before them were drafts of a document, the merger agreement, spread out like a patient under a surgeon's careful eyes.

Clayton glanced outside the door at a young woman, a secretary from a freelance legal services staffing firm. The woman knew every major word processing system in the United States, could take dictation and could keyboard 110 words a minute. These skills were fetching her forty-two dollars an hour though at the moment she was being paid that fee solely to sip coffee and read a battered paperback called *Surrender, My Love*.

He wondered if he'd still have the energy to fuck her in an hour or two, after the final negotiations were completed. Clayton thought it might be dicey; he was utterly exhausted.

Perelli wore half-rim glasses, low on his nose. He looked up and stared into Clayton's eyes. "I should tell you—my people aren't happy about your demand. About ousting Burdick. Even with the giveback."

"What're you saying?" Clayton asked coolly.

"He could sue. Older man, EEOC. He could make a mess."

"We're lawyers. Our job is to make messes go away."

"We'd prefer to keep him for a while. Say, a year. Phase him out."

Clayton laughed. "You don't phase people like Donald Burdick out. Either he's in charge or he's gone completely. That's his nature."

Perelli pulled off his glasses and rubbed the bridge of his nose.

The gesture explained that there'd been considerable rebellion in the ranks at Perelli's firm over Burdick. And Clayton knew that he had to act immediately.

"If you want Hubbard, White—Burdick has to go," he continued casually. He gestured in an aristocratic way toward the window, outside of which Wall Street at night glistened. "If you want Burdick, John, go find yourself another firm."

"You'd walk?"

"And not look back."

Perelli's assistants shifted uncertainly in their chairs.

A moment passed and not a cell in Wendall Clayton's face revealed the electric tension he felt.

Finally Perelli laughed. "Goddamn, you and I're going to make some serious fucking money together." He and Clayton shook hands with finality.

Perelli stood and stretched. "You going to use a special pen to sign the merger agreement, Wendall? Like the President does?"

"No, I'll just use this old thing."

He displayed a battered Parker fountain pen, one he had used for years. Not long after Clayton had started at Hubbard, White he found himself at a closing without a pen. Donald Burdick had shot him a gruff glance and slid this very pen to him. "You should always be prepared, Wendall. Keep that one as a reminder."

Wendall Clayton put the pen away and helped the other men organize the documents while he dictated instructions for the copying and assembly of the execution copies to the *Surrender, My Love* woman. After the firm approved the merger tomorrow, these papers would be brought into the large conference room for the signing of the agreement with Perelli's partners itself. Since so many people had to sign, the logistics of closing the deal were massive.

A half hour later, walking back toward his office, Clayton stopped and turned quickly, aware of someone approaching fast from down a dark corridor.

The person was making right for him.

For a moment he actually thought that Donald Burdick had lost his mind and was about to assault him.

But, no, it was Sean Lillick.

The red-eyed paralegal raged at Clayton. "You fucked her! You son of a bitch!"

"Quiet, you little shit!" Clayton whispered. John Perelli hadn't left yet.

"You fucked her!"

"Who?"

"Carrie Mason."

Clayton regarded the young man with some amusement. "And?"

"How could you do it?"

"Last time I looked, Sean, that girl was over eighteen and unattached." He lifted an eyebrow. "Was she wearing your Art Carved engagement ring? A tasteful but small solitaire? I didn't notice one."

"I don't want your fucking sarcasm, Wendall."

So, the puppy has some teeth. He'd never seen them bared before.

"Calm down, Sean. What the hell is she to you? She's a fat little inbred preppy and you're the point man of the avant-garde. Capulets and Montagues. You have nothing in common except gonads engorged by your differences."

"How could you treat her like that?"

"I treated her very well. Besides, the word 'consensual' comes to mind."

"She was drunk. She thinks you used her."

"She's an adult. What she thinks is her business. Not yours or mine." Clayton glanced back toward the conference room. He lowered his face and asked, "What? Did you think you two were going to move to Locust Valley and have babies? For God's sake, Sean. You're not crazy. Go find some girl with a crew cut, pierced labia and dirty fingernails."

"I hate you."

"No you don't, Sean. But even if you did your hatred is irrelevant. What is relevant is that you need me. Now, the merger vote's tomorrow and I don't have time for this. Learn a lesson, son: If somebody fucks your girlfriend the question isn't who did it and how can I get even—it's *why* did she want to? Think about that."

The boy fell silent.

Clayton could still see the anger and bitterness in his face. In a calmer tone he said, "It happened once. She was drunk, I was drunk. I have no intention of ever seeing her again." This was as close to a sincere apology as Wendall Clayton would ever come.

Lillick seemed to realize this. He wasn't pleased but Clayton saw that he'd pulled the rug out from underneath his rage.

"I'll tell her," Clayton joked, "what a wonderful human being you are."

"I—"

Clayton held up an finger. He said, "Tomorrow, early—in my office? We've got a big day tomorrow. We've got a thousand documents to get ready. The phalanxes will be marching through Rome."

CHAPTER TWENTY-SIX

North of Fourteenth Street, where Taylor Lock-wood had risen from the hot, pungent subway on her way to Mitchell Reece's, the broad sidewalks were sparse.

After she'd put Thom Sebastian into a cab Taylor had returned to her apartment, changed and was now on her way to report to Reece that one suspect had been eliminated—but that she still had no clue where the note might be, the note that he'd need in court tomorrow morning, a little over twelve hours from now.

She zigged around patches of ice, remembering how her music teacher taught her to think of footsteps as musical beats. As she walked she'd break the spaces between the tap of the steps into half notes, quarter notes, eighths, triplets, dotted quarters and eighths, whispering the rhythms.

One two and uh three four . . .

A noise behind her, footsteps on the gritty concrete.

She turned quickly but saw no one.

A block farther. Now the streets were completely deserted. This area, Chelsea, near Sixth Avenue, contained some residential lofts and cavernous restaurants. But this particular street was the home of professional photographers, printers, warehouses and Korean importers. At night it was empty, a gloomy, dark, functional place, and she felt another chill of uneasiness.

One and two and three and—

Suddenly the scenery vanished as the arm went around her chest and a hand clamped over her mouth.

She screamed.

The man started to drag her into the alley.

Goddamn, no . . .

She struggled to free herself but managed only to force her attacker to fall, still clutching her fiercely around the neck. They landed on some boxes and tumbled to the slick cobblestones. The man ended up on top of her and knocked the breath from her body. Choking, gasping, she threw her hands over her face, unable to call for help.

The man rose to his knees. Taylor took this chance to twist away, smelling rotting bean sprouts and chicken bones and garlic from restaurant trash. She saw a fist rise up, about to come plunging down toward her face.

But anger detonated within her and, still breathless, she pushed hard with her legs, slamming into the man's hip and knocking him against a wall. Taylor grabbed the first thing she could find as a weapon—a piece of jagged concrete—and staggered to her feet, about to swing the sharp stone.

Her hand paused as she heard the man's sobbing. The raspy voice wheezed between the sobs. "Why, why, why? . . ."

"You!" she whispered.

Ralph Dudley wiped his face and stared at her at her in raw hatred. He didn't pay any attention to the rock in her hand. He stiffly rose, walked to an overturned trash drum and sat on it, gasping for breath. "Why did you do it?"

"Are you out of your mind?" She pitched the rock away and began brushing her coat off, rubbing at the oil and grease stains. "Look at this! Are you crazy?"

The old partner stared blankly at the ground. "I followed you from your apartment. I don't know what I wanted to do. I actually thought about killing you."

"What are you talking about?"

"You followed me. You bribed my . . . You bribed Junie to find out about me. Then I asked an associate if he'd seen you in my office and he said you had."

Taylor shrugged. "You lied to me, Ralph. You lied about being in the firm a week ago Saturday."

"So?" He smoothed his mussed hair, examined his damaged coat.

"What were you doing in the firm?"

"It's not any of your business."

"Maybe not. But maybe it is. What were you doing?"

"I love that girl."

Taylor said nothing.

"She makes me feel so alive. I hate it that she's in that business. She does too, I know she does. But she doesn't have any choice."

In her mind she saw the cheap red plastic napkin ring.

Poppie . . .

Taylor's fear had changed into pity. The desires to flee, to slap him, to put her hand on his shoulder and comfort him were balanced.

He lifted his head; the cold light, shining down from above, hit his narrow face and made him look deranged and cadaverous. He started to speak then lowered his face into his hands. A dozen cars crashed over a pothole in the street next to them before he spoke. "Why did you do it?"

"Do what, Ralph?"

"Tell Wendall Clayton about us."

"I didn't tell Clayton anything."

"Somebody . . ." He wiped his face again. "Somebody told him."

"Oh, please . . ." Taylor laughed. "That law firm is like Machiavelli's villa. Everybody's got spies."

"But why did you go to the West Side Club? Why did you follow me?"

"There are problems at the firm. I needed to know where some people were at a certain time. I got the feeling you were lying to me so I followed you after dinner. Now, tell me what you were doing at the firm."

He shook his head.

Just as she had with the cop who'd arrested Sebastian, Taylor now lowered her head and said, "Ralph, I can put you in jail for a long time—because of that girl. And I'll do it if you don't cooperate. No bullshit. Tell me what you were doing in the firm."

The look of hatred in his face chilled her but he finally said, "Junie's father died two years ago and left her some money. But her mother and stepfather're keeping it all tied up. They're trying to get it for themselves. I've been spending every weekend and half my nights at the firm, learning trusts and estates and fiduciary law. I'm going to get the money back for her." He wiped tears. "I couldn't tell anybody at the firm because they'd find out she's not my granddaughter and then . . . they might find out the real situation. Besides, I've borrowed against my partnership draw so much the firm'd fire me if they knew I was spending my time on a project that wasn't making Hubbard, White any money."

He looked up, wretched and lost. "I'm really not a very good lawyer. I can charm people, I can entertain clients . . . but this is the only real law I've done in years."

"Prove it to me."

He said stiffly, "I don't think I owe you anything more."

Once again the same dark power she'd felt before filled Taylor Lockwood's heart and she whispered harshly, "Prove it to me or I go to the cops."

A wounded animal, Dudley hesitated. Then he glanced down, opened his briefcase. Shoved it toward her.

She knew little about trusts and estates law but it was clear that these documents—petitions to the Surrogate's Court, copies of cases and correspondence—bore out what he'd told her.

"You were in the firm early Sunday morning after Thanksgiving."

"Yes" he answered as if he were a witness under cross-examination.

"You used Thom Sebastian's key?"

"Yes. I didn't want anybody to know I was in that night. I got there about one-thirty. After I'd been to the West Side Club."

She asked, "Where *were* you in the firm?"

"Just the library and my office. The rest room. The canteen—for some coffee."

"Did you see anyone else there?"

Dudley rocked slowly back and forth on the trash can, under the rain of harsh streetlight. His breath popped out in small puffs as he worried the tear in his coat. "As a matter of fact," he answered, "I did."

■

The loft door was open. She paused in the hallway, seeing the trapezoid of ashen light fall into the corridor. Taylor felt a jab of panic. In a burst of frightening memory she remembered the white car driving them off the road and, though at the time she believed the thief had intended only to scare them, she thought for an instant that the man had come back and killed Mitchell. She ran to the door and pushed inside.

He was lying on the couch, wearing blue jeans and a wrinkled dress shirt. His hair was mussed and his arms lolled at his sides. His eyes stared unmoving at the ceiling.

"Mitchell?" she asked. "Are you all right?

He turned on his side slowly and looked at her. A faint smile. "Must've dozed off."

Taylor crouched next to him and took his hand. "I thought . . . you were hurt or something."

She felt the slight pressure of his hand on hers. He looked at her jacket and jeans. "What happened to you?"

Taylor laughed. "Little wrestling match."

"Are you all right?"

"You should see the other guy." Then she said, "I know who the thief is."

"What?" His eyes returned to life. "Who?"

"Wendall Clayton."

"How do you know?"

"I eliminated Thom and Dudley." She told him about Sebastian's adventure with the police and the old partner's attack on her. Then she said, "Clayton let the thief in that night."

"But he wasn't in the firm," Reece said.

"Yes he was. Dudley saw him. And Clayton's key entry didn't show up because he got to the firm on *Friday.*"

Reece nodded, eyes closing at the obvious answer. "Of course. He was there all weekend, working on the merger. He didn't leave until Sunday. He stayed two nights. Must've slept on the couch. I should've thought about that."

Taylor continued. "I just went back to the firm and checked his time sheets. We would've seen that he'd ordered food in and made phone calls and photocopies but all those records were erased, remember?"

Reece's smile faded. "That doesn't mean he stole the note though."

"But Dudley told me something else. About three-thirty or four on Sunday morning he saw this man, like a janitor, walking through the firm with an envelope. Dudley thought it was odd that he was carrying something like that. He noticed he went into Clayton's office with the envelope but came out without it. Dudley didn't say anything to him—or to anyone else about him—because he was working on something unrelated to firm business.

"I talked to my private detective. He said there is a Triple A Security—the receipt I found in Wendall's desk—and he checked the grapevine. It's in Florida. He said they're a firm that has a reputation for doing labor work. Which he tells me is a euphemism for rough stuff, like stealing documents and bugging offices and even driving people off the road. That's who Dudley saw. Clayton let him into the firm and he stole the note after you went home."

Reece said, "And you think the note's in that envelope?"

"I think so. Like you said, he probably hid it in a stack

of documents in his office. I'm going to search it. Only we have to wait. He was still at his desk when I left the firm and it didn't look like he was going to leave anytime soon. I'll go back to the firm and wait till he leaves for the night."

"Taylor... What can I say?" He hugged her, hard, and she threw her arms around him. Their hands began coursing up and down each other's backs and suddenly it was as if all the compressed tension they'd felt over the past week had been converted into a very different kind of energy... and now suddenly erupted.

The room vanished into motion: his arms around her, under her legs, sweeping her up. Reece carried her to the huge dining room table and lay her upon it, books falling, papers sailing off onto the floor. He eased her down onto the tabletop, her blouse and skirt spiraling off and away, his own clothes flying in a wider trajectory. He was already hard. He pressed his mouth down on hers, their teeth met and he worked down her neck, biting. Pulling hard on her nipples, her stomach, her thighs. She tried to rise up to him but he held her captive, her butt and leg cut by the sharp corners of a law book: The pain added to the hunger.

Then he was on top of her, his full weight on her chest, as his hands curled around the small of her back and tugged her toward him. She was completely immobile, her breath forced out of her lungs by his demanding strokes.

Taylor felt a similar hunger and she dug her nails into his solid back, her teeth clenched in a salivating lust for the pain it was causing.

They moved like this for minutes, or hours—she had no idea. Finally she screamed as she shuddered, her toes curling, her head bouncing against the table. He finished a moment later and collapsed against her.

Taylor lifted her hands. Two nails were bloody. She shoved the law book out from underneath her; it fell with a resonant thud. She closed her eyes and they remained locked this way for a long time.

She dozed briefly.

When she awoke a half hour later she found that Reece

was at his desk, dressed only in a shirt, scribbling notes, reading cases. She watched his back for a moment then walked to him, kissed the top of his head.

He turned and pressed his head against her breasts.

"It's up to you now," he said. "I'm going to proceed with the case as if we can't find the note." He nodded at the papers surrounding him. "But I'll hope for the best."

At three in the morning, wearing her cat burglar outfit of Levi's and a black blouse, Taylor Lockwood walked into Hubbard, White & Willis.

Her black Sportsac contained a pair of kidskin gloves, a set of screwdrivers, a pair of pliers, a hammer. The firm seemed empty but she moved through the corridors in complete quiet, pausing in darkened conference rooms, listening for voices or footsteps.

Nothing.

Finally she made it to Wendall Clayton's office and began her search.

By four-thirty, she'd covered most of it and found no sign of the note. But there were still two tall stacks of documents, on the floor beside his credenza, that she hadn't looked through yet.

She continued searching. She finished one and found nothing. She started on the second one.

Which was when jaunty footsteps sounded on the marble floor in the corridor nearby and Wendall Clayton's voice boomed to someone, "The merger vote's in six hours. I need those fucking documents now!"

CHAPTER TWENTY-SEVEN

█████████ He didn't truly live anywhere but here.

In murky, echoing rotundas of courthouses like this.

In marble corridors lit by milky sunlight filtering through fifty-year-old grimy windows, in oak hallways smelling of bitter paper from libraries and file rooms.

At counsel tables like the one at which he now sat.

Mitchell Reece studied the courtroom around him, where the opening volley in *New Amsterdam Bank & Trust, Ltd. v. Hanover & Stiver, Inc.* would be fired in a short while. He studied the vaulted ceilings, the austere jury box and a judge's bench reminiscent of a conning tower on a warship, the dusty flag, the pictures of stern nineteenth-century judges. The room was unlit at the moment. There was a scuffed, well-worn aspect to the place; it reminded him of old subway cars. Well, that was appropriate; after all, justice was just another service provided by government to its citizens, like public transportation and trash collection.

He sat for a few minutes but grew restless; he stood suddenly and began to pace.

And what, he speculated, would happen if Taylor *didn't* find the note?

He supposed he could find alternatives. But because Mitchell Reece was so very driven, because he was someone who, as Taylor had once said, had left behind reason and logic and even safety in this mad sojourn, he felt a fierce desperation to find that tiny piece of paper.

He wanted to win this one oh-so-badly.

He rose and walked to the soiled window, through which he watched men and women hurrying along Centre Street: attorneys and judges and clients. Everyone was wearing a suit but making the distinction among them was easy. Lawyers carried big litigation bags, clients carried briefcases and judges carried nothing.

He wandered to the judge's bench then to the jury gallery.

Theater.

Winning is about theater, he reflected.

The revelation had come to him early in his career—he was representing a young boy blinded in one eye when a lawn mower fired a rock out of the grass chute and into the child's face. The boy's father had used a hacksaw to cut off the safety deflector panel, believing the motor labored harder with the deflector in place and used more gas. Reece sued the manufacturer, claiming that the unit was defective because there was no warning that users should *not* cut the panel off.

It was understood by virtually everyone that—because the proximate cause of the injury was the father's removal of the device—Reece had absolutely no chance of winning. The bored judge knew this, as did the arrogant lawyer for the defendant and the complacent lawyer for the defendant's insurance company.

Seven people did *not* know the impossibility of the suit, however. One was Mitchell Reece. The others were the six members of the jury, who awarded the snotty, self-pitying little kid one point seven million bucks.

Theater.

That was the key to litigation: a dab of logic, a bit of law, a lot of personality, and considerable theater.

He glanced at the door to the courtroom, willing it to open and Taylor Lockwood to hurry inside, the note in hand.

But of course it remained closed.

After he'd heard nothing more from her after she left to go to the firm at 3 A.M. He'd gotten a few hours' sleep, shaved and showered then dressed in his finest litigation Armani. He'd gathered his documents, called the clients to have them meet him at the courthouse then limoed downtown, where he slipped into the cavernous domed cathedral of New York State Supreme Court.

Well, the matter was out of his hands, he now reflected. Either Taylor would find it and life would move in one direction, or she would not and an entirely different set of consequences would occur.

Mitchell Reece had not prayed for perhaps thirty years but today he addressed a short message to a vague deity, whom he pictured looking somewhat like blind Justice, and asked that she keep Taylor Lockwood safe and to please, please let her find the note.

You've done so much, Taylor; now do just a little more. For both of us....

■

Taylor Lockwood stood in Wendall Clayton's private bathroom.

The time was now 9 A.M. and she'd hidden here for hours, waiting for the partner to take a break so that she could continue going through the remaining stack of papers.

But Clayton had never even stood up to stretch. In this entire time he'd remained rooted at his desk, reading, picking up the phone and calling partners and clients. The news he was receiving was apparently good for his side; it was clear to her that the merger would be approved and that both firms would sign it up later in the day.

Reece would be in court by now, probably despairing that he hadn't heard from her.

But there was nothing she could do other than wait.

Ten minutes passed. Then ten more. And finally Clayton rose.

Thank God. He was going to check on something.

She would grab the remaining stack and flee with it to her cubicle, looking through it there. Then—

Her gut jumped hard. Clayton wasn't leaving the office at all. He needed to use the rest room and was walking directly toward where Taylor Lockwood now hid, a room without a single closet or shower stall where she might hide.

"Bench conference, your honor?" Mitchell Reece asked. He was standing in front of the plaintiff's table.

The judge looked surprised and Reece could understand why. The trial had just started. The opening statements had been completed and it was rare that a bench conference—a brief informal meeting between lawyers, out of earshot of the jury—should occur at this early stage; nothing had happened so far that the two attorneys could argue about.

The judge raised his eyebrows and Hanover & Stiver's slick, gray-haired lawyer rose to his feet and walked slowly to the bench.

The courtroom was half empty but Reece was distressed to see some reporters present. He didn't know why they were here; they never covered cases of this sort.

Someone's political hand? he wondered.

At the defendant's table sat Lloyd Hanover, tanned and trim, his hair combed forward in bangs, his face an expression of blasé confidence.

The two lawyers stood at the bench. Reece said softly, "Your honor, I have a best-evidence situation. I'd like to move to introduce a copy of the promissory note in question."

Hanover's lawyer turned his head slowly to look at Reece. It was the judge, however, who was more astonished. "You don't have the note itself?"

No one in the jury box or elsewhere in the courtroom could hear this exchange but the surprise on the jurist's face was evident. Several spectators looked at each other and a reporter or two leaned forward slightly, sharks smelling blood.

The Hanover lawyer said tersely, "No way. Not acceptable. I'll fight you on this all the way, Reece."

The judge said, "Was it a negotiable instrument?"

"Yes, your honor. But there is precedent for admitting a copy at this stage, as long as the original is surrendered before execution of the judgment."

"Assuming you *get* a judgment," the Hanover lawyer countered.

"Bickering pisses me off, gentlemen." When the jury wasn't listening the judge could curse to his heart's delight.

"Sorry, sir," Hanover's lawyer murmured contritely. Then he said, "You prove to me the note's destroyed—I mean, show me ashes—and then you can put a copy into evidence. But if not, I'm moving for dismissal."

"What happened to the original?" the judge asked.

"We have it at the firm," Reece said casually. "We're having some technical failure accessing it."

"'Technical failure accessing it'?" the judge blurted. "What the fuck does that mean?"

"Our security systems aren't functioning right, as I understand it."

"Well, wouldn't that be convenient, to have the note disappear just now?" the Hanover lawyer said. "Especially since we intend to call into question certain aspects of the execution of the note."

Reece gave a bitter laugh. "Let me get this right—you're saying that you gladly took my client's money but now you're not sure they executed the loan agreement correctly so you don't have to pay it back?"

"Our thinking is that the bank tried to give itself an out because interest rates turned and they want to invest the capital elsewhere."

"Your client missed six months of interest payments,"

Reece said, raising his voice just loud enough for the jury to hear. "How exactly—"

"Was I not making myself goddamn clear? No bickering, no fucking comments on the merits of the case in a bench conference. . . . Now, Mr. Reece, this is very unusual. A suit on a note, especially a negotiable note, requires the original document. Under the best-evidence rule if you can't explain the note's destruction, you're precluded from entering a copy into evidence."

Reece said calmly, "I'd like to make a motion to submit other evidence of the existence of the note."

"Your honor," opposing counsel said, "I would point out that it is Mr. Reece's client that sued on the note it alleges is properly executed. It is his responsibility to present that note. A copy won't show that there's been tampering on the part of Mr. Reece's client."

Reece countered, "Your honor, it is very important that the administration of justice not get bogged down in technicalities. The note is merely *evidence* of the debt owed—and remaining unpaid, I should point out—by Hanover & Stiver. It is true that the best-evidence rule generally requires the original but there are exceptions. We're all familiar with the rules of civil procedure, I'm sure."

"But this isn't a bill of sale, Mr. Reece," the judge said. "It's a negotiable instrument worth hundreds of millions of dollars."

"With all due respect to Mr. Reece," the Hanover lawyer said, "I am reminded of a case once in which a similar claim of a missing note was made and it turned out that the document in question had been sold by the bank to a third party. I would never suggest that New Amsterdam Bank was guilty of such wrongdoing but . . . we can't take that chance."

Reece walked to the counsel table and returned with some documents. He handed one copy to the lawyer and one to the judge. "Motion papers. I move to allow the introduction of secondary evidence of the note. I've briefed the issue in here. If you would like to recess for twenty-four hours to allow my opponent here to respond—"

"No more delays," the judge snapped. "This case has fucked up my calendar enough."

The other lawyer shook his head. "You lost the note, Reece, I'm ready for trial. Your honor, I move for a directed verdict in my client's favor."

The judge flipped through the lengthy brief that Reece had prepared then lifted an impressed eyebrow. "Good work, Mr. Reece. Brilliant analysis." Then he tossed the brief aside. "But it doesn't cut it. No secondary evidence will be allowed."

Reece's heart sank.

"On the other hand, I won't grant a directed verdict for Hanover. What I will do is grant a motion to dismiss *without* prejudice. That will allow Mr. Reece to bring his case in the future. However, given the nature of defendant's financial condition, I doubt they'll have much money for your client to collect, Mr. Reece. You'd better talk to your malpractice carrier. I think your client may look to you for restitution in this matter. And that's to the tune of two hundred and fifty million dollars."

The opposing counsel began the formalities: "Your honor, I move for dismissal of—"

"Mitchell!" a woman's voice called from the back of the courtroom.

The judge looked up, glaring at the intrusion. Everyone in the gallery and the jury box swiveled to watch Taylor Lockwood hurry down the aisle.

"It's customary to ask permission before shouting in my courtroom, young lady," the judge snapped sarcastically.

"Forgive me, sir. I need to speak to plaintiff's counsel for a moment."

Hanover's lawyer said, "Your honor, I—"

The judge waved him silent and nodded Taylor forward.

CHAPTER TWENTY-EIGHT

"I *am* sorry, your honor," Taylor Lockwood said.

Judges were public servants, catering to the will of the people, but as her father had reminded from a young age, you could never be too deferential to jurists or, as he put it even to grade-school Taylie, you could never kiss too much judicial ass.

She walked to Reece and handed him an envelope. Inside was the promissory note, looking as mundane and matter-of-fact as the copy he'd showed her at their first meeting.

Mitchell Reece took out the document and exhaled slowly.

"Your honor, at this time the plaintiff would like to introduce Exhibit A." He handed it to the opposing counsel, who looked at Taylor with a gaze of distilled hate. "No objection." He returned the note to Reece's unsteady hands.

Reece walked back to his favorite space, in front of the jury box. "Your honor, before continuing with my case, I first must apologize to the court and to the jury for this delay." He smiled contritely. The six men and women smiled or nodded back and forgave him; the interruption had added an element of drama to the case.

"Fine, fine, Mr. Reece, let's move this along," the judge grumbled, his chances for a fast escape to golf or tennis ruined.

"One moment, your honor." The Hanover & Stiver attorney bent toward one of his clients, probably Lloyd Hanover, Taylor guessed, to judge from his slick, tanned appearance, which matched what Reece had told her of him. After a bit of conversation the attorney stood up. "Approach the bench again? With opposing counsel?"

The judge gestured them up. The defense lawyer said, "Your honor, my clients would like to present a settlement offer to the plaintiff."

The judge lifted an eyebrow to Reece. Taylor's father had also taught his daughter that settlement was the Holy Grail of judges. Burdened by an endless workload, they infinitely preferred the parties' agreeing to work out their differences rather than slugging it out at trial. The judge might even be able to get in nine holes today.

"We'll entertain it," Reece said stiffly.

The lawyer moved closer to Reece and whispered, "Look, you can get a judgment entered for the face value of the note plus interest but there's no way there'll be enough cash left in the company to collect that much by the time you enforce it. Not to mention your legal fees' eating up a lot of the rest."

"A number," Reece said. "Just give me a number."

"I—"

The judge: "Give him a number."

"Sixty-five cents on the dollar."

Reece said, "Eighty cents on the dollar. U.S. cash, not negotiable instruments or assets or tangible property, even gold."

"We're trying to be cooperative. But we have to be realistic," Hanover's lawyer said. Then he added ominously, "The money just won't be there in a few months."

"Then we'll just have to go a-lookin'," Reece said

cheerfully. "Now, Lloyd Hanover personally guaranteed the debt. I'm ready to interrogate—excuse me, *depose*—every one of his relatives and every business associate of his for the past ten years to find out where he hid the money."

"He didn't hide—"

"We'll look into every deal he's ever been involved in, every charity he ever gave money to, his kid's college funds."

"He's completely innocent of secreting funds if that's what you're suggesting."

Reece shrugged. "Dismissal without prejudice. Eighty cents on the dollar. Cash. And we close within one week. If not, then Lloyd Hanover and everybody he's ever known won't have a minute's peace."

The lawyer held his eye for a moment and strode back to his client, who listened, gave a searing look to Reece then whispered something to the lawyer.

When the man returned he said, "Agreed."

Reece nodded and said, "We'll execute the stipulation now."

"We don't want to take the court's time. I suggest—"

"I think his honor would prefer to spend a few extra minutes now rather than risk being back here in a few weeks for a full-fledged trial. Am I right about that, your honor?"

"You are, Mr. Reece. Write out the stipulation by hand and we'll get it signed up."

The defense lawyer sighed and scurried back to give the bad news to the client.

After the paperwork was completed hands were shaken among comrades, glares delivered between opponents and the courtroom emptied.

In the courthouse rotunda, the New Amsterdam vice presidents and executives clustered together, enjoying their relief. Taylor followed Reece to a small vestibule that contained public phones, which unlike most in the city were in old-fashioned booths with closing doors. He pulled her inside one and kissed her hard. After a moment he released her and leaned back. "What on earth happened? Where were you?"

"I was almost through searching Clayton's office but he came in early to take care of some last-minute things for the merger. I hid in the bathroom."

"Jesus. What happened then?"

"About nine or so he had to use the john. But I unscrewed the lightbulbs before he got there. So he went up the hall. When he did I grabbed the last stack of paper and ran down to my cubicle with them. I found all of this in the envelope the note was in."

Reece took the sheets of paper that Taylor offered. Shaking his head, he looked at them closely. A copy of a letter to the *National Law Journal.* "Re: Careless Security Costs Firm Client." The letter blamed Burdick and the executive committee. There was also a typewritten list with the names of several other clients and cases that Clayton was going to sabotage while, presumably, shifting the blame to Burdick.

From her purse Taylor then took a small tape recorder and held up a tiny microcassette. "This was in the envelope too." She inserted the cassette into the player and hit a button. They heard Reece's voice, thick with static, talking to her about the promissory note. She shut it off.

"Son of a bitch," Reece said. "He bugged my office. That's how he knew we were after him. He's known all along. He..." Then Reece paused and looked at his watch. "Oh, no."

"What?

"The firm's voting on the merger any minute now. We've got to tell Donald about this. It'll change everything."

He grabbed the phone and dug in his pocket for some change.

━━━━━

Perpetual motion does exist.

In business, in fact, where the mere laws of science

mean zip compared with the power of greed and ambition, it's one of the essential principles.

Donald Burdick sensed the undercurrent of this energy surrounding each partner as he or she entered the big conference room. Mostly they were uneasy. They lingered at the door, pretending to leave messages with the conference room secretary, pretending to wait for comrades so they might enter with human shields, or at least with allies to deflect the glare of the partners representing the other side of the merger issue from theirs.

As always, few of the younger partners would make eye contact with Burdick but this morning he felt this evasion was due not to distance in social station but to hostility on the part of his opponents and shame in the hearts of those who had betrayed him.

The Danish pastries on the Limoges china, the coffee in the sterling urn were practically untouched. Burdick, looking down, reviewed a loan document that did not need reviewing. He heard conversations about the Jets and Giants, about concerts, about vacations, about closings, about the faux pas of opposing counsel, about the Supreme Court's latest excursions to Olympus, about rumors of other law firms breaking up.

Finally, at eleven o'clock, Burdick started to call the meeting to order. He was about to ask for a quorum vote when:

"Excuse me," said Randy Simms, whom Donald Burdick couldn't help but picture as a handsome leech.

"Yes?" Burdick drew the word out threateningly.

Simms said, "We're not all present."

Eyes coursing leisurely around the table, Burdick said, "But we have a quorum."

"Well, Mr. Clayton isn't here."

"Either we have a quorum, in which case the meeting proceeds, or we do not, in which case it doesn't. Whom that quorum is made up of is not, to my memory, an issue of any concern in *Robert's Rules of Order.*"

"I'm just thinking that it might be appropriate—"

But the slick young sycophant's words were interrupted by a bold knock. The door opened and Burdick's secretary walked inside with a sealed envelope. Ignoring everyone in the room, the older partner took it, slit the seal open with his gold pen and read the note. He handed it to Bill Stanley, who blinked in surprise.

Burdick said, "If you'll excuse us for a moment please. There's something that needs attending to. We'll adjourn for fifteen minutes. Bill, you come too."

Donald Burdick was as angry as Taylor had ever seen him. He glanced at her and she looked away from his towering fury.

They sat in Burdick's office. Bill Stanley was on the couch, a fat ankle resting on a fat knee, and read over the papers Taylor had found in Clayton's office.

Stanley muttered, "What a stupid, stupid thing to do."

But Burdick was venting at Reece. "Why the hell didn't you tell me about the note?"

Reece said, "It was a judgment call. I didn't want word to get out. I had my own way of handling it."

"You almost lost the case," Burdick spat out. "You almost got yourselves killed."

Reece withstood the anger easily. "Clayton wasn't going to hurt us. I'm sure the car incident was just to scare us. As far as losing goes, well, yes, I took that chance."

"You risked our client because you were afraid you'd lose your job."

The associate fired back, "Of course that was one reason. But it was also because if word got out it would be bad for the firm. In my assessment we had to act covertly."

" 'Covertly.' You sound like a damn spy." Burdick took the papers and the tape recorder from Stanley. "He wanted the merger so badly, he'd do this?" Burdick's anger was giving way to astonishment.

Stanley considered something. "You introduced the note into evidence, right?"

Reece nodded. "Hanover's agreed to settle. We're going to close in Boston next week."

"Well, then Clayton will've heard you found it. He'll know he's in trouble."

Burdick nodded. "That's why he's not at the meeting." The old partner rubbed his eyes. "What a mess."

"Fucking scandal," Stanley growled. "Last thing we need."

"Give me some thoughts on the damage assessment," Burdick said to the rotund partner.

"Probably not terrible." He nodded at Reece and Taylor. "They didn't tell anyone." A piercing glance at Taylor. "Right? You didn't mention it to anybody?"

"No, of course not. When I found those things in Clayton's office I took them right to Mitchell at the court-house. I didn't even call—because I thought the phones might be bugged. Nobody else knows what I was doing."

Stanley nodded and continued, "The problem's going to be talking him into leaving. He knows we're afraid of pub-licity so we're not going to go to the police or going to sue him. Fucking clever when you think about it. He arranges to misplace a note, nearly loses our client and when we catch him red-handed he's practically got immunity from the liability."

Burdick was shaking his head. "We'll find a way to oust him. That man has to . . ." His voice faded as there was an urgent knock on the door.

"Come in."

The door opened fast and one of Burdick's secretaries stood there. Her face was white and her eyes were red from crying.

"What is it, Carol?"

Oh, no, Taylor thought: Just what they were afraid of had happened—word had gotten out that Clayton had stolen the note.

But the tragedy was of a somewhat different order.

The woman gasped, "Oh, Mr. Burdick... it's terrible. They just found Wendall Clayton in the garage downstairs. In his car... He's..."

"What, Carol?"

"He shot himself. He's dead."

TWO

Men of Most Renowned Virtue

"You will observe the Rules of Battle, of course?" the White Knight remarked, putting on his helmet. . . .

"I always do," said the Red Knight, and they began banging away at each other with such fury that Alice got behind a tree to be out of the way of the blows.

—Lewis Carroll, *Through the Looking-Glass*

CHAPTER TWENTY-NINE

Only a few hours had elapsed since Clayton's suicide. But it seemed to Taylor Lockwood that days had passed—given all the conjuring that Donald Burdick had done in the wake of the tragedy.

First, he'd appeared at the merger vote meeting and delivered the news to the partners. Then, leaving the stunned men and women to make what they would of the man's death, he'd returned immediately to his office, where Reece and Taylor had been ordered to remain.

The senior partner had handled an endless stream of phone calls and meetings with his cronies. So far he'd talked to the mayor's and the governor's offices, the medical examiner's office, the police, the Justice Department, the press.

Taylor was startled to see Burdick's wife make an appearance, walking into her husband's office unannounced, without the least acknowledgment of Reece or Taylor. The woman apparently knew all about the suicide and she and her husband retired to the small conference room off his office and closed the door. Five minutes later Burdick returned alone.

He sat down, leaned back in the chair and then asked Reece and Taylor, "Do you have anything else that has to do with Wendall or the theft? Anything at all?"

Reece shook his head and looked at Taylor, who said numbly, "I didn't think this would happen."

Burdick looked at her blankly for a moment then repeated, "Anything else?"

"No," she said.

He nodded and took an envelope out of his pocket. "There was that suicide note in the car, the one the police found. Talking about pressures at work, being despondent." Burdick looked at both Reece and Taylor. He added, "But he wrote another one. It was on his desk, addressed to me."

He handed a sheet of paper to Reece, who read it and then passed it on to Taylor.

> *Donald, forgive me. I'm sending this to you privately to keep my theft of the note out of the news. It will be better for everyone.*
>
> *I want you to know that I truly believed the merger would save the firm. But I lost sight of how far I should go. All I'll offer is this from Milton: "Men of most renowned virtue have sometimes by transgressing most truly kept the law."*

Burdick took the letter back and locked it in his desk. "I'm going to try to keep this note quiet." He nodded at the drawer. "I'll talk to the police commissioner and I don't think he'll have a problem with it. This is Hubbard, White's dirty laundry and no one else's. Publicity would be bad for everyone. Bad for the firm. Bad for Clayton's widow too."

"Widow?" Taylor asked suddenly.

Burdick replied, "Yes, Wendall was married. Didn't you know?"

"No," she said. "She wasn't in Connecticut the other day.

I've never seen her at any of the firm functions. He never wore a ring."

"Well, I guess he wouldn't now, would he? Given his extracurricular activities."

His widow...

The words stung. Before his death Clayton the man had been hidden beneath Clayton the ruthless aristocrat. That he had a wife—and maybe children or living parents, siblings—was a shock.

"The newspapers'll get a watered-down story," Burdick continued. "I've called the public relations company. Bill Stanley's with them now. They're preparing a statement. If anybody asks we'll refer questions to them." He lowered his head and looked into Reece's eyes, then Taylor's. She had the same sense as when she met Reece's gaze, or Clayton's. Or her father's. They drew you in, made you forget who you were, forget your own thoughts. In Burdick's eyes she saw will and confidence, strong as bronze. Her mind went blank. He asked, "Will you back me on this? If I thought there was anything to be gained by a full disclosure I wouldn't hesitate to reveal everything. But I can't see any upside to it."

Men of most renowned virtue.

Reece said, "I won't perjure myself, Donald. But I won't volunteer anything."

"Fair enough." The partner looked at Taylor.

She nodded. "Sure. I agree."

The hairs on the back of her neck stirred.

Widow...

Taylor looked into the conference room, inside which Vera Burdick, her gray hair piled on her head in a stately bun, was on the telephone. She glanced back and caught Taylor's gaze. The woman half-rose and swung the door closed.

Burdick's phone rang and he took the call. He mouthed something about its being from someone at City Hall but Taylor was preoccupied. She was seeing in her mind's eye the real suicide note, tucked away in Burdick's desk. She vaguely heard Burdick speaking to the caller in a low, reassuring tone. She watched his long, jowly face, carefully shaved, his sparse gray hair brushed into precise alignment.

And Taylor Lockwood thought: What the hell had she been doing all along? What did she *think* would happen when she fingered the thief? Had she ever considered the consequences?

Never once.

Renowned virtue.

Burdick hung up the receiver and nodded with satisfaction. "I think we'll get away with it."

Taylor tried to figure out what he meant.

"The Medical Examiner's office is going to rule the death suicide. The AG agrees. And we can keep our other suicide note private."

Reece blurted an astonished laugh. "The ME ruled *already*?"

Burdick nodded then looked at Taylor and Reece with a vaguely ominous gaze, which she interpreted as: Don't be too curious about this.

The partner looked at his watch. He held out his hand to Reece, then to Taylor, who first wanted to wipe her palm. It was damp as a washcloth; Burdick's was completely dry.

"You two get some rest. You've been through a hellish week. If you want any personal time I'll arrange it. Won't come out of your vacation or sick leave. Are you busy now?"

Reece walked toward the door. "I've got the Hanover settlement closing in Boston next week. That's the only thing on the front burner."

"You, Ms. Lockwood?"

"No, nothing," she replied, still numb.

"Then take some time off. In fact, I'd urge you to. Might be best."

Taylor nodded and began to speak but hesitated. She

was waiting for some significant thought to arrive, some
phrase that neatly summarized what had just happened.

Nothing occurred; her mind had jammed.

Get away with it?

"Oh, Mitchell," Burdick said, smiling, as if the suicide
no longer occupied even a portion of his thoughts.

Reece turned.

"Congratulations on the Hanover settlement," the partner said. "I myself would have settled for seventy cents on
the dollar. That's why you're a litigator and I'm not."

He rose and walked to the small conference room,
where his wife awaited him. Burdick didn't open the door
right away, though. He waited, Taylor noticed, until she and
Reece had left the office.

■

They walked in silence to the paralegal pen.

Everyone in the corridors seemed to be staring at her. As
if they knew the part she'd played in the partner's death.

Near her cubicle, in a place where the hall was empty,
Reece took her by the arm. He bent down and whispered, "I
know how you feel, Taylor. I know how *I* feel. But this
wasn't our fault. There's no way we could've anticipated
this."

She said nothing.

He continued, "Even if the police'd been involved the
same thing would've happened."

"I know," she said in a soft voice. But it sounded lame,
terribly lame. Because, of course, she didn't know anything
of the kind.

Reece asked, "Come over for dinner tonight."

She nodded. "Okay, sure."

"How's eight?" Then he frowned. "Wait, it's Tuesday . . .
you're playing piano at your club, right?"

Was it Tuesday? The thought of the leches in the audience and Dimitri's reference to her satin touch suddenly re-
pulsed her. "Think I'll cancel for tonight."

Reece gave a wan smile. "I'll see you later." He seemed to
be looking for something to add but said nothing more. He
looked up and down the hallway to make sure it was empty
then hugged her hard and walked away.

Taylor called Ms. Strickland and told her she was taking
the rest of the day off. She couldn't get the supervisor off the
line, though; all the woman wanted to do was talk about
Clayton's suicide. Finally she managed to hang up. Taylor
avoided Carrie Mason and Sean Lillick and a half dozen of
the other paralegals and snuck out the back door of the
firm.

At home she loaded dirty clothes into the basket but got
only as far as the front door. She stopped and set the laundry down. She turned on her Yamaha keyboard and played
music for a few hours then took a nap.

At six that night she called Reece at home.

"Look," she said. "I'm sorry, I can't come over tonight."

"Sure," he said uncertainly. Then he asked, "Are you all
right?"

"Yeah. I've got the fatigues. Bad."

"I understand." But he sounded edgy. "Is this ... Come
on, tell me, is what happened going to affect us?"

Oh, brother ... you can hardly *ever* get men to talk seriously. And then, at the worst possible time, you can't
stop them. "No, Mitch. It's not that. I just need some R&R
time."

"Whatever you want," he said. "That's fine. I'll be here.
It's just ... I guess I miss you."

" 'Night."

"Sleep well. Call me tomorrow."

She took a long bath then called home. Taylor was troubled to hear her father answer.

"Jesus, Taylie, what the hell happened at your shop?"

No "counselor" now. They were regressing to her grade-
school nickname.

"I just heard," her father continued. "Was that somebody you worked for, this Clayton fellow?"

"I knew him, yeah. Not too well."

"Well, take some advice: You keep a low profile, young lady."

"What?" she asked, put off by his professorial tone.

"You keep your head down. The firm's going to have some scars from a suicide. We don't want any of it to rub off on you."

How can scars rub off? Taylor thought cynically. But of course she said nothing other than: "I'm just a paralegal, Dad. Reporters from the *Times* aren't going to be writing me up."

Although, she added to herself, if they'd told the whole story by rights they *should*.

"Killed himself?" Samuel Lockwood mused. "If you can't stand the heat stay out of the kitchen."

"Maybe there was more to it than standing the heat, Dad."

"He took the coward's way out and he hurt your shop."

"Not mine," Taylor said. But her voice was soft and Samuel Lockwood didn't hear.

"You want to talk to your mother?" he asked.

"Please."

"I'll get her. Just remember what I said, Taylie."

"Sure, Dad."

Her mother, who'd clearly had a glass of wine too many, was happy to hear from her daughter and, to Taylor's relief, wasn't the least alarmist about what had happened at the firm. Taylor slipped into a very different mode with her—far less defensive and tense—and the women began chatting about soap operas and distant relatives and Taylor's Christmas trip home to Maryland.

The woman was so cheerful and comforting in fact that Taylor, on a whim, upped the length of her stay from three days to seven. Hell, Donald Burdick wants me to take some time off? Okay, I'll take some time off.

Her mother was delighted and they talked for a few minutes longer but then Taylor said she had to go; she was afraid her father would come back on the line.

She put a frozen pouch of spaghetti into a pot of water.

That and an apple were dinner. Then she lay on her couch, watching a *Cheers* rerun.

Mitchell Reece called once but she let her answering machine do the talking for her. He left a short message, saying only that he was thinking of her. The words shored her up a bit.

But still, she didn't call back.

Taylor Lockwood, curled on the old sofa, the TV yammering mindlessly in front of her, thought about when she was a teenager and her Labrador retriever would pile into bed next to her and lie against an adjacent pillow until she scooted him off. She'd then lie still, waiting for sleep, while she felt, in the warmth radiating from the empty pillow, the first glimmerings of understanding that the pain that solitude conjures within us is a false pain and has nothing to do with solitude at all.

Indeed, being alone was curative, she believed.

She thought about Reece and wondered if he was different, if he was like her father, who sought company when he was troubled—though it was not the presence of his family Samuel Lockwood had ever needed but that of business associates, politicians, fellow partners and clients.

But that's a different story, she thought wearily.

She lay back on the couch and ten hours later opened her eyes to a gray morning.

She took the next day off and spent much of the morning and early afternoon Christmas shopping. When she returned home, in the late afternoon, there was another call from Reece and a curious one from Sean Lillick. He seemed drunk and he rambled on for a few minutes about Clayton's death, an edge to his voice. He mentioned that Carrie Mason wasn't going to Clayton's memorial service with him and asked if Taylor wanted to go.

No, she thought. But didn't call him back.

Thom Sebastian too had left a message, asking her to phone back. She didn't call him either.

She rummaged through the mail she'd picked up downstairs and found, mixed in among the Christmas cards, a self-addressed envelope from a music company. Her heart sank as she felt the thick tape inside and realized what it contained. Ripping the envelope open, she upended it and let her demo tape clatter out onto the table.

This wasn't the last of the tapes she'd sent out for consideration—there were still about a half dozen out at various companies—but it was the important one, the only tape that had made it to a label's Artists and Repertoire committee.

There was no response letter; someone had simply jotted on her own cover note, "Thanks, but not for us."

She tossed it into a Macy's box with the rest of them and, finally, opened that morning's *New York Times*. She read the article she'd been avoiding all day, headlined:

WALL STREET LAWYER KILLS SELF
PRESSURE AT WHITE-SHOE FIRM
CITED IN DEATH OF PARTNER, 52

Burdick apparently had indeed gotten away with it.

His artistry was astonishing. Not a word about the Hanover & Stiver case, nothing about the theft of the promissory note. Nothing about her or Mitchell or the merger.

Burdick was quoted, calling the death a terrible tragedy and saying that the profession had lost a brilliant attorney. The reporter also quoted several members of the firm—Bill Stanley mostly (well, the PR firm)—discussing Clayton's huge workload and his moodiness. The article reported that in the past year Clayton had billed over twenty-six hundred hours, a huge number for lawyers of his seniority. There was a sidebar on stress among overworked professionals.

She sighed and threw the newspaper away then washed the ink off her hands as if it were blood.

At five-thirty the doorbell rang.

Who could it be? Neighbors? Thom Sebastian assaulting her to beg for a date?

Ralph Dudley simply assaulting her?

She opened the door.

Mitchell Reece, wearing a windbreaker, walked inside and asked her if she had a cat.

"What?" she asked, bewildered by his quick entrance.

"A cat," he repeated.

"No, why? Are you allergic? What are you doing here?"

"Or fish, or anything you have to feed regularly?"

She was so pleased to see him in a playful mood—so different from the shock in his face after Clayton's death—that she joked back, "Just occasional boyfriends. But none at the moment, as I think you know."

"Come on downstairs. I want to show you something."

"But—"

He held his finger to his lips. "Let's go." She followed him out to the street, where a limo awaited, a black Lincoln. He opened the door and pointed inside, where she saw three large bags from Paragon Sporting Goods and two sets of new Rossignol skis propped across the seats.

Taylor laughed. "Mitchell, what are you doing?"

"Time for my lesson. Don't you remember? You were going to teach me to ski."

"Where? Central Park?"

"You know of someplace called Cannon? It's in New Hampshire. I just called the weather number. Four inches of new powder. I don't know what that means but even the recorded voice sounded excited so I assume it's good."

"But when?"

"But now," he said.

"Just like that?"

"The firm's jet's on the ramp at La Guardia. And they bill us by the hour so I suggest you hustle your butt. Go pack."

"This is crazy. What about work?"

"Donald called—he or his wife found out you like to ski so he ordered us to take some time off. He's giving us the trip all-expenses-paid. He called it a Christmas bonus. I've bought everything we need, I think. The store told me what to get. Skis, poles, black stretch pants, boots, bindings, sweaters, goggles. And ..." He held up a box.

"What's that?" Taylor asked.

"That? The most important thing of all."

She opened it. "A crash helmet?"

"That's for me." He shrugged. "Maybe you're a good teacher." He smiled. "And maybe you're not."

CHAPTER THIRTY

The helmet wasn't a bad idea. Reece had been on the bunny slope at the Cannon ski resort in New Hampshire for only fifteen minutes when he fell and jammed his thumb.

One of the resort doctors, a cheerful Indian, had taped it.

"Is it broken?" Reece had asked.

"No, is no fracture."

"Why does it hurt so much?"

"Lots of nerves in fingers," the doctor said, beaming. "Many, many nerves."

Afterward, they sat in the small lounge in the inn.

"Oh, Mitchell, I feel so bad," she said. "But you did a very respectable first run."

"My thumb doesn't feel too respectable. Is it always this cold?"

"Cannon's got the coldest, windiest runs in New England, dear," she said, pulling his head against her neck. "People have frozen to death not far from here."

"Really? Well, we wouldn't want to have too much fun now, would we?"

Reece actually didn't seem too upset about either the accident or the weather. And she soon learned why: He preferred to sit out the day with what he had smuggled with him—files from the Hanover settlement closing. Taylor too didn't mind; she was eager to get out onto the double-diamond trails and kick some ski butt, not baby-sit him on the beginner slopes or worry about him on the intermediates.

She kissed him. "Sit in the lodge and behave yourself."

As she crunched her way toward the lifts, he called, "Good luck. I assume you don't say, 'Break a leg.'"

She smiled, stomped into her skis and slid down the slight incline to the bottom of the lift.

At the top of the mountain, she eased off the chair and braked to a stop just past the lift house. She bent down and washed her goggles in snow. The White Mountains were, as she'd told him, son-of-a-bitch cold and the wind steadily scraped across her face. She pulled silk hand liners on and replaced her mittens, then poled her way into position and looked down the mountain. Her impression had always been that most runs never look as steep from the top as they do from the bottom but as she gazed down toward the lodge, over a half mile straight below her, she saw a plunge, not a slope. Her pulse picked up and immediately she realized how right Mitchell had been to arrange the trip. How important it was to get away from the city, to distance herself from Hubbard, White & Willis, from Wendall Clayton's ghost.

She pushed off the crest of the mountain.

It was the best run of her life.

Suddenly there was nothing in her universe but speed and snow and the rhythm of her turns.

Speed, speed, speed . . .

Which was all she wanted. Her mouth was open slightly in the ellipse that suggests fear or sexual heights. Her teeth dried and stung in the frigid slipstream but the pain only added to her surge of abandon.

Taylor danced over moguls the way girls skip double-Dutch jump rope on playgrounds. Once, her skis left the ground and she landed as if the snow had risen timidly to stroke the bottom of the fiberglass. Trees, bushes, other skiers were a swift-ratcheting backdrop sweeping past, everyone hushed, it seemed, listening to the cutting hiss of her Rossignol.

She was sure she was hitting sixty or seventy miles an hour. Her hair was whipping her shoulders and back. She wished she'd borrowed Reece's helmet—not for safety, but to cut the wind resistance of the tangled mass of drag.

Then it was over. She brodied to a stop near the base of the run, her thighs in agony but her heart filled with a glorious rush of fear and victory.

She did four runs this way, until on the last one, on a big mogul, she lost control and had to windmill her arms to regain her balance.

It sobered her.

Okay, honey, one suicide a week is enough.

At the bottom of the mountain, she kicked out of her skis and loosened her boot clasps. A tall, thin man came up to her and said in a Germanic accent, "Hey, that was a, you know, pretty okay run. You feel maybe like another one?"

"Uh, no, not really."

"Okay, okay. Hey, how about a drink?"

"Sorry." She picked up her skis and walked toward the cabin. "I'm here with my boyfriend."

And she realized suddenly that, by God, she was.

███████

Taylor returned to find Reece in great spirits, the tiny room cluttered with papers and documents delivered by FedEx or DHL. He was on the phone but he motioned her to him and kissed her hard then resumed his conversation.

She sat on the bed, wincing as she pulled off her sweater

and stretch pants, and began massaging her thighs and calves.

It was around that time that Reece hung up the phone and stacked the files away in a corner.

When they awoke in mid-afternoon they went to several antique stores, which weren't the precious collections of cheese dishes and brass surveying instruments you find in Connecticut or New York. These were barns packed with furniture. Rows of dusty chairs and tables and dressers and pickle jars and canopy beds and armoires. Very rustic and practical and well cared for.

None of the shopkeepers seemed to expect them to buy anything and they didn't.

That night they ate in one of the half-dozen inter-changeable inns in the area, their menus virtually the same, they'd found: veal chop, steak, chicken, duck à l'orange, salmon or trout. Afterward, they had a drink in the common room in front of a huge fireplace.

After they made love that night and Reece had fallen asleep, Taylor Lockwood lay under the garden patch quilt of a hundred hexagons of cotton and felt the reassuring pressure of a man's thigh beside her. She smelled the cold air as it streamed through the inch-open window and gathered on the floor. She tried to forget about Wendall Clayton, about Hubbard, White & Willis, about life on the other side of the looking glass.

At 4 A.M. she finally fell asleep.

On Thursday morning Taylor was first in the lift line.

She skied her first run fast, smelling the clean electric scent of snow, the biting perfume of fireplace smoke, hearing the sharp hiss of her turns in the granular snow.

Today, however, the speed had none of the cleansing effect that it'd had on her first day out. She felt alone, frightened, vulnerable. Like the first time her father made her ride her bike without training wheels. He'd put her on the tall Schwinn, aimed it down a hill and pushed. (She'd refused to

scream until the wobbly front wheel hit a curb and she'd
gone over the handlebars onto the sidewalk.)

She made mistakes, skied too defensively and nearly
wiped out bad.

At the bottom of the mountain she loaded her skis and
boots into the rental car.

No, Dad, I'm *not* getting back on the fucking horse, she
thought now.

She drove to their inn and went back to the room,
where Reece was taking a shower. She poured coffee from
the pot he'd ordered and dropped into the musty armchair.

Thinking:

*Where and for a first cause of action, Taylor Lockwood did
willfully . . .*

Outside she could see other skiers heading down the
mountain, some fast, some timidly.

*. . . and with full knowledge of the consequences, without a
warrant or other license, enter the office of one Wendall Clayton,
the decedent, and . . .*

She sipped the coffee.

*Where and for a first cause of action, Taylor Lockwood did
willfully ascertain and make public certain facts about one
Wendall Clayton, the decedent, that caused . . .*

Taylor sat back in the chair, closed her eyes.

. . . that caused said decedent to blow his fucking brains out.

Mitchell Reece, wrapped in a towel, opened the bathroom door and, smiling with pleasant surprise, walked up
to her. Kissed her on the mouth.

"Back early. You okay?"

"I don't know. Wasn't fun. Thumb still hurt?" she asked.

"A bit. I tell you I'm no good at this sort of thing. . . . I'm
much better with simpleminded, safe sports. . . ." He seemed
to be groping for a joke, something cute about sex probably,
but he sensed that she was upset. He sat down on the bed
opposite her.

"So what's up, Taylor?"

She shook her head.

"What is it?" he persisted.

"Mitchell, you know history?"

He motioned with an open palm for her to continue.

She asked, "You know what the Star Chamber was?"

"Just that it was a medieval English court. Why?"

"We learned about it in my European history course in college. It came back to me last night. The Star Chamber was a court without a jury, run by the Crown. When the king thought the regular court might decide against him he'd bring a case in the Star Chamber. You got hauled up before these special judges—the king's privy counselors. They'd pretend to have a trial but you can guess what happened. If the king wanted him guilty he was guilty. Very fast justice, very efficient."

He looked at the coffee, swirled it. He set it down without drinking any more. His face was somber.

She blurted, "Christ, Mitchell, the man is dead."

"And you think it's your fault."

A spasm of anger passed through her. Why can't he understand? "I was so stupid." Taylor looked at him briefly. Wondering how Clayton had felt lifting the gun. Had it been heavy? Had there been pain? How long had he lived after pulling the trigger? What had he seen? A burst of yellow light, a second of confusion, a wild eruption of thoughts, then nothing?

"Taylor," Reece said with measured words, "Clayton was crazy. No sane man would've stolen the note in the first place and no sane man would've killed himself if he'd been caught. You can't anticipate people like that."

She gripped his arm firmly. "But that's the point, Mitchell. You're thinking the problem is that Wendall outflanked us—that our fault was we weren't clever enough. But the *fault* was that we shouldn't've been playing the game in the first place. That firm's like Wonderland—it's got its own set of rules, which don't even make sense half the time but you never think about that because you're so deep in the place. Topsy-turvy. . . . Everything's topsy-turvy."

"What're you saying?"

"That we *should've* gone to the police. And we should've

let the chips fall wherever. So New Amsterdam would've left the firm. Well, so what? And you? You're one of the best lawyers in New York. You would've landed on your feet."

He rose and walked to the window.

Finally he said softly, "I know, I know. . . . You think I haven't been living with exactly what you're talking about?" He turned to face her. "But if I don't lay part of the blame at Clayton's feet, it undermines all my beliefs as a lawyer." He touched his chest. "It undermines all that I am. You know, this is something I'm going to have to live with too. I mean, you did what I asked you to do. But ultimately it was my decision."

So here was another aspect of Mitchell Reece—not all-powerful, not in control, not immune to pain.

She walked next to him, lowered her head onto his shoulder. His hand twined through her hair. "I'm sorry, Mitchell. This is very odd for me. It's not the sort of thing *Ms.* or *Savvy* prepares the working girl for."

He rubbed her shoulders.

"Can I ask a favor?" she said.

"Sure."

"Can we go back?"

He was surprised. "You want to leave?"

"I've had a wonderful time. But I'm in such a funky mood. I don't want to spoil our time together and I think I'd be a drag to be with."

"But I haven't learned to ski yet."

"Are you kidding? You're a graduate of the Taylor Lockwood School of Skiing Injury. You can go out now and break arms and legs all by yourself. With that kind of education there's no telling how far you can go."

"Let me see when I can get the jet."

CHAPTER THIRTY-ONE

████████ Thursday afternoon, Taylor Lockwood stood in front of the Metropolitan Museum of Art on Fifth Avenue, looking up at a brown brick apartment building across the street, about as far from the wilderness of New Hampshire as you could get, conceptually speaking.

She checked the address again and verified that she had found the right building. Inside, a solemn doorman regarded her carefully and then called upstairs to announce her.

She was approved and he nodded toward the elevator.

"Sixth floor," he said.

"Which apartment?" she asked.

He looked confused for a moment then said, "It's the whole floor."

"Oh."

She stepped into the leather-padded elevator and was slowly transported to a private entryway. She smoothed her hair, looking into a brass mirror, a huge thing. The foyer was in dark red and filled with Georgian yellow and white dovetail trim. The pictures were old English hunting scenes.

Plaster scrolls and cherubs and angels and columns were everywhere.

An ageless, unsmiling woman in a plain navy shift answered the door, asked her to wait then disappeared down the hallway. Taylor glanced through the doorway. The rooms were larger versions of the foyer. She looked back into the mirror and stared at herself, at a person who was thinner than she'd expected. Thinner and...what else? More drawn, gaunter, grimmer? She tried smiling; it didn't take.

A shadow passed across her and Mrs. Wendall Clayton stood in the doorway: a middle-aged woman, wearing the stiff, straight-cut, big-patterned clothes that people who learned style in the sixties still sometimes favor. Her straight hair was swept back and sprayed perfectly into place. Her thin face was severe. The foundation makeup had been applied thickly but her skin wasn't good and Taylor could see red patches beneath the pancake.

They shook hands and made introductions.

Taylor followed the woman into the living room. Why the hell am I doing this? she wondered suddenly. What possible point could it have?

I'm here to give you my deepest sympathy.

I'm here to say I worked with your husband.

I'm here to say that even though he's dead don't feel too bad because he tried to seduce me.

Mrs. Clayton sat upright in an uncomfortable satin wingback, Taylor in a spongy armchair.

I'm here because I helped kill your husband....

The widow asked, "Tea? Coffee?"

"No, thank you," Taylor said. And then realized that the woman's dress was red and that this was hardly a household in mourning—the room was festooned with antique Christmas decorations and there was a faint but rich scent of pine in the air. Classical Christmas music played on the stereo. Taylor looked at the woman's cocked eyebrow and her expression, which wasn't one of bitterness or sorrow. It was closer to curiosity.

"I worked with your husband, Mrs. Clayton."

"Yes."

"I just came to tell you how sorry I was."

And Taylor understood then, only at that moment, that uttering those words was all she could do. Watching this stolid, lone woman (Taylor couldn't picture her as one half of the Claytons) light a cigarette, she understood that the spirits of Donald Burdick and Vera Burdick and Messrs. Hubbard, White and Willis themselves had accompanied her here and were laying cold fingers on her lips. She could not, even here, in Clayton's home, do what she desperately wanted to do: explain.

Explain that she'd been the one who'd uncovered the terrible secrets about her husband, that she was the cause—the proximate cause, the law would say—of his death. No, there'd be no confession. Taylor knew what bound her. In this joint venture Hubbard, White & Willis had secured her soul.

"That's very kind of you." After a pause the woman asked: "Did I see you at the funeral? There were so many people."

"I wasn't there, no." Taylor eased back in the chair, uncomfortable, and crossed her arms. Wished she'd asked for coffee to keep her hands busy.

Now she looked around the room, aware of its size. The ceilings were twenty feet high. It reminded her of National Trust mansions and palaces in England. Taylor said, "He was an excellent lawyer. . . ."

Clayton's widow said, "I suppose." She was examining a tabletop. It seemed to be a dust inspection. "But then we didn't talk much about his career."

Taylor was counting the squares in the carpet. Trying to figure out the designs. Finally: St. George and the dragon, she believed.

Beware the Jabberwock . . .

The widow paused. "The truth is, Ms. Lockwood, I'm a little bewildered. I don't know you—though we may have met before. But you seem genuinely upset by my husband's death and I can't quite figure out why. You're not like the little sycophants who've come by since he died—the associates at the firm. They thought they were covering it up but I could see through them—in their eyes you could tell that they were amused at his death. I know they'd chuckled about it over their beers when they were alone. Do you know why they were here?"

Taylor was silent.

"They came because they thought word would get back to the firm that they'd done their duty. They'd made an appearance that might earn them another point or two, get them a step closer to being partner." She pressed out her cigarette. "Which is so ironic, of course, because they didn't grasp the situation at all. They should've been avoiding this house as if it were a leper colony. If word gets back to Burdick that young Samuel and Frederick and Douglas were paying respects to me, well, then, my God, they're in Dutch. At worst, they'd had the bad judgment to pick the wrong side; at best, they were displaying an oblivion about law firm politics.

"So you see, Ms. Lockwood, I am a little perplexed by your sympathy call." A smile. "That sounds appropriately Victorian, doesn't it? Sympathy call. Well, you aren't here to toady. You aren't here to gloat. Your dress and demeanor tell me you couldn't care less about what the Donald Burdicks and Wendall Claytons of the world think of you. You're clearly not one of the little malleable things he picked for his, dare I use the euphemism, girlfriends. . . . No, you're genuinely upset. I can see that. Well, you may have respected my husband as a lawyer and an ambitious businessman. But I doubt very much if you respected him as a human being. And I know without a doubt that you didn't like him."

"You had a loss in your life and I'm sorry," Taylor said evenly. "I didn't mean anything more or less than that." She fell silent, watching this shrewd woman light another cigarette with bony, red hands. It seemed as if the smoke that floated out of her nose and mouth had over the years taken with it her weight and softness.

Mrs. Clayton finally laughed. "Well, I appreciate that, Ms. Lockwood. Forgive my cynicism. I hope I haven't offended you. But don't feel sorry for me. Heavens, no. You're young. You don't have any experience with marriages of convenience."

Well, let's not go that far, Taylor thought, replaying many images: her parents' twin beds, her mother with her glass of wine sitting alone in front of the television, her father calling at midnight saying he was staying at his club. Night after night after night . . .

Clayton's widow said, "I guess you'd say our relationship wasn't even a marriage. It was a merger. His assets and mine. A certain camaraderie. Love? Was there any love between Williams Computing and RFC Industries when they consolidated? To name just one of the deals that took so much of Wendall's time . . ." She looked out over the park, spindly with branches, the residue of snow faintly surviving in shadows. "And that's the irony, you see."

"What?"

"Love—there was never any between us. And yet I'm the one he was most content with. Cold, scheming Wendall, the power broker. The master of control. But once outside of our life, he was at sea. Vulnerable. That's why he killed himself, of course. For love."

"What do you mean?" Taylor heard herself ask, her heart pounding fast.

"He killed himself for love," the widow repeated. "That's the one thing Wendall didn't understand and couldn't control. Love. Oh, how he wanted it. And as with so many beautiful, powerful people it was denied him. He was an alcoholic of love. He'd go off on his benders. With his chippies. His little sluts. And there were plenty of them— women would flock to him. A few of the men, too, I should tell you. How they all would want him!

"He'd spirit them away on carriage rides, buy them roses, have a breakfast tray put together at Le Perigord and sent to their apartments. Wendall goes a-courting. They were all disasters, of course. The girls never quite lived up

to what he wanted. The older ones . . . they turned out to be
every bit as superficial and material and cold"—she laughed
again, dropping a worm of ash in the ashtray—"as cold as I
was. Or he'd pick a young puppy, some ingenue, who'd
cling to him desperately, rearrange her life around him.
Then he'd feel the arms around his neck, dragging him
down. Someone *relying* on him. My Lord, we couldn't have
that, could we? Then he'd dump them. And back he'd come
to me. To nurse his wounds."

Taylor jumped in to steer the conversation back on
course. "What do you mean about his suicide? Killing himself for love?"

"It's the only thing that makes sense. He must've fallen
madly in love with somebody and he was sure she was the
one. When she told him no it must've devastated him."

"But the note he left said he was under pressure at work,
stress."

"Oh, he wrote that for my benefit. If he'd mentioned a
girlfriend, well, it would have embarrassed me." She
laughed. "The idea of Wendall killing himself because of
pressure? Why, he lived for pressure. He wasn't happy unless he had ten projects going at once. I've never seen him
happier than over the past few months working on the
merger, doing deals for his clients . . . and then planning the
other firm."

"What other firm?"

She looked at Taylor cautiously then pushed out her
cigarette. "I suppose it doesn't matter anymore. In case the
merger didn't go through, he was going to leave Hubbard,
White & Willis, take his boys and a couple of dozen partners and open his own firm. It was his alternative plan. I
think he almost preferred that to the merger. Because he'd
be a named partner. He always wanted to have his name on
the letterhead. Clayton, Jones & Smith, or whatever."

Another firm? Taylor wondered.

The widow resumed her examination of Central Park
flora. Then smiled. "That note . . . He could have said in the

note how unhappy he was with me as a wife. With our life together ... But he didn't. I was very touched."

Rising, Mrs. Clayton looked at her watch. "I'd like to talk to you longer." She picked up her Dunhill cigarette case. "But I have bridge club in ten minutes."

████

Aristocratize.

Taylor Lockwood was sitting at Wendall Clayton's desk.

It was late afternoon and a yellow-gray illumination lit the room from the pale sun over New York Harbor. The office lights were out and the door closed.

She looked at the jotting on a faded piece of foolscap.

Aristocratize.

Was that a word? Taylor glanced at the brass, the carpets, the vases, the tile painting, the wall of deal binders, the stacks of papers like the one that had held the note and tape recordings of her conversations with Mitchell Reece. The huge chair creaked as she moved.

Men of most renowned virtue ...

Spinning around once more to face the window, she decided that, whether it was real or not, "aristocratize" certainly described the essence of Wendall Clayton.

There was no reason for her to be in the firm. Technically she was still on vacation, courtesy of Donald Burdick. She could leave at any moment, smile at Ms. Strickland and walk out of the front door with impunity. She was, in fact, due at Mitchell Reece's loft right about now. (It turned out that he could cook after all and was planning to make them a tortellini salad for dinner; he was currently baking the bread himself!) She wanted to lie in his huge bathtub, a wonderful bathtub that had claw feet, to luxuriate in the water holding a thin-stemmed glass of wine and smell him cooking whatever went into a tortellini salad.

Instead, Taylor slouched down in Clayton's chair and spun slowly in a circle, 360 degrees, once, twice, three times.

Alice spinning as she fell down the rabbit hole, Alice buffeted on the ocean of tears, Alice arguing with the Queen of Hearts. . . .

Off with their heads, off with their heads!

Taylor stopped spinning. She began what she'd come here for: a detailed examination of the contents of Wendall Clayton's desk and filing cabinets.

A half hour later, Taylor Lockwood walked slowly downstairs to the paralegal pen. She made certain that no one was in the cubicles surrounding hers then looked through her address book and found the number of her favorite private eye, John Silbert Hemming.

He stopped suddenly, jolted, as he watched her slip out of Wendall Clayton's office, looking around carefully as if she didn't want to be seen.

Sean Lillick ducked into a darkened conference room where Taylor Lockwood couldn't see him. It had scared the hell out of him, as he was walking toward Clayton's office, to see the sudden shadow appearing in the doorway. For a split second all his chic, retro-punk East Village cynical sensibilities had vanished and he'd thought: Fuck me, it's a ghost . . .

What the hell had she been doing in there? he now wondered.

Lillick waited until she was gone and the corridor was empty. Then he too ducked into the dead partner's office and locked the door behind him.

It was excellent tortellini salad—filled with all sorts of good things only about half of which she recognized. The bread was lopsided but Reece had propped it up in a cute way. Whatever its shape, it tasted wonderful. He opened a cold Pouilly-Fuissé.

They ate for ten minutes, Taylor nodding as he told her about the impending settlement conference in Boston during which Hanover & Stiver would transfer the bulk of the principal of the loan back to New Amsterdam. He told anecdotes about some of Lloyd Hanover's shady business dealings. Normally, she liked it when he talked about his job because, although she didn't always understand the nuances, the animation and enthusiasm that lit up his face were infectious.

Tonight, though, she was distracted.

He finally caught on that something was wrong and his voice faded. He looked concerned. But before he could question her, Taylor set her fork down with a tap. "Mitchell."

He refilled their glasses and cocked an eyebrow at her.

"There's something I have to tell you."

"Yes?" he asked cautiously, perhaps suspecting some personal confession.

"I've been looking into a few things. About Wendall Clayton."

Reece sipped his wine. Nodded.

"He didn't kill himself." Taylor picked a lopsided bit of bread crust off the table and dropped it on her plate. "He was murdered."

CHAPTER THIRTY-TWO

Mitchell Reece smiled, as if waiting for a punch line.

Then: "Why do you think that?"

"I went to see his widow," Taylor said. Then she added quickly, "Oh, I wasn't going to tell her what happened—about the note and everything. But..." She paused. "Well, you know, I'm not sure why I went. It was something I just had to do."

He said, "I hear she's a bitch."

Taylor shrugged. "She was civil enough to me. But you know what she told me? That if Wendall couldn't get the merger through he was going to start his own firm."

"What?" Reece frowned.

Nodding, she said, "He had it all planned out. I went through his desk at the firm. I found business plans, bank loan applications. He even had the firm name selected. Clayton, Stone & Samuels. He had a sample letterhead printed up and he'd been talking to a broker about space in the Equitable Building."

Reece too had put down his utensils. "But if he was ready to start his own firm it makes no sense for him to risk his career to push the merger through."

"Exactly. Stealing the note? He'd be disbarred if he got caught. And he'd probably be prosecuted." Taylor held up a finger. "Another thing. Think about the gun."

"The gun he used?"

"Right. I called my detective, my private eye, and he talked to some buddies of his at the police department. The gun he used was a .38 Smith & Wesson knockoff, made in Italy. No serial number. It's one of the most popular street guns there is. 'It's like your McDonald's of firearms' is what John said. But if you're going to kill yourself why buy an un-traceable gun? You go to a sporting goods store, show a driver's license and buy a twelve-gauge shotgun."

"Or," Reece said, sitting forward, "why even shoot yourself? It's messy, unpleasant for your loved ones. I'd think you'd park your car in the garage with the engine running."

She nodded her agreement. "What I think is that some-body else stole the note and planted it in Clayton's office. Then when we found it he murdered Clayton to make it look like suicide."

"Who's the 'he'?" Reece asked.

"At first, I wondered if his widow might've done it. I mean here she was hosting a bridge party right after he died. She knew about the affairs he'd had. So she certainly had a motive."

"And she must have inherited some bucks from him."

"True. But then I got to thinking and it seems that the killer'd need to know about the firm and have access to it. Clayton's widow isn't like Vera Burdick, who's there all the time. Besides, Mrs. Clayton didn't seem that upset with all his affairs."

"Well," Reece suggested, "what about one of them? A lover? Somebody Clayton dumped?"

"Sure. That's a possibility. Or the husband or wife of

somebody he'd had an affair with. But," Taylor added, smiling, "what about some of the people we thought were suspects: Ralph Dudley. Clayton had found out about Junie and was blackmailing him."

"And Thom Sebastian. Clayton was the main reason he didn't make partner."

"He occurred to me, too. . . . And one other possibility."

Reece frowned, shaking his head.

Taylor pointed upward. "Go to the top."

"Donald Burdick?" Reece laughed. "Look, I know the motive's there. But Donald? I can't believe it. Whoever stole the note risked not only my career but risked losing a client as well—if we lost the case. There's no way Donald would've put New Amsterdam at risk."

Taylor countered, "But there *was* no risk. At the very worst, if we hadn't found the note, Donald would've sent his thief to get the note back from Clayton's office and it would've shown up on the file room floor or someplace in time for you to introduce it at trial."

Reece nodded, considering this. "And look how well Burdick covered everything up. The medical examiner, the prosecutor, the press . . . Nobody knows about the promissory note theft. And everything else—the evidence we found in Clayton's office, the real suicide note—I'm sure Burdick's shredded it by now." But then Reece shook his head. "Let's think about this. If it *is* Burdick remember that he's real tight with City Hall and Albany. We can't trust the police. We'll go to the U.S. attorney's office; I've still got friends there. I'll call them—"

"But didn't Donald call somebody in the Justice Department?" she asked. "After they found the body?"

Reece paused. "I don't remember. Yeah, I think he did."

Taylor said, "You're going to Boston tomorrow for the settlement closing. Do you know anybody in Justice up there?"

"Yeah, I do. I haven't talked to him for a while. Let's see if he's still there." He walked to his desk and found his address book and picked up the phone. But he looked at it warily.

"Bugs?" Taylor asked.

"Let's not take any chances—we'll go downstairs."

On the street they found a pay phone and Reece made a credit card call.

"Sam Latham, please. . . . Hey, Sam, Mitchell Reece."

The men apparently knew each other well and Taylor deduced from the conversation that they'd both been prosecutors in New York some years ago. After a few whatever-happened-to's, Reece told him their suspicions about Clayton's death. They made plans to meet at the U.S. attorney's office in Boston the next day, after the Hanover settlement closing. He hung up.

"He's getting his boss and an FBI agent to meet with me."

Taylor felt a huge weight lifted from her. At last the authorities were involved. This was the way the system was supposed to work.

They returned upstairs. Reece closed the front door and latched it then walked up behind her, enfolded her in his arms. She leaned her head back and slowly turned so that they were face-to-face.

He glanced at the table, where the meal sat unfinished: the exceptionally good tortellini salad, the cold wine, the sagging bread. She smiled and, with her fingertips, turned his head back to face her.

She kissed him hard.

Without a word they walked to Reece's bed.

███

So far, not so good . . .

Thom Sebastian sat back in his office chair, pushing aside the documents he'd been working on all morning, a revolving credit agreement for New Amsterdam Bank.

He should have been comfortable, should have been content. But he was troubled.

Wendall Clayton, the man who'd destroyed his chances for partnership at Hubbard, White, was gone—as dead as a shot pheasant in one of the hunting prints hanging in the partner's office.

Good.

But his life didn't really *feel* good. He had a brooding sense that his entire world was about to be torn apart. And this terrified him.

Three times he reached for the phone, hesitated, put his hands flat on his thick thighs and remained where he was.

He peeked under his blotter and saw the notes he'd gathered on Taylor Lockwood over the past ten days or so.

Taylor Lockwood . . . the sole reason that things weren't so good.

Come on, Mr. Fucking Negotiator, make a decision.

But ultimately, he knew, there was no decision at all. Because there was only one thing to do.

The problem was finding the courage to do it.

The next morning Reece called Taylor from Boston.

She was at her apartment; she'd decided it was safest to stay away from the firm. He called to report that the settlement had gone well. The money from the Hanover settlement had been safely wired into a New Amsterdam account and he'd endured Lloyd Hanover's relentless glare and potshots at lawyers throughout the closing.

Reece was on his way to meet with his friend in the U.S. attorney's office.

"I miss you," he said.

"Hurry home," she told him. "Let's get this behind us and go back and ski for real."

"Or," he joked, "go back and shop and eat dinner at the inns."

"I'll get you on black diamond slopes sooner or later."

"What the hell? I've still got one thumb and eight fingers left."

After some Christmas shopping Taylor stopped at a coffee shop on Sixth Avenue, around the corner from her apartment, for some lunch.

Sitting at the counter, she wondered what to get Reece for Christmas. He had all the clothes he needed. Wine was too impersonal.

Then she recalled his collection of lead soldiers.

She'd find one that was perfect for him—just one. A special one, antique, expensive. But where? Well, this was New York, the city that boasted neighborhoods devoted to special interests: the garment district, the flower district, even the sewing machine district. There was probably a cluster of stores somewhere in Midtown selling antique toys.

A man sat down next to her, a large workman in gray coveralls, wearing a baseball cap. There was something vaguely familiar about him and she wondered if he worked in her apartment building; the structure was old and there were always people renovating and repairing.

He pulled out a book and began reading.

Taylor's chicken soup came and as she was sprinkling Tabasco on it the man next to her took a sip of coffee. When he replaced the cup his elbow knocked his book to the floor. It dropped at her feet.

"Oh, sorry," he said, blushing.

"No problem," she said and bent down to retrieve the book. When she handed it to him he smiled his thanks and said, "I like this place. You come here a lot?" A trace of some accent from one of the outer boroughs.

"Some."

"With your boyfriend?" he asked, smiling, ruefully.

She nodded, and let the small lie do double duty: let him know she wasn't interested and save his ego from a flat-out rejection.

"Ah, well," he sighed and returned to his book.

When she left he was working on a double cheese-burger. He waved to her and called, "Merry Christmas."

"You too," she said.

Back at home, she pulled the phone book out from under her bed and looked up toy stores.

Well, let's start at the beginning.

As she stood to get the phone she realized she felt achy, as if a cold were coming on. Her head was hurting a bit too. She went into the bathroom to get some aspirin, swallowed them down and returned to the bedroom to start calling the stores in search of Reece's Christmas present.

Feeling tired...

She reclined on the bed and picked up the cordless phone.

She'd dialed the first digit when she gasped and sat up fast. A churning pain struck somewhere deep within her abdomen. Her face burst out in sweat.

"Oh, man," she whispered. Not the flu, not now....

Recalling that she often got sick around Christmas when she was young. A therapist she'd seen for a while had wondered if it wasn't her dread of a holiday presided over by a domineering father.

"Oh..." She moaned again, pressing the skin above the pang hard with both her hands. It ceased for a moment then exploded in another eruption of agony.

Taylor stood up, adding nausea to the sensation. The room began to spin and she tried to control her fall to the parquet floor. Her head hit the dressing table and she blacked out.

When she opened her eyes she saw claws.

The Jabberwock's claws, disemboweling her, tearing her stomach, throat, the back of her mouth, shredding her flesh...

She squinted. No, no, they were just the claws on the legs of her bed. She—

The pain stunned her again and she moaned, a low, animal sound.

Sweat filled her eyes and ran down her nose. She wrapped her arms around herself and drew her legs up, trying to stop the pain. Every muscle hard as rubber, she tried to will the pain away but this had no effect. Then the nausea overwhelmed her and Taylor crawled to the toilet, opened the seat and held herself up on one arm while she vomited and retched for what seemed like hours.

Her hands shook, her skin was inflamed. She stared at the tiny hexagonal tiles in front of her until she fainted again. Consciousness returned and she struggled for the phone. But her muscles gave out and she dropped again to the floor. From a distant dimension she heard a thunk—the sound of her head hitting the tiles.

She understood now that she'd been poisoned. . . . The man at the restaurant. The workman in the coveralls and baseball cap. *He* was the one who'd stolen the note, the one who'd run them off the road, the one who'd killed Wendall Clayton.

That was why he'd seemed familiar—because she must've seen him in the firm or following her and Reece earlier. Maybe he'd overheard her conversation with John Silbert Hemming. Maybe he'd put a tap on *her* phone at the office or even in her apartment.

She—

Then the poison began to churn again and she started to retch in earnest, unable to breathe, trying to scream for help, slamming her hand on the dresser so that somebody might hear and come to her aid. Perfume bottles fell, makeup, an Alice in Wonderland snowball crashed to the floor and broke, the water and sparkles spattering her.

She began to pummel the floor—until she realized she had no feeling in her hand; it was completely numb. Taylor Lockwood began to cry.

She crawled to the phone, dialed 911.

"Police and fire emergency."

She couldn't speak. Her tongue had turned to wood.

The air was becoming thinner and thinner, sucked from the room.

The voice said, "Is anyone there? Hello? Hello? . . ."

Taylor's hands stopped working. She dropped the phone. She closed her eyes.

CHAPTER THIRTY-THREE

"What happened?" Carrie Mason asked.

The doctor was a woman in her mid-thirties. She had straight blond hair and wore no makeup except for bright blue eye shadow. The medico's badge said Dr. V. Sarravich.

The woman said, "Botulism."

"Botulism? Food poisoning?"

"I'm afraid she ate some severely tainted food."

"Is she going to be okay?"

"Botulism's much more serious than other types of food poisoning. She's unconscious, in shock. Severely dehydrated. The prognosis isn't good. We should get in touch with her family, if she has any. She lived alone and apparently the police couldn't find her address book or any next-of-kin information. We found your name and number on a card in her purse."

"I don't know where her parents live. I'll give you the name of someone who can get in touch with them. Can I see her?"

"She's in the Critical Care Unit. You can't visit now," Dr.

Sarravich said. Medical people were all so serious, the girl thought.

Carrie asked, "Is it really bad?"

She hesitated—a concession to delicacy—and said, "I'm afraid it may be fatal and even if it isn't there could be some permanent damage."

"What kind of damage?"

"Neuromuscular."

"To her hands?" Carrie asked.

"Possibly."

"But she's a musician," the paralegal said, alarmed. "A pianist."

"It's too early to tell anything at this point." A pen and paper appeared, and the doctor asked, "Now, whom should I contact?"

Carrie wrote a name and phone number. The doctor looked at the pad. "Donald Burdick. Who is he?"

"The head of the firm she works at. He can tell you everything you want to know."

■

Taylor's eyes opened slowly. Her skin stung from the sandblasting of fever. Her vision was blurred. Her head was in a vise of fiery pressure. Her legs and arms were useless, like blocks of wood grafted to her torso. The nausea and cramps were still rampaging through her abdomen and her throat was dry as paper.

There was a young woman in a pale blue uniform making the bed next to hers.

Taylor had never been in such pain. Every breath brought pain. Every twitch was a throb of pain. She assumed that the nerves in her hands and legs had short-circuited—she couldn't move her limbs.

Taylor whispered.

No reaction from the young woman.

She screamed.

The attendant cocked her head.

She screamed again.

No reaction. Taylor closed her eyes and rested after the agonizing effort.

Several minutes later the bed was made. As the attendant walked toward the door, she glanced at Taylor.

Taylor screamed, "Poison!"

The aide leaned down. "Did you say something, honey?" Taylor smelled fruity gum on her breath and felt like gagging.

"Poison," she managed to say. "I was poisoned."

"Yes, food poisoning," the girl said and started to leave.

Taylor screamed, "I want Mitchell!"

The girl held up the watch on her pudgy wrist. "It's not midnight. It's about six."

"I want Mitchell. Please . . ."

Taylor tried fiercely to hold on to consciousness but it spilled away like a handful of sugar. She had an impression of struggling to leap out of bed and calling Mitchell in Boston but then she realized that her legs and arms had started to spasm. Then a nurse was standing over her, staring in alarm and reaching for the call button, pushing it fiercely over and over.

And then the room went black.

At 7:30 P.M. the telephone in Donald Burdick's co-op rang.

He was in the living room. He heard Vera answer it then mentally followed her footsteps as they completed a circuit that ended in the arched entrance near him. Her calm face appeared.

"Phone, Don," Vera said. "It's the doctor."

The *Wall Street Journal* crumpled in his hand. He rose and together they walked to the den.

"Yes?" he asked.

"Mr. Burdick?" a woman's matter-of-fact voice asked. "This is Dr. Vivian Sarravich again. From Manhattan General Hospital? I'm calling about Ms. Lockwood."

"Yes?"

"I'm afraid I have bad news, sir. Miss Taylor has gone into a coma. Our neurologist's opinion is that she won't be coming out of it in the near future...if at all. And if she does she's certain to have permanent brain and neuromuscular damage."

Burdick shook his head to Vera. He held the phone out a ways so that she too could hear. "It's that bad?"

"This is the most severe case of botulism I've ever seen. The infection was much greater than usual. She's had two respiratory failures. We had to put her on a ventilator. And a feeding tube, of course."

"Her family?"

"We've told them. Her parents on on their way here."

"Yes, well, thank you, Doctor. You'll keep me posted?"

"Of course. I am sorry. We did everything we could."

"I'm sure you did."

Burdick hung up and said to his wife, "She probably won't make it."

Vera gave a neutral nod and then glanced at the maid who'd silently appeared beside them. "They're here, Mrs. Burdick."

"Show them into the den, 'Nita."

■■■■■■

Donald Burdick poured port into Waterford glasses. His hands left fingerprints in a slight coating of dust on the bottle, which, he noticed, had been put up in 1963.

The year that a Democratic President had been killed.

The year he made his first million dollars.

The year that happened to be a very good one for vintage port.

He carried the glasses to the guests: Bill Stanley, Lamar Fredericks, Woody Crenshaw—all old fogies, his granddaughter might say, if kids still used that word, which of course they didn't—and three other members of the executive committee. Three young partners to whom Burdick was making a point of being kind and deferential.

Three partners who were in absolute terror at the moment—because they had been picked and polished by Wendall Clayton and then leveraged by him onto the executive committee.

The men were in Burdick's study. Outside, wet snow slapped on the leaded glass windows.

"To Hubbard, White & Willis," Burdick said. Glasses were raised but not rung together.

The Reconstruction had began swiftly. Only one of Clayton's lackeys had been fired outright—tall, young Randy Simms III, a fair-to-middlin' lawyer but one hell of a scheming nazi sycophant, Vera Burdick had observed. It had been her delightful task to transmit, through her own social network, rumors of various types of illegal scams the young partner was guilty of. By the time she was through he'd been thoroughly blackballed and was a pariah in the world of New York law and Upper East Side society.

As for the other pretty young men and women associates on Clayton's side . . . they weren't asked to leave, the theory being they'd work even harder to rid themselves of the contamination. These secessionists and collaborators were given the shaved-head treatment then kicked onto the summer outing and hiring committees.

These three Nameless were the last order of business in the Purge.

One of them said, "Your wife, Donald, is a charming lady."

Burdick smiled. They had of course met Vera before this evening though she had never served them dinner, never entertained them, never told them stories of her travels and anecdotes about her famous political friends; never, in short, grilled them like an expert interrogator.

He set the assassination-year bottle in the middle of the tea table.

He said, "Bill knows this but for the rest of you, I have some news. I'm meeting tomorrow with John Perelli. We have a problem, of course. Perelli's position is that Wendall's discussions with him suggest an implicit agreement to go forward with the merger—even though the whole firm's never approved it."

One of the Nameless nodded. Impressed that the man returned his gaze, Burdick continued, "His thinking is that we agreed to negotiate in good faith. The firm has now decided that we do not want to go forward simply because we do not want to go forward. That is *not* good faith. We have an implied contract problem. Look at Texaco and Pennzoil."

Another Nameless: "I know the law, Don." This was a little brash, as the youngster understood immediately; he continued more contritely, "I agree they'd have an argument but I think we hedged well enough so that with Wendall gone the basic deal has changed."

Vera asked bluntly, "Was Clayton's presence a condition precedent to going forward?"

Two of the Nameless blinked, hearing the charming woman nail the legal situation perfectly with one simple question.

"No."

Her husband, smiling, shrugged. "Then, I submit, we still have our problem."

The first Nameless said, "But what would they want as a remedy? Specific performance?"

Burdick decided the man was an idiot and made a mental note to give him only scut work for the rest of his time at Hubbard, White. "Of course not. The courts can't *make* us merge."

Bill Stanley said, "They want money. And what do *we* want?" When no one answered he answered himself, "Silence."

Burdick said, "No more publicity. Under any circumstances. A senior partner kills himself? Bad enough and we're going to lose clients because of that, my friend. Then a suit from Perelli? No, I want to preempt them."

Lamar Fredericks, round, bald and roasted from two weeks of golf on Antigua, said, "Preempt? You mean bribe. Cut the crap and tell us what it's going to cost."

Burdick looked at Stanley, who said to the group, "We'd pay Perelli twenty million. Up to, that is. We'll start lower, of course. Full release and agreement not to say anything to the press. If they do, liquidated damages of a double refund."

Crenshaw snorted. "What does that do to our partnership shares?"

Burdick snapped, "It'll be a cut out of operating profits. Take a calculator and figure it out yourself."

"Will they buy into it?"

Burdick said, "I'll be as persuasive as I can. The reason you're all here is that it would be an expenditure out of the ordinary course. I don't want to present it to the firm. So to authorize it we need a three-quarters vote of the executive committee."

None of them had assumed that this was solely a social dinner, of course, but it was not until this moment that they understood the total implications of the invitation. They were the swing votes and were being tested; Burdick had to know where they stood.

"So," Burdick said cheerfully, "are we all in agreement?"

This was the final exorcism of Wendall Clayton. In these three trim, handsome lawyers resided what was left of his ambitious spirit.

Was his legacy, Burdick wondered, as powerful as the man?

Gazes met. No one swallowed or shuffled. When Burdick called for the vote they each said an enthusiastic "In favor."

Burdick smiled and, when he poured more port, gripped one of them on the shoulder—welcome to the club. He was the foolish partner, the one whose professional life would be a living hell from that day on.

Then Burdick sat down in his glossy leather wingback chair and reflected on how much he despised them for not having the mettle to take Clayton's fallen standard and shove it up his—Burdick's—ass. He then grew somber. "Oh, just so you know: We have another problem, I'm afraid."

"What do you mean?" Stanley's voice was a harsh whine.

"One of the paralegals is in the hospital," Vera Burdick explained. "It's quite serious. I have a feeling she won't survive."

"Who?" a Nameless dared to ask.

"Taylor Lockwood."

"Taylor? Oh, no, not her. She's one of the best assistants I ever had on a closing. What happened?"

"Food poisoning. Nobody knows exactly how she got it."

"Should we—" one of the Nameless began to ask.

But Vera Burdick interrupted. "I'm on top of it. Don't worry."

Bill Stanley shook his head. "God, I only hope it wasn't anything we catered. Could you pass that port, Donald?"

CHAPTER THIRTY-FOUR

████████ Mitchell Reece closed his litigation bag and slid it under the seat of the shuttle from Boston as they approached La Guardia early the next morning.

Still no call from Taylor Lockwood and he hadn't been able to reach her at the firm. He'd gotten only her voice mail.

He wondered what was going on.

But as he stared at the brown and gray expanse of the Bronx beneath him his thoughts returned to Wendall Clayton's funeral, held in an Episcopalian church on Park Avenue. The minister's words came clearly to mind.

I recall one time when I happened to meet Wendall; it was a Saturday evening, late. We happened to be strolling up Madison Avenue together, he returning from the firm, I from some function at my congregation....

The minister had foresaken the pulpit and, like a talk show host, walked down into his audience.

...and we passed a few moments in idle conversation. Though we were in very different places in our lives I saw that there were striking similarities between his profession and mine.

*He voiced some concern for a young man or woman, a lawyer at
his firm, who was suffering from doubts. Wendall wanted to in-
spire this protégé to be the best lawyer they might be . . .*

Hundreds of people. Most of the partners from
Hubbard, White & Willis, many associates, many friends
had attended.

*. . . just as I in my own way deal with spiritual doubt in our
young people. . . .*

Quite a church, Reece recalled. Huge, pointy, Gothic,
solid. All the joists and beams met in perfect unison—high
in the air. It was a fitting place for an aristocratic man to be
eulogized.

Then he thought back to another death at the firm—
Linda Davidoff's. Her funeral, Reece decided, had been
much better. The church was tamer, the minister more upset. It seemed to Reece preferable to get more tears and
fewer words from men of the cloth at times of mourning.

Clayton's Upper East Side minister had been correct
about one thing, though: He and Clayton had indeed been
cut from the same bolt—noblemen and medieval clergy. In
tarot cards pentacles would be their suit. Choose this sign
for dark men of power and money.

Aggressive men.

The minister was seizing an opportunity to preach, just
as Clayton had seized a chance of his own—and had died as
a consequence of his reach.

The sudden grind and windy slam of the plane's wheels
coming down interrupted Reece's thoughts. And as he
glanced out the window, Reece decided it was ironic that he
saw below him the huge cluster of dense graveyards in
Queens—a whole city of a graveyard. He watched until it
vanished under the wing and they landed.

As he walked down the ramp toward the terminal Reece
saw his last name on a card being held up by a limo driver.

"Is that for *Mitchell* Reece?" he asked.

"Yes, sir. You have luggage?"

"Just this."

The man took his bags.

Reece gave him the address of the firm.

"We're supposed to stop someplace else, sir."

"What do you mean?"

"I'm afraid there's some kind of problem."

Reece climbed into the back of the Lincoln. "What kind of problem?"

"An emergency of some kind."

Forty minutes later the driver pulled up in front of yellow-painted doors at an annex to Manhattan General Hospital. It was deserted, except for some big blue biohazard containers and a bloody gurney sitting by itself. It seemed as if a body had just been pulled from it and hauled off to a pauper's grave.

Inside, Reece stopped at a reception desk and was directed down a long, dim corridor.

He found the basement room he sought and pushed open the door.

Gray-faced and red-eyed, Taylor Lockwood blinked in surprise at his entrance and shut off the soap opera she was watching.

She smiled. "Mitchell, it's you! Kiss me—it's not contagious—then see if you can scarf up some food. I'm starving to death."

███████

Suck on ice," Reece said when he returned a few minutes later.

Taylor frowned.

"I asked them what you could have to eat. They said you should suck on ice."

She nodded at the IV. "Glucose. It's pure carbohydrates. I'm dying for a hamburger."

Reece gave her a Life Saver. "You look, well, awful."

"'Awful' is a compliment, considering how I did look. The nurse tells me I've recovered incredibly well."

"What happened?"

Taylor nodded. "I was stupid. I'm sure *my* phone was bugged too, either at my apartment or cubicle. I should've thought about that. Anyway, we got busted—somebody overhead us. And then at lunch yesterday this guy sits down next to me. He drops a book—I mean, *pretends* to drop a book—and when I bent down to pick it up for him I think he squirted botulism culture into my soup."

"Jesus, botulism? The most dangerous food poisoning there is."

She nodded. "I think he got it from Genneco Labs."

"Our client?"

"Yep."

"I was talking to a pathologist here. He told me Genneco does a lot of research into antitoxins—you know, like antidotes."

"So whoever killed Clayton stole some culture—or told the killer about Genneco and *he* stole it?"

She nodded.

"I was feeling a lot better last night but I called Donald and told him I was almost dead, in a coma."

"You what?"

"I wanted word to get around the firm that I was almost dead. I was afraid the killer would try again. I called and pretended I was my doctor." She gave a faint laugh. "I called my parents and told them that whatever they heard I was fine—although I have to say I was inclined to let my father stew a bit more. Carrie Mason's the only one who knows I'm okay."

Reece stroked her cheek. "Botulism...that could've killed you."

"The doctor told me that, 'luckily,' I ingested too *much* of the culture. I got sick immediately and, well, the word they used was, quote, *evacuated* most of the bacteria. Man, it was unpleasant. I'm talking Mount Saint Helens."

He hugged her hard. "We're not going to have to worry about anything like this happening again. I talked to Sam, my friend at the U.S. attorney's office, yesterday afternoon. He's coming down tomorrow with a special prosecutor from Washington. We're going to meet with him at the federal building at three—if you feel up to it."

"I'll feel up to it. Whoever's behind this . . . we're going to stop them. . . ." Her voice faded. "What's wrong, Mitchell?"

"Wrong?" His eyes were hollow and troubled. "You almost got killed. . . . I'm so sorry. If I'd known—"

She leaned forward and kissed him. "Hey, I lost those five pounds I gained at Thanksgiving and then some. Call it an early Christmas present. Now, go on, get out of here. Next time you see me I promise I won't look like Marley's ghost."

CHAPTER THIRTY-FIVE

The girl walked sheepishly into the hospital room, hiding behind a bouquet of exotic flowers that she'd probably hand-selected from an Upper East Side florist.

"Whoa," Taylor told Carrie Mason, laughing at the massive arrangement. "Anything left in the rain forest?"

The chubby girl set the vase on the bedside table and sat in the functional gray chair near Taylor's bed, studying her carefully.

"You're looking a thousand times better, Taylor," Carrie said. "Everybody's like, ohmagod, she's dying. I wanted to tell them but I didn't. Not a soul—like you said."

Taylor gave her a rundown on her condition and thanked the girl for staying with her just after she'd been admitted.

"It's, like, no problem, Taylor. You looked . . . You were pretty sick."

Attempted murder does that to you.

"Well, I'll be getting out soon. May not eat for a week or so but it'll be good to get vertical again."

The girl avoided Taylor's eyes. She stood and arranged the flowers and it was this compulsive activity that told Taylor that she was troubled by something.

"What is it, Carrie?"

The girl paused, her back to Taylor, then sat down again. Tears were running down her cheeks. She wiped her face with the back of her fleshy hand. "I . . ."

"Go ahead. Tell me. What's the matter?"

"I think I know why Mr. Clayton killed himself. I think it was my fault."

"Your fault?" Taylor said. "What do you mean?"

"Well, okay . . . You know Sean."

One of the firm's busier spies. Taylor nodded.

"Well, what it was . . . see, last week Sean asked me out. I went over to his place. And I thought he wanted to go out with me and I was really, really excited about it. 'Cause I've had this crush on him for, like, a while. But it turned out . . . I mean, the thing was he just wanted to go through my purse."

"Why?"

"To get my log-on pass code for the firm computers. One of the operators told me he went on the system with my user name."

Taylor remembered the gum-snapping computer operator and the blank screen that should have had information about taxis and computer time and phone records. This was interesting. She nodded for the girl to continue and listened carefully.

"When I found out what he did I got totally mad. I asked him how could he do that? I mean, he way used me. Anyway he got all freaked out and apologized. But I was so mad . . . Well, I wanted to get even with him and . . ." She again attended to the stalks of weird flowers. "And when I was in Connecticut with Mr. Clayton and you . . . Well, afterward, he came on to me, Mr. Clayton, you know and . . . well, we sort of slept together."

Taylor nodded, recalling that she'd overheard the tryst

from Clayton's den. The poor girl, suckered in by the vortex of the partner's eyes and charm.

"So, Sean found out and he had this big fight with Clayton. It was really vicious. I think Sean threatened to go to the executive committee about what happened and Clayton was afraid he'd get fired and he killed himself."

Taylor was frowning. So he and Lillick had had a fight. It had never occurred to her that *Lillick* might have killed Clayton.

Then she focused on the distraught Carrie once more. She couldn't, of course, say anything about Clayton's death but she could reassure the girl. "No, Carrie, that had nothing to do with it." A woman-to-woman smile. "Wendall Clayton slept with half the firm and he couldn't care less if anybody knew about it. Besides, I talked to Donald. I know why Clayton killed himself. I can't tell you but it had nothing to do with you or Sean."

"Really?"

"Promise."

"Despite what happened, I really kind of like him— Sean, I mean. He's weird, but underneath he's not as weird as he seems to be. We kind of patched things up. I think he likes me."

"I'm glad to hear that."

Taylor decided it was time to get out of the hospital. She feigned a yawn. "Listen, Carrie. I'm going to get some sleep now."

"Oh, sure. Feel better." Carrie hugged her. Then she asked, "Oh, one thing—do you know where the United Charities of New York general correspondence file is?"

"No idea. I never worked for them."

The girl frowned. "You didn't?"

"No. Why?"

"I was down in the pen this morning and I saw Donald Burdick's wife in your cubicle."

"Vera?"

"Yeah. She was looking through your desk. And I asked what she needed and she said she was doing a fund-raiser for the UCNY and needed the file. She thought you had it. But we couldn't find it."

"I've never checked out any of their files. Must be a mistake."

Carrie glanced at the TV and her face lit up. "Hey, look, it's *The Bold and the Beautiful*. . . . That's my favorite! I used to love summer vacations so I could watch all the soaps. Can't do that anymore. Things sure change when you start working."

Well, that's the truth. . . .

Taylor's eyes strayed absently to the screen, watching the actors lost in their own intrigues and desires. When she turned to the doorway to say good-bye to Carrie, the paralegal had already left.

Taylor felt uneasy. Lillick, Dudley, Sebastian, Burdick . . . or somebody else had tried to poison her. They might find out that she was no longer in a coma and try again. She summoned the floor nurse, who in turn managed to track down a resident. The young doctor, seeing the urgency in her eyes, reluctantly agreed to discharge her as soon as the paperwork was finished.

After he'd left, she lay back in bed and looked through her purse for her insurance card.

She found a folded sheet of paper stuck in the back of the address book.

It was the poem that Danny Stuart had given her. Linda Davidoff's poem, her suicide note. She realized that she'd never read it, which she now did.

> *When I Leave*
>
> *By Linda Davidoff*
>
> *When I leave, I'll travel light*
> *and rise above*
> *the panorama of my solitude.*
> *I'll sail to you, fast and high,*
> *weightless as the touch of night.*

When I leave, I'll become a light
that shows our love in a clear, essential way
(After all, what is a soul but love?).
After all is reconciled, and the darkness
      pitched away,
I'll travel light, transported home to you
in the buoyancy of pure and peaceful flight.

Taylor Lockwood thought of Linda, the beautiful, quiet, gypsy poet. She read the lines again very slowly.

Then she read them once more.

A moment later a huge orderly appeared in the door. "Ms. Lockwood, good news: The warden called."

He grinned; she frowned, not understanding.

Then the man delivered the rest of what would be his stock joke. "It's a full pardon. You're free to go." And he maneuvered the wheelchair into the room.

▄▄▄▄

Taylor Lockwood had learned early who the real power centers were at Hubbard, White.

One of the most powerful was a short, round-faced woman of sixty. Mrs. Bendix had used her miraculous skills at memory and association to save the butts of almost every attorney and paralegal in the firm on more than one occasion by finding obscure file folders buried among the millions of documents residing on the gray metal shelves.

She was the doyen of the firm's massive file room.

Taylor now stood over Mrs. Bendix's frothy blue hair as the woman flipped through the three-by-five cards that were her computer. Taylor silently waited for her to finish. Mrs. Bendix—even more so than a senior partner—was a person one did not interrupt. When she was through she looked up and blinked. "I was told you were in the hospital. We contributed for the flowers."

"They were lovely, Mrs. Bendix. I recovered more quickly than expected."

"They said you were almost dead."

"Modern medicine."

Mrs. Bendix was eyeing Taylor's jeans and sweatshirt critically. "This firm has a dress code. You're outfitted for sick leave, not work."

"This is a bit irregular, Mrs. Bendix. But I have a problem and you're just about the only person who can help me."

"Probably am. No need to stroke."

"I need a case."

"Which one? You've got about nine hundred current ones to chose from."

"An old case."

"In that event, the possibilities are limitless."

"Let's narrow things down. Genneco Labs. Maybe a patent—"

"Hubbard, White does not do patent work. We never have and I'm sure we never will."

"Well, how about a contract for the development of bacterial or viral cultures or antitoxins?"

"Nope."

Taylor looked at the rows and rows of file cabinets. A thought fluttered past, then settled. She asked, "Insurance issues, the storage of products, toxins, food poisoning and so on?"

"Sorry, not a bell is rung, though in 1957 we did have a cruise line as a client. I got a discount and took a trip to Bermuda. I ate pasta that disagreed with me very badly. But I digress."

In frustration, Taylor puffed air into her cheeks.

Mrs. Bendix said tantalizingly, "Since you said toxins, food poisoning and so on I assume you meant toxins, food poisonings and so on."

Taylor knew that when people like Mrs. Bendix bait you, you swallow the worm and the hook in their entirety. She said, "Maybe I was premature when I qualified myself."

"Well," the woman said, "my mind harkens back to ..." She closed her eyes, creasing her gunmetal eye shadow, then opened them dramatically. "...Biosecurity Systems, Inc. A contract negotiation with Genneco for the purchase and installation of Genneco's new security system in Teterboro, New Jersey. Two years ago. I understand the negotiations were a nightmare."

"Security," Taylor said. "I didn't think about that."

Mrs. Bendix said, "Apparently not."

"Can you tell me if anyone checked out the files on that deal in the past few months?"

This was beyond her brain. The woman pulled the logbook out and thumbed through it quickly then held it open for Taylor to look at. Taylor nodded. "I'd like to check it out too, if you don't mind."

"Surely."

Then a frown crossed Taylor's face. "I wonder if we could just consider one more file. This might be trickier."

"I live for challenges," Mrs. Bendix replied.

CHAPTER THIRTY-SIX

The New York State Department of Social Services worked fast.

After one anonymous phone call to the police the West Side Club became the front-page feature in the evening edition of every tabloid in the New York area.

Though gentlemen did not read such newspapers Ralph Dudley made an exception this once, since the *Times* wouldn't have the story until tomorrow morning. He now sat at his desk, lit only by a single battered brass lamp and the paltry December dusk light bleeding into his office, and stared at the same article he'd already read four times. A half-dozen people were under arrest and two underage prostitutes were being placed in foster homes in upstate New York.

Good-bye Junie, Dudley thought.

He'd made one last trip to see her—just before he'd made the call to 911, which closed up the West Side Art and Photography Club forever.

"Here," he'd said, handing her a blue-backed legal document.

She'd stared at it, uncomprehending. "Like, what is it?"

"It's a court order. The marshal seized your mother's and stepfather's bank accounts and house and they've put the money into a special trust fund for you."

"I . . . Like, I don't get it."

"The money your father left you? The court took it away from your mother and they're giving it back to you. I won my petition."

"Whoa, like radical! How much is it?"

"A hundred and ninety-two thousand."

"Awesome! Can I—?"

"You can't touch it for three years, until you're eighteen."

"Or whatever," she'd added.

"And you only get it if you go to school."

"What? That's fucking bogus."

It was also untrue. There were no strings on the money once she turned eighteen, as the trust officer would undoubtedly tell her. But she'd have a few years to think about it and might just try a class or two. Junie might just succeed at school; she was, he'd concluded, more savvy than half the lawyers at Hubbard, White & Willis.

She'd hugged him and then looked at him in that coy way that, before this, would've melted him. But he'd said he had to be going. He had an important meeting—with a pay phone. He'd looked at her for a long moment then kissed her on the cheek and left.

He wondered if Junie would say anything about him. She was, of course, in a position not only to destroy the delicate balance of his career, such as it was, but also to send him to prison for the rest of his life.

These possibilities he considered with remarkable serenity, sipping coffee from a porcelain cup. He weighed the odds and decided that she would say nothing. Although she'd been badly used by life and had the dangerous edge of those who learn survival skills before maturity, Junie was nonetheless motivated by a kind of justice. She saw essential good and essential evil, assigned her loyalty accordingly and stuck by her choice.

There were few adults with that perception. Or that courage.

Also, Dudley chose to believe that the girl loved him, at least by her wary definition of that word.

Good-bye, Junie. . . .

He now set the paper down and rocked back in his chair.

Reflecting that for once in his forty years as a lawyer he'd given up charming people and trying to win clients. Rather, he'd mastered a tiny bit of the law. In this small area of expertise he was now the best in the city: restitution of parentally converted intestate distributions (though he himself preferred to think of the subniche as "saving teenage hookers' bacon"). And he was proud of what he'd learned and done.

Still, there was one more potential problem: Taylor Lockwood knew his secret.

He picked up the phone and dialed a number he'd been calling so often over the past two days that he had it memorized.

The main operator at Manhattan General Hospital answered. He asked to speak to the floor nurse about the paralegal's condition.

They'd been reluctant to talk about details but it was clear from the tone—as well as from the gossip around the firm—that the girl was near death.

Maybe she'd died. That would take care of all the problems.

But then an orderly came on the phone. The man listened to Dudley's question and replied in a cheerful voice, "Don't you worry, sir. Your niece, Ms. Lockwood, was discharged today. She's doing fine."

An electric charge shot through him at this news. He hung up.

With Clayton dead, she was the one person who could destroy his fragile life here at the firm. She was the one risk to his budding life as a real lawyer. So much of the law deals with risk, Dudley reflected, some acceptable, some not. On which side did Taylor Lockwood fall?

He rocked back, looking out the window at the tiny sliver of New York Harbor that was visible between the two brick walls outside his office.

■■■■■

As she left the firm by the infamous back door—no longer taped open, she noticed—Taylor Lockwood was aware of someone's presence near her.

She stepped onto the sidewalk of Church Street, which at one time had been the shoreline of lower Manhattan. Now a half mile of landfill had extended the island well into the Hudson and the harbor.

Pausing, she looked behind her.

This was a quiet street, with a few bad restaurants, a girlie bar (ironically next to the rear entrance to Trinity Church) and the dingy service entrances to a number of office buildings. The street was now largely deserted.

She noticed a few businesspeople hurrying to or from one of the gyms near here and some construction workers. A number of vans were parked on the narrow street, half on the sidewalk. She had to walk around a drapery cleaning van to step into the street and hail a taxi.

Of course, there were none.

Then, in the bulbous disk of a wide-angle rearview mirror on one of the vans, she noticed a man looking her way.

She gasped.

There was nothing ambiguous about the recognition this time.

It was the man in the baseball cap, the one who'd sat next to her in the coffee shop.

The killer, the thief.

Okay. He doesn't know you saw him. You can get out of this.

Shaking her head casually, as if discouraged that there were no cabs, Taylor turned slowly back to the sidewalk.

Then instantly reversed herself and, sprinting as fast as her still-weak legs could carry her, made straight for population.

She glanced back once and saw that the man had given up any pretense—he was running after her. He reached into his coveralls and pulled out a long dark object. At first she thought it was a gun but then she realized that it was a knife or ice pick.

Still dehydrated and in severe pain from the poisoning, her muscles began to slow. Judging distances, Taylor realized that she wasn't going to make it to Broadway or one of the other heavily traveled streets before the killer reached her.

She stopped suddenly in the middle of the street and jogged down the concrete stairs to the Rector Street subway stop. This was better than the street anyway—not only would there be people on the platform but the token seller in the booth would have a hot line to the transit police. The killer wouldn't follow her here. He—

But he *was* following, grim determination—to kill her—on his face. A glance back showed that he'd picked up the speed, as if he could sense her fatigue and was moving in for the coup de grace.

"Help me!" she screamed to the startled young woman in the token booth. Three or four people scattered or ducked as Taylor vaulted the turnstile and fell hard onto the platform. One man started to help her but she raged, "Get away. No, get away!"

There were more screams behind her as the killer reached the bottom of the stairs and looked for her.

A businessman hovering nearby saw the ice pick in the hand of the killer and backed up.

Rising to her feet, she ran as fast as she could along the platform to the far exit of the subway. She heard the staticky voice of the token seller call out, "Pay your fare," as the killer jumped onto the platform and started after her.

Sprinting as best she could, she came to the end of the platform and turned to run up the stairs at the exit door.

But it was chained.

"Oh, Jesus," she cried. "No . . ."

Taylor returned to the platform and saw the killer, his face emotionless, walking slowly now, studying her carefully from thirty feet away. Anticipating her escape routes.

She jumped off the platform and dropped four feet into the muck between the rails. Turning away from the killer, she began to run through the tunnel, stumbling over the slippery ties.

He was right behind her, saying nothing, not threatening her or urging her to stop. Not negotiating—there was only one thing he needed to do—kill her.

Taylor got only about twenty feet when, exhausted, she slipped on a slick piece of tie and nearly fell. By the time she regained her balance the killer had made a leaping grab and seized her by the ankle. She went down hard against the solid piece of wood.

Catching her breath, she lashed out with her other foot and caught him in the mouth or cheek with her sole—a solid blow—and he grunted and lost his grip. "Fuck you," he muttered, spitting blood.

"No, fuck you!" she screamed. And kicked again.

He dodged away from her and swung with the pick.

Taylor rolled away and he missed. But she couldn't climb to her feet; he was coming forward too fast, swinging the steel, keeping her off balance.

Finally she managed to stand but just as she was about to start running he grabbed her overcoat and pulled her legs out from under her. She tumbled again to the ground, her head bouncing hard on a tie. She rose, exhausted, to her hands and knees.

"No," she said. "Please."

The killer was up, ready to pounce. But Taylor remained motionless, on her hands and knees, stunned. "What do you want?" she gasped, breathless, spent.

Still, no answer. But why should he respond? It was clear what he wanted. She was the tiny bird that her father had hunted, she was the victim of the Queen of Hearts—off with her head, off with her head.

The weapon drawing back, its needle-sharp point aiming at her face. She lifted her head and gazed at him, piteous. "Don't, please."

But he leaned forward and lunged with the pick, aiming toward her neck.

Which is when she dropped to her belly and scrabbled backward.

She'd been feigning, remaining on all fours like an exhausted soldier, when in fact she had—somewhere—a tiny bit of strength left.

"Ah, ah, ah, ah . . ."

Taylor squinted at him, still in the position of attack, right arm extended, clutching that terrible weapon.

"Ah, ah, ah, ah . . ." The terrible moan from his throat.

In his haste to stab Taylor he'd ignored what was just beyond her body—what she'd been trying to sucker him into hitting: the electrified third rail of the subway, which held more amperage than an electric chair.

"Ah, ah, ah, ah."

There were no sparks, no crackles but every muscle in his body was vibrating.

Then blood appeared in his eyes and his sandy hair caught fire.

"Ah, ah, ah—"

Finally the muscles spasmed once and he collapsed onto the tracks, flames dancing from his collar and cuffs and head.

Taylor heard voices and the electronic sound of walkie-talkies from the Rector Street platform. She supposed it would be the transit cops or the regular NYPD.

It didn't matter. She didn't want to see them or talk to them.

She knew now that there was only one thing to do that might save her. Taylor Lockwood turned and vanished into the darkness of the tunnel.

CHAPTER THIRTY-SEVEN

"Do you mind my saying? . . . I mean, will you take it personally if I say you don't look very good?" John Silbert Hemming asked.

Taylor Lockwood said to the huge private eye, "I lost eight pounds in two days."

"Quite a diet. You should maybe write a book. I'm told you can make a lot of money doing that."

"We couldn't market it—the secret ingredient ain't so appetizing. I'm feeling better now."

They were at Miracles Pub. She was probing at a bowl of Greek chicken soup flavored with lemon. It wasn't on the menu. Dimitri's wife had made it herself. She had some trouble with the spoon—she had to keep her fingers curled; her rings tended to fall off if she didn't.

"Maybe," he joked cautiously, "you should've taken my offer to have dinner. Probably would've been better than where you ended up eating."

"You know, John, I wish I had." Then she said, "I need a favor."

Hemming, who was eating a hamburger, said, "If it's not

illegal and not dangerous and if you agree to go to the opera with me a week from Saturday at eight o'clock sharp, I'd be happy to oblige."

She considered. She said, "One out of three?"

"Which one?"

"I'd like to go to the opera."

"Oh, dear. Still, it makes me very pleased. Though nervous—considering you're balking on the other two. Now, what's the favor?" He nodded toward his plate. "This is a very good hamburger. Can I offer you some?"

She shook her head.

"Ah." He resumed eating. "Favor?" he repeated.

After a moment, she asked, "Why do people murder?"

"Temper, insanity, love and occasionally for money."

The spoon in her hand hovered over the surface of the soup, then made a soft landing on the table. She pushed the bowl away. "The favor is, I want you to get me something."

"What?"

"A gun. That kind I was telling you about—the kind without any serial numbers."

It would be near quitting time at the firm.

The end of another day at Hubbard, White & Willis.

Files being stacked away, dress shoes being replaced with Adidas and Reeboks, places in law books being marked for the night, edits being dropped in the In Box for the night word processing staff.

Four miles away Taylor Lockwood was hiding out in Mitchell Reece's loft. She was concerned that the person behind Clayton's death might figure out that she'd been responsible for the death of one hired gun and had called in a second one who was staking out her apartment right now.

She picked up the scarred gray .38 revolver that John Silbert Hemming had gotten her. She smelled it, sweet oil and wood and metal warmed by her hand. She hefted the small pistol, much heavier than she'd thought it would be.

Then she put the gun in her purse and walked unsteadily

to Mitchell Reece's kitchen, where she found a pen and one of his pads of yellow foolscap.

She wrote the note quickly—he was due home at any moment—and she didn't want him here to deter her from what she had to do.

In her scrawled handwriting Taylor promised that she'd explain everything to him later—if she wasn't killed or arrested—but she begged him to please, please stay away from the firm tonight. After all the deceit and horrors of the past two weeks she'd learned who Wendall Clayton's killer was. She'd gotten a gun and, finally, she was going to make sure that justice would be done.

CHAPTER THIRTY-EIGHT

Taylor Lockwood had never liked this room—the big conference room in the firm.

For one thing, it was always dim—a pastel room so underlit that the colors became muddy and unreal. For another, she associated it with the large meetings in which the paralegal administrator would gather her flock and give them all a rah-rah pep talk, which amounted to a plea not to quit just because the raises this year were going to be only 5 percent.

Mindless, proletariat babble.

Nonetheless, at eight o'clock in the evening, here was Taylor Lockwood, sitting in a large swivel chair at the base of the U, the chair Donald Burdick reserved for himself.

Suddenly the huge teak doors to the room opened and Mitchell Reece ran inside.

He stopped, gasping, when he saw the gun in her hand.

She looked at him with surprise. "Mitchell, what are you doing here?"

"Your note! I read the note you left. Where did you think I'd be?"

"I told you not to come. Why didn't you listen to me?"

"What're you going to do with the gun?"

She smiled absently. "It's pretty obvious, isn't it? I've got to save us."

"The U.S. attorney's coming tomorrow! Don't do this to yourself."

"The cops? The U.S. attorney?" She laughed skeptically. "And what would they do? We don't have any evidence. You and I are never going to be safe. We got run off the road, I was poisoned. I was almost stabbed to death."

"What?"

She didn't tell him about the latest assault just yet. She muttered, "It's just a matter of time until we're dead—if I don't stop things right here. Now."

"You can't just shoot somebody in cold blood."

"I'll claim self-defense. Insanity."

"The insanity defense doesn't work, Taylor. Not in cases like this."

She rubbed her eyes.

"The man who stole the note's dead."

"What?"

"The janitor or whatever he was, the one who put the poison in my food—him. He tried again. He chased me into the subway. But he got electrocuted."

"Jesus. What did the police say?"

"No." She shook her head. "I didn't go to them. It wouldn't do any good, Mitchell. They'd just hire somebody else."

"Well, who is it?" he asked. "Who's behind all this?"

She didn't answer. She glanced up, over Reece's shoulder, and said, "Turn around and find out." She hid the gun behind her back and called, "We're over here. Come on in."

Reece spun around.

A figure emerged from the dull light of the hallway into the deeper shadow of the end of the conference room. Donald Burdick, his posture perfect, like a ballroom dancer's, stepped past the doors, which swung closed with a heavy snap.

The partner called from across the room, his voice ringing dully, like a bell through fog. "Taylor, it *is* you." He nodded at Reece.

"Surprised to see I'm still alive?"

"Your call . . . it didn't make any sense. What's all this about Wendall's death?" He walked to within ten feet of them and stopped. He remained standing. "We thought you were sick."

"You mean, you *hoped* I was *dead*!" She slowly lifted the gun.

His mouth opened. He blinked. "Taylor, what are you doing with that?"

She started to speak. Her voice choked and then she cleared her throat. "I had a speech rehearsed, Donald. I forgot it. . . . But what I do know is that you hired that man to steal the note and set up Clayton's suicide. Then you had him run us off the road and try to kill me—twice."

The dapper partner gave a harsh bark of a laugh. "Are you crazy?" He looked at Mitchell for help. "What's she saying?"

Reece shook his head, gazing at Taylor with concern.

"I went through the file room logs, Donald. You checked out a file for Genneco last week. I saw your signature."

"Maybe I did. I don't remember. Genneco's my client."

"But there'd be no reason to check *this* file out. It wasn't active. As part of a contract negotiation their insurer analyzed their pathogen storage facility in New Jersey. It was basically a blueprint about how to break into the place. You checked the file out and gave the information to your hit man. He broke in, stole some botulism culture and poisoned me!"

"No, I swear I didn't."

"And when that didn't work you sent him to stab me. Well, he's *dead,* Donald. How do you like that?"

"I don't know what you're talking about." He started to turn and walk away.

"No!" Taylor cried. "Don't move." She thrust the gun toward him. The partner stumbled backward, lifting his hands helplessly.

"Taylor!" Reece shouted.

"No!" she screamed and cocked the gun. Burdick backed against the wall, his eyes huge disks of terror. Reece froze.

They stood in those positions for a long minute. Taylor stared at the gun, as if willing it to fire by itself.

"I can't," she whispered finally. "I can't do it."

The gun drooped.

Reece stepped forward slowly and took the pistol from her. He put his arm around her shoulders. "It's all right," he whispered.

"I wanted to be strong," she said. "I wanted to kill him. But I can't do it."

Burdick said to them both, "I swear I had nothing to do—"

She pulled away from Reece's arm and faced Burdick in her fury. "You may think you have the police and the mayor and everyone else in your pocket but it's not going to stop me from making sure you spend the rest of your life in jail!"

Taylor grabbed a telephone off the table.

The partner shook his head. "Taylor, whatever you think, it's not true."

She had just started dialing when a hand reached over, lifted the receiver away from her and replaced it in the cradle.

"No, Taylor...," Mitchell Reece said. He sighed and lifted the gun, the muzzle pointing at her like a single black pearl. "No," he repeated softly.

CHAPTER THIRTY-NINE

She gave a faint laugh of surprise.

Much the same sound that Mitchell Reece himself had uttered when she told him a few days ago that Clayton had been murdered. Then her smile faded and with bottomless horror in her voice she said, "What are you doing?"

His face was stone, his eyes expressionless, but the answer was clear.

"You, Mitchell?" she whispered.

Donald Burdick said, "One of you tell me what's going on here."

Reece ignored him. Still holding the gun on both of them, he walked to the door, looked outside, made sure the corridor was empty and returned. He said to her angrily, "Why the hell didn't you stop when you should have, Taylor? Why? It was all planned out so carefully. You ruined it."

Burdick, horrified, said, "Mitchell, it was you? You killed Wendall Clayton?"

Taylor's eyes closed for a brief moment. She shook her head.

Reece told her, "Wendall Clayton killed the woman I loved."

Taylor frowned then said, "Linda? Linda Davidoff!"

Reece nodded slowly.

"Oh, my God..."

After a moment Reece said, "It was all about a man and a woman. As simple as that." His eyebrows rose. "A man who'd never had time for relationships, a woman who was beautiful and creative and brilliant. Two people who'd never been in love before. Not real love. It wasn't a good combination. An ambitious, tough lawyer. Best in law school, best at the firm...The woman was a poet—shy, sensitive. Don't ask me how they became close. Opposites attract, maybe. A secret romance in a Wall Street law firm. They worked together and started going out. They fell in love. She got pregnant and they were going to get married."

A moment passed and Reece seemed to be hefting the words to select among them. Finally he continued, "Wendall was working on a case one weekend, and he needed a paralegal. Linda'd cut way back on her hours— that's when she'd stopped working for me and Sean Lillick took over. But she still worked occasionally. She did a few assignments for Wendall Clayton and he got obsessed with her. One weekend in September he found out she was at her parents' summer house in Connecticut, not far from his place. He went to see her, tried to seduce her. She called me, crying. But before I could get up there or she could get away there was a struggle and she fell into the ravine. She died. Clayton left her poem to make it look like a suicide."

"This whole thing," Taylor whispered, "it was fake. You lied about everything. . . . Your mother, in the hospital? You weren't going to see her at all. You were going to Scarsdale—to take flowers to Linda's grave."

Reece nodded.

The nail of Taylor's index finger touched the marble. "Oh, Mitchell, it's so fucking clear now." She looked at Burdick. "Don't you see what he's done?" She turned to face

Reece, who leaned against the dark, dried-blood-red conference table, looking gaunt and pale. "You got one of your
criminal clients from the pro bono program—what? A hit
man, a killer, a mercenary soldier? You got him to break into
your own file cabinet, steal the Hanover note and hide it in
Wendall's office. Then you had him bug your own office so
you'd look as innocent as possible. You recorded some conversations then planted the tapes with the note. You had me
track him down."

She thought for a moment. "Then, at Clayton's party, I
found the receipt from the security service: upstairs, where
you sent me to search—after you planted it there.... Finally
I found the note in Clayton's office." She laughed bitterly.
"And after the Hanover trial your hit man killed him right
away—because he couldn't very well be accused of something he hadn't done."

The lawyer made no effort to deny any of this.

She continued, "And his suicide note...It was fake,
wasn't it? Who forged it? Another criminal client?"

The associate lifted his eyebrow, conceding the accuracy
of her deduction.

She laughed bitterly, glancing at the partner.

Men of most renowned virtue...

Reece was gazing at her, impassive as a statue.

Eyes still on Reece, locked on his, Taylor said, "And
Donald was a big help, wasn't he?" She turned to the partner. "Nothing personal, Donald, but you laid a pretty damn
good smoke screen." Her hands were shaking now. The
tears started. "And as for me, well, you were keeping pretty
close tabs on your pawn. All you had to do was look across
the pillow."

A bit of emotion blossomed in his face at this—like the
first cracks in spring ice. Reece took a Kleenex from his
pocket and began rubbing the trigger guard and grip and
frame of the gun. He nodded. "You won't believe me if I tell
you that what happened between us wasn't part of the
plan."

"Bullshit! You tried to kill me!"

His eyes grew wide. "I didn't want to hurt you! You should have stopped when you were supposed to!"

Burdick said, "But Mitchell, how could you risk it? You love the law. You'd *risk* everything for this, for revenge?"

He smiled with a look as bleak as a hunting field in December. "But there *was* no risk, Donald. Don't you know me by now? I knew I'd get away with it. Every nuance was planned. Every action and reaction. Every move anticipated and guarded against. I planned this exactly the same way I plan my trials. There was no way it wouldn't work." He sighed and shook his head. "Except for you, of course, Taylor. You were the flaw. . . . Why didn't you just let it go? I killed an evil man. I did the firm—hell, I did the *world*—a favor."

"You used me!"

Donald Burdick sat heavily in a chair, his head dipping. "Oh, Mitchell, all you had to do was go to the police. Clayton would've been arrested for the girl's death."

The young lawyer gave a harsh laugh. "You think so? And what would've happened, Donald? Nothing. Any half-assed criminal lawyer could've gotten him off. There was no witness, no physical evidence. Besides, you of all people ought to know how many favors Clayton could've called in. The case wouldn't've even gotten to the grand jury."

His attention dipped for a moment to the gun. He flipped it open expertly and saw six cartridges in the cylinder. Then from his pocket he took the note that Taylor Lockwood had written to him, the note about going to confront a killer. He folded it into a tight square, stepped forward and stuffed it into her breast pocket.

She whispered, nodding at it, "I wrote my own suicide note, didn't I? I kill Donald and then myself. Oh, my God . . ."

"It's your fault," he muttered. "You should've just moved on, Taylor. You should've let Clayton stay in hell and let the rest of us get on with our business."

"My fault?" She leaned forward. "What the hell happened to you? Has it all caught up? Finally? Pushing, pushing, pushing . . . years and years of it. Win the case, win the goddamn case—that's all you see, all you care about! You don't know what justice is anymore. You've turned it inside out."

"Don't lecture me," he said wearily. "Don't talk to me about things you can't understand. I live with the law, I've made it a part of me."

Burdick said, "There's no way you can justify it, Mitchell. You killed a man."

Reece rubbed his eyes. After a moment, he said, "You get asked a lot why you go to law school. Did you go because you wanted to help society, to make money, to further justice? That's what people always want to know. Justice? There's so little of it in the world, so little justice in our lives. Maybe on the whole it balances out; maybe God looks down from someplace and says, 'Yeah, pretty good, I'll let it go at that.' But you know the law as well as I do, both of you. Innocent people serve time and guilty ones get off. Wendall Clayton killed Linda Davidoff and he was going to go free. I wasn't going to let that happen."

Taylor said, "The suicide note—Clayton's. 'Men of most renowned virtue . . .' How does it go?"

Reece said, "'Have sometimes by transgressing most truly kept the law.'"

"You meant it about you, then, not Clayton."

Reece nodded solemnly. "It's about me."

"Mitchell," Burdick whispered, "just put the gun down. We'll go to the police. If you talk to them—"

But Reece walked slowly over to Taylor. He stood two feet away. She didn't move.

"No!" Burdick shouted. "Don't worry about the police. We can forget what happened. There's no need for this to go beyond this room. There's no need. . . ."

Reece glanced at the partner briefly but didn't speak. His whole attention was on Taylor. He touched her hair, then her cheek. He nestled the muzzle of the gun against her breast.

"I wish . . ." He cocked the gun. "I wish . . ."

Taylor wiped the thick tears. "But it's me, Mitchell. *Me*. Think about what you're going to do."

"Please, Mitchell," Burdick said. "Money, do you want money? A fresh start somewhere?"

But it was Taylor who raised her hand to silence the partner. "No. He's come too far. There's nothing more to say."

At last there were tears on Reece's face. The gun wavered and rose. For a moment it seemed to be levitating; maybe he intended to touch the chill muzzle to his own temple and pull the trigger.

But his deeper will won and he lowered the black weapon to her once more.

Alice, in this dreadful world on the other side of the looking glass, remained completely still. There was no place to go. All she could do was close her eyes, which is what she now did.

Mitchell Reece, practical as ever, held his left hand to his face to protect himself from the blast—and her spattered blood—and then he pulled the trigger.

CHAPTER FORTY

 In the hushed conference room the metallic click was as loud as the gunshot would have been.

Reece's eyes flickered for a moment. He pulled the trigger three more times.

Three more clicks echoed throughout the room. His hand lowered.

"Fake," he whispered with the tone of someone observing an impossible occurrence. "It's fake?"

Taylor wiped the streaming tears from her face. "Oh, Mitchell . . ."

Burdick stepped forward and firmly lifted the gun away from him.

Taylor said, "The gun's real, Mitchell, but the bullets're just props." She shook her head. "All I had was speculation. I needed proof that you did it."

Reece leaned against the wall. "Oh, my God." He was staring at Taylor. "How?" he whispered. She'd never seen such shock in anyone's eyes—pure, uncomprehending astonishment.

"A lot of clues I finally put together today," she said. "What got me wondering was the poem, Linda's poem."

"Poem?"

"The one that Wendall left as her suicide note. I read it in the hospital and, you know, everybody *thought* it was a suicide note. But nobody really understood what it was about. It was a *love* poem. It wasn't about killing herself, it was about leaving solitude and loneliness and starting a new life with somebody she loved. Anybody who was going to kill herself wouldn't leave that as a suicide note. Danny Stuart, her roommate, said she wrote it just a few days before she died."

He was shaking his head. "Impossible. You couldn't make that kind of deduction, not from the suicide note back to me."

"No, of course not. It's just what put the idea in my head that maybe she didn't kill herself. But then I started to think about everything that'd happened since you'd asked me to help you find the note, everything I'd learned. I thought about you nudging me away from the other suspects and toward Clayton. I thought about what kind of strategist you were, about Clayton's womanizing, about how it would be easy for you to get a gun from one of your clients in the criminal pro bono program. Your trips to Linda's grave . . . I had my private-eye friend check out your mother. Yes, she was a paranoid schizophrenic. But she died four years ago. Oh, Mitchell, you looked me right in the eye and lied. I felt like crying when you told me about your mother!"

Still, he held her eye, not a flicker of remorse in his.

"Then," she continued, "I called the Boston U.S. attorney's office. Your friend Sam hasn't worked for them for four years. . . . You faked that call to him from the street in front of your loft, didn't you?" Her anger broke through. "You're a pretty fucking good actor, Mitchell!"

Then, calming, she continued. "Hard evidence? You yourself helped me there—that first day I met you, when you mentioned that the records in law firms reveal all kinds of information about where people've been and how they spend their time. I went through the time sheets going back a year and figured out exactly what happened. It's all right there: You and Linda working together, taking time off together, logging travel time to clients on the same date, joint meal vouchers. Then Linda's time drops and she takes sick leave and files insurance claims because she's pregnant. And not long after that she dies.

"Then I found the Genneco security system contract negotiation files. And, yeah, it was checked out to Donald. But if he'd used them to get access to the botulism he sure as hell wouldn't use his own name. Then I asked Mrs. Bendix to find any other files Donald had supposedly checked out recently. There was one—an insurance claim. Where a car went off the road and looked like it was going to sink in the reservoir in Westchester but ended up on a ledge of rock that kept it from sinking. In exactly the same place we drove into the reservoir that night. You needed to make it look like Clayton was desperate enough to kill us so he'd be desperate enough to kill himself. Right? Am I right?"

Reluctantly he nodded.

"Oh, sure, a lot of people had motives to kill Clayton. Thom Sebastian and Dudley and Sean Lillick...and Donald here. Even Donald's wife. And probably a dozen other people. But I decided you were wrong—when you told me that motive is the most important thing in finding a killer. No, the most important thing is finding the person who has the *will* to murder. Remember your herald, Mitchell? Preparation and will? Well, of all the people in this firm, you were the only one I believed could actually murder someone. The way you destroyed that doctor on cross-examination...you had a killer's heart. I could see that.

"But even then I wasn't absolutely sure. So I called Donald earlier tonight and we arranged this little play of our own—to find out for sure."

"You don't understand," Reece whispered desperately. "Clayton was pure evil. There was no way to bring him to justice otherwise. He—"

Taylor's hand flew up toward him, palm out. "Justice?"

she raged. "Justice?" She sighed and lowered her head, speaking into the microphone hidden under her collar.

"John, could you come in please?"

The door opened and John Silbert Hemming entered. Reece stared up at the huge man as he gripped Reece's arm tightly and stepped protectively between the lawyer and Taylor.

The man said to her softly, "You could have stopped earlier, before he tried to use that." Nodding at the gun. "We had enough on tape for a conviction."

She was looking into Reece's evasive eyes as she said in a whisper, "I had to know."

The handcuffs went on quickly, with a crisp, ratchety sound.

"You can't do this!" Reece muttered bitterly. "You have no legal authority. It's illegal detention and kidnapping. And that fucking tape is illegal. You'll be subject—"

"Shhhh," John Silbert Hemming said.

"—to civil liability and criminal charges, which I'll pursue on the federal and state levels. You don't know the kind of trouble—"

"Shhhh," the big man repeated, looking down at Reece ominously. The lawyer fell silent.

Seeing Reece standing in front of her, oddly defiant, even angry at what they'd done to him, she wondered if she was going to scream, or slap him, or even reach for his throat with her hands, which seemed to have the strength, more than enough, to strangle him to death.

Reece said, "Taylor, I can make you understand. If you'll just—"

"I don't want to hear anything more."

But she was speaking only to John Silbert Hemming, who nodded solemnly and escorted the lawyer out into the firm's lobby to await the police.

━━━━

She spent an hour giving several lengthy statements to two humorless detectives from Police Plaza. She refused a ride home from gallant John Silbert Hemming but promised that she'd call him about their opera "date," a word that she pointedly used.

"Looking forward to it," he said, ducking his head to step into the elevator car.

Taylor walked slowly back to her cubicle. She was almost there when she heard the sound of a photocopier and noticed Sean Lillick copying sheets of music on the Xerox machine near the paralegal pen. He looked up and blurted, "Taylor! You're out of the hospital? We heard you were totally sick."

"Back from the dead," she said, glancing at the music, the copying of which he was probably charging to a client.

"You're all right?"

If you only knew . . .

"I'll live."

He nodded toward the manuscript paper. "Take a look. My latest opus. It's about Wendall Clayton. I found all of these pictures and papers and things in his office the other day and I'm writing this opera about him. I'm going to project pictures on the screen and get some Shakespearean text and—"

She leaned close and shut him up with an exasperated look. "Sean, can I give you some advice?"

He looked at the music. "Oh, these're just the rough lead sheets. I'm going to arrange them later."

"I don't mean that," she whispered ominously. "Listen up: If Donald Burdick doesn't know you were Clayton's spy yet, he will in about a day or two."

He gazed at her uneasily. "What're you talking about?"

"I'm talking about this: Pack up your stuff and get out of here. I'd recommend leaving town."

"Who the hell're you to—"

"You think Clayton was vindictive, you ain't seen nothing yet. Donald'll sue your ass for every penny of the money Clayton paid you to be his weasel."

"Fuck you. What money?"

"That you've got hidden under your stinky mattress."

He blinked in shock. He started to ask how she knew this but he gave up. "I was just—"

"And one more thing. Leave Carrie Mason alone. She's too good for you."

The kid tried to look angry but mostly he was scared. He grabbed his papers and scurried off down the corridor. Taylor returned to her cubicle. She'd just sat down and begun to check phone messages when she heard someone coming up behind her. She spun around fast, alarmed.

Thom Sebastian stood in the doorway, hands stuffed in his pockets.

"Hey," he said, "only me. Mr. Party Animal. Didn't mean to spook you."

"Thom."

"I was mega-freaked when I heard you were sick. They wouldn't let me in to see you. Did you get my flowers?"

"I might have. I was pretty out of it. I couldn't read half the cards."

"Well, I was worried. I'm glad you're okay. You lost weight."

She nodded and said nothing.

A dense, awkward moment. His voice quavered as he said, "So."

"So."

He said, "Anyway, I just wanted to let you know.... Looks like I'm leaving."

"The firm?"

He nodded. "What I was telling you about, that new firm I'm starting with Bosk? It's going to happen. Tomorrow's my last day here. I've got ten associates from Hubbard, White coming with me. And a bunch of clients too. We've already got fifteen retainer agreements. St. Agnes, McMillan, New Amsterdam, RFC, a bunch of others."

Taylor laughed. "You're kidding." These were Hubbard, White's biggest clients. They represented close to one third of the firm's revenues.

Thom said, "We're going to do the same work Hubbard, White did but charge them about half. They were ready to leave anyway. Most of the presidents and CEOs I talked to said everybody here was paying too much attention to the merger and firm politics and not enough to the legal work. They said the other associates and I were the only ones who gave a shit about them."

"That's probably true."

"The funny thing is, if I'd made partner I'd be under a noncompetition agreement so I couldn't've taken any clients with me. But since I'm just an associate the firm can't stop me."

"Congratulations, Thom."

She started to turn back to her desk. But he stepped forward nervously and touched her arm. "The thing is, Taylor." He swallowed uneasily. "The thing is, I have to say something." He looked around, his eyes dark and troubled. "I've spent a lot of time..." He swallowed. "I've spent a lot of time thinking about you and checking you out. What you found in my office, my notes about you? I shouldn't've done that, I know. But I just couldn't get you out of my head."

Taylor stood up, glanced at her arm. He removed his hand from it and stepped back. "What're you saying?" she asked.

"I'm saying I learned some things about you that're a problem for me."

She looked at him steadily. "Yes?"

"I've learned that you're the sort of person I don't think I'll ever meet again. Who I think I could spend the rest of my life with." He looked away. "I guess I'm saying that I think I love you."

She was too surprised even to laugh.

He held up a pudgy hand. "I know you think I'm goofy and crude. But I don't have to be that way. I *can't* be that way at my new firm. I'm giving up the drugs. That's what I was meeting with Magaly about the night she was killed—the night you got me out of jail. I wasn't going to score anything—I was going to tell her I wasn't going to buy from her anymore. I was doing that for you. Then, that night at the Blue Devil, I was going to ask if you maybe wanted to go out

with me—kind of, I guess, steady." He shook his head at the
old-fashioned word. "I had it all planned out, what I was going to say ... but then Magaly got shot and you had to bail
me out. The whole night went to hell and I couldn't even
look you in face, let alone tell you how I felt about you."

She began to speak but he took a deep breath. "No, no,
no, don't say anything yet. Please, Taylor. Just think about
what I said. Will do that? I'll have the firm, I'll have
money. I can give you whatever you want. If you want to go
to law school, fine. You want to play music, fine. You want
to have a dozen babies, fine."

"Thom."

"Please," he begged, "don't say yes and don't say no. Just
think about it." He took a deep breath and seemed on the
verge of tears. "Jesus, I'm the world's greatest fucking negotiator and here I am breaking all my rules. Look, everything's in there." He handed her a large white envelope.

"What is it?" she asked.

"I did kind of a deal memo."

Now, she couldn't help but laugh. "Deal memo?"

He grinned. "For us. About how we might work things
out. Don't panic, we don't get to marriage until phase four."

"Phase four."

"We'll take it nice and easy. Please, just read it and let
the idea sit for a while."

"I'll read it," she said.

Then, unable to resist, he threw his arms around her
and hugged her hard. He retreated before she could say anything more.

Don't get too interested in her. ... Sebastian's comment to
Bosk. It was a warning from a jealous lover, not a potential
killer.

Taylor lowered her face to her hands and laughed softly.
Thinking: I guess it's safe to say, *What a night.*

Her desk was a mess; Vera Burdick's ransacking hadn't
left it in very good shape. When she'd called Burdick about
Reece earlier in the evening she'd asked him bluntly why his
wife was searching through her things.

"Vera doesn't trust anybody," Burdick had said, laughing. "Samuel Lockwood's daughter? She thought for sure you were working with Clayton, helping him push the merger through—or, after he died, sabotaging me. You should consider it a compliment."

The way a fly should feel complimented that he's a spider's first choice for dinner.

Taylor noticed a blinking red light on her phone. She lifted the receiver and pressed the play button.

"Hey, counselor."

Hello, Dad.

"Listen, hope you're feeling better. 'Cause I've made some plans for us tomorrow. I get into La Guardia in the morning. How 'bout you come pick me up? I've made lunch reservations at the Four Seasons. There's somebody from Skadden I want you to meet. A senior partner. He said they're looking for people like my little overachiever. Now, get a pen: My plane gets in at—"

Click. Taylor Lockwood hit a button.

A woman's electronic voice reported: *"Your message has been deleted."*

She hung up the receiver.

Taylor pulled on her raincoat and walked through the half-lit corridors. The Slavic cleaning women in their blue uniforms moved from office to office with their wheeled carts. Taylor could hear the whine of vacuums coming from different directions. She imagined she could smell sour gunpowder, as if Reece had in fact fired real bullets from the heavy pistol. But she realized, as she passed a conference room littered with a thousand papers, that the smell was only the residue of cigar smoke. Earlier in the evening a deal had perhaps closed here. Or maybe it'd fallen apart. Or maybe negotiations had been postponed till tomorrow or the next day. In any case the participants had abandoned the room for the time being, leaving behind only the pungent aroma of tobacco as the evidence of that success or failure or uncertainty.

The police had gone. Burdick had gone. The partner would need some rest—he'd have plenty to do in the morning. More favors would have to be called in. Taylor suspected, though, that Donald Burdick and his wife would have a sizable inventory remaining.

She continued through the firm, pressed a door latch button and stepped into the lobby. The door swung closed behind her and when the elevator arrived she stepped in wearily.

Outside, Wall Street was nearly as quiet as the halls of Hubbard, White & Willis. This neighborhood was a daytime place. It worked hard and curled up to sleep early. Most of the offices were dark, the bartenders had stopped pouring drinks, cabs and cars were few.

Occasionally someone in a somber overcoat would appear from a revolving door then vanish into a limo or cab or down a subway stairwell. Where, she wondered, were they going? To one of Sebastian's clubs, to pursue some private lust like Ralph Dudley, to plot a coup like Wendall Clayton?

Or maybe just to retreat to their apartments or houses for a few hours' sleep before the grind began again tomorrow?

What a place this was, the topsy-turvy land at the bottom of the rabbit hole. . . .

But, Taylor considered, was this *her* land?

Alice's trips to Wonderland and the Looking-Glass world had, after all, been dreams and the girl had eventually wakened from them.

She couldn't, for the moment, say.

Taylor flagged down a cab, got in and gave the driver the address of her apartment building. As the dirty vehicle squealed away from the curb she slouched down in the seat, staring at the greasy Plexiglas divider.

Thank you for not smoking. 50-cent surcharge after 8 p.m.

The cab was a block away from her apartment when she leaned forward and told the driver she'd changed her mind.

———

Taylor Lockwood sat in the spotlight.

Dimitri twisted his curly hair and leaned over the microphone. (His habitual suspicion left when she told him,

"I'll play for free. You keep the receipts—all of them—but the tips're mine. And, Dimitri: No satin touch. Not tonight, okay?")

"Ladies and gentlemen . . ."

She whispered ominously, "Dimitri."

". . . it is my pleasure to present Miss Taylor Lockwood at the piano."

He hit the switch controlling the faux spotlight. She smiled at the crowd and touched the keys, cold and smooth as glass, enjoying their yielding resilience as she began to play.

After half an hour Taylor looked out into the cockeyed lights, brilliant starbursts beaming at her, so bright she couldn't see the patrons. Maybe the wobbly tables were completely occupied. Or maybe the place was empty. In any event, if anyone *was* in the audience they were listening in absolute silence.

She smiled, not to them but only for herself, and swayed slowly as she played a medley of Gershwin that she herself had arranged, all revolving around *Rhapsody in Blue*. Tonight she improvised frequently, playing jazzy harmonies and clever riffs, allowing the music to carry itself, the notes soaring and regrouping, then flying to risky altitudes. But Taylor Lockwood never let go completely and was careful to alight at regular intervals on the theme; she knew how much people love the melody.

ABOUT THE AUTHOR

Jeffery Deaver's novels have appeared on a number of best-seller lists around the world, including the *New York Times,* the *London Times* and the *Los Angeles Times.* The author of sixteen novels, he's been nominated for four Edgar Awards from the Mystery Writers of America and an Anthony award and is a two-time recipient of the *Ellery Queen* Reader's Award for Best Short Story of the Year. His book *A Maiden's Grave* was made into an HBO movie starring James Garner and Marlee Matlin, and his novel *The Bone Collector* was a feature release from Universal Pictures, starring Denzel Washington. Turner Broadcasting is currently making a TV movie of his novel *Praying for Sleep.* His most recent novels are *The Stone Monkey, The Blue Nowhere* (soon to be a feature film from Warner Brothers), *The Empty Chair* and *Speaking in Tongues.*

Look for his other suspense novels from Bantam Books: *Manhattan Is My Beat, Death of a Blue Movie Star, Hard News* and *The Lesson of Her Death.*

Deaver lives in Virginia and California and is now at work on his next Lincoln Rhyme novel.

Readers can visit his website at *www.jefferydeaver.com* and the site for his latest book: *www.thebluenowhere.com.*